# YOUNGBLOOD

*By
John
Oliver
Killens*

*Foreword
by
Addison
Gayle*

# YOUNGBLOOD

*Brown Thrasher Books*
The University of Georgia Press
*Athens, Georgia*

Library of Congress Cataloging in Publication Data
Killens, John Oliver, 1916–
    Youngblood.
    "Brown Thrasher books."
    Reprint. Originally published : New York :
Dial Press, c1954.
    Title.
PS3561.I37Y6    1982    813'.54    81-16156
ISBN 0-8203-0601-0        AACR2
ISBN 0-8203-0602-9 (pbk.)

Seventh printing, 2000    ISBN 0-8203-2201-6 (pbk.)

*Youngblood* was first published by Dial Press in 1954
and was reissued by Trident Press in 1966.

To Grace and "The Folks"

# FOREWORD

"WE MUST," WROTE the novelist Louis Ferdinand Céline, "tell everything that we have seen of man's viciousness." For the French writer whose novel *Journey to the End of Night* explores the depths of man's depravity and inhumanity, human history was little more than a compendium of one atrocity after another. Unwilling to believe with Theodore Adorno that there should be no poetry after Auschwitz, Céline insisted that the function of the poet was to pass the record of man's failures from one generation to another. There have been few such theses in Afro-American literature, primarily, one supposes, because the many Auschwitzes undergone by black Americans have simply strengthened the desire of black poets to view humankind from many varied perspectives.

Few poets are more representative of this view than John Oliver Killens, whose novel *Youngblood*, published first in 1954, remains one of the classics of American literature. Coming at a point in time when the Afro-American novelist explored, almost exclusively, the northern urban environment, when Ralph Ellison and James Baldwin were impressing many critics with their tales of alienated existential blacks searching for a tenuous American identity, *Youngblood* returns to the terrain explored so well by Richard Wright and becomes a novel that serves as a symbol of the civil rights revolt, then in its infancy. Not willing, like Céline and Adorno, to accept modern history as a paradigm, Killens looked back upon Afro-American history with the penetrating, sensitive eyes of a talented poet, and divined in that history the counter thesis to the proponents of man's extinction and damnation. There were many monuments erected to human endurance in that history, foremost among which was courage.

And as courage is the unifying thesis of Afro-American history, it is also the unifying thesis of *Youngblood*. Around this concept men and women demonstrate their commitment to other human beings or acquiesce, cynically, in the belief that humankind is unregenerate: "Crackers been hard on me ever since I come into the world," announces a harried Joe Youngblood, "can't be no harder. . . . Made up my mind that I wasn't gonna take no more stuff from these crackers. Gon be a man by God, living or dead." Yet courage, as Killens knows so well, is not always so desperately or bitterly exclaimed; indeed, often takes the form of quiet concentrated effort. There is the courage displayed by Joe Youngblood, who refuses to allow a white paymaster to continue to cheat him of part of his wages; there is that displayed by Laurie Lee Youngblood, who lashes her son bloody-red on the orders of a sadistic policeman in order to save him. Courage is also displayed by Richard Myles, young northern schoolteacher come South, in staging a Jubilee—a black celebration of history—in the face of the anger of the white community. There is that of Robert Youngblood attempting to unite black and white workers under the union banner, and that too of Oscar Jefferson, white, who casts his lot with the black community.

Thus, contrary to the twentieth-century prophets of doom, Killens envisions a world not so much "red in tooth and claw" as one overflowing with limitless possibilities. It is a world populated by heroes, men and women who do not accept their fate but challenge it. "You bring your children into a white folks world," laments Laurie Lee Youngblood, "and you don't know what to tell them to live." The statement is not altogether true, and Laurie Lee, like others in her community, must realize that history has not begun with her generation in Crossroads, Georgia, for neither whites nor blacks, that the ways in which men and women confront the terrors of living at present were prescribed by those who confronted similar terrors in the past, that the great Jubilee is as much an exercise in learning how courage was exhibited in the past as it is a reclamation of black culture.

When Oscar Jefferson views the Jubilee he is moved not so much because he has accepted black history as his own, but by the courage displayed by men and women, mortal like himself. Because of his insistent struggle between the magnetic attraction of his white "tradition" and his humanity, he is able to perceive the "Sorrow Songs," as DuBois called the Negro spirituals, as the poetry of the human heart and soul. It is the poetry of the Jubilee, then, composed after numerous holocausts, that espouses the best of the human condition; it is a vehicle of communication between individuals, highlighting a major tenet of Killens's poetry from *Youngblood* to the later novel *The Cotillion*, that the necessity for communication is paramount at this period of man's existence.

For it is this that motivated the freedom riders and the civil rights protesters; this need to construct lines of communication between one human being and another, that produced the rebellions in the streets from Watts to Harlem, and infused the rhetoric of Martin Luther King, Jr., and Malcolm X. Yet, the difficulty of establishing lines of communication cannot be understated: "Rob looked into the white man's face again, and he wanted desperately to trust this white man with the friendly face and the eyes that were crying out loud to be trusted, but how could he trust him in Crossroads, Georgia?"

It is the question raised today by individuals and nations alike, and the answer does not lie, Killens tells us, in a retreat into one's own ego, or into the philosophy of alienation. Existential man may be a product of the paradise lost, but his journey must be toward reclaiming that paradise, not for himself alone, but for all. Such a journey is undertaken by the Youngbloods and the gallant men and women of their community. It is a journey whose byroads, to be sure, are strewn with evidence of human viciousness, with fear, trepidation, and death. Still, it is a journey made by human beings who realize that manhood and womanhood are achieved not so much from reaching or not reaching a prescribed goal as by the courage displayed in moving toward it.

One comes away from the final pages of *Youngblood*, having witnessed the death of the patriarch, gunned down by a white man, believing still in the nobility and sanctity of the human spirit. For the old man's death galvanizes the black community into action, brings a partial reconciliation between Oscar Jefferson and the blacks, and thus symbolically between whites and blacks, and a promise of better things to come: ". . . look all around you at your brothers and sisters," intones the minister after Joe Youngblood's funeral, "thousands of them, and great God-Almighty, fighting mad, and we're going to make them pay one day soon, the ones that're responsible. There's going to be a reckoning day right here in Georgia and we're going to help God hurry it up."

Looking back from our vantage point at the present time, we know that the "reckoning" day spread from the South to engulf the entire nation. The heroism and courage personified in the Youngbloods helped to move this nation toward a terrible confrontation with its own destiny. The mores and traditions that had bulwarked hundreds of towns like Crossroads were attacked and here and there people discovered sparks of humanity in others across the color line. The forces of hatred and racism—the forces of anti-man—were never completely vanquished, though the structure they had erected for centuries tottered precariously upon the brink of extinction. The Rubicon had not then been reached, and even today there is evidence that a resurgence of old traditions is at hand. Those who believe in the inalienable inferiority of other human beings now mount the barricades of bigotry and hatred across America. In the face of this new onslaught against the human spirit, few of the nation's poets, black or white, are to be heard.

Thus the republication of *Youngblood* is necessary at this time. The novel is a kind of Jubilee of its own, calling us back to the fierce struggles of yesterday, while yet envisioning a future in which courage, struggle, and sacrifice will bring ample rewards in human terms. The novel reminds us of the enduring beauty and nobility of people and that human beings can create the great society. It speaks to what is good in the human character and encourages us to be ever hopeful about the human condition. It assures us that heroes and heroines abound still, and that to discover them we need only redefine our definitions. It assures us, in the words of the Negro spiritual, that the "great gettin' up morning" is possible for those with hope and faith.

One suggests, therefore, that even Céline, cynic, malcontent, would find much to admire about the human beings in *Youngblood*. They are noted more for their generosity than for their viciousness, more for their strengths than their weakness, more for their optimism than their pessimism. Throughout the history of this country, men and women very much like them have raised high the banner of freedom and democracy, and given real meaning to the Constitution and the Bill of Rights. It is little wonder, then, that wherever human beings gather in an attempt to rid themselves of oppression, the voices of black poets from Claude McKay to Richard Wright have been heard. Foremost among those voices is that of John Oliver Killens. He has written a novel, timeless in evocations of the rights of humankind and unparalleled in its optimism concerning the human condition. *Youngblood* is a tremendous achievement.

ADDISON GAYLE

*Part One*

# IN THE BEGINNING

*Didn't my Lord deliver Daniel*
*And why not every man?—*

FROM A NEGRO SPIRITUAL
*"Didn't My Lord Deliver Daniel"*

# CHAPTER ONE

LAURIE LEE BARKSDALE began this life along with the brand new century. About one minute after twelve, a black cold night, in Tipkin, Georgia, January the first, nineteen hundred and zero-zero. As the church bells rang and the pistols fired and the whistles blew all over town, the new baby cried. But she didn't cry much. The mother smiled at the father as he walked in nervously from the back porch. The old midwife said, "She sure is a pretty youngun." And the mother's mother wiped her brow and said, "Umph—Aah Lord——" And the mother lay in the bed and smiled. The father's name was Dale. He kissed his wife on her forehead, went to the chest and got his gun, went out on the back porch and shot into the night, till his fingers got tired and his strong hand trembled. Load and reload. He had expected a boy, but it didn't matter much. She sure was a funny looking baby. Just as red as a beet. Didn't favor a thing.

Got to work twice as hard now, Dale Barksdale. Got to give her all the chances you didn't have in spite of these crackers. His face filled up and his throat and his shoulders. He felt weak, helpless, and scared, he felt strong and mighty. As the whistles still blew and the church bells rang and the guns fired out, he raised his gun and BANG BANG BANG. And—a Great God Almighty, what you gonna name this pretty little child?

The years jumped by, and the girl grew pretty and strong and healthy, and Dale and Martha were as proud as punch. Everywhere they went people said—That child sure got a pretty head on her shoulders, and mother-wit too. They would look at Dale and say—Whachoo swelling up so about? She don't look like you. She Martha up and down. Well, Dale would tell them, that's all right about that.

When she was four years old she said a long recitation by heart in church at an Easter exercise, and she didn't seem nervous. Right then and there folks said she was going to be a school teacher.

When she was eight years old, she was pretty as a peach and round and plump, except for her slender hands, her long tapering fingers. Folks told Dale and Martha that God had given their little girl a gift and she was born to play pretty music, be a great musician. And Dale believed it. On her ninth birthday he brought home a second or third or fourth-hand piano and got Professor Larkins to give her music lessons. And how she loved to tickle those keys. So it was church recitals and playing for the B.Y.P.U. and this and that and everything else. When her nimble fingers ran up and down those keys, she made you laugh and sing, she made you cry and shout, she filled your eyes with shamefaced tears.

Dale was good to his children, Laurie and Tim, worked hard like a dog. Folks would say to him—Dale Barksdale, you sure ain't got no sense at all, working so hard. Ain't got the sense you were born with. You ought to sit down and rest a little while. Children these days ain't worth all them sacrifices, I do declare. Grow up to be something, turn they back on you sure as you born to die.

That's all right about that, Dale would tell them. I ain't looking for no rewards. Just want them to do better than I did. Git an education. Be something else 'sides a workhorse for white folks. Thatta be good enough reward for me. And he meant that thing.

Laurie Lee Barksdale: eleven years old now, and her old mischievous grandmother told her that very morning at the breakfast table. "Gal, you jes beginning to smell your pee, you old pretty thing you!" Later that morning she was coming from town. There wasn't a prettier girl her age in all Johnson County no matter the color. Feeling good and walking with bouncing steps through Woodley's Lane, with the sun reaching down into the alley and resting on her face and her neck and her shoulders. Thinking about next Sunday's recital, mixed up with thoughts about the pretty-faced boy in the ninth grade always smiling at her. She was about halfway through the alley. She saw a tall lanky white man walking towards her, but she didn't think about it, till he walked right up to her, and he grabbed hold of her before she knew it in broad open daylight—Lord Lord Lord!

"Turn me loose, man! Turn me loose!" Struggling with an anger and fright and strength hitherto unknown to her. She looked desperately around her—not a soul in sight, but two great big old alley cats on top of a garbage can.

Nicely dressed, middle-aged white man with brown squinting eyes, mixed with whiskey-red. He mumbled to himself as he grabbed her plump buttocks. And he wouldn't let her go. Scared

4

crazy with her heart in her mouth and blood flowing in the well of her stomach. Greatgodalmighty! She kicked him on his shins, she kneed him in his groin, but he wouldn't turn her loose.

"Turn me loose!"

His hand found her young breasts, a recently developed wonder to her. He squeezed them till they hurt. "Come on, yaller bitch, you got something good and I know it. Ain't no needer keeping it to yourself." Grabbing at her skirt and fumbling at his fly.

She could hear other voices now. "Damn I reckin—Thassa fiery little nigger heffer."

"She sure is pretty."

"Leave her lone, Mr. Hill, you old no-good hound."

Breathing and snorting in her face and on her neck and her ears. His breath smelled like whiskey puke. *Upped her skirt and peed on her thighs!*

She raked her fingernails down his long scrawny face, drawing his blood, and she sunk her teeth deep into his arm, and she got away from him. Jesus Have Mercy, she got away!

"Goddamn no-good nigger bitch! Come back here. Doncha run from me." She heard crackers laughing till she turned the corner.

Running and crying most of the way home—Through the heart of Crackertown, across the railroad track and through Tucker's Field, she reached Colored town. She stopped running and crying, and she leaned against an evergreen tree, and she looked at the shanties scattered over the valley, but her eyes saw nothing.

"What's the matter, Laurie Lee?"

"Nothing, Miss Susie. I'm all right, I thank you."

Somehow she straightened up just before she reached the house, because she didn't want the folks to know; wanted nobody in the whole wide world to hear about it. Sneaked around the side of the house and into the woodshed. She looked hard at the axe. She should chop off her legs. Whack them off clean up to her belly. A sharp chill ran across her shoulders and down her back. She stripped off her clothes, and she got into a washtub full of water, and she scrubbed the skin off her young brown body with washing powder and lye soap. Her legs and her thighs were on fire. Standing in the tub now, naked and trembling. One thing sure, she wouldn't tell the folks.

Later that evening after the chickens got quiet and a little old unexpected breeze got busy and stirring, she sat on the back porch listening to her Mama and her Big Mama talk. Looking straight into Big Mama's mouth like she usually did. Big Mama doing most of the talking. "You listen to these-shere rich white folks, honey, talking about slavery was a good thing —talking about good-hearted marsters. Won' no sicha thing. I done told you that a million times. If a marster was good, he wouldna had no slaves—he'da sot em all free. Crackers always talking about the slaves cried when Marster Lincoln sot us free. We cried all right, honey. Aah Lord—we cried. Won' a Negro's eyes dry that time. We cried for joy and shouted hallelujah." She glanced down at Laurie Lee and she rocked back and forth, singing to herself:

> *Free at last....*
> *Free at last....*
> *Thank Godamighty*
> *I'm free at last....*

Listening to Big Mama, Laurie Lee felt like she was being lifted upon a great silvery cloud, going higher and higher, sailing around and around and higher and higher towards a bright purple moon—Big Mama stopped singing and she laughed that short dry laugh of hers and she looked down at Laurie. "Aah Lord, doll baby, all this time and we ain't free yet." Suddenly, all that had happened to Laurie Lee in the alley that day came back to her, the evil old white man and everything else. Her bosom became heavy and her face filled up and she turned her head—didn't want to let on.

"What's the matter, doll baby?" Big Mama asked her.

She started to say, nothing Big Mama, but her voice choked off and her eyes filled up and she couldn't hold it back. Steamed up and boiling right over. Telling it now, bit by bit, then fast and fiercely, pouring it angrily out of her system.

There was a pitiful scared look in her mother's eyes, anxious and terrifying, as she begged and pleaded with the girl—"Don't say nothing to your Papa about it, please, sugar pie. Do, he'll go outer here and get himself kilt, sure as gun's iron!"

Laurie Lee looked up at her slavery-time grandmother, as she sat in her rocker, with her wrinkled-up face drawn tight towards the going-down sun, with those deep-dark, at-the-present-time, completely black eyes. Talking between puffs on

her corn cob pipe. Speaking with a calmness, nurtured painfully in hatred and meanness and born-in-slavery militance.
"Donchoo cry, honey," she said, as she rubbed Laurie Lee's
shoulders with her rough bony hands. "Git mad, yes Godamighty,
but donchoo waste a single tear. Crying all the time don't do a
damn bitter good."

She puffed twice on her pipe, watched the gray smoke, her
eyes almost closing. "Hit's always been thataway, doll baby.
Aah Lord, honey, goddammit—Crackers make way with the
black women folks, and black man bet not even now say a
mumbling word!"

Laurie Lee looked sideways up into Mama's eyes, desperate,
wide and pitiful. Mama—Mama—Mama! She looked up at Big
Mama, felt the strength from the old woman flow into her
young body. She got up and walked through the kitchen into
the big room, and she cried no more.

NINETEEN TWELVE WAS A YEAR AND A HALF—A
COW AND A CALF. It was the year that white men came to
the house and took her piano away, while Big Mama cussed.
And it didn't matter that Mama went around all day long
shaking her head in a helpless fashion, or that Big Mama kept
telling Laurie Lee, Donchoo cry honey, or that Papa was mean
and cross with everybody for over a week, the piano was gone
and it stayed gone. Laurie Lee felt like dying, but she felt like
living, and she kept on living, 'cause it was better than dying.

Laurie Lee got a job that summer working for old Lady
Tucker over in Radcliffe Heights. Taking care of her little old
eight year old girl. It was a real hot summer, burning up, and
old Lady Tucker was fat in the stomach, just as big as a house.

"Laurie Lee—ee—"

Laurie was in the great big beautiful kitchen feeding the
white child and also getting something to eat for herself. What
did that contrary old white woman want this time? Laurie
Lee this and Laurie Lee that—

"You Laurie Lee—ee—ee—"

She could hear Mrs. Tucker coming down the stairs and
shuffling through the hall. Well let her come. Laurie Lee wasn't
going to be running up and down those stairs every time Mrs.
Tucker had an urge to call her. Bring me this and take care of
that—

"Laurie Lee, didn't you hear me calling you?"

Laurie looked up from the plate, stared the white woman straight in the face, then looked brazenly and contemptuously at her big fat belly. Mrs. Tucker changed colors from white to red. She used to be slender and pretty, but lately her stomach hung down and poked out terribly, and her eyes carried great big double rings around them.

"No mam, Miss Sarah, I didn't hear nothing."

"You must be deaf. Need to wash out your ears."

"Yes, mam."

The white woman's eyes roved around the big kitchen, rested on the little white girl, then roved some more, and back to Laurie Lee. "Laurie Lee, you know Becky, I mean Rebecca, she *is* getting to be a mighty big girl." She paused, catching her breath, waiting for Laurie to express agreement, but the girl said nothing, just kept on looking straight at Mrs. Tucker.

"What I mean is, Laurie Lee, it doesn't look right for you to be calling her Becky and she getting to be a young Miss already." White woman cleared her throat.

Laurie Lee cut her eyes over at the little gray-eyed girl, who kept on eating. "She ain't that big, Miss Sarah."

"What I mean is, don't you think you ought to be calling her Miss Rebecca, instead of keep on calling her Becky like you do?"

"No, mam, I don't see it thataway at all."

White woman sighed heavily and breathed deeply, her fat stomach going in and out like an old dog sleeping. She wished the girl would cooperate. It was so darn hot. "How come, Laurie Lee?"

"She isn't nearbout big as I am. Don't see how come I got to be *Missing* her."

"But—but—but you work for her."

"She don't pay me no wages."

Sarah Tucker wiped the sweat from her brow. "Well, Mr. Tucker and I discussed it last night, and we decided that you start calling our big beautiful girl *Miss* Rebecca. That's all there is to it."

Laurie Lee's nose popped out with sweat, as she looked at the sloppy white woman and away again. "I hate that about you," she muttered to the woman.

"What did I hear you say?" The woman shuffled towards her.

"I said I hate that about you. That's what I said. Thinking

I'm going to be calling a little pee-behind white gal *Miss,* you got another thought coming." She stood wide-legged and defiant. Scared, mean and desperate.

Miss Sarah grabbed her by the shoulders. "You *going* to call her Miss Rebecca," she screamed, "you sassy little nigger!" Shaking Laurie Lee by the shoulders now.

Laurie Lee pulled away from the white woman, but the woman stood between her and the door. Laurie's voice trembled. "Don't you shake me," she said. "My Mama don't do that to me."

Miss Sarah picked up the broom leaning against the wall. "Teach you a lesson." She struck Laurie Lee on the side of the head. "You *going* to call her Miss Rebecca. I'm going to tell Mr. Tucker. . . ."

The girl backed up. Red hot all over and covered with sweat. Head going around like a flying jenny. "I hate that hole in your dirty old drawers. Tell Mr. Tucker—You—you better tell Mr. Tucker stop trying to pat me on my behind. I—I'm too big for that . . ." She was ready for anything. The big wide beautiful kitchen was little and stuffy now, and Laurie wanted room and breathing space. The sharp sweaty odor of the white woman surrounded her. Let me out! Let me out!

Miss Sarah let out a gasp and crowded in on Laurie Lee. "Don't you say that about Mr. Tucker! Don't you dare!" Swinging the broom wildly, she hemmed Laurie Lee up in a corner. "Sassy little nigger!" *Swish—Swish* on the head—on the legs—on the shoulders—"Sassy little nigger!"

"Sassy little nig—" Laurie ducked under the broom and closed her eyes and rammed her fist deep into Miss Sarah's stomach. The white woman yelled and fell out on the floor, and the gray-eyed girl opened her pretty mouth and screamed. Laurie ran out of the kitchen through the hall and down the front steps and all the way home.

Mama gave her a good whipping, because she shouldn't have struck the white woman like that in the stomach, knowing she was big and going to have a baby. Took Laurie out in the woodshed to keep Big Mama from interfering. Big Mama broke the door down. Wrestling with Mama all over the woodshed.

"Don' whup that child! Stop whupping that child! Ain' done nuthing wrong. She jes shoulda kilt that evil old bitch!"

That night Big Mama got Laurie Lee off to herself in the

kitchen, with the rest of the folks out on the front porch, and she told Laurie Lee—"Honey, don' choo never let em walk over you—don' choo do it—Fight em, honey—Fight em every inch of the way, especially the big rich ones—like—like them Tuckers. They the one took over where ol' marster left off. They lynch us, they starve us and they work us to death, and it ain-na gonna change till you young Negroes gits together and beat some sense in they heads. So fight em, sugar pie. Aah Lordy, honey."

Laurie looked past the kerosene lamp across the table where Big Mama sat. Her eyelashes blinked as a chill went across her round girlish shoulders. An old candle-fly went around and around the lamp chimney, flapping his dusty wings.

"That's right, honey. Don' choo pay your Mama no never mind. And another thing, baby doll, all this crying and praying and shouting and who-shot-John—Ain' none of it gon change these white folks' heart—they don't believe in it nohow."

NINETEEN TWELVE WAS SOMETHING ELSE AGAIN —Mama died towards the end of the year and Big Mama passed four months following. Big Mama Big Mama Big Mama! The sweet hated smell of death in Laurie's nostrils. Standing in that lonely death-kissed room, smelling those flowers that Big Mama couldn't smell. Big Mama's eyes, those dark-black eyes, staring at her through death-sealed lids, lying there in that dark-gray casket, Laurie saw her part her colorless swollen lips and heard her speak in that strong young-folks voice of hers—"Doncha cry, honey. Don' choo waste a single tear!" And she tried not to cry, awfully hard, but she just couldn't help it. Feeling Miss Susie's arm around her shoulders. "Don' cry no more, pretty thing. She ain' dead. She jes gone away on a little short journey. Gone to that land where she never grow old."

Year after next Laurie Lee's brother, Tim, went to the reformatory for rockbattling white boys and breaking old man McWhorter's window. They kept him there for two whole years, and when he came out he was as mean as a bull dog. Tim Barksdale had been the nicest sweetest boy in the world before that reformatory got hold of him. Friendly and shamefaced and so tenderhearted, he couldn't even wring off the neck of a frying-sized chicken. The only boy in Tipkin that wouldn't tie a string to an old ugly juney bug and listen to him zoon. Laurie Lee never would forget the time one summer when she and her baby sister,

Bertie, and Tim had spent a couple of weeks down in the country with Uncle Leo and Aunt Jenny Mae—

One July Saturday morning, Uncle Leo had gotten up early and said—"What we gon have for breakfast this morning?—Let's have one them nice frying chickens"—He started to sing some funny words to an old church tune: "There's not a friend like a frying-size chicken——GLORY TO HIS NAME——GLORY TO HIS NAME——PRECIOUS NAME———"

Tim laughed at Uncle Leo and said, "That's just what the doctor ordered." He had grown into a nice looking boy, long and slim, and all the girls liked him.

Uncle Leo said, "All right, boy, let's me and you take care of breakfast for a change. You kill the chicken and I'll fry that scound. Show these womenfolks how to cook. They think they so tight when it come to the kitchen. Just go out in the chicken yard and pick out any one of them fryers you want—git the prettiest in the bunch and wring that scound's neck clean off."

Tim said, "All right Uncle Leo." And Bertie and Laurie Lee heard him and they giggled to themselves because they knew Tim had never killed a chicken in all his life. Tim went out into the chicken yard. Aunt Jenny and Uncle Leo had all kinds of chicken.

Five minutes passed and Uncle Leo called out—"Got him ready, boy?"

Tim called back, "Not yet, Uncle Leo." A tremble in his voice.

"Alright, boy," Uncle Leo said, "Christmas is coming."

About five more minutes. "Got him ready, son?"

"Just a few more minutes, Uncle."

"What's the matter, boy—you got to hatch that chicken?" Uncle Leo came out on the back porch. The girls had been watching Tim from the window. They came out on the porch.

A nice-sized fryer popped out of Tim's frightened grasp and Tim chased him desperately, but unconvincingly, across the yard, sweat pouring from all over his body.

"What's the matter, Tim? Hem that fat rascal up and wring his neck off."

"Yessir." Tim followed the chicken and hemmed him up between a corner of the yard and a big fig tree. Chicken mess was all over the yard and Tim was trying to keep from stepping in it. He was the most nice-nasty boy in the whole wide world. He made a half-hearted lunge for the chicken and the young chicken jumped straight up in the air and yelled out loud, striking Tim in his breast, and poor Tim jumped back, giving the chicken just enough room to get by him and the chase was on all over again. Bertie and Laurie Lee were rolling all over the back porch laughing to beat the band.

Uncle Leo walked down the back steps. "What's the matter, boy—you scared of that chicken?"

"No——Sir——he——he——he just slipped by me that time." Tim caught up with the chicken again and this time he grabbed the chicken and held on desperately, both of their hearts beating a hundred miles an hour, his and the chicken's.

Laurie Lee had stopped laughing now, sympathizing with Tim.

"That's right, boy," Uncle Leo shouted, "now wring his neck off——ain't nothing to it——ought to have you down here during hog killing time——Greatgodamighty—"

Tim's face was blank, he looked like he would rather have been anywhere else in the world excepting that chicken yard. He held the poor chicken out at arm's length and his arm went around and around and around. "That's right, boy. That's what I'm talking about——you done killed him now——let him fall to the ground. I knew you could do it."

Tim let the chicken go and the chicken dropped to the ground and kicked around like a chicken with his neck wrung off and then he lay right still. Tim looked around, scared to death, and stooped to pick him up, and the chicken let out a cry and jumped and ran away and it was Tim and the chicken all over that yard. Tim never did kill that chicken or any other chicken. But the one thing Tim wasn't ever chicken-hearted about was white folks. Just as soon fight a white boy as to look at one. And that was what got him into all that trouble. Papa encouraged him in his meanness towards white folks, but Big Mama was the main one. She always told him: "Don't take no stuff offa 'em, Timmie. Not a damn drap." Everybody said that's what led him to the reformatory. And what happened to him in the reformatory? Greatgodalmighty they made that nice boy ugly and mean and heartless and don't-care, and when he got out he wouldn't listen to anybody.

When he came home he started running around with fast no-good women almost twice his own age, and when Papa got after him, he would cuss under his breath at Papa and tell him to mind his own damn business, and he would stay out all night long and some time come home two days later, and he and Papa would argue and shout at each other for hours at a time. But the one thing that stayed with Laurie Lee more than anything else was the time a big field rat jumped out of the wood box in the kitchen behind the stove and started brazenly across the kitchen floor, and Tim, who used to be so squeamish and nice-nasty, met the big rat in the middle of the floor and brought his foot down and stomped that rat, and stood there crushing him till the blood gushed out and his entrails oozed out over the floor. And Laurie ran out of the kitchen into the next room and passed out cold. When she came to herself, Tim laughed at her. "Since when did you get so chicken-hearted and high-toned? In the institution that was our favorite sport—rat squashing. Don't be for that we'da had to sleep with them bastards. I 'member one time a big old rat ran up a boy's pants leg named Yaller Joe. Old Yaller Joe caught that skeester just before he struck gold—way up his britches legs. He grabbed that rat away up on his thigh and he mashed that rat up against his thigh and he didn't turn him loose till he mashed him flat and the stuff ran down his legs into his shoes." Laurie lay on the bed holding her stomach, her head going around and around. "Get out of here Tim—Go away! Go away! Get out of my sight." But Tim just stood there laughing and jeering at her.

A few days later he ran away from home. Just up and left without saying a word. And nobody ever heard from him. With Mama and Big Mama gone on to Glory, there was nobody left at home but Papa and Bertie, Laurie's younger sister.

Laurie Lee graduated from high school in the tenth grade at the head of her class, and she made a big speech at the exercises. She surely had grown into a pretty young woman. She missed Mama and Big Mama more than ever at graduation time. Papa swore he was going to send her right on to college, and if he didn't there wasn't a cow in Texas, but he couldn't quite make it the very first year. He would send her the next year just as sure as you were born. She got a job teaching school right there in Johnson County. She was a darn good teacher, everybody said so, and the school children liked her.

On Sunday evenings the big boys hung around the house like flies around sugar. Some after Bertie, but most of them after the pretty little school teacher. Ray Morrison was the most persistent. He wouldn't be discouraged——didn't care what. He got further than the others, but he didn't get far. Then one day Ray upped and went off to war, and folks said Laurie had chased him away. She laughed at them and said, "Never mind." But she worried about it.

Joseph (No Middle Name) Youngblood was born in Glenville, Georgia, ninety miles from Tipkin on the Central Line, not even a whistle stop, on April Fools Day, and it rained all day long that day, but he never was anybody's fool. Never had any formal education to speak of, he graduated from the School of Hard Knocks. His Papa died when he was six years old, and his Mama passed when he was nine. His only relative, Uncle Rob, who really was his second cousin, told him when he was eleven years old, seated at the breakfast table on a bright September morning, the early-morning sun casting slicey shadows through the shingled roof—"Son, I hate to say it, Lord knows I do, but things is tough and money is sca'ce and times is tight and the old man ain't so sporty no more."

The soft-eyed black boy looked up in the old man's face, stared across the table through a transparent ladder of dusty rays of sunshine reaching from the roof to the table, and he didn't say anything.

Uncle Rob looked at the boy, and his old wrinkled eyes filled up, and the hairy, shapeless bush over his old mouth quivered. "What I mean is, boy, I want you to go fiward and git ahead, but——but——you know what I mean—"

The boy said, "Yessir." It was early in the morning, but hot already, a day no different from any other day.

The man blew his nose two or three times, because nothing was in it. Tried to look tough and stern with his eyes and his jaws. "Doggonnit, boy, you eat like a man . . . Eat us outa house and home . . . I'm telling you, son, just can't afford it . . . I'm right poorly 'long in now . . . 'bout to give up the ghost . . . School be opening fore long——What I mean you won't be going, cause you gotta go to work."

"Thatta be all right, Uncle Rob. I go to work. Get me a job most any old place."

Uncle Rob sucked his teeth and shook his head. "Old man Rickerson just saying yestiddy——Sure could use that boy in the field powerfully much. Need every hand wrestle with that cotton. Time he broke in good. What's the useter waiting? Like I always said————"

Joe Youngblood's face flushed hot and tight, almost giving him away, but it didn't, because his eyes remained quiet like they always did. He'd sooner die than work in old Man Rickerson's cotton field again. One white man whose guts he hated. His mind was traveling a mile a minute, but he didn't say a thing. Late that night long after the town had tucked in and gone completely to sleep, he tiptoed down the front steps, his heart in his mouth, and walked down that long dark lonesome road and the only light he had was the lightning bugs, and he never took a single look back at the one room, fresh-air shack he had shared with Uncle Rob. He hated to put Uncle Rob down, but he just couldn't help it.

He didn't forget Uncle Rob. He wrote to him three weeks later from Waycross, Georgia, sent a little money in the letter, but the letter came back unopened, because Uncle Rob had passed on. Joe sat down and wondered. There was no one left, not a chicken nor a child.

He lived in Waycross, Georgia, working sun-up to sundown, from one job to the next, even did a little sharecropping a few miles out of Waycross, but he hated that kind of work most of all. Grew strong and big and tall by the day. The collard greens and the black-eyed peas and the fat back seemed to stick to his ribs and spread into his shoulders and his arms and his chest, filling them out and the rest of his body. Went to church on Sunday, sang bass in the glee club, played baseball on Saturday afternoons, smiled at the girls and the girls smiled back, thinking he was older than he actually was.

When he was sixteen years old he met a man from Detroit, Michigan. A colored man who drove for a drummer. Met him one night in Hoot's Pool Room. Told Joe in a friendly kind of a way, thought he was talking to a full grown man—"Man, you ain't nothing but a sucker, and I don't mean maybe." Told him about the glories of the Promised Land, Up the Country, where freedom was natural fact, and a man was a man. Colored man get a job 'most any old place—any kind of a job.

And Joe just looked at the man quiet-like and said, "Is it sure 'nough?" A million thoughts running around in his head. Was there really such a place where a colored man could get any kind of a job? Could he ever go to that place?—Good Lord, would he ever?

The man looked at him unbelievingly and said in a kind of sing-song—"Well I done tole you all about it, and it's right there for you, and if you don't get it, it ain't no fault of mine."

And all Joe said was—"Is it, sure 'nough?" His mind was working a mile a minute but his face didn't show it. Plans jumping around in his head already. . . .

Joe dreamed about it and saved and scratched every penny without telling a living soul, because God wasn't exactly living. It was a Saturday afternoon around the last of September when a war was in the world, a great big war, and it was all Germany's fault, and President Wilson promised to keep us out of it, but Germany just wouldn't let us stay out, because she wanted us in, and it looked like we just had to make the world safe for democracy, and everywhere people felt patriotic and they sang that song—*Well I wish I was in Dixie—Look Away—Look Away*——Joe Youngblood walked up to the depot, strapping six feet-two inches, eighteen years old black man, with his clothes tied up in an old beat-up suitcase, his face and his body scrubbed till it hurt, money in his pocket for a ticket to Chicago and a little bit extra to tide him over.

Station Master looked friendly-like at Joe's serious face, smiled and said, "Whew—eee! Boy, you going so far you gon fall off the side of the world."

But Joe didn't crack a single smile.

The station master chuckled. "Boy, where you steal so much money from?"

But Joe didn't smile.

Looking out of the train window now at the fields of cotton and the fields of corn, leaving it behind—Greatgodalmighty! The tall pine trees and the shingled shacks, and the little out-houses with the burlap doors—leaving all that behind a mile a minute. The red clay hills and the country roads, winding and weaving, and the country towns and the big pretty houses and the little ugly houses and the red-faced crackers at the country stations, leaving all that behind, going north every minute, and a lump in his throat and a chill in his shoulders and a knot in his stomach. Feeling good-good-good. Leaning back in his seat in a jim crow coach, but not thinking hard about it being jim crow, because it was taking him up the country. Rocking and reeling and puffing and snorting and clackety clack. Good old, powerful old going-north train.

**16**

The fat man seated next to Joe wiped his face with a big red-and-blue handkerchief, looked out of the window and said to Joe—"In Tennessee now—Just crossed the line."

It seemed to Joe he could feel the difference, out of Georgia already. Proved he was going north. He felt excited like a young kid—Is it really you, Joe Youngblood? You old up-the-country fool. You really going up north? But all he said to the fat man beside him was—"Is we sure 'nough?"

The soot from the engine close by got all over him, in his face and his eyes, on his neck and his hands, blackened his clothes, but he really didn't mind. Joe was hot and sweat poured out of his head and all over his body. He felt dirty and sooty, but that was all right. A barefoot black woman stood in front of a one room shack with her baby in her arms. Both of them waved at the jim crow coach and Joe waved back, his eyes filling up watery-like, and he had never seen the woman before, and never would again, but somehow in the pit of his stomach and all through his shoulders she felt to him like a mother or an aunt or a long lost sister. He took a deep breath and closed his eyes in excited weariness, then peace and contentment, like going home at last and the next thing he knew the train was stopping and the porter was yelling Wayman, Tennessee. He thought he was dreaming as he looked out of the window and saw a bunch of white men coming toward the train with shotguns and rifles. He looked at the fat man next to him, whose eyes were wide and nervous now. Everybody else had worried looks on their faces and he knew he wasn't dreaming. The train slowed down to a nervous stop, started up again, jerked a few feet forward and stopped again, puffing and blowing. And the men kept coming towards the jim crow coach.

They boarded the coach from both ends, rifles and shotguns leveled, as Joe and his kind of people waited. A short, square-shouldered, heavy-set man with a handle-bar mustache was the leader of the bunch. He said, "All right all you niggers, git your stuff and git off. We got jobs for every one of you." Like he was saying to them have a drink of nice cold lemonade.

One Negro said, "But I ain't looking for no job, I'm visiting my folks."

"You wuz visiting your folks, but, boy, you ain't visiting your folks no more, lessen they live on Mr. Buck's plantation."

A couple of white men laughed. The rest were grim. Not

**17**

a Negro had moved. "All right," said the peck with the red mustache, friendly like. "Ain't no hard feelings lessen you boys want to make it like that."

A young Negro with glasses on, looked like a doctor, got up and walked over to the cracker. "Look," he said, "you got the wrong man. I'm not a southerner." Talked proper and straight, looked the cracker in the eye. "I'm on my way home to Chicago. I go to college." Didn't even say please sir.

Cracker looked at him like he had seen a ghost. Cracker batted his eyes, looked away for a moment. "That's what's the trouble, too many niggers going north already. Well, a little stop-over on Mr. Buck's plantation ain't gonna hurt none. Don't need no education nohow."

Joe sat still, face unmoved, everything tumbling down around him. Two whole years of corn bread and syrup, of hoping and conscious scheming, and dreaming and planning and stinching and going without—More than two years——Maybe a lifetime. He had had his doubts all along, but once he got on the train, he had thought that all he had to do was sit back and just ride his way to the Promised Land, never mind what he'd find when he got there. He was more angry than afraid, and wanted to take a stand alongside this nicely dressed Negro, say something, but he didn't know what to say; do something, but he didn't know what to do.

He felt good and strong, though frightened for the young Negro, who turned to the rest of the people in the coach and said—"Are you going to let them get away with this? After all we're American citi—"

The rifle went off. The explosion temporarily deafened Joe. The young Negro slumped down in the aisle, his right arm a shattered, bloody mass at the elbow. Joe jumped from his seat. The cracker with the mustache looked up at him. "See what I mean," he said to Joe, motioning with his rifle towards the young Negro. "Had to shoot one of the youngest and strongest bucks in the group. Won' no needer that neither." He turned to a couple of his men. "Git him offa here fore he bleed up the train. Won't no call for that at all, and Mr. Buck ain't gon like it. See how bad education is for niggers?"

Joe stood there in a silent, helpless, maddening rage, hating the other Negroes for not doing something and hating himself twice as much and double times again. Smothered with hate for this cracker till he could hardly breathe. The jaw muscles of his strong face flexing under the tautness of his black skin. His eyes still quiet except for little, angry crinkles in the corners. Sweat, sweat, sweat——everywhere sweat. Cracker looked at Joe, Joe looked at cracker. First time Joe ever looked at a cracker so straight in the eye. Cracker's eyes shifted.

He licked his mustache and prodded Joe with his rifle. "All right, Goddammit, all you niggers, let's git going."

Joe smiled as he always had a way of doing when he was really good and mad, and he laughed—*"Hingh"*—almost like a dry cough, and he swung his mighty fist, and the man went one way and his rifle the other. But even as the cracker fell he shouted, "Don't shoot that nigger. Mr. Buck won't like it. Just mess him up good fashion."

Fear had gone by now and Joe didn't give a good goddamn, and he swung his fist in every direction, but they cut him down like a strong, sturdy oak. They beat on his shoulders with their guns and rifles, on his head and about his body, till he didn't feel anything, and his knees buckled and they chopped him down, as the sunlight spilled in through the windows along with the smoke and the cinders, and some poor colored fool yelled police.

The lights came on slowly, but everywhere was dark. He opened his eyes. It was night and he wondered where he was— I up north already? Couldn't be on no train . . . Couldn't be up north, because the north is different, and there is something familiar about the way the floor creaks when I move my aching body, the way the moon peeps in through the shingled roof and the smattering of stars. Am I back with Uncle Rob? But Uncle Rob been dead a long time ago. Maybe I'm dead too . . . His body felt like it had been trampled on from head to foot, his shoulders pained like an aching tooth. Dead man couldn't feel. His face was numb. He tried to move his arm, but a pain knifed him so hard he groaned unconsciously. Where the hell was he? It even hurt him to think, but he couldn't help from thinking. Where the hell was he? He heard breathing over here and snoring over there, and the smell of too many people sleeping close together entered his nostrils. *Goddammit, where the hell am I?* Now the moonlight helped him, slivering through the roof and identifying a black face on this side of the shack and a brown face on the other and a body in the corner. Suddenly he

**19**

was vaguely concerned about a young Negro who was going up north to college, and it all came back to him. The train, the crackers with their guns, the young Negro on his way to college, the explosion, the shattered, bloody arm. And after that what happened? What happened?

He lay there thinking, hurting all over. Goddammit, if nothing had happened he would have been long gone by now. He would have been in Chicago already. He felt God or fate or whatever it was, with its long, claw-like fingers, tightening around his throat, cutting off his breath, like it had always done, choking off his life, his hope, his spirit, and he swore under his breath it wouldn't be like that. If only he had caught the train before that particular one, or the one right after. How come them peckerwoods had to pick on that particular train just because he happened to be on it? Wonder what happened to that Negro on his way to college—Sure talked up to them peckerwoods—From way off he heard the long drawn-out crow of a rooster and another one answer from close by. Another one, then another and another, separate and all together. Must be getting on towards morning. Got to think with a clear head, cause one thing sure, I ain't staying on no Mr. Buck's plantation—Onh-onh—I ain't coming. Got to keep a clear head——Got to——Got to——keep a clear head—— hurt—hurt—hurt——pain all over——clear——head—

Noise outside interrupted his thoughts. A flashlight dipped into the shack from one sleeping face to the other. Joe closed his eyes before it got to him. He heard a loud-mouthed cracker say—"Here's that *baaad* nigger. We git through with him his pee gon be like water. We sure got what it takes for a bad ass nigger." He was talking very loud, as if he knew everybody was playing possum. He was all dressed up like a cowboy picture with a black and white holster and gleaming gun.

"All right, all you niggers," he sang out, nudging Joe in the side with his big heavy boot. "All you monkeys—Git up and piss on the rock—it ain' quite day——But it's four o'clock —" Cracker laughed to himself. "Damn sure is one ugly bunch of monkeys, I swan. Smell like billy goats." And the peckerwood laughed again.

"Come on in here, Jim," the cracker called out, "and give these monkeys somethinteat. Goddamn they ugly."

A short, stocky Negro with a narrow mouse-like face came

in the shack with a kerosene lantern. He went out and came back in again with a pot of hominy grits and a pan of corn bread. Then he brought in tin plates and dropped them on the floor. Meanwhile the cracker stood playing with his flashlight, blinking it off and on, throwing its glare from face to face while the angry men grumbled underneath their breaths. Joe's body was so full of pain he could hardly move. He managed to get his right hand up to his face, felt the caked-up blood on the side of his head. He wasn't gonna stay in this goddamn place—guarantee anybody.

"All right, you nigger, quit assing around and git that slop down your craw. You ain't in Atlanta at the Biltmore, goddammit, we got work to do."

Every day except Sunday they went out into the cotton fields, while the rooster still crowed and the old dogs howled and before the day broke, with a stomach full of corn bread and hominy grits and worked and sweated till the sun went down and the chickens had gone to bed. On the ninth day during lunch, Joe sat his pan down and started walking, saying nothing to anybody. He walked about a mile past fields of cotton and fields of corn, row upon row of them, wave after wave, acre after acre, everywhere he looked. Where the hell did old man Buck's plantation end? He walked on further till he saw a big iron gate and he started out of it.

"Hey, you, old nigger, where you think you going?" It was the medium sized man with the handle-bar mustache. Where did these crackers get so many guns? Thought the goddamn war was in Europe.

"Just looking around."

"What you looking for?"

"Nothing particular."

"Git your black ass back to work."

Joe muttered to himself, "You got everything right now, Mr. Charlie. Got the world in a jug, got the stopper in your hand. But my day's coming."

That evening when they knocked off work, they took him and they beat him in front of the other Negroes. Cut his back up like raw hamburger, chopped him down to the ground with a long buggy whip, and he didn't say a mumbling word. They dragged him to the shack, blood pouring from his back, and they dumped him in. Late that night about one o'clock, when everybody was asleep, he dragged himself out of the shack, straightened his battered body up, and he walked till daybreak, thinking while he walked . . . looking back at his own life which had not been anybody's bed of roses.

A hard life—hard work—Everything hard——hard. Thinking as the sun rose higher and he left the dusty highway and took to the woods, that he would volunteer for the army, if they were taking colored men. What the hell—he didn't have nothing to hold him back, not a chicken nor a child—Damn good idea——Make the world safe for democracy——Wonder how you went about it? He walked past cotton fields and corn fields and tobacco, rolling far and wide, as if the entire world were made of cotton and corn and tobacco, a beautiful world to look at. Walked till he was weak from hunger and his legs gave out, his shirt all sweaty and sticking to the blood caked up on his back. Shoulda brought some of them other Negroes with me from old man Buck's plantation. Should have talked it over with them, but what the hell would I'da said. He dropped right where he was—Shoulda brought some of them with me . . . Shoulda talked them into it . . . Gotta learn how to talk to people . . . Went right down to his knees and stretched his great body out on the grass and slept till morning and the sun shone on him.

He sat up and blinked his eyes and rubbed them with his knuckles, becoming awake gradually, hurting so bad he could hardly move. He looked all around him at the trees and the fields, and the dew-kissed grass gleaming in the sunshine, his face and arms wet from the dew. How about going into the *man's* army? Make the world safe for democracy, make the whole wide world safe for democracy—that's all that old cracker he used to work for in Waycross talked about. He could see him now, with his toothless grin and his evil blue eyes. Bald headed old bastard. Make the world safe for democracy—Well to hell with that bullshit. I ain't coming—unh—unh. I ain't got no democracy to make the world safe for, no-damn-how. He got to his feet, walked to the next town, caught a freight back to Georgia and settled in Crossroads.

It was 1918 when Laurie Lee Barksdale met Joe Young-blood, the first Saturday in May at a big church picnic. Big-city man from Crossroads, Georgia. Big powerful black hand-

**22**

some man with soft quiet eyes. It was as hot as any day in the middle of August. A few snowy clouds drifting in a big blue sky, sun shining everywhere. Clean and clear and Sundayish looking.

First time she noticed him was at the baseball game. When he came to bat, he stood there at the plate as cool as a cucumber, wide-stanced and pigeon-toed, and he hit that ball a country mile, way up into the big blue sky and far and wide and away over yonder. When he wasn't at bat or playing in the field, he would stand off and seem to be thinking to himself, but every now and then she would catch him looking at her, halfway smiling to himself, and she would feel funny and steal glances at him when he wasn't looking. The other men on his team would come over to him and say something to him or ask him something, and he would say something but he wouldn't say much. He was a part of the team but he seemed stand-offish. He was the biggest in the bunch, and somehow she sensed his tremendous power.

The people yelled themselves hoarse when he came to bat, and they clapped their hands and waved their arms.

And groups of people from Crossroads, Georgia, shouted at him—"Come on, Joe Youngblood! You got the business!"

And—"Crossroads can' lose—For the stuff we use!" And— "Tipkin can' win—For the shape they in!"

Some of them got together and sang at the top of their voices:

> *Joe Youngblood gon shine tonight . . .*
> *Joe Youngblood gon shine . . .*
> *Joe Youngblood gon shine tonight . . .*
> *Out on the line. . . .*
> *When the moon comes up . . .*
> *And the sun goes down . . .*
> *Joe Youngblood gon shine. . . .*

Everybody talking about Joe Youngblood.

Laurie just couldn't keep her eyes off Joe. He was a big strong sturdy oak tree way up above the rest of the forest. As she watched this man, this stranger to her, her heartbeat quickened, her face grew warm, her mouth tasted different. He stirred her soul. Hundreds of men, women and children laughing and talking and playing all around her. . . .

Later in the afternoon they had glee club singing. The boys

from Crossroads won the glee club contest. Joe sang bass. Great big thundering powerful bass. All the while stealing glances at Laurie, upsetting her poise.

Laurie had not intended to go to the dance that night, but she reckoned she might as well go along with Bertie. No need of acting stuck-up like she thought she was better than anybody else. Everybody was there, including Joe Youngblood. It was hot and close and nobody felt like dancing, but everybody danced except Joe Youngblood. He just stood around looking important, like he was sweet on himself, as Laurie imagined he was. Watching the man play the piano and stealing glances at Laurie, keeping time with the music with his great big feet, and talking and laughing with people when they came up to him.

About middle ways the dance he got up his courage, walked over to where she was standing and held out his hand, didn't open his mouth. She looked up into his soft dark eyes and away again.

"Sorry," she said. "I'm saving this dance for somebody else. He just went to get me some lemonade."

Joe mumbled something and turned away.

Her narrow eyes flickered. Her nose perspired. She grabbed his arm. "All right," she said, "he can wait till we finish. Lemonade won't spoil."

Joe was a smooth dancer, but he was so darn quiet. There was a soft sweet smell of corn likker on his breath, but she didn't mind a bit, although she knew she should have. He danced the next round with her and the next round and the next, till they both got hot and burning up and their legs got tired, but they kept on dancing. She never did go back for her lemonade. A scandalous shame.

Poorly-lit hall, feet scraping over splintery floor, old piano going bomalama bomalama, couple of hundred people dancing and sweating. Eyebrows raising—Look at Laurie Lee—Look at Miss Laurie—unh—unh—Who woulda thunk it?—Well I do declare—Every now and then she would glance up into his calm quiet face, painfully conscious of herself in his arms and their bodies close together from head to feet and the size of this man in contrast to her own little five-feet three. Swaying together this way and that. Stupid—silly—ridiculous—Making a fool out of herself in front of everybody—What did she know about this man? That he was a good baseball player, that he was a smooth dancer, that she felt excitingly comfortable in his arms, that he gave her a sense of tremendous power, stirring her depths, exciting her bosom. The nearness of his body—the nearness of his body—the rhythm of the dance—What did she know about this great big powerful calm-looking black man? Hardly his name. . . .

They walked together to her house that night up the long dusty road with trees and fields on both sides of them and crickets jabbering and an old locust moaning and lightning bugs blinking, saying very little to each other, but thinking so hard you could almost hear them. They stood on her front porch, the black night all around them. It had cooled off a little, and the old dog was stirring around in the backyard. A brand new quarter moon shone silvery and lonesome-like through a big fig tree.

She didn't want to say goodnight. "I had a good time, Joe. A very lovely time."

"Me too, Miss Laurie." Big, soft, beautiful eyes looking every whichaway. Big, strong, powerful, baby-faced-looking man. He was the quietest young man she had ever met.

"Don't call me *Miss* Laurie."

"Yes, mam." Fumbling with his cap in his hand like one of the big boys in her school. Tissue paper inside of his brand new cap sounded like somebody eating salted soda crackers. His feet toed inward and pawing the porch. . . .

She laughed at him lightly, didn't feel like laughing. "When you coming back to visit our little old town?" Saying the words flippantly, making a joke about it.

Joe looked at her and away again. Greatgodamighty, they had danced and danced and danced, and he could have danced all night long with her. She was just a little biddy armful to Joe Youngblood—a pretty little armful—with beautiful narrow slanting eyes that seemed to know everything, and they looked straight through him when he wasn't looking, and black heavy hair beginning high on her forehead, and the prettiest curviest mouth he had ever laid eyes on. She wasn't bigger than a minute but she was stacked up solid and well put together.

He turned his cap around and around. "Next year I reckin —when the picnic is."

"You going to wait so long?" Never felt this way about a man before. The taste in her mouth, the fullness, the warmth like never before. But she knew it didn't mean anything, because he wasn't her type.

His feet toed in worse than ever. "Ain't got nobody to come to see in Tipkin."

"Oh," she said, "so the town too little for you and the folks too country."

"No'm. No, mam, you know it ain't that."

"You can come and visit us then." Ashamed of her own self for being so forward.

"Can I sure 'nough? I mean I sure be glad to." And she knew that he meant it.

"Goodnight, Joe. Look to see you soon." She held out her hand and took his limp one, and she squeezed it hard and he squeezed hers harder.

He cleared his throat. "How about next Saturday night?" An anxious note in his deep rumbling voice, making a great big lie out of the calm in his eyes.

She said, "That would be just fine."

He came to see her every Saturday and sometimes on Sunday. He had to quit the baseball team because it only played on Saturday afternoons. She didn't want to take him seriously at first. He wasn't educated, didn't have any polish. Just a hard-working man. She had no idea he would be so persistent. She didn't know Joe Youngblood. Sometimes they would be sitting around talking, and she would catch herself correcting his English, trying to polish him up, and he would draw himself inward and stop talking to her. She came to appreciate his unaffected dignity, fierce and proud. And after she got to know him better, she learned of the things that happened to him in his young life, jam-crammed-full. She became familiar with his solid power, his stubborn ways. He reminded her of Big Mama. He wasn't talkative like Big Mama—but there was something about him. Something big and fierce like a keg of dynamite inside of him, and his mother-wit that no amount of education could take the place of. She was in deep deep water before she knew it. Subtle, powerful, unsuspected, he slipped up on her.

Sometimes he would take her by surprise and break out in a rash of conversation, and she couldn't stop him even if she wanted to and the stories he would tell her about himself made her blood run cold. But these times were few and far between.

**26**

Her old man liked Joe from the very start. But that didn't mean he was ready to hand his favorite child over to Joe or to anybody else. No-sir-ree-bob. He liked Joe as a man, crazy about him, but not as a son-in-law, past, present or future. Dale Barksdale didn't think there was a man living on God's green earth good enough for his Laurie Lee. But that didn't stop Joe Youngblood a single minute.

Because Joe was as stubborn as a Georgia mule and he never was as slow, or even as quiet as he seemed to be. He was like greased lightning. Once he got started, Laurie didn't have a chance. He took Dale's daughter, the pride of Tipkin, clean away from him and made him like it. They got married in October, and he took her to live in Crossroads, Georgia. People in Tipkin just shook their heads.

## CHAPTER TWO

CROSSROADS, GEORGIA IN the United States of North America. Great big sign down near the Terminal Station says: CROSSROADS, GEORGIA, IS THE CROSSROADS OF THE U.S.A.—Signed GEORGE CROSS, SR.

Few people outside of Georgia ever heard of the place, but it's on the map. And it has a pretty big Terminal Station. The Southbound Rocket stops there every day the Good Lord sends, and that's really something. Crossroads is what you might call a mill town. Eight large factories and a whole heap of small ones. The Courthouse and the County Jail combined stand smack in the middle of town, the biggest building in Crossroads. Right across the street is the white Post Office. That's a pretty big building too. A block down the street is the Opera House, where the first-run moving pictures show every day except Sunday, and the colored folks sit way upstairs in the second balcony. And three blocks away on Oglethorpe Street two big hotels stand, looking each other over, reaching up towards the sky like the beautiful white Courthouse. The streets are paved in this section of town, the downtown district. The pavement runs uphill for several blocks past the big proud handsome tradition-bound mansions with the great massive columns and the perfectly kept grounds, which are more like campuses than residential lawns. So smooth and spacious and pretty and green and inviting and forbidding, shaded by tall and stout and biggedy-looking oak trees.

Then abruptly Jefferson Davis Boulevard levels off, as the pavement ceases suddenly, and the dust and dirt begin and the red clay of Georgia, along with the little white houses of Pecker-wood Town, row upon row of them, all alike, running for more than a half a mile and pulling up short as they meet the nondescript houses of Pleasant Grove. This is Colored Town. The houses here have many colors. Some no color at all.

The Youngbloods lived in Pleasant Grove in Crossroads, Georgia. Ten months after they got married a little girl was born. They named her Jenny Lee, and some colored people signified counting the months on their fingers and grinning on the sly. She was a pretty little skinny old thing with great big shiny eyes, and Joe Youngblood didn't say much about it, but he hoped to himself that they would have a boy on the next go-round and he would have a little meat on his bones. About a year later he got his wish—half of it anyhow. A boy was born and they named him Robert after poor Uncle Rob. But the boy was just as skinny and puny as the days were long, and sickly as the devil. Didn't have any appetite at all. Joe and Laurie Lee worried about him.

The Youngbloods lived in a two room business like most of the other colored folks in Pleasant Grove. The front room was the sitting room for everybody and the bedroom for Joe and Laurie Lee. The back room was the kitchen and also served as bedroom for Jenny Lee and Robby. Jenny Lee slept in a big iron bed and Robby on a pallet. It wasn't much of a house, but yet and still, it was better than the shacks out in Rocking-ham Quarters, which was the only other place in town where colored folks stayed outside of Pleasant Grove, except Monroe Terrace where the well-to-do colored folks lived. At least in Pleasant Grove folks had toilets attached to the side of the houses with running water too. While out in Rockingham Quarters, people were lucky to have outhouse privies.

The girl grew long and skinny and the boy stayed short and thin and sickly. Folks called him Peewee. He wouldn't hardly eat anything at all till he was a little past five years old and then he started to eat everything that wouldn't bite him back. He began to eat all the grits and black-eyed peas and corn bread and snap beans and rice, and sometimes biscuits and syrup, that he could get hold of. And after eating he would strut around the table demanding everybody feel his tight stomach. But Jenny Lee, Big Sister Youngblood, never was a good eater and never would be.

Joe worked at the mills from early till late and came home later, and bringing up the children was Laurie's job. Working in the white folks' houses sometimes, cooking and maiding and general cleaning, staying at home washing white folks' clothes, sewing for white folks, it didn't matter. She still had the job of the family washing and keeping house and caring for the children, watching them grow. Answering questions they were always asking, especially Robby. Mama, what makes a rainbow? Where does the rain come from? How big is the world? Mama, what makes the crackers so mean to us colored folks? Sometimes she would answer and answer, till she got tired and then she would say in a sing-song: *Ask me no questions—Tell you no lies— Give me some pumpkins—Bake you some pies—*And the children would laugh.

One evening after school Robby and Jenny Lee were seated in the front room doing their homework and Laurie was sewing up a tear in Robby's trousers on the sewing machine. There was a sleepy looking fire in the fireplace throwing soft jittery shadows on the big oak bed in the corner and the bare floor scrubbed colorless, and on the center table and Laurie Lee's back, even dancing now and then on the boy's brown face. Robby was a goodlooking curly-haired boy and mighty big for his seven years, especially since he had been such a puny baby. His curly mouth and his high wide forehead were just like his mother's. He looked up from the book in his lap and watched in silence the fire-cast shadows on Mama's back. "Mama, how you know so much about everything?"

"I don't know everything, boy. A long ways from it."

"But how you know so much?"

"You—you learn from school. That's why you go to school. Most things you learn from experience, I reckin."

"Experience, Mama?"

"From life—from living. Remember that old pot-belly stove we used to have in here? Remember how red-hot it used to get? Especially in the winter time. When you were a little boy you would get out of the tub buck naked after taking a bath and back up so close you would burn your behind every time, till you finally learned not to stand so close. Me and your Daddy used to tell you not to stand so close, but you had to learn the hard way—from experience. And that's how most people learn, I reckin."

"I'm going to read a whole heap of books, Mama," Robby said seriously and Jenny Lee laughed. Robby said, "How much do you know, Mama? Tell us everything."

"I know both of you better get them school lessons, else I'm going to give you some more experience right on both of y'all's behinds."

Robby and Big Sister laughed. Big Sister said, "Mama—uh, Mama—" Mama made a funny face. "Mama this and Mama that—Going to change my name to Jimmy John." And the children laughed and Mama did too.

CROSS MILLS INCORPORATED BEAT HELL OUT OF Joe Youngblood, and Joe Youngblood tried to beat the hell out of Cross Mills, Incorporated, single-handed in self-defense. It sure was one hell of a fight.

When he turned twenty-one he got a job in one of the big turpentine stills, handling those great big barrels of turpentine from sun-up to sundown. He worked hard and steady, but he didn't like to take any stuff off any man—black or white. His foreman was a hateful old cracker, that didn't do anything all day long but go from place to place putting his two cents in, giving stupid advice and telling everybody how to do their work. Joe Youngblood didn't like him.

One hot day in the middle of June, Joe was working with Joshua Rayfield and Mr. Pete came by. Mr. Pete was a pretty big fellow with a fat ugly stomach, looked like he was always pregnant and fixing to drop a baby any minute. He stood around watching the two Negroes wrestling with the big heavy drums. The old cracker wiped his face with a big colored handkerchief.

He took a deep breath and wiped his face again. "Why you boys don't sing while you work? Make it much more easier."

They didn't say a word, didn't even turn around, kept right on working. They were stripped to the waist, and the sweat on their black backs glistened in the midday sun. Cracker looked up at the sky, shaded his eyes from the sun, stuck his fat nose in the air and sucked in the sharp sweet smell of fresh sticky turpentine. He beat the ground with a big black stick.

"Why don't you boys sing while you work?" Mr. Pete repeated.

And Joe gave his partner a quick knowing look. Josh's eyes fluttered nervously as he looked the other way.

Mr. Pete pressed his thin lips together and his blue eyes darkened. "Singing is a big help. Give rhythm to your work."

The men said nothing. Their faces were grim and drenched with sweat.

"That ain't no way to tote no barrel. One of you should—" A fly lit on his big pimply nose. He waved it away, forgot what he was going to say. "Uh—ah—uh—"

When they put the barrel down, Mr. Pete was right on their heels. Joe was madder than an old rattlesnake. Day in and day out, from week to week, and year to year, the same old thing. He had taken about as much as he could stomach from this old cracker. Joe was a quiet man ordinarily, didn't have much to say, but don't let that quiet fool you, and don't get him started. Heat and anger moved around in his hot face like something alive.

Joe turned to Josh and said in that soft booming bass of his, "Josh Rayfield, you got more nerve than a brass-ass monkey. Standing around all day long in people's way, not doing a goddamn thing but giving orders—making crazy suggestions. You don't like the way I work, do it your own goddamn self."

Josh looked Joe full in the face, searching desperately for something. There wasn't the trace of a smile on either of their faces. Mr. Pete's face turned red like he had been drinking some of that bad Georgia corn. He backed up a little, but he didn't go anywhere.

"Tell you right now," Joe continued, "I don't like for no sonofabitch standing over me while I work. I ain't no slave. Just tell me what you want me to do, then go on about your goddamn business."

Mr. Pete cleared his throat, beat the ground furiously with his big black stick.

Joe shook his finger in Josh's face. "Be something else if you was working along with me, but you don't do nothing all day long but meddle in this and that and stick your big fat ugly nose in the other."

Pete Donovan cleared his throat again. Josh Rayfield just

looked at Joe, didn't utter a sound, scared of the quiet calmness in Joe Youngblood's voice and in his face, didn't know whether to smile or look serious. His light brown eyes were opened wide, asking questions. He was caught in a trap and didn't know how to get out.

Joe kept talking in a soft even cadence. "Be something else if you was talking something had some sense to it. Just run off at the mouth all day long and never say a goddamn thing. Most stupidest joker I ever did see—Crazy sap-sucker."

Peter Donovan's bulbous face was on fire with anger. "Watch your language, ol' nigger."

Joe turned around and looked at the cracker, an ominous smile on his smooth black face, but Mr. Pete misunderstood Joe Youngblood's smile. "How you, Mr. Pete? Didn't hear you walk up. Didn't know you was around—Swear to goodness. Josh, how come you didn't tell me Mr. Pete was here?"

Josh said nothing; his eyelashes flickered.

"You one nigger too smart for your own good," Mr. Pete insisted.

"What's the matter, Mr. Pete?"

His big fat stomach went in and out like a pregnant woman in the very last stages. He was breathing hard. "Don't give me none of that what's-the-matter. You one of these smart ass niggers."

Joe looked down into Mr. Pete's fat face. Where had he heard those words before? Bad ass nigger. Smart ass nigger— He tried to remember. It was as if everything that happened had been done before—Bad ass nigger. Feeling his entire body grow hot with anger. Control yourself, Joe. Don't get in no trouble with white folks.

He heard Mr. Pete mutter something like—"Gotta teach you a lesson." And before he knew it, the old red-faced cracker struck him across his broad sweaty back with his long black stick and drew back to hit Joe again.

Joe saw a white blinding flash and before he knew it he grabbed the cracker by the arm, snatched the stick out of his hand. "Look, Mr. Pete, ain't nobody's body gon beat me with no stick just-dry 'long-slow. I wouldn't give a good goddamn if it was President Coolidge. Further you stay away from me better me and you gon get along."

Mr. Pete stood his ground, puffing and blowing, turning redder by the second. "I don't have to get along with you, old nigger. You got to get along with me."

Joe looked at the cracker hard and mean. "I ought to take you and—" He muttered the rest of it under his breath— "mop up the ground with you. Stick your ugly head in one of these barrels of turpentine!" He threw the black stick just as far as he could throw it. He turned around and went back to work.

Mr. Pete stood there for a moment just to show he wasn't scared, then walked away mumbling.

Josh Rayfield looked at Joe Youngblood, terribly frightened concern in his eyes. "What's the matter with you today, Joe Youngblood? You losing your mind? Ain't never heard you talk that much long as I knowed you."

"There's a heap you ain't heard."

"You hadn't oughta went that far with that white man, Joe. Ain't gonna get away with it either."

"Man, get outa my face," Joe Youngblood said.

About three-thirty that afternoon, the *Man* sent for Joe. One of the white boys from the office came over to him. "Mr. Jefferson wanna see you, Joe."

Josh looked up and said, "Uh—uh."

Joe put on his blue denim shirt, feeling it soak into his sweaty back and he walked towards the main office. He was so damn mad he could taste it in his mouth. Just please don't let Mr. Will or any other peckerwood call him nigger—not again today—not to-god-damn-day—no-sir-ree—or else it was just going to be too-bad-Jim. If Mr. Will called him a nigger he was going to sweep up the goddamn floor with him. He wasn't going to take any shit off another cracker this day of our Lord. He walked straight in the office and up to the desk where Mr. Jefferson was sitting.

"You send for me, Mr. Will?" Standing before white bossman, straight and proud and mad and mean. You got your family to think of, Joe. Don't say nothing out of the way.

"Yes I did, Joe. Hear tell we having trouble with you." Mr. Will was a short and skinny little white man with coal-black hair and hard gray eyes and a smile that seemed to be frozen on his face, and everybody knew it was anything else but a genuine smile.

Joe didn't bat an eyelash.

Mr. Will messed around with some papers on his desk, looked up at the big black man. "Hear tell you giving us a whole peck of trouble, Joe. How about it now?"

"I ever give you any trouble, Mr. Will?"

"Can't say you have. Leastways, not until now."

"I do my work good?"

"Far as I know, Joe." Mr. Will leaned forward in his swivel chair, and he pounded his desk with his tiny fists. "But I don't care how hard a worker you are, boy, you just can't be going around sassing out our foremen."

Joe kept quiet, bursting wide open.

"Mr. Pete is your boss and you got to respect him. That's all there is to it."

Joe didn't move a muscle.

"Got anything to say, boy?"

"No sir." *Boy—Boy*—He had a boy almost as big as this skinny little sawed-off peckerwood.

"All right, then, Joe, goddammit, let you off this time, but you better watch your step. Go on back to work and report to Platform Number 3 tomorrow morning."

The next morning Joe went over to Platform Number 3 and he took one look and he knew what the deal was. The platform was long and deep and wide, higher up off the ground than he was tall. Big barrels of turpentine stacked all over the platform. He had to take them to the warehouses, twenty-five, fifty and seventy yards away. They were the biggest barrels in the entire factory. He stood around looking, controlling his anger.

White man came over to him. "You Joe Youngblood?"

"Yes, sir."

He looked Joe up and down like he was sizing up a horse. Little biddy old cracker. Biggest thing about him was his misshapen head, big and long and shaped like a watermelon. "Well, let me tell you in front, boy, we don't 'low no messing around. You know what the job is, so get to work."

Joe looked around him. "Where's my helper?"

"Helper? Ain't no helper. Big and bad as you is, you don't need no helper."

Cracker looked at Joe. Joe looked down at the cracker. Cracker turned and walked back to his office.

Joe sat down under Platform Number 3 staring at the white

man's back and his watermelon head, feeling his aloneness and helplessness mounting. There was no way in the world to get back at crackers. They had a million ways of slapping you down, and there was nothing you could do about it . . . Thinking about his pretty little wife and their skinny little girl with the big brown eyes, and the handsome boy. One of these days he was going to pick himself up and his family and be long gone, but some folks said it wasn't any different up-the-country. Sometimes he didn't know what to believe. His big broad chest was filled to the brim, his throat and face. He felt a sensation, familiar to him now, of being choked and stifled, slow strangulation. Laurie would be out in the backyard now, with Jenny Lee and Robby in school; Laurie, busting suds, washing white folks' clothes. He remembered when she had been pregnant with Robby. Worked right up to the last minute before he was born. Couldn't hardly get up close to the tub with that great big baby moving around in her stomach.

Go along, Joe. You ain't got no win with Mr. Charlie. Looking up at the stout heavy drums, pulling off his shirt, the powerful cords of his muscles quivering. His head beginning to throb and ache from an overwhelming anger. Being mad all the time ain't gon do no good either. You ought to be done got used to white folks by now, and the way they run things.

Joe grabbed the first drum, his back buckled momentarily. Aah —Lord. Usually he told himself that his day was coming, but lately he wondered if the day would ever come for his kind of people. Thinking wondering hoping doubting aching sweating hating. The fresh smell of turpentine felt good to his nose. He walked toward the warehouse with the barrel on his back.

## CHAPTER THREE

IT WAS A trifle before six in the morning. Laurie Lee had been up and stirring since five. Joe had left for the mill a few minutes before with his lunch under his arm and the taste of Laurie Lee's kiss on his lips and the children's on his smooth cheek. He had grunted when each one of them had kissed him as he always did. "Umph—Lil Bits—" when Laurie kissed him, and "Umph—umph—Lil Bits the Second—" when Jenny Lee kissed him, and—"Boy, you almost big as I is—" when Robby kissed him, awkward and shy. And as he left he had mumbled something like—"Goodbye. See you tonight. Can't be good be careful." And then the big man had gone out into the cool, nippy darkness of the early morning.

Lil Bits and Lil Bits the Second and Robby Youngblood sat at the kitchen table with serious looks on their faces, as if eating warmed-over hominy grits and meat grease were a thing of deep significance. Laurie had steaming hot coffee with her grits. The children had hot water tea. The boy was quiet, his eyes cast down on the food on his plate as he went about the business of eating with no fooling around. But Big Sister's eyes were flighty and nervous, shifting from the uninteresting plate before her to her mother's face, to the piles of soiled clothing over the kitchen floor, to Robby's face, to Skippy-the-cat-Youngblood asleep and breathing deeply in her bed in the corner, and back to the plate and starting all over again. Laurie watched Big Sister, started to say something to encourage her to eat, changed her mind about it.

She looked at her boy with that special look she unconsciously reserved for him alone. "Well, Mr. Man, soon as you through eating, start a fire out there under the wash pot and fill those tubs with water." She turned to Jenny Lee. "We going to let you do the dishes and straighten the house, my young Miss."

Jenny Lee looked up at her mother, sideways at Robby, then back at her plate, muttering half aloud—"I all the time have to wash the dirty old dishes."

Big Sister hadn't eaten anything at all. She just sat there stirring the grits around and around and batting her big eyes and her long black eyelashes. She hardly ever had any interest in eating.

"How come Mama's big girl isn't eating her breakfast?"

Jenny Lee mumbled—"Nu-nuthing." Looking down at the lumpy old grits in her plate and the meat grease, the smell of which almost turned her stomach, tiny bubbles of sweat popping out on her nose.

"Come on, Lil Bits the Second, eat your grits. Make you big and strong, doll baby. Stick to your ribs."

She looked up in her mother's face, her eyes batting fiercely like they always did when she was good and angry. "How come we always got to have lumpy old grits for breakfast, Mama? Don't even have no butter to go with it."

"They good for you, sugar pie. Stick to your ribs. Put meat on your bones."

Jenny Lee's mouth poked out a mile and a half. "Ain't good for them Richardsons," she said. "You used to work at their house, never did see no hominy grits on their table. No fatback, no—no—no black-eyed peas, none of that old mess! How come we all the time gotta—"

Mama wiped the sweat from her nose and forehead. "Alright now, don't want to hear anymore of that sass, young miss. Just pick up that spoon and eat them grits, and I don't mean maybe—Many a poor child be glad to get a plate of grits this morning. You ought to be thankful to God."

Big Sister's big dark eyes flashed angrily at Mama. "I ain't thankful to nobody that make me eat grits and meat grease every morning. I can state you that."

"Shut your mouth," Mama said. "I'm not going to stand for no children of mine to sassy me. Now you just go ahead and eat those grits, and I don't want to hear another word out of you."

Her big eyes batting, Big Sister began to stuff her tiny mouth with the hated old grits, spoonful after lumpy spoonful, till her jaws poked out and grits and grease ran back through her quivering lips. She began to gag and her wide eyes deepened, and she vomited back into her plate, spattering over the table and on her pretty gingham dress that she had to wear to school. Bitter tears spilled down her thin little face. And she kept on cramming her mouth full of grits.

"Stop!" Laurie Lee shouted to her. "Stop it—I say!"

But the girl kept filling her mouth with the greasy old grits, lump after lump, and her stomach kept throwing them back onto the table. She was crying and vomiting and cramming her mouth, all of the time her eyes on her mother.

"Stop it, I said! Stop it this minute!"

Big Sister dropped the spoon, stared fiercely at her mother. "You made me do it. You told me to eat them. You told me I ought to be thankful to God."

"Hush, girl, hush now," Laurie said. "Hush this minute." She wet a rag and wiped Big Sister's face and especially her forehead and around her mouth and the front of her dress.

Big Sister muttered, "When I get grown I ain't never gon have no grits on my table. Never make my children eat no hominy grits and grease."

"Shut up, girl," Mama said. "I'm not going to tell you to hush anymore." She looked at Robby and back at Big Sister, whose big sassy eyes were filled with defiance.

There was a knock on the front door. "Wonder who that early bird is so soon in the morning," Robby said, looking over at the kitty cat in the corner.

"Your leg broken?" Mama asked him. "Go to the door and see." Then sighing heavily, she looked through the front room —*"Who—that?"*

Somebody called back from the other side—*"You that—"*

Robby came back through the house to the kitchen with old lady Sarah Wilson, a tall, big-boned hunched-over old woman, with a yellowish face and green eyes like a cat. She had a cup in her hand. "Morning, Laurie Lee—Morning, Big Sister."

"Morning, Sarah."

"Morning, Miss Sarah."

She looked at Jenny Lee. "What's the matter with you, honey? You look kinda peaky."

Big Sister looked up at old lady Sarah, shifted her eyes and cut them at her mother, looked down fiercely at the wooden table.

"Kinda poorly this morning myself. Had a bad night last night," Miss Sarah said to Laurie, rubbing her side. "Rheumatism came near killing me. I do declare."

"Hush your mouth," Mama said.

"I tell you, Laurie Lee, woke up this morning, couldn't move this here arm."

"I know it's the truth," Mama said sympathetically, wondering what old lady Sarah wanted to borrow this time.

Old lady Sarah was seated by now, and she looked around at the piles of clothes on the floor. "Don't reckin I'm gon do no washing this morning, Laurie, don't feel up to it. Gon rain anyhow I do believe."

Mama got up and went toward a pile of clothes. "Gonna get me an early start this morning ahead of the rain. Sometimes when bad weather finally gets here it spends the week." She sat down again and looked nervously at old lady Sarah.

"This here's pneumonia weather sure's you born," old lady Sarah said. "If we gon have winter time, wish to God we would have it and be done with, stidda first warm and then cold." She reflected somberly. "Better leave that in Jesus's hand though. Man ain't got nothing to do with it. Woman ain't neither."

Finally Mama got up again and said, "Well, you going to have to excuse me, Sarah. I got to get ready to get down with it. Don't pay me no mind, though. Stay as long as you like. Look in the safe and get anything you need—if we got it."

"Just want a cup of sugar, honey. Just one little old cup. Pay you back Saddy. Don't know how come—just can't seem to get started in the morning lessen I have my coffee."

Mama gave her a cup of sugar, and the old lady didn't hang around much longer. And after she had gone, Robby looked at his mother and said, "That's one woman could borrow the sweetening out of gingerbread without breaking the crust."

Mama laughed. "Never you mind, young man. Best you get out of here and get that fire started and don't worry your head about Miss Sarah." She gave him a light tap on the behind, squeezed his more-than-ample buttocks, hard and mannish already.

Big Sister was scraping the breakfast dishes, her mouth poked out. Laurie sat at the table looking at the *Morning Telegram* for a few minutes, then laid the paper aside. "Well, better get a move on if I'm going to beat that rain." Some Monday mornings, when she thought about the long hard lonesome day ahead of her, she felt tired before she began. Especially this particular morning because she hadn't slept well last night—backaches and stomach cramps had kept her awake. It was the worst part of the month for her. But just thinking about it wouldn't get those clothes out there washed. No—Sir—ree—Bob.

By the time she got out of doors a blazing fire had already been started, and there was a continuous popping and crackling of the burning twigs beneath the black pot as sparks flew about all over the place like lightning bugs. Her eyes looked dreamily at the flames that pierced the semi-darkness. A dark gray lizard crawled from underneath the house and ran across the yard and up the chinaberry tree. She looked up at the sky, a dark ominous blanket. The cold, damp morning bit into her limbs. Her nose sucked in the moist air. She put the white folks' clothes to soak and sprinkled washing powder in the first tub. It was Monday morning and all over Pleasant Grove from many a backyard, trails of smoke were climbing skyward as if Monday were the day to send signals to the Lord.

**39**

"Before you go to school, Robby, be sure you and Big Sister put some of that pasteboard in the bottom of your shoes, you hear? Might be raining before you get back."

"Yes'm."

"Got to take both y'all's shoes to the shoe shop. Lord Jesus, if it ain't one thing it's another."

She had kissed the children goodbye, but before that, she had pulled at both of them, fixing their clothes on them just right and looking at their necks and behind their ears. "You comb your hair, Robby?" "Yes'm." "You comb back in the kitchen? Let me see." "Yes'm."

The children gone, the day stood before her, a long and lonesome highway. Somehow she was in low spirits this morning. She stopped rubbing the clothes and looked detachedly at her hands. Seeing them as they used to be, long, slender and tapering, when people used to say God had given her a gift and that she was born to play pretty music. Professor Larkins said she was the best pupil he ever had. Big Mama used to sit in the front room proud as you please. She would wipe her old eyes and rock back and forth. "Play it, honey—Play it, sugar pie—Play it till the keys jump off." But look at your hands now—knobby, calloused, out-of-shape, muscle-bound hands, big ugly knuckles. Conditioned by the washboard and the scrubbrush and the flat iron and the needle and working too damn hard for white folks all your young life. And you don't hardly remember one note from the other.

Working fast while she daydreamed, she had the first round of clothes in the second tub already. The knuckles of her hands were sore, and her entire body was soaked with perspiration and chilled with the sharp morning dampness, aching all over to the very bone. As the sweat poured from her brow, burning slightly, into her deep narrow eyes, and spilled down into her mouth, salty taste and all, and the girlhood dreams of making something different out of her life, of really being somebody —a piano player, a school teacher, of even leaving Georgia maybe—fading now—fading, as so many times before, into the dewy mist of the early morning, she thought about her father, how hard he worked, and the words he used to preach, "Don't want my children to be work-horses for white folks——" and she made herself smile. All she and Joe had to look forward to was work work work.

"Hey, there, Laurie Lee. How you this morning?"

Laurie straightened up, wiped her face with the bottom of her skirt. Jessie Mae Brunson looked over the fence at her. "I'm all right, Jessie Mae. No use complaining. How you this morning?"

"So-so, honey, so-so. Nothing to brag. Don't feel like no powerhouse. Saw that widow 'oman knocking on your door before day this morning. I was taking my paper off the front porch. She sure visits early. That's the borrinest 'oman in Cross County. I tell you the truth."

"She always pay back."

Jessie Mae changed the subject. "Don't see no smoke coming out of her yard this morning. That 'oman is something. She puts the clothes to soak on Monday, wash them on Tuesday, put them to boil on Wednesday, rench them on Thursday, hang them out on Friday, and take them in on Saturday. She must iron them on Sunday. I don't see her in church."

Both of the women laughed. "Lord, I declare, Jessie Mae Brunson. You ought to hush your mouth." Jessie Mae handed a cup over the fence to Laurie. "Looka here, I wonder if you could spare a cup of grits this morning. Pay you back Saddy."

Jessie Mae back to her wash bench and Laurie back to hers. And wringing out the white things from the second tub and putting them in the big black pot. She had just put the last white piece in the pot of boiling water when a drop of rain hit her in the face. She held out her hand for further proof. She didn't have long to wait. Suddenly the wind began to blow, and the fire under the pot licked from one side to the other, and a far-away rumbling in the sky gave further warning. Laurie worked furiously. If she could just get the first tubful done, she could hang them in the kitchen, and at least she would get that much accomplished. All at once the wind seemed to be blowing all of the rain out of the sky directly into Laurie's backyard. She heard Jessie Mae yell in the yard next door. The fire went out, and soot and leaves and dust and dirt got into everything.

Back in the house Laurie Lee sat at the table looking blank-faced at the *Morning Telegram,* reading nothing. Skippy Young-blood got up from over by the stove, stretched herself and walked over to the woman and rubbed her body against the woman's leg. She reached down and caressed the soft, black fur of the kitty cat, thought about her children. Robby growing bigger by the minute. He had found Skippy on the street and brought him home a few days after the rat had jumped in the bed and bit Jenny Lee. Laurie Lee was always thinking about the children when she was at home like this all by her lonesome. . . .

Just the other Saturday she had been going to the Big Store with the children to do the weekly shopping for groceries, and they had met Mr. Jenkins, Head Deacon of the Pleasant Grove Baptist Church, coming from the store. "Howdy, Laurie Lee. You sure is got some real fine younguns. Yes indeedy. Girl just as pretty as a speckled peach, and this here boy, Lord have mercy, he you up and down. Look like you just said *spichew* and spit him right out." And Laurie had smiled with shamefaced pride and said—"Thank you, Deacon Jenkins. You think so?" The Deacon said, "You mighty right. Course they gits it honest. There sure ain't no flies on Laurie Lee Youngblood." And he turned to the boy standing pigeon-toed behind his homemade wagon. "I do declare, Peewee, you sure is growed. 'Member when you wan't nothing but a little old runt. Just wouldn't git up and grow no kind of how. How old you, Peewee?" Robby looked down at the dark gray earth. "Seven years old," he mumbled, and Laurie Lee knew he wanted to say ten. "What! GreatGodAlmighty—Boy, I ain't asked you what number shoe you wear, just only asked you how old you is." All of them laughed and the tall lanky deacon wiped his eyes. "Well, goodbye, Laurie Lee. See you in church. Tell Deacon Youngblood I say—Hey." And he laughed some more, as he reached in his pockets and gave the children a nickel apiece.

Everywhere she went everybody commented on what fine children she and Joe had, even some white folks, but it was more than a notion bringing them up. The cat turned and walked back past Laurie Lee, rubbed her soft body against Laurie's leg. The woman smiled. The rain coming down outside harder than before, and she looked up at the ceilings where the yellowish pancake rings were forming and water seeping through and gathering slowly and hesitating before leaping downward. She went around putting down pots and pans throughout the house to catch the weather which would be coming in with a vengeance any moment. She came back and sat down at the table. She got up again and went into the front room to the sewing machine.

## CHAPTER FOUR

JOE YOUNGBLOOD STOPPED for a moment and straightened up his hot, weary body to its full six feet four. The sun was hiding behind a big dark cloud, and there was a light chill in the winter air. A shiver ran across his naked sweaty back. Better put my shirt on.

He had been working at Platform Number 3 all by himself for a good while now. Mr. John was a different kind of foreman from Mr. Pete. He worked you like a dog, but he didn't stand over you every hour in the day. The big heavy drums beat Joe down to the ground, but he kept on going, minding his own business, staying in his place and breaking his back. He had to think of his family—think of his family. He couldn't afford to be getting in any trouble with white folks and run the risk of losing his job. Jobs for colored men were getting scarce as hen teeth.

He was buttoning up his shirt when he heard quick footsteps coming from behind him. He turned around and saw Mr. Pete. He took a deep breath. Oh Lordy-lordy.

Mr. Pete walked right up to him. "Hello, Joe."

"How you, Mr. Pete."

"How you doing on the job?"

"I'm doing all right, I reckin."

"Just wanted you to know, I'm foreman of Platform Number 3 starting today. I'm the boss of all the workers that work in this section, including you."

Joe just looked at him, didn't move a face muscle, eyes like still water.

"How you like that?"

"Like what, Mr. Pete?"

"What I just told you."

"Ain't nothing for me to like or not like. Ain't none of my business."

Mr. Pete stood for a moment beating the ground with his stick and looking at Joe. "Well I just wanted you to know I'm the boss over here now. You taking orders from me, and I ain't gonna stand for no messing around." He looked at Joe hard for a moment, scratched his big nose and turned and went on about his business.

That evening after Joe knocked off work he went to see Mr. Will and asked to be transferred to another platform or another kind of job. Mr. Will refused. Told Joe he had to learn to work with any and everybody. "Who running this place, boy, me or you? You better learn yourself how to act around white folks."

He walked home that evening, tired and weary, disgusted with the whole damn world. The sun had gone down long ago, and darkness was settling over the town, but it was still hot like the middle of the day. There wasn't a piece of breeze anywhere. Why didn't the white folks leave him alone? I don't mess with nobody. Why the hell don't they leave me alone? I work hard and I mind my own business—Joe used to walk with his shoulders thrown back, tall and proud, but now he walked like a tired old man—I'm a young man—I'm still a young man!—His broad shoulders sagged as if he were carrying a barrel of turpentine around with him everywhere he went —I'm young I'm young and I got a young wife and two young children and one of these days I'm going to pick right up and leave this town—But what guarantee was there that New York would be different—or Chicago—or Detroit, Michigan? He couldn't take his family running all over the country like a pack of wild animals. Georgia was as much his home as it was the crackers'.

Mr. Pete came every day, hanging around, dipping in, advising this and advising that, but Joe didn't let on that he minded at all. He kept right on working. Talk till your tongue gets tired, Mr. Pete. Beat up your gums, Mr. Charlie, till the blood runs out.

One day Mr. Pete came over right after lunch. Joe was pulling off his shirt, getting ready to work. Joe walked to the platform and the white man followed. Joe turned around and waited.

Mr. Pete cleared his throat. "Joe, how come you so solemn? Don't never hear you singing on the job or nothing."

Joe wondered if he was supposed to answer Mr. Pete.

"Why don't you smile some time, Joe?—Show your pretty white teeth."

"Ain't nothing to smile about." Joe picked up a barrel. He didn't want to start anything with this old cracker. Lord knows he didn't.

Mr. Pete followed him around. "Can't understand you at all.

Don't never sing or laugh or grin. Make me think you ain't happy."

Joe had put another barrel on his shoulder and almost bumped into Mr. Pete, just as the old cracker was saying—"A nigger ain't supposed to look straight faced all the time—"

Joe said, "Up—excuse me," as he jumped quickly aside and let the barrel drop accidentally-on-purpose, aiming for Mr. Pete's feet, but the old cracker jumped like a scared chicken. The barrel struck him a slight glancing blow on the leg and he hobbled towards his office.

Shoulda dropped it on that goddamn fat head of yours. Joe licked his lips, relishing his own anger. "Can I help you, Mr. Pete?"

Mr. Pete cussed out loud, kept hobbling towards his office.

After the cracker had gone, Joe got scared. He looked around him at the great big buildings and the low squatty buildings, long and wide, and the great red smoke stacks reaching up above the rest and smoking up the sky. They all ganged up and leered at him.

Late that evening Joe was walking across the yard of the great big plant. Thinking about Mr. Pete and white folks in general. If he could just stay out of their way, he would be better off. He had to learn how to get along with them. After all these years he should have gotten used to it. Goddammit— He didn't want to ever get used to it, but month by month and year by year they were taking the sting out of his bite and he realized it. The big buildings cast dark shadows all over the yard. His tired body ached from top to bottom. He'd like to be able to walk right out of this big old ugly yard and never come back, never see another smoke stack or a platform or a barrel of turpentine the longest day he lived. But where would he go and what would he do? Thinking about Laurie, Big Sister and Peewee, and the scarcity of jobs for a colored man.

It was just about first dark, as he turned the corner near an old empty warehouse. That's when the gang of white men jumped him. They dragged him into the dusty warehouse, but they had their hands full. They beat him till he lost consciousness. "Learn this nigger how to act around white folks.—Next time you see a white man you better take off your cap and bow your head and skin your jaws, you hear, old big ugly black nigger!"

**45**

When Joe regained consciousness, he felt like something the elephants had walked on. He was broke as a ghost. They had taken every penny he had in his pockets. He didn't go home, and he didn't stop at Mr. Will's this time. He went straight to Mr. Cross Jr. Next to Mr. Cross Sr. he was the great big boss, the solitary heir to Cross Mills, Incorporated. Told him everything that happened.

Mr. Cross Jr. looked Joe up and down. He had those natural-born cold-blue eyes just like his father, Mr. Cross Sr. He didn't crack a smile. He asked Joe who did it. Joe said he couldn't say for sure, because it had happened in the pitch-black darkness. But he told Mr. Cross that Mr. Pete must have put them up to do it.

Mr. Cross Jr. said well you can't go by must've. Got to have the straight facts. Then the biggest handsomest white man in Crossroads, Georgia reared back in his swivel chair and smiled sympathetically his beautiful smile, and told Joe Youngblood —"I'll look into this, Joe, and if I find out who did it, they'll hear from me. Don't you worry at all. You just keep your nose clean, boy."

Joe Youngblood said, "Yes, sir. Thank you, sir."

And that was that.


## CHAPTER FIVE

A BEAUTIFUL DAY all day long with winter merging into summer quietly and calmly, almost unnoticed, and at the same time, it was not so quiet, it was not so calm, not so unnoticeable. The almost forgotten warm rays of sunlight and trees half-filled with green leaves, and the birds in big squadrons coming north and going north, and many of the kids going barefoot already—some of them never wore shoes—and things Robby had not heard all winter long alive and chirping again, and the rough old March wind almost overnight quieting down to a small whisper, still causing a slight chilliness in his shoulders, and the sun rays giving a warmth to his face and his neck and his shoulders. He walked along dreamily and by himself, with his jacket open and his shoes untied and his shirt-tail out, because he had been slower getting dressed this morning than ever before, and Big Sister had left him.

He had doodled and dawdled and couldn't get started, and nothing Mama had said had been sufficient to arouse him. Sat in the toilet twenty minutes daydreaming, spent almost a half an hour at the wash basin. "Hurry up, Robby. You better get a move on. You going to be late to school, you hear. Messing around all morning like you got all day. Don't unstring your shoes—tie them up. What's the matter with you? Going to send you out of here without any breakfast, you don't mind." Well Mama usually understood him, give her credit, but not this morning, because he didn't understand it himself. But Daddy was a man and used to be a boy. Maybe he would understand.

Miss Josephine didn't understand either and she was the nicest and the prettiest teacher in the state of Georgia. Because when he and four or five other children came straggling into the room after class had begun, she stopped to make a little speech about she didn't want them to form a habit of being late to school, because they wouldn't be able to keep up, and besides it was a very bad habit for a person to form in life, not being on time, and she wasn't going to have any *C P T* (Colored People's Time) in her classroom. But she did not keep anybody after school for being late, so maybe she wasn't so dumb after all.

At recess the kids were out on the school grounds racing and romping and tearing, as if they had been in jail for a century and had been suddenly released, wild and uncontrollable. A tar-paper-shingled-roof house down the street caught afire, and the fire engines came too late, and the teachers had their hands full with children standing around the fire and ducking in and out among the engines, and laughing and yelling and shrieking to the top of their voices.

Rob walked across the school grounds and into the outhouse where he found Fat Gus Mackey and Benjamin Raglin, his two best buddies. They were trying to get a contest going.

"Bet I can stand further away than you can."

"Whatcha bet?"

"Betcha anything—a million zillion. There's my buddy——Robby Youngblood, the Kid himself."

"Betcha can't neither."

The outhouse was overrunning with school boys. It was a long wooden box with neatly cut holes to fit buttocks of varied sizes. Every seat was occupied. Fat Gus was a big, broad-shouldered boy, almost as wide as he was tall. He always carried himself like a big shot. He was smiling and you could see the gap in the center of his upper teeth, and the other boys didn't have any gaps in their teeth. "Soon as that kid gits down, I'm gonna prove it to you. I'm the champeen pisser at Pleasant Grove School. I got all of you'ns waters on. Bet a great big fat man."

Ben Raglin disputed him. "You ain't no sucha thing. Yours ain't no longern mine. Bet I can piss just as far as you can any day in the week." Ben was copper colored and slenderly built, big eyes like a girl. He was one of Robby's best buddies, and he had a pretty sister named Ida Mae Raglin.

Fat Gus looked up at a skinny little boy squatted over a hole at the end of the outhouse. His face was drawn in a mask of seriousness and his eyes ran water. "That boy sure having a hard time. If he don't hurry up and git down from there, I'm gonna try my luck anyhow. If he get a little wet, it ain't my fault. Musta think he in Pleasant Grove Baptist Church." He turned to the frightened kid. "Gotcha pews mixed, aintcha, boy?"

Ben and Robby bent over laughing, Fat Gus keeping a straight face, like he always had a way of doing. He looked up at the boy again.

"I don't know this old boy," he said to Ben and Robby. "He new around here. Must be from the country. Jes moved to town."

He looked up at the boy. "Where you from, sonnyboy?"

"Dub-Dublin, Georgia."

"Dublin, Georgia—How far out of Dublin? I bet you come from Plum Nelly, Georgia."

The little boy looked at Gus scared and puzzled.

"Plum out the City," Gus said, "and Nelly out the State."

The boys laughed and laughed, bending over and holding their stomachs.

"He don't hurry up and get down, I'm gonna piss on him all the way back to Plum-damn-Nelly."

Robby stopped laughing because he didn't want the outhouse odor to enter his mouth. It was bad enough in his nostrils. "Don't pee on him, Gus." Robby was never exactly sure whether Gus was serious or just fooling around.

"Well, he better make haste, cause I don't do to fool with." Gus fumbled with his fly.

The little fellow's eyes widened. "Be through in jesta-jesta—— jesta——" He got down and out of the outhouse in a hurry, almost slipped in the hole, even forgot to clean himself.

"Now—Let's go," Gus said to Ben. "I let you pee first. Go head."

Robby stood there watching, almost overcome by the dense outhouse odor, holding his breath as long as he could, then breathing quickly and holding his breath again, lips pressed together.

Ben turned to Robby. "Come on, man. You get in the game too."

Robby barely opened his mouth, didn't want the terrible scent to enter. "I don't want to."

"Aw come on. What's the matter—scared we'll beat you?"

"Naw, it ain't that. Just don't like to wet up these seats. Folks have to sit on them."

Gus looked at him with contempt and amazement. "Aw hell, don't nobody sit on these things nohow. You crazy, man? This here's a squat house."

"I just don't feel like playing that game. I don't have to pee anyhow." He kicked at the ground. "A man can't pee any time he gets ready."

And Ben said, "Me neither."

Gus backed up against the wall and hit the bull's eye like a true champeen, barely wetting the seat. "You assbuckets make me sick! Nothing but a bunch of pansies. Don't know how come I mess with you nohow."

Gus walked back to where Ben and Robby stood. "Let's get outta this damn place. Smell like a goddamn shithouse." He held his nose between his fingers. "One thing sure, you come in here every day in the week you never catch a cold. Keep a clear head the balance of your days."

The other two laughed, but none of them moved.

Gus looked at them with a mock-serious expression on his face. "Hear tell in the white folks' school they got running water in the shithouse, and pretty white seats for them dainty white asses, smooth and everything. Real high class."

"You reckin so?" Ben said.

"Hell, yes. What you talking about, man? White folks got everything. Niggers ain't from doodly-squat."

Robby swallowed the hated smell of the outhouse. His face grew warm, his fists clenched. "You ain't from doodly-squat?" he asked Gus.

"Me?" Fat Gus asked, a surprised look on his face. "I ain't no nigger. I'm a Chinaman. Didn't you know that, man? I come from way over yonder. Gonna start me a tunnel and dig my way back home one of these days."

"Mama say you oughtn' never say nigger," Robby told Gus heatedly. "How you gon keep them pecks from saying it, if you gonna do it all the time your own self?"

Ben said thoughtfully, "You mighty right. A colored man ought to have better sense than to call himself a nigger."

Fat Gus looked from Robby to Ben and back again, a tone of respect in his eyes, taken down off his high horse for the moment. He reflected over what Robby and Ben had said, then scowled at them both—"Mama this—Mama that—Mama-Mama-Mama—" The two boys stood there facing each other, Fat Gus trying to out-stare Robby with a mean arrogant look, but Robby's narrow eyes wouldn't be out-stared.

Ben looked at both of them and began to sing—"Oh it ain't gonna rain no more—no more—It ain't gonna rain no more—How in the heck can I wash my neck—When it ain't gonna rain no more—" Gus shifted his eyes to Ben and said—"That ain't the way the song go, man. It goes like this." He cupped his hands over his mouth and wiggled his broad behind.

"Uh—It ain't gon rain no more—no more
It ain't gon rain no more
How in the hell
Can the white folks tell
When it ain't gon rain no more?"

All three of them laughed, Robby included, despite the odor that overwhelmed him. He laughed at Gus with his mouth wide open. Fat Gus stopped laughing and looked seriously arrogant at Robby and Ben.

One of the bigger boys climbed up the side and was looking over at the girls on the other side, jeering and laughing and whooping at them. Suddenly the big kid fell back into the boys' outhouse, shouting—"Miss Austin!—Miss Austin!" who had a reputation of being the strictest and the meanest teacher at Pleasant Grove School.

The boys laughed and shrieked as Biff Roberts yelled—"Yeah! Yeah! She can't get me—one sure thing, she can't come in here!"

But the laughter was cut short as Miss Austin, with that quick jerky movement of hers, suddenly appeared with a long hickory stick in her hand flailing left and right, till she reached

Biff, hitting him on the legs and arms and behind as the outhouse cleared instantly, and the kids ran off laughing and yelling louder than before.

And now Robby sat in Miss Josephine's room, elbows on his desk listening to Miss Josephine and glancing sideways at Ben Raglin's sister. A pretty girl, color of brown honey, Robby's age, with long, black plaits down her back and big brown eyes that knew Robby Youngblood was staring at her. She was roundish and plump. He wondered what time it was and how long it would be before school let out. He had always liked to go to school more than most boys. Take Fat Gus, he played hookey all the time, more absent than present. But Robby was funny that way. Used to cry to go to school with Big Sister when she first started.

When he first started to school, he liked to play with the children, but some of them wanted to fight all the time, and he never wanted to fight. A few times he came home crying to Mama, and she would be very upset, because he hadn't fought back. "Don't come crying to your Mama. I feel like giving you another beating. Give you something to cry about. You just got to learn to take care of yourself. I can't go everywhere with you. Your Daddy can't either." He would realize how concerned she was and would wish deep inside of him he had not come home crying, and had fought back like a man, as Mama said he should. But the next time and the next time and the time after that, he would come crying home to Mama just like before. And each time he would make up his mind never to ever do it again.

Sometimes he would get in a scrap on the school grounds and Jenny Lee would walk up. Without hesitation she would jump right in and start slinging her skinny arms like a windmill. She didn't seem to care how big the boy was that happened to be fighting Robby. Many a time the fierceness and gameness of her attack would make a much bigger boy back down in shame, and amazement. Some of the children would say, "That Jenny Lee Youngblood is really something—She don't do to mess with." Others would say—"Ya-ah—Ya-ah—Robby is a sissy—His sister has to fight for him—"

One day a boy jumped on Robby right in front of his house, and Mama heard the racket. When she saw the boy hitting Robby and him not fighting back, she ran out to where they were and started shouting to the top of her voice at Robby. "Hit him—hit him—he's no bigger than you are. Hit him Robby. I mean it—hit him. Don't cry, hit him back!" He never remembered Mama so angry and excited before. And Robby wanted desperately to hit back. He put up his arms and swung lightly at the boy, barely brushing him on the shoulder. The boy swung as hard as he could, striking Robby in the face, in the stomach, once on his mouth. Robby backed into the hedges bordering his front yard, got his bare legs scratched up. "Don't watch me," Mama told Robby. "Hit him—hit him hard!"

The boy wound up and hit Robby in his mouth again, and this time Robby tasted his own salty blood. He wanted to cry, but somehow he didn't. He glanced at his mother, saw the look in her eyes, and his whole being revolted in anger and militance. Then the tears did flow, and he waded into the other boy, struck him flush on the jaw, hard and vicious this time, and once in the stomach, and he kept on swinging with that tremendous strength of his, feeling the perspiration soaking his entire body, and his own fist sinking in the fat cushion of the other boy's stomach. The boy turned and ran.

"See," Mama said. "What I tell you? All you got to do is put up a fight and anybody'll think twice before they mess with you." And later she told him, "Don't you ever be a bully, son. Never pick a fight, but don't be a coward either. I mean never! It won't get you anywhere. That's one sure thing. Me and your Daddy always did fight back."

Rob heard Gus Mackey ask Miss Josephine could he sit with Robert Youngblood and share Robert's speller, because he hadn't brought his to school that day. Robby wanted to tell the teacher not to let Gus sit with him, not that he was selfish, but because he knew Gus would not let him pay attention. It was hard enough already, with the sunlight slicing in through the windows, mixing up with a soft March wind, giving him that want-to-be-outdoors feeling. But Miss Josephine said, "All right Gus, make sure you behave yourself. We're glad you're taking an interest in your lessons for once, aren't we, Robert?"

And Robert Youngblood grunted.

As soon as Gus sat down he looked in the book and spoke out of the side of his mouth like one of those cowboys at the picture show. "Boy, you sure is one ugly boy-child. Tell me one thing—Is ugly got the mug on you?"

Robby pretended to ignore him, acted like he didn't even hear. He had listened to this ugly routine many times before. Thinking now to himself—If I'm ugly, what the hell are you? "One thing sure," Gus told him in a half whisper. "You ain't gon die no natural death, you just gon ugly away. Going around telling people you nine years. Ain't no way in hell you could get that big and ugly in nine little years." And when Robby made no reply, Gus looked Miss Josephine in the eye with a honey-melting innocence in his wide open face and reached under the desk and gave Robby a vicious pinch.

Robby jumped and gave Gus a quick jab in the short ribs and said, "If you don't stop messing around I'm gonna tell Miss Josephine to make you go back to your own seat."

Just as Robby opened his mouth, Miss Josephine called on him to go to the blackboard, but he didn't hear her, because he was talking. And with Gus sitting next to him, eyes wide and attentive, looking like the most virtuous angel in the Good Lord's Heaven, Miss Josephine told Robby to stay in after school was out. Robby cleaned the blackboards, took the erasers out and beat them, brought in three scuttles of coal, swept the classroom, wondering all the time what Gus was doing, a sneaky rascal, probably somewhere playing ball and laughing at Robby.

Then Miss Josephine had him write on the blackboard twenty-five times—I WILL PAY ATTENTION IN SCHOOL—I WILL PAY ATTENTION IN SCHOOL—And after he had finished, he had to erase it.

Walking along the dusty street, contemplating the newness and greenness and aliveness of everything, the new smells in the air with old familiar undertones not entirely forgotten. Brand-new butterflies and honey bees and bumblebees and green flies with their big ugly heads and wasps and grasshoppers and devil-horses. Spring was the time of the year that made Robby count the minutes before recess time and squirm the time away before school let out in the afternoon—Made him count the remaining days before summer vacation—Made him miserably sleepy during the last hour of school, but he always came alive after school was out. Loving school as he did, he didn't understand his own reactions.

He went through Drayton's Alley and across Johnson Place, which bordered on Peckerwood Town, cut across the field and stood looking up the steep embankment where the railroad track lay still and gleaming. He wondered had the Mary Jane Special gone past already. He hoped not, because he loved to hear that far-off Who-Eee and to look towards the sound and see that old train coming out of the south gleaming in the sunshine, a big black monster— *Who—eee—Eeee—Greatgodalmighty!* Loved to see it fly past him like the wind. Loved to wave at the lucky people on the train, and especially the engineer with the white smiling face, and to be waved back at. That was something he was going to be when he got to be a man—An engineer—Hadn't ever seen a colored engineer, but he was going to be one. Mama said she reckoned he could be one, when he pressed her very hard about it. He stood looking up the embankment, a frown on his face, his feet toed in more than usual, oblivious to everything now except the anticipation of the Mary Jane Special. It was so fast and so special, it didn't even stop in a great big town like Crossroads, Georgia. Just zooted right through. A path had been trampled out from the bottom of the hill to the top where the railroad track lay and down the other side, and Robby had started absentmindedly up the path when—

"Hey, little old nigger, what you think you doing?" Hearing it vaguely at first, his mind preoccupied with that pretty old Mary Jane and WHO—EE—EEeee—

"You deef, nigger? You hear me talking to you." A rock whizzed past Robby's head, humming softly in the wind.

He turned and looked back down the trail. A white boy about his size, red hair, barefoot, a malicious grin on his face, stood staring at him. Robby didn't say anything. The white boy picked up another rock. Then Robby said, "Leave me alone now. Ain't nobody messing with you."

The white boy sneered at Robby. "Oh, so the cat ain't gotcha tongue after all." Talked with assurance like a boy twelve or thirteen years old. Walking towards Robby with a big rock in his hand. "Better get your black ass over to niggertown in a hurry."

Robby wanted to run, and he didn't want to run. Wished Mama or Daddy were here or maybe Gus or even Ben Raglin. Not to help him fight if it came to that, but just being close by would have meant so much. He looked the white boy up and down as he approached, rock in hand. Just about my size and build. Well I ain't gonna turn my back and run so he can hit

**5 4**

me in the head with his rock. I ain't gonna run nohow. He balled up his fist. "Ain't bothering you now. Better leave me alone." He remembered what Mama used to say to him when he used to stand at the window at home and watch the rain come down and a sharp flash of lightning would make him back away from the window. "If the lightning's going to strike you, son, it'll find you. Running from the window won't do any good. Running away never does any good. We have to stand up and face things in life." And he would clamp his tongue with his upper teeth and force himself back to the window.

"Don't you know ain' no niggers allowed on this side of the tracks?" He was close upon Robby now. The white houses of Peckerwood Town stood up in full view behind him. Over in a green field white boys were playing baseball.

Sweat popped out on Robby's nose. His lips trembled. "Dare you throw away that rock and call me nigger."

The boy said Humph and threw the rock away and spat on Robby's trousers, shouted niggerniggernigger, and that's how it started. Robby's eyes narrowed, almost closing; he felt a fullness in his bosom and heat around his collar, as he threw his right fist at the white boy's head. The boy ducked and Robby felt a blow in his stomach that knocked the wind out of him and another blow on the side of his head that deafened him. He closed in on the white boy, trying to get in a good one, but he didn't succeed. The white boy kept pounding—to the face, in the mouth, on the head, in the stomach. Robby was in pain and he felt like turning and running, but he wouldn't, just couldn't, because he had to stand up and fight. He grabbed desperately for one of the boy's flinging arms and moved in close and encircled the boy's waist with his arms, summoned all of his strength to bring pressure on the middle of the boy's back and bending it as they went down, Robby on top. He pressed his upper teeth hard on his lower lip and put his elbow on a side of the boy's face and pushed down hard with all his might, grunting out loud. Making an outline of the red-haired boy's profile in the dusty red clay. The white boy squirmed and wiggled and cursed, still muttering goddamn nigger, and with the strength of a bull turned his body and he and Robby began to roll back down the bank, over and over and over, as the pretty, big-black monster roared past like a streak of lightning, with its mournful whistle and its clackety clack clack, and dressed-up people looked out of Mary Jane's windows at a little brown boy and a little red-faced white boy in a big little factory town in Georgia called Crossroads, playing with each other, grappling and rolling and kicking up dust.

They rolled down the path to the bottom of the hill and stopped, Robby ending up on top again. "I show you who's a goddamn nigger," he said, puffing and blowing, scared and angry and mean and desperately biting his lower lip, and bumping the white boy's head against the ground as hard as he could.

Then he swallowed his heart, as he felt himself being pulled backwards and up to his feet and spun around. The white boy scrambled to his feet and hit Robby in the middle of his back and turned and ran towards the baseball field. Robby fell forward in the arms of old Lady Sarah Wilson who lived next door to him in Pleasant Grove. His back felt like it was broken in two.

He straightened up and looked the woman in the face. "Why —why—why—you—you——"

She yanked him roughly by the arm and partially dragged him up the hill. "Be shame of yourself," she said, her lips trembling with anger and exasperation, "fighting in the streets like that. Tell your Mama skin you alive."

Robby tried to pull away from her. She gave him a hard slap on the neck. "Gon tell your Mama. You just as sassy as you can be."

"Bu—but I wasn't bothering that boy. He—he—picked—"

"Don't make no difference. Got no business fighting white boys."

"Mama told me anybody pick on me fight them back."

"Your Ma ain't told you to be fighting no white boys and I know it. Better learn your place now while you young, else you heading for the chain-gang just as sure as you born."

They argued like two grown folks till they got a few doors from home, and Robby looked at the houses and thought about Mama, and, although he was sure Mama would back him up, yet and still, Mrs. Wilson was a grown person, and grown folks usually stuck together where children were concerned. He began to feel more hurt than ever, and the spot on his neck where she had cuffed him began to pain him unbearably, as likewise did the middle of his back where the white boy had struck him, and as his house came into view, his whole being filled up and overflowed, and tears of apprehension and hurt and self-pity and indignation streamed down his face.

"Ain' no needer crying now," Mrs. Wilson told him as she pulled him up the ramshackle steps.

Mama was standing at the ironing board when they came in the door. The room had a sharp, scorchy smell of clothes being ironed mixed with the smell of charcoals burning in the fireplace. She sat the iron on the board, put her hands on her slender hips. "Now what in the world?"

"Caught this young man fighting like a wild tiger. Knowed you wouldn't like it, Laurie Youngblood, so I broke up the fight and Robby sassed like he was my own age. Lord, do pray —A sin and a shame how this boy carried on—Fighting a white boy. Stood right up to me and told me you told him to fight anybody he wanted to."

Mama looked at him. He was crying now without restraint. "Mama—Mama, I wasn't bothering that boy." Catching his breath and sucking the tears back up his nostrils. "Ju—just minding my own business, and—and—he picked a fight with me, and—and called me a black nigger and—and spit on me and like that and—and I wasn't gonna take no stuff offa him. Mama—Mama, you told me—"

"You see," old Lady Sarah interrupted, "what I tell you? That boy think he white and blaming it all on you. Jesus, did you ever?"

Robby looked sideways at Big Sister standing in the kitchen door, big brown eyes opened wide, sympathizing with Robby.

"I did tell him to fight back," Laurie finally stated.

"But you ain't tell him to fight no white boys and I know it—Had one of them red-head Jones boys down on the ground."

"I didn't tell him there was any difference, Sarah Wilson."

"Well, you better tell him now fore it's gone too far. Better put some sense in his head. Act like he think he white."

"He doesn't think he's white." Laurie spoke slowly now, carefully choosing her words, a slight trace of heat in her voice that she tried to restrain. "He knows he's a Negro. And he knows he's just as good as any white boy that ever lived."

"Well did you ever?" old Lady Wilson exclaimed. "Honey you gon be sorry one of these days, just as sure as you born to die."

Laurie's face grew warm, she was so angry with this widow woman she could have struck her on the head with a red-hot iron. "I can't help what you say, Sarah Wilson. I'm never going to tell my children white folks better than they are, cause it's a lie, and I know it and—and By God, you know it too."

Old Lady Sarah backed up towards the door, her big-boned shoulders hunched forward more than ever, her old withered body trembling. "Well did you ever? And right here in front of these poor children. Ain't no good coming of it, Laurie Lee Youngblood. Lord in Heaven knows it ain't."

And after old Lady Sarah had gone and Robby was in the kitchen eating his dinner with one hand and rubbing Skippy Youngblood on his head and his back with the other, and Skippy purring and wagging his tail, and every now and then looking at Robby, and Big Sister sitting on the bed studying her lessons, Laurie thought to herself as she stood at the ironing board—Did I do the right thing? She tried to think calmly. I know I shouldn't have talked to old Lady Sarah like that. Apologize to her tomorrow, maybe tonight. But Sarah had no right to do what she did. Not that Laurie resented other grown folks correcting her children, but when it came to telling them not to fight back against white children, then she definitely drew the line.

But even now, as she stood looking at the shadowy fireplace she felt old and tired and she thought to herself that it wasn't that simple and it wasn't that easy. Teach them they're good as white folks, teach them to fight back and what would that get them?—It got Rooster Mason the hangman's noose—It got Joe-Boy Collings the lynchers' rope—Not even to mention her own brother, Tim. Tim—Tim! She never would forget what the reformatory did to her baby brother. Maybe after all's said and done old Lady Sarah was right—Maybe she was leading her children in the wrong direction—Not teaching them how to live in white folks' country—Blinding her children to the facts of life. Be polite around white folks now—Stay in your place— Take off your hat and smile when they want you to—Doesn't hurt anything—White folks aren't so bad—A colored man just got to know how to act around them. Big Mama used to say, don't ever grin in a white man's face and don't cry either. But who was right and what you going to teach your children?

All her life she had heard folks say colored man get out of

his place he get smack into trouble. But how could she tell her children to go through life bowing and scraping to white folks and turning the other cheek and running and dodging like a rabbit in the woods? She drew a deep breath. Lord Jesus Have Mercy—She was by no means sure of herself.

She carried the iron in her shaky hand and placed it on the charcoals, took another off, mopped her face with a big white rag—Remembering the time a few years ago on a Saturday morning around about Christmas. Reckon how come that came to mind?—She and the children had been shopping. They were in the five and ten—F. W. Woolworth. Everything was red and green, decorated pretty for Christmas. That day Big Sister stuck close to Laurie, but Robby felt devilish and ran all over the store. Laurie kept calling to him to stick close to her so he wouldn't get into anything. Never would forget it—He was going through a stage when he would try to smile or grin or laugh her out of getting him to do anything he didn't want to do.

She would say, "Robby, if you don't come back here and stop running all over this store, you better." And he would turn and look at her with his big curly head cocked to one side, and a pretty, impish smile on his face and his narrow eyes widened, and say something like "Mama—Mama—Mama," then continue to do whatever he was doing as if she hadn't spoken. Sometimes, like that particular Saturday morning, she would let him get away with it. Running all around the store, he took up with a little white girl just about his size. Pretty little thing with greenish-blue eyes and golden-brown plaits bouncing on her shoulders. Laughing and squealing and shrieking, they would run up one aisle and down the next. White folks in the store watched the kids unsmilingly. Laurie didn't know how to cope with the situation, feeling a certain tension already, thinking that she should put a stop to it, not exactly knowing how and rebelling against the thought—Two five-year-old kids having such a good time and not knowing the difference. The white girl's mother wore a tolerant smile.

Once Robby left the girl and ran up to Mama out of breath, eyes shining, full of fun and happiness. "Mama—uh—Mama, she's my sweetheart." And ran away again, not noticing the painful, uncertain look on Laurie's face. Every girl he met those days he claimed as his sweetheart.

They ran back towards each other and put their arms around each other and expressed their enjoyment with a kiss. A horrified look wiped the tolerant smile from the face of the little girl's mother, as she ran up to them and snatched up her child, almost wrenching her arm out of the socket, dragging her away to a safe distance. She leaned down and said something to the child and shook her finger in his sweetheart's face. Robby looked at Mama, undecided, and before Mama could get herself together, he ran towards his sweetheart, probably to protect her from the mean old lady. Just as he was almost upon them, his brand-new sweetheart turned on him and licked out her tongue at him and yelled, *"Nigger—Nigger—Nigger!"* He stopped short, Laurie's boy, knowing definitely that this was not part of the funny game they had been playing.

Laurie stopped ironing and looked at the flickering fire in the fireplace. Aah—Lord—That morning she had seen the lynch rope and the mob and the chain-gang and *Greatgodalmighty* the reformatory! And she never would forget the look in his face, as he stood in that store like he was caught in a trap, his mouth open and his eyes asking questions, hurt and bewildered. How he had backed up, turned and had run back to his Mama, curvy lips contorted and quivering, tears in his narrow angry eyes.

She folded the white folks' white shirt carefully. She shook her head. Jesus Have Mercy, she said to herself. You bring your children into a white folks' world, and you don't even know what to tell them how to live. . . .

When she told Joe about it later that night—About Robby fighting the white boy and old Lady Sarah dipping in—Joe sat there in the front room for a while and didn't say a word. "She didn't have any right to do it, Joe—Old Lady Sarah?"

"I don't know, Laurie Lee," he said, wiggling his toes on his big bare feet and massaging his knee. "It's hard to say. Don't know how to raise your children these days. Teach em they good as white folks—Teach em not to take no stuff— that's good, cause that's the way you want em to be—Yet and still—where will it lead em? Run em right up on a dog-gone snag—I know what I'm talking about—"

"But, Joe—Joe—isn't that what we working and sacrificing for—so they can grow up and be real men and women—and not to think anybody better than they are?"

He rocked back and forth in his chair. He was tired and weary—beat down to his socks—a hard day behind him and another coming up—It was a question that haunted him day and night—How do you live in a white man's world? Do you live on your knees—do you live with your shoulders bent and your hat in your hand? Or do you live like a man is supposed to live—with your head straight up? He loved his wife and he loved his children—fiercely and tenderly.

He shook his head from side to side. "It ain't easy, Laurie Lee. Ain't easy atall. It's hard to say which is the right road to follow. Lord know it is. Get the short end of the stick either way the wind blows."

She looked at Joe with a fright in her eyes, a terrible fright. He had always walked with his shoulders back and his head in the air—big and powerful and straight and proud and that's how she wanted him always to walk—but she had noticed changes in him lately—little, by degrees. And Greatgodalmighty, what did it mean?

## CHAPTER SIX

IT WAS ONE of those red-hot days in August. Ninety-nine in the shade and there wasn't any shade. A humid heat that soaked Joe to the skin and sapped his great strength like juice from a pine tree. He just wasn't anybody's hot weather man. Never remembered such a hot day as this though. He set one of the drums down and looked up at the blinding sun, shading his eyes with his hand. Wish that sun would go behind a cloud for just a few minutes anyhow, but there were no clouds anywhere in the sky. His only hope came from a murmur of thunder rumbling out of the west every now and then. He hoped that the bear wouldn't grab hold of him today, but he couldn't be sure, because the heat was murderous.

Weatherman predicted in the *Morning Telegram* hottest August 6th in the history of Crossroads. Joe thought about the prediction and felt weak all over. Wouldn't be so bad, if he had a partner to help him, like the rest of the platforms, with those big heavy drums of turpentine. He had tried every way he knew to get off this particular job, but it looked like he would be handling these heavy goddamn barrels for the rest of his life.

He eased one of the barrels onto his naked weary back and stumbled forward. He could hardly make it. Beads of sweat crawled like live things down his back and all over his body. His powerful legs trembled. He set the barrel down and went back for another. He put it on his back and walked forward about five steps, and things began to dance before his eyes, and the buildings moved around, and heat waves seemed to steam up toward him from the hot dusty earth, and his eyes blinked desperately, but the old bear had him. He struggled for his bearings, tried to straighten himself out. White dots flashed before his eyes—and a swimming in his head—fighting, struggling, grunting, puffing—Wasn't no bear going to get him today—not if he could help it—He stumbled over a rock and the whole weight of the barrel fell upon the small of his back and he felt something snap, and pain pain pain—unbearable pain and going going gone. The old bear got him.

They found him lying there cooking in the sun, and they took him home in style in a big ambulance, and he stayed laid up for three whole months.

The only white man that visited him was Mr. Cross Jr. Told Joe not to worry about a single thing. Had him moved to the Colored Ward in the City Hospital. Got the best doctor in Crossroads to attend to Joe.

## CHAPTER SEVEN

ONE DAY AFTER Robby and Jenny Lee came from school Mama told Robby Mrs. Cross Jr. had been by the house and wanted to know if he would be interested in a job every afternoon bringing in coal and splinters and sometimes sweeping up the backyard, and stuff like that.

Ever since that barrel of turpentine fell on Joe's back, the Cross Jrs. had been real extra nice to the Youngbloods. Just as fast as the Cross Juniors' daughter would grow out of her clothes Jenny Lee Youngblood would get them, and Mama would do them over so they looked brand-new—looked like they were tailor-made for Big Sister. They were eating dinner and Robby looked down at the blackeyed peas and looked up at his mother again.

"Well—What you gonna say about the job, young man?"

"Yes, mam," he said, "I'd like that right smart."

"That's what I thought, and that's what I told her. She wants you to start tomorrow afternoon."

"Yes, mam." He sat there reflecting. Money in your pockets —Helping out at home make ends meet—But money in your pockets—He looked up at his mother. "That's over on Oglethorpe Street."

"Did Mizzez Santy Claus bring me anything, Mama?" Big Sister asked.

"Mrs. Santa Claus? Oh, don't be so sassy, child. Look in there on my bed. Never see such an ungrateful child in all my born days. You ought to be thankful Mrs. Cross Jr. gives you all these beautiful things. She doesn't have to, you know."

"She sure don't have to," Big Sister said. "Humph—I don't want no charity from white folks."

Laurie Lee smiled to herself as she watched Big Sister going into the other room batting her big angry eyes. Lord Lord Lord—If you could spend pride for money the Youngbloods would be rich as the Vanderbilts. She looked around at Robby again.

"It's the big white house on the corner of the alley. One of the places I worked when your Daddy was in the hospital. She say you don't need to come home first after school let out. You can eat your dinner right over there every day."

"Yes, mam." This job was more enticing by the minute. He hoped the white woman liked him. He wanted to hold this job a long long time. But there was bound to be a catch somewhere.

Mama seemed to know what he was thinking. "Now you just act like a big boy. Do your work good. Be polite. Mind your own business. And don't put your hand on anything. Sometimes they leave things lying around just to test you out. White folks think all colored folks steal."

"Yes, mam." That was easy. If that was all he had to worry about he would keep the job a long long time.

"And when she talks to you, don't look down at the floor. Look her straight in the face, and speak right up."

"Yes, mam."

"Mrs. Cross isn't what you call a stomp down cracker. She used to be a Yankee. She comes from the north."

"Yes, mam."

Big Sister came back into the kitchen with one of the dresses held up against her and reaching far below her skinny knees. She strolled about the kitchen swinging her little hips from side to side. "I'm really gon strut Miss Lucy next Sunday," she said, "and I don't mean maybe." Robby giggled and Mama started to laugh and they both stood there looking at Big Sister and laughing and laughing and Robby pointing at Big Sister and laughing till his stomach hurt and Big Sister stopped strutting and looked at Robby and Mama, and she really didn't want to but she couldn't help from laughing.

When Laurie spoke to Joe about Robby's job later that night, he looked up from his Bible and said—"That's good." And he looked at Laurie closely and he asked her—"Whatchoo looking so funny about? Work ain' never hurt nobody."

Laurie Lee Youngblood thought about the way *work* had hurt her Joe, all kinds of ways, inside and out—She had been thinking about it a lot these days. Work had beaten him down like a man beating a horse with a buggy whip. Work had made him almost a stranger to her and the children. Whipped the spirit right out of him, broken his back in two. She smiled at Joe with a frown on her face—Work ain' never hurt nobody—

Joe looked into the empty fireplace, glanced at his Bible. "Sure that's right," he said. "You must be thinkin that boy too good to work. I was his age I'd been taking care of myself I-don'-know-how-long." He looked down again and lost himself in his Holy Bible, or so Laurie thought.

Actually he didn't see a word on the page. It's all right, he thought to himself, it's alright for the boy to get a job after school—just so it didn't get his mind offa school. One thing sure, when the boy grow up, I don't want him to have to wrestle with any turpentine barrels. Joe's lips began to move again, driving himself back to the righteous words that lay before him in his Holy Bible.

Robby walked down the leaf-filled alley and pushed the big wooden gate open, listening for it to squeak, but it didn't squeak. He looked at all the leaves in the yard, thought DOG-

GONE they don't ever stop falling. It had rained one night a few weeks ago and ever since then the leaves had been falling, golden brown, and the green grass had begun to change its color, and the leaves would be falling everywhere till all the trees in the world were bare. It was a big backyard and a great, big, white beautiful house. He walked up the long white stairway and across the back porch and knocked at the door. A Negro woman came to the door and cracked it open.

"What you want? Oh, you the Youngblood boy—come for the job?" She was an elderly lady with dark-brown skin, and her light-brown eyes were friendly-looking.

"Yes, mam."

"Come on in then. Have a seat in the kitchen. I go fetch Miss Ruby."

"Yes, mam." He sat in a corner, his eyes traveling all over the big, white beautiful kitchen with the bright blue border. It seemed to have everything a kitchen should have and more besides—Two big stoves! A coal range and a gas stove. He looked at the big electric clock over the ice box. He swallowed hard, his stomach quivered. He had a feeling he was being watched, spied upon. His eyes searched the room, darted over towards the open door to the hall and he thought he saw a head of hair disappear quickly. Maybe he imagined it.

He looked away again, then back to the door quickly and this time he caught her. A yellow-haired girl, a couple of inches taller than he, stood in the doorway looking at him as if he were something in a three-ring circus. He wanted to say what the hell you looking at? She stuck out her tongue and ran back up the hall. Robby sat there turning the leaves of his school book, wishing that Mrs. Cross would hurry and hoping that he wouldn't have any trouble with the big white girl with the yellow hair.

"So, you're the Youngblood boy and you came for the job," Mrs. Cross Jr. said as she walked over to him. She was a tall, good-looking woman with yellow hair like the girl he had just seen. She walked with long strides like a man, and she talked different from most of the crackers he had heard. Talked nice and proper, from deep in her bosom.

"Yes, mam." He didn't like the way she looked at him as if he weren't there at all.

"Well, stand up, boy, and let me get a good look at you."

He got to his feet and made himself look her full in the face like Mama always taught him. Serious-faced.

"How old are you?"

"Ten years old."

"You're mighty big for your age. I guess you'll do." She turned to the cook. "What do you think about him, Pauline?"

The Negro woman looked at him with pride in her eyes. "He look like a smart boy to me, and he sure is pretty. And he sure do come from the best kinda family."

Mrs. Cross Jr. laughed. Then she took him around the house and told him what his job would be. Take in coal and splinters every evening and lay the fire in the giant-sized fireplace in the living room that was twice as big as both rooms at his house put together. Wanted him also to keep the backyard in shape. "Think you can do it?"

"Yes, mam." He wanted to ask how much she was going to pay, but he didn't because she might think he was sassy.

"Well go in the kitchen and get something to eat and then get to work. Don't worry about the yard this evening, it's so late already."

Just before he left that evening, she smiled at him and told him he had done a good job, and when he finally asked her how much she was going to pay, she laughed and said a dollar a week, and she thought they were going to get along all right and he said Yes mam. He didn't see the big yellow-haired girl again that evening.

Later that night he talked to Mama and Big Sister about the job. "Yes mam, indeed. I like it right smart."

The flame in the kerosene lamp danced to the tune of a soft autumn wind that blew into the room. The yellow fire licked from side to side, smoking up the chimney, almost going out. Mama turned down the wick, smiling at her boy. Big Sister looked at him, sitting there, trying to look calm, bursting with pride. "Humph—I reckin you think you a grown man now."

He threw a side glance at her.

Mama said, "He might not be a grown man, but he's a mighty big boy."

Robby looked at his mother, shadows from the flickering light dancing on her face. He felt good and comfortable, filling up and overflowing. How would he say it? How would he express his deep deep feelings? He looked at Big Sister, and he knew she was proud. A little biddy old breeze drifted into the kitchen from the backyard and it tickled the anxious sweat on his brow. Mama's face looked so pretty and serious and pleasant and lovable and everything else.

"Mama—Mama—If—If I do my work good and—and I keep my job, maybe you won't have to work so hard."

Laurie looked at her big boy till she couldn't any longer, and she turned her head towards Jenny Lee, and she got up, and walked over towards the stove, Aah Lord—Lord Lord—

And Robby wondered about the yellow-haired girl, hoping he wouldn't have any trouble out of her.

And the children *were* growing up in the Youngblood family. No more bathing in the same bath water at the same time in the same tin tub. They stopped doing that a long long time ago. No more looking at each other dress and undress. They were the same people they were two months ago or two years ago, but somehow they were different. They were growing up.

Big Sister didn't grow much taller or fatter, but she was growing just the same. She didn't ever put on Robby's britches anymore, stopped trying to act like a boy all the time. She was getting so she liked pretty clothes like a grown-up lady. She got a job after school taking care of two white children out in Rayburn Heights, but she didn't keep it long, because the white woman said Jenny Lee was too sassy. Laurie Lee shook her head and smiled. She could imagine Big Sister, about as big as a minute, mouth poking out at the white woman, eyelashes blinking. "Aah Lord, Sister, you're a Youngblood and a half. You sure take after the Barksdales too. Big Mama'd be tickled over both my children. They sure don't take any stuff off of white folks."

Jenny Lee, walking towards the kitchen, looked back at her mother. "Humph," she said. "You can say that again. Ain't no cracker gonna walk over no Youngbloods don't care how rich he is."

Robby grew like a stalk of tall sugar cane. He got bigger by the minute and sturdy and powerful. He was getting along fine with his job after school. Had not had any trouble at all. And he ate like a horse. He ate more food at the Cross house than he did at home. There was so much more of it. All kinds of good food and dessert at every meal. Sometimes when Mrs. Cross Jr. would be standing around in the big kitchen watching him eat, he wouldn't eat very much. She would smile at him. "Boy, you eat like a bird. Don't see how you grow so big." And Robby would think to himself—If she only knew.

Her little yellow-haired girl was something else again, always meddling and teasing, giving him trouble. One Friday he was down under the house getting a scuttle of coal. Betty Jane came up behind him and covered his eyes with her hands. He took a deep breath and tried to pull away from her, but she managed to keep her hands over his eyes. He felt her body hard against his and he smelled her young sweat, sharp and sweetish. "Guess who," she demanded.

This time he pulled away from her and stood facing her. He had almost caught up with her in height, but not quite. She was round and plumpy and tall to go with it. Her eyes were blue and her mouth was cherry. She was too darn friendly. She was the freshest girl that he'd ever seen and she was white and he was black and he wanted to keep his job, and he hated her guts.

"How come you so shame-faced?" Betty Jane asked him. Standing there looking at him with her hands on her hips, her red lips pouting.

"Ain't nobody shame-faced." Sweat on his forehead and his neck and shoulders, narrow eyes almost shut.

"If you aren't shame-faced you're a scary cat then."

"I'm not a scary cat." Why didn't she take her white self back upstairs and leave him alone? Leave him alone!

"Let's rassle then." Before he could get out of the way, she put her arms around him and tried to throw him down. She was as strong as a mule, but he was as strong as two mules. He didn't want to throw her down, and he didn't want to let her throw him down. Breathing in his face and on his neck and his ears. Sweet, pungent smell of youthful sweat. Making him feel funny and scared and mad, hating her guts. He had to get loose from her, but he didn't want to get loose from her. She was nice and friendly and he didn't want to be afraid of her. His heart was pumping a hundred miles an hour, conscious of her nearness from head to toe. He heard somebody coming down the back steps. His heart stopped beating. He pulled desperately away from her, grabbed up the scuttle and dashed out in the backyard and up the steps, leaving a trail of coal behind him. He almost bumped into Miss Pauline, as she came down the steps.

# CHAPTER EIGHT

MAMA LOOKED AT him when he came in the house from the Crosses' that evening, stopped what she was doing. "What's the matter with you, Robby?"

His narrow eyes narrowed and his face looked funny and somehow he knew that his face looked funny. What did she mean—What's the matter with him? How could she know? "Nothing the matter." His face aflaming.

"You feel alright?"

"Yes, mam. I'm doing just fine. Nothing the matter." His head was like a merry-go-round.

She felt his forehead, making him angry and shamed. "How you doing on the job?"

"I'm doing just fine. Here's the money." Anxious to have the subject change.

"You keep it this week, son. Every bit of it. You getting to be a mighty big boy."

He wanted very much to say—You take it Mama, and he wanted also to hug and kiss her, but he said, "Yes, mam."

Big Sister came in a little later from taking care of a little white girl that afternoon. He looked at her in a different way, stranger to him, his own little big sister. Noticing things unnoticed before, the things that were beginning to make her look more like Mama than ever before. One of the big boys, maybe it was Gus, told him the other day, that Adam swallowed an apple and it lodged in his neck, but a woman was greedy and Eve swallowed two apples and they lodged in her breasts. That was one of the differences between a man and woman, a boy and a girl, Mama and Daddy. But Mama wasn't greedy, never had been. And everybody in the world was greedier than Big Sister. Yet and still there was a difference between man and woman, a great big difference.

Lying on his pallet that night, everybody else asleep. A soft buzzing rhythm from the next room. That would be Daddy snoring, calling the hogs. He turned on his pallet and he listened so hard to the stillness of the night he could hear the quiet ring in his ears. What about Ida Mae? What *about* Ida Mae? Maybe she would like to rassle with him. He closed his eyes, tried to fall asleep, his nostrils picking up the strange familiar odors that came with the night. Ida Mae—Betty Jane

—His eyes getting heavy—Ida Mae was the prettiest girl in the world—girls girls girls—He wasn't any sissy——To heck with girls———Sleep sleep sleep———Turn this way and toss the other—

Saturday morning. Robby Youngblood was the last to stir. He was usually the first, except for Daddy, who went to work almost before the chickens got busy. Mama watched him get up and fold up his pallet.

"Come over here to me, Robby. What's the matter with you?"

He walked shakily over to Mama, his lips puffed from sleep and his narrow eyes swollen, a sour moldy taste in his mouth. She felt his forehead and looked hard at the dark half-circles under his eyes. "How you feel?"

"I feel all right." Let her leave him alone.

"How you sleep last night?"

"Oakie doakie." Restless and nervous under her gaze.

She smiled at him. "Tell you what we do. You get dressed in a hurry and get washed up and run to the Big Store, get a can of Calumet Baking Powder, bake some good old buttermilk biscuits especially for you."

Outside the store he met Fat Gus. "Whatcha know, good kid?"

"Nothing to it," Robby answered. They walked into the Big Store.

"Hey, you boys, wanna make some money?" the white grocery man in the Big Store asked.

Robby looked at Fat Gus. "What we got to do?" Fat Gus asked.

"Wanna make some money?" the white man insisted.

Another white man chuckled. "That there one look just like Jack Johnson."

Robby and Gus stood there in the front of the store looking at one another, wondering what the devil these crackers were up to.

Finally Gus said, "Yeah, we want to make some money. What we got to do?"

The smile disappeared from one of the grocers' faces. "Did you say—yeah to me, boy? You better say—yes sir." He smiled again. "Come on in the back, both of y'all." He spoke over his shoulder to another white man behind the counter. "Take care of everything, Joe, you and Jesse. Me and Roy got some business to tend to out in the back."

They followed the two white men through the back of the store to the backyard, Robby dragging behind the rest. The smell of the Big Store lingered in his nostrils. It was early yet, but the bright morning sun cast ragged shadows all over the yard. What were these crackers up to?

One of them, Mr. Brad, opened up a pasteboard box. "We got a real surprise for you boys." He pulled out a pair of boxing gloves. "We gon have a little boxing match, and the one that wins gets the prize—fifteen great big old cents." He threw one pair of the gloves to the other white man, Mr. Roy.

Mr. Brad walked over to Robby and handed the gloves to him. Robby drew back. "What's the matter, Jack Johnson, you yeller?"

Robby could hear the other white man speaking coaxingly to Gus. "Come on, fat boy, just a little sociable bout. Colored boy ain't never earned fifteen cents this easy." Cold sweat gathered on Robby's neck as he saw Gus hold his hands out to the other white man. He didn't want to fight Gus. Fat Gus was his buddy.

He didn't say anything. He just shook his head and licked his lips.

"Come on, Jack Johnson. You holding up the war. Your buddy ain't scared. How come you?" The man grabbed Robby's hand and started putting on the gloves. Robby resisted at first, but then he figured what the hell. They didn't have to hurt each other. He didn't want to appear to be more scared than Gus. Being scared didn't have anything to do with it anyhow.

The man brought them together. "Let the best boy win."

Gus was fat, but he was light on his feet and could jump around fancy. They sparred at each other. Gus cut a few steps, but they didn't pass a lick.

"Come on, boys. Les mix it up. Quit that waltzing around. Git rough with each other. Y'all ain' no kin."

"Ain' nobody gon win if you keep that up."

Gus tapped Robby on the chin lightly. Robby connected with Gus's short ribs. Neither hurt the other. They were working up a sweat now. Dancing and jumping around, hitting each other—on the jaw—on the arms—in the sides—tapping each other lightly—puffing and blowing. Robby dodged out of the way of a blow aimed for his chin, and he ran into a stiff jab to his stomach. Almost took his breath away. "What's the matter?" he muttered to Gus. "You fighting or playing?"

"Now you coming," Mr. Roy yelled. "I'm bettin on Fat Boy. You can have your Jack Johnson."

"Come on, Jack Johnson. That's the way to do it."

Gus had hit Robby two stiff ones in a row—intentional or otherwise. Robby let Gus have a hard one on the tip of his chin. They were hurting each other now, and Robby felt like crying, because Gus was hurting him, and he was hurting Gus, and they were good buddies. He didn't cry though. He wanted to quit, but he didn't know how.

"Come on, Jack Johnson! Half a dollar my nigger win." A half dollar hit the ground, kicking up dust.

"Taking candy from a baby—Come on, Fat Boy!" Another half dollar kicked up the dust.

Robby's lower lip was bleeding, and he tasted his salty blood. He wanted desperately to stop fighting. Wished that Gus would suggest it. Hating these crackers and every last one of them should be dead and in hell. Hating Gus for letting the white man talk him into fighting so easily.

"Thatta boy, Fat Boy. Now you coming! Let him have it in the nuts—Y'all ain' no kin. Least I don't reckin."

"Come on, Jack Johnson—Draw his goddamn blood!"

Gus hit Robby over the heart. Robby stumbled and fell, but he got up again. They were dead on their feet. Tired, weary and exhausted, hurting all over. Sweat raining from every pore in their bodies. Robby could barely raise his arms. Dust and salty sweat came together in his angry eyes. Gus hit out at Robby, missed him completely, almost fell down.

"Come, fat-black, stop assing around. Knock the shit out of that little yaller bastard! Draw his goddamn blood! He think he bettern you cause his skin a little lighter. His mammy muster been messing with the policy man."

Gus danced around slowly, hit Robby over his heart. Robby was hurting all over, aching and tired and hot and sweating, and the white men shouting at them like they were two puppy dogs. Anger and hatred mounting, filling up to the brim. Boiling over with meanness and hate-for-white-folks, every-last-one-them, goddamn their souls—and goddamn Gus!

Mr. Brad's eyes stretched wide and wild, his mouth hanging open. "Come on now, you little black bastards. First one draw the other'n's blood get a nickel extra. Come on, goddammit."

Robby stumbled away from Gus's left, and an open-handed blow struck him on the side of the head and sent him clear across the yard. Temporarily deaf, then ringing in his ears. He felt himself yanked roughly by the shoulder and he heard Mama's voice.

"Two grown men. I guess you mighty tickled. You want some fun, pick on your own damn kind! You ought to be ashamed but I don't reckin you got that much mother-wit. Uncivilized savages! Low-down, filthy peckerwood trash!"

She yanked the gloves off their hands, almost disjointed their arms.

The two white men stood with their mouths wide open, but they were not grinning. Mr. Brad looked like a man caught in an act of masturbation.

Laurie held Robby with one hand, reached out and grabbed Fat Gus with the other. "Come on, you too." She partially dragged them through the store. Tears spilling freely down Robby's face. When they reached the sidewalk, she turned to Fat Gus. "You go on home to your mother, and I'm coming all the way out to Rockingham Quarters just to tell her what happened. Neither one of you ain't got the sense you were born with. I get through with Robby, he be sorry the day he ever seen a pair boxing gloves."

Gus stood looking at Laurie, his eyes big and scared. He had never seen Robby's mother like this before. Usually she was soft and easy. He was scared half-to-death.

"Go along with you," Laurie shouted at him. "And don't stop till you get there." He turned and walked quickly up the tree-shadowed street.

"And you, my young man, just wait till I get you home. The very idea. Me waiting to fix some biscuits specially for you. Worrying about you. Thought you had taken sick or something, cause you been acting so funny. You out in the back of the Big Store fighting Gus Mackey for the pleasure of white folks."

Robby felt worse than ever before in his life. Felt bad all over. His stomach wrenching like he wanted to vomit. His throat felt like broken glass scratched it. His face was tight and filling up tighter. "I'm sorry, Mama—I-I-I'm sorry, Mama —Ain't gon do it no more, Mama."—Crying, choking up, sobbing—Face flooded with salty tears—

"Ain't no need of crying now—Get you home give you something to be crying about—Promise you that—" Laurie getting madder by the minute, unreasonably angry with her favorite child and she desperately tried to control her anger. "Can't never get you to fight just—just drive along slow—But you just tickled to death to fight for white folks—" Anger, meanness, hatred, spilling out of Mama like never before. "All they got to do is say the word—Just whistle at you and pop their finger—"

Robby stumbling along the dusty street, Mama practically dragging him, hurting him where she clutched him by the shoulder, but hurting him a hundred times more everywhere else, deep down inside of him. Wishing that he could blot this day completely out of his life, hating biscuits and Fat Gus and baking powder and boxing gloves and white men and everything else. Maybe he would be better off dead.

Mama pushed him inside of the front room ahead of her and dragged him towards the kitchen, Big Sister watching them wide-eyed with excitement.

"Pull off every rag you got on. I'm gon skin you alive this morning of our Lord—"

Big Sister looked almost as frightened as Robby. "Wha—wha—what's the matter, Robby?" Scared to talk to Mama, never having seen her like this before.

Robby looked at his sister, his swollen lips trembling, face contorted.

Mama said to Big Sister, "Go out in the yard, girl, and get me a switch off that chinaberry tree, and if it ain't big enough, I show you what's the matter—"

"Don't whip him buck naked, Mama. Please don't whip him buck naked—Please—Please, Mama!"

"Girl, you don't get out of here and get me a switch, I'm going to beat you buck naked." Looking over at Robby. "Pull off your clothes, boy. I mean every last stitch!"

He pulled off his shirt, his fingers working nervously, his heart beating fiercely. He fumbled with his trousers. Mama had never whipped them stripped buck naked.

Laurie looked out of the back door. "Jenny Lee Youngblood—You better bring me that switch—I mean in a hurry."

The girl came through the kitchen door with a switch in her hand. "Girl, you better get outa here, bring me a *big* switch, else I'm gon use it on you—I don't want have to get a switch myself—I might come near killing him—" The girl ran back out of the kitchen door.

She brought Mama a great big switch and Mama stood there pulling the leaves off of it, stripping it down to the naked bone, looking at Robby in the middle of the kitchen stark buck naked like he came into the world, trembling all over, like a fit had grabbed him.

She walked over to him with the switch in her hand.

"Get down on the floor."

Big Sister closed her eyes and turned her back to them, and she started towards the kitchen door.

He looked so helpless and pitiful and innocent and picked-upon as he lay down on the floor, and angry as Laurie was, she didn't want to fight him. She wanted to love him, because she really did love him. They were making her fight him—making her fight him—Goddamn the white folks! She looked down at him and she wanted to strike him all about his face, beat the pitiful look from his eyes and the resemblance for her that seemed more striking than ever before, and she drew back her arm, but her heart filled up, bursting wide open, and her throat choked off, and her love came down, and she dropped the switch, and she picked up her boy.

"Doll baby—baby—Robby, my son—Oh Lordy-Lordy! Jesus have Mercy!"

"Mama—Mama—Ma-ma—Mama!"

A great big sob slipped from Jenny Lee's lips, and she cried out to her mother, "I love you Mama!"

Robby dreamed every night the Good Lord sent. From knee-high to a mosquito, ever since he could remember, it was dream-dream-dream, about this and that. And when all was quiet and dark that Saturday night, when the heavy breathing and snoring broke the stillness along about three in the morning, the boy on the pallet was no longer in Pleasant Grove in Crossroads, Georgia. Maybe not in Georgia at all. Two mighty armies gathered in a great wide open space. Weighted down with all kinds of arms—swords, guns, knives—Everything! On one side was massed a great White army with ugly ghost-like faces, evil and leering. And on the other side the great great Black army, proud and handsome and fierce and brave and everything else. And Mama was there and Daddy was there and Jenny Lee and Ben Raglin and Ida Mae Raglin and Fat Gus Mackey and everybody else. But most of all, Robert Youngblood was there, strong and mighty, leading the Black army to victory. There was shooting, there was sword-fighting and cutting and killing and cannons roaring and blood all over the place. And sometimes he was in Crossroads, Georgia, and sometimes he was fighting up and down the streets of a great big city. Sometimes the faces of the people were familiar. Sometimes they were strangers—It was as plain as day, it was all mixed up—White faces soaked all over with blood and black faces too. He awoke and sat up on his pallet, cold sweat on his face and his neck and all over his trembling body. He looked around him in the darkness, wondering where he was, getting himself together. He felt his pallet, his ears picked up the faint snore coming from Big Sister in the bed. He could see the old stove on the other side of the room and the big kitchen table. Relief flowing through him like a glass of ice water. Glad he was home again, tickled to death it was only a dream. He lay there trying to figure out who won the battle. Glad it was a dream—glad it was a dream. He twisted and turned and he scratched his itching body. Why in the devil were white folks so mean? And why in the hell did black folks let them get away with it? WHY? WHY? WHY? He thought and he thought till his head got groggy and sleepy with thoughts. He turned over on his stomach and went back to sleep.

Sunday morning he tried to piece his dream together. But everything was vague and misty, a big wide wall standing between him and his dream, and last night it had been so real and terrifying. He sat at the unpainted table in the kitchen. A big heavy clumsy-looking table, scrubbed clean and colorless like the kitchen floor. The greasy smell of bacon and hot hominy grits and freshly-cooked coffee had almost chased the sharp musty sleepish bedroom odor out of the kitchen window. A big black man sat at the head of the table. A man with soft gentle eyes and a set look about his face, with double-barreled shoulders like a buffalo. It was a pleasant face, unexcitable. A deceptive face, that was the hiding place of a whole factory of nervous tensions and subtleties, a powerful steel spring, coiled and ready.

Sometimes Joe Youngblood would be just sitting studying to himself—Sometimes he might even be talking to Laurie Lee or the children or anybody else, but his mind would be long gone—a million miles away. He often wondered how it would have been if those crackers hadn't stopped that train that time he was headed for Chicago. Seemed like a hundred years ago —One thing sure, he wouldn't have married Laurie Lee cause he never would have known her—He wouldn't swap Laurie Lee Barksdale Youngblood for a million Chicagos. When he broke loose from Old Man Buck's plantation and landed in Crossroads, he was hard to get along with—mad with the world. It wasn't long before he started saving up his money to get on that northbound train again, but it took such a long time, because he made so little. He would've gone though, if he hadn't met Laurie Lee that summer in Tipkin. Even after he married he often thought about taking his family up north. But Ray Morrison said it wasn't any different up the country— said a cracker was a cracker wherever you went, and he ought to know. Ray had lived in all those big cities up there after he had got out of the army. Laurie Lee was against it too. "I don't feel right about moving up north," she had said many times. "I was born in the south. This is as much my home as it is any of these evil old crackers. Why should we be running away? Suppose we find the same old thing up there. What we going to do then? Just keep on running the rest of our lives?"

Laurie looked across the table at him drinking his coffee out of a big white bowl. She smiled at him. "Doctor told you drink one cup of coffee a day, Joe. You here using a great big old bowl."

His soft eyes twinkled almost unnoticeably, and the rest of his face remained calm and serious. "Ain't drinking but one little old cup neither." He shook his head. "Little Bits—Little Bits." He was a noisy drinker, and when he had drunk almost half the bowl, he took the overflow that was in the saucer and poured it in the bowl, and without looking up he said to Jenny Lee—"Little Bits the Second, how about pouring me a little hot coffee in this here cup. It's a heap too sweet like it is, and it's done gone and got cold already."

Laurie shook her head at the still serious look on her husband's face. "Lord, Joe Youngblood, you sure are a mess and big pile of it."

After Jenny Lee poured the coffee for her father and sat

down to the table again, Robby looked up from his plate and said to her, "That dream I drempt last night was something terrible—I mean to tell you!"

The girl's eyes widened. "What was it about, Robby? Tell it to us right now."

Joe Youngblood had a deep bass voice, soft and booming. A man that talked quietly, but came out like murmurings of thunder on a clear summer day. "Wait till the sun comes up, boy," he said. "Dream be bound to come true if you don't."

Laurie looked at her husband. "Joe, you ought to hush that foolishness. What you want to tease the children like that for?"

A slow smile moved across the big man's face. The boy sat there brooding over a dream he dreamed last night. The girl with hominy grits on the floor of her open mouth, her big eyes wide and expectant.


## CHAPTER NINE

*Not that Mama say so*
*Not that Mama know*
*Not that Mama say so*
*Cut that butter so——so*
*Cut that butter so——so*

"*So—so—so—*" The song ended unevenly. "*So—so——*" The game ended abruptly. The children broke the circle and ran in all directions, some of them aimlessly. But Jenny Lee, with a pretty, hand-me-down-from-white-folks dress that Mama re-made flapping just above the knees, ran towards Benjamin Raglin and grabbed him by the hand. He pulled away without even looking at her and ran around the side of the house towards the backyard. Four-by-four Gus Mackey, bursting out of his patched-up Sunday-go-to-meeting suit, observed what happened and walked over to her. Stood looking at the skinny girl batting her big pretty brown eyes. He wanted to say something and Big Sister knew it, but the cat had his tongue.

It was Jenny Lee's and Robert Youngblood's birthday party. Laurie Lee made up her mind she was going to give the children a birthday party this year, if they never afforded one again. And it didn't matter much that they were not born on the same day or even within the same month.

"Let's play 'Sally Walker,' " somebody said.

Lawn dresses you could see through—Gingham dresses stiff with starch—Cheesecloths—Much too long, old-lady-looking dresses—Pretty dresses, some not so pretty—Hand-me-down dresses that looked like hand-me-down dresses—Front yard full of them, likewise the backyard. Nobody cared what the boys had on.

The sun was setting amidst a multitude of colors over Peckerwood Town. A slight breeze mixing with the lingering heat. Singing, laughing, playing, in the front yard and the back. Black legs, brown legs, yellow legs—running and jumping— Thin legs, fat legs. Laurie sat on the front porch for a moment with Sarah Raglin and Jessie Mae Brunson, waving a paper fan in front of her face and her neck and over her shoulders. She had been up since before day in the morning getting everything in order. Baking a big, three-layer coconut cake, giving the house a good general cleaning, making the ice cream and the punch, looking after the children who didn't need much looking after but still—

A circle formed down in the yard, a ring of children going round and round and the song began—

> Step back gal—
> Don't cher come near me
> All those sassy words you say

She stopped fanning and looked absently at the reading on the fan, advertising the Mansion Funeral Home, and she turned to Sarah Raglin. "Lord knows, Sarah, me and Joe ain't able to afford this party, but I believe Negroes just got to make big sacrifices *sometimes,* so their children can get a little pleasure and enjoyment out of life. They get grown so quick, and life is so hard."

> Say little sissy
> Won't you marry me——

Sarah Raglin rocked the chair back and forth and shook her head. "It's the truth, Laurie Youngblood. It's the truth, so help me."

> Sissy in the barn——
> Join the wedding
> Prettiest little sissy
> I ever did see

Jessie Mae Brunson shook her head and laughed out loud. "That Mackey boy sure is a mess. Big fat rascal. He right after Big Sister like a mannish puppy, got his eyes on her like a hawk watching a chicken and she ain't paying him no never mind. Lord, I declare—Childrens is a mess."

The three women laughed heartily. "Lord have mercy, Jessie Mae Brunson, you ought to be shame of yourself." And they laughed some more. Laurie had already noticed the goings-on between Ben and Big Sister and Gus.

"Let's play 'Little Sally Walker.'"

"Naw, I don' like that game."

Fat Gus said, "Yeah-yeah, that's the game to play." He looked around for Jenny Lee, wanted her to join in the game, but she had disappeared. He walked around to the backyard, didn't see her amongst the children playing Rat ball, came back and joined Sally Walker and forgot about Jenny.

> *Little Sally Walker*
> *Sitting in a saucer*
> *Crying and a-weeping*
> *For all she has done*

The sun was setting now in all kinds of deep pretty colors, and a soft breeze got into the dresses and played with them like big balloons and made them flap this way and that. The laughing—the playing—the running—the jumping—the singing —the dancing—the happiness.

The games went on. "I'm in the well—five feet deep." "Who you want to pull you out?" "Mister Robert Youngblood." And Robert Youngblood gave Willabelle Braxton five quick kisses that tasted good and felt kind of funny, and he sat in the chair in the midst of the children, and Willabelle giggled, and Ida Mae's face burned—*Hunph*—

"I'm in the well—six feet deep—" If I say Ida Mae to pull me out everybody will know I love her. But I want to say Ida Mae Raglin—I want to—"Who you want to pull you out—" He said Ida Mae Raglin. Ida Mae's eyes looked down at the ground, looked up again, and her sweet face spread in a shame-faced grin that was pretty to look at. She kissed him six times and he felt delightfully funnier than ever before, and now everybody knew she was his sweetheart. "In the well six feet deep—who you want to pull you out—Mister Robert Youngblood" and six more kisses—

Fat Gus was in the well now with his big fat self, and somehow Jenny Lee knew that he was going to say that he wanted her to pull him out and she could feel her face growing warmer and warmer. "How many feet deep?" Fat Gus said, "Fifteen feet deep"—"Fifteen feet deep!" somebody exclaimed. "That's mighty deep!" A couple of the boys whistled, and all of the kids laughed except Jenny Lee. Her face was on fire, and she wanted to run away from the crowd, but something wouldn't let her.

"Who you want to pull you out?"

"Jenny Lee Youngblood."

There was giggling all around her, and she felt herself being pushed toward Fat Gus. And while he kissed her, the children were counting—"One—two—three—fourteen—fifteen—"

Jenny Lee was in the well now. Willabelle Braxton came over to her and whispered—"If you don't want to be in the well, I'll take your place." Jenny Lee didn't answer. She just stayed in the well. "How many feet deep?" She stared at the ground. She wanted to say fifteen, but didn't dare, because she knew that the children would laugh and whistle. "How many feet deep?" the children insisted. "Ten feet deep," Jenny Lee blurted. "Who you want to pull you out?"—"Ben—Benjamin Raglin—" And after Ben had pulled her out with ten quick kisses that seemed to her like a hundred and ten, she pushed through the circle of kids and ran around the side of the house.

It was getting a little late and twilight cast dark shadows on the yard already, and Laurie figured it was time to serve the refreshments and blow out the candles and cut the cake. She was feeling good, because everything had gone off so nicely, and everybody had had a good time, with only one or two fights, and a couple of the bigger boys had been caught in the toilet smoking dried tree leaves rolled in newspaper paper, but things like that were to be expected. She went into the kitchen and opened the safe and reached up to the top shelf for the great big beautiful birthday cake. Funny, the plate felt so light—And when she looked in the plate, she let out a small, smothered scream, that was unintended. Nothing left of that lovely, three-layer coconut cake but crumbs and broken candles. Oh Good Lord no! Robby couldn't have done a thing like this, not to mention Big Sister. She felt sick inside and faint in the head. She went in the front room. The well had been moved from the yard to inside of the house, and Robby was in the well again, seated in a straight chair in the middle of the circle of children. "Robby, come here." By the way she spoke and the look on her face, he knew she didn't mean tomorrow, so he got out of the well unkissed and followed her into the kitchen. She sat down at the table. She could hardly talk. "Rob-Robby, where's the cake?"

His face was blank. He pointed towards the safe, at the same time he saw the empty plate on the table. "Ma-Mama— What happened to the cake?" Staring at the look on Mama's face now. "Ma-Ma-Mama, I didn't do it, Mama. I wouldn't do a thing like that. Raise my right hand to God."

"Hush your mouth," she said. "Don't you use the Lord's name in vain."

"Bu-bu-but, I didn't do it, Mama." He shook his head and his eyes were wide, then narrowed in indignation. "I wouldn't do that, Mama. You ought to know I wouldn't."

She looked at her son, wanted to strike him in his face that looked so much like her own, wanted to hurt him real bad for looking so innocent, and she almost burst out crying, drew a deep breath and God Jesus Have Mercy! And she sent him in a hurry to the Big Store for a dozen ten cent store cakes.

Later that night, long after the party was over, and everything had been straightened up, and Joe had come home and eaten, and the children had gone to bed, they sat in the front room talking about the party. Seated before the fireplace as if there were a fire. "But before that, Joe," Laurie Lee said, "everything was so nice and all the children had such a good time. You just ought to could've been here."

Joe rubbed one big bare foot with the other and took a couple of puffs on his pipe. It was good and restful for him to be sitting talking to Laurie Lee after such a hard day. His wife was still mighty pretty to look at and strong and fine and understanding—always understanding how tired he was. And she talked so pretty. The party the party the party—He wished he had been able to be at the party and help Laurie out and watch the children enjoy themselves—He had never had a birthday party himself in his whole lifetime—Sure wish he could have been at his children's birthday party, but actually, it was better this way—a little bit better—to sit and listen to

Laurie Lee tell him about it and nod his head and smile and puff on his pipe and make a pretty picture of the party up in his head and rock back and forth in his chair and rest those weary bones of his. Sitting there listening to Laurie Lee, slowly slowly slowly his mind went on a trip—drifting drifting—as he sat there listening and thinking—not hearing Laurie Lee now—daydreaming in the nighttime—

Sometimes he felt like a hundred years old. There seemed to have been so many many years. The years of marking time and getting nowhere, the cold mean-hearted years, the seemingly hopelessly wasted years—included among them the year that after he got out of the hospital he wasn't going back to working in the plant anymore, but he went back just the same. And also the year that he asked for a lighter job and *They* obligingly gave him one and *They* cut his $8.95 almost half in two, and he begged to go back to the barrels once more and *They* obligingly gave him his old job back. One of those years all mixed up with the rest of them now he made up his mind he was going to go into some little old business for his ownself —tired of working for a boss—open him up a little old grocery store and his neighbors would patronize him because he was a colored man and his family had always been friendly neighbors, or open up a cleaning and pressing place or maybe an ice cream parlor, but he never was able to save enough money—

Joe sought refuge further and further into his Holy Bible like a man hiding in a deep deep cave from the rest of the world. And his Bible never let him down, because he could find just about anything he wanted in his wonderful book— from *Go down Moses way down in Egypt land and let my people go* to the *Patience of Job.* But the only thing about it, he had to come out of his cave every single day into the world where the barrels of turpentine were—still were—And Bible or no Bible, Time didn't wait for nobody's body—a natural fact. Everything changed—Change Change Change—But nothing seemed to change for Joe and Laurie Youngblood—except maybe for the worse—

And he knew he had changed. After he came out of the hospital he never was the same again. He wasn't the same on the job, and he damn sure wasn't the same around home. He used to help Laurie around the house, don't care how tired he was. He used to play with the children, used to keep up with how they were getting along in school, used to talk with Laurie and help her worry about the million problems around the house. He still worried alright, but he worried by himself and he didn't help Laurie worry anymore.

Sometimes—not just sometimes—but tonight right now, as he sat looking at Laurie Lee, an old familiar glow seized hold of him and flowed like newly-gotten old-time religion all through his great body—spiritually, physically and every other way—but the moment passed and the tiredness and the awful awful pain in his back and terrible hopelessness grabbed him again. Sometimes he wished he could just sit there peacefully and fall asleep with his Bible in his lap and never wake up again and never again bother about the struggle and the pain and the worry of the world—Just lay down his burden down by the riverside and study war no more.

But next year was going to be different. I'm gonna straighten up. I mean that thing. Straighten up how? Never mind that—Some kind of way—Beginning with the New Year— Laurie Lee's birthday—Laurie Lee was born on New Years Day —Laurie Lee Laurie Lee—His family—his family—the room coming back in the focus of his eyes and the birthday party back to his mind—the birthday party.

He laughed softly. "You mean to tell me that little big old fat scoundrel Gus Mackey really stuck on Little Bits the Second?"

She looked at him worried-like. She smiled at him and nodded her head. "One thing I can't figure out though is about that cake. The way Robby told me, I just can't believe he did it. Yet and still—"

"Ooo—oo—oop—Mama!—up—oop—"

"God Jesus—What in the world!" Laurie ran into the kitchen, Joe right behind her.

Big Sister was sitting up in bed with her head bent over vomiting into her lap. "Ooo—oop—" Each vomit was so deep it shook her whole body and seemed to throw up all of her insides. She looked up at her Mama and Daddy and her eyes were red and deep and almost closed and her thin body shaking.

"Lord have mercy—what's the matter, baby?"

"Mama—Mama—oo—oop—" She looked up at Laurie, her big eyes deep and hollow. She shook her head. "Mama—Mama —I didn't mean to do it—I'm so sorry, Mama—"

Laurie Lee sat on the bed and took the girl in her arms. "Joe get them salts out of the safe and get me a glass of water and wet me one of them rags and bring it here. This child is sick—mighty sick!"

Laurie Lee smelled the sour odor of coconut eaten and thrown up again, saw the stringy yellowish coconut vomit on the bedclothes. She closed her eyes—Big Sister ate the birthday cake! Of all the people in Crossroads, Georgia! Tears were spilling down Big Sister's cheeks. "I just meant to get one little biddy piece, Mama, but it was so good—so good, Mama. I didn't mean to do it, Mama, but it was so pretty."

Robby sat up on his pallet on the floor rubbing his sleepy eyes. "Wha-what's the matter with Big Sister?"

"She's sick, son, very poorly. Got to get her a doctor."

His nostrils quivered, picking up the smell of the coconut vomit, as he watched Big Sister vomiting her insides. His stomach became nervous and he was paralyzed with fear, as he thought about Skippy, his cat, and how she had vomited one evening the same way as Big Sister, and Daddy had said wasn't anything the matter with Skippy, she was just bigged and going to have a baby, but the next morning Robby had found her dead on the back steps.

He didn't want them to know what he was thinking. "Mama—Mama—Big Sister gonna be all right?"

"What you say, boy?" his Daddy asked him.

"Didn't say nothing."

"Stop telling your lies—I heard you say something."

He looked up at the big man, tears spilling down his face.

"What you crying about?"

"I ain't crying, Daddy."

"Don't lie to me, boy. What's the matter with you?"

"Big Sister gonna die like Skippy?" he blurted, crying now, not trying to hold back.

The man looked down at him in a helpless fashion. "Big Sister ain't gonna die, son. It ain't gon be like that."

"Big—Big—Big Sister bigged—She gon have a baby?"

"What?—Boy, what's the matter with you? Shut your mouth."

"But-but Skippy was sick like Big Sister and you said she was gonna be alright, you said she was just bigged, and-and she—she—" His voice broke off and he lay down on his pallet and pulled the cover up over his face, but he couldn't get the picture from before his eyes of Skippy vomiting and Big Sister vomiting and Skippy stiff and hard the next morning and Big Sister and Skippy and Skippy and Big Sister, til Big Sister had on Skippy's face and sometimes the other way around, Big Sister's body hard and stiff and mouth dripping greenish-red blood. Skippy buried in the cold, wet ground. It was awful—awful—awful!

Another vomit raked her insides, throwing up coconut, epsom salts and everything; her face had broken out in little red spots. "I'm sorry, Mama. I'm sorry—I was going to tell you who did it—Mama—Mama—I was going to tell you—yes I was, Mama—"

Joe stood looking on, helpless.

And Mama said, "That's alright, Big Sister. Don't worry none about that. Mama understands." And looking up in Joe's quiet-looking face and thinking about Big Sister never eating much, just enough to keep going, always forcing her food and playing with it, eating the little she did eat mostly to please Mama, always hating the darn old grits and the black-eye peas and the fat meat and the collard greens—poor folks' food. Mama rubbed Big Sister's knotty little stomach and wiped her skinny face and her forehead with a wet rag, and LORD JESUS HAVE MERCY—

## CHAPTER TEN

"YOU AIN'T MAD with me, is you?" Fat Gus asked. Standing in front of the schoolhouse after school. Big ugly wooden two-story building, used-to-be-white, but now dirty gray, even black in places.

Robby looked at Gus. They hadn't spoken to each other since their fight in the Big Store, not even at the party. He was moved by the anxiety he recognized in Gus's eyes and the tone of his voice. He and Gus had always been buddies. He remembered when they were younger, and they would be running around and playing with other children in front of Gus's house out in the Quarters. In those days Gus never seemed to be able to keep his fly buttoned. Gus's mother would come and stand in the doorway and watch them play for a while and then she would call out—"Gus—You Gus—" and when Gus would finally look around, she would point to his fly and flick her tongue out and back in again, and Gus would look down and button up his britches, and the boys and girls would howl with laughter. Robby's face warmed and he stared past Gus and over across the street at a little ugly unpainted house, watched a little black boy go up the steps and into the house. He stared at Gus and away again. "I'm not mad with anybody."

"I ain't mad with you," Gus told him, pulling up his baggy pants to keep them from falling, didn't have on a belt. "That sure was a nice birthday party."

"I'm not mad with anybody," Robby repeated. It wasn't his fault that Gus got invited to the birthday party. Mama had insisted.

"Gimme five then," Gus said, holding out his fat hand.

They stood there looking at each other, shame-faced, pumping each other's arm.

Walking along together now, saying nothing, feeling kind of good, still shame-faced. Robby looking up at the sky, wide and blue and deep and even, broken here and there by clouds that looked like snow-covered mountains, as he imagined snow-covered mountains would be. He stumbled and almost fell down but Fat Gus caught him. "It sure is a pretty day," he said to Gus Mackey.

"You ain't lying a bit," Gus said. "That sure was a mighty nice party. I mean to tell you it was."

They turned in Tennessee Avenue. Robby knew that Gus was every-now-and-then glancing at him on the sly, but he didn't let on. They followed a pathway between two houses and through a backyard and took a short cut across Rockingham Field. Gus picked up a rock and threw it up toward the sky. "How you like your new job?"

"I like it alright. Just fine."

"Bet it ain't as gooda job as my newspaper route."

"Betcha it is."

"How mucha make?"

Robby hesitated. Sweat popped out on his curvy nose. "A dollar and a half." He barely muttered it. Why did he lie to Gus about a thing like this?

"Come again?"

"A dollar and a half." Almost shouting it.

"That ain' nothing. I makes an average of two dollars and a half. Sometimes three."

"I get dinner every day," Robby argued. "Just as much as I can eat. All kinds of good food."

"Bet you have to work like a goddamn horse."

"Naw. Isn't much to do. Specially this time of year."

"Bet that old white woman stand over you all the time."

"Naw, she doesn't. She doesn't give me any trouble at all. Nobody messes with me but that old white gal—Miss Ruby's daughter. She always messing with me. Old tomboy want to rassle all the time."

Gus stopped walking and looked at Robby. "Man, you crazy, she don't wanna rassle. She got something else on her mind and it ain' no rassling—I can state you that—and you can put that in your pipe and smoke it."

They stood looking at each other in the middle of Rockingham Field, serious-faced, like two grown men, green grass all around them, blue sky over them, slight breeze making the green grass shimmy. "What you mean?"

"You know what I mean. You ain't as dumb a stud as you make tend to be."

Robby just looked at Gus, didn't open his mouth. Gus smiled at Robby and laughed out loud. "She wanna give you something, and she ain't gon take it back."

Robby's face flushed hot and his neck gathered sweat. He swallowed hard. "Man, what you talking about?"

"You know what I'm talking about. Tryna play dumb. She wanna play Mama and Papa." Gus made a circle of his left thumb and forefinger, and took his other forefinger and stuck it in the circle and moved it back and forth. "You know what I'm talking about."

Robby looked at Gus and away again, kicked fiercely at a rock. "You—you crazy as a bedbug."

They had started to walk again. Robby didn't want to think about Betty Jane, but he couldn't help himself, couldn't overcome the strange, unexplainable feeling that came over him when his mind made a picture of her. The yellow hair hanging carelessly around her reddish-white face and the laughing blue eyes and the devilish mouth and the long body and the legs and the knees and the wrestling, and—and the body against body. The funny feeling, different and separate from the hatred and the fear, yet at the same time all mixed up together.

"Boy, you bet not get that white gal bigged. You be in a whole heap of trouble. I mean. These pecks string your ass up so fast you won't know what hit you. And you bet not let Ida Mae find out you messing around with a white gal or any other gal. You better watch your step, and I don't mean perhaps!

Robby just walked along listening to Fat Gus. His whole body sweated. He never knew when to take Gus seriously. He didn't want to talk about it anyhow. Play Mama and Papa. Didn't want to think about Daddy doing that to Mama, only half-believed it, completely rejected it most of the time, even though somehow he really did believe it. That's all Gus talked about every day in the week. Mama and Papa. They walked between two houses and continued along Mulberry Street, where the big chinaberry trees stood between the houses, naked babies, brown, yellow and black, on front porches and playing in the yards.

Gus started to sing.

> *Beef steak, poke steak*
> *Make a little gravy*
> *Your thing, my thing*
> *Make a little baby*

Gus laughed out loud, looked sideways at Robby, having a good time at Robby's expense. Picture in Robby's mind now of Mama and Daddy late at night, bed springs squeaking, but Robby wouldn't believe it. Lying on his pallet in the dark of the kitchen one night, late late late, his eyes gradually getting used to the pitch-black darkness, whispering voices in the next room—bed springs whining out a squeaking rhythm, hard breathing, moaning and groaning, seemed loud enough to Robby to wake up the dead. Mama's voice—Joe! Joe! Joe!— Everything quiet except his own heartbeat—scared—scared— scared—Swallowing hard the dark, sleepy bitterness—Must've been dreaming—Damn my Daddy!—Dream—Dream—Dream —Stay awake all night so you won't have to dream—Damn my Daddy—Damn my Daddy!

They were walking on pavement now past the big pretty houses where the rich white folks lived. Walking along Orange Street, around the beautiful, white-folks-only park, up Pine Street, past the Catholic Church, most beautiful church in Crossroads, Georgia.

"It sure is real pretty inside of that church." Robby deliberately changing the subject.

"How you know?" Fat Gus asked him.

"Miss Fannie says so. And she ought to know. Cleans it up every Saturday."

"Oh, I thought you was Father Youngblood."

On Oglethorpe Street now in front of the house where Robby worked. "So this is where you work."

"Onh honh."

"Well, I be looking at you. Keep your eyes on that wild-ass white gal. I mean you better damn sight keep your eyes offa her. Well, take it easy." He started to walk away, turned around and came back. He looked at Robby. "Me and you still buddies?"

"Course we are." Wishing Gus would hurry and leave him alone.

Gus spat on the sidewalk. "I sure is sorry about us fighting at the Big Store."

"I am too. Let them peckerwoods make us fight each other."

"Yeah," Gus agreed, "that's what I was thinking about. Well, I be looking at you." He turned and his big body ambled down the street. And Robby felt good, but he really felt bad and scared and angry, and mad with Gus but not about the Big Store.

He walked down the alley and opened the big white gate, listened for it to squeak, but it never did. Looking up at the house—big, white and awesome. Turn around, go back out the gate, don't ever come back, forget about the job, get away from these white folks while getting is good. His face filling up. To hell with that—He wasn't running anywhere. Walking up the steps—the long white steps. . . .

He ate his dinner, couldn't tell you what he ate, thinking all the time about what Gus had told him. He chopped up the splinters, filled the scuttle with coal, thinking most of the time about the yellow-haired girl, hating her guts, confused about his hatred. Feeling nervous and funny and jumpy as a cat. He went into the toilet down under the steps. When he finished, he pulled the chain and buttoned up his fly and turned around and there she was standing in the door smiling at him friendly-like. First thing he thought about was what Gus had told him. His mouth swallowed hard, tasting the dryness, and a great fear gripped him. Goddammit! He didn't want to be afraid of anybody.

"Hello, Robby."

"Hello," he muttered, wishing desperately that she would get out of his way, some strange curious part of him not wanting her to go. The tiny little room gave out an awful smothering heat.

"How was your birthday party?"

"It was okay." He didn't want to be scared of this girl, white or no white. Damn her whiteness! Looking at her this time in a different light, nothing he was able to put into words or thought. Gus was just lying, kidding like he always did. Rassling wasn't nothing but plain old rassling. But how come he had such a funny feeling?

"How come you didn't invite me to your old party?" She asked him as if she really meant it. He didn't answer her, just narrowed his eyes at her. She knew how come. The way he figured it, she was just making fun of him, and he hated her for it. Let her leave him alone—leave him alone!

She held her arms up. "Look," she said, "I got hair under my arms. I betcha a nickel you don't have any."

He saw the light colored hair under her arms, just beginning to sprout, but he didn't say a word. Swallowed his spittle.

"And that ain't all," she said very proudly, her blue eyes serious. "I also got hair in-between my legs."

"Don't do it!" he whispered. He wanted to knock her down and run right over her, but he stood stock-still and watched her as she pulled up her yellow dress, and pulled down her pink panties and he stared at her little triangle of dark, yellow hair, dirtyish looking, and the very very whiteness underneath her clothes. She pulled her panties back up and stood laughing at his funny serious face and pressing down her dress. "Bet you don't have any hair except on top of your head." Making herself laugh now, her eyes uncertain.

"Go on upstairs!" he told her. "Go on upstairs and leave me alone!" He had broken out into a sweat all over his body, and his face and neck were covered with sweat.

She stared at Robby, trying to figure him out.

"Leave me alone," he shouted softly. "What you trying to do —make me lose my job?" He hated her because she was white and dangerous and she had the color of skin that everything and everybody had taught him to hate ever since he could remember.

She didn't say a thing, didn't laugh anymore, just stood there and stared at him like she couldn't move even if she wanted to.

"What you trying to do?" he asked her. "Get me into trouble?"

"I'm sorry, Robby. I'm really sorry."

She just turned around and left him. And he listened to her footsteps going up the back steps and across the porch. He didn't move a muscle till he heard the back door open and close again. Picking up the scuttle, cussing softly to himself. Confused, sweating everywhere, his neck, his face and under his arms, eyes filling up, face and shoulders, scared and angry, thinking hard and fiercely and feeling his age like never before.

## CHAPTER ELEVEN

BETTY JANE RAN up the back steps, her heart beating double-time and her face filling up and her yellow hair flopping all over her face. She stopped on the porch and got herself together before entering the house. Ruby, her mother, mustn't suspect anything at all. She heard voices in the kitchen, Ruby and Pauline. She walked softly and nonchalantly past the open kitchen door and started up the carpeted stairway to the second floor. Halfway up the stairs she broke into a run.

In her room now with the door closed behind her. Staring into the big mirror at the big-for-her-age, developed-more-than-average, twelve-year-old girl. She watched her bosom expand and contract, feeling a great fullness in her big-girlish breasts and her shoulders and her face. She didn't want to get Robby into trouble, and the last thing she wanted to do was to cause him to lose his job. She felt so ashamed about what she had done. Her ever-changing body was so strange and awful, sometimes she didn't know what to do with herself. She walked from the mirror and sat on her bed.

The boys in the school were so different from Robby, the big boys his size. For over a year now she had been painfully aware of them, the boys that were thirteen and fourteen and fifteen, some of them even a little bit older. First it had been wrestling with her and boxing and hitting and pulling and pushing and hurting. But lately there was pinching and feeling-on-the-sly and patting, and squeezing and getting her frightened and angry and confused and excited and inquisitive as she ran headlong into life. Ever since she was a little red-head baby she was always running without caution smack into life, and stumbling over life, and getting up and crying a little, her hair turning gradually into a golden-yellow, and running away with life all over again. She never seemed to understand that she was the most special girl in Crossroads, Georgia, in spite of the fact that her father was always reminding her, and now recently reading books when mother wasn't looking, about men and women and love and the facts-of-life and Jean Harlow and Clark Gable. And books that Ruby had hidden from Daddy about the Abolition movement and Votes for Women. Paying more attention lately to the dresses she wore and fixing her hair. Almost a half year now since the day she came home from school frightened to death by her big step towards womanhood, yet not quite as frightened as she thought herself to be. Fear mixed with pride and calm and fulfillment, and Ruby had had to talk with her woman to woman, and the tears of relief. From month to month—period to period—calm and fulfillment mixed up with the fear, the awful anxiety.

Sure she knew that Robby was different from the boys in her school and in more ways than one. Robby was colored, brown—black—Negro—A million other words and names used to describe and scorn and ridicule and keep them in their place. Lazy, good-for-nothing, study about nothing but rape, but Pauline worked harder than Ruby ever worked. And Ruby had told her many years ago that most of what they said about Negroes were lies based on ignorance and prejudice, Ruby not being what you would really call a southern lady, not yet a while, still a Pennsylvania Yankee, whose mother before her had been a militant suffragette and had known Frederick Douglass and Sojourner Truth. Betty Jane called her mother Ruby, usually when Daddy wasn't around and not out of disrespect, but with love and affection. Sharing many rebellious moments together. Ruby, herself, in full flight from the reality of her position as the Second Lady of Crossroads, in the County of Cross. Better known as Mrs. Cross Jr.

Lying on the bed now, and crying into the pink and yellow

spread. Sitting up and wiping her eyes and brushing the thick yellow hair out of her face with her hand, thinking hard and feeling fiercely, because she didn't want to hurt Robby, but who did he think he was anyhow? Trying to understand why, when she was around him, she was so painfully pleasantly aware of his nearness. What harm was in it? Oh, what harm could be in it? Yet if Mother knew you even went anywhere near him, she would run him away and skin you alive! Yankee or no Yankee—Thinking about Pittsburgh and New York where she had spent a few summers—Maybe up there she and Robby could be friends and it wouldn't matter—But how could she be friends with Robby anywhere, if he didn't like her in the first place? Hating him now—hating him for his color and he dared to tell her to go upstairs and get away from him. Hating him fiercely because he was pretty and brown and proud and black and attracted her terribly.

"What's the matter, darling?"

She didn't really hear her, not the first time.

"Betty Jane, what's the matter?"

Betty Jane jumped up, startled and angry. She looked at her mother and brushed down her dress and pushed her hair back from over her face. Ruby Cross walked over and sat down beside her and put her arms around her and pulled her close. "Tell Ruby what happened."

"Nothing, Mother. Nothing—nothing." Trying to make her voice sound steady and calm.

Ruby trying to be patient and tolerant, as she always tried to be with her big girl. "There must be something, darling. Come on now, what are you crying about?"

She wanted to tell her mother, needed terribly to put her confidence in her very best friend. Confused, scared, fearful of the consequence, to her and to Robby. She didn't give a kitty what happened to Robby—Yes, she did. Knowing for some time now, and feeling sharply at the moment that Mother wasn't the Yankee she used to be, three, five, six years ago— Used to argue with the people who came to the house, years and years ago. Betty Jane used to hear Ruby arguing heatedly with Daddy far into the night after the company had gone. And Betty Jane would listen and ask questions afterwards. Ruby used to tell her there wasn't any difference between colored and white. "I'm not going to let them make an ignorant cracker out of my big girl," Ruby used to say and she really meant it.

One night she had heard Ruby and Daddy argue long after the company had gone. Daddy had been very loud that night, probably more than a little bit drunk.

"Shuuu—shuuu," she had heard Ruby say. "You wake up Betty Jane."

"I don't give a *continental*. Time you woke up and quit that damn superior foolishness about giving the colored people a break. Sick and tired of you embarrassing me all the time. After all, enough of a thing is enough and too much is good for nothing. I've been patient, pretty goddamn patient."

"Yes, you have been patient, George, so noble and patient but-but I just can't see it you all's way. I—I—"

"Tonight was the last damn straw—When Bob Middleton asked you if it would be all right with you if your daughter grew up and married a nigger, and you looked him straight in the face and said it would be left up to her."

Betty could barely make out what her mother had said in reply. "You know I didn't mean that exactly, George. He—he had me in a corner—I—I—"

Her Daddy continued, voice calming down a little. "Look, Ruby, I don't give a goddamn about your racial equality and your woman's independence. There's nobody in Georgia that treats the colored man better than I do. Ask any of them who their best friend is. There's only one thing involved as far as I'm concerned and you gotta understand this. And that is what we represent—What the Crosses represent—What my father owns, which we will own when he passes, is based on the established southern way of life—Racial segregation—prejudice —The whole shebang. That's what's at stake—and don't you forget it." Ruby Cross *used* to stand right up to him. . . .

Ruby's voice raising ever so slightly now, her arm squeezing Betty Jane's shoulder. "You don't have to be afraid of your mother, darling. Tell me—Tell me, what's the matter."

Betty Jane drawing further and further inward. How could Ruby know that she was afraid of her at this very moment? How could she know? "I told you nothing the matter." Hot all over and covered with sweat and cramps in her stomach now.

Ruby putting two and two together, seeing Betty Jane walking quietly past the kitchen door a short while ago. Where had she been and what had happened to her? She was afraid of what her two-plus-two added up to, unprepared to raise the question on her mind, because the question on her mind might have nothing to do with what bothered her daughter. Afraid to put ideas into Betty Jane's head not already present. Maybe something happened to her at music practice. Didn't think much of that Professor Kilgore anyhow. "Something must be the matter, dear. You wouldn't be crying just for nothing at all."

"I-I-I just don't feel so well. That's all, Mother."

She felt the girl's forehead, much warmer than usual. But she knew the girl was lying. "You got a headache?"

"Yes, Mama. My head hurts me awful." She wasn't exactly lying, Betty Jane told herself. She wanted to tell Ruby about the cramps in her stomach.

Ruby Cross looked at her girl, wondered how she could break through this wall that had sprung up between them. She felt tired and aged, as pieces of breeze crept through the windows past the pink curtains and caressed her hot face. She stood up and walked towards the big mirror and back towards the bed. What was the matter with her anyhow? Getting all heated up and bothered over nothing. It would be better to let it drop for the moment, but supposing it was something more serious than she dared to suspect—Suppose it was—Suppose it was—was—!! She looked down at the girl, examined her dress, her legs, her face, noted the disarrangement of her hair and her swollen eyes. Her breath grew short and quick. Her imagination began to gallop like a Cross County race horse. She saw Robby, expanded and grown into a giant, big and black and burly and fiendish and horrible and ugly and hired-by-her and running amuck and ape-like and dangerous and hired-by-her!

"What did he do to you, darling? What did he do?"

The girl looked up at her mother, her blue eyes wide, frightened and bewildered. "Who, Mother? Who? What?" Holding her stomach and wanting to tell Ruby about the cramps in her stomach.

"That big black—black—" She reached down and grabbed the girl and pulled up her dress and pulled down her panties. And everything went blank as her eyes looked at the red stain on her baby's drawers! Blood rushing to her face now and throbbing her temples and pounding her heart. "What happened, darling? Where did he go? My own fault for hiring the sneaky black bastard!"

Betty looking down at herself and up at her mother. "Nobody did nothing, Mother. You know what this is. Comes every month."

Standing now, Ruby Cross, the mother, puffing and panting, ashamed before the terror and innocence and disgust and hatred in Betty Jane's eyes. Feeling like a fool and naked and exposed and indecent, and a sour, nauseating taste in her mouth. She put her arm around her girl. "I'm sorry, darling." She felt Betty Jane's body quiver with revulsion, and she hated herself and the South and her husband and the pretty black boy and the yellow-haired girl and southern womanhood and everything else.

"I'm sorry—sorry—Betty Jane darling, I'm sor—"

The girl pulled away from her and ran out of the room and down the back stairway.


## CHAPTER TWELVE

HE WALKED ALONG Middle Avenue and he kicked at a rock. Three-thirty in the afternoon, and it was hot and sticky, and the streets were dusty. Get over to Betty Jane's in a hurry, do his work just as quick as he could, shouldn't take too long, then head for the ball game a-mile-a-minute. He had to get to that game, because they needed him bad, the way he figured. That Betty—Jane—Betty Jane Cross—hadn't seen her since he-didn't-know-when, just snatch a glimpse here and grab a glance there. Usually she kept herself clean out of sight, avoided him completely. That suited him perfect, because he didn't care if he never saw her again, he kept telling himself.

Miss Ruby acted kinda funny here-lately. Sometimes he would catch her giving him dirty suspicious looks, but he wouldn't let on. Other times she was nice and extra-sweet to him. Couldn't figure that long tall white woman out.

He came in the yard and ran up the steps. He didn't have much to do this afternoon. Get in a couple of scuttles of coal for the kitchen range and chop up some splinters and run the old brush broom over the backyard. After that he would be long gone. Wonder where Betty Jane kept herself these days? To hell with Betty Jane. First thing he did was to sweep the yard, and he knew Betty Jane was watching him from the second-floor window, but he didn't let on, just kept sweeping. His face tightened, and saliva slid down his ticklish throat, funny feeling all over, but he didn't let on, not even to himself. And how did he know it was Betty Jane? Could be Miss Ruby. She always watched him so closely here-lately. But he knew it was Betty Jane—Nobody else but that yellow-haired girl, with the fresh-looking face and the devil in her eyes.

He finished sweeping the yard and he chopped up the splinters and he brought in the coal, and he stood looking around the big pretty kitchen. Wonder where was Miss Pauline? It was Friday afternoon and Friday was payday. And where was Miss Ruby? He wanted to get his money and be long gone.

Betty Jane came into the kitchen barefooted, walking softly on her toes. Funny little fearful little grin on her face. His whole body stiffened, and it hurt him to swallow, and he felt a tension like never before. Standing motionless, waiting, tasting his mouth.

She walked over towards him and she spoke in a whisper. "Hello, Rob."

"Hello." He hardly recognized his own gruff voice.

Looking him up and down like he belonged to her. "What's the matter with you?"

"Nothing the matter." Sweat on his lips and his nose and his neck.

"You and I friends?"

"I reckin so."

"I like you." She smiled at him in a friendly fashion, little worried wrinkles in the middle of her forehead. "I really do like you, but you act so funny."

He didn't want her to say that he acted funny. "What you mean act funny?"

"You don't ever be friendly. Don't ever want to talk. Act like you scared."

"I ain't scared of nobody. Just don't want to get in no trouble, that's all." He hated her for saying that he was scared, and always acting like she was so brave, and throwing her whiteness and richness and the freedom that went with them all over the place.

"Don't nobody want to get you into no trouble. Just want to be buddies, cause I really do like you."

She was close up on him and all around him and pretty blue eyes, clear and shiny and worried and smiling and sassy

**9 8**

and fresh and yellow hair and her skin was white, reddish-pinkish-white, and leave him alone goddammit! And her little firm bosom pushing out her blouse, and her skin was the color they lynched you about, and he hated her color. Looking at him as he stared at the stove.

"I just wanted to tell you good-bye, cause we going off on vacation Sunday, and we're not coming back till the first of September. Ruby upstairs taking her nap, and Pauline got the afternoon off. Sickness in her family."

She stopped talking and waited for him, but he said nothing.

"Just wanted to give you a little good-bye kiss." And before he knew it she kissed him quickly and firmly and full on his mouth, and he felt her body trembling from her head to her feet and he trembled too.

They both stood there and their hearts stopped beating, as they heard Miss Ruby coming down the back stairway. The girl squeezed his hand and ran out the side door through the big dining room, and he looked around him, but he didn't have anywhere to run.

Miss Ruby came into the kitchen with those long strides of hers, and he was glad to see the sleepy look on her face, hoping she wouldn't notice the scared look on his face which he couldn't wipe off. The smell of the girl was still in his nostrils, the taste of the girl was still on his lips, a terrible fright in the bottom of his belly, his hands on fire. Eyes narrowing narrower to hide his great guilt from this tall, monstrous white woman. What was he guilty of? He hadn't done anything. Her sleepy-looking eyes went all over the kitchen and back to him again. She never looked unfriendlier to him.

"Well, boy, you finish your work?"

"Yes'm." Swallowing hard, because there was nothing to swallow.

She looked down at him, and he felt himself growing smaller and smaller, and he wished he could get so small that she wouldn't be able to see him at all. Feeling hot and cornered and closed-in-upon.

"I reckon you waiting around to get what's coming to you."

"Yes'm." What did she mean by—get what's coming to you?

"You don't need to come back any more after today, because we're going away for the summer. Won't be back till the first of September."

Robby said nothing. He wanted to say something, couldn't

think of anything. He wanted his face to look like he was surprised and concerned.

"Well, what you say, boy? You like your job?"

"Yes'm, Miss Ruby. I like it right smart."

Miss Ruby looked at him, and her face seemed to become soft and kind, and she smiled at him like she really wanted to be friendly, but she was white and rich and he was suspicious and scared and confused. He tried to remember that she was a Yankee and different and he tried to relax, but he just couldn't do it.

"We'll look to see you again around the first of September. Hope you have a real good summer."

"Yes, mam, I thank you, and the same to you."

"Thank you, sir," she said, mocking his voice and smiling at him and making him smile a scared nervous smile.

"Well, let me see—How much do I owe you?" She reached in her little change purse and she took out three brand-new dollar bills and she handed them to him. She didn't owe him but one.

"Does that cover everything?" she asked.

"Yes, mam," he answered. "Thank you, mam."

And standing there in that big wide blue-bordered beautiful kitchen, she shook his hand and they said good-bye.

## CHAPTER THIRTEEN

"Wher—rrr—eee." He looked up from the book he was reading, his ears jumped to attention and his eyes took note of Big Sister standing before the mirror.

There it was again. "Wher—rrr—eeeee." Longer this time with a mellow, lingering tone. It sounded like Fat Gus, but it might be Ben or even Bruh Robinson.

Robby answered back the best he could. He never could whistle like most of the boys. He had tried all the methods. Like Fat Gus who whistled with his tongue on the roof of his mouth. Or like Bruh Robinson with two fingers in his mouth and pressing his tongue against his front teeth, and every other kind of way, but he just couldn't whistle. He stood up and put the book away, watching his sister still before the mirror. "Humph," he teased as he started toward the door, "getting so you can't pass that old looking glass without looking at yourself. You just as ugly today as you were yesterday or the day before. Never seen anybody so vain before in my life."

She looked back at him with a friendly kind of contempt in her eyes. "Humph your ownself—That's as much as you know about it—*Little Brother*—You look at this looking glass more than I do. You just slyer with it."

"Wher—rr—ee" Short and impatient, or so Robby imagined it.

He made a funny face at his sister and went out of the door. He had noticed though that lately Big Sister had begun to put on lots of airs, and he didn't understand it. He wasn't even sure when it had begun. It was especially confusing to him, because it was mixed up with a new tomboyishness that was not so sofistercated or whatever-you-call-it. Sometimes she wanted to follow him everywhere he went, embarrassed him with the other fellows. Trying to do all of the things that everybody understood only a boy could do, took for granted a girl shouldn't even attempt. Climbing trees and fences and spinning tops and flying kites and shooting marbles and knuckles and wrestling. Lately she was almost as bad as that Betty Jane Cross. Every time Ben Raglin came to the house she wanted to wrestle with him and box and tussle. And yet there were times when you couldn't touch Jenny Lee Youngblood with a ten-foot pole. Just as high-tone and airish as one of them moving picture stars. He didn't understand it. Using Mama's perfume, always had her head stuck in one of those moving picture magazines that Mama brought home from the white folks' houses, and sometimes she talked so proper he could hardly understand a word she said. There were other changes too, noted shyly by Robby, and slyly, physical changes.

"Hey, Robby, wake up, Christmas is coming." Fat Gus stood on the sidewalk impatiently waiting, as Robby walked dreamily down the front steps.

They stood looking each other over like full-grown men. "Whatcha know, stuff?" Robby Youngblood said in as nonchalant a manner as he could assume.

"Don't know a thing," Fat Gus answered, looking at Robby with a twinkle in his eyes like a man of the world talking to a little country boy. He shifted his great weight from one foot to the other. "Guess what?" he asked Robby.

"What?"

"Chicken butt—Go behind and lick it up."

Robby Youngblood laughed.

"Wanna go swimming?"

"Where bout?"

"Out the Big Road—Cracker Rayburn's Place."

Robby was silent, thinking about it. In the back of his mind he could hear his mother. "Don't want to hear tell of you going near that swimming hole, Robby. Get drowned before you know it." Every year some kid got drowned at Rayburn's, or shot at by Cracker Rayburn. "You go out there, Robby, I'll skin you alive, and I don't mean maybe."

"What's the matter, you sked?" Fat Gus asked him.

"What you mean scared?" Fat Gus had a way of getting next to Robby, an easy, effortless, friendly kind of a way.

"Sked—sked—You know what I mean. Sked to go swimming. Sked your Mama won't like it."

Robby wiped his forehead with his sleeve. "Leave Mama out of it."

"Sked of the white folks then. Sked of Cracker Rayburn."

"I'm not scared of no Cracker Rayburn."

"Your Mama at home?"

"Naw, she working over Mrs. Richardson. They having a big party over there tonight."

"Goddamn—White folks sure have a ball. Don't do nothing but frolic all the goddamn time."

"Mama sure gonna bring home a lot of good something-to-eat tonight."

"Well, let's go if you going," Fat Gus said.

Robby turned to go back in the house. "Be right with you."

"Where you going now?"

"Get me some tights."

"You crazy, man? Don't need no tights. We swim bare-ass—buck naked. You act like you got something to hide. You ain't got no pussy in 'tween your legs—Least I don't reckin."

Heat collected on Robby's neck. His face grew warm. "Alright," he said. "I just thought maybe—," and he started back out of the front yard with Gus.

"Course," Gus told him, his big eyes widening, "you *could* ask Jenny Lee if she wanted to go swimming."

Robby didn't even answer, kept walking out of the yard past the bright green hedges clipped short and even.

"I bet she got a beautiful stroke. Bet she can really kick her legs." Fat Gus smiled sweetly.

"Man, I don't play that mess," Robby mumbled to Gus.

They walked out Johnson Avenue toward Evergreen Street and across Shofield Field, heading towards the Big Road, as the sun beat down out of the clear blue sky, and the heat waves steamed up out of bright green grass.

Just as they turned the corner to hit the Big Road they met four other guys. Ben Raglin and Bruh Robinson and Skinny Johnson and Sonny Boy Blake.

"Well, goddamn," Sonny Boy yelled. "Look who Fat Gus brought along with him."

Fat Gus laughed. "What you expect? He my ass-hole buddy, ain't he?"

"I don't know about that, but I know one thing, he sure got a pretty sister."

All the boys laughed, even Ben Raglin. "That ain't no lie. She *ii-is* that."

Robby's face became even hotter than it already was. That was another thing new about Big Sister. The older boys were beginning to tease him about her, and they could tease damn hard.

Ben Raglin put his arm around Robby's shoulder and they walked together with the rest of the boys out the Big Road. He could say to Robby—How's Miss Laurie? And Robby could say to him—Just fine. How's Miss Sarah getting along? And nothing else would be implied, but if Gus or Sonny Boy or even Bruh Robinson said the very same thing, it would make a world of difference and you could make anything out of it you wanted to make; the sky would be the limit.

The summer in their blood made all the boys feel good. As they walked along they threw rocks at the trees and at great big rocks and they told dirty stories and all of them laughed, and they sang, and they sparred with one another like inside a boxing ring.

They left the dusty road and hit a trail through the woods. Cross County Woods was screaming out loud and crawling with summer, practically jumping. Every kind of bird that ever existed was flying around everywhere and singing like crazy. And everything imaginable (snakes included) zooting through the grass that was thick and high and you couldn't see in it, and crickets and locusts yelling to beat the band. And yet to Robby there was something soft and quiet and pretty and nice about the Cross County Woods. About a quarter of a mile into the woods they met Biff Roberts and his skinny little yellow-faced friend, Jerry Wilson. Jerry wore glasses. "What'-chall doing out here by yourself?" Sonny Boy asked.

"What you think we doing? We going swimming just like you all are." Biff didn't like the insinuating way Sonny Boy raised his eyebrows and the tone of his voice.

"Y'all ain't been playing with your wee-wees, is you?" Fat Gus asked.

"I don't have to take that kind of stuff offa you, Gus Mackey," Biff said.

The other boys giggled. "Leave him alone, Fat Gus," Robby said. Gus and Biff never got along together. They were always on the verge of fighting each other.

"They better leave they fists alone," Fat Gus said.

The boys laughed. Biff made a break towards Gus. Gus stood his ground—broad-shouldered, flat-footed and dangerous-looking. They stared at each other. Biff—red-faced, puffing and blowing. Gus with a calm smile on his wide-open face.

"Go ahead and fight—y'all ain' no kin."

"Aw come on, cut it out. Let's go swimming."

"Don't tell him nothing," Fat Gus said. "Fool him, Devil."

"One sked and the other'n glad of it," Bruh Robinson yelled.

Skinny Johnson picked up a handful of dirt and started to hold it up between them to see which one would knock it in the other one's face. Robby pulled Fat Gus away. "Come on, Gus, you come by my house and said you wanted to go swimming. So come on, let's go."

"All right," Fat Gus said, "but you better tell that half-white sonofabiscuit he better stop jumping up in my face."

Ben Raglin pulled Biff Roberts away. Biff made a big show of resisting Ben, muttering threats under his breath.

They went through the woods toward Cracker Rayburn's Place and they seemed to have forgotten that anything had happened. Fat Gus walked beside Robby, whistling *"I be glad when you dead, you rascal you."*

They came to a clearing surrounded by tall pine trees that reached towards the sky and all kinds of vines climbing all

**104**

over the place. It was roped off neatly with a double-barbed wire fence. Three big signs hung from the fence:

NO TRESPASSING
THIS MEANS YOU

Sonny Boy walked up to one of the signs and he spat on it. Skinny Johnson did too. "Sorry Mr. White Folks," Sonny Boy said, "us colored boys can't read a scratch. We just gonna take a little old swim if you don't mind, Mr. Charlie. We ain't gonna poison your pretty little water."

Everybody laughed. Fat Gus said, "To hell with Cracker Rayburn. I had Mizzes Cracker last night. She didn't say *No Trespassing.*"

Laughter all around him. Robby laughed till his throat and his nostrils got strangled and tears stood in his eyes. He heard a rustling noise in the grass behind him. He looked around quickly. Sometimes Cracker Rayburn would slip up on the boys with his sawed-off shotgun. Sonny Boy looked at Gus and said, "Now aintchoo something? Boy I bet you wouldn't know what to do with it if Old Lady Cracker offered it to you. Be so sked you wouldn't know what to do."

"Your dear-rold mother didn't say that last night. She didn't say I didn't know what to do."

Sonny Boy eyed Gus, made his face look serious. "Look out boy," he said good-naturedly. "You better watch that stuff. You know goddamn well I don't play no dozens." He picked up a rock.

"Pat your damn feet then," Fat Gus told him. "Louis Armstrong plays it." All the boys laughed.

Sonny Boy looked at Robby. "You play the dozens, Pee-wee?"

"Naw, man, you know I don't play no dozens." Robby stopped laughing.

"Well, if you don't play em, don't be enjoying em. Signifying is a damn sight worse than stealing."

Ben held up the bottom of the barbed wire while the others crawled under. Robby held the wire up for Ben.

Robby looked at the creek, flowing freely, clear and blue and greenish and mossy in places, and on the other side you could see big shiny rocks all the way to the bottom, and a wonderful, not-fully-grasped feeling swept his whole being. He licked his lips and swallowed a great fullness. This belonged to him and to Ben and to Gus and to Sonny Boy and Bruh —and even Biff—And to hell with Cracker Rayburn and all the little Rayburns. He looked around him and he started to undress as fast as he could. "Last one in is an old dirty dishrag," he yelled to the rest.

Fat Gus shouted as he ran naked towards the creek. "Last one in I had they Ma last night."

Robby took a running start and dived in the water going straight to the bottom and touching a rock and swooping up again on the other side of the creek. Then he turned and swam back to the other side with swift overhand strokes and throwing his head from side to side. "Race you over past that old willow tree," Ben called out to Robby.

"Bet you a million dollars, leave your ass in the dust."

*"On your mark—Get set—Go!"*

Fat Gus and Bruh Robinson were turning upside down and diving to the bottom and seeing who could stay under the longer. Small clouds had gathered quietly in the sky and the sun moved slowly in and out from behind them. One minute the woods would be filled with bright sunlight, and another minute the tall trees would cast shadows on the short trees and all of the trees would cast soft calm shadows on the ground and the grass and the bushes and across the old creek. They had been swimming for over an hour, when all of a sudden a big grayish-black cloud blotted out the sun, and the woods turned quickly from daylight to darkness. You could hardly see the shadows. A deep ominous rumble came out of the east.

Sonny Boy said, "Uh-uh."

Robby looked up at the sky and he said to Sonny Boy, "What's the matter, man, you scared of a little old thunder?"

Before Sonny Boy could answer a streak of lightning flashed across the sky and the clouds opened up and the rain came down by the great big bucketfuls. The boys yelled and they got out of the water and snatched up their clothes and got underneath the barbed wire—every man for himself—and they dashed towards a shack about fifty yards away and, as they entered, could hear things scampering all over the place making room for them. Ben Raglin pulled a pack of cards out of the pocket of his trousers and they started to play a game called Strip Buck Naked.

Sonny Boy's eyes wandered up towards the roof of the shack. "Goddamn," he said. "We'd'a done better we hadda stayed outside. We get drownded messing around in this sonofabitch."

The boys laughed quietly. Fat Gus looked up from the cards in his hand. "What you bitching about? It's damn sight better'n that outhouse you live in."

The boys looked up and snickered. Sonny Boy's eyes twinkled. "Watch out there, Fat Ass. I done told you I don't play that."

Fat Gus looked up at Sonny Boy and flashed a broad friendly smile. "How is your mother, Sonny? Goddamn, she a sweet lady. I'd do anything in the world for her. I swear to my Jesus."

The boys' giggling spread, went up and down. Fat Gus glanced around him with an innocent look on his wide open face, caught Robby's eye and gave him a quick wink. Robby held his head down bursting wide open, laughter oozing out of him.

Sonny Boy looked at him. "I done told you, Peewee. You don't play it, don't enjoy it."

The lightning flashed sharp and a loud clap of thunder came almost at the same instant. It sounded as if it had struck something nearby. The boys got quiet, appeared to be concentrating solely on the card game. Ben Raglin looked up at the roof. The rain was pouring in now all over the place. They had had to move their card game a couple of times.

Ben spoke aloud to no one in particular. "What would you do if you had a million dollars?"

"Who—me?"

"Any y'all. Don't make no difference."

There was silence around the circle. You could hear the rapid-fire barrage of the rain coming through the roof. You could hear curious sounds of crawling in corners, making you think about snakes and lizards and rats and everything else.

"———had a million dollars I be *lon—ong*—gone," Gus said. "Tell Crossroads, Georgia, kiss my royal hindparts."

"Man—You better be long gone. Colored man with a million dollars last in this town 'bout long as a snowball in hell."

Skinny Johnson had yellowish color and very bad eyes that

were kept half closed all the time. He turned and spat behind him, looked at Ben through squinting eyes. "Donchall ass-buckets know Mr. Charlie ain't gon stand for no millionaire Negroes? Y'all talk like a fool. Who got all the money? The white man. And god-dammit he gon hang on to it. Be a fool if he didn't."

Ben looked at Skinny. "I said *If,* man *If. If* you had a million."

Skinny spat again. He was always spitting, like a man who chewed tobacco. *"If,"* he repeated. "If the dog hadn't stop to shit he'd a caught the god-damn rabbit."

"If I had a million dollars," Sonny Boy said fiercely, "I'd buy me a million guns, and give every black man I come across a gun a piece. Get all these Negroes together and go gunning for white folk. I bet that'd be something. Get through, Mr. Charlie's ass be dragging the ground." He took a package of cigarette butts out of his pocket and lighted one.

Robby looked at Sonny Boy, as the rain continued to pour outside, and he heard Fat Gus say, "Be sure to count me in. That's just what I'd like." And it seemed to him as he listened to Sonny Boy and his narrow eyes narrowed, that Sonny Boy must've been eavesdropping or standing around peeking into a dream Robby had had about black armies and white armies.

"If I had a million dollars," Robby said, as he swallowed the dampness that stuck in his throat and his face broke out into a damp cool sweat, "I'd buy me a great big old house, prettiest and biggest house in the whole wide world. I'd have enough room in it for all my family and all my friends to live in. I'd have me a swimming pool in the backyard and a basketball court. I wouldn't never let my Mama work again." His tongue was getting thick. "And my Daddy neither. I'd buy me a factory and I'd give everybody jobs black and white, but I would make the colored men the foremen over the white men. I would pay them all good wages, and I wouldn't work them so hard."

Skinny Johnson spat again through his teeth, another thing Robby couldn't do, spit through his teeth. "Damn," Skinny said, "wonder if this rain ever gonna let up."

"Damn," Ben said, "I sure would like to take a trip up north. They say things mighty nice up there. New York City, place like that, Chicago, Illinois,—Detroit, Michigan. Say a Negro can get most any kind of a job. Go to all the pitcher shows, eat anywhere. Course I don't believe everything I hear, but I sure would like to try it out. See for my ownself."

The boys were quiet, looking at him. A piece of raindrop hit him kerdap on the nose. "I got a Aunt and Uncle in Washington, D.C. Sure would like to pay them a visit."

Fat Gus said, "Man, that ain't nothing but a whole lot of crap. Mr. Ray told me and he know everything about things like that. Ray Morrison is a smart colored man. He say a cracker is a cracker all over the country, and a Negro is a Negro. And he been everywhere. He say Washington, D.C. is specially bad, like Mississippi."

"It couldn't be like that. It's the nation's capital. That's where the government is."

"I wouldn't give a good goddamn if it's the nation's *capital*. I reckin he ought to know. He's sure been there." Gus looked around at the rest of the boys. He had all of their attention. The rain sounded like it would beat the roof in. "This is really supposed to be true," he said. "You can ask Mr. Ray if you don't believe it. A colored man from Alabama went into one of them Washington restaurants one morning—see. He was a rough stud and didn't mean to take no shit. There wouldn't be no stuff if they didn't start no stuff. He had on his togs and he was sharp as a rat-tud. And that's sharp on both ends." The boys laughed softly. "As I was saying, when I was so rudely interrupted, he went into this uppidy restaurant in Washington, D.C. and the cracker waiter walked over to him and asked him was he looking for somebody—see. The Negro said I ain't looking for nobody, I want something to eat. Cracker waiter told him we don't serve no niggers in here. Colored man looked at the waiter and told him—Man, I don't want no niggers for breakfast. Just give me some stew beef."

The boys laughed and stomped their heels and held their stomachs and they slapped their thighs and some of them coughed. Sonny Boy laughing a high shrill laugh, sounded just like an old dog howling from far away.

Sonny Boy stopped laughing and said, "Man, he nacherl born had that cracker's waters on."

Skinny Johnson was choking with laughter. He cleared his throat long and loud. "That nigger was something, I reckin."

Fat Gus looked at Skinny. "Man, dontchoo know bettern to be talking about *nigger*? I'm surprised at you. Cantchoo say Negro? Jes cause you yaller, that don't make you white."

Skinny didn't know what to say or what to do. He looked at the rest of the fellows whose faces were serious now, turning over in their minds what Fat Gus had said. And something turned over and over in Robby's stomach, as he remembered, at first vaguely, him and Fat Gus and Ben in the stinking outhouse at school and-and-and he had corrected Gus about saying nigger and Gus had said Mama this and Mama that—

Gus didn't even look in his direction now, kept his eyes on Skinny. "How you gon make white folks stop calling you nigger, if you say nigger your own goddamn self?"

"A colored man that call his ownself a nigger is a goddamn fool," Bruh Robinson said, as if it were a fact he had just discovered this very minute. "It's just like committing suicide," Robby said. "Suicide's worse than first degree murder."

He wiped his eyes with the back of his hand. He had heard Uncle Ray tell a whole heap of tales, but he'd never heard the one about stew beef in Washington. He sat there still laughing with a picture in his mind of the Negro in the Washington restaurant. He thought about what Gus and Bruh and he had said about colored folks saying nigger, and he felt good about it— His mother was the smartest woman in the world—didn't care what color. All of a sudden he knew a very very good and warm and comfortable feeling, like sitting by a pot-bellied stove on a cold winter day with your stomach full of food. He looked around him at the other boys, and he felt close to them; a glow inside of him flowing through his body like so many cups of hot water tea, heating his insides. Looking into each one of their faces and thinking to himself, maybe it would always be like this, couldn't they be buddies forever and ever?

Ben Raglin looked at Robby and he shook his handsome head. "Goddamn—goddamn—A colored man catch hell everywhere he go."

Robby looked at Ben and especially at Ben, and he wanted to say to Ben and all the rest of them the things that he was thinking right then and there. He wanted to tell them that if they kept being buddies even after they became grown men and never stopped being buddies ever, then white folks wouldn't be able to touch them with a ten-foot pole. He wanted to tell them, as his face filled up and a frog caught in his throat, and a brief chill danced swiftly across his broad shoulders, but thought to himself that maybe he was wrong, and maybe they wouldn't listen because he was the youngest. He wanted to say that sticking together was the most important thing in the whole wide world, but he didn't say a word.

Bruh Robinson looked up at the roof and around at the boys and up at the leaky roof again. He cupped his big hands around his mouth, and he started a sing-song:

> *If you white*
> *You right—*
> *If you yaller*
> *You meller—*
> *If you brown*
> *Stick around—*
> *If you black*
> *Goddammit—get back!*

Robby looked at Bruh Robinson and he laughed a dry laugh like his father laughed sometimes. "Hey, Bruh, say that again and go more slow."

Bruh looked at Robby and the rest of the boys. "Boy, I'm gon say it one more time, but all y'all listen good, cause I'm just like Shakespeare, I don't in generally repeat myself."

> *If you white*
> *You right—*
> *If you yaller—*
> *You meller*
> *If you brown—*
> *Stick around*
> *If you black*
> *Get back—*

Skinny looked at Bruh seriously. "You can' fool me," he said. "Didn't no Shakespeare write that poem."

Fat Gus said, "Hell naw, man, Snakeshit wrote it. He smarter than Shakespeare."

The boys giggled at Gus.

"Whoever wrote it," Robby Youngblood said, "they sure told the truth."

"Ain' no stuff," Ben Raglin said. "A black man sure gets a hard row to hoe. Ain' no lie—especially a black woman."

Robby said, "I heard them say they got colored schools—colleges—right here in Georgia, where they don't allow a dark skin girl to attend. You got to be high yaller—almost white."

"Great God Almighty—you reckin so?"

"Give me a black gal any old time," Fat Gus said. "The blacker the berry the sweeter the juice."

"I likes me one of them teasing browns. Know what I mean?" Skinny said.

"Teasing browns—Boy, you don't know nothing about no women—wouldn't know what to do with one if you had her all by your ownself."

Skinny Johnson looked fiercely at Gus. "Black folks don't do nothing but study evil. Black woman sleep with her fists balled up."

"Did your dear old mother have her fists balled when she slept with that white policy man, you half-white, shit-colored sonofabitch?" Fat Gus said.

Skinny jumped to his feet and he grabbed up a rock about the size of his fist. "You don't talk to me like that goddammit!"

Ben said quietly, "Put the rock down, Skinny. We ain't doing nothing but kidding each other. All of us buddies."

"Yes," Robby said. "All of us buddies."

"Don't tell him nothing. Just let him keep on making them country breaks at me," Fat Gus said, blinking his eyelashes. "Let the devil fool him."

Skinny walked away muttering to himself, threw the rock in a corner.

Robby swallowed the damp dusty air. He started to say Mama say, but he was a big boy amongst big boys, so he spoke for himself. "Ain't no difference—black, yellow or brown—All of us Negroes. One color ain't no better than the other. We need to stick together, don't care what color." He swallowed again, harder than before, and a cold sweat broke out on his serious brow, but it felt real good talking to the boys like this—very very good. And especially the looks of respect in their faces.

"You can say that again," he heard Fat Gus say.

Every minute a new leak started somewhere in the shack and it didn't look like it would ever stop raining. Maybe they would have to spend the night. Great God Almighty! Suppose Cracker Rayburn caught them in there.

Ben Raglin said, "Wonder what kind of teacher they going to get to take old man Mulberry's place."

Robby said, "I sure hope he's a good one. Me and Gus'll be in his room."

"Yeah," Gus said. "I hope he got some git-up about him. Old man Mulberry didn't have sense enough to pour piss out of a tin can—teaching school—He didn't go any further than the fourth grade his own self."

"Don't talk about the poor old man like that," Robby said. "He did the best he could. He's dead and gone so let him rest easy."

"But he up in Heaven with a colored choir singing for white folks," Fat Gus said.

All the boys laughed.

"I ain't glad old man Mulberry dead," Sonny Boy said. "But I sure hope they don't get that choir up again—singing all those old-fashioned spirituals for Mr. Charlie's pleasure."

Robby remembered last term when the big rich white folks and a few poor ones turned out at the auditorium—and the practice practice practice, the weeks of practice. Old Man Mulberry was in his glory. Every afternoon he had the Pleasant Grove School Chorus practicing—"Steal Away Steal Away Steal Away to Jesus." And the night the Big Rich White Folks came with their pleasant smiles on their rich white faces and the singing, the beautiful singing that made you feel funny and special, and the clapping of the pinkish-white hands and the smiling white faces, the false polite smiles—the knowing smiles—and the words spoken by the white folks under their grinning breaths, and some out loud, meant to be overheard— "Darkies sure can sing like nobody's business"—"They sing so good cause they ain't got no worries"—"There ain't nothing in the world like colored folks' spirituals"—Robby had felt there was something wrong, something nasty and dirty, about colored children singing Negro songs for the pleasure of white folks. And Mama had said that Negro spirituals were the most beautiful songs in the whole wide world, but colored folks ought not to be made to sing them for white folks' pleasure—especially colored children—She told Mr. Mulberry—

"They say that new teacher going to be from up the country —New York City."

Fat Gus got up and walked back and forth switching his broad behind. He raised his voice to a very high pitch and he smacked his lips. "I do hope you young men will be able to *understand* the new teacher. You know how we *tawk* when we come from New Yawk."

The boys laughed at Gus.

Ben said seriously, "I hope he don't come down here putting on a whole heap of airs."

Skinny said, "Man, you know he gon put on some of them ten cents airs. Wish I was gonna be in his class. I show that sonofabiscuit a thing or two."

Robby closed his eyes, trying to make a picture in his mind of what the new teacher would be like. "Give the poor man a break," Robby said. "Wait till he gets here and see what he's like."

"To hell with the teacher."

"I'll be in his room," Biff Roberts said. "I'll show him a thing or two. Be sorry he ever heard of Crossroads, Georgia."

"Whatchoo know about it?" Fat Gus said.

"I reckin I ought to know," Biff said. "I been to New York. All them Harlem Negroes got their ass on their shoulders. Think they better than the colored down here."

"Wait till he gets here," Robby argued. "He might be the best teacher we ever had." Hoping it would be true. His mind's eye saw a tired old man who had gotten too slow for the pace of a great big city like New York, but he hoped it wasn't true.

Fat Gus got to his feet. He spoke softly like a full grown man. "I think Robby Youngblood is right. I think he's ten times smarter than you, don't care where you been. I think we ought to wait and see what the teacher is like, before we say we gon do this and we gon do that."

"My father said—" Biff began.

"To hell with your father."

"Anyhow," Biff said, his cheeks turning red, "I don't have to wait. I know them Harlem darkies to a tee. They think they better'n us down here."

"Did your dear-rold Mother think she was bettern us when she slept with that cracker before she hatched you?"

Biff jumped towards Gus and they both went down to the floor, Biff on top. They rolled over and over grunting and puffing. The boys watched quietly—serious faced. Skinny edged over towards the corner where he had dropped the big rock and he picked it up and put his hand behind his back. He moved towards the center of the floor where Gus and Biff

**114**

were fighting. Gus was on top of Biff now and he picked Biff's head up and banged it against the floor.

"Dontchoo ever try to jump me again, you half-white, chickenshit sonofabitch."

"Don't talk about my folks then," Biff shouted.

"I'll talk about your folks—I'll talk about your folks—Your pa ain't nothing but a white folks' colored man. Your mother is a—"

Skinny jumped towards Fat Gus with the rock in his hand. "Look out, Gus!"

Robby had been half-way keeping an eye on Skinny and when Skinny leaped towards Gus, he jumped towards Skinny and hit him knee-high with a flying tackle. The rock went one way and Skinny went the other. "Stay out of it," Robby said, after catching his breath. "Ain't nobody going to gang up on Gus."

The other boys moved in now, Ben and Sonny Boy, to break up the fight between Fat Gus and Biff. "Alright," Sonny Boy said, "goddammit—you guys wanna fight all the time, join the goddamn army."

Robby stood his ground, kept an eye on Skinny. The boys pulled Gus and Biff apart. "Tell him to stop messing with me," Biff said, his voice quivering as if he were about to burst into a cry.

After it was over they sat quietly listening to the rain which seemed to be coming down even harder than before. Robby was sorry the fight had started. Before the fight there had been such a warm close feeling between them, and now it was gone. He looked around at the other boys. He wanted desperately to recapture that feeling again. He reached around in his head for something to say to them. "That's the trouble with us Negroes," he said. "We always fighting each other instead of the white man."

They looked at Robby and they looked at each other. Ben Raglin shook his head in agreement. Bruh Robinson said, "You right about that."

Fat Gus looked at Robby and they caught each other's eye, and Robby thought about Fat Gus and him fighting in the back of the Big Store, and he thought that Gus was thinking about the same thing. "I didn't start no fight with Biff," Fat Gus said. "He started it."

"That's alright about who started the fight." Robby looked at Fat Gus. "Enough to make anybody want to fight. Always talking about each other's mother." He cleared his throat. "Everybody want to jump on the schoolteacher before you give him a chance. He's a colored man too. You all always want to fight everybody but Mr. Charlie." It seemed to Robby that his voice was changing, right before his ears. He was really growing up. He looked around at all of their faces. "Let's us get together and stay together and let's be buddies. —All of us buddies—"

The boys shook their shame-faced heads up and down, most of the boys.

Suddenly the rain began to slacken and soon it would stop, because pieces of sunshine came in brightly through the holes in the roof along with the rain, and the shack lit up as if somebody had pulled an electric cord.

Bruh Robinson looked up at the sun-filled roof. "Damn," he said. "The sun shining and the rain still raining. The Devil must be whupping the hell out of his wife."

## CHAPTER FOURTEEN

### EXTRA!

GEORGE BENJAMIN CROSS SENIOR DEAD! A great big headline that took up the whole front page of the *Crossroads Daily Telegram*.

### EXTRA!

Robby Youngblood was in his nightshirt. He looked both ways to see if anybody was on the street so early in the morning. Doggone that paper boy—always throwing the paper to the other side of the porch. He walked over quickly and picked up the paper and he meant to hurry back into the house before somebody saw him in his nightshirt, but his eyes caught the headline and brought him to a stop.

*George Benjamin Cross Senior dead!* He heard somebody walking on the street and he looked down at himself and he ran back inside of the house. He walked through the first room to the kitchen. Mama was at the stove. Big Sister was washing up. Daddy had already gone to work.

"Old man Cross is dead," he said. "Mr. Cross Sr."

"Mr. Cross Senior dead—" Mama said. "Stop fooling, Robby."

"Is he really dead?" Big Sister asked.

"I'm not fooling," Robby said excitedly. "He really is dead. See for yourself. Don't take my word." He sat down at the kitchen table looking at the paper, and he felt a little proud, because he was the first in the house to know.

Mama and Big Sister came and looked over his shoulder. Big Sister said, "Everybody goes when the wagon comes." And she shrugged her shoulders.

"Hush your mouth," Mama told Big Sister. "Go on now and finish washing up."

Mama walked back over to the stove. "Read it to us, Robby."

Robby coughed nervously. "Death came quietly in the middle of the night to Crossroads' first citizen."

"Everybody *do* have to die, don't they, Mama?" Jenny Lee insisted.

*"Does,"* Mama corrected. "Yes, Jenny Lee, everybody has to die sooner or later."

Robby cleared his throat in annoyance at the interruption. "George Benjamin Cross Senior, founder and builder of the County of Cross and the City of Crossroads, passed away last night in the middle of his sleep—"

"He done lived his three-score-ten anyhow," Jenny Lee said. "He was living out somebody else's time."

"You better hush your mouth, girl," Mama said. "Quit interrupting your brother."

Robby kept reading, louder and louder, about the death of the biggest man in Crossroads, Georgia. The *Telegram* was full of it. The editorial page said he was one of the pillars of the Southern tradition. Pictures all through the paper—kindly-looking pictures of Mr. Cross Senior at various stages of his long useful life. Pictures of Mr. Cross Jr. too. And Mrs. Cross Jr., and even Betty Jane. He gazed at the picture of Betty Jane Cross and his face grew warm. She would be coming home now from Long Island Sound. He felt somehow that he was a part of all this, and yet on the other hand that he was outside of it. He put the paper down and put on his trousers and went out the back door on his way to the toilet. He knew that Big Sister was right—that everybody had to go sooner or later, but when a great big white man like Mr. Cross Sr. died, it took you by surprise and made you stop to think real hard. And what difference would it make in Crossroads, Georgia?

Outside now, he looked up at the sky where the sun was coming up just like it had done yesterday and the day before and last year this time. Nothing seemed different. After he was dead old man Cross wasn't any better off than Skippy. Skippy was buried in the ground and Mr. Cross would be buried in the ground and that was that. Dead was dead, no matter who you were, except that cats didn't go to Heaven. He sat in the toilet thinking that he would watch all day long to see if there was any difference in Crossroads, Georgia, now that old man Cross was dead.

He had come back in the house and had washed up and dressed and was eating his breakfast. He looked up and around. "Mama, is old man Cross already in Heaven, or does he have to wait till he's buried in the ground?"

"How you know he's going to Heaven?" Big Sister asked. "Did the Good Lord speak to you out in the toilet?"

He looked sideways at Big Sister. She was getting just as sassy as the devil here lately. He didn't know what was getting into her.

Mama looked at him and said, "I don't know, sugar pie. Nobody's ever been back to tell the story."

"Mr. Cross Senior was an evil old man," Robby Youngblood said.

Mama had to go over in the Heights to do some sewing that day and Robby Youngblood walked all the way downtown just looking around listening to people.

In Jesup's Barber Shop he heard colored people talking about old man Cross.

"All that money and he couldn't take it with him," Booker Roberts said.

"Wonder did he leave anything to his servants," Joe Jesup said, looking up from clipping a bald-headed man's hair. "Is the will been read?"

"He wasn't such a bad cracker."

"He was bad enough."

"Maybe things won't be so bad for the colored man now.

They say Mr. Cross Jr. is a little bit different. Lived up north, you know. Went to school up there."

"Yet and still, a cracker is a cracker," Joe Jesup said, "don't care where he went to school."

Dick Dixon looked up from the checker game. "Y'all colored folks worried about old man Cross—this and that—He ain't paying none of you any rabbit-ass mind."

"Ain' nobody worried—"

"Bet he up in Heaven now getting fixed up—looking around to see how many colored servants he gon need. He gon be real mad with Saint Peter when he find out they don't allow no colored folks in Heaven *eee—tall.*"

The men laughed. "A cracker is a bitch." Some of them stomped their feet. "Dick Dixon, you better hush your mouth."

Joe Jesup winked his eye at Robby. "Your Ma know where you is boy?"

"Yes, sir," he lied.

"You better git outa here and git for home," Joe Jesup said.

Robby left the barber shop, walked up Harlem Avenue and turned into Oglethorpe Street. He stopped walking. He saw two crackers standing near the post office. He stood near them listening to them, without their knowing. "It sure was a shock," one of them said. "He died in his sleep. Didn't suffer at all. They say it was heart failure."

"Yeah," the other cracker said. He was a chunky-shouldered cracker. He wasn't really short, but he was built stocky from the ground on up.

"I sure is sorry," the first cracker said. "Young Cross Jr. too easy on niggers. They liable to git clean outa hand. I seen him shake a nigger's hand once."

"Don't make me no bit of difference," the second cracker said. "It don't put no more money in my pay envelope one way or the other."

The first cracker looked hard at the second cracker. "You better hush your mouth, Oscar Jefferson. You talk like a nigger-lover." He looked up and caught Robby's eye. Robby started to walk away. "Hey, nigger boy, look up at that courthouse clock for me and tell me what time it is. My eyes kinda gitting bad on me."

Robby's eyes flashed angrily at the long tall white man. "I

know good and damn well you ain't talking to me," he said to the cracker and he walked down the street.

"Now what you reckin the matter with that boy?" the first cracker said to the other one.

"He mad with you cause you called him a nigger," Oscar Jefferson said.

"What's wrong with that? He's a nigger, ain't he? My eyes ain't that bad."

Oscar Jefferson laughed. "You talk like an ignorant fool," he told the other cracker and he scratched his head. "That boy sure do remind me of somebody else. I swear fore God."

Old man Cross Senior's body stayed above ground five long days, and every one of those days was no different from the rest. It didn't thunder or lightning and there wasn't any earthquake. The sun came up every morning and stayed up all day long and it was hot with very little breeze if any at all. His funeral was held on a Tuesday afternoon and the factories were shut down all day that day. All of the stores downtown excepting some on Harlem Avenue wore black crepes in mourning for Crossroads' first citizen. People stood on the street and watched the funeral procession with its long black beautiful cars. Robby stood on Popular Street, not far from the church. He saw the family dressed in black coming out of the church. He saw Mrs. Cross Jr. and Mr. Cross Jr., tall and thoughtful-looking. He saw many other people of the family, and the big shots that came from all over the state, all over the south. The papers said they came from all over the country. Important-looking people. And he also saw Betty Jane getting into one of those long black cars. He almost did not recognize her at all. She looked so small and subdued and tense and sad, and there was nothing about her that he actually remembered. Her bigness, her sassiness, her know-everythingness, her over-all aggressiveness. He thought that she had glimpsed him as she got into the car, thought he saw her face light up for a moment. Then she sank back into the plushy cushions and disappeared from view.

The week following the funeral he heard that the Cross Juniors were going to move out to the edge of town to The Crosses, which was the name of old man Cross's giant estate on the Eastern Highway.

Robby could hardly wait for school to open and to see what the new teacher was going to be like. Would he be a young man or an old man or an in-between man? He wasn't worried so much about how the boys in the school would treat him, but he had heard Mama say she hoped the new teacher from New York City didn't get in any trouble with the crackers down here, because up-the-country Negroes weren't used to taking all kind of stuff from white folks. And that was a natural fact.

*Part Two*

# NO HIDING PLACE

*I went to the rock to hide my face*
*The rock cried out—No hiding place—*

FROM A NEGRO SPIRITUAL
*"No Hiding Place"*

# CHAPTER ONE

"WHAT THE HELL am I doing in this jerkwater town?" the young black man with the lightish brown eyes asked himself, looking out of a window of the dirty train as it pulled jerkily into the station.

*"Crossroads, Georgia—Crossroads, Georgia—"*

The old gray-haired Negro porter, whose feet were so big and flat and bad that he limped when he walked, came up the aisle to where the young man was seated. "This is your stop, son," the old man said. "Good luck to you in your school-teaching job. You'll need all the luck in the world I reckin."

"You telling me?" the young man said under his breath. But he said to the old man, "Thank you, sir." All of the built-up confidence oozing out of him, now that he had actually arrived. And he reached up and pulled his bag down from the rack. It was a handsome brand-new leather bag with engraved initials R.W.M., given to him by his father.

The train shuffled slowly into the station blowing and snorting like a tired old workhorse and in spite of his nervous anxiety Richard Myles smiled, thinking of the stories his father used to tell him, when he was a boy in Brooklyn, New York, not very many years before.

His father had pushed him onward and upward ever since he could remember. His mother liked to tell about the first time his father had laid eyes on him, a new-born baby in a Brooklyn hospital. "He's going to be a lawyer—He's going to be a lawyer—" his father had said excitedly to the nurse, and then had added in a shame-faced afterthought—"How's my wife? How's Mrs. Myles?"

His father had come originally from a little town outside of Birmingham, Alabama, where he had taught in a country school for thirty dollars a month. His father had wanted to be a lawyer, a professional man. He wanted security, wanted to own a home, wanted human dignity, wanted everything at once. But Charles Henry Myles worked as a porter in the New York subways. Most of the time he worked on two jobs at the same time. He tried to study law through a correspondence course after coming home late at night from the second job, but it didn't work out, because there was a limit to a human being's energy—even Charles Myles's.

When Richard Myles was seven the Myleses started to buy a home. It wasn't much of a home, one of those old-fashioned brownstones, already used up by well-to-do white folks, shaken apart by the subway that ran underneath. Every time you looked around it was repair this and fix up that and patch up the other.

Sunday nights, black men and brown men and light-complected men would collect at the Myles's home and drink coffee and eat cake and sometimes drink home-made wine and talk about white supremacy and the American government like dangerous revolutionaries, and Charles Myles was the most vocal of them all. None of these men were native New Yorkers. They came from South Carolina and Georgia and Mississippi and Barbados and Trinidad and other points south. He always took these occasions to show his son off, waking him up sometimes in the middle of the night.

"Leave him alone. Let the boy sleep," Clara Johnson Myles would say to him. The mother was a handsome dignified woman from South Carolina.

In patched-up pajamas the boy would stand there before the men rubbing his eyes, angry with his daddy. "Say the Gettysburg Address," his father would command him. And the little boy would stand there trembling with sleep, wondering why his father tortured him like this, trying to remember how it began. "Go ahead, son. Say it for the gentlemen. It won't take long. You can go back to sleep." Turning to the men. "He can say it all right—as well as any grown man. Go ahead, Richard Wendell, say it without stopping." Richard Wendell Myles stumbling through the great speech with his mouth poked out and sleepyhead tears standing just on the other side of his light brown eyes. "Go on back to bed, son. See, I told you he could say it. You ought to hear him say it when he's really wide awake. Imagine that? Seven years old!"

Some nights Clara would sit there, the only woman, listening to these men talk about conditions of the Negro north and south and praising Marcus Garvey and damning Marcus Garvey, and praising Frederick Douglass and praising Booker T. Washington and damning Booker T. Washington, and she would take out her anger on the West Indians who happened to be present. "So much idle talk," she would say. "You Negroes ought to go out to Bedloe's Island every day and kiss the Statue of Liberty. If things are so bad here, why don't you carry yourself back to the West Indies. British subjects—You never had it so good in all you life." The men would look at her with surprised injured looks on their faces, change the subject for a few minutes, then back to it again, this time including the damn evil British.

Once when Richard was in the eighth grade, he brought home his report card containing five A's and one B. His father looked at him with pride-filled eyes, shook his head and said, "Son, you're falling down on the job. You just got to do better. What you mean bringing me this B in history?" One day seated at the dinner table after coming home from one of his jobs, Charles Myles looked up into the face of his son and said to him— "Boy, remember this—Whatever you be, be the best there is. If it's digging a ditch, be the best ditch digger, I don't care what it is be the best there is. If it's shooting craps be the best crapshooter."

When Richie was thirteen years old, the Grand Lodge of Harlem sponsored an oratorical contest for one-year college tuition scholarships for Negro high school youth. Charles Myles entered his son in the contest. Every night after he came home from his second job he would drive his precious son. "Don't talk from your mouth. Speak from down here. Speak from your diaphragm—All right now, repeat that first line again." On and on till Clara would break it up. "Let that poor boy go to bed and get some sleep. Don't you know he got school for tomorrow? If you want to kill yourself, don't carry him along with you."

"Everything I do, Clara, is for his own good." The father's little eyes assuming a deeply-hurt, misunderstood, picked-upon expression.

It was a real rough winter that year, and living at the Myles's house was almost as bad as living outside. The subway had shaken the poor house aloose, and the weather came in like it paid the rent. One night about a week away from the date of the oratorical contest, Charles Myles came in from work and as he sat at the dinner table, he looked over at his son, who sat in a corner with his head in a book. His tired eyes lighted up. "How you doing, Richie boy?" The boy tried to hide his annoyance, as he took his eyes away from the book. "I'm all right, father." And at that moment, he felt a tickling in his throat that caused him to cough. "What's the matter, Richard? Was that you just coughed?"

"Yes, father."

The man dropped his fork and jumped up from the table. "Oh, my God! It can't be! How you feel, son?"

"I'm all right. Just got a funny feeling in my throat."

They doctored on Richie and they put him to bed, and there wasn't any practice for the contest that night. But the next night Charles Myles sat at the boy's bedside and went over his speech with him, likewise the third night. On the fourth night he asked the boy how he was feeling, and Richard said much better, and his father said are you sure, and Richard said yes and he coaxed the sick boy out of his bed. He went over the speech with the boy for almost an hour, and Richie's head began to feel dizzy and the room seemed to dance. Myles felt his wife's angry eyes heavily upon him. His small eyes shifted toward Clara for a second and looked back just in time to see Richie slump quietly to the floor.

"Great God Almighty! Son—What's the matter?" He jumped toward the boy.

"What you think the matter?" Clara shouted. "You crazy jackass, you trying to kill the boy! You think more of that darn contest than you do your own son."

He went for the doctor but it was the next morning before the doctor came. He said the boy was mighty sick with the flu and would have to stay in bed. Give him this three times a day and give him the other, and keep him perfectly still. And after the doctor had gone, Clara said to Charles, "I'm so glad the doctor got here before you left for work, so you could hear what he had to say. You wouldn't've taken my word for it. I guess you know now there won't be no oratorical contest as far as Richard is concerned."

He looked at his wife, his small eyes begging her to try to understand him. "You talk like I don't have the boy's interest at heart, Clara. If anybody in the world loves Richard Wendell Myles, I certainly do."

"Never mind who loves him. I guess you understand he won't be able to be in any contest. I hope you got that through that blockhead of yours." Charles looked back at his wife as he went out of the door, late for his job, muttering to himself— "The doctor didn't say he wouldn't be able to participate."

That night Richie hardly slept a wink. His feverish body ran hot and cold. His head felt like it weighed a million tons, aching all over like a rotten tooth. His nostrils were clogged, and he breathed hard through his mouth. His throat was inflamed, felt like it had been scratched by broken glass. His chest hurt and his right side was painful. One of the many times he awoke during the night, he felt like he was choking and he gasped for breath. His mother rushed in from her bedroom. He heard a faint snore and he looked on the other side of his bed where his father sat slumped in a chair asleep with his mouth open, a battered cigar hanging from his lips, dead to the world. A faint smile crinkled in the corners of the boy's feverish lips.

The following morning the fever abated, and he began to sweat like never before. He seemed to be draining himself of all the water inside of him. He threw all the bedcovers from on top of him. His body began to cool. That night his father took his temperature. It was down to 99.5. "How you feel, son?" It was the night of the contest. "Much better, father."— "That's good, son. Mighty good." Fifteen minutes later. "Feeling better, Richard Wendell?" Caressing the boy's forehead. "Yes, father, much better."

"Why don't you leave the boy alone? For Heaven's sake."

"All right, Clara. All right—All right." Taking his cheap watch out of his fob pocket and glancing at it slyly and nervously.

"Never saw a man like you in all my born days." She walked slowly out of the room and upstairs to her girls, leaving him alone with *his* boy.

The man got busy. He coaxed his boy tenderly out of bed with soft sweet words, and he quietly got the boy's clothes together, dressing him up in his Sunday blue serge, and they went out into the night where the snow packed high six inches deep, and they caught the subway going all the way to Harlem. It was long past midnight when they got back home, but they saw a dim light in the window downstairs, and Richie felt his father's hand tighten on his shoulder. The tall graceful woman met them at the door. She took the boy in her arms and she looked at her husband with hate gleaming fiercely in her usually calm eyes, but she didn't say a word. She undressed the boy like he was a two-year-old baby, and she gave him some medicine and put him into bed. "Clara, you should have been there. He was grand—He was wonderful—I tell you, I never was so proud before in my life. My son is going to be a great—" She turned on him. "Your son—your son—I suppose he doesn't belong to me at all—I suppose I didn't have nothing to do with bringing him in the world—I'm just only his mother—If it was left up to you he wouldn't be nobody's son—wouldn't live to be a man. But you outdid yourself this night of our Lord. You crazy vain old ignorant jackass."

"He won the prize—He won the prize—He won first prize! Don't you hear what I'm saying?"

She shook her finger at him, her lips trembling and her eyes flashing. "If anything happens to that boy in there, I swear to God, I'm going to have you arrested for first degree murder!"

The boy took a turn for the worse. The doctor came the next day. He took one look at the boy and he turned to the parents. "What happened to this boy? What have you been doing to him?" The parents said nothing. He turned to the boy again and he worked for over an hour with his sleeves rolled up like a real working man. Then he turned to them again. "Well, Mr. and Mrs. Myles, you got a sick boy on your hands now. He's got pneumonia, and he's got it in both sides, he's got double pneumonia. If you don't follow my instructions to a tee you won't have any son."

The father gasped. "Oh Lordy-Lord!" When the doctor left the father broke down, cried like a baby. "It's my fault, Clara —It's all my fault! Lord have mercy on my soul, I don't deserve such a wonderful son—Lord knows I don't!" He didn't go to work that day nor did he go for two whole weeks. Most of the time he sat by Richie's bed watching him waver between life and death, and swearing at himself and bursting into tears and praying to God whom he didn't really believe in. He wouldn't let anybody else do anything for Richie, excepting the doctor. He nursed the boy slowly back to health. But when he finally went back to work he didn't have a job, either one of them. And before he landed two regular jobs again, the mortgage people had taken away his home. It was months later that Richie overheard his father say to his mother—"Better lose the house—Better lose a million houses than to lose my wonderful son." And Clara said—"Humph!"

That summer Richie's father pushed him into taking music lessons, piano and voice, and Richie didn't do much with piano, but the teacher had tremendous hopes for his baritone voice, and the next winter he sang regularly in a church choral group and the high school glee club. The following year Charles Myles got a job working way up in the Bronx as a clerk in a big wholesale store, and he held down a part-time night watchman job somewhere in Brooklyn. When the other boys and girls in school would sometimes talk about where their fathers worked, Richie would be especially proud to say that his father worked as a clerk, because it sounded like his father was something special, and also because some of the white kids were always speaking of their fathers as doctor this or lawyer that, and some of the colored children never liked to say what their parents did for a living. Because chauffeuring and butlering and cooking and domestic servicing in the white folks' houses were nothing that you boasted about. But his father worked with his head and a pencil.

One day coming from school he made up his mind, just like that, to go to see his father on the job. Instead of going home he caught the subway all the way to the Bronx to his father's store. He walked into the big store, the very biggest he had ever been inside of, brilliantly lighted, high ceilings and everything. He tried to move around the store without attracting any attention. He saw an important-looking white man seated at a desk, but he didn't see his father—not yet awhile. Maybe it was the wrong store—But it had to be the right one—and where was his father? Maybe he worked behind one of those doors marked private. He would just have to ask one of these white men. He swallowed hard and walked up to a white man seated at a desk. His face didn't look unfriendly to Richie. "Could you tell me where I could find Mister—Mister Myles—Mr. Charles Henry Myles?"

The man looked at Richie through horn-rimmed glasses, scratched his pinkish half-bald head. "Mr. Myles—Mr. Myles— Oh, you mean—I see—Go right through that big door over there and walk all the way to the back."

He opened the big door and looked in, and it seemed like he was in another store altogether. Dark and gloomy with packages stacked up high all over the place. He swallowed hard and he felt something go down his throat and move through his chest and settle slowly in the pit of his stomach. He didn't see his father at first, not before he heard somebody yell—"Hey, Charlie, how long it's gonna take you to bring that goddamn stuff over here, boy?" He didn't see the boy that the great big giant of a white man was yelling at, but he knew it must be some other Charlie, couldn't be his father. Then he did see his father, little black man in overalls with a package on his back much bigger than he was. He knew the feet, both of them toed outward as he walked. His face grew warm like a fever had seized him, his eyes filled up, and he felt a watery something pushing out his cheeks. He was caught in a trap, but he could not wrest his eyes away from the little black man bent almost in two by the big heavy package. And he watched the man as he took the package over to the big white man and dropped it on the floor at his feet, puffing and blowing, wiping the sweat from his face. *My father—My father—My father—* He heard the white man say, "Put it over there a little further, Charlie." And as his father bent his body and put his shoulder against the package, the white man reached over and goosed his father—*His father—His father—*

His father jumped and turned to face the laughing white man. "What's the matter, Charlie? I be a sonofabitch if you ain't the goosiest boy I ever did see." Laughing all the while. But Father didn't laugh. He looked at the white man, anger gleaming fiercely out of his little dark eyes. "DON'T YOU DO THAT! Don't you ever do that to me again. I'll take up the first thing I get in my hands and knock hell out of you. I'll tell Mr. Young, if this has to keep up, he can have his damn job. Sick and tired of it, anyhow!" Richie heard the white man's voice vaguely—"Now, Charlie, you don't have to be like that." Richie was trembling all over with shame and excitement as he slipped back out of the door, but somehow a small piece of pride started to grow somewhere inside of him and pushed outward and upward, growing fast and fiercely, as hot salty tears fell down his cheeks. When he was outside in the spring once again, he wiped his eyes, and his face smiled with a certain knowingness, and somehow he could almost feel himself growing. He thought now that he knew what it meant to be a father like his father, feeling that he had never fully appreciated his father before. Wondering at the same time why his father had lied to them about being a clerk and also if even Mother knew the whole truth. But the feeling that dominated all the other feelings was the pride-filled feeling and the love for his father, as the tears flowed freely again down his cheeks, and he felt like a little boy and at the same time a man, a big knowing man. The following week Richie got a job working after school in a neighborhood grocery store.

Richie finished high school second in his class. Charles Myles slapped his son on the back. "You won it, son. I know you did. They stole it away from you because you're Negro. I know you were first, Richard Wendell Myles." Richie looked at him. "Aw now, father."

Charles insisted that his son go right on to college, but Richie wanted to get himself a regular job, even if for a little while only, save up some money, then maybe he would be able to go to college. "Richard Wendell, I don't want you to stop one minute from going to college. Don't think about work now. Plenty of time for that when you've prepared yourself to do the kind of work you want to do. What kind of work could you get to do now? What would they pay you? See what I mean?" The boy looked across the dinner table at the father.—"I can't do it, father, I just can't let you work yourself to death so I can take it easy."

"Son, listen to me. Going to college is just as hard a job as going to work every morning. Any time you work your brain instead of working your muscle it's harder, and much more important. Son, this is everything I have worked for and—Look Richard Wendell, you got the first year's tuition already in the bank. You won it in the contest—" The young high school graduate looked down at his plate, looked around at the others, his sisters and his mother. He knew it would be a losing argument, because on this particular question, they all went along with his father. These days and time a man had to be educated in order to get along— especially a colored man—He just had to be prepared for the opportunity when it came along—Because opportunity only knocked once—He closed his eyes wearily. He had heard it all before on so many occasions, and he had also heard his father contradict himself so many many times. A colored man doesn't get any fair breaks in this country, he would say. No opportunities at all. And in the next breath—If a man's got it in him, he's bound to succeed. All you got to do is to be prepared. He knew that he would finally give in and he would go to college as his father insisted, and his father would push him onward and upward, till one day he would put his foot down and he wouldn't be pushed around anymore, onward or upward or anywhere else.

*College wasn't so bad after all.*

It was learning to drink and to hold your liquor, learning all there was to know about women, and how to be suave and sophisticated, and hearing young Negroes talk callously about the absurdity of God and the hereafter, and learning to pretend to forget sometimes that you were a Negro at a Negro college. It was fellowship, it was idealism, it was individualism. It was studying harder than ever before; it was books—books—books; it was the liberal approach, it was the radical approach, it was brand new terms like "reactionary" and "conservative"; it was the Howard Theater and the latest jazz tunes. It was the grandeur of the broad green campus. It was men and women. It was all this and a hell of a lot more. It was real life, but it wasn't really life —at least not at first. It was a great big package of sophisticated make-believe.

"Apply yourself, son. Don't forget that. Integrate yourself in the life of the University, but above everything else, apply yourself. It's very serious business," Charles Henry Myles counseled his son. But before he could really apply himself, he had to find himself first, and that was not easy. He had to figure out why he was there, aside from being prepared when the opportunity presented itself. There just had to be other reasons, besides the one the men BS-ed about in the "bull-sessions" that went on and on. "I'm going into the medical racket. Be one of them bullshit doctors. Make plenty money."—And if it weren't that it was the lawyer racket, the teaching racket, the preaching racket, better known as the glory train. Some of the fellows called it the gravy train. Racket Racket Racket.

The President of the University told them in the chapel, assembled, in his deep rich voice: *Young men and young women, you are fortunate to be sojourning within these time-tested walls. You have a very serious responsibility to yourself and your family and above all to your people*—Richie felt a warm glow of response inside of him, and he looked around him and he saw

**134**

serious young faces and anxious faces and cynical faces and he thought about his father and he felt separate from the students around him, and at the same time a part of them, and his family and their families and all of the family-sacrificing it had taken to get most of them there. The million tons of white folks' clothes that had been washed, the packages lifted, the elevators run— The President's voice brought him back to the chapel—*You must prepare yourself for service to your people*—

Father came down from New York every weekend he could afford to come, and many times when he couldn't afford it. He came once around the time for final exams, and he asked Richie if he could help him get ready for them. Go over some of the problems with him. Richie was glad that his roommate was out of the dormitory at that moment. He told his father No thanks. They argued quietly about it, but he was firm. He told his father he didn't need to be wet-nursed any longer. This was his end of it. Charles looked at Richard as if he had never seen him before.

The second year of college, Richie had a new roommate— Randolph Wainwright. Randy seemed to know something about everything. He came from Chicago, his father was a railroad man. He got Richie interested in Student movements and activities on and off the campus. Some of the students called Richie's "old lady" Randy the Radical. Richie had angrily challenged his first roommate about calling him Old Lady all the time, and his roommate had told him to pay it no mind. "It doesn't mean a thing. Roommates always call each other Old Lady. That's because they're supposed to look out for each other—take care of each other. That's what old ladies are for, isn't it? The trouble with you freshmen you're too damn sensitive."

Randy Wainwright filled Richie's head with all kinds of radical stuff, like the trade union movement and the working class and the Negro Problem, and he seemed to Richie to have more answers to life than all of those men who sat around his father's dining room table put together. He shoved books under Richie's nose that he'd never seen before. He had never even heard of some of these dangerous books—Booker T. Washington's *Up From Slavery, The Life And Times Of Frederick Douglass, Black Reconstruction* by W. E. B. DuBois and Karl Marx's *Das Kapital* and Carter Woodson and many many more. One day Randy walked into their room and he sat down beside Richie on his bunk and he looked over Richie's shoulders to see what he was reading. "That's a real radical book you reading, Old Lady. Better watch that stuff. First thing you know you be doing something about it." He slapped Richie on his back and he knew he was annoying Richie.

The next afternoon Randy tried to get Richie to go down on U Street with him to help some other colored people picket a drugstore. Richie said he was too busy, he had a rough schedule in school that week. Randy smiled and bowed and left the room, leaving Richie with a guilty feeling. The next day Randy asked him, "How about it, Old Lady?" Richie told him he was still busy, he really was busy. Randy went to the table and he fumbled amongst a pile of books till he found the one he was looking for. He leafed through the pages. "Listen to the Great Man. I mean Fred Douglass. *'If there is no struggle there is no progress. Those who profess to favor freedom, and yet depreciate agitation, are men who want crops without plowing the ground. They want rain without thunder and lightning. They want the ocean without the awful roar of its many waters.'* That's what I'm talking about," Randy said, and handed Richard the big book. "You intellectuals don't ever want to do anything but read." The next day Richie went to the picket line by himself with all kinds of fears and misgivings. But it wouldn't hurt to go just once. He didn't have to make a habit of it. Nobody he knew would see him on the picket line. He would try anything at least one time. It was an evening in late November and freezing cold and snowing steadily since early morning. The Better Jobs for Colored Committee had a campaign going against a chain drugstore company to get them to hire Negro pharmacists and clerks in Negro sections of the city. That was the first time he met Hank Saunders. She carried a big sign that read "DON'T BUY WHERE YOU CAN'T WORK," and he carried one that said—"THE POLICY OF THIS DRUGSTORE IS ANTI-NEGRO—PASS IT BY."

"Boy—Am I tired," Richie said to the little slender brown-skinned girl with the big medium-brown eyes. Making conversation to hide his excitement. "You just got here," she told him. "What you mean you tired?" They separated, walking to opposite ends of the front of the drugstore, turned and walked back towards each other. A short fat white man from the drugstore stood under the snow-laden awning watching the picketers. "How long have you been at it?" Richie asked her. "Off and on since one o'clock. This is the way I spend my only day off." She laughed at the funny look on his face. He thought to himself—She isn't afraid of a picket line. Why should I be? When they passed each other again he asked her where she worked. She said she worked in a big downtown restaurant, where did he work, but before he answered she was gone again. The next time he passed he asked her what was her name. She said, "Who the hell are you—The Police?" When they passed each other again she said her name was Henrietta Saunders. Her best buddies called her Hank. And then she asked him, "Who are you? Where do you work? And everything else about you." When they were relieved around nine o'clock by a Negro man and a white woman, Hank suggested coffee. They sat in a booth across from each other waiting to be served, and he held her numb hands because she told him to see how cold they were, and he kept holding them, as the warm blood flowed back into both of their hands and throughout their bodies.

The next time he met Hank was on a picket line in front of a downtown theater in a demonstration against *The Birth of a Nation,* which the Committee claimed was anti-Negro. After the demonstration they sat in a joint back up on U Street with other students and young people having coffee and laughing and talking. He was seated next to Hank. Randy looked over towards them and said, "What're you up to with Hank, Old Lady? One thing sure, she's the girl to knock some of the bourgeois out of your head. She's time enough for anybody." All of them looked at Richie and laughed. He glanced at Hank and looked down at his milkshake. Hank smiled at Randy. It didn't appear to ruffle her at all. Randy continued. "I don't know what you got I don't have. I tried to talk to her for the longest kind of time. She never would hold still for me." Randy laughed and so did the rest of them. Hank looked at Richie. "Don't let young Karl Marx get you down. You ought to know him by now. He's your roommate, isn't he?" Richie nodded his head and smiled at Randy. "Don't you worry about the mule going blind."

He walked Hank home that night, and he put one of her cold hands in his topcoat pocket and pressed it hard and she responded and he felt a great warmth go all through his body. He looked at her standing in the doorway of her 2 by 4 room, and he swallowed the moldish air of the dimly-lit hall and whispered—"Hank—," and clumsily tried to take her in his arms and go into the room

**137**

with her. She pushed him from her and she smiled at him. "Don't let it get you down," she told him. "Don't let your old lady get next to you like that."

"What the hell are you talking about?"

She laughed at the serious look on his face. "Take that pout off your mouth," she said in that clear clipped tone of hers. "Don't take it so serious. Just because your old lady was signifying a while ago, that doesn't mean you got to make it come true."

"Hank—Hank—"

"Pay it no mind," she told him. "You can forget all about it."

"Hank—Listen. I don't give a damn about what Randy said. I don't care what anybody says—I just like you and that's all there is to it." He wanted to tell her that he loved her, but it would have sounded so trite and empty, and he knew she wouldn't have gone for it anyway. He smothered Hank's reply as he pulled her towards him, heard her and felt her breathing hard upon his neck, found her lips, firm and hard at first, then yielding under the pressure of his, becoming soft and pliable, her arms around his neck —Only for the briefest kind of a moment. Then she muttered— "Well" and pushed her frail body away from him and told him goodnight.

Randy looked up from a book he was reading, watched his roommate for a moment without saying anything, cleared his throat. "How you and Hank getting along these days?"

"What do you mean getting along?"

"You know what I mean," Randy teased. "How's the wonderful romance progressing?"

He looked across the room at Randy. "Don't you worry about it." He liked Randy Wainwright more than anybody else on the campus, but sometimes Randy got under his skin.

"I ain't worried, old lady. I'm just tickled to death—me. I think you two make a wonderful match, but I doubt if your old man would agree with me."

"What's my father got to do with it?"

"Your dad is really a wonderful guy. He—he's a fabulous character. Got more stuff than a Christmas turkey. I-I love the guy. I guess that's where you get all your stuff from. But he's got plans for you, and Hank doesn't fit in them."

Richie stared at Randy with a distant look on his face. "You don't know what you're talking about," he said, thinking about Hank now, sweet-faced Hank, strong-willed Hank, slender Hank, sassy-faced Hank, tender and fragile and weak-bodied, and strong-minded. What would his father think of Hank? He remembered the last time his father and mother had visited him. "Son," his father had said, "Richard Wendell, I want you to be independent. Be a lawyer like you want to be. Set your course now, son, before you start the voyage and don't let anything take you off of it!" Clara Myles had said, "Leave the boy alone, Charlie. Some of these things he has to make up his own mind about. Don't you think he's capable?"

Randy spoke as if he hadn't heard Richie at all. "Your father has more stuff on the ball than five or six people, but he's still blinded by all these bourgeois illusions. Most Negroes with a little education think they gonna be rich some day, gonna be better off than the average run of Negroes." He smiled at the quizzical look on Richie's face. "You got those illusions too, old lady."

Richie looked down at his slippers. "What the hell has all this got to do with Hank?"

"Your old man ain't going to permit anything to stand in the way of your becoming a lawyer—Hank or nobody else. Women is something he's got lined up for you five or six or seven years from now. Man, you gon be a *big* colored man." Richie's face grew warm, and he got up off his bunk and walked out of the room, hating Randy and his know-it-all smile and the bourgeois-illusions, and the system-of-things that had worn his father to a frazzle, and his own confusions, and everything else.

From Meridian Park you could stand on its balcony and see the entire governmental section of town spread out before you. It was a beautiful city to look at. You could let your eyes wander from the shining dome of the Capitol building and carry them on a straight line across the great Mall to Washington Monument and bring them to rest on the Lincoln Memorial. You could let your lucky eyes travel slowly and gradually or you could complete the process in half of a second. He thought he felt a chill pass through his body, not caused by the night air. He put his arms around her and pulled her lean body more closely to him as he gazed out at the city before him. "It's a beautiful city, Hank. So clean and so beautiful."

"I used to think it was pretty," she said wistfully.

"But it is pretty. It—it's beautiful. New York doesn't com—"

"Its beauty is only skin deep."

"What do you mean—only skin deep?" he asked uneasily.

"My mother always told me pretty is as pretty does and outside beauty was only skin deep. According to that this is the ugliest dirtiest city in the whole damn world." He didn't want to
think about that side of it. Maybe at the moment he didn't want
to think at all. Just wanted to gaze upon the outside beauty, and
forget that he was a Negro gazing at the outside beauty, but let
him be an American like any other American and drink in the
simple, quiet snow-white beauty of the city like anybody else
would. But she never let him forget—Always bringing up the
color question. She never seemed to get tired of it. "It's like a two-
faced man," she said. "A goddamn hypocrite. Like a no-good
whore all dressed up with paint on her face. Ugly underneath as
home-made sin."

"Aw, Hank, don't let's always look at that side of it." His arm
tightened around her.

"All right, Richie, but it just makes me so damn mad to think
about it. This country came out of its mother's womb with a fresh
lie in its mouth. All men are created equal—But George Washington had slaves and—and even Thomas Jefferson."

They were quiet. He knew what she was talking about, and he
didn't really disagree with her. He thought about the other day
when he and Randy had gone to the opening day of the baseball
season at Griffith Stadium and Herbert Hoover had thrown the
first ball out and the New York and the Washington baseball
players had marched with the officials out to center field where
the flag was raised, and how hard he had tried to feel what he
had imagined all the white people felt when everybody stood up
to sing the Star Spangled Banner. His eyes lingered dreamily on
the Lincoln Memorial, a couple of miles away, and he spoke almost unconsciously. "Took my father and mother down to the
Memorial last Saturday. Took them by the Monument and the
Cherry Blossoms down on the Speedway and past the White
House—over to the Capitol—House Office Building."

"Why didn't you let me know?" she asked. "You knew I was
off Saturday. I told you last Wednesday."

A feeling of guilt and hypocrisy and two-facedness and skin-
deepness made his face grow warm and tight. "I don't know why
I didn't let you know," he lied. "I must have forgotten."

They came out of the Lincoln Theater on U Street and walked
along quietly and closely together, and she invited him to go by

her place for coffee. They had been to forums together and movies and picket lines and parties and Meridian Park a couple of times, but he had never gotten further than the door to her apartment. When they got to her room she put on an apron. Her room was a combination bedroom-living room-kitchen with the community bath at the end of the hall. She was over by the stove. "Get some soda out of the icebox, and mix up a couple of drinks, Richie. Whiskey's in the cupboard. I'll be getting this mess together over here."

"Oh, we going to have a party, honh? Anybody else invited?" Looking up at the picture of Frederick Douglass hanging on the wall and around at a home-made bookcase with hundreds of books from floor to ceiling up against the opposite wall.

"I'm surprised at you, son. Don't you know—Two makes a party—Three makes a crowd?"

After they had eaten, they sat across from each other, looking down at the drinks they were sipping. His eyes came up from his drink and he made himself stare brazenly at her. "Didn't know you were a drinking woman," he said, mockingly.

"Only on very special occasions." She smiled and then added —"I could write a book about what you don't know about me. In fact that's exactly what I'm going to write my book about." He laughed and he took another drink and he was feeling woozy, because he wasn't used to drinking and he sat there taking in her beauty that wasn't anything you could point to definitely, but was a composite thing. Except maybe her big expressive medium-brown impertinent eyes. She looked small and weak and helpless, but at the same time hard as a rock and willful and determined and sometimes even more know-it-all than Randy Wainwright. He watched her get up and walk over to her Victrola and put on a record by Duke Ellington, and he listened dreamily to the sweet seductive melody. She walked deliberately over to him and asked him for this dance sir. Holding her in his arms he felt so comfortable it was almost painful, and then he was disturbed by thoughts of his conversation with Randy about Hank and his father and his future. To hell with Randy. "Are you the Sophisticated Lady?" he whispered in her ear.

She laughed at him. "Now how could I be sophisticated? I've never been to college."

"Stop pulling my leg," he told her fiercely.

The music stopped and she went to change the record. They

141

continued to dance and she asked him what were his plans after college and he hesitated, as he thought about Randy and he thought about his father, and he told her he didn't know, but his father wanted him to be a lawyer and she said *wonderful*. "You're going to be in school a long long time. Very very good." They danced silently, he didn't know what to say, wished they didn't have to talk at all, just dance—dance—dance—with her in his arms. She looked up in his face and she told him she graduated from the School of Experience. "I learned everything the hard way, Richie. And I hate some things so hard and so fierce it scares me sometimes. The things that lynched my father in South Carolina for being a man and the things that killed my mother— worked her to death in the white folks' houses. And I hate all of them and every bit of it, and I'm gonna fight against it till the day I die. I'm not sophisticated like the nice girls on the campus, Richie. I'm mean and hateful and—and sometimes I don't think I even love my own self." Her voice broke off and he thought that she might burst into a cry—hoping fiercely that she wouldn't—at the same time knowing that somehow she couldn't. The music had stopped without their being aware of it, and they stood near the middle of the floor in each other's arms and he felt a great overwhelming compassion and he wanted to be everything to her, help her to hate and to fight the things that she hated, mixed with guilty thoughts about his own sheltered life and his conversation with Randy, and an undefined obligation to his father. He tightened his arms around her and pulled her closer to him, felt a slight tremor go through her body, and—*Hank—Hank—Hank* and wanting to protect her and above all a growing heat inside of him, a sweet mounting heat that moved through his shoulders and swelled in the middle of him, an awful aching, feeling his maleness like never before. His lips found hers and there was a sweet something in the kiss that seemed to calm both of them, especially her. She pulled away from him. She walked towards the scratching Victrola and changed the record. He followed, but she walked around him and went and sat down. "We'd better forget about it. Skip it—Forget the whole thing." She lit a cigarette and took two long drags.

"For—forget about what?"

She waved at the smoky air and looked down at the floor. "Forget about my plans for the night. Forget about me taking advantage of you and stealing your cherry, and you letting me do it and telling me that you love me and that you will always love me. Let's forget the whole thing. It's the oldest BS in the world, and you don't have to go to college to get it."

His face grew warm, and he thought he must be wearing a ridiculous expression. At the same time he knew she wasn't nearly as tough as she made herself sound. "I don't know what you're talking about, Hank. I never tried to fool you. I never said that I loved you."

"Then don't say it. And you think I would sleep with you if you didn't say it and—and really mean it? What do you take me for? You think because you're a college boy you can have your way with me—I'm—I'm just an insignificant restaurant worker." She waved the cigarette smoke from her eyes.

He looked through the swirls of smoke at her little brown serious face and for the moment he wished she were not so direct in her manner, wished she were more like the sophisticated helpless romantic women in the novels he had read and the movies he had seen, the artificial women. He didn't know what to say to her, but he wanted her then and there and he wanted her badly, and he had never experienced such a terrible want. "Hank-Hank, I don't know what to say. I—I—"

"Don't say anything. Forget all about it." She stood and held out her arms to him. "Let's not waste the beautiful music." Then she laughed and shook her head. "Nope, we'd better not dance again. Not tonight. Make us feel so unnecessary. Let's just sit and talk about stuff and things." She stared at him seated across from him. "So your father wants you to become a lawyer. Well, I'm for that. Yes sir—one hundred percent. And you would make a good one too—with your sweet talking voice and your pleasing personality—" She went on and on like an old phonograph record as he got up and turned off the victrola. "With your brilliant brain— Randy told me all about what a bright young man you are—but he didn't have to tell me, because I knew it all the time—Anybody can see you would make a brilliant lawyer, darling—"

"Hank—Hank—"

"And one thing sure, you don't need any woman around standing in the way, especially one of those uneducated ones, cause an ignorant Negro woman is nothing but a millstone around a colored man's neck." She laughed out loud at his serious face.

"Dammit—Hank—Cut it out!"

"The trouble with you," Hank said, "you get excited so quick. You take life too serious."

"Hank, did you ever think of yourself going back to school? Why don't you go to college? I mean you don't have any responsibilities, no dependents or anything."

"Darling, my school days are over. I don't have any money and they don't give scholarships out to colored girls just like that, don't you know? And besides, I got a responsibility where I work, and I don't mean to the boss. That man thinks he's got slaves on a plantation but we going to give him the biggest surprise he ever had. We're going to get the butter from the duck. We're organizing a union of fifty black folks, mostly women. It's starting slow and we're doing it quietly at first, but one bright day he's going to think lightning struck him. And that's my work, and it's just as important to me as college is to you." She turned the glass up to her lips till the last drop drained out of it, and she rose abruptly and went over and put on another record. "On second thought, maybe we should dance."

Her lean body heavily against his own, and every now and then she losing step and stumbling and excuse me darling and his heart beating mad and wild and crazy in his chest and a nervous human swelling growing in the middle of him overcoming thought and reason and morality-as-he'd-been-taught-it and everything else, and the keen awareness of her little plump bosom against his chest and the softness and the firmness—and—and— "Excuse me, darling—I must be drruunk—"

After the music stopped she led him stumbling towards the couch, and they sat there for the longest kind of time in silence, her body leaning against his and resting on his shoulders and in his arms. His arms tightened around her and her whole body seemed to melt into his, and the moment was filled with a powerful sweetness he had never imagined. He turned roughly towards her and his lips found hers and he kissed her fiercely and his hand became bolder than ever before, exploring the softness and the firmness of her young womanhood, his inexperienced hand tenderly exploring. He felt her whole body tremble and it seemed to be quivering inside of him. "Love you—love you—" he said without knowing. She uttered a sigh that was almost a shout. "Richie! Richie!" and she pushed herself away from him. "Don't, darling—don't—" He wanted her to remain where she was in his

**144**

arms—on his lips—in the throbbing beat of his heart—and everything else just as it was . . . no conversation . . . no nothing . . . but love love love. . . .

But she pushed herself away from him and looked up into his face. "What—what do I mean to you, Richie?"

"Everything—Everything in the world."

"You shouldn't say that, Richie."

"Why? Why? It's the truth—it's the truth—"

"No, darling, not for you it isn't. The truth for you is the—the college and law school and your future as a lawyer. Your father, your career—I would be in the wa—"

He smothered her small fiery voice with a kiss. "The truth, darling is you, and everything in this world that you stand for. You you you—" And he really thought he was telling the truth, he knew he was, as he crushed her lips with his rough awkward kisses and soft tender kisses, and he wanted her now now now, and he just had to have her. . . .

"No, Richie, no!" Standing up and backing away from him and shaking her head angrily. "Let's be calm and reasonable about it." She sat down on the couch, and he saw a single tear slip from her eyes and trickle down her cheek. He knew she was holding back an ocean of tears. He wished she would let herself go just this once and cry cry cry. . . .

"Reasonable—" he said fiercely. "I *am* being reasonable. I wish you would be reasonable, and just a little bit human." He sat down beside her and took her into his arms again. She became suddenly as alive as he was and the great fire within her reached out quickly and swept all over him. "Yes, Richie, yes, I do love you, darling!" And outside on the street an automobile honked and the wind was blowing and it had started to rain, and inside was love. And after the loving—tired—spent—they fell asleep in each other's arms.

Later that morning, Sunday, back on the campus, Randy came into the room from breakfast and he stared at Richie sitting on the side of the bed and he turned his back and started to sing— *"Old Lady—Old Lady—Where you stay last night—Your clothes don't fit you and they don't hang right—"* He kept it up till Richie jumped from his bed. "Goddammit, Randy, what you take me for—a kid or something? I don't dip in your business. Stay out of mine!"

Randy turned to face Richie. "Look, Old Lady, Hank means a

lot to me and a whole lot of other people in this town, especially to the women down at the restaurant. So you better be serious about her, and all this business of men ganging up on women and talking about them like the guys do here in the dorm, and tricking them and laughing about it and this piece of ass and that piece of ass, it just doesn't go with Hank, because I wouldn't stand for it a goddamn minute!"

"I'm serious about Hank, Randy," Richie said. "Don't you worry about it."

It had been near the end of May, the first time Charles Henry Myles met Hank Saunders. He was polite and gallant and solicitous all through dinner that Saturday night and afterwards the three of them had taken in a movie on U Street. "The campus isn't too far from here," Charles Myles told his son, as they stood on S Street in front of where Hank lived after taking her home. "Let's walk. It's such a beautiful night." Richie knew what was coming. "Okay, father."

"Henrietta's a very nice girl, a very fine young woman," Charles Myles began, as they walked along S Street. "I think so, Father."

"Does she live with her family?" He said No, and, as a matter of fact, she didn't have any family, and his father said it was very unfortunate. Richie didn't say a word. "She doesn't attend the University?" his father said and Richie said No. "She attends the Normal School?" his father asked.

They had turned into the neon brightness of U Street, still busy with automobile traffic and people of varied complexions on foot. "No, Father. The fact of the matter, she doesn't go to school at all."

"Oh, I see," Charles said quietly. "She works in the government." They had stopped walking and the son turned and faced the father. "What is all this song-and-dance about, Father? Come on out with it. I'll tell you all about her. She finished high school —Couldn't afford to go to college. She works like a slave all day long in a downtown restaurant, but she's got more to her than fifty of those color-struck women up at the University." His voice broke off momentarily. "She's wonderful, Father. She's so unselfish and good, and she's got a strong mind—and I've learned more from her than a million colleges."

The father's eyes shifted nervously. "I see," he muttered as they started to walk again. "No need to get excited, son." They walked along in silence for a while and they turned up Georgia Avenue. "Well, you have all the time in the world for women, Richard. The thing to do is to prepare yourself and let nothing stand in the way of it. Nothing at all. When you get something up in your head, son, nobody can take it away from you. Profession—profession—When you become a lawyer it's time enough then to look around at the women. You can have your pick then. You can get a woman on your own level. One that is prepared to go up the ladder with you. Meanwhile you have to be careful, Richard Wendell. Keep yourself under control of yourself all the time. Some women are tricky."

Richie was almost blinded by the sweat that dripped down into his angry eyes. "You don't have to talk about Hank like that, Father. I don't want to listen to it. You don't know what you're talking about and I'm not going to hear a bit of it."

"Son, Richard Wendell—"

"Look, Father, I don't want to hurt your feelings. Don't want to get mad with you—but—but—let's just drop the question of Hank."

"All right—All right, son, just be careful, that's all."

"Look, Father, you married Mother when both of you were very young. Are you sorry about it? Are you sorry? Honh? She didn't trick you. And she didn't go to college."

"Son, all I'm saying is, achieve your goal first. Get your education. Get yourself a profession—achieve independence and security. I didn't want to tell you, son, but the candy store—the candy store—we had to close it up—lost everything—Didn't want to worry you—I'm out on the pavement again looking to the white man to give me another job. Help make him richer. . . ."

He avoided his father's eyes. In his mind he could see his proud father when he had quit his job and had opened up the little candy store a block from the subway. "I've been struggling and fighting and reaching after security ever since I first came up-the-country a young man. It's just as far out of reach as it ever was. It's—it's like something unreal, never intended to be. I'm tired son, and I'm not even an old man yet and your mother is sick. Both of us just plumb worn out."

He looked at his bleary-eyed father and he felt something trying to fill his own eyes and moving in his shoulders and his throat and his face and he turned his head and wiped his eyes on the sly and put his arms around his father and they walked through the gate and on to the campus.

He didn't go back to the University the next year. He went instead to City College. His father said he couldn't afford to send him to college outside of the city, but Richie knew that to be only part of the reason. Richie always had been lax about letter writing, but he drove himself to write Hank regularly—during the fall term anyhow. But after he became oriented to the different life at City College, he became involved in so much darn activity, he hardly had time to take care of his studies, let alone write letters. He took a job in a down town hotel, joined a union. His father objected to his hotel job, wanted him to concentrate fully on college life and getting an education, but Richie wouldn't listen. Some nights he worked so hard at the hotel, he fell asleep in class the next day. But he wasn't discouraged. Sometimes when he would receive a long letter from Hank, he would hurriedly drop her a penny postcard, till finally she began to write postcards to him in retaliation. One Friday night he ran down to Washington and spent the weekend and she looked very bad and had lost weight and developed a cough. Randy Wainwright told him she wasn't doing well at all, because she kept so busy and she wouldn't take care of herself, and she wouldn't listen to anybody but Richard Wendell Myles. His father raised hell about his going to Washington.

The letters were frequent for a while after that, but he got so mixed up with liberal and radical students at City College, Negro and white, rushing him off his feet. Electing him to this committee and chairman of the other. Sometimes making a figurehead of him—Sometimes he refused to be window dressing for them. The letters sloped off again and finally discontinued. He sang a baritone lead in the Glee Club. His father pushed him to join the debating team and he excelled in that. He developed into a public speaker, speaking from his diaphragm like his father had taught him, and everybody wanted him to speak this place and the other. He joined this and the other organization. Everybody was interested in the *Negro Problem*.

One weekend, out of sheer desperation, Hank swallowed her pride and came to New York to see him, borrowed the train fare. But he was up at Cornell at a Students' Conference. She never wrote him again, and his father didn't tell him that she had come to town and had telephoned him from Pennsylvania Station. They never saw each other again.

And now he was a man a long ways from home with a brand-new leather bag walking down the steps from the train platform and walking through that part of the station marked COLORED and people staring at him, because his face was new and important-looking, especially around the eyes, and he looked up-the-countryish. He heard somebody whisper out loud to somebody else, "I bet he's that there new school teacher from New York City. Bet a fat man he is." Well at least he was expected. As he came out of the station and took a quick nervous look at Crossroads, Georgia, a brief flash of fear quivered in his stomach and his eyes blinked uneasily in a bright September sun. He saw the big sign hanging outside of the station. CROSSROADS, GEORGIA, IS THE CROSSROADS OF THE U.S.A. Signed GEORGE CROSS, JR. He heard the train he had just left pulling out slowly for points further south, and his father had offered to buy him a round trip ticket, but he had refused. He was hundreds and hundreds of miles from home and he asked himself again—"What the hell am I doing in this jerkwater town—Crossroads, Georgia?"

## CHAPTER TWO

SUMMER IN CROSSROADS was a thing of the past. School opening time. No more sneaking out to Cracker Rayburn's to swim, no more baseball, ratball, walking through the woods, picking wild blackberries and muscadines and selling them to white folks out in the Heights. No more spending a whole summer's day out in the Quarters where Fat Gus lived, Robby and Gus just messing around all day long. Rockingham Quarters was the ugliest spot in town. One and two-room shacks huddled close together and scattered apart and little and ugly and rusty, and they seemed to be sinking into the black dusty earth. The other day Robby was out in the Quarters, and he and Gus were sitting on the other side of the outhouse behind Gus's backyard smoking dried tree leaves on the sly. Fat Gus had looked up and around. "Goddamn if Rockingham Quarters ain't the worstest damn hole in the world to live in." Robby had already smoked a couple of cigarettes, and he was feeling grown-up and biggedy, drunk from the dried tree leaves and the smell of the human manure from the outhouse. He said to Gus in a sudden streak of outright meanness, "How come you and your folks live in this goddamn hole? How come you don't live in Pleasant Grove?" He saw a flash of hurt in Gus's eyes and regretted the question. "Why do you live in Pleasant Grove?" Gus asked softly and bitterly. "It ain't no bargain. Why don't you live in Crossbranch Heights with the other rich white folks?"

Later they were inside the outhouse. Gus was standing up on the privy box. "Boy, you better learn how to do these steps if you want to be a sheik with the women-folks like the Kid," he said, as he danced all around the privy holes. He was as fat as a hog but limber as a grasshopper. All of a sudden he made a mis-step and his leg disappeared. He let out a yell you could hear all the way to Mr. Cross's courthouse and back, and Miss Lulabelle came a-running. She pulled him out and took him by the hand and he really was a mess and dripping and hollering to beat the band. Miss Lulabelle stripped him and threw that fat scound into the washtub and got her some lye soap and washing powder. And Robby laughed till the tears rolled down his cheeks and his stomach ached. *But all that was over because it was school opening time.*

It was the very first day of school, and the children had just come back into the classrooms from recess time and the brand-new teacher from up-the-country—New York City got up from behind his desk, and he stood before the class with his hands in his pockets and his eyes wandered nervously all over the room. He looked scared and uneasy, as if he were facing a bunch of wild tigers.

But somehow or other Robby liked him immediately, and right then and there he felt like going up to the teacher's table and whispering to him, "Don't be scared. We're not going to bite you. Don't go running and jump out of the window. What do children look like where you come from?" He watched the young teacher's eyes blinking nervously, and he waited for the man to open his mouth and say something to them. Robby looked down at his desk, and when he looked up again, the teacher wore a big handsome smile, and that seemed to make everything alright.

The young teacher put his hand on his chin, put it back in his pocket, nervous as an old setting hen, and then he spoke. "You know I have a confession to make." He certainly did have a beautiful voice, strange and deep and pretty and important and up-the-countryish. "They say truthful confession is good for the soul. Well let me confess. You're the very first class I have ever taught, but I think it's going to be a whole lot of fun—for all of us I mean. And I have a sneaking suspicion that every last one of us is going to learn something—including the teacher."

Children stirred in their seats and giggled out loud.

Robby looked out of the side of his eye and he could see Biff Roberts with a scowling frown on his face. Well let him frown— This new teacher would be time enough for Biff. Bet a fat man he would.

——"Whenever there is something I say that you don't understand, I want you to just raise your hand and let me know about it. I also want you to feel free to express any opinion you might have on any question." Richard Myles's anxious eyes traveled over the classroom from face to face. Was he being too hi-falutin? Wondering if he sounded like a fool to the children. He wanted to win them just as soon as he could. And yet he already sensed a certain hostility, or maybe distrust, on the part of some.

The door opened behind him, and before he turned around he was aware of the anxious looks on the children's faces. Mr. Blake, the principal, stood in the door smiling and beaming, and he stepped aside as two white gentlemen walked past him into the classroom. The first white man was a long, tall, business-like, expensive-looking man. The other one was short and fat and red and sloppy and reminded Richard Myles of an unmade bed. The first white man walked up to the teacher.

"Myles, my name is Mr. Johnson. I'm the superintendent of the Cross County Board of Education. And this here is Mr. Jeffries, one of my assistants, in charge of colored schools. You be seeing quite a lot of Mr. Jeffries. Yes indeedy."

Both of the white men broadened their smiles in as friendly fashion as they could manage. Richard Myles looked them straight in the face, his eyes wide and arrogant, wondering what was expected of him. Should he hold out his hands and say glad to meet you? White folks didn't shake Negroes' hands—not down here. He wanted to return their smiles, start off on the right foot, but he just couldn't make his face cooperate. He was aware of the stillness behind his back, the quiet of the children.

The important-looking white man cleared his throat. "Well, we just came by to see how you were getting along. Welcome you into the flock, so to speak." The other white man laughed out loud.

"How you think you going to like being with us?" Mr. Johnson asked. "We a little different from up north where you come from."

"I think I'm going to like it all right." Myles turned his head and glanced at the children. Fishing around in his head for something to say to these important white men. "We're going to have the most outstanding class in Crossroads, white or colored." Wondering what the hell made him say that. It didn't make any sense.

Mr. Johnson's face turned red as a beet. "Well, that's just fine," he said, getting himself together. "Yes indeedy. Like I always say—Niggrahs and white folks can get along together almost anywhere. All that's needed is a good understanding in front."

Myles could feel the heat gathering in his collar, wondering if his face gave his feelings away. He stared Mr. Johnson so coldly in the eye, that the white man's blue eyes shifted up towards the ceiling. "All anybody ever needs is a good understanding."

The sloppy white man smiled at Richard Myles and laughed out loud, a look on his face that said to Richard Myles—Smile, boy, smile—show us those teeth—laugh why don'tcha—what the hell you so serious about?

Mr. Johnson spoke to Myles in a pretended whisper, but loudly enough for the children to hear. "Have to watch yourself with these bucks, Myles. They get wild and out of hand sometimes."

Richard Myles stared blankly at the cracker. He felt the listening silence of the children behind him. Maybe he should pretend he didn't hear Mr. Johnson. Washington, D.C. was such a long ways off and New York City seemed a million miles away. He looked brazenly into the white man's face, his arrogant eyes deliberately widening. "Are they any wilder than the bucks across town?"

Mr. Blake, the Negro principal, moved around nervously, clearing his throat and smiling politely. "Our new teacher has to get himself acclimatized."

Mr. Johnson glanced sideways at Mr. Blake and looked back at Myles. His face was redder than an over-ripe carrot. "You better talk to him, Blake. Learn him how we do things down here."

"Yes, sir, indeed. He'll be all right. Just needs a little seasoning—that's all."

**1 5 2**

They were gone—They were gone and he stood before the class collecting himself, overcoming his anger, wondering now if he had made a stupid mistake, coming south to teach. He wasn't going to be able to take it. He knew he wasn't. Should've listened to his father. If only he didn't have to come into contact with white folks, he could make it. He just had to keep himself under control—He was too hotheaded. He put his hands in his pockets and looked at the class and he made himself smile at the children, and most of the children smiled right back.

School had let out and the children had started home, and the sun was playing *Ten Ten Double Ten* behind a dark gray cloud. "Man I reckin," Fat Gus said. "That teacher is something. You see how he talked right up to those crackers? He didn't take no shit." He looked around him slyly. "Excuse my language, Ida Mae. Swear fore God—didn't see you atall. You too, Willabelle."

"Humph," Willabelle said. "I hate that about you."

Robby cut his eyes at Ida Mae, as they walked up the street in the middle of the dusty road. He looked at Fat Gus. "That's what I'm talking about," he said. "Mr. Myles sure was time enough for them crackers, and I don't mean maybe. Did you see how that Negro looked at them pecks?"

Fat Gus said, "And we *gon* be the best class in the whole damn country. We got to help Mr. Myles make it come true. That's what I'm talking about. He's my man!"

"You'll be a great big help," Biff told Gus. "Can't spell *it*."

"Now ain't you something?" Fat Gus said to Biff. "You thickhead sonofabiscuit eater. They had to burn down the school house to get your big ass outa the first damn grade. Excuse me, Ida Mae."

"I know one thing," Ida Mae said. "Teacher sure is cute. And his voice is so deep and pretty and romantic. And anybody can see he's a real smart man."

"Cute," Robby said, scowling contemptuously. "Cute! Humph."

"He ain't no cuter'n somebody else I know. I can state you that," Willabelle said, eyeing Robby Youngblood and smiling at him like she always had a way of doing.

Biff Roberts kicked a rock with his brand new shoe, stirring up the red chalky dust of the road. "Shit—I don't see where he so forty. Somebody better put some sense in his head."

"What you mean, man?" Robby asked Biff.

"Hell—my Daddy met him when he first came to town. Interviewed him for the *Telegram* Colored Page." Biff's father was editor of the Colored Page of the *Daily Telegram*. "And like Daddy say, told me again, just this morning—that's one colored man too big for his britches. Thinks he better'n us colored down here. I know what I'm talking about."

Gus looked at Biff. "You red-headed sonofabitch, whatchoo talking about?"

Biff's mouth poked out. He ran his hand through his thick red hair, and he balled up his fist. "Talking about that new teacher—that's what. You hear me, you ain't deaf. Anybody can see he thinks he's white. Damn sight better get some business in his head. Just like all them up-the-country Negroes. Just like I told you—"

"He's right—he's right," another boy said. "Negroes up the country always think they better than us."

They were standing in the middle of the red dusty road—Pleasant Grove Avenue. The sun had come out and was going back in again. Fat Gus plopping one of his big bare feet smack in the middle of a big pile of something a horse had put down just a short time before. Fresh and golden brown and still smoking and smelling like a stable. Ida Mae Raglin turned her head. The stuff oozed up between Fat Gus's toes, as he wiggled them around. Robby tried to keep a straight face, but it turned his stomach and Fat Gus knew it. He kicked some of it in the direction of Biff who was all dressed up in a brand-new suit.

"Now ain't that a bitch? If anybody think they white, it's you, you half-white, shit-colored bastard," Gus said. "I 'member when you went to New York on your vacation that time. Didn't stay long enough to get your goddamn feet wet. Come back here with your nose in the air and your ass on your shoulder, and you talked so proper couldn't nobody understand a word you said."

"Don't you kick that stuff on me—I mean that thing!" Biff was jumping around like he was doing a dance. The rest of the children spreading out now, giving Gus plenty of kicking space, some of them laughing.

Gus scooped up a big load of the stuff on the top of his feet and walked towards Biff.

"Donchoo—Donchoo!—" Biff turned and ran up the road. "I'll get you for this," Biff yelled back. "I'll fix you goddammit if it's the last thing I do. I'll get you for this. I'll fix you goddammit!"

"You can't fix me," Gus yelled after Biff. "The Good Lord already done fixed me the day I was born. Left my ass in a helluva fix."

The children laughed.

"Let him alone, Fat Gus."

Robby Youngblood sitting in the classroom, dreaming in the broad-open daytime. Mr. Myles really had a new way of teaching. Nobody ever taught like him before—not in Crossroads, Georgia. Who ever heard of letting children ask the teacher questions, and even disagree with the teacher sometimes? The other teachers wouldn't let you do doodly-squat. Spent most of the time telling you what you better not do. Can't do this—Can't do that. Mister Myles made you feel you had some sense in your head, and what you thought amounted to something, even though you were only a kid in school. Then again he taught things that hadn't ever been taught before in Crossroads—And one of those things was Negro History—GreatGodAlmighty! All about things colored people had done. It was a whole lot better than a moving picture show. Made you feel like your folks amounted to something from way back yonder. Didn't care what Biff or any of the others said about that old young-ass teacher don't know what he talking about, making up all that stuff about Harriet Tubman and all those people, Mr. Richard Myles was the newest and the best and the smartest teacher in the whole wide world. He was even better than Miss Josephine, Robby thought guiltily, feeling like a traitor.

"And now let's take up where we left off yesterday—Negro History—"

Mr. Myles barely parted his lips when he talked. The words seemed to slide right out of his mouth, and yet they came out as clear as a Sunday church bell. Robby was glad to see Ida Mae pay more attention to the teacher than in any of her previous classes. She didn't gaze slyly at Robby as much as she used to, and he was naturally a little bit jealous, because she was his supposed-to-be girlfriend, but that was alright about that. She sat there with her big eyes on the teacher, pulling at her hair that she didn't wear in pigtails anymore, and fidgeting around in her seat. And when the young teacher's eyes swept the faces of the children and came upon her, she looked nervously down at her desk.

"They don't want us to know about Negro History," Mr. Myles was saying. "You see, if they can keep us believing we have been over here three hundred years and never did anything worth while, then we won't have anything to make us believe that we will ever do anything worth while. You know what they say about us." He raised his deep voice to a very high pitch, making it sound like one of those stomp-down red-faced tobacco-spitting crackers. "A niggrah ain't nothing—Ain't never been nothing—Ain't gon never be nothing."

Most of the children laughed, somehow knowing he wanted them to laugh and to be angry too. Biff Roberts took a rubber-band out of his pocket and a paper clip and he improvised a sling shot. He put it inside of his desk, and he eased his broad behind up off his seat, held it for a moment, a sly expectant look on his round freckled face, and he sat back down again. He looked around him, tried to attract attention to himself, and he held his slender nose pinched between his fingers like a clothespin, and he pointed to a boy seated next to him. A few children snickered.

Mr. Myles paused, his big eyes moved from face to face. "Z iii nnng—Bop," a paper clip struck the blackboard, barely missing Mr. Myles's head. He didn't let on that anything had happened, went right on talking.

"This country was built off the backs and the sweat of our fathers and forefathers."

"How about the mothers?" Gus Mackey asked, and somebody whistled and the children giggled.

When Mr. Myles talked about Harriet Tubman and Frederick Douglass and Nat Turner and all those people that Robby had hardly if ever heard of before, he listened to the teacher with his mouth open and his narrow eyes almost shut and a warm feeling moved throughout his body. Life-like picture of Harriet Tubman, little Negro woman, standing up against the mean white slave-holders—Great big evil hateful-looking white men—Big and ugly and fierce and hateful—outsmarting them—making trip after trip back into the south—leading hundreds of Negroes up north to freedom—A price on her head. She really was something! He fashioned for her a life-sized picture and gave to her his own mother's face. Pictured a railroad running underground, long and shiny, beautiful black train, Harriet Tubman the conductor and the engineer too. Harriet Tubman and Laurie Lee Youngblood. And yet he understood that it wasn't really that kind of railroad.

Biff raised his hand. "I hear my Daddy say sometimes, that

most colored people ain't got no get-up about them—lazy as the devil—ain't worth the powder it would take to shoot them with."

A funny look on the teacher's face. He could hear children giggling all over the room. A broad knowing smirk on Biff Roberts' face.

"Well, William, what do you think?" Mr. Myles asked him. "Are most colored people you know lazy and no-count?"

"I don't know, sir, but that's what I hear my Daddy say sometimes, and I ain't studying about disputing his word."

Robby raised his hand, painfully conscious of his heart pumping fiercely and a nervous sweat popping out on his forehead. "My Daddy works hard, and my Mother does too. She works all the time." Sweat breaking out all over his neck. "She—she—she just like Harriet Tubman. She doesn't take no stuff off of no cracker living." A great big bubbling-over pride for his mother swelling inside of him, a taste in his mouth that felt good good good.

Later that evening at home with his mother. "Mama, you know about Harriet Tubman and the underground railroad?"

"I reckin I do know a little about her, but I don't know much because there isn't hardly anything written about it that I ever got hold of. She was a mighty woman. Big Mama used to tell me all about that underground railroad. Lord Lord Lord."

"Mr. Myles knows a whole heap about the underground railroad and Harriet Tubman," Robby said heatedly. But why did Mr. Myles know more than his mother? His mother was smart. He knew his mother was smart—tell anybody.

Mama laughed. "Your great grandmother was a lulu. She used to tell us all about slavery. She told us about how the slaves used to gather in one of the cabins for prayer service and at the same time make plans against the master. One of the white overseers used to crawl underneath the house and listen to what the slaves were talking about. One night one of them was under there and Big Mama, she heated her a pot of boiling hot water while the Negroes kept singing Swing Low Sweet Chariot, and she sat on the floor right above where this cracker was lying on his belly and she turned the pot over and when that hot water hit that scoundrel, he let out a yell you could hear all the way to the Big House and back. Such a scrambling under that house Big Mama say you never heard before. Lit out across that field like a wild buck rabbit." Mama was laughing and Robby was laughing and

Big Sister was laughing. Tears streaming down Mama's cheeks, thinking about how Big Mama used to tell that story. "Big Mama say she didn't see that skeester for over a week, and when he did come around, she asked him—Where you been keeping yourself here lately, Mr. Josh?—That cracker turned a million colors and walked away from her mumbling and cussing under his breath."

After they all had a real good laugh, Robby repeated, "Mr. Myles sure do know a heap about Harriet Tubman."

Mama laughed. "I reckin that Mr. Myles of yours is a real smart man alright."

That night, late that night, in the cool of the evening, he dreamed a dream about a railroad that ran underneath the ground and came out on top to put Negroes on and went back under. Ran under hills and valleys and rivers and woods, and picked up passengers all along the way, and Laurie Lee Youngblood was the conductor and Robert Youngblood was the engineer, and the train was long and black and beautiful, like the Mary Jane Special, but longer and blacker and even more beautiful. And black folks got on at every stop—Everybody headed for that thing called Freedom.

And Freedom was a great big black beautiful something—big and black and oh so beautiful—And what was Freedom? And where was Freedom? And who was Freedom? Freedom had a black face and Freedom had a white face. It was a warm chilly feeling that moved through your shoulders and filled up your face. A soft cool morning in the early spring, when the sun comes up quietly and slowly and all of a sudden bursting wide open and singing out loud with a brand new greenness all over the earth and filling up the trees and birds singing and baits and worms and crickets and grasshoppers too, and the whole wide world come suddenly alive. Freedom was a doctor, a lawyer, a chicken-house cleaner and Robby Youngblood driving the Mary Jane Special and the South Bound Rocket and working in the Big Store—You and Fat Gus—Freedom was a hardworking man like your father with his shoulders thrown back and his head up high. Freedom was your mother and Mr. Myles too. And Freedom was you and Freedom was sassy to low-down crackers and Freedom was Freedom. . . .

The next day after school let out, he hung around until the others had left, and he asked the teacher—"Wonder where I can get me one of them books about Negro History? They don't have none down to Burden's Book Store. They ain't never heard of no Negro History."

The young teacher smiled. "I don't imagine they have. But I'll bring one tomorrow and lend it to you if you promise to take good care of it."

The teacher brought a book written by a man named Carter G. Woodson—a black man who had written a book all by himself! And Robby would read it at home every chance he got. And after he went to bed and she thought he was asleep, Mama would grab the book and she wouldn't turn it loose till sleep grabbed her. She would always put the book back exactly where Robby left it before going to bed. But he knew that Mama was reading the book, because sometimes Robby played possum.

"Hey, Laurie Lee. How you doing these day?"

"Fair, Carrie Belle. Nothing to brag about, but no use complaining."

"It's the truth, honey. It's the God's honest truth."

Laurie Lee stood on the dusty sidewalk, watching Carrie Belle Watson come down her front steps. She looked up at the sky which was a dark grayish cover blending with touches of blue here and there, and directly above was a big black zig-zaggy cloud that hung from the sky like bottom-heavy draperies.

"This weather is really something," Laurie said. "Don't ever know what to expect. Wish that weatherman would make up his mind."

Carrie Belle was leaning on the wooden fence that bordered her front yard. She was a big heavy woman and Laurie was always afraid that one of these days the fence was going to give way under her weight. "This weather is a mess, but you better leave it alone, cause the weatherman ain't got a thing to do with it. That's the Good Lord's problem."

Laurie Lee laughed.

"Looka here, child," Carrie Belle said, "what you think of this here new school teacher from up the country?"

Laurie looked up at the big woman's round heavy face. "Robby's in his room you know. He's his teacher."

"Heard tell he was. Well I declare."

There was a slight pause of loaded-down silence. Laurie knew that Carrie Belle was waiting eagerly.

"Robby thinks he's just fine. Plumb crazy about him. I thought

**159**

that boy loved Josephine Rollins, but he's just wild about this new teacher from New York."

"The way I heard it he ain't so hot. One of these hankty up-the-country Negroes. Think he better than us down here."

"I don't know about that. Haven't had time to pay him a visit. You know he told the children that the parents were welcome to come to visit the class just any old time. Just sit and look and listen. Be glad to have us. Be glad for us to make any suggestions. He even sent us a note—an invitation. Now how good is that?"

"Tell me he's one of these good-looking colored men and he know he's good-looking."

Laurie laughed. "I don't know about that either. I only know he seems to be a John-Brown good teacher and he's teaching them things they never heard about before, and they really do love him. The other day Robby wanted to get next to me about something, told me he was going to run away and live with Mr. Myles. He loves that man like he was a woman or something. Always talking about him. I declare before God I'm a little bit jealous."

Carrie Belle Watson was clearly disappointed, but she wasn't the kind to give up easily. The fence seemed to sigh as she took her weight off of it and put her hands on her hips that were twice as broad as Laurie's were. "You don't mean to say so— Child, I heard he wasn't no good riding or walking. It's all over town, he asked the children to express their own say-so about everything. Told them plain he didn't know nothing 'bout teaching. Poor little yunguns have to teach their ownself. Did you ever hear tell of such a thing in all your born days?"

"Well I tell you, Carrie Belle—You can't believe everything that goes around. You know how people run off at the mouth specially in Cross County. They talked about Jesus Christ way back yonder—they crucified him and nailed him to the cross, and Lord in Heaven knows there never was a better man."

"Laurie Lee Youngblood—you better hush your mouth."

Laurie picked up her black leather shopping bag that wasn't really made of leather. "Well, Carrie Belle, I got to be moving along."

"Alright, honey. Take care of yourself and give my best to Joe."

"Thank you, Carrie Belle. You do the same."

As she walked up the dusty street, she didn't look back, but she knew that Carrie hadn't moved from the spot, knew that she would stare after her until she turned the corner. In her own mind Laurie wasn't as sure of herself as she sounded when she talked to Carrie Belle Watson. Thinking very fiercely that maybe the new school teacher might really be heading for trouble, and maybe somebody should go to him and talk to him and explain how things were done in the South—How colored folks got along with white folks. Lord have mercy—how could she talk to this smart educated colored man, when she wasn't sure she said the right things to her own fleshborn children? She was angry and confused and she had a helpless kind of a feeling, wondering if other colored people in town were talking against Mr. Myles like Carrie Belle Watson was doing.

Richard Myles lay in the darkness of his room on top of a sheet with the cover thrown back, because the night was warm— not exactly warm. Well—well—well. Richard Wendell Myles— way down south in Crossroads, Georgia—the Crossroads of the U.S.A. Away down south in Dixie—Away Away—Listening to the sounds outside that to him were not so familiar—the fierce competition between the bullfrog and the locust and cricket and many other things he couldn't even identify. Yet it was a quiet kind of noisiness different from Brooklyn, and no subway trains shook the house from underneath. Staring through the darkness up at the white ceiling, thinking about the Borough of Brooklyn in New York City—hundreds and hundreds of miles away from where he was now in this clean little room in Crossroads, Georgia. Sometimes it felt like a million miles. When he had arrived in Crossroads, the town had resembled nothing he had imagined. It had been like getting aboard a train and taking a long trip across the border into another country. And he had been here for over a month now, but the strangeness had not worn off.

If only the white folks would stay out of the way, he would be all right, because if they didn't get in his way, he wouldn't get in theirs. The children in his class were swell except for a few. Well —more than just a few were sullen and distrustful and a little bit cynical, but none were bad or malicious, excepting maybe Mr. William "Biff" Roberts and a couple of others. Most of them liked him anyway, and he liked them, especially Ida Mae Raglin and Robby Youngblood and Augustus Mackey and Booker T. Jefferson—and—and—He wondered if Robby Youngblood had really been reading the history book he had lent him. He would give Robby plenty of books to read.

White people—There must be at least one or two decent ones in a town this big. There just had to be.—But what about the older Negro people in town? What did they think about him? He had to get to know them better than he did—had to visit more often—had to make himself visit. Only yesterday he had met Rev. Ledbetter in town and the pastor walked up to him and shook his hand and told him that he heard he was doing a real good job and he hoped he would be with them a long long time. The pastor was friendly and Richard felt guilty, because he had not set foot inside of a church since he arrived. When the pastor left him, he invited Richard to come around to the church and see them sometime. "You won't be under no obligation to join, if that's what you scared of. You and me in the same stock and trade, you know that, Professor. I try to teach a little my ownself. Teach them how to live in this great big world that the Good Lord gave us."

A soft cool breeze floated into the room past the white billowing curtains of his window and caressed his slim naked body, crawled all over him, tickling the little black blades of fur on his arms and his chest and his legs. Wonder what Randy Wainwright was doing? Randy the Radical. He didn't know if Randy were dead or alive. Dead—Dead—Washington, D.C.—Washington, D.C. and . . . and Henrietta Saunders and his first picket line and Meridian Park . . . The City . . . The City with the skin deep beauty . . . The City The City with the skin deep beauty. Hank—Hank—Was Hank really dead? Even now he couldn't believe she was dead—buried in the cold earth—her beauty, her littleness, her bigness, her spirit, her militance, her warmth, her powerful love, her intelligence—everything about her dead. Never to smell—see—hear—love. Love. He didn't know a damn thing about love. He hadn't appreciated Henrietta Saunders, or he wouldn't have left her to die in Washington, D.C., a place that she hated worse than Mississippi.

Hank had ignored all of the danger signals, just like Hank would, and she had worked when she should have been in a hospital. Worked day and night till she fell on the job one day. They took her to the hospital then, but it was far too late. She didn't linger long. She died the spring of the year Richard was graduated from City College, and Randy wrote Richard a bitter letter announcing her death and wishing him a shining legal career. Richard let his father read the letter. That was the time his father broke down and cried openly, and told Richard about Hank coming up to New York to see him, when he had been up at Cornell attending a students' conference. Richard hadn't fully realized it at the time, but that was when his legal career went up in smoke. That was when father's bright boy became a full-grown man. That was when father stopped running his favorite child's life. Maybe that was why he was in Crossroads, Georgia. Maybe Hank sent him. . . .

## CHAPTER THREE

SHE TURNED THOSE narrow slanting kind of eyes of hers with the heavy-laden eyelids and looked at the old hand-me-down-from-white-folks clock over the mantelpiece, with the long hand on X and the short hand on III.

Lord—Lord—The children would be coming through that door any minute now. And what would it be today? Yesterday it was Robby coming in with his big toe bleeding. She wiped her face with a big white rag as she stood over the ironing board pushing a hot flatiron. *White folks' clothes*—She hardly had time to do her own family's. *Work—work—work*—night and day. It was hard, mighty hard, but she would stand over the white folks' clothes out in her backyard till her back broke if it meant a better life for her children.

The charcoals glowed under the irons in the fireplace, throwing nervous shadows on the big bed and the center table and the bare floor that was scrubbed colorless, and now and then dancing on Laurie's face, even shadowing the home-made bookcase in the corner that Laurie and Robby had built and painted with such great care and industry. A clean overwashed smell about the room mixed with a very different, scorchy kind of a smell of charcoals burning and clothes being ironed and also drifting in from the kitchen a sharp burnish odor of sausage and rice cooking, one of the children's favorite something-to-eats, and—and—

Feet pounding up the front steps. "Mama—Mama!" Big Sister yelling.

An anxious look on Laurie's face now, as she heard the creaking porch cry out from old age and "Mama—Robby! Mama!" Laurie held the iron suspended in the air.

The front door swung open and the skinny little girl ran into her mother's arms. Big brown eyes, wide and tear-swollen. Tracks down the sides of her face made by dust and tears and Georgia dirt. She tried desperately to talk, but sobs and tears strangled her and kept her from talking.

"What in Jesus's name, Big Sister? Where in the world you been?"

"Robby—they—they locked him up—white boys—fi—fighting!" was all Laurie could get out of her. Big Sister's dress was torn and her black, curly plaits scrambled and twisted, looked like the devil had gotten hold of her. Her nose sucked inward at each breath, thin face bloated like a balloon.

Laurie's voice was steady, face impassive. "Sit down, child. Get a hold on yourself. Now, what's the trouble, baby doll?"

"Mama — Uh — Mama — Uh — Robby — peckerwoods — Mama — Mama!" Big Sister burst right out into fresh tears and sobbing.

Laurie put the iron back on the charcoals and hurried to the kitchen for a glass of water. She brought the water back and took a swallow herself, before she remembered, and she handed the glass to Jenny Lee. She drank some of the water and set the glass on the ironing board.

"Alright now, girl, take your time."

Big Sister took a deep breath, her flat chest pumping as if each were her last breath. "They—they locked Robby up!"

"What they? Who locked him up?" Mama still trying to remain calm, trying hard to keep cool.

"You know, that old long tall policeman, Mama, name Skinny McGuire. You know, Mama—He—he told me to come get you. They got Robby down to—" Fresh salty tears made wider tracks on the girl's face, spilling down to her quivering lips, and trails of cloudy water ran from her nose.

Laurie's face maintained a desperate calm. She took the rag she had been holding the iron with and wiped Jenny Lee's face, letting her blow her nose. "Don't cry anymore, Big Sister. You never were anybody's crybaby, you know that. There now, tell me, honey, how come they locked him up?"

"Cause he jumped on them white boys. That's how come!"

**164**

Getting the story from Jenny Lee was like cleaning a Sunday chicken. "White boys—what white boys? How come he to jump on them?"

"Cause they jumped on me first. Wasn't doing nothing to them white boys, Mama. Wasn't doing nothing but walking up Planters' Alley all by my own self. But I fought 'em back, Mama. It was just too many of them."

"Where was Robby? I mean wasn't he with you?" Why the devil didn't the girl tell the story right along without stopping?

"No'm—My class let out early—so I started home by my own self. Th—them white boys, 'bout four of them, they double-teamed me, and—and—and threw me to the ground. I tried to bust one of them peckerwoods wide open, but it was too many of 'em. Hands under my dress—yelling—yelling—" Big Sister's nose sniffling, her hands rubbing her great big eyes, her meager breast pumping in and out. "Yelling—yelling nigger pussy—nigger pus—"

Laurie couldn't make out what Jenny Lee was saying, because she was crying and talking at the same time. Mostly crying and sniffling and choking up. And Laurie bit her own lips and her eyes batted and she remembered bitterly another time in another place and another alley and a drunken white man—Remembering also Big Mama—Aah Lord Honey, goddammit—White man make way with black woman and black man bet not even now say a mumbling word! And looking down at Big Sister she almost shouted—*No! No! God-Jesus—No!* But she, the mother, had to control herself. "Alright, Big Sister, alright."

Laurie picked her up and laid her on the bed, upped her dress and found scratches on her skinny thighs and between her legs. Her drawers had been ripped and torn.

Laurie bathed her trembling legs and privates and put iodine on the scratches. "Now, doll baby, it's alright now. It's alright, Big Sister. It isn't so bad, honey. Now don't cry anymore. Tell Mama what happened to your brother?" She stroked the girl's skinny thighs. Slow, deliberate motions, back and forth—back and forth.

Between sobs and sniffling Jenny Lee got out—"That time— Mama, Robby caught up with me—started beat up them peck-erwoods—and—I helped him too—Time Skinny McGuire came up—grabbed me and Robby—let them pecks get away—Didn't lock them up, Mama!"

No, Laurie thought to herself, almost quietly, he wouldn't lock up the pecks. It wasn't to be expected. She took off Jenny Lee's shoes and pulled the sheet over her up to her neck. "You alright now, Big Sister."

She got ready to go downtown to the courthouse, moving quick-like, but without obvious excitement. When she was ready, she went to the fireplace and took an iron off the charcoals, walked around the room with it, not remembering why she had picked it up, then it came to her, and she breathed a deep sigh and *LordJesusHaveMercy* and she took the irons off the charcoals and sat them on the hearth. She took the ironing board down from its perch atop of two straight chairs and leaned it against the wall.

She went to the bed and kissed Jenny Lee on her sweaty forehead, now a network of anxious wrinkles. "Alright now, honey, I'm going down to the courthouse and get your brother. You just lie still and rest yourself. You feel better before we get back, get yourself some dinner, hear? Robby and me be back before a cat can wink his eye."

"Bu—but—but can't I go with you, Mama?"

"No, doll baby, you just lie here in Mama and Daddy's big old bed and keep yourself quiet."

"Wa—wa—wanna go with you, Mama. Don't leave me here by myself. Pl—please, Mama! Please!" Big Sister's eyes were wide with a pitiful fright, her lips tremulous and pleading. Fresh, salty tears pouring again.

Laurie's firm little bosom began to fill up and push outward, then inward again, breathing hard and painfully. Godalmighty— Her children had never been what-you-call crybabies. That was one of the things she had instilled in them, transferring to them through her from Big Mama.

"Now, Big Sister. It's alright. You're at home. Nothing in the world's going to bother you. Just you keep quiet and when you feel like it, get your dinner, hear? Mama fixed a surprise for you, doll baby. Something you and Robby really love. You smell that sausage and rice?"

Laurie smelled it. A sharp compelling odor of smoke, flavored with burning sausage and rice. God Jehovah! She ran into the kitchen, reached for the smoking pot and dropped it back on the stove. A blistering pain bit into her fingers like they had been thrust into an open flame. She shook her hands and put them in her mouth, grabbed the dish cloth and snatched the pot from the stove and sat it on the table. Sharp, fierce pin-point throbs shooting from her finger tips through her hands and up her arms. Sausage and rice charred from the bottom up to almost halfway the pot. Stifling and coughing like a spasm, fumes and tears in her eyes, she flung the back door open. The sun came in past her, thick, white and yellow. Everything that had been pent-up inside of her pushed upwards and outwards forcing its way to the surface, overcoming all her resistance, like mighty tidewater from the depths of the ocean, deep deep inside of her, up-up-up—, choking at her breasts, her throat, in her nostrils, her eyes, her deep brown, narrow, heavy-laden eyes, filling up her face, upwards and outwards, her cup ran over. She sat at the big awkward kitchen table, her head in her arms. Her shoulders shook, her legs trembling. The tears broke out of prison.

She got off the bus and walked through Jeff Davis Square. The sun had disappeared and a soft wind blew dust and trash and bits of the *Daily Telegram* along the pavement, some of it hitting her in the face, annoying her. She was in front of the courthouse now and awed by its big size. (All of ten stories.) A big white fearsome giant. Negro people called it Mr. Cross's Courthouse. She noted the big sign chiseled in the center of its huge white face. JUSTICE FOR ALL, it said in big pretty letters. Laurie rubbed the dust from her eyes as she went up the long marble steps and into the courthouse. Her face didn't give away the nervous trembling in her stomach, as she walked amongst the big majestic Georgian columns. Walking with her shoulders erect, left one slightly lower than the right like she always walked when she was going about her business. She met a policeman in the long marble corridor on the main floor and he told her where to find officer McGuire.

"Thank you, sir."

The policeman acted like he didn't hear her say thank you, sir, but she could feel him watching her as she walked down the corridor, looking at her supple body, at the quick, pleasant-for-him-to-watch movement of the pair of hips inside of her dress. Her face burned in anger. It wasn't the first time. Many white men had done so in the past, even more boldly. Skinny McGuire —Skinny McGuire—Now that she thought it, they said he wasn't the meanest cop in the world when it came to colored folks. Maybe—*Lord Have Mercy*—Maybe—Thinking now, as she approached Room 12, about her brother, Tim. Just wasn't nothing like himself, when he came out of that reformatory place. She didn't know today whether he was living or dead. She thought about Robby and she thought about the reformatory, and something caught in her throat and her face filled up and *Lord Heavenly Father* don't let them do it to him—*Please please please no reformatory no reformatory*—Room 12 Room 12—Please Lord, don't let them do it—not to my Robby, Lord, not to my Robby . . . Breathing deeply now, trying to calm herself and quiet down a great fear that had built up inside of her. She couldn't go into the room like this. They mustn't suspect. She wiped her face and took a deep sigh and knocked on the door.

"Howdy, Laurie," Skinny McGuire greeted her friendly-like.

"How you, Mr. McGuire?"

Another man in a gray suit, wearing a big fuzzy hat, sat at the other end of the room behind a desk. He looked up as Laurie entered. Skinny pawed the floor with his right foot and scratched the tip of his long beaky nose. He didn't have any shoulders at all. Looked like his arms were coming right out of the sides of his neck. Everything about him was skinny—scarce and skinny. Hair, face, nose, ears, body, legs—everything.

He picked something out of his nose and flicked it on the floor, looked at it for a moment, then flushed embarrassment. He cleared his throat and spoke like he had memorized a speech. "Gotcha boy down here—fighting white boys—Little white boys coming home from school—Serious offense, Laurie—Don't be you and Joe's younggun, wouldn't let him off so easy—Y'all some mighty good colored folks and we don't wanna see your boy git into no trouble—I go git him now." His greenish-blue eyes had been traveling everywhere except into Laurie's face.

"Thank you, sir," Laurie said in a restrained overflow of gratitude. She didn't like what she knew he meant by "Good colored folks," recognized how close it was to saying good something else, but she was glad anyhow. GreatGodAlmighty she had to be! Lucky though, it had been Skinny McGuire who arrested her boy, instead of one of those hateful cops that liked to lock Negroes up and beat them up too. She kept her eyes on the floor all the while Skinny was gone for Robby. The eyes of the other white man were stabs of uneasiness thrust into her back and spreading throughout her body.

The boy came back in the room with Skinny. He looked proud

and rebellious. She almost smiled at how he looked so much like her. Boy child favor his mother born for good luck they said. She certainly hoped so, but she didn't really believe it. Standing there just about caught up with Laurie in height. Going to be tall and powerful like his Daddy. He stood pigeon-toed just like Joe Youngblood. His eyes brightened, widened, crinkled at the corners. Now that Mama was here, nothing really serious could happen to him. And Mama saw it in his eyes and the way he held his mouth and understood what it meant and felt good over it.

"You know what to do," Laurie heard Skinny's voice saying vaguely, bringing her back to the reality of the courthouse office. She turned and saw Skinny taking something resembling a buggy whip down from behind the door, detachedly watched him handing it towards her. She didn't move, just stood there overcome, like she was struck dumb and paralyzed.

"You know what to do," he prompted. "He's gitting off light at that. Most colored boys woulda got some time. Ain't no lie. Reformatory's fulla them."

She knew what to do alright. Now it was clear to her what they expected. And the alternative, the reformatory, *God—Jesus Have Mercy!* Asking her to either break off his leg, or beat his brains out. She saw Robby's face as Skinny handed the whip to her. There wasn't the slightest doubt in his mind that his mother would refuse to take it. His eyes narrowed arrogantly, mouth set in a kind of curved-upward pout, shoulders back, legs apart, feet toed inward. Nothing could touch him. God knows she would not have taken the whip if she dared! The man under the fuzzy hat coughed and cleared his throat. Another look at Robby and she swallowed and pressed her lips together and made up her mind not to lash her son in front of these white men, no matter what. But the memory of Tim reared up before her and the reformatory itself, the mean, hateful-looking, dirty gray buildings, the Negro-hating people who ran the place, almost entirely filled up with Negro boys. The same ominous fear crept into her which had always been with her as a young girl, when they would come all the way from Tipkin to visit her brother at the Cross County Institution. The fat, red-faced superintendent with the sneering eyes, and the sneaky-looking assistant superintendent and the evil-looking guards and everything else. . . .

She saw the fear and confusion in Robby's face as she accepted the whip, a knife being stabbed in her own heart, shoved

**169**

all the way to the hilt and twisted. It was an ugly, murderous looking whip, an oversized razor strap sliced into three pieces. An obvious shiver passed through her body. Her legs trembled. Shame and pride gone now before these white men, replaced in her eyes by a terrible, humiliating fear. She turned to officer McGuire, handing the whip back to him. "Can't I take him home and whip him, please, sir, Mr. McGuire?"

Skinny wouldn't confront the desperation in the woman's face. He looked down at his big feet, then over at his desk. "You know that ain't the way it's done, Laurie. You know bettern that."

"But I'll give him a good whipping, Mr. McGuire. I'll give him a good one soon as I get him home, please, sir!"

She wished the boy were temporarily deaf, didn't want him to hear her pleading to white folks like this. Like getting on her knees, like stripping buck naked in Jeff Davis Square. "Please, sir, Mr. McGuire, I'll give him a whipping he never forget the longest day he lives—I'll skin him alive. I'll. . . ."

The man at the desk did some long and drawn-out throat-clearing, muttered something to himself. Skinny flushed red in the face. His keen voice hardened. "Lissen, woman, don't be for me, you be here begging me not to send him to the reformatory. After all, he was fighting white boys, garldernit!"

She wiped her face with her arm, and she turned toward her boy, who was looking a hole in the cement floor. A feeling of complete lifelessness had seized her entire body. Skinny's voice was apologetic. "Make him pull off his jacket."

"Pull off your jacket, Robby," she said, avoiding his bewildered, unbelieving eyes.

"You don't know what I did, Mama." He made no move to take off his jacket. "You don't know what they got me in here for."

"Yes I do, son. Your sister gave me the whole story. Now take off your jacket." She didn't want to look at him.

"But—but—but—Mama, I didn't do nothing wrong. Those—those—white boys were. . . ."

"Yes I know, Robby. I know all about it. Now, will you please —please—pull off your jacket!" It was hard enough for her as it was, with these white men standing over her and surrounding her. She wanted him, her own, to understand and cooperate. Hurry and get it over with.

The boy looked up into his mother's harassed face, his eyes

asking questions. He didn't know his mother acting this way. Laurie was a different person, a total stranger who wore Mama's face. Don't be a bully she always said. Don't pick a fight, but don't be a coward either. You can't run away from life, she always said. You're as good as any white person alive and much better than a whole heap of them. But this was his mother, the person he trusted above everybody, loved a thousand times more than anything or anybody in the world, and without another word, his tongue slipped over his lip and he swallowed hard, as he began to unbutton his jacket, his lips working noiselessly, hands trembling slightly. A quivering hardness in his stomach, a nervous fear he didn't want these people to know about.

The little office that wasn't particularly stuffy had suddenly become unbearably hot. Sweat crept all over Laurie's body like something alive and exploring. She would rather have bared her own body to the lashes of these white men than to do this thing to her son. Her face was a total blank as she raised the whip above her head. The plainclothes gentleman had lighted a cigar and was puffing it a mile a minute. It seemed to Laurie that hundreds of cigars were being puffed all over the little office. She was turned away from the white men, and she felt their eyes upon her like so many loaded pistols aimed at the middle of her back. Her arm was as light as yeast dough. The boy's body was drawn tight like a trap drum. The first blow made a three lane welt across his back, but he only winced, didn't utter a sound. She raised her arm again and she felt like taking the whip and lashing these white men until every bit of breath left their bodies. She wished that every white person in the world were at this very moment under her power. She would lash the life out of them one by one with a smile on her face.

*Whack!* Another red trail across her boy's back. And he didn't cry, just winced and moved his body sideways. *Whack—Whack!* After awhile it seemed that she was out of her own body. Standing there watching another woman who looked like her. Her eyes following each flight of the whip, up and down. Her own son receiving each murderous lick and she powerless to stop this crazy, beast-of-a-woman. Paralyzed from head to foot, except her eyes, which she couldn't close. She couldn't even cry out!

Her boy's eyes narrowed, almost closing, his lips curved and set, giving forth a grunt now, as each blow knifed his body. She saw Joe at the mill wrestling with a barrel of turpentine. She felt a contemptuous anger towards him. He had it so goddamn easy. Just lifting those heavy drums, while she lashed their son in front of white men for defending his sister against a bunch of little no-good crackers trying to rape her. She vaguely heard the plainclothesman in the corner say, "Damn! Tough little nigger buck! Tough as whit leather!" If he'd only cry out—Show some sign of pain, instead of that look on his face of grown folk's sassiness.

WHACK! The whip bit into his flesh like an angry rattlesnake, cutting the welts open; blood seeped out and spread over his back. A tremble started in Laurie's legs and ran upwards all over her body. His eyes were wide now, pleading for her to stop. The sweat had dripped into her own eyes, and mixed with tears forming there, almost blinded her. There was a mechanical motion about her now, as if she didn't know what she was doing. She might have been whipping the trunk of a dead tree. Her arm grew tired. She was at the top and inside of a deep deep well, holding on with her fingertips—WHACK—Fingers blistered, arms giving way—Any minute she would be falling down—down into the bottomless well—couldn't hold on any longer—She didn't want to hold on. . . .

She turned towards the crackers with her arms at her sides and her eyes begged them to let her stop whipping him. Her angry lips quivered. "No more—no more—please—no more!"

One of them said—she wasn't sure which—wasn't sure of anything by now—"You ain't hurt that boy yet—He ain't even cried—Reformatory fulla boys like him—You better give that sassy buck a good whipping—you don't want him in the reformatory."

Her arm was a mold of cement as she saw the blood flow freely now, nasty and spattering, some of it on her dress. Her own blood, from her own flesh and she was drawing it! Everything was blurred in white for her now. The room with its white walls seemed to be closing in on her. Skinny and the other white man blended into the white mass of the office. The desks, the floor, the hat rack, everything the color of cotton blossoms now, and closing in. The cigar smoke a big, white, choking cloud. For a moment even the boy before her was white and the blood on his back.

Robby began to whimper like a puppy suffering slow and deliberate torture. It seemed she was somewhere far far away, as she heard him, beaten to the floor and kicking like a dying animal. "Don't whip me anymore, Mama! I do anything you say! Please—Please—Mama! Don't whip me anymore! Oh, lordy, Mama! It hurt so bad! Don't kill me, Mama! Mama! Mama!" She tried to raise her arm, but the strength and the will had deserted her. She turned towards Skinny.

"That's enough, Laurie, he done learned his lesson, I reckin."

Laurie gave the blood-dripping whip to Skinny and reached for Robby's jacket. She was dead through and through, but she wanted to get out of this courthouse without any messing around. The smoky atmosphere of the white office closed in on her more than ever.

The other white man's voice cut the air like a buggy whip. "Make him say he ain't gonna fight white boys no more." His big mouth was smiling, a flash of gold teeth upper-center.

Laurie slipped the left sleeve of the jacket carefully over Robby's arm and started towards the door, not tarrying a second to button up his jacket.

The voice rose to a higher pitch. "Tell her make him say he ain't gonna fight white boys—*I said!*" The smile on his big mouth widened as he lit another cigar.

Laurie kept walking with Robby towards the door. It seemed a million miles away.

"*Skinny!* Tell her make him say he ain't gonna fight white boys —*Goddammit!*"

Skinny called out to Laurie, his thin face drawn thinner and red as a beet.

"Don't go yet, Laurie."

Laurie turned, she and Robby standing in the open door. She could feel her boy's whole body trembling. Her mouth tasted like the bile from a chicken.

Skinny said, "Tell him say he ain't gonna fight white boys no more."

Her eyelids heavier than ever, the narrow eyes empty now. "You tell him," she said. "I've done all I'm going to do."

The man with the broad, golden smile and eyes like steel balls adjusted his fuzzy hat, got up from the desk and walked around and rested his big bottom on the edge of it. "What the hell's wrong with you, Skinny? You let a nigger woman talk to you like that?" His big hand rubbed nervously between his legs, like a little boy playing with himself.

Skinny's long face turned various shades of red and popped

**173**

out all over with sweat. "Woman, you don't want no more trouble. Tell the boy what I say. Galdernit, you want him to go to the reformatory?"

She turned to Robby. Her voice sounded like somebody else's voice. "Say it, Robby."

The boy didn't open his mouth, kept looking at the floor.

"For Jesus' sake, say it, son, say it!"

He didn't look up. She barely heard him mumble, "Not gon fight whi—boys en—more."

The office was quiet and smoky. The plainclothesman said, "Whip him and make him say it."

Laurie looked empty-eyed, from the plainclothesman back to Skinny. The pleading tone had left her voice entirely. "I can't do any more. I'm sick and tired. I'm not going to do any more." She looked him full in his bony face, took the boy by the hand and walked out of the door. She heard Skinny's thin voice say— "She done had enough, Mr. Paul."

The plainclothesman played with himself and laughed like he was enjoying a funny picture at the moving picture show. "Officer of the law—Goddammit, Skinny, I believe you turning into a chickenshit nigger lover."

Anger made Skinny's jaws suck inward. "That's alright, Mr. Paul. More'n one way keep niggers in line. I skin my cat, you skin yourn's."

They walked down the steps of the courthouse, empty-eyed, heads swinging beneath their slouching shoulders. Laurie looked sideways at Robby, put her hand on his curly head. He pulled away from her.

Halfway down the great white steps she saw the big man approaching them. Mr. George, coming up the steps—His own great white steps. Biggest man in Crossroads, Georgia, fact of the matter, in all Cross County. Harvard graduate, traveled in Europe, inherited the town from his father. George Benjamin Cross, Jr. was different from all the other white folks in Crossroads. He wasn't anybody's small town hick and you could tell it. The way he walked, with his broad shoulders thrown back and his long legs striding like a man who always has important business to attend to. Blond giant, square-jawed and healthy-looking—Blue eyes that could afford to be warm and friendly on occasions to the common man, even to colored folks. Didn't even talk quite like a southerner. A reputation to most people of being a good man, if, God forbid, you never crossed him.

**174**

"Hello, Laurie," he said, with that magnanimous, I'm-the-big-dog-and-can-afford-it smile in his eyes and face. He kept walking, didn't even break his stride.

Laurie saw him and didn't see him, hardly realized he had spoken, didn't answer the big man. But after he had passed, she turned on the steps. She had a good mind to call him, to tell about what had just happened in his courthouse. Maybe he'd do something. Because some Negroes said he wasn't like the average cracker, that he was just as hard on poor white man as he was on a Negro. And he didn't look the other way when he saw a colored man on the street, and after all Robby still worked for the family after school three times a week. But somehow or other her mouth wouldn't form the words, just refused to call out his name. It wouldn't do a drop of good, something told her. Yet as she watched him, undecided and desperate, her mouth opened and she heard her own voice call after Mr. George. She called him twice.

The big man turned and answered—"Yes—?" The way they do when they spend a few years up North. He stood waiting, mouth opened to a kindly smile. And she walked back up the steps, dragging the stubborn boy after her, while Mr. George Benjamin Cross, Jr. waited and the sun broke through the cloudy evening in heavy slices onto the white marble steps.

"Well—"

"Mr. George—I er—I hate to—That is, I want you to know how they treated me and my boy in your courthouse." It made her angry to be stuttering in front of this big white man. Wasn't like her at all.

"This isn't my courthouse, Laurie. It's your courthouse. It belongs to the people, everybody's courthouse." Deliberately smiling his million-dollar-smile.

"Never mind that," Laurie said. "They sure didn't treat us like it was any courthouse of our'ns. That's what I'm talking about."

He balanced his weight from one long leg to the other. "What'd you do? I mean what did he do in the first place?" He looked down at the boy. "What'd you do, boy?"

"Didn't do anything. That's just it. Didn't do a blessed thing. You know my boy is a good boy, Mr. Cross."

The smile widened slightly, telling Laurie without so many words—Sure—Sure—Negroes never do anything. And Laurie wished she hadn't detained him. "He didn't do anything that wasn't right. Some white boys jumped on my daughter and my boy came along and defended her, his own sister. Ain't nothing wrong with that."

"Fighting white boys—"

"Skinny McGuire locked up Robby and when I came down to get him, he made me whip my boy till the blood came."

Mr. George looked up at the dark clouds and the parcels of sunlight, his mouth widened and eyes squinted, looked down again at Laurie and the boy. "Well—" He cleared his throat. "I'm sure he's none the worse for it."

"You ought to see the big welts and gashes on his back." Laurie's voice was calm now, edged with anger and bitterness.

"Well—I wouldn't worry too much about it, Laurie. Keep him out of mischief. You'll get over it, won't you boy?" The boy didn't answer, kept his eyes on the marble steps.

The big clock struck six times and Mr. George looked at his watch and said he was sorry but he had an appointment and to drop in some time to see him and was gone just like that, beautiful, handsome, smile and all.


## CHAPTER FOUR

REACHING THE SIDEWALK he pulled away from her, pushed both hands deep into his pockets.

"Robby! I had to do it, son. Couldn't help myself at all. They'd've put you in that reformatory like they did your Uncle Tim, and God in Heaven knows I just couldn't stand it. Understand me, Robby—son. God in Heaven knows, that reformatory is the worst place in the whole wide world." Her swollen eyes begged him.

Before long night would come, but the sun still shone in little silver streaks through dark-gray purplish clouds, and the wind blew trash and dust in their faces. Robby didn't say anything to Laurie Lee, didn't even look in her direction. He just pushed his hands deeper in his pockets and stared great big holes in the paved sidewalk.

They sat on the bus in silence, as it twisted and turned through the downtown section. Robby hadn't opened his mouth since they left the courthouse. She explained it to him, but he acted like she was speaking a foreign language. Now they were going through

Peckerwood Town. She studied his face till she couldn't any longer. A young bitter face with dark puffs under those narrow eyes, curvy lips pushed harshly upwards, his high forehead scowling like a grown man's forehead. She turned her head angrily and looked out of the window at the row upon row of little white houses that looked all alike.

A heavily-mustached colored man in the aisle studied the boy's face, and he looked at Laurie. "What's the matter with him, lady?"

"Nothing," Laurie Lee said, strangled by the unshed tears flowing inside of her. "He's alright now." She massaged the back of his head and his good strong shoulders. He shook his shoulders and pulled angrily away from her.

By the time they got home the slight wind had quietly blown up a drizzling rain, but Laurie and Robby were hardly aware of it. The evening sun had come out again and the rain looked silvery dropping through the sunshine. The shadow of the un-painted rusty-looking house enveloped them as they entered the yard.

Jenny Lee's face lighted up as she saw that Mama had brought Robby home with her, just as she had promised she would. She ran to her brother, murmuring his name, all of the torment, the fear and the suffering of the last, lonely, by-herself hours flowing from her little bosom and out of her lip-trembling kisses as she smothered his face. He stood motionless, arms at his sides, narrow eyes widened and empty, face impassive, as if nothing would ever touch him again.

There was a mechanical tone to Laurie's voice, like a worn-out Gramophone. "You eat your supper?"

"Yes'm. I wasn't very hungry. It sure was good though," she added quickly. "I threw the burnt part away."

Laurie pulled off Robby's jacket and a sob slipped from Big Sister's lips. Her eyes widened in astonishment, mouth hanging open. Laurie doctored the boy's back silently, explaining nothing.

"They—They—They did that to him, Mama! They—They got to him before you got there!"

There it was again—as if Jenny Lee were Skinny and were handing her the whip, saying—Make him pull off his jacket. She wished she could say to Big Sister—Yes, they got him before I got there—She wished to God she could. "No, girl I did," Laurie stated.

"No'm—No'm! They did it—them crackers, Mama—I know they did it!"

Laurie took a deep breath. "They did nothing of the kind, girl. I did it myself."

Jenny Lee looked unbelievingly at the long, bloody welts on Robby's back. "You—you—you did that to Robby? You—you —you hate us too?"

Tears spilled down Big Sister's face, as she ran into the kitchen. Laurie finished doctoring the boy's back and gave him another shirt. He stood before her, head down, already beyond her shoulders in height, feet toed inward, hate burning fiercely in his narrow eyes. She was angry with him for not understanding. Yet somehow she wanted to take him in her arms and with her overpowering love blot out everything that had happened that day. She looked him up and down and she made herself smile, as she remembered the other day when she and Robby had been going down Apple Street together, and Joe Jesup, the barber, had asked him how old he was. And when Robby had said eleven, Joe had stood away from him, measuring Robby's size with his eyes— "Who—wee," Joe had exclaimed. "Boy, you never be eleven no more till you get a hundred and eleven." A feeling of anger rising again inside of her towards him and Jenny Lee, as he stood there with his head down, accusing her, his mother, as if she hadn't sacrificed for them every single hour since they came into the world. And always praying that, God Willing, they should have a better life than she had. But now she stood there almost hating him, wanting somehow to beat him into understanding. God-Almighty damn the white folks! They're not satisfied with treating you like it's still slavery time, they turn your own children against you!

She went to the center table and took off the lamp chimney. Darkness was lowering itself over Crossroads, creeping gradually into the house through all of the windows. She blew her breath into the lamp chimney and wiped it inside and out with a rag. When she turned she caught her boy staring at her, searching, accusing. Their eyes met and held each other's momentarily, moved away simultaneously. How could she explain it to them? Was there an explanation?

"Come on," she said to him. "Let's get something to eat."

The odor of burned food still lingered in the kitchen. She watched him forcing the food down as if it were straw. The sau-

**178**

sage and rice stood in her mouth, spreading over the floor of her mouth, refusing to go down.

"You're not eating anything, son."

"I'm not hungry."

Laurie was aware of Big Sister seated at the other end of the kitchen on the side of her bed, her eyes upon the book in her lap, but her ears and her mind taking everything in.

"But you must be hungry. You haven't eaten a thing hardly, and I fixed it especially for you. This part is not burnt, darling. Your favorite—"

"Don't feel like eating!" he muttered as he left the table and ran into the other room.

She walked to the door. He was lying on her bed, his face buried in the spread. Crying for the fear and insecurity and confusion that had suddenly seized him. Weeping for the love and respect and devotion that she had beaten out of him . . . Because he felt lonely and mad and betrayed and forsaken and loveless like a motherless child. His shoulders shook and shook and shook. Mama turned against me! Mama Mama Mama . . . Mama turned against me! The spread became wet with his hot salty tears, and he made no attempt to control himself.

And she understood it. In his own house he could cry and cry and cry some more. And he didn't have to spare Mama, because there was nothing between him and her anymore. She walked over to the bed and rubbed his head gently. He shook his head and squirmed away from her, as if her hand were a red-hot poker.

She sat in the rocker near the fireplace. The rain beat an off-time rhythm on the window and the roof. Sleeping weather. Rain all night, rain, and maybe I'll be able to get me some sleep. She rocked back and forth with a nervous motion.

"Robby, come over here. You come in here too, Big Sister." The girl came into the room. The boy didn't move.

"What you want?" he asked, after she had called him a couple of times.

She wasn't going to stand for any sass out of him, courthouse or no courthouse. "You come over here and see what I want," she said. "I want to talk to you—both of you."

The boy came, taking his good time. They sat on the floor in front of her. She didn't know how to begin. It was like groping around in a strange dark house, clumsy, stumbling, uncertain, even afraid. "Robby . . . er . . . Both of you I mean—you don't understand about . . . about what happened at the courthouse today. You—you—" It wasn't like Mama to stammer this way.

"How come you do it, Mama?" the boy asked her. Usually he didn't interrupt her like this.

She looked past him at the cold fireplace. She got up and walked over to the center table and turned the wick up higher in the lamp. It was about that time when nightfall meets the end of the day, not completely dark, and the kerosene lamp had little or no effect. The lamp chimney smoked, she turned the wick down a mite. She came back and sat down in the rocker. A nervous rock back and forth and then . . . "Well, it's not so easy to explain. You see—I mean—The white folks in this town and all over the country I reckon, especially down south here, they think they're better than all the colored people. You all know that—both of you. They got the world in their hip pockets and they aim to keep it that way. They gon keep the colored man under their feet as long as we let them. And they aren't going to stand for us fighting back fair and square."

Nothing in the children's faces moved, not a lip nor an eyelash.

"Did I do wrong, Mama?"

Sitting there, both of them, as if they were the white prosecutors and she the black prisoner. Well, By God, her house was nobody's white folks' courtroom. But she tried to be calm with her children, talk to them evenly, explain. "It isn't a matter of right or wrong. It's just that. . . ."

"But—did I do wrong?" His young face was pulled hard and tight. Uncompromising.

"In the eyes of the white folks—yes."

Big Sister looked her mother in the eyes, sassying her with an open-faced look. She batted her eyes, then narrowed them like her brother's. "You wanted them white boys to rape me—that's what it is."

Laurie opened her mouth, her lips moved, but no words came out. Like a vicious kick in the middle of her stomach. She closed her eyes . . . *Lord Lord Lord* . . . She could see the drunken white man in Woodley's Lane as plain as day and her legs seemed to ache and tremble like the limbs of a tree, and the big cats on top of the garbage can and she saw Mama and Big Mama on the back porch in Tipkin that night many years ago . . . Big Mama and Mama gone on to Glory . . . *Lord Lord Lord* . . . and she wanted those white boys to rape Big Sister . . . she, Laurie Youngblood, their mother.

Robby looked hard at his mother and said, "I want to know how come you whipped me—How-how come?"

"Because," she answered in a weary tone that said, this is all I'm going to say about it. This is all, so clean out your ears and get it straight. "Because if I hadn't done it, they'd've put you in the reformatory. You'll get over the whipping, but if they put you in the reformatory you'd never get over it. I told you that already, Robby."

The boy reflected. Reformatory—reformatory—He knew all about the reformatory—knew it was a bad mean evil place especially to colored children—He knew all about Uncle Tim too. And ever since he'd left that courthouse he had been trying desperately to picture the reformatory in the worst kind of light, but he couldn't realize anything horrible enough for his mother to whip the blood out of him for the pleasure of white folks. Mama couldn't help doing what she did. You know she couldn't. But yet and still Mama was everything—the strength, the love, the knowledge, the comfort, the power and the glory, and Mama was Mama. The hurt and the pain of the whip on his back, and the blood, but much more than that the shame, the godawful shame, sharper and fiercer than any pain in the whole wide world.

Nothing made sense to him anymore, especially his mother. He felt like he had been put out of doors, thrown out into life on his own; no help, no guidance. Go for yourself. Nobody loves you— Nobody gives a good goddamn. Root, hog or die! His lips pressed together, his slanting eyes narrowed, almost closing. His mother shivered like she was having a chill. He made sure she had finished talking this time and then he said—"I don't like white people. Hate every one of them. See every last one of them in hell on the chain gang!" Without looking at her again, he walked quickly into the kitchen.

She started to tell him to come back, to say to him he shouldn't hate all white people—that all white folks weren't like that. Give him some kind of hope. Tell him hate was a mean thing and tell him all the other things her Christian upbringing had always taught her. But she didn't say anything, because at that moment she hated the whole human race, maybe God Almighty himself. Watching Big Sister follow her brother into the other room, she felt a terrible pounding inside of her head with a dull monotonous beat.

Joe Youngblood got home from the turpentine mill shortly afterwards. His husky body was soaked to the skin, and as usual, exhausted and beaten to the ground by the big heavy drums, his used-to-be-soft eyes vacant and dull, mouth drooping, his body and clothes smelling like turpentine and the goddamn mill. He didn't pay attention to things around the house. He was too doggone tired. Laurie gave him something dry to put on and she gave him his supper.

He sat down heavily at the big wooden table with a *Whew!* And she watched him as he sat there, working his jaws silently and breathing heavily through his big handsome nose, and swallowing his food with a muscular movement that went from his jaws to his neck and down through his broad shoulders. Working hard even at the enjoyment of eating. He looked up at Laurie, half smiled. "Sure taste good. Know what it taste like?" he asked. "It taste like more." Deep booming voice.

"Burned it a little." She smiled back, making herself smile. She didn't used to mind the noise he made eating, but lately it had begun to get on her nerves.

"Don't hurt none a bit. Make the flavor more better. What don't kill you, 'll darn sure fatten you."

She smiled again. The children were in the front room. She knew they wouldn't say anything if she didn't. Because of late, they didn't know the big man that well. He was just their father. Laurie didn't say anything to him about what had happened that day. She didn't feel like talking about it, going through the whole experience again. Not tonight. She would tell him tomorrow night . . . Maybe she would.

But sitting with him later that night after the children had gone to bed—seated before the fireplace, listening to the sleepy old rain beat out a lazy rhythm and the water striking the pots and pans throughout the house—watching the man whom she had met years and years ago at a church picnic in Tipkin where she came from—the smell of his pipe making her think of a courthouse room filled with cigar smoke although the smell was different—and watching him placidly smoking his pipe and reading his Holy Bible and breathing evenly, her entire body grew warm and she felt an eruption of anger towards him. His face was relaxed and his full pleasant lips worked hard, following his eyes along the pages of the Bible, and now and then a sucking noise from the pipe, and breathing restfully through his nostrils. He was big and strong enough to whip any white man in Georgia.

But what made her so damn mad, as she sat there watching him and his pipe and his Bible and his busy lips, Joe hadn't even sensed anything at all. Just came home, washed up, put on dry clothes, ate supper, picked his teeth with a broom straw, picked his favorite corn with a penknife, got out his pipe, got his slippers, made from old shoes with the toes cut out, and now he was reading his Holy Bible.

As she watched him she felt her whole being filling up-up-up, and she couldn't contain it, couldn't keep it inside of her any longer—and why should she? Why should he always be spared everything? She watched his face, lips busy, his jaws relaxed. Doggone his hard-working, easy-going time—knowing full well Joe Youngblood wasn't easy-going. A long ways from it.

"Had a rough day today, Joe." Laurie consciously controlling herself.

His eyes didn't leave his Holy Bible more than a second. "I done told you before, sugar. You ought to take it more easier. Can't do everything in one little old day." He didn't like to be interrupted when he was reading his Holy Bible.

And she knew he didn't like to be interrupted. Making her even angrier than before. "I don't mean that, Joe. They had Robby down to the—the—Made me come down there and whip him right in front of their eyes. Whip—whip—whip him till—till" —Her face filled up, her throat choked up, her voice broke off.

He had heard what she was saying, but actually he had only half-listened to her. He looked up from his Bible, glanced anxiously at her, then back his eyes went to his Holy Bible. He felt a great aching weariness all through his limbs; his poor back was killing him. He looked up at the ceiling, took two slow puffs on his smelly old pipe. His face barely changed its expression. "Like I always says, Laurie Lee—Like I read here in the Good Book just yestiddy—Don't spare the rod and spoil the child."

Her mouth was temporarily paralyzed. He had thrown a bucketful of ice water on her, leaving her speechless. She wanted to kick him, beat him, swear at him, spit on his Bible, hurt him real bad, call him—call him a *White folks' nigger,* but when she finally spoke, all that came out was—"I don't feel so powerful, Joe. I think I'll go to bed a little early tonight."

He looked at her as she got up from her rocker, concern in his

**183**

face for a half a minute. "What's the matter, Laurie Lee? You eat something didn't agree?"

She didn't answer him, didn't say a word, because she knew Joe wasn't really a mean man, and she knew he really loved her and the children.

The hours had long ago dragged past midnight. The rain had ceased now, but there was still the plinkity-plunk music of the rainwater dropping from the ceiling into the pots and pans. The Youngblood house was completely black. An entire darkness filled with the heavy breathing and snoring of people asleep. A familiar sharp odor of sleeping people with mouths opened and relaxed. The loud conspicuous tick-tock of the clock over the mantle. A strip of moonlight cutting-into-halves the tattered window shade, piercing the darkness, and casting a pale streak of light on the bed and across Laurie's face and up against the wall. A lonely, stay-up-late cricket disturbing the peace outside. But Laurie Lee Youngblood was not asleep.

She heard Joe snoring and she looked over at him, studied his face. *Spare the rod and spoil the child!* Joe wouldn't have said it if he had heard the whole story. She knew that he wouldn't have, and yet she felt the fiercest kind of anger toward him. She felt like beating him in that pleasant face of his till it was welted and bloody like Robby's back and it never would look pleasant again.

She sat up in bed and looked around her in the darkness. Sweat on her face and neck, and the clock and cricket seemed to be inside of her head. She had been asleep and it was all a bad dream . . . the courthouse, the white men, the white boys after her daughter, the blood on Robby's back . . . on her dress . . . and the smile on Mr. Cross Jr.'s face. Nothing like this had actually happened. Dream—Dream—Dream—How she wished it were only a dream! She lay back in the bed beside Joe. Great-GodAlmighty! This was the way she showed her love and affection to the children. You're no good, Laurie Youngblood. No good . . . No good . . . Got no pride about you . . . Uncle Tom . . . Scared of white folks . . . White man speak, you jump like a puppy dog . . . Got no business with such fine pretty children . . . And this is the way you teach them to live in the white folks' world. . . .

Turning from side to side in the bed beside Joe. If she could only fall asleep . . . Maybe in the morning when she woke up, she would find out it was all just a dream. Joe's heavy snoring chimed

**184**

in with the cricket, the clock, the rainwater, accentuating the hard brutal reality. She could hear the plainclothesman with the fuzzy hat on—"Tough little nigger buck—Tough as whit leather"—Her arms like cement, and Robby's face, and blood everywhere . . . The shame and humiliation before those white men and in front of her boy. She felt like she had been robbed of her womanhood! *Lord—Lord Lord!*—And to hear Robby break down and cry for mercy in front of those white men—Robby! Robby! Robby! No wonder she couldn't explain it to him and Big Sister. Lord Jesus, I would never do it again. Hope God to kill me I wouldn't. There must be some other way to fight this thing. Rather they lash the last drop of blood out of my children than to make me raise my hand to strike them once. Never . . . Never . . . Lord Jesus Never!

Joe Youngblood was awakened by the soft quiet weeping of his restless wife. He turned sleepily toward her, gathering her into his mill-strengthened arms. "What's the matter, Laurie? Can't you sleep?"

"I'm all right, Joe. I didn't mean to wake you up. I'm all right now." He lay there conscious of her vigorous body against his, her firm breast against his broad hairless chest. Knowing that everything was not all right, also suddenly realizing that he had let her and the children down earlier that night with *Don't spare the rod and spoil the child.* Now sleepily reaching around in his brain in quiet desperation for words to comfort and reassure her, simple words to make her know how he felt, but much too tired and sleepy to think clearly, everything mixed up and misty like a fog in the early morning. His back wasn't what it used to be, and those goddamn drums were no Sunday School outing.

Laurie Lee lay there breathing deeply and anxious, seeking strength and courage from his muscular body. Telling herself now that she should have told him the whole story about her and Big Sister and Robby and he would have acted differently. His arms good and strong to her, his thighs smooth and hard. She wanted him to say something to her, any little something, anything at all, to let her know he shared the hardships of their lives. Wanted him to take her now, as she was, physically and spiritually—Wanted desperately to feel him inside of her and a part of her, blending one into the other, their love, their strength, their power, their understanding, one and one and one and indivisibly one. She lay in his arms breathing hard and fierce like she had been running up a long steep hill, and then her breath cut off momentarily. His body smelled like fresh coffee cooking. She felt his tobacco breath in her face, heard him snoring again, like a man calling hogs. . . .

Joe! Joe!
Poor Joe Youngblood

She wrested herself angrily from his arms, powerful even in sleep, and she got out of their bed and stumbled through the dark into the next room and got into the bed with Jenny Lee.

Big Sister, breathing evenly in her sleep, never knew until morning. But the least disturbance always woke Robby. And lying there in the middle of the floor on his pallet, he heard his mother weeping—quiet bitter weeping like he had never heard before. His eyes stared through the darkness, and his throat contracted, swallowing the night air. His face filled up, he wanted to go to her and find out what the matter was, but he was confused and mixed up, thinking about that afternoon in the courthouse room . . . Angry with her, hating her, but deep down inside of him loving her in spite of himself, and feeling sorry for her and wanting to comfort her and get comfort from her. He turned over on his stomach and pulled the cover up over his head, but he couldn't shut out the sound of her weeping.


## CHAPTER FIVE

THE LETTING-OUT bell rang and Mr. Myles said would Robert Youngblood remain a few minutes after school. The other children left and Robby sat still, his eyes on his desk, as he heard Mr. Myles walking over towards him. He looked up from his desk and over towards the door and he saw Ida Mae hanging around outside. Mr. Myles was standing over him and followed Robby's gaze to the open door. "You want to come in, Miss Raglin?" She ran off quickly down the hall.

"What's the matter, Robert?" the young teacher asked.

"Nothing the matter."

"Are you and I friends—buddies I mean?"

"Yes, sir. I reckin so."

"Friends don't talk with their eyes down. They look each other straight in the face. They don't act like they're afraid of each other." Robby didn't say a word, kept looking at the floor. "Do they, Robby?" It was the first time Mr. Myles had called him Robby instead of Robert.

"No, sir. I don't reckin they do." Robby's eyes came up and he tried very hard to keep them up. He wanted Mr. Myles to be his friend always. He needed a friend, a really honest-to-goodness friend that never would betray him. "I'm all right, Mr. Myles. Nothing's the matter with me." He wanted to tell Mr. Myles in the worst kind of way. He opened his mouth but he just couldn't make the words come out. He couldn't tell Mr. Myles, of all people, because he had been so proud when he had spoken in the classroom about how like Harriet Tubman his mother was and the way she didn't take any stuff off of crackers, and he knew Mr. Myles had been proud too, and he couldn't tell anybody about his mother. He heard Mr. Myles as if off in a distance saying that something must be troubling him, he looked so worried, and he hadn't been paying attention in class, and maybe he was having trouble at home. Robby saw Mama's face, and it would serve her right to tell Mr. Myles and everybody else, but he just couldn't do it. He felt his face filling up and he had to get away to himself, his eyes filling up now, and he didn't want the teacher to see him cry. "I have to go, Mr. Myles. I really got to go." He walked hurriedly out of the classroom, leaving his books, and he ran down the hall and tears flowing now, and he heard himself say to himself, I'll run away from home—I'll run away from home, not fully realizing what he was saying. He stood in the front yard of the school. *Run away from home!* The idea frightened him half to death.

Ida Mae came up behind him and gave him a bang in the back of his knee with her books, almost making him fall to the ground. She stood before him, her big eyes serious. "What's the matter with you, Robby?" He glared at her angrily. He looked down at her legs, pretty and roundish and long and covered with black woolen stockings up to her knees. She was his girl and a man ought to be able to tell his girl anything, and she was smarter than all the other girls. "Ain't nothing the matter with me," he said.

She pressed her pouting lips together, put her hands on her hips like a grown-up woman. "Robert Youngblood, you can't fool me. You just don't want me to know, that's all."

She's your girl—Go ahead and tell her. He looked down at the dark grayish earth, looked up into her sweet anxious face again.

A cool piece of breeze tickled the heat around his face, and he suddenly felt a desperate agonizing need of comfort and friendship and love and understanding, the feel of human arms around him. Go to Ida Mae . . . stand in her arms . . . Hug her tight and she hug you . . . Tell her everything. A shiver passed over his body and left him. "Well," he said, making himself say it, standing wide-legged and mannish, his feet toed inward even more than usual, "I haven't got time to be talking to you. I got to be going."

"Where you going?"

"None of your business. Tend to your business and leave mine alone."

Her big eyes widened. "Robby Youngblood, you don't have to act so uppidy. I declare before God!" She left him quickly and ran across the road, catching up with some other girls, and when she reached them, she turned around and gave him a look, a beautiful warm hurtful look in her great big beautiful eyes. His eyes followed her and he wanted to call her back to him. He looked around him. He was really going to run away from home, but where would he go? Where would he go? His mind messed around with this question for a very brief moment. To hell with it. He would go anywhere. Maybe Atlanta or Savannah, or even New York where Richard Myles came from, a place where they wouldn't treat him like he was a dog or a slave just because he was colored. If he could grow up to be like Mr. Myles, then he was all for going to New York. Mama would be sorry and hurt and would cry after him. So it didn't matter where he went as long as he went. The thought of Mama crying and unhappy made him feel very funny, took some of the sting out of his running away. He looked up at the sky where big dark clouds blocked out the sun, and he started walking up Pleasant Grove Avenue. It was chilly and damp. Well if Mama cried, that's just too bad. No better for her. One day after he became a man, he would come back and bring presents and they would be glad to see him, and no white folks had better look at him hard. To hell with that, he wasn't ever coming back.

He walked till the muscles of his legs cried out. Through Green Street, across Davis. Cut through the empty field where the Black Sox played. A positive idea of where he was going had not formed yet. He was running away, that's all, and Mama would be sorry. Through Peckerwood Town, red-faced white folks on their little white stoops looking at him like they would a stray dog, and their children playing in the front and the backyards and his hungry stomach growling like an angry bulldog, and he kept walking . . . walking. . . .

And now he had walked through Peckerwood Town as darkness fell and then through the rich white folks section, and it had gotten real late and dark like midnight. He was walking down hill now and out of the residential section, entering the business district where everything had long ago bedded down for the night.

The sound of his bare feet on the pavement was loud and frightening. A man walked toward him and he ducked into an alcove between two store windows. The man passed by whistling, and Robby wished he could whistle too. Frightened more than ever, he left the streets, and took to an alley walking down the middle of it. He looked neither down nor to the sides, kept his eyes straight ahead of him. His ears picked up the sound of great big rats that had taken over the alley for the night. He could hear them pilfering trash-filled crates and garbage cans, squealing and running all over the place like it belonged to them. He wanted to run fast and be out of the alley, but he kept walking at a steady gait and tried to whistle. A big white cat gave a loud wail like a baby crying, and streaked across the alley in front of him. Robby's feet left the ground and they took him as fast as possible out of the alley into a wide place on the other side of which was a railroad yard. He slowed down to a walk, crossed the plaza and entered the yard.

That's what he'd do—catch himself a freight and end up notelling-where. Riding the rails wasn't hard to do. That's how Fat Gus's brother came to his grandmother's funeral. All the way down from Cleveland, Ohio. Maybe he'd ride all the way to New York. He stole past a little old building that resembled an outhouse. It stood in the middle of the yard and a dim reddish light shone from a small window. He ran across the yard toward a group of boxcars and stood for a moment surrounded by them. He saw an open one and tried to make himself crawl up into the jet-black darkness, but it didn't come off. Anything might happen if he climbed up into this thing. It was like a big black canyon gaping at him ready to swallow him up. A salty perspiration dripped down into his eyes, angrily burning them. Almost anything might be in there looking out at him, waiting for him. Nothing's in this old boxcar, he told himself. The cool night breeze made his hot body shiver. If he was going to run away from home, he couldn't be scared of every little thing, he argued with himself, and finally he drove himself up to the door, a great sweat draining from all over him, and he pulled up by hands and knees and feet and fell forward, holding his breath, into the boxcar. He lay there breathing hard and sometimes thinking that his breathing would stop altogether. He didn't move for the longest kind of time. His tiredness, nervousness, fright, hunger and loneliness, his hatred of white folks, his hatred of his mother, his love for his mother, all of it merged into a mighty stream, that kept swelling up till it burst inside of him. He cried silently till he fell asleep.

The sun reached into the open car and shone brightly on his young tired face. His eyelashes blinked. His arm came up and shielded his face. His body stirred quietly. His narrow eyes opened, closed and they opened again. He started to his feet, but he was so weak he fell down again. His stomach growled like an angry old bulldog. He got up and looked around him in the empty car. Where was he? He thought about Mama. He was running away from Mama—That was it! His mouth tasted bitter and stale, and he could taste the disagreeable odor of his breath like a whole host of bedbugs, dead and bloody. His face was stiff as an ironing board.

He walked stiff-legged to the door and jumped to the ground. He looked around at the damp early morning. He had better get out of here, before he got into trouble with white folks. These freight cars here weren't going anywhere. He began to walk and he walked while the sun climbed higher and higher. And he kept on walking, aware of the town waking up for the day. He heard the sleepy-head cloppiddy-clop of the milkman's horse, and he saw the milkman walk up the paved and the graveled walks and leave bottles of milk on the rich white folks' porches, and he saw newsboys delivering the *Daily Telegram*. He saw people on their way to work early in the morning, mostly Negro women, on their way to make everything nice and easy for rich white folks when they woke up. He didn't let these women see him.

He stopped walking and stretched himself and his whole body trembled from his head to his feet, and the muscles of his legs seemed to be drawing up on him. He shook his legs and started to walk again. Where would he go?—What would he do?—Go over near the railroad where the tracks run along the edge of Peckerwood Town and grab himself a whole heap of freight train. That was the place. He had seen hoboes do it many times. He didn't know anything about how to be a hobo. Hell, it was easy. He wasn't

going to be a regular hobo anyhow. Just hack himself a ride till he
got where he was going. Just so it took him out of Crossroads,
Georgia. His feet carried him across Rockingham Field and
through Drayton's Alley heading for the railroad. He saw a group
of Negro men sitting in a clearing at the foot of the embankment
that ran up to the tracks. He walked over toward them with his
eyes upon the ground.

"Hey, Young Blood, what you want around here?"

Robby stopped short. How did these men know his name so
well? Maybe Mama had already been here looking for him. He
glanced about him uneasily. "My name ain't no Youngblood."

"That don't make no never mind," the man said. "Don't care
what your name is, you Young Blood to us. You ain't no Old
Blood—you must be Young Blood."

It was the long-legged skinny one, who sat in the middle of the
semicircle of them. He was dressed in patched-up overalls and a
beat-up lumber jacket. He looked at Robby out of coal-black eyes.
"What you looking for around here?" the man asked Robby.
"You lose something?"

"No, sir," Robby answered.

"What you doing round here then? You don't see no other
children round here, do you?"

Robby was scared, but he made his voice sound tough like a
full grown man. "I'm doing the same thing you doing around here.
Going to grab me a freight."

"Boy, you better get outa my face and get your young ass back
home before I kick the shit outa you."

Robby looked down into the man's dark eyes and the eyes
were angry and the man wasn't kidding. "I haven't got any
home," he said to the man. "I don't live in this town. I'm passing
through it just like you are."

"Leave the boy alone, Scotty," somebody said.

"Boy, don't you stand up there with your bare face hanging
out and lie to me like that."

"I don't have to lie to you, man. You ain't none of my daddy,"
Robby told Scotty, making himself look the man in the eye. The
other men snickered.

Scotty looked Robby up and down. "You kind of sassy too,
ain't you, Young Blood?"

Robby didn't answer. Was this a trick—calling him Youngblood? Did the man really know him?

"Alright—alright," Scotty said, "ain't none of my business. Sit down and rest a little while. Make yourself at home. But I tell you right now—This ain't no life for no pissy-ass cry-babies. Ain't no good life for nobody's body."

Robby sat down on the red-clay earth in the middle of the men. He listened to them talk and tell stories and one of them would try to tell one bigger than the others. A real fat man with jet black skin and serious eyes sat next to Scotty. He kept his eyes on Robby most of the time. The other men called him Skinny.

Skinny drew a circle in the red dusty earth. "Where you headed for, Young Blood?"

"Going to New York."

Skinny looked hard at the boy and laughed softly. "I don't blame you, Young Blood. I'm gonna shake this Georgia dust off my heels too, and I ain't gon want to see any part of the South no more, not even in a picture show."

Another man laughed. "Skinny, you sure is hard on the South, I swear 'fore God."

Skinny didn't laugh. "I ain't hard on no South. She hard on me. Last southern town I spent any time in was in Mississippi. We called it Laughing, Mississippi. Man I'm telling you. If a colored man walking up the main street he had to walk in the gutter when a white man pass. They got a big old garbage can in the middle of each block. If a colored man see anything funny and he wanna laugh he have to run to that can and stick his head in it."

Some of the men laughed. "Man, you ought to stop that stuff."

"I ain't lying," Skinny insisted. "They got a great big sign in one uppidy section of town, it says—WHITE TRASH READ AND WALK FAST—NIGGERS READ AND HAUL ASS."

The men laughed and Robby laughed too, but Skinny didn't laugh, and Robby looked into Skinny's fat face and tried to figure out if the man were serious.

Scotty was smiling but his eyes weren't smiling. "Remind me the time I was passing through Tipkin, Georgia, about a hundred miles down the road from here. I went into one of them little stores on the outskirts of town and asked the man for a can of Prince Albert Tobacco. He say what you say, boy? I say I want a can of Prince Albert. He say 'nigger you better say Mister Prince Albert.' "

The men laughed and chuckled with a funny-kind-of-harshness that shouldn't be in a man's voice when he laughed. Robby wondered about it, because when a man laughs his heart should be in it and the laughter should be all over his face, including his eyes.

Robby felt Scotty's eyes taking him in, and it made him uncomfortable, made him feel like he was younger than he actually was. His neck collected a coolish kind of heat, and he wished Scotty would stop looking at him.

"So you going to New York."

Robby said nothing.

"I'm talking to you, Young Blood."

"Man, I already told you I'm going to New York."

"New York ain't much better than Georgia or Mississippi."

"And that's the truth," another man said.

Scotty looked at Robby and laughed out loud. "Man, I'm telling you—These Young Bloods of the colored race ain't gon take no shit like us old heads. They gon make things move or *else*. These old crackers might as well get used to the idea. I know what I'm talking about. Ain't that right, Young Blood?"

Robby's face felt a great warmth in it. "You ain't no Old Head," he told the youngish hobo.

"Old enough to know better," Scotty said with a short dry laugh.

It was getting late and the children passed on their way from school and Robby sat in the middle of the men hoping that none of the school kids would see him, and yet at the same time longing to be a school child again, a terrible longing to be going home from school, but to hell with that, he was going to New York, and Crossroads, Georgia knew what it could do. The sun was over and away to the west, and it wouldn't be long before it would be going down. A swift wind blew across Schofield Field, kicking up trash and dust, and golden-brown leaves ran around the field chasing one another. The sun was temporarily hidden by a cloud and a chill was in the air. Somebody suggested, "Let's get us some of that trash and twig over there and make us a fire. It's getting kind of cold."

Skinny looked at the man who made the suggestion. "You crazy, feller. That's all them crackers need to attract their attention. Police catch you in this town they beat your head till it rope like okra. This is a bad cracker town. I know what I'm talking about."

"We ain't got much longer to stay here anyhow," Scotty said.

**193**

"Our train be coming through here in a few minutes." He looked at Robby. "You know how to get aboard a freight, Young Blood?"

"Sure I do," Robby said quickly. "Ain't nothing to it."

"I mean when it's moving, not standing still."

"Sure I do."

"Alright, Young Blood, but you got to be careful." He winked his eye at Robby in a friendly way.

About ten minutes later Robby heard a train whistle, and he looked towards town and he saw swirls of smoke reaching toward the sky, and a funny kind of feeling gripped him in his stomach and his body grew warm. The men got up and picked up their bundles and started towards a spot where a broad path led up the embankment to the tracks. Scotty walked along beside Robby and Robby was grateful. He heard the shuffling noise of the train coming closer, as smoke and cinders began to fill the air, and he smelled the train coming. He saw the black engine as it rounded the curve and the red boxcars following it, and the bottom seemed to fall out of his stomach and a panic seized hold of him and he wanted to turn and run as fast as he could away from the track and the train and the smoke and the cinders and not stop running until he reached home, but he couldn't run away. He didn't have any home!

He felt Scotty's bony hand on his shoulders, and he looked up into Scotty's slender face and he thought he saw a warm kind of friendship in Scotty's black eyes. "Ain't nothing to be scared of, Young Blood. It won't be going fast at all. You just stay close to me, and when you see me jump, you jump and grab hold the edge of the car, and I'll pull you in."

Robby didn't have time to say thank you. The train was almost up to them now, and they gathered close together at the foot of the embankment, and when the engine passed, they began to trot, spreading out a little, and broke into a run up the path to the top. Robby ran alongside of Scotty and his heart was beating a hundred miles an hour. The train was going slightly upgrade and had not picked up any speed at all. The men ran for the first open car and they started jumping in. Just before Robby jumped he tripped and stumbled over Scotty's foot and he fell down, and Scotty didn't seem to realize it till he was already in the car, and when Robby got up he heard Scotty's voice through the noise of the train picking up speed—"Go on back home to your Mama. Can't even hack a ride on a slow-ass freight train."

Robby's knees were cut and bleeding from the gravel near the tracks and his eyes filled with tears. Wondering if Scotty had tripped him on purpose.

He got to his feet and looked around him. He started to walk, didn't have any idea where he was going. One sure thing, he wasn't going home . . . wasn't going home . . . He didn't have a friend in the world. The train gave out a long lonesome whistle from far away, and he thought that maybe Scotty would have been his friend, but he was long gone now on the northbound train, and he never would see Scotty again. Mr. Myles was his friend. To hell with Mr. Myles. He didn't have a friend in the whole wide world.

## CHAPTER SIX

HE WALKED NOW without any sense of direction like a boy sleepwalking. He stopped and looked around him to see where his feet had taken him. He was standing in front of a large wooden-frame two story house with a great big persimmon tree in the front yard and an old oak tree on the edge of the sidewalk. He knew where he was, but he didn't know why—Why had he come here where Mr. Myles lived without telling himself, and how had he done it? Couldn't have been an accident . . . Mr. Myles was his friend, he argued with himself.

He stood in the chilly darkness in the shadows of the wide-spreading oak tree, and he looked at the big house, trying to make up his mind to go in the yard and walk up the steps and knock on the door, but he wondered if coming to see his teacher was such a good idea after all. Mr. Myles would know then that his mother was not the good strong woman he had pretended she was, and he would think Robby was a great big liar, and Mr. Myles wouldn't lend him any money to go to any New York City. He would probably take him home to his mother. As he looked at the big awkward house covered with the trembling shadows of the trees, all of the hunger and pain and self pity and frustration and loneliness came down upon him, and his face filled up and all through his body, and he didn't know which way to turn. A light came on in the front room upstairs and Robby hid behind the oak tree. He stood there until he felt weak all over and his head went around like a merry-go-round and his legs got wobbly and he leaned against the tree to keep from falling, and he saw Mama and he didn't see Mama, because it was some other woman standing in the courthouse room with the whip in her hand, and he saw Daddy and Big Sister and Mr. Myles and Ida Mae and Mama and Betty Jane, and Mama with a kind face and Mama with an ugly face and Mama with a white face. His hands went out and he grabbed at the oak tree and his knees buckled as if GreatGod-Almighty Jack Johnson had hit him and he fell to the ground.

He didn't know how much later it was, but he heard somebody calling his name, vaguely he heard a voice strangely familiar, and somebody leading him up long narrow white steps, he stumbling most of the way, being picked up and carried now. And washing his face and hands and then they went into a big clean kitchen and sat him down to a table with food. Warm food finding its way down his weak hungry body, hurting his insides at first, but at the same time soothing him inside like a cup of hot milk in the cold wintertime. He looked up into the light brown eyes of the man from up north, listening to the deepness and richness of the voice with the accent foreign to the people of Georgia.

"Did you get enough to eat?"

Robby looked down at the table. "How did I get—how come I came—I mean I didn't mean to come to your house, Mr. Myles. Didn't want to bother you. . . ."

"You didn't bother me. You came to me because you needed a friend and you knew we were friends. I'm glad that you came. Remember yesterday?—in school? We agreed we were buddies."

Yesterday . . . yesterday . . . yesterday seemed such a long time ago to him—Yesterday before he ran away from home—before the dark dark night and all night long sleeping scared in a boxcar, before the colored hoboes in Schofield Field and Scotty and Skinny and falling near the train and powerful hunger doubling up his belly . . . Yesterday ended when Ida Mae left him on the school grounds . . . Yesterday was a hundred years ago.

He looked up into the teacher's smiling face. "Yes, sir, but—"

"Did you get enough to eat?" the teacher asked again.

"Yes, sir, I thank you."

"There's plenty of it left, so don't be bashful."

"No, sir." He looked down at the plate and he knew that the

teacher was staring at him and shaking his head and mumbling to himself, angrily muttering. The boy looked up and he caught the man's eyes and he looked down again and he loved this man and his face filling up again and his eyes growing misty and trying hard to be a big man, awfully hard—No crying here please please please——

He tried to talk to the teacher, to explain away the tears, but he just couldn't make it.

"Don't try to talk, Robby. Finish your food. I know all about it. I talked with your mother already. I just left your house about an hour ago."

He looked up at the teacher, his narrow eyes opened wide and his eyelashes fluttered, and Mr. Myles seemed to know what he was thinking.

The teacher shook his head from side to side. "Your mother is wonderful," he said to the boy. "A tremendous woman."

"Thank you, sir." How could his mother be wonderful and do what she did?

"Don't thank me—It's an absolute fact. You know that better than anyone else. She's everything you said she was and more besides."

"But she—she—"

"I know all about it. She did what she believed was the best thing for you. Didn't have much of a choice, did she?"

"But—but—"

"She's still a great fighter," the teacher told the boy, thinking about another great fighter he had known, a young Negro woman by the name of Hank Saunders. He turned his face away from the boy. A picture of Hank disturbing his mind, militant Hank with great big brown impertinent eyes. Hank dead—Hank no more —"I'll be right back," he mumbled and went out of the room.

Later he took the boy home to his mother. "Don't want to go home. Don't want to ever see Mama again." But he was too feeble, too exhausted, too bruised and beaten and much too young to offer any really strong resistance to Richard Wendell Myles, his teacher and friend.

Mama looked like a dried-up sweet potato when Robby walked in the door. He could see the life flow back into her face when she first laid eyes on him. Ran to him, hugged and kissed him and crying all over him—Robby! Son! Robby! and Jesus Have Mercy! But he wouldn't let on that he felt anything. He just stood there with his narrow eyes widened and curvy lips pressed against one another, his hands in his pockets. Let her suffer . . . Let her suffer! No better for her.

The father stood near the fireplace in his towering height. His face was solemn and his eyes were quiet. "Thank you, sir," he said to the teacher. "Our boy is a good boy."

And gawky Big Sister stood in the doorway to the kitchen in her patched-up nightgown with her mouth hanging open and her big wide open eyes asking questions.

Mama hugged the boy with all her might, shook him nervously. "Son—Son—don't run away from home—your family loves you —your family loves you."

He didn't say a word.

She looked him over from head to feet. "Son, you really been through the mill. Jesus Christ Have Mercy—what happened to you?"

He didn't say a word.

She looked around her. "Have a seat, please sir," she said to the teacher. "Excuse me for just a few minutes. Big Sister, heat me a kettle of water, honey, right quick right here on the fireplace."

She took her boy into the kitchen and she closed the door and she stripped him down tenderly, piece by piece, and she looked at his knees and the bruises all over his body, and the welts on his back that she had inflicted and she couldn't help from crying all over again. He wanted to cry too, filled up to the brim, but he couldn't, just wouldn't let her see him cry. She bathed him gently from his head to his toes.

Standing in the tub, tall and big and just like he came into the world. Bathing his broad, mannish-looking chest softly and tenderly. "Does that hurt, son?" And under his arms, and Mama aware of the sharp new smell of his great exhaustion mixed up with the smell of his reaching towards manhood. Her narrow eyes were open wide, eating him up from head to feet. The boy squirmed angrily under her gaze. Barely touching the wounds on his back now, the deep ugly gashes made by the whip. You did this, Laurie. Nobody but you. You did this to him. . . .

He let her bathe him, because at this point he was unable to struggle against her anymore, and the hot soapy water and his mother's tender touch were soothing to his young weary body. But he had not forgiven her—not by a long shot. He didn't care what Mr. Myles said about her being a tremendous woman or whatever you call it, she was still the same woman who whipped the blood out of him for the pleasure of white folks. He hated himself for letting her bathe him. He let her bathe him because he had to let her bathe him.

He snatched the rag from her and turned his back to her. "I can wash in between my legs my own self."

And when he was done, she wiped his body with a big white towel and put peroxide on his wounds and she put him to lie in Big Sister's bed.

Laurie came back into the front room and sat down in her rocker, and when she finally calmed herself, she spoke rather softly to the young, pleasant-faced, medium height man from up-north New York City, whom her Robby seemed to love more than anyone else. "He's a good boy," she said.

"I know he's a good boy," the teacher agreed. "He's more than a good boy."

"He sure does think the world of you," she said, smiling thinly. "Makes me jealous sometimes, I do believe."

The teacher smiled and looked down at the hearth. His face flushed warmly, feeling now that he had to explain it. "He came to me—He came to me because he had tried to run away from home and failed. He—he was hurt very badly, beaten down to the ground with no place to turn. Too young to do what he tried to do. He wanted to come back home to you, but he was too proud to take the short cut—so he took the long way around. You know, I don't believe he fully realizes, even now, precisely why he came to my place, but deep down inside of him he knew—he knew I would bring him home."

"You reckin so?" she said very softly, as if she were talking to herself. She glanced at Joe and looked back at the teacher again. "Yes . . . yes . . . I reckin you're right. He wanted to come home. He really did."

Joe Youngblood breathed hard and cleared his throat. The teacher's big eyes were troubled and nervous. "He wanted to come home to me and Joe," she whispered, "and Jenny Lee too. He wanted to come home but he was just too proud. Always was proud and a little bit stubborn. He sure gets it honest." She rocked quietly back and forth, and suddenly she turned to the young teacher. "It was all my fault, Mr. Myles. Nobody else's fault but mine. I ran him away from home. I beat him down to the ground! LordSaviorHaveMercy!"

"No—Mrs. Youngblood, it wasn't your fault. You mustn't—"

"Go—Go in there and look at his back—look at the great big welts on his back—You'll see whose fault it was—I put them there—I beat the blood out of him! And he always had so much confidence in me—LordJesusSaviorHaveMercy!"

"I know, Mrs. Youngblood, but it wasn't your fault. Robert himself knows better than that. He may be all mixed up right now, but deep down inside of him, he knows it wasn't your fault. Let's put the blame where it really belongs." Mr. Myles's big light-brown eyes, usually happy and arrogant-looking, were angry and serious. "It's the white folks. The crackers. It's the *southern way of life*." He looked at Mrs. Youngblood, and he glanced at Robert's father and he thought about his own father and mother, and a picture flashed in his mind of his own father, little man bending over a great big package and a white man goosing him. His Father and Mother, old and worn out before their time came. His big eyes narrowed and his face grew tight. "I'm beginning to believe it's the whole American way of life—north and south. They get you to fight your boy, Mrs. Youngblood, beat his wonderful spirit out of him, beat out of him everything you ever taught him. That's what they want to do."

"Yes," she said almost calmly. "Yes, that's it. Lord Have Mercy, you sure know how to put it. But I promised myself on bended knees—I swore to my God on high—I'll never never do it again." She looked up into the young man's face, as if she thought she could find the answer there to all of her problems. Embarrassment warmed the blood in her cheeks. If—If only Joe would talk to her like this—show her some feeling and spirit like he used to—some understanding . . . She looked at the small yellow flame in the lamp on the center table, and she got up nervously and turned up the wick. She sat down again and she watched a dusty-looking candlefly circling the lamp chimney around and around. Suddenly she looked up in the young teacher's face. "What can we do?" she demanded of him. "What in the name of God can poor colored folks do?"

"We have to fight back," he said, and even as he said it, he felt the awful inadequacy of words—just words—and a little bit ridiculous, sitting there in the front room with this beautiful woman and her big silent husband, his slender hand fumbling with the edge of the center table.

She looked at him with a blank face. He mistook the look in her eyes for a kind of contempt for him, the school teacher, educated and uplifted—academic. "Fight," she repeated softly, because she didn't want to offend the up-the-country teacher, who understood so much for such a young man. "Fight—Our middle name is fight, Mr. Myles—Been fighting ever since I came in the world—but where does it get us? Fight," she repeated softly and gently. "Like saying to us that we got to eat."

"Can't just do it on an individual basis," he said, trying to keep the heat out of his voice. "I mean we have to band together—got to organize ourselves. We can't fight this business one by one."

Joe Youngblood looked down at his big pigeon-toed feet, a guilty feeling flowing through his huge body. Laurie Lee was every inch a fighter, everybody knew it, so the teacher must be talking directly to him. He thought about a couple of nights ago, when Laurie and he had been sitting in the same place they were sitting right now, and she had told him about her and Robby down at Mr. Cross's courthouse, and all he could think of to say with his tired beaten-down ignoramus self was *Don't spare the rod!* Laurie Lee must think she had a damn Uncle Tom for a husband. But where did this up-the-country school teacher get off making him feel little and cheap in front of his wife? It was so easy for him to talk about fighting. New York City was a damn sight different from Crossroads, Georgia.

Richard Myles felt that he had to say more. He was a teacher, at least he was supposed to be one, and yet he didn't want to sound academic like a teacher. "We have to look at this from a long range point of view—" That wasn't what he meant to say.

Joe's booming voice interrupted the teacher. "I know you a smart man, Mr. Myles, and most of the things you said is the gospel truth. I appreciate everything you done for us and the boy, but I want you to know something. I been fighting ever since 'fore you was born, and every time I fight back I get knocked down and beat up. Laurie Lee'll tell you—I never did take no stuff offa no crackers. But—but——but everything's against me. Them barrels of turpentine beat me down to my knees every day the Good Lord sends and every time you talk back to them crackers, they slap you down and walk right over you—make it hard for you—" He was talking a whole lot more than he had intended, but he wanted fiercely to let the young teacher know where he stood, and he was talking for Laurie Lee to hear him as much as he was to the teacher. "It's alright to talk about fighting. I believe in fighting, but—but a colored man just ain't got no win.

"It's a known fact," Joe said doggedly, breaking out in an angry sweat, "these colored folks down here just don't stick together. You get them together and you think they with you, and the first time the white man bark out loud they scatter like jack rabbits. I know what I'm talking about." He didn't exactly believe all he was saying, but so much hurt and confusion had lingered deep down inside of him for such a long time, he wanted to get it all out of his system, and he wanted to hear what this bright young teacher-man from New York City had to offer.

Laurie's narrow eyes flashed with excitement. "That's not true, Joe. We just don't try it often enough."

"Mr. Youngblood, we just got to stick together," the young teacher said. "It's the only way out." He looked the big man in his dark quiet face. "Sure, I know, we got Uncle Toms and handkerchief-heads among us. We always had them—ever since slavery. But they don't amount to a hill of beans. If the rest of us get together, we can roll right over them."

Joe looked at the young teacher and down at the hearth, cleared his throat.

"One sure thing," the teacher continued, "we don't have any win if we fight single-handed. They just pick us off one by one. Another sure thing, nobody is going to give us any freedom on a silver platter."

A soft smile moved over Joe Youngblood's face and he shook his head from side to side. "You right about that, Mr. Myles. Ain't no lie. Got to fight these pecks every day in the week. Ain't nobody can dispute your word on that."

Joe leaned back in his chair and gazed up at the grayish ceiling, stared long and hard at a brown circular spot left by the weather when it rained very hard. He reached way back into the far corners of his life's experiences, the long-ago-years, the in-between-years, the right-now-years. He watched himself, an eleven-year-old boy walking all alone down that long dark lonesome road in the middle of the night away from Uncle Rob's fresh air shack, and ever since then, even before, it had been fight fight fight, always alone, and nothing but fight and everywhere fight . . .

**202**

Getting on that train bound for Chicago . . . Wayman, South Carolina . . . Mr. Buck's plantation . . . evil old cracker with the handle-bar mustache . . . fight fight . . . Crossroads, Georgia and the barrels of turpentine whipping him every day like a slave driver, breaking his back half in two, and the cracker foreman always picking at him and the paymaster cheating him out of his pay every week and making him like it . . . In between was the baseball team and the Pleasant Grove Baptist Church and the Pleasant Grove Glee Club . . . then Laurie Lee Barksdale . . . Laurie Lee Barksdale . . . Laurie Lee Barksdale Youngblood and love and happiness and facing things together, and children and family—Still there was the barrels of turpentine and the cracker foreman and the fight went on and on and on, whether he wanted it or not, even as the happiness and the family increased . . . Somewhere along the line he had slowly but surely given out of steam, like a tired old workhorse, the juice of his spirit had been sucked from him like sap from a pine tree. But he had always had Laurie Lee and Jenny Lee and Robby at the end of each day. He had taken them for granted. . . .

He puffed unconsciously on his corn cob pipe which had gone out without him knowing and he got a long bitter drink of black spit and tobacco and it choked in his throat and bit at his tongue and he began to hiccup with tears in his eyes. "Excuse me folkses" and he went to the kitchen for a dipper of water. When he came back he sat down again and he looked at Laurie, and he didn't fully understand it, but somehow he realized that he couldn't take his family for granted any longer, and a great fear seized him and his body grew warm and his blood ran cold and he struggled hard to keep his shoulders from shaking. He had to make a fight for them . . . Somehow the white folks had reached into this part of his life and were undermining it—GreatGodAlmighty he had to fight!

"Yes—Sir," Joe heard himself say almost in a whisper, "got to fight alright—got to keep on fighting—" His voice became louder now like the deep resounding roar of the thunder—shaking his big head up and down—"We got to fight," he said. *We? —We?* Yes, he thought—*We*—We—You mighty right—*We*—We—We got to band together and fight—He looked at the teacher. "We got to get together and fight these peckerwoods down to the ground."

The young school teacher shook his head and he looked at Joe and at Laurie Lee and down at the bare, scrubbed-colorless floor, and he wanted to say more—but maybe he had already said enough for tonight, and how would he say it without sounding like a know-it-all. He felt like anything else but a know-it-all. . . .

"We're not exactly alone in this," he said. He cleared his throat. "We have friends all over this country—colored and white —The N.A.A.C.P." Thinking out loud. "We could use a branch of the National Association for the Advancement of Colored People in this man's town."

"Where the white friends at?" Joe Youngblood asked.

"In the labor unions—th—the white workers—and some of the more educated liberal-minded white people." He read the doubt in both of their faces.

Laurie smiled at the teacher, a thin bitter smile. "I sure do hope it's true," she said. "But I sure don't know where our good white friends hiding. Lord Have Mercy."

Joe Youngblood said, "I sure want to see them crackers that's my nacherl-born friends. They must be kinda shamefacey. I was flat on my back for three whole months. Onliest white man came to see me was the rich white man—Mr. Cross Jr. He was the one that befriended me when I really needed a friend. Maybe it's different in New York City, but down here in Georgia the poor white peck is the black man's worstest enemy. Labor unions—These pecks down here won't let you get one foot in the door. White workers. Humph—Anybody'll tell you. It ain't the rich man that lynches the colored down here. It's the poor crackers. If they my friend they sure got a real funny way of showing it. I sure do wish they would come out the bushes and make themself known. I be looking for the high sign sure as you born."

The fire had gone completely out in the fireplace. The big ugly clock sounded loud over the mantle. Richard Myles got up. Ideas about an N.A.A.C.P. in Crossroads going around in his head already. Were there any white friends in Crossroads, Georgia? He could hear the boy twisting and turning in the bed in the next room. He wanted to say more, but it was getting late, and he knew that Mr. Youngblood went to work early, and neither of them had hardly slept the night before, and he thought they wanted to be alone, the woman and her husband, to talk and discuss it. So he took both of their hands and he felt a great warmth flowing from them, and he said good-night, and they said thank you and good-night and to come back to see them, and he knew they wanted to

**204**

talk with him again, a whole lot of talk, about colored and white, and he said he would be back to see them again—Very very soon.

After he left they sat there looking at the shadowless fireplace and the dead powdery ashes. It was time to get to bed but they didn't want to go. Joe was puffing on his smelly old pipe. "That young feller sure-as-you-born got a heap of thoughts in his up-the-country head. He a smart colored man, and I don't mean maybe. Colored folks really got to get together. Ain't no lie." He got up from his chair. He wanted desperately to walk towards her and he wanted her to get up and move towards him. She sat in the rocker and looked up in his face. He made a couple of steps towards her.

"First of all, Joe Youngblood, me and you got to get together more than we been," Laurie Lee said. "A whole heap more."

"Laurie Lee, I know I been—I realize I ain't done my—"

The boy interrupted them from the next room. "Don't hit me again, Mama!—Please, Mama, please! Oh Lordy, Mama!"

Laurie jumped up from her chair and ran into the kitchen. Joe followed. Robby was lying on his back, his young face twisted in pain and fear, his eyes stretched wide. He turned over on his stomach—"Please, Mama, please! Don't kill me, Mama!"

She reached out and she touched his head with the tip of her fingers. "It's alright, Robby. Everything's alright. You home now. Everything's going to be alright from now on."

His body lay quiet under her tender caresses. She pulled the cover over him up to his neck and she tucked him in. She kissed him on his broad forehead. Joe stood looking on, helplessly looking, his big hands hanging heavily down by his sides, his chin on his chest.

Laurie looked from the boy up into Joe's face, and she saw the great hurt in his soft quiet eyes. An overwhelming flood of anger and resentment washed right over her, and from now on she wanted Joe and her to walk through this hard life together, really together. But the anger against him mounted within her, gained domination. *Don't spare the rod and spoil the child!* She started to say something mean to him, but she didn't trust herself. She was too filled up. She heard him mutter Laurie Lee Laurie Lee, as she passed him on her way to the front room. Was that all he could say—Laurie Lee Laurie Lee?——Well shame on him! Yes!—Yes!—Yes!—Shame on him! He had to come better than that, a whole lot better! She got her nightgown and undressed in the kitchen. She thought about what the teacher had said.——Here she was fighting Joe Youngblood instead of the white folk . . . taking it out on him . . . But I can't help it tonight, Lord . . . I just can't help it . . . *Spare the rod!* . . . Laurie Lee Laurie Lee. . . .

She stood in the middle of the kitchen floor near her girl on the pallet. Go to Joe Youngblood—right now—tonight—don't wait another minute—He's ready now—Ready—ready—ready—— Her bosom filled up as if it would burst. Slight pieces of breeze moved around the kitchen and around her nightgown, cooled her heated body. She looked at the outline of her boy in the bed and she knew Joe was ready, but she couldn't go to him. She shook her head angrily and she got into bed beside her big boy.


## CHAPTER SEVEN

IT WAS ALMOST half-past one, a Saturday afternoon, and as Joe stood in the colored section of the payline, he thought about Laurie. He looked up at the clear-blue November sky, and he blinked his calm eyes in the face of the sun that came in large healthy slices down through the big ugly buildings of Plant Number 3. He thought about the little sawed-off white paymaster, always cheating him out of his pay. Big and gray and white and red-bricked were the buildings, and tall and wide and as ugly as home-made sin. And powerful and mean and frightening and hated-by-Joe and casting shapeless shadows, and red giant smokestacks smoking up the sky, and awfully ugly. His eyes blinked again, the sun and clear sky coming into sharp contrast with the big ugly buildings of Plant Number 3. Sun didn't have any business shining that hot and pretty in November no–dadgum-how. Anybody that would cheat a poor colored man out of his hard-earned pay ought to be dead and in hell on the chain gang, and that's just where Joe Youngblood would try to send this cracker if he pulled that stuff on him today. He could almost hear himself persuading himself——Don't back down today, Joe. Don't back down.

Laurie Lee . . . Laurie Lee—*Doggone Doggone*——It seemed like every time he turned around here lately, he was thinking about Laurie. Every minute on the job. It had been that way ever since that dadgum business with her and Robby at Mr. Cross's courthouse, and particularly after the night the teacher brought Robby home. You sure were a big help, he told himself, time and time again. *Don't spare the rod and spoil the child* . . . You ought to be ashamed of yourself . . . He remembered how she looked that night when he said it, and the way she looked at him the night Robby was brought back after he ran away from home when she told him—"First of all me and you got to get together more than we've been." Great God Almighty, Joe Youngblood, you got the prettiest, you got the smartest, you got the fightinest, the most intelligent colored woman in Crossroads, Georgia. You got the best everythingest kind of woman in Cross County don't care what color. That's what you got. And you ain't no man— You ain't nothing but a dadgum handkerchief head, and you don't deserve a woman like Laurie, cause you don't appreciate her. You supposed to be a man, but she got more fight in her in one little minute than you got all day long.

That old peckerwood paymaster better not try to cheat me to-day, like he usually do, cause I ain't taking no stuff today—don't care if he got fifty guns underneath that counter. He heard the other men in the payline laughing and talking and grumbling and cursing, heard them vaguely and absent-mindedly, because his mind was on that evil old paymaster, and mixed up with thoughts about Laurie and the children and home, and what home was, and what it could be, and what he could do to help make it be—

He was getting near to the little cubby hole that was the pay-master's counter, and he felt his whole body growing warmer and warmer, and his face began to tighten. He wasn't going to take any stuff off this peckerwood paymaster—not this afternoon of our Lord and Savior, Jesus Christ.

Ray Morrison yelled at him from near the foot of the colored line. "Hey, Joe Youngblood what you so nervous about? It'll be there when you get up to the counter. Don't be in such a hurry. All you gon do when you get it anyhow is strike a bee-line for home and dump it into Laurie Lee's lap."

Joe didn't say a word. He could hear the colored men giggling and laughing, and some of the white, and he smiled to himself, but he was thinking about the paymaster and how he had a way of cheating Joe every single payday, always giving him a fast short count. But not today——onh onh. It wouldn't be like that.

Laurie Lee—Laurie Lee—Since the business at the courthouse, Joe had paid more attention to things around the house. Just last

Saturday night after supper, Joe said to Robby——"Say, man, let's me and you work together. Know what I mean? You clean all the shoes, and I press the Sunday-go-to-meeting britches. What you say to that? Put a crease in them scounds so keen cut your dadgum fingers off."

His boy, surprised and smiling, responded quickly. "And I'll put a shine on them shoes so bright see your dadgum face in them."

Joe smiled at Robby, a good strange feeling swelling inside of him. "Watch out there, boy. Like to heard you cuss that time."

"I mean it, Daddy. Put a real shine on them."

"Sure, Mister Man, that's what I'm talking about. Women folks be taking care of the kitchen, while we taking care of the pressing and shining. Won't have to be rushing around tomorrow morning getting ready for church."

And lately Joe had taken to asking the children how they were getting along in school and like that, showing interest in them, and the other night he had even washed the supper dishes. Laurie had smiled and walked up to him and felt his broad forehead and said to him—"What's the matter, Joe? You feel alright?"

Another one of the men in the line, Jack Linwood, a loud-mouthed feller, broke into his thoughts. "Old Joe gon run home with his money like a bat out hell, and when his old lady reach for it, he say—*Don't, woman, don't*—And she say don't what, Doll Baby? And old Joe say—*Don't leave a damn penny.*"

Joe heard the men laughing out loud now, but he didn't feel like laughing, and his whole body was tense. Getting close to the pay counter. Every week this old cracker would short-change him. Fifty cents here and seventy-five cents there. Sometimes he got real bold and went over the dollar mark. Sometimes Joe would mumble something to the cracker, and the cracker would say— "Go 'long, boy, don't waste my time. I don't make no mistakes." Sometimes Joe wouldn't say a single word, and he would feel his whole manhood being robbed from him, draining him of his manhood, like a giant leech sucking all the blood out of him. Other times he didn't even count the money until he got home. But Laurie never knew about this. What if she ever found out? He saw her now, her still-beautiful-to-him face with the narrow, deep-set eyes, her strong, youthful, wiry body. She was at home now, doing something, working. She always worked, and he was beginning to appreciate the fact that her job was never done. He

**208**

was going to share it with her. Share everything with her. A few days after the courthouse business, he had started to tell her how he felt, that he was sorry about *Don't spare the rod,* and things would be different; tell her he understood——But he had never told her, not in so many words, because it was hard for Joe to find the right words.

Closer and closer to the counter. He had broken out into a cool dampish sweat. He wished and prayed that the paymaster wouldn't try to cheat him today. Not a goddamn cent, because he wasn't going to hold still for it, and he knew he wasn't, and he didn't know what the results would be. Joe smiled bitterly when he thought about the new colored teacher that Robby and Laurie were so stuck on. Talking all that foolishness about some white folks were the colored man's friend. He liked the teacher too, and the young man meant well, and he had a whole heap of sense in that young head of his'n, but he just didn't know these crackers down south. Only one man stood between him and the paymaster now. He didn't want to get into any trouble with white folks. He wanted to live a long time, and he didn't want to cause his family any trouble, God knows he didn't, but neither was he going to let any cracker or anybody else take food out of their mouths. Just wasn't going to stand for it any dadgum longer. Mr. Mack had everything on his side—the court, the judge and the police too. He could shoot Joe dead as a dog, and he wouldn't even be locked up in a jail overnight. In his entire life Joe had never heard of a cracker being executed for killing a Negro.

He was in front of the pay counter now, facing the cracker. The little white-haired white man smiled at him, began to count out his money. "How you, Joe?"

"I'm alright, Mr. Mack," Joe mumbled. Please, don't let him try to cheat me this time, Lord. Talk to him, Jesus.

The cracker was supposed to give him nine dollars and thirty-five cents, and he counted it out to himself, and he pushed it toward Joe, all in currency—nickels, dimes and quarters. Made Joe hot as a six-shooter, hoping all the while that everything was there. Maybe he should wait till he got home to count it. Didn't need to count it anyhow. Mr. Mack knew how to count a whole lot better than he did. Had plenty of experience. Besides what good would it do? He saw Laurie's face before him and all around him, watching him with her deep narrow eyes.

The cracker said, "Alright—alright," as Joe stood there deliberately counting his pay, his face drawn tight and his eyes quiet, his hands trembling slightly. He counted it over twice, but it didn't add up to but eight dollars and fifty cents.

Joe's tongue slipped over his bottom lip and he cleared his throat, and his feet toed inward and his shoulders hunched forward. "Mr. Mack, you made a mistake."

Mr. Mack looked up at Joe and away again. He said, "Move along, boy. Move along now. Sign that paper and go 'long with you. Ain't got no time for no discussion. Got to pay off everybody."

All the men were listening, the colored and the white. Joe could hear the silence ringing in his ears. He said, "Yes, sir, but you made a mistake. You need to give me eighty-five more cents. That's what I'm talking about." Go ahead on home, Joe. Don't argue with this cracker. What's eighty-five cents any-god-damn-how? But Joe didn't move. Something wouldn't let him.

Mr. Mack said, "Go 'long, boy. I done told you—you better move along now. You holding up the works."

The big ugly gray and white buildings surrounded Joe, closing in on him. Joe said, "Yes, sir, but how about my eighty-five cents? I work hard for my money."

Peckerwoods standing around looking and listening, and Negroes too. Mr. Mack turning ten different shades of cracker red. He was as mad as a mad dog, but he wasn't as mad as Joe Youngblood was. He said, "Nigger you insinuating? You mean to stand up there and call me a liar?"

Joe was sweating like a bull now. He knew Mr. Mack had a gun underneath the counter. He felt the water draining from all over his body, trickling down his neck, crawling from his armpits. He said, "I ain't called you out of your name, Mr. Mack. I just want my money. I worked hard for it, and I aims to get it."

The cracker batted his eyes.

Joe pushed the money back towards Mr. Mack. "Here's what you gave me. Count it your own self." Sweat dripped down into Joe's quiet eyes, burned them a little. A mechanical smile spread over his face. A dangerous smile, and Mr. Mack knew it was a dangerous smile, and not to be confused with any other smile. Joe didn't give a good goddamn now. He was ready to pull this red-faced peck across the counter and get amongst him for awhile, and Mr. Mack knew it. Ready to sweep up the whole damn yard with him.

Mr. Mack's ears glowed redder than the rest of his face, as he counted the money slowly. "That's right—that's right—Well, I declare," he mumbled to himself. "How the hell did that happen?" And he looked up at Joe, and he skinned back his jaws and showed Joe his yellowish dingy-looking teeth, as he gave Joe the correct amount this time.

Joe's face was blank as he counted the money and signed the payroll, trying desperately to keep his hand from trembling.

Mr. Mack grinned his dingy-looking grin. "Alright now, boy, watch your talk around white folks. Go 'long now before I lose my temper."

Joe turned around and bumped into Ray Morrison, who had been standing behind him without Joe's knowledge. They walked off together, a couple of other Negroes left their places in the payline and followed them. Jack Linwood and Charlie Roundtree. The white men watched them as they walked silently together towards the gate. Walking in the midst of them, Joe felt Ray and Jack and Charlie all around him. Feeling them fiercely in his face and shoulders and his arms and his legs. All of their strength seemed to come together in his single body. Joe heard one of the men standing in the white payline say in a real friendly voice— "Howdy, Joe." Plain as day and it made him feel funny, but he didn't look back. Plenty people named Joe, white and colored. Joe kept walking with Ray and Jack and Charlie towards the big white gate.

"You did the right thing, Joe." Ray Morrison broke the silence. "We got to stop taking shit off these no-good crackers."

Joe grunted. "You can say that again." The tension oozing out of him now, slowly, like air out of a slow-leaking tire, but he was still afraid.

They had almost reached the gate. Joe turned around and looked at the others, and he felt a great warmth towards them, and his eyes began to fill and he smiled at them.

"What y'all following me around for? I don't need no dadgum nursemaids. Better get on back there and get y'all's money before they shut that pay counter down."

The men looked at Joe and at each other and turned to go back.

Joe walked towards the gate. His feet felt light, and his back felt naked and exposed and unprotected, and he was scared, but he felt good too, feeling like a man was supposed to feel. He would tell Laurie what happened, and she would be scared, but she would feel good too. Greatgodalmighty he knew she would.

# CHAPTER EIGHT

JOE WALKED ACROSS town through an uppidy white neighborhood of wide green lawns and pretty bungalows towards Harlem Avenue. Walking with his broad powerful shoulders thrown back like he used to walk; like Laurie remembered he used to walk. Smiling to himself and every now and then glancing nervously behind him. When he thought about the way those three Negroes got out of line and walked with him to the gate, he felt so good he was bursting wide open. It took plenty of nerve—whole heap of nerve. He hoped they got paid off without any trouble.

*Walk together children—Don't you get weary*—That was one of his favorites when he used to sing in the Pleasant Grove Glee Club——*There's a great camp meeting in the Promised Land*—— He used to sing a bass that wouldn't stop for the red light. Couldn't figure out that white voice that said Howdy Joe after he left the pay counter. Sounded just like old Oscar Jefferson. Had he really been saying Howdy to him, Joe Youngblood? Maybe he had only imagined it. Daydreaming . . . But his mind didn't conjure up Ray Morrison and Charlie Roundtree and Jack Linwood. Damn sure didn't.

*Walk together children*——If all the colored folks walked together all the time—if—if—He heard footsteps behind him pounding the pavement. His face tightened, his whole body stiffened, his back felt broader than ever before, and it tried to contract itself in self defense, but he didn't break his stride, kept right on walking. His feet wanted to break into a run and be around the next corner in a great big hurry. The street was quiet like Sunday and almost empty, and clean and clear, and a brilliant sun was directly above him and seemed to turn on an extra ray of sunlight and focus its beams on poor Joe Youngblood. Footsteps behind him got closer and closer, and Joe tried to look through the back of his head, didn't want to turn around as if he were expecting something to happen. His fists balled up rigid and hard, but he kept on walking at the very same pace, as sweat poured out all over his body. Was it one person behind him, or two or three? Walking and waiting and waiting and walking. The block was like a long lonesome highway, the more he walked the longer it became. Then he heard the footsteps become dimmer and dimmer, tapering off, and he almost stopped walking, as he turned sideways and he saw two white men going up the front steps of a pretty red bungalow, talking to each other. Them crackers ain't paying me no rabbit-ass mind. He felt a great relief flow through his body like a soft autumn breeze and he halfway smiled. Hurry up, Big Feet, and take Joe Youngblood to Harlem Avenue. He felt the need to be among his kind of people, felt it awfully bad, and he quickened his steps. He had to struggle hard to keep from breaking into a run, because how would it look for a Negro to be running in a white section of town? Wouldn't be dignified anyhow.

He heaved a deep sigh as he turned into Harlem Avenue, the only paved street for colored people in all of Crossroads. It was the street where the colored businesses were. The Ritzy Hotel, Fat Jack's Pool Parlor, Jesup's Barber Shop, Harlem Grill, South Side Pool Room, Jenkins Funeral Home, the New Lenox Theater——shoe shine parlors, newspaper stands and all like that. Colored people walking up and down the street like it belonged to them. You home now, Joe, and they can't get to you.

"Hey, Long Goodie," Bessie Brown said. She was always picking at Joe whenever she met him and his wife wasn't around, pretending she was sweet on him. Maybe she was. One sure thing——she was mighty good-looking. A pretty black woman.

"Hey there, Bessie Mae." He was feeling good and he flashed her one of his unusual smiles. "What you know good?"

"You got the business, Long Goodie." She put her hands on her slim curvy hips and she laughed at him. "Lord I declare—— What's gonna happen next? Didn't know you could smile that pretty, Mr. Youngblood——especially in any woman's face besides Laurie Lee Youngblood. You must be hit the numbers."

"Go along, woman," he said, laughing back at her. "Got to go in here and let Joe Jesup cut my dadgum head off. Be careful now."

"Alright, Long Goodie. Be seeing you when your troubles get like mine." She strutted off down the street and he walked into the barber shop smiling to himself and shaking his head. Some folks said Bessie Mae Brown was a no-good woman, said she even messed around with white men. One sure thing she really was pretty.

He had to sit and wait his turn. Saturday was the worst day in the week to get a haircut, and Harlem Avenue was crowded too. He found out from Joe Jesup where he stood in the line among the haircut-getters and he sat down in one of the waiting chairs and he got up again and walked to the door. He looked up and down. The street was even more crowded than it had been a few minutes ago. Negroes coming into the big city from the outlying countryside. Coming in by the wagonloads and in beat-up flivvers and trucks and tin lizzies and every other kind of way they could come—From the East, from the West, from the North and the South. Scrubbed-clean and all-dressed-up in brand-new overalls, some even wore suits, pants and jackets matching. They would be coming in like this till night began to fall. He could hear a Victrola playing down the street—loud and pretty—*Got to see your Mama every night or you can't see your Mama at all—— Kiss your Mama———*. Coming in town to shop around and attend to business, and go to the show and dance at the Saturday night dance and have a good time and let off steam. (Some came to town for one thing, some came to town for the other.) Harlem Avenue was jumping. "Lord Lord Lord," Joe Youngblood sighed. "There damn sure is a whole heap of us."

It was his turn now and he walked from the door over to the barber chair, and he stretched his long body in the chair as Joe Jesup adjusted it for Joe Youngblood's size. "Man, I don't believe you gon ever stop growing. Look like to me every time you git in this chair you done got bigger and bigger. I was Laurie Lee I'd starve you to death."

"You was Laurie Lee I wouldn't ever feel like eating." He lay wearily back in the chair and he tried to relax, hearing Joe Jesup chuckling and laughing.

"Come on, Brother Jesup, stop messing around and give the man a haircut. You know what I like."

The buzzing noise of the clippers almost put him to sleep. He watched a good-looking baby-faced country boy get down from the chair next to him dressed to kill from head to foot in brand new overalls. The young fellow paid the barber and he looked in the mirror long and hard, and he threw up his arms and stretched his slim body. "Whoo—weee," he shouted softly. "I would holler but the town too small." He looked around him and walked out of the shop. The man who got into the chair behind him shook his head and looked at the boy's back. "Ain't that a damn shame. You can get the feller out the country but you can't get the country out the feller. He comes from so fur in the sticks he ain't never heard a train whistle. He on his way down to the railroad tracks right now to see the trains come in. Crackers catch him down there and run him loose." The men around him laughed and giggled.

Joe laughed a little bit and looked up at Joe Jesup, and his nostrils picked up the smell of people close together standing and sitting and the sickening odor of barbershop hair tonic all mixed up with the scorchy smell of the potbelly stove in the center of the shop. His ears took in the busy chatter of various conversations running together. His eyes wandered over near the stove where two men were engaged in a hot checker game and a circle of men stood around looking on. Joe watched the steam from the pan of water on top of the stove climb lazily up towards the ceiling.

"Lord have mercy, Brother Jesup," he said. "When you reckin white folks gon get offa our necks?"

Joe Jesup looked at Joe Youngblood and spat tobacco into an old spittoon. "Brother Youngblood, these here crackers ain't gonna git offa our necks till we git together and knock their ass off."

"You told the truth then," Joe Youngblood agreed.

He held his clippers up over Joe's head, he spat tobacco again and his face drew up into an angry seriousness. "I mean it, Bruh Joe. Mr. Charlie gon always keep his foot on our neck till we git together and stick together, steada one group over here and the other over yonder and nobody not doing a damn thing for the race. Most of the leaders kissing Mr. Charlie's hindparts. We ————"

A man looked up from playing checkers. "Talk to 'em Brother Jesup. I ain't got the heart."

Another man walked in from the street. "Preach it, Brother Jesup. Tell 'em about it."

And Joe Youngblood closed his eyes and sighed in agreement with Joe Jesup, halfway wishing he hadn't started the question. It might be dark before his haircut was finished, because when Joe Jesup got off on the question of white and colored he really got excited. Joe Youngblood wanted to get home to his family very very bad. Stick together——that was it——that school teacher from up the country said the same thing——*Walk together children.* He was so damn tired of working and waiting and walking by himself——If all those folks out on Harlem Avenue now—if all the colored folks in Crossroads, Georgia, walked together down the same highway, business would have to pick up . . . He was tired and nervous but somehow he had a good warm kind of feeling, and he wanted to get home, and it didn't look like Joe Jesup was ever going to stop talking.

"Alright, Brother Joe, you ain't in no pulpit. Finish the man's haircut," Joe Youngblood said. "Other people waiting."

When Brother Jesup finished with him, Joe Youngblood walked out of the barber shop, and he made his way over to the Harlem Grill, and he bought two bottles of Bevo, which was the strongest kind of brew you could buy legitimately in Crossroads, Georgia. He bought two bottles of Try Me sodas for the children. He went by the fish market and bought two pounds of mullet, and he started for home. Rent was due on Monday morning, and with winter coming on, coal had to be bought, and Joe felt guilty about spending money foolishly so close to rent day, but he did it anyhow, because he felt so good about what happened in the payline, and he wanted his family to feel good too. He wanted to really be a part of his family and he wanted them to be a part of each other. The closer he got to home, the faster he walked, like an overgrown kid full of excitement. When he reached his block he slackened his pace, and a calm spread over him.

He walked through the front room into the kitchen. "Alright —Alright—look what I brung. Who gonna kiss the handsome man first?"

Big Sister ran into his arms and gave him a kiss and he said "unnnh—unph—Lil Bits the Second," and he put her on one of his shoulders and the boy came in from the backyard and he hoisted him up to the other shoulder and he asked Laurie if she wanted to hang from his neck.

She laughed and her eyes were brimful of happiness and she went to him and gave him a kiss, and she said to the boy, "Be careful, Robby, don't hurt your Daddy's back. You almost as big as he is already."

Joe didn't sit and blow till dinner was ready like he usually did. He took the fish out in the backyard and he scraped the scales off them and cleaned the insides of them and prepared them for cooking. "I'm gonna cook these fish this day of our Lord. Show you folks how to really fry fish."

Laurie Lee stood at the table stirring the meal and water for the cornbread and she wondered what was the matter with Joe. Wondering if the boss had given him a raise or something. It couldn't be that, because something had happened even before today, and Laurie had noticed a change in Joe for quite some time. He was more like the Joe Youngblood she had married. But why? Why? Maybe he was covering something up. Another woman? Her face grew hot, she felt ashamed and cheap—as long as she had known Joe Youngblood, she ought to be ashamed——She put the spoon down, wiped her hand on her apron, and she went in the next room to get herself together, because she was so happy she felt like crying. This was the way the family should always be.

Joe Youngblood sat at the head of the table, eating noisily the mullet fish and cornbread and collard greens and drinking his Bevo and watching his family enjoy their dinner. He took a swallow of Bevo and his lips lingered on the mouth of the bottle making a sucking sound, it tasted so delicious, and the kitchen was filled with the good smell of fried fish, and he thought this was the time to tell them about how he had called the paymaster's hand, how he, a black man, had stood up to Mr. Charlie. He felt like boasting before his family, not really boasting, but he felt so proud and he wanted to share his great pride with them. Let Laurie Lee know what kind of husband she had. Let the children know who their father was. What should he tell them? How should he begin? He wasn't much at speech-making and he wanted it to be just so. He wanted to include Ray Morrison and the other Negroes and to give them credit. And Oscar Jefferson— Oscar Jefferson. He turned it over in his mind, and he saw himself again in the payline with the sun shining on him through the big ugly buildings, and he felt the same tension as he saw the little white man standing before him on the other side of the counter, and thinking about the gun Mr. Mack always kept under his counter, he realized how close he had been to his death, and no telling what they would have done to his family, if he and the little cracker had really got into a fight, and even now as he sat at his table, he realized that the thing might not be over. Crackers might be plotting against his life this very moment. The good feeling rushed out of his body replaced by fear and worry, and his shoulders grew warm and a cold sweat popped out on his face and his whole body shivered.

"What's the matter, Joe?" Laurie Lee asked, her narrow eyes wide and anxious.

"Nothing the matter," he said, forcing a great big smile on his face, but he knew that she wasn't deceived by him. He put the bottle to his mouth again. He had no taste for the Bevo now—it was as bitter as gall, and everything else was spoiled for him. He tried to think of something to say to make them believe that nothing was the matter. He wanted desperately to maintain the happiness he had seen in all of their faces. He couldn't tell them now about him and the paymaster—Not this minute——Maybe after it was all over and the danger had passed. Maybe then. He made himself smile.

"Hey, Rob, how you like the way I fried that fish, man?"

Joe had started to call his son Rob instead of Robby lately, and it made the boy feel he was really growing up. "That's the best mullet fish I ever sunk my teeth into, Daddy. You must be the best fish fryer in Crossroads, Georgia."

Joe Youngblood laughed. "Well, I wouldn't go that far son. I reckin your mother got me skint a dadgum mile. But if I ain't the best in town I'm a stomp-down good one." Still, thinking about Mr. Mack and the gun under his counter and wondering if he would be living next week this time or even tomorrow.

Joe washed the dishes, and he pressed the Sunday-go-to-meeting trousers for him and the boy, and Laurie wondered what it was all about.

As darkness fell, a chilly dampness crept into the house, and Joe said to Robby, "Getting chilly in here, Rob. Tell you what let's do. You bring in the kindling and the wood, and I'll fix the fire."

"That's alright, Daddy, I'll bring in the kindling and fix the fire too."

They sat before the fireplace, and it felt good and warm and friendly. The sharp scorchy smell of the burning wood and the dancing shadows around the hearth and the smell of his pipe and the look on their faces. Joe put his hand out and placed it on his big girl's head. He ran his rough gentle hand through her hair that was thick and black just like Laurie Lee's. Lord Lord Lord I got a fine-looking family, and nobody better not mess with my family, white or black. He stretched his body and lay back in his rocker and he closed his eyes. He wanted to preserve this moment forever and ever. If he could always have peace and love and devotion in his home, he could take anything these crackers handed out. He felt the boy's eyes on him, and he sensed that Laurie was a little bit tense, and Jenny Lee squirmed underneath his hand, but when she felt his hand leaving her head, she said, "My head itches, Daddy. Please scratch it a little."

**218**

"What your head needs is a good washing, girl. You ain't got none of them boys in it, is you?"

All of them laughed, and they were laughing when somebody knocked bam bam at the door. Joe jumped from his chair, and he sat back down.

"What's the matter, Joe?" Laurie Lee asked, concerned with the bubbles of sweat on his forehead and the look on his face.

"I'll get it, Daddy," Robby said getting up from the floor.

"That's alright, son, I'll answer the door. No—no——sit still, son." They watched him as he walked to the door. "Who that?" he asked in his deep rumbling voice.

"You that," somebody answered back and pounded upon the door once more louder than before. "Open up or I'll break it down."

Joe opened the door quickly and stood looking down into Ray Morrison's face. "Man, you better watch that stuff," he said softly to Ray. "That's the best way in the world to keep from growing old."

Ray Morrison said, "What the matter, cousin? You must've thought the *MAN* had come for you."

Laurie said, "Hello Ray, you scoundrel beast. Haven't you got any better sense than to be banging on people's doors like that in the night time? Robby, go get your Uncle Ray a chair out the kitchen." Ray Morrison was their adopted uncle.

"Laurie Lee Barksdale Youngblood——prettiest Georgia peach ever been produced. Joe Youngblood, you are a lucky man ——doggone your time. You hear what I say?"

They were all seated by the fire, the two men facing each other. "You should have seen your face when you opened that door while ago," Ray said to Joe. Then something seemed to break through in his thoughts and he pointed at Joe and he started to laugh, and Joe looked at him and they both were laughing. They laughed and they laughed as Laurie and Jenny Lee and Robby watched them and wondered to themselves what was so funny.

"What's funny?" Robby asked. "What's the big joke?"

And they looked at Robby and they laughed some more. They finally stopped laughing and Ray said, "Excuse me, folks. I know it ain't polite to laugh when everybody don't know what the joke is. Y'all know what happened today—" The merest wink from Joe's quiet eyes and a quick nod of his head from side to side cut

**219**

Ray short, and he never did finish what he was going to say about Mr. Mack and the payline.

Laurie Lee asked, "What did you start to say, Ray?"

Ray looked at the ceiling. "I don't know what it was I started to say. Couldn't've been much 'count."

"You started to say something about what happened or something——"

He shook his head. "I declare I forgot."

He didn't fool Laurie Lee, but she dropped it for a moment. She looked at the children. "Getting kind of late. You all better heat you some water and take your bath in the kitchen."

"You stay in here, Big Sister. Let Robby bathe first."

"I let her bathe first, Mama."

"What did I say?" Mama asked him and gave him a look.

"Yes mam," he said.

The children took their regular Saturday night baths in the big tin washtub, and they sat around a few minutes afterwards, till Mama told them it was time to go to bed, and then they said their prayers and kissed all the grown folks goodnight.

Uncle Ray said, "Goodnight——sleep tight——don't let the bedbugs bite."

And the children laughed and said, "Try not."

After the children had gone to bed, Laurie Lee settled back in her chair and asked Ray—"Did you remember what you were going to say a little while ago?"

Ray's face was blank. "Say about what?" He glanced at Joe.

"You know what. You started to say something and then you claimed you forgot what it was."

He shook his head. "I can't remember, Laurie Lee. Just sitting here now trying to call it back to mind, but I just can't do it. I declare before God it couldn't've been much."

Laurie wasn't taken in by the innocent look on Ray Morrison's face, but she dropped the subject. Ray sat there with them for awhile talking about first one thing and then another, and then he got up and said he had better be going.

"You don't have to be in such a big hurry," Laurie Lee said.

"Hurry? I been here since I don't know when. I got to get home and take my Saturday night constitution. Got to get ready to go to church in the morning."

"Ray Morrison, you ought to be ashamed of yourself, telling

**220**

that great big something-ain't-so about the Sabbath. You haven't been to church in so long you'd knock at the door."

The powerfully built medium-height man smiled at her. "I'm going to church one of these Sundays. You'll be surprised. Maybe that's what I need to change my luck."

"You need prayer, Ray."

"Prayer ain't gonna do no good as long as crackers are crackers. That's what I'm talking about. Reminds me of the story of the man who had to go through some thick woods to get where he was going, and there was known to be a whole heap of very bad bears in these woods. The brother was scared. His preacher told him all he had to do if he met a bear was to get down on his knees and pray to the Lord and no harm would come to him. Halfway through the woods the man met a great big old bear. The brother got right down on his knees and started praying. The bear gave the man one big swipe on the behind with one of his paws and the brother lit out and he didn't stop running till he was back where he started from. The preacher said, well I see you're safe and sound, brother, so you must've taken my advice and prayed. The good brother said, 'Well Reverend I tell you, prayer might be alright in prayer meeting, but it ain't worth a damn in bear meeting.' "

Laurie Lee and Joe laughed and laughed, as Ray sat there with a serious look on his devilish face. "You better hush your mouth, Ray," Laurie Lee said. She liked to encourage him without seeming to, when he talked about religion, because deep down inside she had some of the same ideas.

Ray laughed and nodded towards Joe. "Ask Deacon Young-blood about prayer and these crackers. These crackers are great big polar bears. I'm gon get me a gun."

Joe went out of the door with Ray and he walked out on the porch closing the door behind him. It was a black night without moon or stars. It was cloudy and a sharp biting chill was in the air. Joe walked down the steps with Ray and they stood in the yard, and Joe put his arm on the other man's shoulder. "I didn't want Laurie Lee to know what happened between me and Old Man Mack."

"That's what I figured, but how come?"

"Didn't want to worry her—She might get scared."

"Don't you worry about her getting scared," Ray told Joe.

"That wife of yours don't take no stuff, white or black. She's truly brave."

Joe felt his neck growing warm and damp in the cool night air. "I don't mean scared—just don't want to upset her. You know."

"She wouldn't be upset. She would be proud as everything. But that's your business. My business right now is my Saturday night bath. See you in church." He started to walk out of the yard.

"Wait a minute," Joe told him, and Ray turned around.

"I—I just want to say I sure do appreciate how you fellers stuck by me this afternoon."

"You kidding?" Ray said and he turned and he walked up the dark street towards the lone street light at the corner.

Joe watched him go into the black night, past the street light into the darkness, wanted to call him back again, because there was so much more to be said about sticking together and way back in his mind he wanted to find out if Ray heard the white man say Howdy Joe and didn't it sound like Oscar Jefferson and what did it mean?

When Joe came back into the house, Laurie gave him a look, but she didn't say a word. She went into the kitchen and looked at the children. Robby stirred on his pallet, as she went back into the front room and closed the door. The boy lay there wavering between sleep and wake, looking up at the black ceiling which seemed to be descending slowly upon him, but he knew that it wasn't. Thoughts running together about this afternoon and the evening and Mama and Daddy and Jenny Lee and Ray Morrison and Mr. Myles and Ida Mae and Mr. Cross's courthouse and Scotty long-gone, and the fish Daddy fried and a good feeling of happiness almost complete, and sleep pressing down heavily on his eyelids, heavy heavy heavy, and smelling the cool night air and the lingering odor of the fried mullet and the conflicting odor of bedroom and kitchen rolled into one. The smell of fish wasn't so attractive when there was no more to be eaten. His sleepyhead thoughts were interrupted by the soft deep thunder of his Daddy's voice.

"Sick and tired of that there cracker cheating me all the dadgum time."

Robby sat up on his pallet, eyes straining in the darkness and his ears bucked up like an old jack rabbit. He couldn't make out what Mama said.

"Every damn week that man cheated me."

**222**

"Sin and a shame before the living God."

He could hear his mother plainly now with his ears fastened to the keyhole and his eyes focused fiercely on the outline of Big Sister in the bed across the room.

"I was so mad I didn't know what to do. He hadn't paid me my money, there'da been two dead people in Crossroads tonight, maybe more, cause I just wasn't gonna stand for it, didn't care what."

Robby looked through the keyhole at his father's legs and feet and the shimmering reflections from the fireplace, his mother rocking back and forth. "You better watch that cracker from now on, Joe. Make it real hard for you."

Excitement had lifted Robby's heavy-laden eyelids, opened his ears wider and chased sleep out of his entire body.

Daddy said, "Crackers been hard on me ever since I come in the world. Can't be no harder. Sick and tired of them peeing in my face and telling me it's raining outdoors. Made up my mind after you and Robby was down to that courthouse that I wasn't gonna take no more stuff from none of these crackers. Gon be a man by God, living or dead."

Mama's rocker went back and forth. "You right about that, Joe. And I'm one hundred percent behind you, and I want you to know it. Yet and still you just got to be careful."

Daddy didn't usually talk so much. "Lordy Lordy," he said. "After all you'd been through that day down at the courthouse, I come telling you something about *Don't spare the rod and spoil the child.* You shoulda put me outdoors. Got to thinking about that thing the next day couldn't get it outa my mind, couldn't hardly sleep for a whole darn week."

Daddy was standing with his hands behind him and his back to the fireplace, and Mama stood up and walked over close up against him. "Let's forget about that, Joe."

Daddy grunted. "What made it so damp and cool was the way those Negroes, Ray and Charlie and old big-mouth Jack, backed me up. Took real courage and it won't their business. They could've got in a whole heap of trouble. Never will forget it the longest day I live."

"When a Negro's in trouble with the white man it's every Negro's business. But it sure was nice and it took a lot of courage. That's the way, to stick together all the time. That's what Robby's teacher was talking about."

**223**

Daddy said, "Something funny happened. Really funny. When we was leaving that payline heading for the gate I coulda sworn I heard somebody in the white line say 'Howdy Joe,' and I coulda sworn he was talking to me——Sounded like it might be old Oscar Jefferson. Made me think about what that school teacher told us—said some white folks was the colored man's friend. Course there was more Joes standing in that payline than Joe Youngblood. Yet and still it made me think."

Mama said, "Oscar Jefferson is a pretty nice old cracker." He was wide awake now and he could hear the happiness and excitement overflowing in his mother's voice.

Daddy reached down and kissed Mama briefly on her lips, and Robby felt a sweet funny taste in his own mouth, and he felt a little guilty about eavesdropping on his mother and father.

Daddy said, "Ain't got nothing for no no-good Georgia cracker to do—I mean that thing——"

Robby smiled unconsciously and his eyes lit up and he felt a great fullness flowing through his body—Daddy Daddy Daddy—and he got up and walked back to his pallet and lay down again. Looking up at the ceiling, sleep trying its best to move in and take over, but thoughts of Daddy and Mama kept him wide awake, and especially Daddy and Uncle Ray and the rest and Oscar Jefferson, but especially Daddy. If only Mama was like she used to be, and Daddy was always the way he is now——think think think far into the night. Sleep moving in now pressing on the eyelids, dark wide ceiling coming down towards you, lower and lower ——Turn over on your stomach and fall fast asleep. . . .

In the next room his Mama and Daddy sat in their rocking chairs. The fire in the fireplace growing feeble by the minute, throwing peaceful shadows onto the hearth. Daddy wanted to get up and put another piece of wood on the fire before it went out, but he didn't want to disturb the sweet peaceful silence. He looked at Laurie and grunted out loud. She smiled and he smiled, and he got up and put another piece of wood on the fire. They sat back watching the slow process of the new piece of wood joining with the pieces almost burnt out and suddenly bursting into a bright flame of beauty reaching outward and upward.

Laurie blinked her eyes and looked up at the clock. "Lord have mercy, it's getting late already. Better fix my bath." She heated water and brought the tin tub and sat it in the front room near the foot of their bed. He sat in a chair with his back towards her as she pulled off her clothes and stepped into the tub, heard the swishing sound of the washrag and the flapping sound of a body in water, Laurie Lee's body, imagining that she would be washing her arms now and under her arms and this place and the other. He felt a glow of warmth throughout his body, a feverish heat that was almost a stranger. She had a good strong young beautiful body and he fashioned it before his eyes, as if he actually gazed upon her standing in the tin tub. He heard her stepping out of the tub and he knew that she had picked up her towel and was drying herself. She put on her gown and sat combing her hair, long, black and heavy.

He walked over to her and let his big hand get lost in a paradise of thick black silver-streaked hair that fell beneath her shoulders and flowed down her back. "Laurie Laurie Laurie . . . Laurie Lee Laurie Lee. . . ."

She looked up at him and smiled mischievously. "Go along now, Joe and behave yourself."

"You mean go'long and bathe myself." Joe Youngblood laughed.

He smiled down upon her, and he picked up the tub and the great big man tiptoed through the kitchen and threw the water out the back door, came back and prepared for his bath. She was in bed now with her back turned to him bathing near the fireplace. She heard all of his bathing noises that she already knew by heart. His big powerful frame always made the tin tub look ridiculously small.

He finished bathing and he put on his nightshirt and threw the water out the back door, and he turned the wick down and blew out the lamp and he came to the bed and looked through the brand new darkness at her lying there with her face to the wall, and she seemed to be breathing so deeply in sleep. He got down on his knees and mumbled his prayers. He pulled back the cover and got into the bed and he lay there a moment before he reached out to her. She turned towards him and came into his arms, and he felt a warmth greater than he ever imagined.

She felt the strength of his long hard body. This was her Joe Youngblood. Joe Youngblood had been on a long long journey, but he had come home at last. Tonight tonight—Greatgodalmighty! And in the black of the night they started on a journey together. It was like she remembered years ago; a more glorious journey than ever before. Together together in love and in body, in love and in spirit, in peace and fulfilment——Together together in love and in love. . . .

*Part Three*     **JUBILEE**

*One of these mornings about five o'clock*
*This old world's gonna reel and rock*
*Pharaoh's Army got drowned—*

FROM A NEGRO SPIRITUAL
*"Oh Mary Don't You Weep"*

# CHAPTER ONE

OSCAR JEFFERSON WAS the strangest cracker in Crossroads, Georgia. Joe Youngblood just couldn't figure him out. He looked like a cracker, he talked like a cracker, but sometimes he didn't quite act like a cracker. A couple of weeks after that Saturday at the payline, Oscar and Joe walked out of the main gate at the same time, and Oscar said Howdy Joe, and Joe knew instantly that it was the same voice that said Howdy to him on the payline, and Joe said Howdy right back to Oscar and they walked up the street with white folks and colored all around them getting off from work. They walked almost a block without saying another word, a million thoughts running around like mad men in Joe Youngblood's head. Finally Oscar spoke again. "Powerfully funny weather we having this winter." And Joe looked around and up at the dark sky and all he answered was "Yes indeed." The next time they walked out of the gate together was two and a half weeks later and after the friendly exchange of Howdies and the silence in between Oscar said, "That Mr. Mack Turner, your paymaster, he's my foreman on the job. He's more than a notion. He rides my ass like William S. Hart." Joe weighed the words carefully before he answered. "You don't mean to say so?" ———"We don't set horses atall," Oscar said. "Always fighting like cats and dogs. He's meaner than a rattlesnake, but I don't take no shit offa him." Joe Youngblood said, "Well I declare." And that was that. Crackers gave them dirty looks and Negroes gave them suspicious looks.

He was a curious cracker all right, and a little bit different, but he was a cracker. Born and bred way down yonder in South Georgia. It was an awfully hot night in the middle of August when Oscar was born in Wilcox County on Old Man Wilcox's farm, and somewhere on the great plantation an old dog howled all night long that night. Oscar heard his father many times laughingly tell the story about how worried his father's ignorant mother had been about the howling dog. Straggly-haired and toothless and mumbling to herself, "It's a sure sign of death." Getting down on her knees and praying and getting up again and listening to the howling dog. She told John Jefferson, her son,

"Whyn'tchoo go out and find that damn dog and shoot his brains out?" He looked at his mother and shook his head. She put a dip of snuff between her gums and her bottom lip. "Go on, son. Git your shotgun. I ain't never heard a dog howl like that without somebody dying."

Oscar came into the world about four in the morning, fine and healthy and fat as a pig, and the doctor said the mother would live. And even as John Jefferson thanked the doctor he could hear the dog howling from afar and he thought to himself——What a crazy old fool his snuff-dipping mother was. Later that day about eleven o'clock, with the new baby yelling in his mother's arms, Grandma Jefferson, weary and exhausted, sat down in her rocking chair with a tired smile on her wrinkled face, dropped off to sleep and never woke up. And the joke was on her, John Jefferson would tell you.

Oscar Jefferson hated John Jefferson, his father, almost since the day he was born. But he loved his mother and she was the prettiest and the saddest thing you ever laid eyes on—Martha Jefferson was. Ossie grew into a quiet brooding boy and his eyes were always on the move especially when he talked to his Pa. His father used to tell his mother when he was a little boy—"That boy is just like a rolling stone, and he ain't never gon gather no moss." His mother would say "Leave Ossie alone. You just don't understand him, that's all. I ain't never seen you gather no moss, except for somebody else—Charlie Wilcox. You one of his head men, but what you got to show for it, except a three-room shack full of old fashioned second-hand furniture?"

Even as he grew up he didn't take to the field work like his brothers. He would slip away every chance he got. One day, when Ossie was fourteen years old, he and a colored boy named Jim, Oscar's best buddy, slipped away from the work and went out to the Eastern Fork. It was as bright as a day in late September could be, a blinding brightness and hot as hell. They had been swimming and were lying on the bank letting the sunshine soak into their bodies. Ossie felt a vague apprehension of his father coming over to this side of the plantation and catching him in the act, but in spite of this, he had an over all feeling of warmth and well being and goodness to the world at large. There wouldn't be many more days in the year like this—warm enough for swimming—and he was making the most of this one. His eyes observed the death-like paleness of his body soaked almost color-

**230**

less by the water, drained of its redness. He was a white man. He turned sideways and his nervous eyes took in Jim's long chocolate-colored body, traveling all over Jim from head to foot, marveling involuntarily at the various shades of darkness in Jim's smooth skin; observing also the secret places where the short black hair was beginning to grow. Jim was nice, but he was the sassiest colored boy on the whole plantation.

"My old man catch me out here with you," Ossie said laughingly, "he'd skin us both alive."

"Your old man's a fool," Jim said and laughed at Ossie. "If sense was dynamite, he wouldn't have enough to blow up his little pecker."

Ossie felt his face growing hotter. "Watch your talk," he said weakly. He felt he just had to say something to keep this colored boy in his place, but he didn't really feel it inside of him, because he hated his father's guts, and he agreed unwillingly that John Jefferson was a first class fool, but after all Jim was colored, and didn't have any business talking disrespectful about his father, a white man, so he had to do something to put him in his place. But what could he do? In a fair and square fight, Jim could beat him. So there wasn't any sense in starting anything. Better change the subject. Pretend he had forgotten. He sat up on the dark grass, blinking his eyes in the brilliance of the sunlight. He heard himself say to Jim—"You talking about my Pa like that— I ought to get up from here and knock the hell out of you." Jim laughed. "You got that wrong, Ossie. You all mixed up. You hit me, buddy, you ain't gon knock no hell out of me. You gon knock hell in me and then I'm gonna up and knock the hell out of you." He laughed softly, making Ossie's color come back to his cheeks.

"I ought to kick the shit out of you," Ossie said against his will. He was no coward or goddamn nigger lover.

"You raise your foot to kick me," Jim said, "they be calling you Peg Leg Jefferson to the last day you live. Don't care if you go clean to New York City. You won't never need to buy but one shoe for the rest of your life. Break your damn foot off up to your pussy." Jim sat up and he started to laugh softly and he seemed to be bubbling over with laughter. That's the way Jim was, sassy as the devil and covering it up with laughing all the damn time. Well he wasn't going to take that kind of shit off any black sonofabitch.

"Kiss my ass," Ossie said and he turned his naked body away

**231**

from Jim and lay on his side, hating himself and the feeling inside of him.

"I'll kick your ass," Jim said, almost pleasantly, and then Jim
started laughing again. "Peg Leg Jefferson—Hahahahahaha—
Hehehehehe—Peg Leg—"

Ossie leaped upon Jim's long lanky naked body. "Don'choo
be calling me no Peg Leg Jefferson." He was a-straddle Jim's
chest bumping Jim's head against the ground. "You goddamn
sassy-ass nigger." Fiercely angry with his own whiteness which
made him start a fight with Jim, when all the time, he would
rather just lie on the bank in the brilliant late-September sunlight
at peace with the world and especially with Jim. Jim had always
been his best buddy. Taught him to swim, taught him to hunt and
a whole lot of other things.

He felt himself being pushed upwards and backward and before he knew it Jim had wrestled him over to the water and had
thrown him in. The cold water striking his hot sweaty body almost cut off his breath. He went under once, but he got himself
together and climbed out of the creek. Jim stood tall, black, naked
and waiting. Why in the hell didn't Jim recognize that white people were better than Negroes? He leaped at Jim again and they
fought and wrestled like fools all over the grass as the sun beamed
down and sprinkled its heat and light all over the place. He felt
strong as a bull as he wrestled with Jim, their hot sweaty naked
bodies up against one another, but somehow Jim rolled him
over and over and threw him into the cold water again. Every
time he got out of the water he would cuss and jump upon Jim and
the fight would be on all over again.

Jim had him down on the ground now, and they were breathing hard and gasping for breath. "Listen," Jim said, "goddamn
your peckerwood soul, I ought to kill you. The next time you
make one of them country breaks at me I'm gon kill you just as
sure as you born to die. Who the hell is your Daddy not to be
called a fool. He *is* a fool and you is too. I thought you had a little
biddy sense but you just as bad as the rest of em. Listen goddammit, you ain't no better than me, you hear me?" Jim's
words beat their way through the heat and the anger into Ossie's
unwilling ears. "Just cause your skin is white and you live in a
three-room shack and I live in one room, that don't make you
no better than me. You ain' got as much sense as I got and you
damn sure can't beat me. You poor white trash and I'm a Negro
—so what goddammit have you got to be so glad about?"

That night Oscar's Pa threw evil looks at him all through supper, but he didn't say a word to him. After supper his Pa left the house. Martha asked her youngest son, "Ossie what you been up to? I seen how your Pa was looking at you." He said Nothing, but she picked the story out of him because he loved her so much. They loved each other. "You went swimming, didn't you? I know you did, cause I seen how curly your hair was when you came to the house. Who you go with?" He told her he didn't go with anybody. Went by his own self. "Ossie, you better stay away from that no-good triflin Jim Kilgrow. That sassy nigger git you in a whole peck of trouble. Don'choo be fooled by that pretty-looking way of his."

John Jefferson came quickly and unnoticed into the house. "So that's where you wuz—running around with that Kilgrow buck. I get through with you you won't wanna see another nigger the longest day you live." He pulled his belt off quickly and crowded the boy into a corner. Ossie's whole body trembled, as he made up his mind that he wasn't going to take another beating from his Pa. He had taken too many. His decision scared him almost to death. "Donchoo hit me, Pa," he made himself say. Pa went crazy. He hit the boy viciously on his forehead with the buckled end of the belt, and he dropped the belt and lunged toward the boy and rammed his head up against the wall. "Don't hit me again, goddammit!" He beat the boy about the head with his fist. "Ain't no bastard son of mine gon talk to me like that! I'll kill you dead as you got to die!"

Martha ran to them. "Leave him alone!" And she grabbed her husband, but he gave her a lick that sent her frail body over to the other side of the room. "I'll attend to you later!" he yelled. "You no-good nigger-loving whore!" He flung Ossie to the floor over by the stove, and Ossie buried his teeth into his Pa's arm till his mouth ached and he tasted blood. His Pa cussed and reached out for a piece of firewood. "You hit my baby," Martha's shrill voice shouted, "and I'll blow your damn brains out, if you got any in that big ugly head of yours!"

John Jefferson got up off the boy and walked toward Martha. "Give me that gun, Martha. Ain't no sense of you getting yourself upset like this," he said in that whining voice of his.

Ossie crawled noiselessly over toward the kitchen door. When John got close enough to his wife he jumped towards her and snatched the shotgun and he swung around to the spot where he had left the boy, but Ossie jumped out of the back door and ran across the backyard and fled through the dark field. "Run, Ossie, run!" he heard his mother shouting but she didn't have to tell him. He ran across cornfields and he ran through the cotton and he didn't stop running till he reached the darkness of the colored quarters.

When he came to the Kilgrow shack, he walked around the side of the house. His heart began to pound and pound. Why had he come down here to the colored quarters? Why had he come running to Jim Kilgrow? If he hadn't gone swimming with this sassy nigger he wouldn't've gotten in trouble with his Pa. He stayed in hot water with his Pa, Jim or no Jim. He noted the lamp light in the window, heard the movement of people inside, remembered that afternoon with Jim sitting black and naked and heavy on his chest and whispering violently into his ear—"I'll kill you—goddamn your peckerwood soul—" He was scared and confused and angry and he didn't want to knock on the door, but there was nowhere else for him to go. This was the one place Pa would not look for him. Wouldn't admit to himself that one of his own would go running to niggers for help. He knocked timidly on the door.

"Who that?" He knocked again. He heard movement of feet inside the shack. The back door opened and the long lanky form of Jim's father loomed in the doorway. "Who that out there?"

"It's——it's Oscar——Oscar Jefferson, Big Jim." Breathing deeply.

"Who?"

"You know me, Big Jim. Oscar Jefferson—Mr. John Jefferson's boy." Even as he said it, he wished he hadn't. All the Negroes on the plantation hated John Jefferson more than they did any other white man. "Whatchoo want down here this time of night, white boy?" And Oscar said he just wanted to see Little Jim about something. Big Jim said, "You better git on back up to where you belongs and leave us colored folks alone."

Ossie stood there in the darkness looking at the tall lanky black man, and he tried to think of something to say to make him know he came as a friend. He heard another voice from the house and his heart leaped inside of him. "That's all right, Pa. I'll see what he wants" . . . "Don'choo go out there in that dark, boy. Wait till I get my gun."

"That's all right, Pa. I know him. He white all right, but he ain't nothing to be scared of." He walked past Big Jim out into the night. "Whatchoo want?" he said, looking at Ossie with that arrogant expression he wore around white folks. "Didn't you get enough of me this afternoon?" He laughed softly. "You in my neck of the woods now, boy. Down here your color don't mean a goddamn thing."

Ossie looked around him in the darkness and he looked past Little Jim toward the doorway where Big Jim stood with his big gun gleaming. Goddamn the Kilgrows! Why didn't they act like it was known everywhere that all Negroes acted around white folks. They weren't even yeller complected Negroes. They were just big, black and bad. To hell with them! He wouldn't ask them any favors. He turned and started toward the side of the house. "Now wait a minute, Ossie. What you come down here for?" He turned toward Little Jim again, his heart beating heavily against his chest. Jim walked toward him laughing softly like he had a way of doing when there was nothing funny. "What's the matter with you, boy?" He sounded to Ossie like a white man talking to a Negro instead of the other way around.

"Jim—Little Jim—Jim," he stammered, "me and Pa had a fight just while ago. He came near killing me——"

"Seems to me you always getting in a fight. You must be trying to go for who-tied-the-bear."

Ossie made himself overlook Jim's off-hand manner because he recognized that underneath it, there was something altogether different. "He jumped on me about me and you going in swimming this afternoon." All the time he had stood there talking to Jim he had forgotten his bruises, had been oblivious to the throbbing pain in his head. Now as he stood there it all came back to him. He felt weak all over. "Look where he beat me all over the head. He was trying to kill me, I do believe." Jim didn't move. "Look," Ossie pleaded.

Jim came closer and he touched the side of Ossie's head where the blood had caked. "So what you want me to do about it? Do I look like the doctor or the police or something?"

Ossie noted a change in Little Jim's voice from hard to soft. "I thought maybe y'all might have a little peroxide or tuppentime or something and maybe y'all might let me stay here tonight."

"Why didn't you go to your almighty white fr—" Jim began. He stopped and stared through the night at Ossie. "Wait till I speak to Pa about this." He walked towards the doorway.

Ossie stood waiting, listening to mumblings of argument between Little Jim and Big Jim, an overwhelming mixture of anxiety and weariness and pain and confusion ganging up on him and the relief and compassion that warmed his cool body and soothingly cooled his hot tired body when Little Jim turned from his father and said in a gruff and unfamiliar voice—"All right, Ossie, come on in the house and let's see what we can do." And then Big Jim's voice—"Naw, wait a minute, son. Y'all stay out here a little while. Let me go in the house and tell Ma about it. She the boss lady."

And later that night after the black tender hands that soothed his wounds and after the black serious faces that wanted to trust him but couldn't, after the hot heavy soup had soothed his insides, he lay there in the black cool noiseless night on the floor near Little Jim's long lanky body. He would fall asleep for ten or fifteen minutes or maybe a half an hour and would wake up again and would lie there wondering whether he had been asleep at all. His eyes got used to the darkness, and he could see the brown army-looking blanket that hung across the middle of the room, separating the space where he and Little Jim and the rest of the children lay from that part of the room where Big Jim and Mamie Kilgrow slept. He wished he could sleep. He wished Jim would wake up so they could talk to each other. A million thoughts raced around in his head. Everything seemed dream-like and unreal to him, especially the part of him, lying down with black folks and breathing the air of their house and the breath that came from their sleeping nostrils, he a white man, Mr. John Jefferson's son.

He remembered when he was much younger one day his father came in for lunch complaining good-naturedly about how he had to bust a hole in the head of one of them sassy niggers. His mother had asked his father did he have to kill him. And his father had said of course he did. "You let one of these niggers get away with sassying a white man and every last one of em'll get outa hand." One of Ossie's brothers, John-the-Second, said, "Why don't we just go outa here and kill all the niggers and let it be done with?" "What!" the father exclaimed, laughing uproariously. "Why the whole plantation would go to hell in a week. You don't think you can get as much work outa poor white trash as you can outa niggers, do you? Hell naw. Just have to make an example outa one or two real bad niggers to let the other lazy bucks know you really mean business." Then Pa had reached out and run his hand good-naturedly through John-the-Second's hair. Ossie turned and looked through the darkness at Jim lying very close to him with his back turned toward him. Jim turned in his sleep toward Oscar, and Oscar could feel Jim's warm breath coming through the night into his own white face.

Jim opened his eyes and looked through the darkness at Ossie. "What's the matter, man? Can't you sleep?"

Ossie swallowed the night air. "Your folks sure wuz nice to me——" And Little Jim told him it wasn't anything. His folks were nice to everybody. "Taking me in like this and treating me, a whi——, treating me like I was they own son——I ain't never gon forget it——" His voice choked off.

He could hear the toughness leaving Jim's voice. "Look, Ossie Jefferson, it really ain't nothing. My folks are Christian folks. I tell you how my Daddy feels about it, and I reckin my mother. He don't trust a white man living or dead, but if one of them is ready to take one step forward, Pa'll meet him halfway." Ossie could hear Little Jim's voice toughening again. "But even if Pa ever trusted a cracker, he would always keep his gun cocked and ready."

Ossie lay there letting Jim's words sink into him——"I'll pay your folks back one of these days, and I don't mean maybe."

"Naw, Ossie, naw. It ain't like that. You don't owe us nothing. Just think about it the next time you get ready to call a colored man a nigger and try to get it through your head that the white race ain't no better than the black." His voice was hot and angry and fierce now as if he and Ossie were about to fight. "Don't never stand around with your hand in your pocket when they throw a lynching party. In other words, be a human being stead of a no-good ignorant cracker."

Ossie swallowed. "We're buddies, ain't we? I—I—I mean—— can't we be buddies?"

"It's oaky doaky with me. But I tell you right now, I'm just like Big Jim. I keeps my gun cocked and ready." He laughed softly like he had a way of doing when nothing was funny.

Later that morning, very early, Ossie Jefferson stirred. He had been asleep this time for about three or four hours, but it was still before daybreak. Outside the house and up on the roof and everywhere else there was a yelling out loud of early morning noises. The birds chirping, the crickets, the locusts, everything chiming in with a howdy-do-you. He had forgotten about the early morning noises. The dogs howling softly, the hens cackling quietly

**237**

and off in the distance the roosters were crowing. He lay there listening as if he had never heard them before, and he wondered about it, because these were the noises that went on every morning, and he knew that they did, but he had gotten used to them and had become deafened to them. Now it seemed that everything was singing out loud like Christmas Carols and he wondered how anybody could sleep through it all. He looked over at Jim and he smiled grimly in the still lingering darkness. He got shakily to his feet and picked up his shoes and tiptoed out of the back door, and he sat on the back step and put on his shoes. The early morning air soothed his tired body and nipped at his nostrils as he walked a good distance from the house and relieved himself. He looked up at the sky and he breathed long and deeply, sucking into his body the coolness and the greenness and the sharpness and the newness and the cleanliness of just-before-day-in-the-morning.

Ossie came back and stood in the doorway looking into the shack at the Kilgrows. He heard a stirring in the shack and he backed away from the door. He walked quietly around the side of the house and started for home. He wanted to stay till they all woke up and to thank them again, but he knew they would insist that he stay for breakfast and he figured they had hardly enough for themselves. He would come again and thank them. He would come again, again and again, unless they objected. He started walking toward the east where his home was and his father awaited him, and also where the new day was borning. The sun getting up golden-yellow and fiery-red from a soft cotton quilt and a bluish gray blanket and his Pa waiting for him and the Kilgrows with their guns cocked and ready. And he was a man, a boy growing swiftly into a man, and his father was a man, and goddamn his father!

After the night he spent in the Bottom Ossie and his Pa had sort of signed an unwritten truce and Pa didn't try to beat him anymore. It was part of the agreement that he wouldn't be caught messing around with the Kilgrow boy, and Pa kept close tabs on them all day long every day. The only time Ossie and Jim got together was when Ossie would slip down to the colored quarters after dark. Sometimes they would sit there on the back steps in the dark and talk about everything under the sun. Sometimes they would get in the doggondest silliest arguments, come pretty close to fighting, because everything they talked about, didn't care what it was, the color question seemed to always be just around the corner. And Little Jim wouldn't ever give in nary a goddamn inch. Kept a chip on his shoulders all the doggone time.

One night they were sitting in the dark on the back steps and Ossie was feeling mighty good and he thought about what good folks Jim's folks were, even if they were sassy as the devil, and he had such a nice feeling about everything. He looked sideways at Jim and straight out into the yard again, and he said to Jim—— "You know some folks say your old man is the strongest colored boy on the plantation, and I b'lieve it's the truth."

Jim didn't say a word at first, just looked up at the night full of stars. When he spoke his voice was filled with calmness that was somehow edged with tension and Ossie could detect it. "You know, man, what you just said remind me of a story I heard the other day, about a colored man in Waycross." Jim spat tobacco juice out into the yard. "This colored man—He was a great big colored man—He was walking down the street in Waycross minding his own business, when this cracker came up to him and said ——Hey, boy, where you going? And the colored man looked at the cracker and said——Mr. White folks will you tell me something please sir?——How big do mens grow where you come from?"

That was all that Jim said. He just sat quiet and spat tobacco juice out into the yard, and Ossie sat there feeling somehow like a bump on a log, looking for the joke in the story Jim had told him, searching for the hidden meaning that must be so clear to Jim, not knowing whether he was supposed to laugh or what he was supposed to do. Thinking about his whiteness and Jim's sassiness and goddamn Jim's sassy black soul!

One day he stepped on a nail in the field, and after he pulled it out of his heel, he hobbled home to put something on his foot. When he went in the house he saw Charlie Wilcox sitting there with his biggedy self like he was completely at home laughing and talking with Ma. Charlie was a big ugly white-haired man with evil gray eyes and jet black eyebrows. He looked at Ossie as if the boy was something the cat dragged in. His mother looked at him with a guilty flush in her cheeks. "What you doing home so soon, Ossie?" Ossie mumbled something angrily and limped into the next room and looked for the peroxide. Ma came in to him and she bathed his feet and looked after his wound, and the tenderness of her touch almost melted him down, and when she was done she burned his angry face with a kiss. He was so mad with her he felt like striking her in that sweet sad face of hers. Because he felt somehow that she had betrayed him, sitting there laughing and talking with Charlie Wilcox, who as far as he was concerned was meaner than his father, with a bad reputation with the women on the plantation, colored or white, married or single.

He went around almost a week without speaking to his mother unless he just had to. Then one night she came to him out in the front yard, almost like a sweetheart would slip out to see a young lover. "What's the matter with you, Ossie?" she asked him. "Walking around puffing and pouting like a little old baby boy." He told her there wasn't anything the matter. "Must be something," she said. "You and me always been closer together than anyone in the house. Now we don't hardly talk to one another. I thought you was my bestest friend, boy." They stood out there in the dark arguing and fussing like a couple of children. She told him not to worry about what folks were saying all over the plantation. "Ain't nothing between me and Charlie Wilcox, and ain't nothing gon be. I wouldn't have that hound on a Christmas tree."

He felt a great relief flow through him. "But-but-but, Ma how come he comes around here when Pa ain't around?"

"I can't keep him from coming around. It's his plantation."

"If Pa ever find out, itter be hell to pay," he said fiercely, almost feeling proud of his father.

She put out her arms and held him close to her like she used to. "You think your Pa don't already know?" she said and laughed a dry laugh. And, when he stood there looking at her with his mouth hanging open, she added, "Your Pa is a Superintendent of Wilcox Farms and he gon always be high-sheriff-in-hell don't care what happen to his wife or anybody else in his family." And she kissed his cheek softly and left him there and walked back to the house.

And he stood there letting the awful meaning of his mother's words sink into him. There was one thing he had always given his father credit for—and that was being a man—no matter how hateful and cruel or ignorant a man——But a man by God! And a man didn't let anybody mess with his woman, job or no job. That was the southern code—Superintendent or no goddamn Superintendent——He had heard Pa shout nigger nigger nigger a million times and what a threat they were to southern white womanhood and southern womanhood had to be protected and southern womanhood and southern womanhood and southern womanhood, and first and last southern womanhood, till he had believed that this was the one principle John Jefferson would never go back on.

He came home one evening from work just as the sun was going down and a storm was making up and the wind was blowing every whichaway, and he felt a weariness all through his body and nervousness in the bottom of his stomach. Thinking about Ma——Ma and Charlie Wilcox and the way she prettied up more than she had in a long time and the sassy don't-care look she was giving Pa at the supper table every night, and it looked like she thought she was getting young again instead of growing old as she should have known she was. He didn't want his mother to ever grow old and ugly, but he didn't want her to act like a young girl either. He felt an uneasiness running all through him as he approached the house. He walked up on the front porch, his feet taking note of the sand and dirt and trash the wind had blown onto the porch. He looked through the open door and his anxious heart leaped inside of him——"Ma——Ma"——soft and natural at first, but when she didn't answer, he shouted her name. He walked through the sandy-dusty house, and he looked around the house and out in the chicken yard and the woodshed, and he ran to the nearest house. It was a two-room shack where the McWhorters lived. Old man Mack was twice as old as his pretty wife, and Ma came over here some time just to chew the rag with Lillie McWhorter. As he neared the house, he temporarily forgot about Mama, as he thought about Miss Lillie Ann, pretty and bright-eyed and baby-faced and plumpish and she liked to tease the young boys, him in particular. He imagined her saucy face before him and he felt a heat growing inside of him and against his will his manhood swelling in the middle of him and he took a big swallow of the dirt and dust that the wind was blowing. He always hated to go around Miss Lillie Ann, but somehow he liked to be around her. He walked up to the front door which was standing open, and he knocked. There was no answer. He knocked again and still no answer. He called her name——"Miss Lillie Ann——Miss Lillie Ann——"

There was no answer at first. Then he heard a young woman's voice say, "Come on round to the back, son."

"It's me, Miss Lillie Ann——"

"I know who it is. Come on round the house."

Her voice made his blood boil. He walked around the house. "Where you, Miss Lillie Ann?"

"Come on over here——" The wind was blowing steadily, and now that he was in the backyard he knew where her voice was coming from. He stopped in his tracks. He started to say something but the words choked off. "Come on over here and tell me what you want." Her voice came from the outhouse and he walked toward it as if drawn against his will by an unseen something. "You seen my mother?" he asked, as he stood outside of the outhouse, nothing between him and Miss Lillie Ann's sacred privacy but a flimsy burlap curtain. "What you say?"

"I say——you seen Ma?" he shouted. And at that moment the wind seemed to blow with a vengeance and a purpose, as with one great puff it blew the burlap curtain upward and held it up and flapping like a flag, giving Ossie an unexpected terrifying glimpse of gleaming white thighs and plump buttocks and drawers below white knees. He stood for a moment in an awful fascination and he wanted to take his eyes away and he wanted to turn around and leave, but he just stood there, and she didn't seem to be ashamed at all. The burlap curtain fell back in place and he backed away. "I'm sorry, Miss Lillie Ann, I'm——"

"Whatcha sorry about? Ain' no harm done. If you ain' ever seen it before, you don't know what it is nohow." As he ran around the side of the house the wind blew her embarrassed laughter into his ears. "Don't tell everything you know," he heard her shout through the wind and the laughter.

He ran to the next house and he asked them if they had seen his mother, and he went from one house to another, but nobody had seen her. When he got back home, Pa and his brothers were there and a lamp had been lit. "Your Ma ain't here, boy," his father said in a husky voice that was usually whining-like.

"I know, Pa."

"Whatchoo mean you know?"

"I mean I was already here. I went down the way a piece looking for her." All of the brothers stared at him and his father did too, as if he were responsible for her disappearance.

"You know where she is, Ossie?" his father said.

"No, sir. I—I—I asked everybody, but ain' nobody seen her."

"She must be somewhere," John-the-Second said. Pa looked at him with a funny expression.

"Didn't even fix the supper yet," Jesse Jefferson said. He was the brother next to Ossie in age.

The father cleared his throat. "Well we ain't gon find out nothing just standing around here. Les————"

Just about that time there was a noise in the front and they looked and they saw a tall black man with a white woman up in his arms and they all were speechless until Pa said————"Why that big black sonofabitch!" And Ossie saw at once that Little Jim was the big black sonofabitch and the white woman was Ma. Pa leaped toward the porch and Little Jim put Ma down quickly and jumped off the porch and disappeared in the darkening twilight.

"Git him! Git him! Don't let him git away!" Pa shouted. He stopped on the porch, looking down at Ma. He started back inside the house————"Where's my gun?"————He came back and picked Ma up and took her inside of the house and lay her on the bed. She was bruised and bleeding and groaning like a puppy dog. She opened her eyes and she looked all about and she called Ossie by name. "What happened?" Pa asked.

"I think I broke my leg or something," she muttered.

"What happened!" he demanded.

She closed her eyes and Ossie heard her mention something about rape, and his heart sank down to the bottom of his stomach as his father reached around the side of his bed for his shotgun. "Big black sonofabitch!" Ossie felt like he had been hit in his belly with a piece of stove wood. He looked into her frightened eyes and at her face that was bruised and bleeding and her quivering lips and he thought about the big black sonofabitch, and he was almost glad it had happened, because now he didn't have to doubt anymore, all niggers were alike, and he didn't have to take any shit off a sassy nigger again as long as he lived, and he felt like he had been suddenly liberated from a hated obligation. But he looked at his mother's piteous face and he thought about Little Jim, tall and lanky and black, somewhere out there in the stormy darkness and he didn't know whether he would laugh or cry.

Pa cussed again. "Big black sonofabitch!"

Ma opened her eyes and sat up on the bed. "Who? What black? Where you going, John?" Her big black eyes were wide and anxious.

"I'm going to find that nigger. Where you think I'm going? You see to your Ma, son? I guess you can do that."

"It wasn't him, John. It wasn't him at all. It was Charlie Wilcox."

"Charlie Wilcox!" Pa exclaimed. "Charlie Wilcox! Woman, whatchoo talking about?"

"It was Charlie Wilcox," Ma said fiercely. "He came by here and told me Ossie was hurt over by the Eastern Fork and he couldn't be moved and he was calling for me. And Charlie Wilcox took me in that horseless carriage of his'n——"

Pa stood there looking at Ma with a look of unbelief and amazement and almost hatred. "You know what you saying, woman?"

"——And he—he took me way out there t'ward the Fork, but just before we got there he turned off into the woods and tried to have me but-but-but I wouldn't do it and I scratched him up and he went crazy-like and he-he-he jumped on me and beat me up. I got up and I ran from him and I tripped up and I musta broken my leg or something cause I couldn't git up and I couldn't go nowhere——"

The other brothers were coming back into the house. "Black bastard got away."

"He didn't look like no Charlie Wilcox to me," Pa said. "Looked like Jim Kilgrow to me, and I'm gonna Kill his Grow if I git hold of his black ass tonight."

"John!" she said. "John! You listen to me. Don't be for Little Jim I be still laying out there by the Fork. He came along and picked me up and brought me home. You ought to be thankful."

"He brung you all the way from the Fork in them black arms of his'n?"

"John—John—"

"When I git through with him he never pick up another white woman in his dirty black arms I betcha."

"But John—John, he helped me. He helped me. Whatcher gon do about Charlie Wilcox?"

John Jefferson's anger was cooling now. He was thinking deliberately. "I don't believe it was Charlie Wilcox at all. You just trying to protect that nigger. I always knowed you was stuck on him." He looked around the room at the boys. "Come on, boys, let's go nigger hunting. John-the-Second, you run over to the Bradys. Tell 'em to meet us down at the Junction and stop by Jack Gibbs and tell him and his boys. Dan, you know where we keeps the rest of the guns. Git em out the closet. Jesse, you go tell

Mack. Tell him to come a-running. Let's go nigger hunting." He said to Ossie, "Guess you better stay here and take care of your Ma. That's just about your speed I reckin."

After they had gone into the stormy night, she called him to her bed, and she told him Little Jim hadn't wanted to bring her home, but she had begged him, because she was scared of being left out there all night long, and it was all her fault. "Little Jim is a nice boy. Lord Have Mercy, Ossie, what we gonna do?" He stood there looking at his mother and thinking about Little Jim somewhere out in the stormy night and white men with shotguns and lanterns and bloodhounds, and his mother asked him what could they do—They could do nothing!

She told him to run down to the Bottom and take the short cut across the branch and run all the way and tell Little Jim he'd better get out of sight, all of them better, and tell them she was going to tell the truth when the sheriff got there. "But tell him if they ketch him tonight ain't gon be no needa no sheriff."

"But, Ma—How about your leg? Pa told me to stay here with you."

"I don't reckin it's broken after all," she said. "Just sprained it a little. Your Pa don't care if both of em broken. He just innerested in catching Little Jim. You better get going." She tried to make her bruised face smile.

Ossie's eyes filled up and he leaned over and kissed her on the cheek and he left her quickly. The wind had blown up a wild crazy rain, and he ran through the storm and the wind and the rain and he fell in the creek and he kept on running, and he thought about Miss Lillie Ann sitting out there in the outhouse talking to him and her behind showing and he wondered why he should think about a thing like that, and he kept on running till he almost reached the Kilgrow house and he started to walk, catching his breath and soaking wet and his clothes sticking to him. And thinking maybe Pa and the rest had gotten down here already and what would he do if they had? He might even get killed by mistake by his own father or brother. He went around the side of a shack before he got to Jim's and he skirted the back-yards till he came to their house, and he stood there for a moment in the protection of the bushes. The house was black dark. He looked around and made sure that the others had not beaten him down there. He walked from behind the bushes and started across the yard, when Bi—Yi—and Ziinnn—nnng—A shotgun

**245**

fired out and a bullet whined softly past his ears and he dropped to the ground and crawled back behind the bushes.

"It's me—It's me, don't shoot again! I'm a friend." He lay there in the rain that kept pouring and he thought about what a crazy situation he was in—A white man down there by himself in the colored quarters and unarmed, and the Kilgrows inside with the lamp out and their guns cocked and really really ready. And the rain pouring and the wind blowing and soaked to the skin and his teeth chattering and he might be killed by the very people he was trying to help.

"Who that out there?" Big Jim shouted. "State yerself in a hurry."

"It's me, Big Jim. It's me—Ossie Jefferson."

"Goddamn, boy, what the hell you doing out there in this kind of weather?"

Ossie walked from behind the bush and started across the yard. "You better whoa there, boy. Dontcher come another step, or I'll blow you a new one."

He halted. "Anybody come with you?"

"Naw sir-ree-bob. Come all the way down here by my own-self to give Little Jim a warning."

"Is you got a pistol?"

"Naw, Big Jim. I ain't got nothing but me. I swear to my Jesus."

"Come on in out of the rain then if you sure about that, but don't act nervous."

When he got inside he found out that Little Jim wasn't there, and they pretended not to know what he was talking about, but he knew they were lying, and he knew that they knew that he knew they were lying. And he knew that Little Jim had been there and gone.

When he got back home Miss Lillie Ann was there and she had taken care of Ma, and Ma was resting but not asleep.

"Did you git down there before they got there?" Ma asked him.

"Yes, Mam. I got there and was gone before they got there. I told them what you told me to tell them."

Ma asked him a lot of questions, and all of the time he could feel Miss Lillie Ann's smiling eyes heavily upon him, and he couldn't help but think about the shameful secret they shared between them. Ma told him to put something dry on before he caught his death of dampness. He went into the kitchen, but before he could get undressed, Miss Lillie Ann came in and she laughed at him, told him he looked like a jaybird in whistling time. He tried to laugh as he watched her messing around over by the stove. She told him he better take off his wet clothes before he caught the pneumonia. He said he was waiting for her to get out of the kitchen. She laughed at him. "Well I declare—you and your shame-facey pride. Boy, I knowed you before you knowed your ownself. I ain't paying you no mind at all. Just heating some water for you to take a bath." She walked past him and pinched his cheeks. "All right, young man. You can take off your clothes now. I'm going in to there and see how Martha Mae doing. Let me know when the water gets hot. I'm coming in here and give you the best old bath." She walked out of the kitchen laughing to herself. "Lord, Jesus, I reckin." He didn't say a word. His face was flushing and the blood ran hot inside of him.

Ossie didn't sleep hardly a wink that night. He lay awake thinking about his father and brothers and the rest of the men who were out there in the storm that had let up now. He pictured them with their dogs and shotguns and lanterns and hunting all over the place and terrorizing the people down in the Bottom. And he wondered about Little Jim and where he was out there in the black hiding like a hunted animal and maybe they had already caught up with him. Maybe there was no such person as Little Jim anymore—just a long tall black body lying somewhere in a pool of blood or hanging somewhere riddled with bullets— He could hear Little Jim's sassy voice. "——Next time you get ready to call a colored man a nigger——" He never would say nigger again, never! never! He also remembered what Little Jim had said that night about lynching, but what could he do? What could he do? His body was shivering from his head to his feet.

He finally fell asleep and when he awoke he heard men talking in the next room and out in the yard, and men and dogs growling. "We'll git his black ass. Dontchoo worry, Martha. If we don't git him there ain't a cow in Texas." The sheriff came early in the morning before day and he talked with Martha and he talked and he talked, but he couldn't get Martha to change her story. Ossie was prouder of his mother than he had ever been of anything in his whole life, and mixed with this pride was hatred and anger against his father and Sheriff Hines and Charlie Wilcox, who didn't come around at all, and the other men who stood around his mother's bed for hours trying to get her to say Little Jim tried to rape her. He didn't feel like working that day, but he

**247**

went anyhow because he didn't want to become involved in a new posse that was forming, and he couldn't stand to sit around home and watch them torture his mother. When he came home for lunch they were still after her. He walked into her room, and she looked up at him and he saw a look of wildness in her face that he had never seen before, and he walked over to the bed and put his arms around her and she cried in his arms. He turned around and looked at the sheriff and the deputy sheriff and John Jefferson. "Why don'tchoo let her alone?" he shouted.

"Ain't no needer gitting excited, son," Sheriff Hines said quietly. "We just trying to do the right thing. Your mother is a little upset, and she don't rightly remember exactly what happened, and we just trying to freshen her memoration."

His mother's body trembled in his arms. "Well, she done told you all she know. Done told you the truth. So let her alone and let her get some rest."

The sheriff looked from the son to the father and back to the son. His eyes were hard and cold. "Look, son, we white folks, all of us, and we don't have to git all het up about a thing like this. The point is to git the nigger and bring him to justice. You ain' no nigger-lover is you, boy?"

He stood up from the bed and he shouted at them. "I ain't sked of any of you! And I wantchoo to leave my mother alone—goddammit!"

"All right, son. Take it easy." Sheriff Hines played with his gray mustache and he looked around at the boy's father. "Can we git a little something to eat around here? I'm hongry as a horse."

And they went in the kitchen and they ate the food Lillie Ann had prepared, and after dinner Ossie left for the field again with the helpless knowledge that they would go back in the bedroom and start to work on his mother all over again. After dinner they took turns from one to the other, the sheriff, John Jefferson, John Jefferson, the sheriff—The sheriff had started working on her again, when they heard somebody running outside and John looked out of the window and saw his son running toward the house. Ossie had been working in the field and working and thinking and hating and loving and thinking so fiercely that his head began to hurt, and all of a sudden he had stopped working and started running across the field toward home. He ran into the house and into her room and he leaped at the sheriff and—"Leave her alone!

Leave her alone goddammit! I don told all y'all to leave her alone—She done told you the truth!" He fought the sheriff from the bedroom into the kitchen. But they ganged up on him, his father included, and they took him way out in the backyard to the woodshed, and they tied him up in the woodshed and they locked the door.

The preacher came to the house and he put his hand in Martha's, and he got down on his knees and prayed for her forgiveness and for her tarnished soul. He stood and looked down on her. "You must repent," he said in solemn tones. "You must repent and I will call on the Lord to wash you white as snow." He was a great big tall handsome man with a deep scary voice.

"I done told the truth—God in Heaven knows I done told the truth. It was Charlie Wilcox—Charlie Wilcox——"

He looked at her sternly and she could see the meanness pouring out of him now. "There's only one truth," he said. "And that is—Every nigger man alive is after raping a white woman, and God wants you to help put a stop to it. If you don't repent and tell the truth, you going to hell and tarnation. I'm going to pray for you in Church on Sunday and ask God to forgive you if you tell Him the truth this evening. But effen you don't open up your soul to God and me, I'm gonna preach you straight into the jaws of hell."

She looked at the preacher and she hated them all—John—Rev. Poultry—Sheriff Hines—Old man Mack—every last one of them. But she was afraid of this man of God who had the power in him to send her to hell. She turned her back to them. "Get out of my room," she shouted feebly. "Every last one of y'all get outa my sight." But they kept after her and finally they were just faces to her—evil, white, men-folks faces, standing before her and shouting at her and growling at her, one by one. John Jefferson and Rev. Poultry and Sheriff Hines and Mr. Mack and finally Charlie Wilcox came, and Mama shouted "There he is! He's the one done it! He's the one!" Charlie Wilcox shook his big ugly head. "It's a bad experience for her," he told John Jefferson. "She's losing her mind, I do believe." He motioned to the sheriff and John Jefferson to step in the next room with him and afterwards he left. And they started on her all over again. And she hoped that Little Jim had gotten away because she didn't know how long she could hold out against them. She wouldn't let them break her down—Wonder where was Ossie?—She wouldn't let them break her down! But it seemed like they had been after her for hours and hours and hours and days and days and the swimming in her head and maybe they were right . . . Maybe it was Little Jim after all. . . .

The preacher cleared his throat and John walked around to the other side of the bed and he sat down and grabbed hold of her shoulders and he tried to shake some sense into her head. "Look," he said to her, "goddammit, you listen to me. If you don't tell the right story, Rev. Poultry gon tell the whole congregation how you been going with this nigger for the longest kind of time and then he gon preach you straight into the jaws of hell and Dr. Roscoe gon find out about you being crazy and how long you been crazy—" "John—John—Please—John—God Savior Have Mercy——" She was crying without trying to keep from crying and shaking her head crazily and John raised his big hand and slapped her once—twice—three or four times. "Listen, woman, goddamn you, if you don't straighten up, the sheriff gon carry you to Milledgeville and you gon spend the rest of your life going to hell in the booby hatch. And we gon ketch the nigger and take care of him anyhow—so you might as well tell the right story—" He shook her shoulders till she was limber as a dishrag and she fell backward and she turned and pushed her pale face into the sheet and she cried cried cried.

When Ossie got himself loose in the woodshed, he took an axe and broke down the door. He ran across the yard with the axe in his hands and before he reached the house he could hear the sheriff laughing and talking around in the front, and he walked past the serious-faced white men gathered in the yard, and he went to his mother's room. "What happened, Ma?"

"Whatchoo doing with that axe?"

"What happened, Ma?"

She looked up in his face and he could see that she was tired and beaten and scared and sick and everything was wrong with her. "Ain' nothing happened. I just told them the right story and they let me alone. They gon catch that nigger tonight, if he ain' already left the plantation. I just made up that story about Charlie Wilcox to protect that black skunk, Little Jim, cause I knowed you was so crazy about him. That oughta teach you how not to be a nigger-lover."

He looked at her and she stared back at him, and he knew that she was lying—in her eyes—in the don't-care expression around

**250**

her mouth—They had made a liar out of her, and now she could look at him almost calmly—He stared at her and there was a wild crazy look that seemed a permanent part of her now, and she resembled nobody he never knew.

He heard her voice—endlessly— "—came to me sudden like Jesus had spoke to me—You got to back up the white man, Martha Mae Jefferson—You got to tell the truth and spite the devil—You got to help your men protect the precious God-given gift of white womanhood—"

He took the axe and drove it into the floor with all his strength. He wasn't thinking about it not being fair to Little Jim or anything like that. He was looking at his mother and hating what they were making out of her—the way they were using her— He was hating his mother, despising his father and Charlie Wilcox and Sheriff Hines and everybody else.

He turned from the bed, his mother still talking like somebody who would never stop talking, and he went to the kitchen and he sat and he ate and he ate, and he ate twice as much as he usually ate, didn't remember at all what he ate. The men outside were leaving now—voices dipping in and out of the kitchen—"Better come on, boy, and join the party"—"Meet us down by the Junction"—"Greatgodamighty, son, you still eating?"—"Eat like you been working on the railroad"—And now they had all gone and he still sat there at the kitchen table and it was dark outside, but he didn't light the lamp. He got up from the table and he put on his jacket and his heavy shoes and he started towards his mother's room, but he changed his mind. There was nothing left—nothing—nothing. He didn't have any mother—He walked out of the house and down the road in the direction of the Junction—He heard somebody calling his name softly, thought it was his mother at first, and he kept walking, and she called his name again and he turned and saw Lillie Ann—tall and slim and white-faced against the blackness of her hair and the darkness of the night. He went, knowing why he went and why she had called him. He was getting to be a man, and he felt a mannish swelling inside of him, and it was going to happen to him tonight and goddamn Ma and Little Jim and Pa and Big Jim and Charlie Wilcox and the whole shooting match—There was nothing he could do about it anyhow—So God bless sweet Miss Lillie Ann McWhorter . . . There was nothing he could do to help Little Jim—nothing—nothing—

And inside of the shack she pulled off her clothes quickly, as he stood watching, and she came towards him—"Off—quick— Make haste!" she shouted in a whisper.

"But, Mr. Mack—"

"To hell with Mr. Mack," she told him. "He gone nigger hunting!" And furiously she helped him undress and they went to bed and they made love even as he had dreamed it—maybe it was a dream—and afterwards she cried in his arms and goddamned the men, every last one of them, especially Will Mc-Whorter—He lay there next to her with a belly full of love, feeling like a grown man, and he could whip his father any day in the week—and being a man, he felt he had to make a gesture of taking the man's part. "You hadn't ought to talk about your husband like that," he said in a gruff voice. "You hadn't ought to be laying in bed with a married woman," she mimicked.

He lay there quietly thinking of an answer. He knew that he should be getting up and out of this man's bed and away from this man's wife while the getting was good, but he just wanted to lay back and sink further into the white sheet and the covers and her body and drown himself in love-making and the sharp strange odor of the love-already-made. Why couldn't he just lie there forever?

She had stopped crying and she whispered to him fiercely, "All Mack takes me for is a cook and a whore. He old enough to be my grandpappy anyhow. He don't near 'bout satisfy me neither. He just gits on top of me for two or three minutes and satisfy his ownself and then drop off to sleep."

He listened, sympathizing with her, not fully understanding, but the dominating feeling he had was one of being a better man than Old Man Mack and possibly his father and all the other men out there in the night looking for Little Jim—Little Jim—Little Jim—maybe they had caught him already . . . Maybe he was already strung up and riddled with bullets. And he laying up with another man's wife. Maybe they hadn't caught him. He got up out of the bed and reached for his clothes. He had to get going——

She yelled at him, "You just like all the other men. Get what you after and you ready to leave. I suppose you going nigger hunting too?"

"Why not?" he asked her with a new kind of sarcasm his manhood was giving him. "Us men-folks got to protect white womanhood, ain't we?"

He left her and he didn't look back although he knew she had come to the front door and stood naked watching him as he went away into the night taking with him her taste in his mouth and her smell in his nostrils, not giving a damn about what he might be leaving behind inside of her. He walked down the road through the dark night, having no idea of where he was going. But he was going. Maybe they hadn't caught Little Jim after all. . . .

He was nearing the Junction and he saw a man approaching him with a shotgun and lantern. He could tell by the way the man walked with a slight limp that it was probably Old Man McWhorter. He felt his body growing warmer than before.

"Where you been, son?" Mr. Mack asked him. "How come you wan't there? I thought you would be one of the ring leaders. Your Ma was always so attached to you. She was such a good woman." The way Mr. Mack spoke sounded to Ossie like his mother was already dead, or somebody that used to be and wasn't anymore.

"Had to tend to something else," Ossie said. "Had to take care of Ma. Somebody got to stay behind and take care of the womenfolks," he added sarcastically. "How come you left the rest?" Maybe Mr. Mack knew about him and Lillie Ann.

"Everything all over 'cept the shouting."

"What's all over?" Ossie asked, his heart beating wildly.

"Well, the nigger got away."

"Got away!" His heart thumping like it would jump out of his bosom. He could hear his heart beating.

"Yeah, somebody claim he was seen way up the Wilcox County Road. But don't worry none we took care of the situation." He spat out in front of him. "We burned the rest of the Kilgrow niggers out. Course one of your brothers got shot in the leg but twan't nothing serious. Boy I'm telling you that was a sight to see. Just as soon as one of em would run out of the house, we would knock em off like a bunch of black birds. Killed every last bugger of them. The way I figger, it was a eye for a eye, a tooth for a tooth."

Ossie started to say—But my mother wasn't killed, but he wondered about it, and he looked at Old Man Mack whom he had known all his life, as long as he had known Big Jim and Little Jim, and in a way he was glad he had gone to bed with Lillie Ann, and he thought about the Kilgrow shack burned to the ground and the Kilgrow family and the night he had spent at their house, and he and Little Jim talking far into the night, and now he knew what happened to Negroes who kept their guns cocked and ready. He had let Little Jim and Big Jim down and Mamie too and he wasn't any better than the rest of the crackers but what could he have done about it? What could he have done? And his mother —his mother! He felt an awful sickness in his stomach and a full-ness in his throat and his face and he wished he hadn't eaten so much and he thought he was going to be sick in front of Mr. Mack. And his eyes filling up. He should go down to the Bottom and kill his father!

He turned away from Old Man Mack. "I got to be going," he said.

"You'll find them down there drinking corn licker and watch-ing the fire burn out."

But when he reached the Junction, he didn't take the road that led to the Bottom, he took the one that ran to the right and out of the plantation.

And now it had been many years since the night Oscar had walked all alone up the Wilcox County Road, and he had not seen anybody connected with the plantation since then, and he had thought he had succeeded in forgetting all about it, till that Saturday afternoon he saw Joe Youngblood in the payline. He had seen Joe many times before and thought nothing of it, but that particular time he had thought about Big Jim and then Little Jim, and listening to Joe talk back to Mister Mack and stand up to him, the years he had made himself forget reached out and grabbed him—the night he had spent in the Bottom and the talk with Little Jim far into the night and the sassy Kilgrows with their guns cocked and ready, but especially his father goddamn his soul to hell, and his poor sweet mother. And knowing Mr. Mack kept a gun underneath his counter, he had been scared and anxious for Joe. And in spite of himself he found himself taking sides with a black man against a white. Mr. Mack was his foreman and picked at him every day in the week and reminded him of his evil father although he looked nothing like John Jefferson. Maybe all straw bosses reminded him of the Superintendent of Wilcox Farm. He wished the business with Joe in the payline had never happened, because now some of the men were talk-ing about him, calling him a nigger-lover.

Over the years Oscar had become a family man with a wife and three children, a respectable church-going Hardshell Baptist white working man, and just like the rest of them when it came to Negroes. But yet and still he thought about the plantation quite often these days and his poor sweet mother and hateful father and his stupid brothers, and he wondered whatever became of Little Jim. He thought he had succeeded in forgetting the night when he went to bed with Lillie Ann McWhorter while his father and brothers burned the Kilgrows out and shot them down, but now it seemed he would never get rid of that guilty feeling.

## CHAPTER TWO

ROB WOULD STAY after school and ask Mr. Myles about it. That's all there was to it. A long time had passed since Mama had beaten him down at the courthouse, and he was getting older and growing up and he understood what made Mama do it, and he pretended that everything was just as it used to be between him and his mother. He wanted to forget that day in Mr. Cross's courthouse forever and ever but he just couldn't do it.

A few days ago at recess time he had been standing on the school grounds daydreaming about Mama, when Biff Roberts and Skinny Johnson had come up to him.

"You and your Mr. Myles this and Mr. Myles that. He ain't any better than anybody else. Just as big a *sambo* as old man Mulberry used to be." Skinny Johnson leered at Rob, his eyes almost closed.

"You bet not be talking like that in front of the teacher's pet. He doesn't allow anybody to talk about Professor Myles from New York City," Biff said to Skinny.

Rob stood there looking from one of them to the other. It was a Monday in January and a chill in the air and the children chased each other all over the grounds to keep their bodies warm. Crying, yelling, laughing, fighting——

Biff said, "Your Professor so tough with the crackers, how come he gon be in charge of Jubilee Day?"

Rob felt an uneasiness all through his body. "You all bet not go around putting that lie out on Mr. Myles."

"If it's a lie how come Mr. Blake told my father when he was at the house for dinner yesterday?"

Rob's hands clenched unconsciously. "You all aren't telling

nothing but a pop-eyed lie. They haven't had Jubilee since Mr. Myles been here."

"They sure gon have it this year. You don't have to take my word for it. You can read it yourself on next Sunday's Colored Page. It'll be right in there for everybody to see."

"Your *Pa* is a damn Uncle Tom. Mr. Myles isn't," Rob shouted at them and walked away from them. But they followed him all over the school grounds till he turned upon Biff in particular. "What you following me all over everywhere for? You want to start something? If you do, I'm ready for you." He balled up his fist and Biff and Skinny decided suddenly to leave him alone.

But he had carried it around with him all week since Monday, and he had taken it home with him and had dreamed about it, and it couldn't be true, but it *was* true, because he heard it everywhere. And now it was Thursday and he wasn't going to walk around in doubt any longer. He was going to stay after school and ask Mr. Myles.

The letting-out bell startled him, bringing him sharply back from his daydream world. He sat at his desk, watching absently, the children gathering up their books and filing out of the classroom. His eyes dwelled particularly on Ida Mae Raglin as she walked toward the door with the rest of the children.

After they had gone Mr. Myles came over to Robby and he sat on top of one of the desks. He smiled at Robby. "Well, Mr. Youngblood, what's on your mind?"

Robby looked up into the teacher's friendly face and away again. He cleared his throat in a nervous agitation.

"How's your family?" Mr. Myles asked him.

"Just fine, thank you." He wouldn't beat around the bush, he would just out-with-it and let it be done with, and besides he and Mr. Myles were friends, so he didn't have to hem and haw with the teacher.

"What's on your mind? Anything in particular?"

"Yes, sir." He was aware of the boy and girl on the other side of the room cleaning the blackboards. He lowered his voice. "I-I-I hear them say——They—They say they going to have that spiritual singing to-do for white folks again this year."

"Nothing's wrong with spirituals."

"I know ain't nothing—isn't anything wrong with them," Robby said heatedly. Mr. Myles had a way of looking at you as if what you were saying were the most important thing in the world. He watched the words as they started out of your mouth.

**256**

"Well, what's the problem?" he said to Rob.

"It's alright to sing them," Rob argued, "but not for them white folks that turn out every year to poke fun at us. That's what I'm talking about. Spend all that time practicing and singing just for a bunch of rich white folks."

Mr. Myles still smiled but his voice had a little bit of irritation in it, unusual to Rob. "Well, there's nothing I can do about it. I wouldn't worry about it anyhow if I were you."

"You think it's alright?" Rob asked in bitter disappointment. "You think it's alright Uncle-Tomming for white folks?"

"I didn't say it was alright. I simply said there was nothing I could do about it. What do you want me to do?" He loved this boy like a son, more like a younger brother.

"I hear them say you going to be the one in charge." It was the first time he had ever had a real disagreement with Mr. Myles, and it put a funny feeling in his stomach and his body grew warm and outside Ida Mae was waiting for him and the great big boys probably picking at her——Maybe she was waiting.

"Well, what about it, if I am? If I didn't do it, another teacher would. What do you want me to do?" It seemed to Rob that even Mr. Myles's voice had changed and now it had a strange harshness in it.

"Anyhow," Rob argued, "let somebody else do it. Don't let it be you. Everybody around town'll sure be disappointed in you. They think that you one colored man in Cross County that wouldn't Uncle Tom for white folks don't care what."

"Negroes in town don't like Jubilee Day?" Mr. Myles asked Rob. Mr. Blake had told him that Negroes liked singing the spirituals for the white folks. "The trouble with you, Myles, you don't understand the psychology of the lower class southern Negro," Mr. Blake had told him.

"Shoot naw, Mr. Myles. And especially the students. That's the one thing we hated about Mr. Mulberry. You ought to see how them crackers look—grinning like they looking at monkeys in a circus."

He looked at Rob and he thought about Brooklyn, hundreds of miles away, and Hank Saunders dead, and he thought about Laurie Youngblood and Joe Youngblood and he looked again at the boy in front of him—a boy that was growing into the handsomest youngster in Cross County and big and serious-minded like an adult and still growing in all kinds of directions. Growing gradually and quickly away from his shyness.

"As long as we help the white make monkeys out of us, they gonna always do it. I don't understand you at all, Mr. Myles. You'd be the last person I would've thought—Look, it ain't nothing against the spirituals, it's the way the crackers make us use them—Don't you see what I mean?"

"Of course I do."

"Don't you be in charge of it anyhow, Mr. Myles. Too many people taking pattern after you."

"I'll see what I can do," he said vaguely, knowing fully well there was nothing he could do. He could refuse to have anything to do with it like Robby suggested and not come back next year. He could resign his teaching job and go back to Brooklyn where he came from——If he didn't do it, somebody else would——

The boy didn't wait another second. It was as if Mr. Myles had said—Take my word for it. There will be no Jubilee Day. Rob said, "Yes, sir. I'll be seeing you."

Richard Myles wanted to call him back and say that he wasn't sure what could be done, but he didn't say a word. He sat for awhile where Rob had left him, until the two children had finished cleaning up the room. When he left the schoolhouse he caught the bus into town. He walked across the wide square toward the post office. He still hadn't gotten used to Crossroads, Georgia, and he thought he never would. Everybody walked as if they were already beyond the Pearly Gates where the streets were paved with gold and flowing with honey and life was peaceful and wonderful and pretty, so what was the use of getting excited or being in a hurry, the colored and the white. The accent of the so-called educated South was soft and slow and easy and sweet and dripping with honey. "Colored and white get along just *fine.*" The last word lingering soft and sweet like an unanswered question. And sometimes it seemed even to Richard that the relationship was smooth and peaceful and totally without friction or resentment from either side.

He came out of the post office and started back across the Square. He saw two crackers standing near the corner. He felt their hostile eyes heavily upon him. "New York City—" he heard one of them say contemptuously. Over in Pleasant Grove he always knew a secure kind of feeling of being at home and among his people. But the moment he came downtown to attend to any kind of business, he was back in that foreign country again. Because he sensed that beneath the surface of the complacency and the politeness and the peaceful relationship, there was a great big rattlesnake poised for the strike, like a streak of lightning chained and ready. Beneath the surface of the How you Mr. Jamison and the Howdy Josephus, his sensitive ears could hear an almighty rumble like a storm making up in the midst of the quiet.

He caught the bus heading back to the colored section. It went up Jeff Davis Boulevard past the beautiful mansions where the rich white folks lived. It was a beautiful town if you just looked upon the outside beauty in the white folks section. He rode through the whiteness of Peckerwood Town. Crossroads, Georgia was the most tranquil city in all the world. On the outskirts of Pleasant Grove was where the colored folks lived that were a little better off than the other colored folks. Since he had been in Crossroads, they had even put pavement on Monroe Terrace. All the homes on the Terrace had electric lights and telephones and bathrooms with real bathtubs. The three colored doctors lived on this street and the two dentists and a couple of mail carriers and school teachers and a pullman porter and William Roberts lived in the middle of the block in a big brick two-story house with a built-in garage. William Roberts Sr. was Biff Roberts' father and the editor of the colored page of the *Daily Telegram*. When Richard Myles first came to town most of the colored people on this street told him all about how much progress was being made in the south and especially Crossroads. And all the intelligent Negro had to do was to prepare himself and make the best of it.

He got off the bus and walked to the end of the street where Reverend Ledbetter lived. He liked Reverend Ledbetter. He liked almost everybody who lived on the Terrace, but they made him nervous sometimes, the way they always made a point of exaggerating to him the progress that the Negroes were making in the south especially in Crossroads and the liberalism of the educated and well-to-do white folks. Every time he talked with any of them, they would pour it on thicker than ever, as if they had to justify to him their being born in the Southland and staying in the Southland. They embarrassed him. It was as if he brought their insecurity to the surface, aroused them from their tissue-paper smugness against their will. They made him feel like an outsider trying to get the inside dope and they trying to show him the bright side only.

He was seated in the Ledbetter living room now, and the personality of the pastor was everywhere in the modest room that was comfortable and livable with a serenity all its own. And books all over the place. The pastor came in.

"Well—well—well—My learned friend from the big city."

He reminded Richard somehow of his father. He was a small black man with tiny eyes, but they didn't have the nervousness that his father's possessed. They were always calm and self-assuring.

"How are you, Reverend Ledbetter?" Richard never understood why a man of the pastor's intelligence and drive was content to stay in a small town like Crossroads. He could have a big church in any big city.

They sat facing each other, looking each other over. Reverend Ledbetter smiled. "Well, what is it today? Getting more material for your book?"

"What book, Reverend Ledbetter?"

"I have tried to figure out why a brilliant young man like you would waste your time in a place like this, and I came to the conclusion that you must be collecting material for a book about *us*. If you are, you just wasting your time on Monroe Terrace. You need to spend some time over in The Quarters, and with the working people in Pleasant Grove, and also the young people you in touch with every day at school. They're the ones gon really change things with the help of the Good Lord. We folks up here on the Terrace, we're scared of our shadow." He looked at Richard's questioning face and laughed as if he were enjoying a private joke. "Yes—sir—ree"—

"But why—why? You would think—I mean the people on the Terrace have more education——"

"Why? Why? We're just scared—that's why. Scared we'll lose this little bit of security the white man handed down to us. We teach school in the white man's school system. We carry mail for the white man's post office. We take care of the colored folks in the white man's newspaper. We got a paved street. We got a nice home with right pretty furniture. We're business men. We're doctors. Sometimes I think we more scared of the Negroes over in the Quarters than we are of the white folks." He stood up nervously and at that moment painfully reminded Richard of his father, but he sat back down and a calm moved over him.

"Look—You know where Monroe Terrace is located? Our Street is two blocks long. It runs to the west smack into Peckerwood Town, but north of us is the rich white folks and south of

**260**

us is the black folks. And here we are in the middle. And you know what it is to be in the middle." He laughed and he slapped his knee with his hands. "Yes—sir—ree—You don't know——"

"Yes," Richard said. "Yes—But you——"

"I'm the only feller on the street with any kind of independence. My support comes from the people south of the border. A Negro preacher is in a better, more independent position to serve his people than any other colored professional man in the United States. Two powers we have to answer to, and that's our congregation and God Almighty, and ain't neither one of them white. I tell all the other preachers—I tell them all—they don't have to be scared of the white man——They don't owe him nothing—Not a thing——Everything they owe is to God and the black folks." He was getting excited and he realized he was getting excited. He smiled at Richard and lowered his voice again. "Well, you didn't come here to hear me preach a sermon. If you liked my preaching you would come to church more regular."

There was a brief silence before the young man cleared his throat. "I wanted to talk to you about the Negro spirituals and Jubilee Day."

"What about them?"

"The children don't like it. They don't like all that spiritual singing for the white man."

"There is nothing wrong with the Negro spirituals, son. They're some of the most beautiful songs ever conceived by man, and they weren't conceived for the pleasure of white folks, I can state you that."

"That's just the point," Richard said.

"Now I can understand the stylish people on this street being ashamed of the spirituals," the Reverend said. "Some of them shame of everything colored. Think everything we invent or anything we do is no-count. To let them tell it they don't like jazz—too high class for the blues, and ain't got nothing for the spirituals to do. But the young folks in the school they should be taught to be proud of the spirituals. And you——"

"We don't mind the spirituals, Reverend Ledbetter. We just don't like the use that is made of them on Jubilee Day. We want to sing spirituals when we want to sing them. Not for the pleasure of a bunch of white folks that think they're dealing with a bunch of monkeys." He could see the worried face of Rob Youngblood, hear his angry voice.

"Never mind what the white folks think, as long as we know what the spirituals mean, why should we always be worried about what the white man thinks?"

Richard looked down at the carpeted floor. Maybe he was whipping a dead horse. Maybe he and Rob Youngblood were wrong. "But—but—the colored folks would prefer that we forget all about Jubilee Night. It's the white folks——the Board of Education's demanding it. I've been to Mr. Blake, and he says it's something that was done every year before I came and the Board of Education say they're going to start doing it again. No ifs, ands or buts. He says it's out of his hands and he can't see where it does any harm anyhow."

The little preacher went to his desk and he came back with a big book in his hand. "Here is a book, son. Here is a book. Next to the Bible it's my favorite book. Next to the Holy Bible." It was the *Life and Times of Frederick Douglass*.

"I have read this book," Reverend Ledbetter said. "Exactly nine times, through and through, from cover to cover. Exactly nine times, and I'll probably read it nine more times, the Good Lord willing that I live long enough. This is one of the greatest testimonies to the equality of man and the human spirit." He waved the big book in his right hand. "This is a monument to the God-given right of every man to be free." He stopped and laughed. "Reverend Ledbetter, what the devil has all this got to do with Jubilee Day?" he said to himself.

"I have read that book, sir," Richard Myles said. They sat for awhile, saying nothing. The preacher appeared to be lost in his thoughts, listening to something from another world.

"Frederick Douglass wasn't ashamed of the Negro spirituals," he finally said, "and he wasn't ashamed of the colored folks' religion, but he didn't give a hoot for the hypocrisy of the white man's religion."

"Nobody's ashamed of the spirituals, Reverend Ledbetter. The children don't object to the spirituals as such. They just want to sing them on their own terms."

Reverend Ledbetter sat there with the great book on his knees, rubbing it nervously with the palm of his hand. Suddenly he slapped his other hand on his other knee. "The children are right," he said aloud to himself. "The children are right."

Of course the children are right, Richard thought to himself.

The preacher jumped up as if something had bitten him, and

again he reminded Richard sharply and painfully of his father in far-away Brooklyn. He sat back down. "We'll do what the children want us to do," Reverend Ledbetter said. "We'll have a Jubilee on our own terms. A real Jubilee. We can have a Jubilee Day these crackers round here will never forget. Make them wish they had never thought it up. Get the point? Ain't nothing Uncle-Tom about the Negro spirituals. They the fightinest songs ever known to man. We'll tell the people how they came into being. Fix a program around the history of the spirituals."

Richard stared at the preacher. The impact of the preacher's suggestion had him speechless for a moment.

Reverend Ledbetter continued. "You know how to do it, son. Tell them what 'Swing Low Street Chariot' really means. Tell them all about that underground railroad, son. I'm glad they put you in charge. You're really the right man for the job." Reverend Ledbetter looked at his big pocket watch. "Excuse my manners, son. I just got to run down to the church for awhile. Got a real important engagement."

"A very good idea," Richard Myles said with a tremble in his voice. "An excellent idea."

He was roused by the preacher's melodious pulpit voice, which was a little different from his regular voice—richer, fuller, deeper. "Can't you hear them singing, son? Way back yonder—Can't you just hear them? My father and your grandfather?—Make you proud to be a black man. Great God Almighty! Just one verse:—

> *Green trees A-bending*
> *Poor sinner stands a-trembling*
> *The trumpet sounds within-a my soul*
> *I ain't got long to stay here*
> *Steal away*
> *Steal away*
> *Steal away to Je—sus*
> *Steal away*
> *Steal away home*
> *I ain't got long to stay here———*

"Steal Away To Jesus," he repeated. "Son, as far as the black man in slavery was concerned, wasn't no Jesus in Georgia. Jesus was in Heaven and Jesus was up above that Mason and Dixon line. GreatGodAlmighty, Jesus was freedom." He laughed at himself. "When is this here Jubilee business?"

**263**

"It's the last Friday night in February."

"Got plenty of time. Sorry I got to rush you. Come back to see me next week after you talk to yourself and get it clearer in your own mind."

"Yes, sir."

They shook hands and said good-night and started toward the door. Richard walked out into the early evening. The pastor called after him, "Don't talk to too many people about it outside of your own self. If you do, Marser Charlie get the news before daybreak."

He heard the preacher laughing as he walked down the steps, and at that moment he had a wonderful full-blown feeling about Negro preachers and Negro churches and black folks' religion and black folks everywhere no matter their color, and his people marching through the pages of history down through the years with Frederick Douglass and Harriet Tubman and his people over in Pleasant Grove and out in the Quarters in their ugly shacks and in Joe Jesup's Barber Shop, his people in far away places like New York City where his father lived and where he came from, and even those on Monroe Terrace and and and he loved his people—and proud proud proud———

## CHAPTER THREE

AFTER HE LEFT Reverend Ledbetter's house, he didn't catch the bus home. He walked all the way through the early evening and the darkness falling fast, and a sharp chilly breeze blowing through the town. The boldness of the preacher's suggestion gradually sinking into his whole being, and the possibilities—the possibilities ———But why hadn't he thought of it? He had thought only in terms of going through with the white folks' version of Jubilee Day; either that, or giving up his job. The answer had been there all of the time just out of reach. With all he had learned about religion keeping the people from thinking, Reverend Ledbetter was one of the boldest thinkers he had ever met.

The next evening, as he sat in his room, mulling it over in his mind, he wished for somebody to discuss it with. There were so many ifs, ands and buts about it. Maybe he would be just stirring up trouble between colored and white. He couldn't just sit alone and plan, because maybe the idea wasn't as good as it sounded, and other people might not think like the preacher.

He put on his topcoat. He would go to the Youngbloods, place the whole thing before them, and see what they thought. He gathered up the notes he had made. Marser Charlie wouldn't get any news from the Youngbloods—he hoped.

It was a dark cold night and they were seated by the fireplace when he got there, and he could tell they were surprised, but very glad to see him.

"Thought you weren't gon never get back to see us." Joe smiled at the teacher. "I declare I thought you had put us colored folks down."

"I keep so busy," Richard Myles said self-consciously. "I meant to come long before now, but I just kept putting it off. You know how it is." He could feel Robby's eyes heavily upon him.

"You know you always welcome," Mrs. Youngblood said.

Joe gave him a chair and Richard Myles sat with them, and he glanced at the boy and then at the girl, and Jenny Lee's face flushed painfully for everyone to notice, and she tried to pull her dress further below her knees than it already was, and the young teacher smiled his own embarrassment.

Joe Youngblood took the poker and poked at the fire in the fireplace. "Kinda chilly out there tonight, ain't it?"

"Yes, indeed," Richard Myles answered. "It's colder than chilly."

"What you need this kind of weather is little old tarty every now and then to keep that old blood warm and carrying on." Joe smiled slyly. "Ain't got nothing like that in the house is we, Mrs. Youngblood? Got anything for snake bites around here?"

Rob laughed out loud, and the rest of them laughed.

"I don't believe we got that kind of medicine on the shelf this time," Laurie Lee said. "I reckon I can stir up a few cups of coffee though. That ought to help a little." She got up from her rocker.

"Don't bother, Mrs. Youngblood. Really, don't go to any trouble."

"Isn't any trouble, Mr. Myles. No trouble at all."

"Set still, Laurie Lee. I'll take care the coffee. You talk to the teacher. He didn't come here to keep company with a great big old hard head like me." Without another word, he went in the kitchen. Laurie Lee watched him with her narrow eyes widened in genuine surprise. She thought about the night the teacher had brought Rob back home and the talk they had had far into the night and she shook her head unconsciously, and she smiled at the teacher.

Richard Myles sat there staring into the sleepy-looking fire. He glanced at Rob. "Are you ready for that history test tomorrow?"

"Yes, sir."

Big Sister looked boldly up into Richard Myles's face for one brief second. "To let him tell it, he got everybody's waters on in your class, Mr. Myles. That's all he talk about—Negro history." Her face flushed warm again, and she got up quickly and went into the kitchen where her father was.

Mr. Myles and Mama laughed.

"You just telling a great big something-ain't-so," Rob said.

And the grown folks had coffee and bread and home-made jam and the children had hot water tea and bread and jam, and they all sat relaxing before the fire and talking about first one thing and then another, and Big Sister glancing self-consciously at the nice looking, pretty-talking young teacher, but most of the time her eyes looking holes in the floor near the hearth, and Rob fidgeting like ants were in his britches, and the quiet noises of the fire in the fireplace and the shadows on the hearth.

Joe cleared his throat and told Richard Myles, with everynow-and-then a tremble in his soft booming voice, about the argument he had with the paymaster and the way the Negroes gathered around him and the cracker saying "Howdy," and the cracker since then walking out of the gate with him and talking to him friendly-like. "Yes, sir," Joe said, smiling and slapping his big thighs, "I got to thinking and studying about what you said when you was here that night, and I said to myself, that Professor Myles must be one of the Major Prophets sent down here on earth by Great God Almighty." Joe laughed out loud and all of them laughed including Richard. Then everything got quiet again.

And Rob just couldn't hold it any longer. "What you going to do about Jubilee Day?" he asked Mr. Myles. The Youngbloods looked at Rob in surprise.

"What would you say, if I told you we *were* going through with it?"

"You mean you going to have it?"

"That's exactly what I mean."

"And you going to be in charge?"

"What would you say, if I asked you to take part in it?" Mr.

Myles smiled at the angry disappointment on Rob's face, and it made the boy angrier.

"Me?" he shouted. "I wouldn't be in it for a million dollars. I can't sing nohow."

"I think everybody is going to enjoy this Jubilee Day—All the colored folks I mean. After you spoke to me, I went to see Reverend Ledbetter and discussed it with him, and he said we ought to have a Jubilee Day, but we ought to have the kind colored folks will be proud of. Teach the white folks a lesson."

"You mean there won't be any spirituals?"

"There'll be plenty of spirituals, but we're going to build a program around the spirituals."

"And you talked Reverend Ledbetter into it too?" Rob said angrily.

"I didn't talk him into anything. It's his own idea. Wait a minute. Listen—We're going to give the meaning and the history of the spirituals. We're going to tell them, the white and the colored, how the Negro spirituals came into being." He looked around into all of their faces that were fixed upon him now. And he told them how the Negro spirituals were born in the fields on the great slave plantations and in the slave cabins, and wherever else slaves could get together to pass the word along, sometimes right under the nose of the master. He hazily outlined the program to them, which had been forming in his head the last couple of days, becoming clearer to him as he talked to them, trying to read the meanings of the expressions in their faces as he went along, and when he finished there was a silence in the room that was painful to him, and the crackling of the burning wood in the fireplace sounded like angry shots from a pistol.

Joe looked at Laurie and cleared his throat. "Never knowed spirituals meant all them things you say they mean."

Laurie Lee's rocker went back and forth, her narrow eyes narrowed in a deep meditation. "This is the kind of Jubilee Day we've been needing for the longest kind of time. This the kind of religion the colored man needs everywhere."

Joe said to the teacher, "Don't get me wrong, Professor Myles. I'm behind the proposition every step of the way, but how you know the spirituals mean the kind of things you say they mean?"

"Learned it from Negro history—from Frederick Douglass—from Paul Lawrence Dunbar—Carter G. Woodson—from Reverend Ledbetter right here in Crossroads—and from the Negro spirituals themselves—Just about all of the spirituals back there in slavery had double meanings. The slaves weren't fools. They knew what would happen if they came right out and said what they wanted to say."

"If they didn't have double meaning," Laurie Lee said, "they just ought to have."

"Listen," Richard Myles said. "Listen to the words." He began to sing in his rich baritone, self-conscious at first.

> *Swing Low Sweet Chariot*
> *Coming for to carry me home,*
> *Swing Low Sweet Chariot*
> *Coming for to carry me home.*

He heard Joe's thundering bass join in. *If you git there before I do, tell all of my friends I'm coming too,* and Laurie Lee's soprano, and before the first verse was finished the children were singing.

"You know where home was," Richard Myles said after the song had ended. "It wasn't only in Heaven. It was up north to freedom."

"Great Day in the morning," Joe said. "Many times as I done sung that song, it ain't never sounded that good before."

"It hasn't felt that good either," Laurie Lee said, thinking about Big Mama.

They sang a couple of more spirituals including Joe's favorite, "Walk Together Children," and the room was filled with a Jubilee spirit. Joe got up and turned his back and wiped his eyes on the sly, and he blew his nose. "I declare I believe I'm catching a fresh cold. That tarty sure would come in handy."

Laurie Lee nodded her head and smiled at the teacher. "You say Reverend Ledbetter going to take part in it?"

"He certainly is. It's his idea to begin with." Thinking to himself it would be a good idea to get the minister to participate in the program itself, and not just the planning. . . .

"That'll be good—mighty mighty good."

Rob was so filled up he could hardly speak. "Wh-wh-what you want me do do? I got a pretty nice voice for calling hogs, but it isn't good enough to sing in any chorus."

"We have something special for you to do," Richard Myles answered. "You're going to have something to say before each number. You're going to be the narrator. You're going to give the history and the background. You and Reverend Ledbetter and I will work out the content."

"Me!" Rob sat there with his mouth open.

"You don't reckin we'll have any trouble with the crackers," Laurie Lee said anxiously.

"Can I be in the chorus?" Jenny Lee asked. "I can sing pretty good. Can't I, Mama? I coulda been in it last year. I just didn't want to."

"You don't reckin there'll be any trouble. Do you, Mr. Myles?" Laurie Lee repeated.

"I sure do want to be in this Jubilee Day," Jenny Lee insisted.

"Quiet girl," Mama said. "Haven't you got any manners?" She looked at Mr. Myles.

He looked briefly into the depths of her anxious eyes. "I hope there won't be any trouble, Mrs. Youngblood. But you folks would know the answer to that question better than I would."

"If the crackers don't like it, shame on them," Jenny Lee said, batting her big eyes. "Can I be in the chorus? I got a good voice."

"There'll be so many Negroes there, won't make no difference what the crackers like," Joe said.

Laurie Lee looked anxiously at Rob and then at the teacher. "But what about afterwards? What about you, Mr. Myles and what about Rob?"

"Don't worry about the narrator," Rob said.

"I'm thinking about what will come after. These crackers won't take nothing like this lying down. They might make trouble for Rob, and they'll sure be giving you your walking papers, even if they don't do you no bodily harm."

"I've thought about that, but as far as I am concerned, if they do send me away, it will be well worth it." He didn't want to leave Crossroads.

"We won't let them!" Jenny Lee said.

Joe Youngblood stood up and he poked at the fire again. He stared up at the ceiling. He remembered the last time the teacher was there in the same room, and the fire in the fireplace seemed to be the same, and the smell of firewood burning, and the feeling everywhere. He remembered the words spoken about standing together and what Laurie Lee had said. He had thought about them enough since then. He cleared his throat and looked down into their faces. "Look like to me if the colored stick together, ain't gon be no need to worry about what the crackers gon do."

Laurie Lee looked at Joe. "You right about that Joe—Yet and still—You right about that Joe," she repeated. "And especially if Reverend Ledbetter is going to be in it. Get all the church folks and the lodge folks behind you, crackers can't do nothing. Crackers don't ever start anything unless they outnumber you a hundred to one. Whatever they start we'll sure God finish."

"And one thing we aren't going to stand for," Jenny Lee said. "We're not going to let them send Mr. Myles away."

"You'll be in the chorus," Mr. Myles told her. "No doubt about it."

The Youngbloods laughed.

Rob had a feeling that he would burst wide open any minute, he was so filled up. He got up and walked over to Mr. Myles and he held out his hand. "I knew you would find some kind of a way Mr. Myles, and I want you to know us Youngbloods are with you one hundred percent."

Richard grabbed the boy's hand, and he squeezed it so hard he himself was embarrassed. He stood up to go, and he wanted to say to them not to tell anybody about the plan right away, but he didn't know how to say it, because he didn't want them to think he didn't have confidence in the Negro people of Crossroads, Georgia. He shook all of their hands, and when he was about to leave, he said, "Up to now you're the only folks that know about the plan besides Reverend Ledbetter and me."

Laurie Lee smiled. "And nobody else going to know about it from us. You tell too many Mr. Charlie'll know it."

All of them laughed including Richard Myles.

He felt good when he left them, and, as late as it was, he walked through the brisk night to the Terrace where Josephine Rollins lived carrying with him an unexplored feeling of being a part of the Youngblood family. He missed his family in far away Brooklyn, and he needed the Youngbloods.

He liked Josephine Rollins more than a little. They liked each other. And he told her about the Jubilee plan as they sat in her prim little living room facing each other, she in her light blue bathrobe with the bottom edge of her nightgown showing, her soft friendly eyes heavy with sleep. When he finished talking she said he was just going to stir up a whole lot of trouble. White folks and colored got along fairly well in Crossroads—better than most places down here. And they talked about it till it got quite late, early in the morning. He tried awfully hard to keep the anger out of his voice, and he was twice as angry with her as he would have been with anybody else because he liked her so much. She told him Mr. Blake wouldn't allow it anyhow, and he said Mr. Blake wouldn't have to know about it ahead of time. Nobody had to know about it, not even the children in the chorus. They became angrier and angrier with each other, polite and angry. And when she said people from up north do more harm than good, he asked her was it true what they said about the Southern Negro being happy and contented. At that point she got to her feet and said it was getting quite late and thanks for taking her into his confidence, but she was not going to be in this colored folks' mess. "I'll just play the piano like I always did, during the practice and Jubilee Night. I'm not going to run and carry tales to the *man,* so don't worry about that. I'm just going to forget you paid me a visit." She wouldn't look into his eyes now. Her usually sweet voice was husky and strange. She walked toward the front door and she stood there as they said good-night, the ceiling lamp casting soft reflections on her dark sweet face.

It was two or three days later before the practice for Jubilee Day really got under way. From then on every afternoon at two o'clock, the children in the chorus would happily leave their classes and go to the auditorium for Jubilee practice. He told them the first day this was going to be the best Jubilee Day in the history of Crossroads and Pleasant Grove School, and he wanted them to practice hard and this was one Jubilee the Negro people of Crossroads would be proud of. Josephine Rollins played the piano and helped him with the children in the chorus as if nothing had happened. Maybe his going to see her that night had not happened at all. Maybe he'd dreamed it.

The day before the Jubilee the children in the chorus marched all the way downtown to the city hall auditorium where the Jubilee was to be held. They marched two abreast and full of pride and happiness and devilment through Peckerwood Town and down Jeff Davis Boulevard past the great big mansions where the rich white folks lived, and they practiced in the great big auditorium. Richard Myles had convinced most of them that this was one Jubilee they would be proud to be a part of. Reverend Ledbetter announced it from his pulpit every Sunday morning and all through the week, and he sent the announcement out in his weekly bulletin. "Your children will not be singing for the benefit of our white friends, welcome as they are. They will be singing for us. The Great Lord be praised. They will be singing for our fathers and our fathers' fathers back through the ages and for generations to come. So come on out on Friday night, Brothers and Sisters. Come on out and bring *everybody* and join in the great Jubilee————"

Richard Myles found himself leaving the auditorium the evening before Jubilee Day, with Josephine Rollins. The final practice had just ended and the children had left, and they had stayed behind looking after first one thing and then another. She was tense and all tuned up to a very high pitch, which she tried to disguise. They walked down the long white marble steps and she looked sideways at him and away again.

"Well, professor, I reckin you got everything in order. You ready to take your flock right smack up to the Pearly Gates?" She gave a quick laugh.

He felt a sudden flash of anger toward her. After all those weeks of practice, she had not once mentioned the new kind of program she knew he and Reverend Ledbetter and Robby were feverishly planning. She had never even alluded to it by a word or a look or the bat of an eyelash. She had just been her same soft sweet-faced cooperative self throughout the entire practice period. And now he wasn't in the mood for flippancy on anybody's part, but especially hers. He wondered how the children would take it when he told them about the special part of the program tomorrow evening before it began. He was really worried about how the audience would take it, especially the crackers. "I think everything is ready," he told Josephine. He said goodnight and turned quickly away.

Before he got home it started to rain and it rained all night long till about seven in the morning. The sky was dark and gray with clouds everywhere. Before he left for school Reverend Ledbetter phoned him.

"Well, my learned intellectual fighter, have you been on your knees this morning?" The Reverend was mimicking his own pulpit voice.

"No, sir, I haven't as yet. I thought that was your department," Richard said in the same joking spirit, edged with a little nervous anxiety. "You've had a whole lot more experience along those lines."

"Bad as some of these crackers are and bad as that weather outside looks, it's going to take a whole heap of knee-bending."

Even after the preacher hung up Richard seemed to hear the rich peals of laughter reaching toward him through the telephone and washing away his early-morning nervousness.

The sun came out about two thirty in the afternoon and it stayed out. The program was supposed to begin at eight thirty sharp. The children were to get to the auditorium at seven. When Richard Myles arrived people were already there standing on the outside, colored and white, mostly colored and mostly country people. It looked like in-town-Saturday-afternoon. Wagons and trucks parked nearby, and talking and laughing like being on a picnic. He walked through a crowd of people and he heard somebody say—

"There go the professor. He the one in charge."

And hostile glances from the red-faced peckerwoods.

"Is that Professor Myles?"

"From New York City—"

"Where Rev. Ledbetter?"

When he went backstage some of the children had already arrived. Rob Youngblood was there. "How do you feel, Robert?"

He looked Richard Myles full in the face. "I'm ready," he said.

The children drifted in from seven to seven thirty. By a quarter to eight most of them had arrived. Richard Myles called them together, and they lined up just as they would when the program began. When he began to speak to them the air was so tense, you could actually feel it moving around. He hoped that the children were not as nervous as he was.

He thanked them for their cooperation and for the confidence they had shown in Miss Rollins and him. "I know what most of us think about previous Jubilee Days and about singing Negro spirituals for rich white folks who come along for the laughs. And we promised that this one would be different, but you had to take our word for it, because we couldn't say anymore than that then. Now we can tell you." He could see their beautiful children faces, dark-eyed and bright-eyed and confident and nervous, and black and brown and light brown faces, all turned toward him in anxious expectancy.

"This Jubilee Day, along with the glorious spirituals and throughout the program, we are going to give the history and meaning of the spirituals, most of which were born in the struggle of our forefathers against the inhumanity of slavery. There was never anything Uncle-Tom about Negro spirituals and we're going

**273**

to prove it tonight. We're going to give the white folks a real education. All of us are going to be teachers tonight. We're going to teach history and we're going to make history. Robert Youngblood will be the narrator."

A murmur went through the chorus, and he wondered nervously had he put the thing over.

"You have done wonderfully in practice, and now with a noble purpose in mind, the purpose of Freedom which we haven't won yet, you will do even better than ever before. Any questions?"

He looked into their anxious faces. His stomach flip-flopped as he heard Biff Robert's voice coming from the back line of the chorus. "I don't know about all that history and meaning stuff, Mr. Myles. I believe it's just going to stir up a whole heap of trouble with the white folks."

"We'll just speak the truth," Mr. Myles said. "The truth never hurt anybody, unless he is guilty of something."

"I don't know about that, Mr. Myles. All I know is, ain't no use of stirring up trouble between colored and white."

He should have been prepared for this, Richard Myles thought. This boy could disrupt the entire business if he tried hard enough. He had focused all of his anxieties and anticipation on the crackers and Uncle Tom Negro adults, had taken the children for granted.

"I don't know about the rest of them," Biff Roberts said. "But I don't want to get in no mess—get put out of school—sent to the reformatory—We ain't nothing but innocent children. You shouldn't be putting us in the middle of everything. I don't know about the rest, but you can count me out."

There were wide-eyed looks of fear and confusion on the children's faces. All of the planning and work, the weeks and weeks of practicing and planning and worrying and the work. . . .

He saw Jenny Lee Youngblood step out of the front line and look toward the back of the chorus. "Get on out of line then," she shouted. "Ain't nobody scared of these crackers but you. Everybody in town knows your whole family ain't nothing but a bunch of Uncle Toms from your daddy on down. Mr. Myles spend all his time studying how to bring the race up, and you trying to tear it down. Get on out if you so scared of crackers. Anybody else scared get out too. I'm standing by my own."

There was a frightening moment of painful silence and then Richard Myles heard the "Me too's" coming from all over the chorus and he wanted to go to big-eyed Jenny Lee Youngblood and pick her up and give her the biggest hug anybody ever gave her, as she stood there with the other children, an angry pout on her upturned mouth.

"Ain't nobody scared," Biff Roberts said.

Richard Myles asked were there any more questions. There was nothing but mumbles. "Anybody want to drop out?"

"I'm with you, Mr. Myles," Rob Youngblood said. "Crackers don't scare me."

"Me too," Bruh Robinson said.

"Me too."

"Count me in."

"How about you, William?"

"Ain't nobody scared," Biff Roberts answered.

Myles could feel the perspiration pouring from him all over his body. "Thank you," he said. "I guess that's all. Relax until the bell rings at eight fifteen. Then assemble in your places. Good luck, God bless you," he added with the greatest sincerity.

Every now and then he would look out from behind the great curtain at the audience assembling. They came in dribbles at first, then at about ten minutes after eight, they began to flow in. By eight-twenty-five every seat was taken, except a few vacants in the section roped off for white folks up front on the right. Even so there were almost a hundred white people present, most of them dressed like important looking people. He saw the Mayor come in with the Superintendent of the Board of Education. All the children in the chorus had arrived but five or six, and they could start without them, except that Willabelle Braxton had not come yet and she was the best alto in the entire chorus. As he stood there thinking about how the Mayor and the Superintendent would react to his program, he felt somebody poke him in the ribs and he jumped nervously. He turned and looked into the smiling face of Josephine Rollins.

"Don't worry about a thing," she said. "The folks are here to-night. They are standing along the sides. Fred and Harriet's folks I mean."

He laughed nervously.

"What time are you going to start the program by?" she asked him. "Eastern Standard or Colored People's Time?"

He looked at her sweet face and he laughed a good laugh this time, suddenly feeling a great relief flow through his body. "We're going to throw *C P T* out the window this night of our Lord," he burlesqued. Both of them laughed.

Willabelle Braxton came in out of breath and she was very very sorry, and he said it was all right and he briefed her quickly about the meaning of the program.

Mr. Blake came over to them from the other side of the stage. "Everything in readiness?" he asked, a nervous look beneath the customary beam of his countenance.

"Everything ready to roll, Mr. Blake," Richard said. He glanced at Josephine Rollins. "Almost everybody is on time, including the audience, and we're going to start as close to eight thirty as possible."

"Well," Mr. Blake said, "I'm sure it will come off all right with you and Miss Rollins taking care of things." He smiled at Miss Rollins and he cleared his throat.

He might as well tell Mr. Blake now, this minute. "I think you're going to find it rather interesting," Richard Myles said. "We're doing it just a little bit differently this time. We're going to give a bit of historical background."

"Historical background?" the principal said with a worried look. "Historical background—Well I guess it can't hurt any," he said to himself. "Good—Good—You should have told me about it before now. I guess it's all right though."


## CHAPTER FOUR

AT EIGHT-THIRTY-EIGHT the curtains parted and the children stood up, and Richard Myles came on the stage with Josephine Rollins and a silence fell gradually upon the audience. Miss Rollins sat down at the piano and began to play the National Anthem, and everybody stood up and sang the first verse—

> *Oh say can you see by the dawn's early light*———
> *What so proudly we hailed*————

Reverend Ledbetter walked out from the wing, the people still standing, and he raised his arms and he asked the blessings of the Lord on the gathering, "We are come, oh Lord, to pay tribute to black men and black women and to sing Negro spirituals which our fore-fathers gave to this great country in the days of slavery a-way down in Egypt Land————"

And when the Amens died softly away, and some of the lights went off all over the great big beautiful auditorium, Robert Youngblood, seated at the left of the chorus, stood up and walked with proud nervous dignity towards the center of the stage. He was all dressed up in his Sunday-go-to-meeting dark blue suit. He looked out beyond the footlights at the upturned faces, and, in a brief second, he glimpsed his mother and his father and Ida Mae Raglin and Fat Gus and a thousand other faces, and black and white faces—brown and light brown. He cleared his throat and he looked bleary-eyed at the paper in his hand and he opened his mouth and worked his jaws but nothing came out. But sweat broke out all over his face. He licked his lips and tried again, and the sound of his voice shocked the fear out of him, for the moment at least.

"In the words of Frederick Douglass, the greatest of all Americans, past or present, the Negro spirituals were tones, loud, long and deep, breathing the prayer and complaint of souls boiling over with the bitterest anguish. Every tone was a testimony against slavery, and a prayer to God for deliverance from chains. Thus were the Negro spirituals born." His young voice trembled. He cleared his throat. "The first of these spirituals to be sung by the chorus is 'Nobody knows the trouble I see.' " He turned and walked shakily back to his seat, his heart pounding heavily, and he heard Miss Josephine start the introduction and the chorus standing and the children's voices and the soprano voices and Willabelle Braxton and her alto voice and the tenor voices and Jenny Lee's voice and the voices that tried to be baritone and bass, and soft and clear and pretty and sometimes too loud, and the girls in white dresses and the boys in white shirts and dark trousers and the whole thing wonderful. . . .

> Nobody knows the trouble I see
> Nobody knows but Jesus
> Nobody knows the trouble I see
>  Glory Hallelu—yah
> Sometimes I'm up—sometimes I'm down
>  Yes my Lord
> Sometimes I'm almost to the ground
>  Yes my Lord.

After it ended he heard the chorus sit down and Mr. Myles took his place and Rob walked back to the center of the stage. He could hear the Amens clearly now and the Yes My Lords coming from all over the auditorium, and he felt the spirit, and all eyes were on him. He lifted his voice.

"In the evil days when slavery was in the land, the Negro people were oppressed so hard they could not stand. They wanted to be free, and they took every chance they got to run away from their shackles and their chains. With their white and black friends up north they organized an underground railroad that reached from deep in Dixie all the way to Canada and they made up religious songs about it, as they joined together their faith in God with their uncompromising determination to be free, and they sang those songs right under the noses of the slaveholders, and one of those beautiful songs is 'Swing Low Sweet Chariot.' "

> *Swing low sweet chariot—Coming for to carry me home*
> *Swing low sweet chariot—Coming for to carry me home*
> *I looked over Jordan and what did I see*
> *Coming for to carry me home*
> *A band of angels coming after me*
> *Coming for to carry me home*

The chorus had lost the shakiness in its voice. It was clear and as pretty as a Sunday church bell. And Rob was caught up by the songs and the meanings and the spirit of the people and the Amens and the sobs that he heard in the audience, and he completely forgot about his nervousness. He walked pigeon-toed to the center of the stage.

"Coming for to carry me home," he repeated. "Home was in Heaven, but Home wasn't only in Heaven. Home was up north in the Promised Land. Away from the chains of slavery—Away from the lash of the whip—Away from man's inhumanity————" Rob heard his people's voices all over the auditorium—"The Lord be praised" and "Merciful Father" and "Yes—Yes—Yes."

"And every chance a slave could get he would get on board that Glory train and—'Steal away to Jesus.' " He heard Jenny Lee's voice and heard Willabelle's, and the other children coming and going like the rolling billows of an imagined ocean, and the sweet mournful harmony made his stomach turn head over heels, and he felt the fiercest kind of love for his people————

> *My Lord he calls me*
> *He calls me by the thunder*
> *The trumpet sounds within-a my soul*

**278**

> *I ain't got long to stay here*
> *Steal away—steal away*
> *Steal away to Jesus*
> *Steal away—steal away home*
> *I ain't got long to stay here.*

After he introduced the next number and went back to his place, he fought himself hard to keep from crying, when he heard Bruh Robinson leading the chorus. *Didn't my Lord deliver Daniel? Why not every man?*

Chills went up and down Rob's back, as he walked to the center of the stage again, and heard people crying in the audience, and over on the left he saw two men holding a shouting woman.

"In the evil days of slavery men and women were sold like cattle. From an auction block. But when Abraham Lincoln signed the Proclamation of Emancipation a new song was born."

> *No more auction block for me*
> *No more—no more*
> *No more auction block for me*
> *Many thousands gone . . .*
> *No more peck of corn for me. . . .*
>
> *. . . . . . . . . . . .*
> *No more drivers lash for me . . .*
> *Many thousands gone*

And then the intermission.

Mama told Robby, "Boy, you really put it on!"

He wanted to put his arms around her and kiss her, but he wouldn't because sometimes he still wanted to be mean to her and angry with her.

Sarah Raglin said, "Willabelle Braxton, honey, you got a voice like an angel."

Richard Myles had very little to say. The children and the response of his own people to the children singing had filled him up with a spirit and strength he had never possessed before, but nevertheless he had been aware of the angry expressions in the white folks' faces, and some of them leaving all during the first half of the program, and at the intermission the way they left in groups was an ominous threat. And the Superintendent of the Board of Education seated with Mayor Livingston. He had seen these two high-ranking white gentlemen talking to Ben Blake in the back of the auditorium, and he could just imagine what they were talking about.

Mr. Blake was fuming when he came backstage. "Why wasn't I told about this in the first place?" he yelled.

"Didn't want to bother you with details," Richard Myles said calmly. "I was sure you would like it."

"Like it?" he said. "Like it! It—it—it's an insult to the citizenry of Crossroads. That's what it is!" he shouted. He lowered his voice so others wouldn't hear. "I came around often. I watched the practice regularly. I didn't see—"

Laurie Lee Youngblood came over to them. "I must give my congratulations to all three of you. Mr. Blake, this is the best Jubilee ever been anywhere. And I'm not just saying so cause Rob and Jenny Lee are in it. I know you just as proud as you can be. Everybody say it's just the best ever." She didn't wait for an answer from him.

He turned back to Richard and Josephine. "Well, anyhow," he said softly but doggedly, "just leave out the background during the next half, and let them just sing the spirituals."

"But the audience likes it the way we're doing it. They wouldn't understand," Richard said with a make-believe calm.

"Man, do you think we're playing ring games?" Ben Blake exploded. "Do you know that Mr. Johnson is out there and the Mayor of Crossroads is out there with him? I'm not playing, man. Leave it out! Leave it out!" His desperate eyes begged Richard Myles to be reasonable. "You standing there looking so smug and righteous!"

Richard Myles didn't feel any smugness or righteousness, and he wished Josephine would have something to say, at the same time afraid of what she might say. "At the beginning of the second half, I'll have to explain to the audience that you thought it wasn't proper," he said to Mr. Blake.

"Don't you dare! What are you trying to do to me, Myles?" He turned to Josephine. "You take over, Miss Rollins. You know how it's done. Just let them sing the good old spirituals."

Richard Myles felt his belly contracting and fresh perspiration all over his body. He didn't dare to look in her direction. He didn't want to hear her but he heard her say with a calm in her voice—"I like it the way it's going now, Mr. Blake. I helped to plan it this way. It's honest and it's Christian and truthful. It's just about the best thing ever happened in Crossroads."

Two Negro women walked across the stage towards them, beaming with smiles, as the bell rang for the end of the intermission, and Mr. Blake walked off mumbling to himself that he was going to have both of their jobs, and they would be sorry they ever messed with Ben Blake.

"You shouldn't have done that," he said to Josephine. "You shouldn't have implicated yourself like that."

"What do you take me for, Richard Myles?" she asked him angrily.

"You heard what he said. You may lose your job."

"So what? *You* may lose *your* job."

He looked at her sweet face which seemed to have acquired a new defiant kind of beauty, and an unreasoning happiness drowned out the doubts and fears ringing in the ears of his mind. He started to say something like I love you, Josephine. But he just said thanks.

She said, "Don't thank me."

The bell rang again to begin the second half, sharp and impatient.

The children were in their seats, the curtains parted and a quiet came gradually over the audience. Robert Youngblood recited "O Black and Unknown Bards" by James Weldon Johnson, and Carrie Lou Jackson led the chorus in—

> *Sometimes I feel like a motherless child . . .*
> *. . . A long ways from home. . . .*

There was unashamed weeping now throughout the audience and a few people shouting here and there, as the chorus sang like angels in a beautiful black Heaven. It was wonderful. It was glorious.

> *I got shoes—you got shoes*
> *All of God's chillun got shoes*
> *When you git to Heaven gonna put on your shoes*
> *Gonna walk all over God's Heaven.*
>                    and
> *Bye and bye I'm gonna lay down this heavy load. . . .*

It was getting closer and closer to the end of the program, and each time Rob would get up to introduce a number, he was lifted higher and higher and filling up to the overflowing. He tried to keep from looking out at the people in the audience. He had seen all of his friends and acquaintances out there at one time or another. He had even looked in the white section and had seen some real big people who were getting the surprise of their lives. Some of them left at the intermission. But many had remained. Even a few red-faced crackers were still in their seats. His knees weren't shaking any more and his voice had stopped going froggy on him. He became aroused by the sound of his own voice and the words that he spoke.

"And there was a great white man by the name of John Brown, an angry God-fearing man, who hated slavery and gave his life at Harpers Ferry so that black men and women might be free. White and black stood together, died side by side. And there was a little black woman named Harriet Tubman, a friend of John Brown, a woman of greatness. Harriet Tubman overpowered her whipping boss and escaped from slavery. But she wasn't satisfied with just her own freedom when she crossed over Jordan. She couldn't sit still till the South was free. She went back south, she went down in Egypt Land, time and again, and she led the He-brew children to freedom. And they called her Harriet and they called her Moses. The next selection by the Pleasant Grove School Chorus will be 'Go Down Moses.' "

He almost burst out laughing, and at the same time crying, when he heard Fat Gus's mother, Miss Lulabelle, who was seated in the front row, say—"Moses been going down too damn long now—He need to git up off his devilish knees and stand up and fight!"

> *When Israel was in Egypt Land*
> *Let my people go*
> *Oppressed so hard they could not stand*
> *Let my people go*
> *Go down Moses—way down in Egypt Land*
> *And tell old Pharaoh*
> *To let my people go.*

The last spiritual they sang turned the auditorium inside out. There was humming by the people in the audience and weeping and patting of feet and Amen-ning and a spirit so strong that it reached out toward the children in the chorus and lifted them up and carried them away toward the Evening star and the River of Jordan, and they sang as they never sang before, and it em-barrassed Rob to see the tears spill down the young teacher's face.

*O freedom*
*O freedom*
*O freedom over me*
*And before I be a slave*
*I'd be buried in my grave*
*And go home to my Lord*
*And be free.*

As Richard Myles turned toward the audience and motioned for everybody to stand, he was still worried and anxious about the crackers who left in droves and groups during the intermission and some of the evil white expressions on the faces of some who still remained, and they might start trouble any minute and they might have guns, and it would be all his fault, and he looked out towards his own people and he saw Laurie Lee Youngblood's face and Joe Youngblood's and hundreds of black and brown faces, and he remembered what Laurie Lee Youngblood had said the night he had talked with them about Jubilee Day—Crackers don't ever start anything unless they outnumber you. Whatever they start we'll sure God finish. He felt growth and understanding and an overpowering strength, as he raised his arms to his people, and Josephine Rollins played the introduction to the National Negro Anthem, and everybody sang, except some of the white folks.

*Lift every voice and sing*
*Till earth and Heaven ring,*
*Ring with the harmonies of liberty:*
*Let our rejoicing rise*
*High as the listening skies,*
*Let it resound loud as the rolling sea.*
*Sing a song full of the faith that the dark past has taught us,*
*Sing a song full of the hope that the present has brought us,*
*Facing the rising sun of our new day begun*
*Let us march on till victory is won.*

Reverend Ledbetter came forward and raised his arms and every head bowed, including most of the white folks.

"We thank you, O Heavenly Father, for this great gathering here tonight of black and white citizens, children of the Heavenly King. We hope that all of them have been caught up by the spirit of the Negro spirituals, the spirit of peace on earth, good will to all men no matter their nationality or religion. We are humbly proud, Dear Father, of our spirituals, for they are some of the most glorious songs ever sung in the name of your Son, Jesus. But we want the world to know, O Merciful Father, that we, your black sons and daughters, haven't sung any songs like we're going to sing them one of these days—In that Great-Getting-Up-Morning, when we all cross over the River of Jordan, when all men on earth will be truly brothers in the sight of God and man, O Lord. We're going to sing a song we never sang before—We're going to sing like nobody ever sang before————"

After it was over and the lights on bright all over the big auditorium, many of the people came backstage, and the congratulations, and the handshakes and the hugging and the kissing. And Mr. Blake standing there with the rest of them, not knowing what to do because it was plain to see that all the people were just crazy about the Jubilee Program.

Big Sister ran up to Mr. Myles in front of everybody and put her arms around him and kissed him on the mouth. "Mr. Myles! Mr. Myles! It was really wonderful!" And many of the grown folks laughed at her.

Everything became suddenly quiet, as two white people walked across the stage toward Richard Myles. Mrs. Cross and her daughter walked right up to the young teacher and the tall handsome yellow-haired woman held out her hand in the sight of everybody. "Magnificent, Mr. Myles. It was simply magnificent. The most moving thing I have ever experienced." Everybody heard. And the big rich white girl standing beside her mother with her pinkish face red and glowing like the first rose of summer. Mrs. Cross Junior asked for Rob Youngblood, but he was nowhere to be seen at the moment. After the white folks left, the stage became noisy with the jubilee spirit all over again, until another white person came, a long skinny ugly man with a broad pink forehead and a friendly smile and along with him a broad-shouldered blond-haired man that dragged behind the skinny one and seemed embarrassed.

"Good evening, Professor," the long skinny one said to Richard in a southern drawl that was somehow cultured and different from the average cracker. "I'm Doctor Riley and this is Dr. Crump. We're from the University. We sure did enjoy your program immensely. It was a real revelation."

"Well, thank you a lot," Richard Myles said. He couldn't think of anything else to say, he was so surprised. The skinny man shook hands warmly with Richard. The stocky one's hand was limp. They both stood there for a moment amongst all those colored folks and their faces flushed and they both looked embarrassed. Richard Myles finally said, "Well we're certainly glad you liked the program."

"Yes, indeed," Dr. Riley said, and both of them smiled and said goodnight.

Rob and Mr. Myles and Josephine Rollins left the stage together. People still stood around in the auditorium laughing and talking, a few of them white. Joe Youngblood came over and shook the teacher's hand and he and two other men stayed close to Richard as they went down the aisle toward the door. They approached a group of red-faced pecks. Let them scowl their ugly heads off, Richard thought to himself. One of them, a square-shouldered, heavy-set cracker, left the group and walked toward Richard and Rob and Joe and the rest. Richard Myles felt his own body stiffen, but he kept walking in the middle of the others, as if nothing at all was about to happen. The auditorium got suddenly quiet again.

The chunky-shouldered cracker stopped walking toward them about five feet away and stood blank-faced and waiting with his hands in his pockets, and Richard Myles and Josephine Rollins and Robby and Joe and Laurie Lee and Jenny Lee and Lee Patterson and Clyde Waters kept coming. When they came up to the cracker they stopped.

The cracker's face turned redder than it already was. He looked into Richard Myles' face. "That was a mighty nice program," he said in a husky crackerish drawl. "And I sure did enjoy it mighty mighty much."

Richard Myles said, "Thanks" when his voice came to him. The cracker turned to Joe and said How you Joe and Joe said Howdy and the cracker said—"A mighty nice program, yes indeed." And he turned and walked back to the other crackers who scowled more than ever, and one of them spat on the pretty marble floor and said "the goddamn sassy ass niggers. . . ."

Richard and the rest continued toward the door. When they got outside Joe said, "That was Oscar Jefferson. That's the one I was talking to you about. Real funny old cracker."

Before he could say anything in reply, he looked down the long wide white marble steps and he saw a gathering of mean-looking white men at the foot of the steps. They were waiting for him and he knew it. He felt his whole body suck in the cold night air and his body growing quickly from warm to hot. But the group he was with didn't hesitate a moment. Then he felt an excitement seize hold of him and relief ran through him as he saw a large group of men move past the crackers and come up to meet them—black and brown men. Just before the men reached them, Joe Youngblood stepped forward to meet them and he said a few mumbled words to a couple of them, one was Ray Morrison, and they moved in quietly and surrounded the group and went down the steps and past the crackers. Joe Youngblood whispered softly to Richard Myles, "Ain't gon be no whole lot of who-shot-John tonight, cause we got the business. If they start anything, we'll sure God finish it."

They took them to where Reverend Ledbetter's car was waiting, and Jenny Lee and Laurie Lee and Rob and Josephine and Richard and Joe piled in, Reverend Ledbetter driving. As they pulled away from the curb, Richard Myles heard another car motor warming up and he sensed the other car pulling out behind them.

Joe's deep booming voice broke into his thoughts. "Don't worry about nothing. Them the members of Frederick Douglass Lodge —five-hundred-and-six. We got the cat by his natural tail."

Richard Myles laughed as they rode through the night toward the Youngbloods' house, where that afternoon Laurie Lee had prepared sandwiches and lemonade.

## CHAPTER FIVE

AFTER THEY REACHED the Youngbloods' they sat around nibbling sandwiches and drinking lemonade and laughing and talking.

"I'm telling you," Reverend Ledbetter said. "This was one night in Crossroads, Georgia I wouldnt've missed for nothing in the world. I know the Good Lord way up there in Heaven must've smiled down on the folks of Crossroads, Georgia tonight. You shall know the truth and the truth shall set you free."

"Did you see the looks on some of them crackers' faces?" Laurie Lee said.

"Did you all hear Miss Lulabelle?" Rob asked. "When she said Moses been going down too much now, I thought I would pop."

Reverend Ledbetter laughed and laughed as Rob told them the story about Miss Lulabelle and Go Down Moses, and everybody laughed. Reverend Ledbetter said, "I heard Sister Lulabelle, son. And I heard that Sunday School word she used. But when I heard her, I knew there wouldn't be any trouble from the crackers. I knew our people were in a fighting mood. The spirit was in them. If my friend from New York had given the word, they would have marched on Atlanta where the Governor is. Our people were ready."

"If *you* had given the word," Richard Myles corrected him. But Richard was feeling good and he couldn't keep his eyes off Josephine Rollins and Jenny Lee Youngblood couldn't keep her eyes off of him.

Reverend Ledbetter said, "I saw Ben Blake backstage talking to you all. That colored citizen looked mighty scared to me."

"That man looked like an accident going somewhere to happen," Jenny Lee said.

"You better hush that sassy mouth of yours, girl," Mama said to Big Sister and laughed.

The preacher looked with fatherly affection at the young teacher from New York City. "That colored man might make trouble for you, Richard. He can be more dangerous than a barrel of these crackers."

"What was that white folks' colored man talking to you all about?" Laurie Lee asked Richard.

"Nothing much," he answered.

"Nothing much," Josephine said. "He just said he was going to have both of our jobs."

"He was just excited," Richard said, his eyes lingering on Josephine.

"He was excited all right. That Negro is as treacherous and as deadly as a rattlesnake. I know what I'm talking about."

"We'll have something to say about that, won't we, Mama?" Rob said excitedly. He was so filled up with Jubilee spirit that he loved everybody, especially his mother. "Won't we Reverend Ledbetter?" he insisted.

"Look here now," the Reverend said. "If Ben Blake said he was going to have your jobs we better get ready for him. We better go to see that gentleman bright and early Monday morning.

What you say, Sister Youngblood, and you, Brother Young-blood?"

"That's what I say," Laurie Lee said, "but why wait till Monday?"

Joe looked at Laurie and nodded his head. "What's the matter with tomorrow?"

"I think Monday'll be soon enough. And I'll preach at the back-slider in church on Sunday. He'll be there. He always comes. That'll give us time enough to get more people together. And don't forget to bring Sister Lulabelle along. She'll be time enough for Benjamin Blake." He slapped his knees and he had a good laugh.

He got up to leave and he said good-bye to everybody and he told Richard and Josephine not to worry about a thing. "They can't defeat the strength and the purpose of the Negroes in Cross-roads and the Negro church. See you tomorrow, God willing, Sister Laurie, and we'll see how we going to get this delegation together."

"All right, Reverend Ledbetter."

He looked about at the rest of them. "How does that jazz song go? Please don't talk about me when I'm gone?" Everybody laughed and said good-night.

After he had gone, and the children had gone to bed, Joe said, "It's a sin and a shame and he's such a fine man and we couldn't offer him a little bitty nip of good old cough medicine."

They laughed and Joe went into the kitchen and he came back with some Georgia corn whiskey, and some of Laurie Lee's home-made blackberry wine, and they all had a drink, and they sat around talking, and Richard Myles thought of his family in far away Brooklyn, and they seemed so very far away but in a way they didn't seem so far after all.

It was much later when Richard and Josephine left the Young-bloods. Late and dark and cold and very few street lights in the colored section. They walked along very close to each other and talking about this and that and everything else.

"This was *some* night," she said. "I never will forget it as long as I live."

"It really was some night, wasn't it?" he said. She had such a soft voice and such a sweet face and a whole lot of strength that was unsuspected.

It was cold and very dark, but somehow he felt her hand coming out through the night towards him, and his met hers and nothing was said, but in that brief moment everything was said.

He heard an automobile coming up the dusty street behind them, and all of a sudden he was conscious of the terrible stillness. There seemed to be nothing awake in the whole wide world except him and Josephine and the automobile. Just before it caught up with them, its headlights turned on full-blast and glared at them, and whoever was driving raced the motor as the car passed by them. Richard could hear his own heart beating. The automobile went a few yards past them and stopped and backed up till it came back to them. He felt Josephine's fingernails digging into his hand. He heard the strange familiar cracker voice that was alien to him, the long arrogant drawl.

"What your name, boy?" the white cracker face behind the steering wheel asked.

He had to control his temper, and if need be he had to even be as polite as Mr. Blake to these ignorant crackers, because he wanted to live, but how could he? Especially after tonight and with Josephine Rollins standing by his side.

"That's the nigger that shine shoes for old man Bakerfield," the other policeman said, and laughed.

Richard Myles could feel an awful tremble traveling the length of Josephine's body as her nails dug deeper in the flesh of his palm. "What you niggers doing on the streets this time of night?" the first cracker asked.

"What's the matter with you, boy? The cat got your tongue? Y'all ain't been going around looking for something to steal—is you?"

He saw himself being taken to a lonely spot and shot down like a dog and there was no telling what they would do to Josephine. He had to think of her too. But he simply didn't know how to be submissive.

He felt a mighty anger growing inside of him, a helpless anger. Angry with himself as well as the crackers. He should have anticipated it. On an empty quiet street and this time of night, these crackers could do anything they wanted to him and Josephine. But he couldn't Uncle-Tom for them even if his life depended on it, which it certainly did. And especially in front of Josephine Rollins, and yet he really wanted to live.

"That nigger so scared, he can't open his mouth," the second policeman said with a laugh.

"He either scared or sassy. I don't know which." The cracker shined a flashlight in Richard's eyes. "What's wrong with you, nigger?"

Josephine stepped quickly between him and the crackers in the car. "We just going home from work, Mister Officers. I take care of Judge Holliday out in the Heights and he was powerfully sick tonight. I had to work so late my husband came for me."

"Who asked your black pot to boil? You better learn how to speak when you spoken to," the first cracker told Josephine.

"Yes, sir, but I didn't want to stay so late, but he needed me so bad and he said it would be all right."

The cracker shined his flashlight in Richard Myles's face again. "What you say your name was nigger?"

"His name is Zeke Johnson and my name is Maybelle and we don't mean no harm. We just hard-working colored folks."

"He don't look like no Zeke Johnson to me," the cracker cop said. "He look like that school teacher nigger from New York City. Goddamn Jubilee singer."

"No, sir. Some folks always saying Zeke favor that school teacher. But Zeke don't know nothing about teaching no school. He ain't nothing but a hard-working colored man."

The first cracker let his flashlight play on Josephine insultingly from her head to her feet. "You better leave old man Holliday's hot chocolate alone," the second cracker policeman said. "The Judge don't stand for no foolishness."

The first cop played with his flashlight from Josephine to Myles and back to her again. "Let you niggers go this time, but you better watch your step."

Richard Myles heard the car start slowly in first gear purring like a big black cat and take off up the dusty street. They watched it till it went out of sight. They walked through the night and they didn't say anything to each other. There was nothing to say. He felt that between the two cracker policemen and Josephine, they had castrated him of his manhood.

They turned into the Terrace and walked in silence toward her house, and when they reached the door, she turned to him suddenly and she leaned against him and he could feel her hot tears spilling on to his cheeks, and he put his arms around her and felt an overwhelming passion for her even as he hated her fiercely for collaborating with the white folks.

**290**

"How could you do it?" he whispered to her angrily, knowing fully well why she had done it, and yet he took his mighty anger out on her. What the hell did she expect him to say? Thank you, darling for saving my life?

She tried to answer him but couldn't say a word.

"Why didn't you let them lock me up or shoot me or something? Anything would have been better than what happened." He didn't want to be unreasonable with her, but something inside of him drove him on.

"Don't be like that Richard," she begged him. "It was the only thing in the world I could do and you know it."

"You made the worst kind of an Uncle Tom out of me, and you didn't do such a bad job of tomming yourself."

"You don't have to be like that," she said angrily. "If you wanted to be so brave, where the hell was your voice? I didn't have my hand over your mouth." She looked briefly into his eyes and she knew she had stuck the knife deep inside of him and deliberately twisted it.

Even at that moment he wanted to take her into his arms and kiss away the conflict and confusion between them, because there wasn't really any conflict between them, but instead he turned angrily away from her and started back down the steps. "Richard!" she shouted, almost without knowing. And when he turned back toward her, she went into his arms. "Let's not fight each other, darling," she said.

He held her in his arms now, and kissing her wet lips and her sweet face and her dark eyes and tasting the hot salty tears and his own face filling up. "I don't want to fight you, Josephine. God knows I don't ever want to fight you."

Her lips reached up toward his again, and another kiss, and after she caught her breath, she said, "I never knew anything would be like this—could be like this, Richard. . . ."

He wanted to say I love you, Josephine, and leave it simply just like that, but his mouth wouldn't form the words, as he remembered Hank Saunders and how easily and truthfully the right words had fallen from his mouth that night in her room on S Street in Washington, D.C. God-knows how many years before. But Hank was no more, and Josephine was here and real and soft and firm and alive and warm and everything about her pulled him towards her.

"Josephine, darling—I—I——"

"It's getting late, Richard," she said. "You'd better be going. And do be careful, and get home just as quickly as you can."

"Josephine—I—"

"Those cracker policemen might double back on you. You can't ever tell."

He sighed. "Okay—Okay. But don't you worry. I'll hurry home all right."

She looked out into the cold black night. "I sure do wish you could spend the night here. You could sleep in the sitting room on the davenport. Mama wouldn't mind, but if anybody caught you leaving here early in the morning, that's all my neighbors on the Terrace would want. You know how it is in a town like this."

"Yes, I know," he said quietly. "I have to go home."

He took her into his arms and kissed her again, and she looked up into his troubled eyes. She said, "Darling, if you going to live down here with us any length of time, you just got to learn how to fight these crackers and stay alive. You have to learn from us down here, because we sure have had plenty of experience. You got to learn that sometimes a good run is a whole lot better than a *bad* stand."

"I really do have a lot to learn," he said, as he drew her closer into his arms again and their bodies hard up against each other and wanting each other desperately.

"I wish I could keep my arms around you all night long," she said. "But this is one of those times when a good run is in order. You better get home just as fast as you can."

They kissed again, and he stood there till she opened the front door and started inside, and he kissed her again and again. And she smiled and said, "Ever since you've been in our city, Richard Wendell Myles, you've been stirring up something." He laughed. "One sure thing, I couldn't stir it up unless it was already here to be stirred." He kissed her again and as he went down the steps, he heard Mrs. Rollins' anxious voice. "That you, Josephine? Where you been this time of night?" He smiled as he drew his topcoat more closely to his body and walked down the steps. When he reached the sidewalk, he turned and he saw that she had turned on the light in the living room, and she stood in the doorway waving good-night with a smile on her face. He walked through the cold dark night thinking about Josephine and the Jubilee Day and Reverend Ledbetter and the Youngbloods and the people in the audience at the Jubilee Program and Joe's Lodge members and people people people, including Mrs. Cross Jr. and daughter and the two white men from the University and Joe Youngblood's cracker acquaintance. And Josephine was sweet—God! She was sweet! And maybe he loved her . . . maybe she loved him. . . .

Saturday afternoon Laurie Lee went to see Reverend Ledbetter and Carrie Belle Watson and Ray Morrison and his mother, Miss Sadie, and Lulabelle Mackey and a whole host of other folks, and those she didn't see Saturday afternoon, like Sarah Raglin and others, she and Joe caught them in church Sunday morning. Most of them agreed to meet her on the schoolhouse grounds early Monday morning.

Carrie Belle said, "Maybe we ought to wait and see what happen first. Maybe ain't nothing going to happen at all." Lulabelle Mackey said, "I'll be sitting on the school steps when the sun come up."

The Youngbloods sat at the Sunday morning breakfast table. They had just finished eating. Jenny Lee was still wrestling with the hot grits and bacon. Joe Youngblood sat at the head of the table. He took his eyes from the Sunday paper for a moment. "You better hurry up and eat your grits, girl. They'll be done got cold if you don't make haste."

"Yes, sir."

He looked back at the paper. He turned to the colored page. "Let me see what the *Black Dispatch* got to say about the Jubilee program."

Jenny Lee stopped eating. Everybody's eyes were focused on Joe.

"Well I be—that no-good skunk."

"Read it, Daddy. Read it out loud."

Joe Youngblood stared at the main editorial on the Colored Page, and he cleared his throat. "The planners of Friday night's Jubilee program almost succeeded in tearing down all the good will that exists in Crossroads between the colored and the white. Crossroads, Georgia is one of the most liberal cities in the great state of Georgia. We don't pretend that things are as they should be, but we have made progress in our own plodding way . . . The Colored Page of The Morning Telegram does not argue, as some do, that our problems down here concern only us who were born and bred in the South. We say now, as ever, it concerns

**293**

the whole of the nation. But this does not mean that people can come down here from New York, and overnight know more about the problems and solutions than we who have lived with it all of our lives. We say to the young trouble-maker from New York City—Friday night's Jubilee program is not the way. It is not the way to peace and harmony and progress between the two races."

Laurie Lee Youngblood shook her head. "It's a sin and a shame."

Joe Youngblood smiled. "I keep studying about that Oscar Jefferson. Most curious cracker I ever did hear tell of. When I saw him coming toward us the other night, all I could see was a red neck cracker and I said to myself—*Now* Mr. Myles going to find out how friendly the poor pecks is. But he's one cracker I can't figure out at all—can't make head or tail of. He ain't hardly got no more education than me and he sure ain't rich—ain't got a pot to cook in."

Monday morning Mr. Blake sent for Josephine Rollins to come to his office. She came to the office and she sat in a chair in front of his desk and he came from behind his desk and stood over her and he put his fatherly arm around her shoulders.

"You have nothing to worry about," he told her.

"Nothing to worry about?"

"Nothing at all, my dear. You can have your job just as long as you want it. I was just a little upset the other night—that's all."

"I'm glad there won't be any trouble, Mr. Blake."

"I was just upset and angry. You can understand. You can understand that, can't you?"

"Yes, sir. I guess I understand."

"I know you didn't have anything to do with planning that radical program. You were just so excited the other night, the music was so beautiful and moving, you said you helped to plan the program out of some misguided sense of loyalty to Mr. Myles. Isn't that it, Josephine?" He felt her squirming underneath his touch and he took his hand from her shoulder.

"That's not exactly true, Mr. Blake. I knew about the program."

"Well, why didn't you come and tell me, my dear? After all, I am the principal and you have known me longer than you have Professor Myles, as they call him. You have known me almost as long as you have known yourself."

"I didn't think it was necessary," she answered him. He was revolting to her—the nice-nasty way he was handling her. But she wanted to be calm and not to get excited. She wanted to find out what he was up to.

"Well anyway, you don't have to worry about your job. I'm in your corner. I can tell them that with you it was a case of mistaken judgment, but that now you realize your error."

She should keep her mouth quiet, she thought, and save her own job. It wouldn't do any good for her to lose her job just because Richard Wendell Myles might be losing his. She had to be sensible. She had her weak-hearted mother to take care of. Besides, what Mr. Blake and the crackers didn't know wouldn't hurt Richard Myles and it surely wouldn't hurt the Negro people. She wouldn't be betraying Richard, if she saved her own job just by keeping her big mouth shut. But she heard herself saying, "I don't know of any error I made, Mr. Blake. I think Jubilee Day was a wonderful occasion. I haven't changed my mind since last Friday night."

"Well, what good will it do to tell the whole world about it? You're entitled to your own opinion, my dear. It's a free country, you know. Just keep quiet about it, and I can still save your job. I wish I could say the same thing for Professor Myles."

She was being a fool, she told herself angrily, a sentimental fool, and letting her emotions run away with her, as she stood up and glared at Mr. Blake. "I'm in it, Mr. Blake. If he goes I go. I'm in it to the end."

"You're a fool," he said. "A crazy little fool! You haven't even got the sense you were born with."

"Mr. Blake, that's just a matter of opinion." She walked out of the door of the principal's office.

He sat in his chair behind his desk for a moment, breathing hard and angrily, perspiration all over his broad forehead. "Goddamn little quiet easy going fool." She was his favorite teacher, and she knew she was. She always had been, and he wanted her to be his favorite in more ways than one, especially since the sudden death of his faithful wife. He had ten times more to offer her than the young upstart from New York City. He got up and went to the classroom next to his office and he sent a boy to tell Professor Myles to come to his office. Mr. Myles came about ten minutes later. "Did you send for me Mr. Blake?" he asked.

Before Myles could sit down, Mr. Blake jumped to his feet.

"Don't come in here with that innocent look, Mr. Myles. You know perfectly well why I sent for you. Ever since you've been at this school, you've been trying to tear down everything I've built up."

"Mr. Blake—" He had never seen Mr. Blake in this kind of state before, completely out of control of himself.

"I'm not going to stand for it, Mr. Myles. I can tell you right now, I am not going to stand for your tearing down the prestige and the good will I have tried so hard to build up all through the years."

"I'm not trying to tear down your prestige or good will, Mr. Blake. I don't know what you're talking about."

Mr. Blake lowered his voice, "Look at it my way, Mr. Myles. I was born and bred in Georgia. I know these white folks down here just a little bit better than you. People like Mr. Roberts of the *Telegram* and me and a few others have worked hard and almost from scratch to build the kind of good healthy relationship between colored and white that exists in Crossroads. It's one of the best in the state. While we don't do all the yelling and shouting and demanding some folks think we should do, we get things done quietly and without fanfare."

Richard listened quietly, wondering to himself what Blake and Roberts ever got done.

"We're working now on a new school for Pleasant Grove—a brick school. It was practically in the bag. But after Friday night, we don't know what to expect. The Mayor and Mr. Johnson been giving me hell all week-end long. They don't do to mess with."

"Jubilee Day won't harm our chances. I guarantee you, Mr. Blake. It can only help them. The more pressure you put on these crackers, the better you make it for the colored people."

"You don't know these southern white folks, Myles. You got to make them feel like the good white father. That's the only way you can get anything out of them."

"The Lord giveth, the Lord taketh away. Blessed be the name of the Lord. I just can't see your way, Mr. Blake. That's the whole trouble down here. We don't need to ask for tolerance anymore. We need to demand what is rightfully ours. We contributed as much to this country as anybody else. And we're never going to get anything for keeps unless we fight for it."

"You're young, Mr. Myles." The hostility had left Mr. Blake's voice completely. "I used to think the way you do, but it didn't

**296**

get me anywhere. So I changed, and now we're getting somewhere in Crossroads. We have in this town what you might call an era of good feeling. Not one single lynching in Cross County last year. . . ."

Richard Myles stared at Mr. Blake as the principal talked, realizing for the first time that the man was expounding a philosophy that he really believed in, lived by. *No lynchings in Cross County in the last year.* He thought about Rob Youngblood and Laurie Lee Youngblood and Jenny Lee and Mr. Cross's courthouse. No lynchings in Crossroads. "I think the people liked the program, Mr. Blake. The colored people. And even some of the white. How do you account for that?" No lynchings in Crossroads. He thought fiercely about the Friday night, and how those cracker gentlemen of the Law had lynched him of his spirit and manhood and dignity in front of Josephine—It was the kind of day to day lynching that every Negro in Georgia experienced. It was the worst kind of lynching.

"Don't talk to me about the average Negro," Mr. Blake said angrily. "It's just like Bill Roberts told me yesterday. Negroes are just like a basket full of crabs. You put a bunch of crabs in a basket, they'll stay in there all week long and never get out, cause the minute one of them try to climb to the top, the others will reach up and pull him back down."

Richard Myles could feel his anger rising. He didn't want to fly off the handle with Mr. Blake, because the principal was an older man than he was, and had more experience, especially in the South, and nothing was as simple as ABC. And he was the principal and had to answer directly to the powerful crackers. It was easier for Richard to be militant than it was for Benjamin Blake. "I don't know what you're talking about, Mr. Blake. I see nothing about the Jubilee program that could possibly be construed as pulling anybody down. As far as that parable about the crabs is concerned—People are a little bit different from crabs. It's not those at the bottom that pull down the others trying to get to the top. That's not the problem at all. Some of those that get half way up turn around and when they see the millions of black hands reaching up to them for a helping hand, they take baseball bats and beat them on their knuckles. But the most important question is to concentrate on the man who put you in the bottom of the basket in the first place. He's the main one seeing to it that we don't get out. They lynch us every day, Mr. Blake! They lynch us

**297**

with these jim crow schools. They lynch us with Pleasant Grove and Rockingham Quarters. They lynch our human spirit and dignity all the damn time. They lynch our children. They lynch me. They lynch you! Don't tell me about no lynchings in Crossroads." He looked at the other man's weary looking face. He stopped.

"You think you're the smartest colored man in the world, don't you, Myles?"

Myles didn't answer.

"You think you're smart, don't you, Myles?" he repeated. "You're not satisfied with creating trouble with the white folks, now you trying to put me in bad with the colored. I've been a leader in this community for eighteen years. I've been a pillar of the Negro church."

"Nobody is trying to put you in bad, Mr. Blake."

"I suppose you didn't go around over the week end plotting against me behind my back. Organizing a delegation to jump down my throat early this morning. Mrs. Youngblood and Mrs. Mackey and Rev. Ledbetter and the rest of them jumping on me before I could get in the office good. You Harlem Negroes think nobody's got any sense but you. But I tell you one thing, Myles, you won't get away with it. I worked too hard in this community to have everything torn down overnight." Mr. Blake's face was covered with perspiration. He was standing now and waving his arms and shaking his fingers. "I give you a fair warning, Richard Myles, you better walk a chalk line from now on, because I'm going to be out to get you, delegation or no delegation."

Richard sat there listening to Mr. Blake. He wanted to explain to him that he was not trying to tear anything down. He was trying to build. The only thing he was trying to tear down was the myth of white man's superiority. Mr. Blake sat down again and he stared at Richard Myles like a man in a trance.

"Excuse me, Mr. Blake, I have to get back to my class."

Mr. Blake didn't hear him.

## CHAPTER SIX

DEPRESSION WAS A funny sounding word the first time Rob heard it—strange and foreign. And the looks on people's faces when they said the word were filled with worry and fear and anger. All kind of people, colored and white. *Depression.* What did it mean? What was a depression? Rob had heard the word for a good while now—How many years? . . . *Depression.* He heard the grown folks say it with frowns in their faces. Heard them talk about it seated before the fire in the cold wintertime. Heard them mumble about it in the grocery stores and the meat markets, everywhere he went. It was a brand new word to everybody when it first came out. He was beginning to know it was an awful word. And a union had come into the town, almost unnoticed, and the union men were talking to the workingmen and signing them up, the white ones only. And everywhere things were different from what they used to be, and people were too—Poorer and angrier and meaner and harder to get along with. And yet somehow things were not altogether different—nor people.

With everybody talking about the Depression and Hard Times and this and that and the other thing, they still had the biggest Sunday School Picnic last May that anybody ever remembered, and everybody had a good time like they always had—Grown folks and children. Early in the morning, the children in their summer-best, gathered at the Negro churches all over town and rode in chartered buses through town, singing songs, to the picnic grounds down by the river. And there was running and romping and tearing and sweating all over the place till you got so hungry you could see biscuits walking on crutches. Playing baseball with a real hard ball and races and laughing and having a good time all the way round—the girls and the boys. At about one o'clock the children started moving toward the long tables under the trees where the food was spread by the Sunday Schools, and you looked for the banner that signified where your Sunday School was. The Friendship Baptist Sunday School, The Pleasant Grove Baptist, The Tabernacle Chapel AME, and all the other churches —and sometime you saw a familiar face that located your table before you saw the banner. All kinds of good food— Sandwiches, fried chicken, potato salad, ice cream and cake— and barrels of ice cold lemonade, made in the shade and stirred with a spade. After the eating and drinking, then the running and romping and tearing all over again, and courting on the sly. And the girls looked prettier than ever on Picnic Day, especially Ida Mae. The grown folks came about two o'clock in the afternoon, excepting those in charge who had been there all along with the children. They brought with them great big baskets of something-to-eat, and they spread blankets and table cloths on the green grass and food food food. At about four the grown folks went around collecting the children for the family spread, but Rob Youngblood never needed any urging. And the children sat and ate with the parents, as if they hadn't seen any food since last Picnic Day. And all during dinner and afterwards, Mama and Daddy and all the other grown folks had just as good a time with each other as the children had. They sang together like people in a real glee club.

> One of these mornings 'bout five o'clock
> This old world's gonna reel and rock
> Pharaoh's army got drowned
> O Mary doncher weep.
> O Mary doncher weep, doncher moan
> O Mary doncher weep, doncher moan
> Pharaoh's army got drowned
> O Mary doncher weep

And a whole heap of other songs. After that, Mama went from family to family, picking at the children and laughing and talking with the grown folks, especially the women. She brought Miss Lulabelle back to the Youngblood gathering to taste her fried chicken and potato salad. Later in the afternoon the men played baseball, hard baseball, and Daddy broke up the game in the fourth inning when he hit a home run all the way to the river, and there was no more ball. But even down on the Picnic grounds, you could hear grown folks talking about the Depression, making up serious jokes about it and laughing about it. But the Depression didn't put any damper on the Picnic, even though it was there before Picnic Day and during the Picnic, and after the Picnic it didn't go anywhere.

And the harder the times got the meaner the crackers, but not all of them. Just before school closed around the last of May, Dr. Riley, who taught in the Medical School at the white University, invited Mr. Myles to bring the chorus out to the University, and they went and they sang before a nice size audience of students and teachers, and Rob was the narrator and they taught those educated crackers a thing or two about Negro History. And everybody was nervous at first but after awhile everybody relaxed except a few mean-faced crackers and it was truly wonderful. In the middle of August, all of the chorus that could be rounded up went in a truck all the way to Glenville, Georgia one Sunday with Miss Josephine Rollins in charge and gave their program at a big revival meeting, and there was big eating everywhere at the Big Meeting, and barbecue cooked over a pit all night long and fried chicken and potato salad, and preaching and shouting and old-time religion and quite a few corn-lickered breaths and a wonderful feeling all over the place. And now the summer was slipping quietly away, making way for the fall, but the Depression was here last summer and the summer before and would be here when the next one rolled around. And Rob Youngblood hated the union, didn't care what Mr. Myles said about the subject, because they wouldn't let his Daddy and Ray Morrison and other working men like them join. It was a cracker union, and he would tell Mr. Myles what to do with his union when the teacher came back from New York City at school-opening-time.

That fall the cracker union went on strike, and after the first week Cross Mills put a great big ad in the *Daily Telegram* blaming the strike on the radical Yankee union and the misguided workers and calling on all the able-bodied colored workers to remain loyal and stand beside their tested friend, George Cross Jr. The company was doing the best it could for the workers and Hard Times were everywhere, and with so many people out of work all over the nation, this irresponsible trouble-making union had the nerve to call a strike and make more men idle. All the unemployed could come and get work, and Cross Mills, Incorporated would not discriminate. Anybody who wanted a job could certainly have one, white or colored. And especially the colored who were not allowed to be members of the union anyhow.

It was the strangest sight ever seen in Crossroads. White men gathered near the plant gates all over town carrying signs up over their heads; silent, angry, red-cheeked white men, some of them shouting and cussing. And colored men walking silently past them every morning and every evening, going in and out of the gates, and company trucks going all over the outlying countryside and bringing men into town to work at the mills, most of them colored. And white men shouted at them and cussed at them and called them scabs and black bastards and strike-breakers and darkies and everything else but children of God. The colored men got mean and nervous, and it looked like all hell might break

**301**

loose any day any hour any minute. Joe and Rob went and talked to Mr. Myles about it, and they called a meeting of all the colored workmen they could round up and they asked Mr. Myles and Rev. Ledbetter to come to the meeting.

They got together in the meeting hall of Frederick Douglass Lodge Number 506, over two hundred colored men, and it was hard to keep order, and they voted to let Reverend Ledbetter chair the meeting and let Joe Youngblood be the Sergeant-at-arms. They talked and argued and a couple of times came near to fighting till it got very late. Joe Youngblood said there wasn't anything that could be done but keep going to work. Don't anybody look for no trouble, but if trouble comes, just close ranks and stick together. Don't listen to the cracker calling you names. Don't bother the cracker unless he bothers you. Ray Morrison said To hell with the crackers. If they start anything we'll finish it. Bibb Mackey, Gus's pa, with the hunger still lingering in his face from being so long out of work, said Just let one of them try to take his job from him, he'd die and go to Heaven before he'd stand for it. Some of the brothers said Amen, and one of the brothers said Old Bibb Mackey sure is taking a heap for granted—going to Heaven —That devil gon bust hell half in two. Some of the men laughed. Rev. Ledbetter told them strikebreaking was an evil thing. It pitted working man against working man, and God was against it. It always leads to war and violence which the Prince of Peace was also against. "But there doesn't seem to be any choice. The white working man wouldn't let you join up with him, the boss man offers work and pay for your work, ain't either one of them any friends of ours, so the only thing you can do is to make the most of a bad situation. Work while you can and try to keep the peace as long as you can. God bless us all." Richard Myles told them he agreed with Rev. Ledbetter in just about everything he said and most of what the others had said. "But I think we should also have in mind what will happen after the strike. Many of us will be laid off and the white will get their jobs back again with the same conditions they had before and nobody will win but George Cross Jr." One brother interrupted him yelling, "How you know so much about it?" Bibb Mackey jumped up and yelled and waved his arms like he was shouting in church. "I don't care if we get laid off. Work now! Work while we can! Let them crackers stay out on strike till hell freezes over! A colored man be a fool not to take this opportunity to put some clothes on his children's back.

Yeah be a strikebreaker. Break one of these no-good pecker-wood's head he mess with me and try to keep me from working!"

After the meeting broke up Joe and Richard Myles and Rob and Rev. Ledbetter and a few others stood around outside of the hall, and Prince Robinson, Bruh Robinson's father, walked up to them. "What you think we ought to do, Professor?" And they stood there talking till it was way past midnight, and at first none of them agreed with Richard, not even Rob or Joe or Rev. Led-better. But he argued with them, one man called him an Uncle Tom, but he told them that the same thing had happened all over the country, Negroes being used as scabs and strikebreakers and laid off soon as the dirty work was over. And crackers and Ne-groes hating each other more than ever before. And Hack Dawson said That was all right, let the white trash hate us. "They ain't putting no bread in our mouths." But before they parted they agreed that it wouldn't hurt for a few of them to go around to the union and sound them out and see if something couldn't be worked out, like joining up with them now and remaining in the union afterwards.

The following morning they went to the union headquarters strictly on the faith they had in Richard Myles. When they walked into the office everything stopped. The crackers looked at them as if they were ghosts, anger and meanness and whitefolks' arro-gance spilling out of their reddish white faces. The Negroes with a quiet nervous dignity, a couple of them confused and frightened. "Well, what you boys want?" one great big brown-haired cracker said. The room was thick with fear and hatred.

The Negroes didn't say anything at first. They glanced at Rich-ard and Rev. Ledbetter. And finally Rev. Ledbetter spoke and then Richard Myles and told the white union folks what was on their mind. Oscar Jefferson said it made real sense and he was all for it. "Ain't no way in the world it can do any harm." And a couple of other crackers nodded their heads. But one of them, a half-pint four-eyed cracker, said that he wouldn't walk in the picket line with no nigger even if his mother's life depended on it. And another one got up and pulled out his gun and pointed it at them. "If you niggers don't git outa here talking about some kinda social equality, I'm gonna lose my goddamn temper."

And later outside Rev. Ledbetter said, "Well my good brothers it's a sad fact, but I'm mighty afraid it's the gospel truth. The South isn't ready for the union movement, just like they ain't ready for the Good Lord Jesus." And the other men shook their heads. And Richard Myles said heatedly, "It isn't the whole South that's not ready. The colored are ready. It's the damn poor ignorant crackers that're dragging their feet. Excuse me, Reverend." Reverend Ledbetter shook his head.

Early one Tuesday morning about a week later, Joe and Ray and Bibb Mackey and Hack Dawson and a couple of other Negroes were approaching the main gate on their way to work when they were hailed by a couple of crackers. "Hey, you boys, clear outa there. Ain' no working today." But Joe and the other colored men closed in on each other and kept walking silently, looking straight ahead. "Hey, Boys! Can'tchoo hear? There's a strike going on—No working today." Joe felt sweat draining from all over his body, but like deaf men, hearing nothing, they marched toward the gate. By this time there were more white men—five—six—seven and the numbers increasing. They headed Joe and his buddies off and stood in the way and kept them from moving forward.

"Say, lissen, you boys. Donchoo know there's a strike going on?"

Joe bit his lip. "Colored men not striking," he said.

"Oh yeah you is—from this minute on."

Ray Morrison said, "Hell, less go to work." And he moved forward.

A great big cracker gave Joe a shove. "You big black sonofabitch!" And Joe hit the cracker with all his might and drove him to his knees. Ray kicked him viciously under the chin. Teeth sprinkled the dirt like dingy pearls. The other crackers held back momentarily, and then somebody yelled "Niggers! Niggers! Niggers!" And other striking crackers came on the run. Joe and Ray and a couple of the others fought their way all the way to the gate, and in the nightmare of sticks and clubs crashing about his head and shoulders, and drawing his blood in two or three places, he saw the face or maybe the image of Oscar Jefferson somewhere near the gate and he heard a cracker yell—Come on, Oscar! What's the matter with you? Let's kill these niggers! And he saw Oscar briefly, backing away and shaking his angry head, and Joe's white friend turned and ran away from the gate across the wide yard into the early fall morning where day was breaking fast and furious. Joe and his buddies were greatly outnumbered by now and the crackers were really closing in and a couple of his buddies had turned and fled. Joe saw a cracker lunge toward him with a dagger-like knife, and he thought it was over, but he stepped quickly aside with a fast hip motion, and he caught the cracker with all his might solidly against his exposed chin and he heard something crack, but they kept closing in and there is no telling what would have happened to the colored if the police had not come in two carloads and broken it up. Joe Youngblood thought it was the strangest thing how the cops seemed to take the colored men's side. And from that morning on the police were there to see that the colored men got in and out of the gates all right.


## CHAPTER SEVEN

HE STOOD LOOKING down into her great big beautiful eyes. He switched their school books from one arm to the other. It was still fall and early November and summer had lingered till the very last minute and leaves turning golden brown and falling softly and being swept up in piles in the backyards and front yards and the sharp scorchy smell of the golden leaves burning, and swirls of gray smoke reaching towards the sky, burning the summertime out of their souls and out of their systems. They were in front of her house and she looked up into his serious face and away again. They would graduate next June, because Pleasant Grove School didn't go any further than the tenth grade. The white schools went the full twelve years like everybody knew schools were supposed to go.

"I came by here yesterday," he tried to say casually, "and saw Miss Sarah sitting on the front porch. She was burning leaves right there in the front yard."

Ida Mae smiled sweetly, the way she had a way of smiling, her big eyes moving every which a way. "I know," she answered. "Mama told me when I got home."

"Humph," he said. "I know where you were alright. I know where you were. But I didn't tell Miss Sarah where you were."

"It wasn't none of your business to tell my mother."

"You don't have to act like that," he said. "I know you came home in Biff Roberts' old automobile."

"It ain't old," she told him, smiling with her eyes, in a way that made him sick in the stomach. "It's a spank brand new one, if anybody wants to know."

"He's telling everybody at school that he didn't take you straight home. Took you for a ride out the Cross County Road."

"He sure has got a great big pretty car, and he knows how to drive it, I mean to tell you."

"It doesn't belong to him."

"He might not've paid the money for it, but his daddy lets him use it any time he gets ready."

"He's telling everybody you're not my girl anymore, 'cause he's done taken you clean away from me."

"Ain't neither one of you my daddy. He's been dead ever since I can remember. I'm not anybody's girl but Mrs. Sarah Mae Raglin's."

He felt an awful taste in his mouth. How could she smile at him like that when she knew she was being mean to him. She was just a heartless woman. That's all there was to it. "If that's the way you feel about it," he said, "I don't care if you went all the way to Macon and back with him. If you so crazy about automobiles." He handed her her books.

"Humph," she said, as she took the books from him. "I hate that about you. I know you don't care. Just as long as you can run all the way out to that old white gal at the Crosses. That's all you studying about. And I know all about Willabelle Braxton too. If you think you the only pebble on the beach, you got another thought coming, Mr. Robert Youngblood."

Her big eyes were wide and full of trouble, just as he remembered them the day she left him on the school grounds the day he ran away from home how many months or years ago, and he wanted to say to her—be my girl friend—be my sweetheart—don't ride in Biff Roberts' car again—of all people Biff Roberts—But he didn't know how to say what he wanted to say. He heard himself say, "If that's the way you feel about it, you can ride all the way to New York City." He wanted her to say, "I love you, Rob Youngblood, riding or walking. I don't care about a brand new Buick."

But she didn't know how to say that either. She made herself give him a don't-care smile that made his stomach turn-head-over-heels. "I hate that about you," she repeated. "You don't have to tell me how far I can ride. Mr. William Roberts says any time I want to take a ride all I got to do is whistle. So put that in your little old pipe and smoke it." She turned and strutted haughtily away from him toward the front porch, leaving him with an ache in the middle of him, and at that moment he wished he had never seen her ever in his life, and he swore to himself that he would make her sorry for what she had done to him. He walked toward the bus stop, and he would be a woman-hater, that's what he would be, for the rest of his life, but how could he hate them when he loved them so much? He would make himself a woman-hater. That's all there was to it.

He sat on the bus. Mr. Myles had come south last fall with a V-8 Ford, and he would get Mr. Myles to teach him to drive, and he would use the car sometimes and take any girl he wanted to for a ride. Mr. Myles would let him use his car. He would show Ida Mae—He had been staying away from Rockingham Quarters, because he didn't want to get tangled up with Willabelle Braxton. He had stayed out of Betty Jane's way every afternoon out at The Crosses for various reasons, but one of them was that he wanted to be a one-woman man, and Ida Mae was the woman . . . Now, in a streak of self-righteousness, he tried to make himself believe that this had been the main and the only reason, as he sat on the back of the white folks' bus.

When he reached the Cross estate the sun had completely disappeared and the world had changed suddenly from day-time into a night-like darkness. He hurriedly swept the big backyard, raking up the leaves. He had a helpless feeling of leaves falling everywhere and raking leaves and burning leaves and leaves still falling. A piece of rain hit him on the face. He really had to hurry. When he finished raking the leaves into piles, he set them afire and he stood there totally involved with the breathing deeply of the sharp scorchy odor which he always loved to smell. He knew he was being watched by someone behind one of those big windows in the house, and he was angry with Ida Mae and he didn't care how many times she went riding with Biff, and he really had to hurry, because the sky was dark and the rain was coming. He heard the rain coming, and he looked across the vast green estate and he saw the rain coming from way over yonder by the western gate like a swarm of big bumble bees. He went under the house and he got the logs for the fire in the big living room, working furiously, and he chopped up some kindling and he went upstairs to the big living room and he made the fire. He hadn't seen Betty Jane. He hoped he wouldn't see her and she wouldn't see him.

He had finished his work, and, as he walked down the back

stairs, he heard the rain falling by the bucket-fulls, as if it would beat the top of the house in, and it was putting out all the fires in all of the yards in Crossroads where the brown golden leaves were burning, and it was Friday and pay day for him and no school tomorrow, and he wouldn't be seeing Ida Mae Raglin. Every Friday, he ordinarily went and waited in the kitchen for Miss Ruby to bring him his money for the week, but his mind was so taken up with girls, and Ida Mae Raglin and Betty Jane Cross and Willabelle Braxton and women women women, that he forgot about it being Friday and pay day, and he didn't stop on the first floor but he continued down into the basement and stood underneath the back porch watching the downpour and smelling the rain and the greenness and the freshness and the wetness of the rain seeping into his being, and goddamn the women, excepting his mother.

"Hello, Rob."

He turned quickly, but he knew without turning that she would be staring at him and smiling friendly at him and looking him up and down as if he belonged to her. "Hello, back at you," he said with a don't-care attitude that had nothing in common with the sudden tension that had grabbed hold of him.

She walked toward him and he wanted to turn and run out into the pouring down rain away from her, but he wasn't scared of her, he argued with himself.

She stood inches away from him and he was conscious against his will of her being a girl and him being a boy, a woman and a man. "You sure have grown, Rob Youngblood. I do declare you have. I remember when you first came to work for us, I was bigger than you were, but now you done passed me by. I declare I believe you can eat off the top of my head." She gazed up into his tightened face, and her blue eyes smiled at him. "It sure is raining hard, isn't it?"

"That's the weatherman's business," Rob grumbled.

"I reckon it's the Good Lord's business." She laughed. She was trying to joke with him about him and his people, but he didn't appreciate it and he hated her for it.

"I swear," she said, "you the most serious boy, I ever did see. You don't ever smile about nothing. Don't you know anything funny?"

"Ain't nothing funny between white folks and colored," he told her. "I don't see a damn thing to laugh about between me and you." It felt good swearing at her like that, but it really wasn't a very good feeling.

Her blue eyes were worried and her white face frowned up at him, and he wished she wouldn't look him so straight in the face. "I'm not like the rest of them, Rob. I don't think like the rest of them. I don't feel like them."

He wanted to put her straight once and for all. He wanted to hurt her feelings good-fashion. "As far as I'm concerned, a cracker is a cracker. And a Georgia cracker at that," he threw in for good measure.

"I'm not a cracker," she protested angrily. "I'm not a cracker and you know it!"

"I don't know no such howdy do." He threw his mannish sarcasm at her like spitting into the whiteness of her face. "You are a cracker—Your mother and your daddy are crackers and their mothers and fathers before them come from whole line of crackers." He was frightened but somehow he received an awesome kind of pleasure from talking to her like this.

He looked at her and he saw a small tear being washed out of one of her eyes and rolling down her cheek. White folks really were something. One minute she wanted him to laugh for her benefit, and now she was trying to make him break down into tears.

"I'm not like the rest of them. I don't feel like they do," she repeated.

"You mighty right you ain't like the rest of them." He laughed at her. "You Miss Ann—Mister Charlie's pride and joy—You belong to the biggest cracker of them all." He looked at her and he forgot about the rain and the time and the place and the danger involved, and he laughed and he laughed and he threw his scornful laughter all over the place. And then he really heard footsteps this time coming clearly down the back stairs and cutting off his laughter and wiping the arrogant smile from his face.

Betty Jane turned quickly and ran back through the corridor of the basement toward the front stairway, and he stood there frozen, having no place to run except out into the rain which was coming down heavier than ever before. The reality of the footsteps moved him into action. He hated running away even now, and he wanted to stand and face whatever was coming. He hadn't done anything wrong, but he found his body taking him quickly out into the downpour—running like crazy through the rain toward the servants' quarters, and hating white folks and everything white. He ran to the room in the rear of the house on the first floor where he always went when he had to wait any length of time for Mr. Jim Bradford, the colored chauffeur to take him home when the weather was bad. He closed the door quickly behind him, his breath coming to him fast and furious. He threw himself, wetness and all, onto Mr. Jim Bradford's bed, and he puffed and he blew, and the dampness cut through his limbs and his body like a sharp angry knife. He felt his anger and his fright and his wetness merging inside of him, and he was a grown man and he had told off Missy Ann and he wasn't going to cry. He wasn't going to cry—He wasn't going to cry! But the anger and the fear and the wetness and the cold and the heat inside of him coming together building building and it was just too big and it was just too powerful and filling up his shoulders and his face and pushing out of his eyes and no matter how big he was or how grown, he couldn't help from crying.

He heard footsteps coming down the hall of the servants' quarters. He jumped up quickly and wiped his face. His wet limber body grown suddenly rigid. Wasn't anything to be afraid of. It was Mr. Jim Bradford or another one of the servants. The footsteps came to the door and stopped and he stopped breathing. And knocking on the door and "Rob! Rob!"

His heart stopped beating at first, but he breathed heavily and a great relief ran the length of his body when he recognized the voice. The door opened and she came in and closed it behind her. She stood there wet and sticky and pale and she looked like the rain had washed all the redness and pink from her face leaving her so white that she didn't seem to have any color at all. She walked toward him water dripping from her raincoat all over the place. He stood watching her, transfixed. When he had heard her voice outside, he had thought for a frantic split second that it was her mother's voice, and when he had seen it was she, he had been almost glad to see her, as if she were a long lost friend, but it came to him now like a shock that he was in a room alone with a white woman and not just any old white woman but Mr. Cross's girl-child, and she was the kind they really lynched you about. "What the hell do you want in here?" he asked her. "Get away from me!"

She pulled off her raincoat and threw it on a chair. She ran her hand through her wet straggly yellowish hair and shook the water from it. "Rob—Rob Youngblood, why do you hate me?"

"What you think? You expect me to love you?" He was afraid of being in a room alone with her and his body was chilled to the bone from the wetness and he wanted to take off his clothes and wrap himself up in the cover of Mr. Jim Bradford's bed, and he wished she would get out of the room and leave him alone. "I tell you one thing," he said, "the further you stay away from me the better I like you."

"But why? Why?"

"Why—" he repeated. "Why—" he mimicked. "Because you're white—Goddammit—that's why!"

She came toward him as if she didn't hear him. She unbuttoned his jacket. "You're just as soaking wet as you can be, Rob Youngblood. You're going to catch your death, you're not careful." She pulled his jacket off him and she felt his shirt and she unbuttoned it, talking as she worked. "Ruby told Pauline to tell you to stay for supper, because she would be late coming from town and when she did get back she would pay you off and get Jim to drive you all the way home." She pulled off his shirt as if it were the most natural thing in the world, and he felt his body grow hot underneath her touch.

She gazed at him as he stood before her naked to the waist almost trembling with fear, hating her all the more because of his fear and hating himself for being afraid.

"There's nothing to be afraid of, Rob."

She took a blanket from Mr. Jim's bed and she put it around his shoulders and he felt a warmth go all the way through him— And what if Ida Mae saw him now, and what would Mama or Daddy think and Big Sister too—To hell with Ida Mae and Biff Roberts and his great big Buick—He stood watching her as she wiped the dampness out of her yellow hair and she brushed it back with Mr. Jim's brush, and she came toward him and she looked up at him and she smiled a sad smile and she didn't look arrogant to Rob anymore.

"You feel better now, Mr. Youngblood?" She reached up and pulled the blanket closer around his shoulders, and he smelled the soft scent of her hair mixed with the dampness and the sharp sweetish odor of her warm body, and the worried look in her beautiful eyes and the nearness of her body and her breast pushing heavily against her blouse, and he was a boy growing swiftly into manhood and she was a girl reaching desperately toward womanhood, and at that moment it didn't matter that he told himself he hated her or that she was trying to get him in trouble, or that they were out at the Crosses in the heart of Georgia, or

**3 1 1**

that he was black and she was white and Mr. Charlie's daughter —She was a girl and he was a boy, and that was all that mattered at the moment—He reached out toward her and took her into his arms and he kissed her awkwardly and clumsily on her wet pink lips and he felt her body tremble and her knees buckled like something had hit her and both of them almost fell to the floor— Even at that late moment he heard a warning voice like a white danger signal—but it was all too late—with his manhood asserting itself all over his body, and his inexperienced hand wandering and blundering and discovering new wonders and Rob! Rob! Rob! a smothered gasp, and her arms tightening around his neck, as the door to Mr. Jim Bradford's room opened noisily, bringing them quickly back to this world.

He jumped away from Betty Jane and stood looking into the horrified eyes of Mrs. Cross Jr. Her hair was wet and dripping and her eyes had the look of a woman gone crazy, as she stared first at him and then at her daughter. She tried to make words with her mouth but her tongue was tied. Rob was so frightened he was unable to move. He could feel the lyncher's rope around his neck choking off his life. He swallowed the hard bitter spittle in his mouth.

"You—you—you—" Ruby Cross muttered and she reached out quickly and seized a poker from the fireplace and she hit at him wildly glancing his shoulder.

"Ruby! Ruby!" he heard Betty Jane cry out, as he dashed past her mother and ran down the hall and out into the cold driving rain. And he ran and he ran with the cold rain lashing his hot frightened body, ran past the big white house and up the long driveway that led to the gate through a funnel of giant trees and wet leaves falling heavily and the Good Lord's rain pouring down on him harder than ever before—

## CHAPTER EIGHT

IT WAS LIKE the passing of a hundred years before he reached the front gate in the pouring-down wind-driven rain that seemed to fall harder by the minute. He threw his weight against the big iron gate to push it open, but the gate wouldn't budge. He tried and he tried, and he puffed and he grunted and he cursed out loud, with the rain falling down striking him in the face and blinding him and the tears that flowed from an anger he could do nothing about. There was the sudden realization that the gate was locked!

He looked up through the rain at the tall wide white gate and he cursed out loud again. He reached out and his hands gripped the gate and he began to climb. Up he went, his feet were like hands feeling around desperately for places to grab a hold on the wet slippery iron. At the same time he wanted to get over the fence as quickly as possible. He felt unprotected, like standing out in the open with ten thousand crackers pointing rifles at his back. When he was about three quarters of the way up the ten-feet high fence, his foot slipped and he thought he was gone and his other foot slipped. He hung desperately by his hands. He got himself together and somehow he managed to get over the top and when he started to go down the other side, he said to hell with it, and he closed his eyes and jumped and he landed in muddy water up to his ankles and it spattered all over him and he cursed again. He got up and started walking.

Through the sound of the rain his sharp frightened senses picked up the evil scary noise of a white man's car coming up the road behind him, and he saw the beam from the headlights break the darkness in front of him, and his fear grabbed hold of him suddenly and violently, and he threw his numb body into the ditch on the side of the highway, with ice water in it up to his waist, and he almost drowned, but he righted himself somehow, and he kneeled in the water up to his eyes. He watched the car pass him by without stopping. He got out of the ditch and continued to walk up the highway again. He was cold and wet and sick and angry, and he felt like crying, and he was not a man, but a boy after all, and he didn't want to die, Lord have mercy, and he wasn't to blame any more than Betty Jane was. She was more to blame. She was more to blame, but it was his own damn fault, because Fat Gus had warned him plenty of times. He was glad for the rain because it was raining so hard nobody could see him, he told himself. He walked through the white folks' section and he passed by Ida Mae's house and he wanted to stop, because he knew that they would help him, because she was his girl and he was her feller, and Ben was his buddy and Mrs. Sarah was one of Mama's best friends. He saw a light in the front of the house and he stood in the rain staring at the house, but he wouldn't go in, because how could he explain to Ida Mae what had happened? And besides she wasn't his girl anymore. He avoided the streets and he walked through all of the alleys that came between Ida Mae's house and his. But after a while there were no more alleys and three long wide muddy blocks of street stood between him and his house where his family was and the fire in the fireplace and the food on the table, and he felt a sudden sense of comfort as if his home had arms and had reached out toward him and had spoken to him with his mother's voice and his father's voice and even Jenny Lee's and said nothing could harm him. If he could just get home—just get home. The rain had slacked up a little bit now, and maybe it would stop. When he was about a block and a half away from home the thought came to him that maybe home wasn't such a safe place to go to. That would probably be the first place they would look—It *would* be the first place! He stopped walking. He wanted to see Mama and Daddy and Jenny Lee too, and he might not ever get to see them again, if these crackers caught up with him. And he was wet and cold and his home was just a little bit over yonder and he wanted his mother. Besides, he didn't think they had gotten to his house yet. And in spite of everything he wanted to go home. He walked up muddy First Avenue for a block and he turned right on Macon Street and he walked a block and then almost to the other end of the second block. He walked softly into somebody's yard, he didn't remember whose, and around the side of the house and he jumped the back fence, and he crossed backyards and jumped fences till he got to his house. He stood in Mrs. Drafton's backyard and he stared through a hole in the fence into his own yard and he looked all over it but he couldn't see anybody. He climbed over the fence into his yard, and he walked across the yard toward the back door, his heart in his mouth, expecting anything and everything. But if he could get across that yard and into that back door without anything happening he would be home!

When Rob had broken past Mrs. Cross Junior and had run down the hall of the servants' quarters, she had run after him as far as the door, and she had watched him run through the blinding rain. She had thrown the poker in her hand after him. She turned and ran back to the room where her daughter was. Betty Jane lying full-length on Jim Bradford's bed, her face buried and crying into the sheet. Mrs. Cross Junior ran out in the hall to the telephone to call the police. She picked up the receiver and put it back down again. She stood there for a dizzy moment, her head in a whirl.

She came back into the room and walked over to the bed and she took the girl and shook her angrily.

"So that's what it was! So that's what it was all the damn time! Sixteen years old and in bed with a boy—and a nigger at that!"

Betty Jane sat up and looked at her mother. She had never seen Ruby like this before, and she was terribly frightened and she thought she must have committed the most evil sin in the world, but how could it be sinful? The tears spilled down her pale cheeks and her heart jumped as if it would leap right through her mouth. "I'm sorry, Ruby. I'm sorry! Sorry!"

"Sorry? Is that the best you can do? Is that all you can say?" Ruby had gone temporarily crazy. Whack! Whack! She slapped Betty Jane on the side of her face and the girl's yellow head went this way and that. "Your father said you were getting too damn grown. How long has this been going on? How long? How long?"

"It was the first time, Ruby," Betty Jane sobbed, shaking her head from side to side. "It was the first time, I declare before the Lord!" Ruby slapped her again and again, but she could hardly feel the blows, because she felt such an overwhelming fright, mixed up with a feeling of unforgivable guilt and shame. If she could undo what had been done, she wouldn't care how many times her mother slapped her, or how hard.

"You hot pants hussy! You hot pants hussy! How long has this been going on? Your father knew what he was talking about. Do you realize what you have done?" She shook Betty Jane till she was limp as a dish rag. She looked at Betty Jane, her daughter, and so much like her, and the pitiful frightened look on her face, and she wanted to beat her up so badly that she never would have anything to do with a man again as long as she lived. But somehow her senses came gradually back to her and fragment of thoughts. . . .

Call the police—call the police—get George on the phone. "My baby! My baby! It's all my fault—all my fault!" All the time she was trying to figure which way to turn, her head in a whirl. She tried to think calmly. "Your father was right all the time—right all the time, but I just couldn't see it." She had to be calm. She was Mrs. Cross Junior and her head was still going around and around, but she had to remember she was Mrs. Cross Junior and she had to be calm—think calmly. But how could she? It was her daughter, not anybody else's daughter—My daughter wouldn't consort willingly with that nigger—She couldn't have done it!—He had been trying to rape her. And this might not even be the first time! Betty Jane might even be pregnant with a black nigger child already! She shook her head crazily. Massaging Betty Jane's back and shoulders now, almost without knowing, and the girl moving gratefully under her touch. "He was going to rape my baby and he's going to pay for it—trying to rape my baby and he's going to pay for it!" Betty Jane heard Ruby from far away say the word *Rape,* and again she heard the word coming closer and closer, digging its way into her consciousness— *Rape! Rape! Rape!*

Ruby's head was clearing and things were gradually coming into focus. *Rape! Rape!* Ruby herself despised the word. When she got through with Robby Youngblood he wouldn't try to rape another. She would tell George that he was right about niggers. She would tell everybody. She would make her peace with the Southern Tradition, because now she understood everything clearly. But even as she told herself, she knew it would not be so easy. She didn't dare tell George. Their relationship was already precarious. He would blame her and kick her outdoors, and she would be disgraced, and what would she do and where would she go? She couldn't tell George—not now—not now—She didn't dare tell the police either, because if she did, the whole Cross family would be disgraced. White trash could afford to be disgraced like this, didn't have anything to lose in the first place, but they were the Crosses, the almighty Crosses.

She picked up the girl's raincoat and put it around her. "Let's go to the house, honey." The girl went like a person sleep-walking. They ran and stumbled through the rain to the house, and she took Betty Jane quietly up the back stairs. She bathed Betty Jane from her head to her feet. "He was trying to rape you—— trying to rape you!" . . . . "No, Ruby no!" She put a nightgown on her and put her to bed.

"Don't say anything to anybody about it, darling. Don't ever say anything. I'll get Lola to bring your dinner to you, if you feel like eating. We'll tell everybody you have a little headache."

And Betty Jane lay there thinking fiercely about her and Rob out in Jim Bradford's room, and it had been bad and evil and sinful and she was ashamed. But it had been so good and sweet and almost Holy, how could it be bad? She felt an awful warm feeling running all through her, and she thought it really and truly must be love. She started saying aloud to herself, "Rob wouldn't rape me. Rob wouldn't rape me!" She was afraid again and she started to cry and she needed Ruby, but she couldn't have Ruby, because she just couldn't say Rob tried to rape her. She just couldn't say it. And she knew now that Ruby, like Daddy, was nothing but a cracker, and she hated Daddy and she hated the crackers, and she hated both of them, Ruby and Daddy, "And I love Rob Youngblood!" she heard herself telling herself over and over.

When Ruby went downstairs she took some aspirins for the pain that pounded inside of her head. She didn't know which way to turn. She wished she were a thousand miles from Georgia and the goddamn Crosses and had never seen or heard of the South. She forgot to take food up to Betty Jane. She put on a coat and took the black Packard that Jim Bradford usually drove, and she drove toward town through the wind-blown rain. She had no idea where she was going.

It seemed like a mile across his backyard, his ears picking up all of the backyard noises, and ready for the sound of shots ringing out. His whole body warm and tense with fear, and cold and wet. It seemed like a million miles across his yard, but he finally made it. He opened the back door and walked in the kitchen, and before he could close the door behind him, he heard his mother's voice. Mama! Mama! Mama! He had closed the back door and had almost walked across the kitchen, when he recognized the other voice as Mrs. Cross Junior's. What was she saying? He stopped dead still and he swallowed the warm stew-beefish smell of the kitchen. The middle of his stomach quivered like gelatin. A trail of water followed him as he tiptoed over to the door, his heart beating heavily against his chest. The door opened suddenly in front of him, and before he could move everybody had seen him.

"Robby! Rob!" Mama's voice. For a split second he expected white hands to reach out and grab him from all sides. He backed away. Where were the rest of them? Why were there only Mama and Daddy and Jenny Lee and Mrs. Cross Jr. in the room?

"Ain't no need to run, son," his Daddy said. "You in your own house."

**317**

"See," Mrs. Cross Junior shouted, "he was about to run away. That should prove to you how guilty he is."

"Doesn't prove anything," Mama said. "Proves that he's smart and knows what kind of justice to expect from you white folks. Ain't nothing you can say to make me believe my boy raped your daughter." She looked in the kitchen at her frightened boy. "Close the door, son, and take off them wet things and get a towel and dry yourself good and put on something dry. Get yourself something to eat."

"I didn't rape nobody, Mama." It was the first time he had spoken.

"I know you didn't, son. Don't you worry."

"You mean to deny that I caught you with my daughter in the servants' quarters?" Mrs. Cross looked at Rob as if he were a mad dog, and a red hot hate was in her angry blue eyes.

"I say I didn't rape her. That's what I said." His whole body trembled from fear and cold and wetness.

"Close the door, Rob, and get yourself dry," Mama said.

Mama and the white lady stood facing each other. The lady was a whole head taller than Mama. Big Sister stood near the door to the kitchen. Joe was standing near the fireplace. He said, "Excuse me," softly and walked across the room and into the kitchen where their boy was, closing the door behind him.

Laurie Lee looked the white woman up and down. She became before Laurie Lee like any old dried-up straggly-haired ignorant cracker. "I thought you were different," she said to the woman. "I thought you were different because you came from the North. Thought you had some intelligence about you. But you just as bad as the rest. You're worst than the rest."

"She's my daughter," Mrs. Cross said. "She's my daughter! Don't you understand?"

"And he's my son. And when your hot-tail daughter say my son raped her, that's a big lie she could've helped from telling."

"If any raping was done," Jenny Lee said, "that old white gal did it."

Mrs. Cross stared at the little Negro woman before her and she glanced at the girl near the door who was almost a woman. She didn't know what to make of these Youngblood Negroes. Didn't they understand that if her daughter were intimate with their son, it had to be rape? She hadn't been able to make Betty Jane understand, but she had thought these Youngblood Negroes would be easy. She thought Laurie Lee would have gotten to her knees and begged her to have mercy on the boy.

A cold fear gripped Laurie Lee's heart like a vise, as she eyed the white woman up and down, and she fought back the tears that gathered inside of her, and she tried to figure the rich cracker woman out. She started to ask the woman, what the girl was doing out in the servants' quarters in the first place, but she didn't say anything.

"You ought to be thankful to me," Mrs. Cross Jr. said. "You're lucky it's me and not some poor white ignorant trash. You might be dealing with a lynching mob."

Laurie Lee's mind was adding things up a mile a minute like an adding machine. Why had this white woman come to her before she went to the police? She didn't come as a friend. "I'm always thankful to God," Laurie Lee said to her. Maybe the police were outside just waiting for her to give them the signal, but it didn't seem likely.

"He's a dangerous boy," Mrs. Cross Jr. said. "And he should be made to pay for his crime, but all I want you to do is to put him away so he won't be able to do any more harm."

"Put him away?"

"Have him put in the reformatory, that's all."

*Reformatory!* The word sent shivers of fear all through her body. She thought about Tim and she felt a murderous anger toward the woman. Sweat popped out on her quivering lips. "Have him put in the reformatory for what?"

"For raping my daughter, that's what. It's rape, you understand, and I could just say the word and get him lynched or electrocuted. But you don't have to give them the real reason. The authorities I mean. Just sign some papers saying he's a bad boy and unruly and you want him put away. I'll put in a word and see that it's all taken care of. Nobody'd ever know what the real reason was."

So that's what it was, Laurie Lee thought. The police had not been notified, and wouldn't be notified, if she cooperated and had her son put in the reformatory. The reformatory! She had to think fast—had to think fast—The reformatory was almost worse than the electric chair. The reformatory! Tim! The reformatory! Everything would be done quietly and her boy would be safe— his life would be safe. "I wouldn't even think of doing it," Laurie Lee said.

"You don't have much choice," the rich white cracker woman said. "All I got to do is have him arrested for rape and his life wouldn't be worth a nickel with a hole in it."

Laurie Lee could hear her heart pounding heavier and heavier and she was scared to death and so filled up she felt like killing this white woman on the spot. At the same time it became clearer to her what the white woman was up to, and the whys and the how-comes moved hazily into focus, and she made up her mind once and for all to call this rich white woman's bluff. She didn't have any choice. Cross County Institution wasn't any choice. "Go ahead, woman, and have him arrested. How come you come to me? How come you didn't do it in the first place? Ain't no love in your heart for me or Robby. Tell me one thing—What was that hot-tail heifer doing out in the servants' quarters with Rob? He didn't drag her out there. Tell me how come?"

"Don't you dare imply—"

"You want it done all quietly, don't you?" Laurie Lee said. "You no-good cracker. And you want me to help you."

"Don't you dare call me that, you—" She raised her arm as if to hit Laurie Lee.

"You lay your hands on me, sister, it'll be the last black woman you'll ever lay hands on. I guarantee you."

"You can say that again," Jenny Lee said.

"What are you but a no-good cracker?" Laurie Lee asked her. "You're worst than any poor white cracker trash that ever was born. You come down here from up north supposed to have some intelligence and decency about you—"

The white woman's face was white as biscuit dough, her lips without color. "Don't you talk to me like that. I could have him—Don't you know what rape is? You're Negroes. All of you are Negroes! Niggers! Niggers!"

Rob and Daddy had come back in the room.

"Niggers—niggers—rape," Laurie Lee repeated. "You're just like the rest of the cracker women, aren't you? You're worst than the rest. That's what you are. Cause you know better. You sell your body and soul to hell with your eyes wide open just to live in the biggest house in town—to wear pretty clothes and strut Miss Ann." The meanness and bitterness emptied out of Laurie like a pot boiling over. "I'm black but I'm the one free and you're a slave. You understand? Mr. Cross Junior's beautiful white slave.

**320**

You're a slave and a whore to every white man in the state of Georgia!"

"You've gone too far!"

"You're the one that's gone too far, you two-faced devil. I know what you're up to. You know my boy didn't rape your daughter. The white man has taken all of your dignity from you. Isn't a drop left in you. And now you ready to sacrifice the dignity of every poor black man in the United States. The blood of every Negro ever been lynched is on your lily-white hands, and you ready to make my boy one in that number. If you think I'm going to help you, you're a liar and the truth isn't in you."

Laurie Lee took a deep breath. She was aware of Joe standing near the hearth again, and Jenny Lee Youngblood over near the door, and Rob near the door, tall and frightened, and the big rich white woman standing before her pale and trembling.

Mrs. Cross Junior looked old and white and confused, and she didn't look handsome and superior anymore. Her legs were wobbly and she reeled as if Laurie had hit her with something. She leaned on Joe's rocking chair and she sank down into it. "I've had enough of this," she mumbled. "I'm not going to talk to you anymore. I'm going straight to the police."

Laurie Lee stood over the woman. She was still scared to death, her heart in her mouth, but she wasn't going to back down now. "You're not going to any police. You can't stand the notoriety. That's how come you came here in the first place. You don't want nobody else to know about it. I know what you're up to."

Mrs. Cross Junior looked up at Laurie Lee and around at the rest of them and her face aged terribly, and she tried to get up but sank back in the chair, and she tried to say something, but it didn't come out, and she cried like a baby.

Laurie Lee watched her and her heart cried out in sympathy to her, because she was a woman and the woman was a woman, and she was moved to go to her and offer her comfort, but she remembered why the big rich white woman was there, and she didn't bat an eyelash and she wouldn't be moved, telling herself that Mrs. Cross Junior, and all of them like her, were white *first* and womenfolks *last*. Shame on her. Shame on her.

Mrs. Cross Junior couldn't sit still. She seemed to be trying to get to her feet, crying and weeping. She tried to get up and she slipped forward from the chair to the floor near the hearth, and she lay full length her long legs sprawled, crying and sobbing, Mrs. George Cross Junior.

Joe bent forward.

"Don't you put your black hands on that white woman!" Laurie shouted softly. "I wouldn't care if she had fallen in the fire—don't you put your hands on her! And you neither, Rob."

Laurie looked down at the hysterical woman—crying and weeping, and her heart wanted only to remember that Mrs. Cross Junior was a woman, but her mind wouldn't let her. She turned to Jenny Lee. "Come here Big Sister." She and Big Sister, about as big as two minutes, struggled and strained and puffed and blew with this great big hysterical white woman, Joe and Rob looking helplessly on, till they had her lying on Laurie Lee's bed, and they covered her up, and they got her to drink some water, and she lay there till she came to herself.

When Mrs. Cross Junior had gone, Laurie Lee closed the door and she walked across the front room into the kitchen, and she stood near the table, her whole body trembling, and she sat down at the table, her head in her arms, and she cried and she cried. And when she was through crying she wiped her eyes and her face on the bottom of her dress. "Come here to me, Rob."

He came in the kitchen and stood near his mother.

She looked at him standing before her. He was twice as big as she was, but his face still wore that babyish expression, and he looked so much like her about the eyes and the mouth, and he looked so frightened and innocent, the way he had a way of looking when he knew she was angry with him. She got to her feet and she gazed up into his soft narrow eyes, and she drew back her hand and slapped him on the side of his face and she didn't want to do it, but she kept slapping him and hitting him as he backed away from her. "Just fifteen years old and can't control yourself," she shouted.

Rob's face wore a shocked expression. "Mama! Mama!"

"Fifteen years old and you can't control yourself—and a white girl—*White girl!*" She lowered her voice. "White girl—white girl. Are you tired of living, son? Is this what me and your Daddy been struggling and sacrificing for?"

She had him in a corner and he stood there with fear and shock and pain in his eyes and he was almost twice as big as she was, and he let her hit him till her arms got tired and her anger ex-

**322**

hausted, and she took her bewildered boy in her arms and smothered him with kisses and cried all over him. And he thought about how she had stood up to the big rich white woman and wiped up the floor with her, and he felt an overwhelming pride that almost consumed him, and Mama the tenderest woman in the whole wide world and he loved her more than ever before.

She gave him food, and she sat at the table across from him watching him eat, but he didn't eat much. "Son, I know you didn't rape no white gal. I know you didn't do it. But that doesn't make any difference to these crackers. Not a dime's worth of difference. I thought you had some sense in your head. Rob, listen to me, son. Stay away from these white gals. Don't go near them. This is a white man's country, and he'll kill you quicker'n a cat can wink his eye, about looking at his women. It's an old old story."

"You don't have to tell me, Mama. I know."

"Well you sure don't act like it."

Laurie Lee and Joe talked to their children far into the night about the ways of white folks. And they figured that Mrs. Cross wouldn't go to the police or to anybody else, but they couldn't be sure, and they couldn't take any chances on a thing like that. Mama and Big Sister and Rob packed Rob's things about two in the morning and got him ready, while Joe walked through the night to Mr. Myles' house and told him what happened, and asked Mr. Myles would he drive Rob to Tipkin, Georgia.

It was about three fifteen before day Saturday morning when Rob and Mr. Myles turned south on the Southern Highway and headed towards Tipkin in Mr. Myles's V-8 Ford. Rob didn't fall asleep all the way to Tipkin. He and the teacher talked and talked. One of the things the teacher said with the sun coming up and shouting over in the east when they were about a half an hour this side of Tipkin was that he would take Rob to New York with him after school closed to spend the summer, if Rob wanted to go.

Rob stayed in Tipkin with Grandpa Dale and Aunt Bertie about three weeks and a half. He received a letter from Mama with a train ticket in it to come back home. Mama had found out from Pauline Jones, the cook at the Crosses, that Betty Jane had had a bitter fight with her mother and told her mother it wasn't Rob's fault and wouldn't budge an inch, and had been sent up north to live with Mrs. Cross Junior's relatives. And that was the end of that—They hoped.

Rob was graduated from high school in the spring—he and Ida Mae. Ida Mae came first in the class with the highest mark and Rob came fourth. The next afternoon Richard Myles and Josephine Rollins and Rob Youngblood drove all the way across the state line to Aiken, South Carolina, and Richard and Josephine got married. Three days later early one morning before daybreak, Rob and Richard and Josephine left Crossroads, Georgia in Mr. Myles's V-8 Ford heading for New York to spend the summer.

*Part Four*　　│　　**THE BEGINNING**

*And before I'd be a slave*
*I'd be buried in my grave*
*And go home to my Lord*
*And be free—*

FROM A NEGRO SPIRITUAL
*"O Freedom"*

# CHAPTER ONE

THE NIGHT BEFORE Rob had left home for New York, they had stayed up real late, his folks, getting him ready and laughing and talking. Mama had said with a funny look on her face, "Boy, you coming back home in the fall of the year? I reckin you think you your own man now. You get up north there for a while, you ain't going to be studying about us poor colored folks down here in Georgia." He had looked into her eyes, and he had known that his mother was making a serious joke like she had a way of doing sometimes. "I'll be back when summer's over, Mama. Don't you worry." But at the last moment before they left she had stood with him near Richard Myles's automobile, and when she had kissed him good-bye, she had hugged him extra hard and whispered roughly—"If you like it, Rob—if it agrees with you—if you want to stay up there, don't let nothing make you come back. Don't come back, Rob, if things are really better for colored up there, don't come back. We'll understand." And he had turned from her quickly and from Jenny Lee and Daddy, feeling a great big shame-faced wetness standing in his eyes. Remembering Daddy many years ago, before he was born, heading up north, and Mr. Buck's plantation.

The first day he had arrived in New York—the very first hour he had been at Richard Myles's home in Brooklyn, Richard's father had talked a hole in Rob's head and filled it back up again —"How'd you leave the Governor of Georgia, son?"—"Glad to have you. Heard a lot about you." . . . "Stay up here. Get yourself a good job. Go to college. Get a profession. . . . Teach in the school system." They had arrived in New York on a Saturday morning and Mrs. Myles had fixed breakfast for them. Richard had laughed at his father and finally had gotten up from the table and walked over behind his father's chair and kissed the older man on his bald head. "Take it easy, father. You can't do it all in one hour. Rob'll be here two or three months, at least. Besides we had a hard trip and all of us are tired."

"All right, son. All right, Richard Wendell. Just so glad to have you home."

But at the end of the summer he came back home in the Ford

V-8 with Richard Myles and Josephine Myles. He came back to Crossroads from New York City because the City had given him a Great New Hope. He had stood in the crowd and seen a new prize fighter named Joe Louis, a colored fighter. He had seen Negro and white people working together, instead of against one another. He had belonged to a union. He came back home because the City had given him a Great Disappointment. He had seen Harlem and angry black faces and tough smiling brown faces and lean hungry faces and long black breadlines and Nationalist street meetings and Communist street meetings, and firetrap houses and rat trap houses, and southern cussing and West Indian accents. He had had a wistful idea that Negroes were free in New York City before he saw Harlem. He had come back home because there had been a big strike where he worked, and the colored and white workers had stuck together and the Puerto Ricans too, but they had lost the strike, because so many hungry bastards were out of work and came in off the street and worked as strikebreakers, and he was fired when the strike was broken. He came home because he lost his job and times were hard in New York City, and it was cheaper to live in Crossroads, Georgia and his folks were there.

And he had come back home from New York, because there was a lot of Laurie Youngblood in his blood and Joe Youngblood too, and especially, Laurie Youngblood, and if the lightning wants to strike you, son, you can't run away from it. You got to stand up and face things in life. Georgia was just as much his as it was the crackers'. And his friends were in Crossroads—Fat Gus Mackey and Ben Raglin and Bruh Robinson, and even Richard Myles, and he was in love with Ida Mae Raglin.

The first couple of weeks back home he went everywhere looking for a job. There were no jobs to be had at the mills. Joe didn't want him to work there anyhow, because Joe hated the mills and the work was too hard, even harder than before, and too backbreaking. People were getting laid off right and left.

Joe didn't work at the mill himself anymore. He was laid off shortly after the strike ended and the striking crackers went back to work, even as Richard Myles had prophesied. Mr. Mack told him in the payline the day he gave him the pink lay-off slip —"It ain't that, Joe. We don't want you to think it's got anything to do with the strike. It's just Hard Times everywhere." And ever since, Joe hadn't held down a regular job. It was work a week here and a month over there and first one thing and then another. And Joe stayed idle most of the time.

The second Sunday Rob was home he read in the paper where a job was vacant as a shipping clerk in a downtown store, and a colored boy was wanted. He took a bath late Sunday night and he got up early Monday morning with his Daddy and washed up again but not all over, and he put on his Sunday-go-to-meeting suit and a bright necktie, and he stood in front of the store for an hour and a half before it opened up. He was the fifth in line. After the first four were interviewed and turned down, he walked up to the desk with his nervous kind of dignity. The white man looked him up and down, like sizing up a horse. "What you want, boy?"

"I come to see about the job that was in the paper."

"You won't do."

"But I can be a shipping clerk. I finished high school right here in town."

"You looking for a job?" the cracker scowled. "You so dressed up, nigger, and look so important, you look like you come in here to hire me this morning, steada me hiring you." The cracker looked past him and motioned to the next boy. Rob felt like knocking the word, nigger, back down the cracker's Adam's-appled throat.

Walking out of the store, cursing the white man under his breath, and cursing Georgia and cursing the South, and at that moment he forgot about what Harlem really was like, he forgot about jobs in New York that were not for Negroes, he forgot about the restaurants and hotels where Negroes weren't allowed, he only remembered that New York was North and New York was different from Crossroads, Georgia—the Union, the Subway and the ride on the ferry and the Statue of Liberty and the buildings that washed their faces in the clouds, and colored folks didn't have to sit in the back, and Joe Louis Barrow the greatest prize fighter since old Jack Johnson, and President Roosevelt, and he wished he had stayed up north and taken his chances. Goddamn these crackers in Georgia!

He walked all over town looking for a job, and everywhere he went, folks were looking for jobs. It seemed that everybody in the world was out of work. He didn't like to hang around the house watching his mother slave over white folks' clothes. Sometimes he would go out to the Quarters and hang out with Fat Gus when he wasn't job-hunting. Fat Gus still had his *Telegram* route and he also sold the *Pittsburgh Courier,* and now he was hustling a few numbers on the side. Fat Gus told Rob one day—"I swear before God you just can't keep a poor colored man down. These folks out here ain't got a pot to piss in or a window to throw it out of, but every damn day some of 'em manage to scrape up a few pennies to play the numbers. Your peoples is a mess."

The town was strange to Rob when he first got back. In three months time it seemed to have contracted to one half its size. It was a hick town all right, but he had never before suspected it —the one and two story buildings that generally defined the downtown business districts, the unpaved streets in the residential sections, except where the well-to-do white folks lived, and Monroe Terrace. And the people seemed different, slow and unhurried, and unbusiness-like, colored and white people. One day he was on the bus, and he watched it come slowly to a stop, and the people didn't stop talking or whatever they were doing, till the bus stopped completely and then they would start getting their packages together. He thought about the swiftness of New York City and the elevateds and the subway trains and the taxi-cabs and people walking fast like they were going somewhere, and speed speed speed, and he shook his head. Even Mama and Daddy were somehow different—Almost like country people. And even pretty Ida Mae Raglin. . . .

He didn't see much of Ida Mae, because she taught school in the country and came to town only on the weekend. He would sit with her in the swing on their front porch where an old oak tree stood in the yard and leaned toward the house. And Miss Sarah would be back in the house somewhere or down at the church or visiting somebody. Ben would be gone to the Saturday night dance or somewhere courting.

Rob wanted to ask her all about her school, and she wanted to ask him about New York City. "I thought you had forgotten about us girls in Crossroads," she said. "Up there in great big old New York City running around with those big city girls. I bet you were something."

"That's a great big joke," he said and he laughed, but he thought to himself, that Ida Mae was different too. She was country—She *was* country—that's all there was to it, and he had never thought of her as country before. She had that sweet southern slow-motion twang, while the girls in New York talked faster and sharper and more business-like. But he thought she was the prettiest in the whole wide world, and nobody in the world could take that away from her. She was pretty and sweet and smart and nice and everything else.

"You seen Willabelle since you been back?"

"No," he said self-consciously. "How's she doing?"

"She doing all right, I reckin. She works down at the Oglethorpe Hotel. She works as a maid."

Sitting there talking about this and that and the other thing and holding hands, and sometimes talking about nothing at all. It got very late and Miss Sarah had signified over a half an hour ago. She had come to the front door and said, "I'm going to have to say good-night to you, Rob. Gonna lay these weary bones to rest. Got to get up early and get ready for church in the morning. I guess you used to staying up all night long way up there in that great big city."

"No, Mam Miss Sarah. Good-night, Miss Sarah."

And after Miss Sarah went back in the house, he laughed and he reached out and found Ida Mae's hand and squeezed it tight, and a warmth seized hold of him and made him bold and he put his arm quietly around her shoulders and pulled her clumsily toward him. He knew her face so intimately, he could see its outline clearly in the midnight darkness. Her big brown eyes, sometimes almost black, and big and wide and concerned like they were always asking questions . . . Her lips looked like they had been carefully molded and stuck onto her mouth. Her face was roundish, almost round. Rob's throat contracted as he swallowed the bitter sweetness of her beauty. His lips searched desperately for her mouth, as he felt her resisting for a brief moment, and then her arms around his neck and her soft sweet lips hard against his, both of their breathing short and fast like running up a steep hill, and he was aware of her breathing softness up against his chest, and nothing was ever like it before. And leaning against each other now and catching their breaths. "Ida Mae!—Ida Mae!" A shouted whisper.

"It's getting late, Rob. You better go now, before Mama come out here and run you away."

They were standing now. "Ain't nobody scared of Miss Sarah." He painfully laughed.

"Ben'll be coming around the corner any minute now."

"Let him come."

"You don't know Ben anymore. He acts so funny here lately. Acts just like he thinks he's my Daddy or something. You don't know. He's really a mess."

He pulled her to him and he found her lips again and he pushed his body hard against hers, and he was a man and he loved Ida Mae————"I tell you one thing," he said. "I'm crazy about school teachers."

"I 'member how crazy you used to be about Josephine Rollins."

"I mean this one right here on this porch."

She said, "Rob, you ought to hush." She said, "You know what they call me out to that country school? The big fellers that live around there? They call me Miss Sweetening."

He said, "Humph, I'm coming out there one of these days and see what's going on. But they sure didn't name you wrong at all. I have to give them credit."

He could see her pretty smile in the darkness. "Sure enough, Rob, it's really getting late, and Mama won't like it."

"All right, I'm going," he said, and they went into each other's arms again, and her sweet lips soft and anxious for his, and his body trembling against her body, and "Good-night, Rob."

"Good-night, Darling. Good-night, Miss Sweetening."

Later that night he lay on his pallet, tossing and tumbling, his toes sticking out at the end of the blanket, because his legs were so long. He had to get a job. He couldn't lie around here living off Mama and Daddy. Jenny Lee had a job working in the white folks' house. Daddy working every now and then . . . But everybody working excepting him. And it was a goddamn shame, him a grown man, lived and worked in New York City, and here he was still sleeping on a pallet in the room with his sister. And how could he expect Ida Mae to be his girl and even think about marrying him, when he didn't have enough gumption to get himself a job?

Every day he walked and walked till his feet got weary, and he walked some more. And Mama would look in the paper every morning, and she asked everybody everywhere she went about a job for Rob, and it got to the point that Mama would tell him about a job almost apologetically, and he would go and see about it, and sometimes he would stay all day, and when he got home, he would say—"No, I didn't get the job today. Boss Charlie didn't like my looks."

Sometimes Mama would say, "Well, tomorrow is another day, son."

**332**

"Tomorrow is another day," he mimicked. "Tomorrow is another day. You think I like to be loafing around, don't you? You think I'm not really looking for a job."

"I don't think no such a thing, son. You know I don't. I know you want to work. Jobs are just so scarce these days. Hard Times everywhere." And she went to him and put her tender arms around him, making him feel like a little boy again, making him remember easier years, making him remember his mother's love for him, job or no job. And he wanted to put his arms around her, as she melted him down, but he wasn't a little boy any longer, he was a man, a full-grown sixteen-year-old man. He pushed her away from him. "Mama, don't!" and he went out the front door slamming it hard.

One Saturday night Rob and Ida Mae were sitting in the swing on the Raglin front porch, and they had been in a gay lighthearted mood, and he had kissed her tender lips, that always seemed to give and take so sweet and firm and soft.

"How're you, Miss Sweetening?" At least with her he was always happy. All week long he looked forward to Saturday night and Ida Mae Raglin.

"Very well, I thank you, Mr. Youngblood."

He looked down into the merry laughter of her eyes, and if every night were Saturday night, and he could be with her like this, he wouldn't mind so much the walking every day from place to place looking for a job. He could feel the moonlight coming onto the porch through the old oak tree. He could see the yellow moonlight in Ida Mae Raglin's big brown eyes.

"I'm going to change your name, Miss Sweetening. And I'm not going to be long in doing it. Going to change your name from Miss Sweetening to Mrs. Youngblood, if you don't mind, just as soon as I get me a job."

She laughed again. "I'm not worried about you getting a job, Mr. Youngblood. I know you got what it takes if anybody has. Like Mr. Blake told me the other day when he visited my school. If a man really wants a job he can get one. Most of these men walking around here just using the Depression as an excuse for not working."

The happiness flowing warmly inside of him froze into ice. His arms were like pieces of iron around her waist. He tried to make his lips smile and think of something to say to her, but it didn't come off. There was nothing to say.

She said, "What's the matter, Rob? I didn't mean it that way."

"How did you mean it?" his husky voice asked.

"I mean—I mean if there's a job to be had, I know you will get it."

"You didn't say that."

"I know I didn't but that's what I meant. Let's don't fuss, Rob."

He didn't want to fuss with her. It was the last thing he wanted. But he thought about the hundreds and hundreds of men he had seen in the last few weeks—feet patting the pavement, standing in front of the factory gates, in the endless breadlines—the looks he had seen on their lean hungry faces—the hope, the despair and the desperation, colored and white, and the other day he had seen Oscar Jefferson looking for work, and the men with families to take care of—the boys all over Crossroads—the desperate faces way up north in the great big New York City—"You meant what Mr. Blake meant. That's what you meant. You meant that all of us out here every day just pretending to be looking for a job. We ain't nothing but a bunch of no-good loafers."

She said, "No, Rob, no! You know I didn't mean that."

He said, "Well, let's forget about it."

And they dropped the subject, and they sat there talking about this and that and everything else till it got kind of late, and Miss Sarah paid her respects. A little bit later they kissed good-night, he and Ida Mae, and he left her there standing on the porch, and he didn't look back like he usually did, and he wouldn't come back till he found himself a job. Maybe he would never come back.

He got so he didn't want to see Mama or Daddy or even Jenny Lee. He thought they were all criticizing him to themselves and to each other behind his back. Sometimes he would stay out so late that everybody would be in bed and asleep, when he came in. Only Mama was never asleep. He began to make a point of leaving home early and getting home late. Some nights he didn't get home at all. He hung around the pool rooms and the gambling joints. He was a lanky six feet one now and nobody would guess he was only sixteen, except for the babyish look on his face which hadn't gone anywhere. He was still the spitting image of Laurie Lee Youngblood.

Joe Youngblood worried about the boy and he went one Saturday night to see Deacon Jenkins who was head bellman at the

Oglethorpe Hotel, told him how badly Rob needed a job and the Deacon told Joe he would see what he could do, but he couldn't promise anything definite, because times were tight. "We just put on old Fat Gus Mackey on the night shift the other day. If I'da knowed Pee Wee was looking for a job, it'da been just the thing." About two weeks later Rob landed a job at the Oglethorpe Hotel. Old Man Bob Morris had dropped dead from a heart attack right there on the job with a great big suitcase in his hand bigger than he was.

The white chief clerk told Rob the first day on the job—"It's an honor to work at the Oglethorpe Hotel, boy. The best people in the whole state of Georgia stop here. Some of the most important people in the country."

Rob stood before the white man, staring him in the eyes, but he felt an uneasiness, all dressed up in his monkey suit, and the white man in his handsome business suit. "Yes, sir," he said.

"We demand the highest efficiency from our boys—from the whole staff. Politeness is our motto. That's the password—politeness. Every employee must be on his toes every minute in the day. Understand?"

"Yes, sir."

"You know Leroy," the clerk said, "he'll show you the ropes."

He looked blankly at the white man—Leroy? He was supposed to know Leroy.

"He's the head bellboy," the white man continued, and then Rob knew that Leroy was Deacon Jenkins, head bellboy of the Oglethorpe Hotel and head deacon of the Pleasant Grove Baptist Church, where his father had been a deacon under him all these years. Ever since he could remember he had never heard Leroy called anything but Deacon Jenkins.

Deacon Jenkins took him around for about an hour, showing him this and telling him the other. The deacon had "hotel" feet. They were so bad he seemed to be walking on red-hot coals. "All you got to do, Pee Wee, is just watch your P's and Q's, and be polite. You can make it. You have any trouble just come to me. I known you before you knowed your ownself. I told you mother just yestiddy I'd look out for you, and I'm sure gon do it." He was one of the few people in town who still called Rob Pee Wee.

Rob ran himself ragged the first day, all over the big hotel from one fancy room to another, and he thought that this must be one of the biggest and swankiest hotels in the United States, and he wondered how it compared with some of those great big ritzy hotels in New York City. Every time he would come back downstairs the bellboy at the post would send him upstairs again. And all day long it was white folks calling after him—Boy, bring me this—Boy do that—Take this, boy, and bring me the other—Come on, boy, I ain't got all day—And boy boy boy all day long and Yes sir—No sir—Thank you sir—And he had been a boy so long—so long—Now he was ready to be a man—Long overdue.

It was about three thirty in the afternoon the first day, and he had been running and sweating and lifting and carrying and Yessirring and bowing. His legs were so tired and hurting he could hardly lift them up and out of the soft deep carpet. At the beginning of the day he had marveled at the deepness and the softness and the richness of the carpets, but now his feet were so heavy it felt like the carpets were reaching up and pulling at his feet and holding on to them like red Georgia mud. He came back downstairs and before he could grunt, the man at the post sent him in a hurry with a pitcher of ice water to Room 831. "Mr. Badcock ain't no snake like some of these crackers. He don't give no nickel tips. He's a very rich cracker," Elmo Thomas told Rob. "And if you give him a 'A'-number-one job, he'll treat you all right. Give you a great big tip. But if you mess up, that cracker will kick you square in the ass."

He took the pitcher of ice water from Elmo, and he started quickly toward the elevator, sweat pouring from all over his body. He pictured Mr. Badcock as a big fat hard-to-get-along-with cracker, but he would give him an 'A'-number-one job, so the cracker would give him a great big tip.

"Boy, you really hustling today," the service elevator operator told Rob. "You must be making a million dollars. Make me wish I was young again."

He got off on the eighth floor and walked quickly up the hall glancing at the door numbers as he went. 805, 806, 807 . . . 815, 816. It must be way around to the other end of the hall. He wanted to get there in a great big hurry. It was his first chance of the day to earn a big tip and he didn't want to mess up. Just before he got to the other end of the hall he looked at the pitcher to see if the ice and the water were still in the pitcher and if everything was all right, and he thought painfully that maybe he should have brought up a couple of glasses with him. He stopped dead still. Suppose there were no glasses in 831. It would be just his luck. He should've thought of it downstairs, but Elmo had shoved the pitcher in his hands so quickly and talked so fast, that he didn't have time to think of anything but Mr. Badcock's great big tip and the kick in the ass if he messed up. Well anyhow, there wasn't time to go back downstairs for glasses. When a rich cracker like Mr. Badcock wanted water he wanted it in a hurry. He turned the corner at the end of the hall. 822, 823, 824, 825. He hoped there were glasses in 831. There had to be glasses, or he was up the creek without a paddle. He was in front of 830 and he turned toward 831 across the hall, and *damn* Mr. Badcock. He wasn't scared of no cracker, rich or no rich. He knocked on the door. He hoped there were glasses.

A long, tall poor-white-trash looking man came to the door. "What you want, boy?"

"Here is your ice water, Mr. Badcock, sir." One of the things he hated most about the job was the sirring and the mamming and the bowing and the scraping and the calling-him-boy.

"Badcock?" the peckerwood said. "My name ain't no Badcock. I didn't send for no ice water."

"But this is 831," Rob said desperately, forgetting to say please sir.

"831? This ain't no 831. This is 829. Boy you must be drunk or losing your mind. Can you read numbers?"

"No, sir—yes, sir—excuse me, sir." He thought he would sink right down into the plushy carpet as his eyes went up to the number over the door—829. What in the devil was wrong with him?

The cracker looked at him like he was looking at the biggest jackass in the world and he laughed at Rob. "Beeinst you brung it up here, boy, I might as well take it. Little ice water would come in handy along about now."

"No, sir," Rob said in warm desperation. "I got to find Mr. Badcock. He waiting for the ice water."

"Well go git him another one then. You done interrupted me," the peckerwood said, "the least you can do is give me the ice water." He reached for the pitcher, and Rob backed away. He and the cracker were about the same height.

"I can't give you this pitcher," he told the peckerwood. "If I don't get it to Mr. Badcock in a hurry, he'll raise all kind of hell with me. Make me lose my job."

The peckerwood looked him up and down. "Mr. Badcock," he said good-naturedly. "All right then, boy. You better git this ice water to him in a hurry. With a name like that he must be worser than a barrel of rattlesnakes."

Rob went back across the hall and he looked at the number on the door and it was 830 just as he had seen it before, and it was the last door on that side of the hall and the one he had just left was the last one on the other side, and this was the last floor in the building. He was sweating now all over his body, and he didn't know what to do or which way to turn, and he tried to picture himself back downstairs talking to Elmo, and he thought that maybe Elmo had said 830 instead of Room 831. He must have said 830, because there wasn't any 831 in the house. He raised his arm and knocked on the door.

"Who's that," a woman's voice said.

The voice startled him, and he heard all kinds of white danger signals in his mind, and he started to back away from the door, when it opened and a white woman stood there looking him over. She was wearing a thin bathrobe and she just had it thrown on carelessly, and it fell away in front of her and she didn't have anything on but the robe. But he didn't know whether she was blonde, red head or brunette—he just knew she was white, the sort they lynched his kind about.

"I'm looking for Mr. Badcock," he said in a husky voice.

"Don't no Mr. Badcock stay here," she said, looking him up and down like she was sizing up a stud horse.

"Mr. Badcock called down to the desk for a pitcher of ice water for Room 830," he argued fiercely, sweat breaking out all over his face. The way she looked at him he felt like dashing the ice water into her face and hitting her on the head with the pitcher.

"Ain't nobody with that kind of a name ever lived here," she said.

"Who that out there, Livonia?" he heard a man's voice call out from the direction of the bathroom.

She didn't move from the door. She just looked over her shoulder. "Nobody, sugar pie."

He turned and ran back down the hall, spilling the ice water as he ran, his heart running wild and leaping like crazy and the lynching mob and the lynching rope running after him. A door opened up ahead of him and he had to stop running. He walked in a hurry until he turned the corner, and he ran to the service elevator.

"You better take it easy," the elevator operator said. "You working too hard. You ain't gon git rich on this job." He stood looking at Rob with the door still open.

"Come on," Rob said. "I'm in a great big hurry."

"Take it easy, man," the operator said. "Don't let these crackers run your tongue out."

Rob closed his eyes and he could hear footsteps coming down the hall, white footsteps. "Man, let's go down—goddammit!"

He heard the elevator door close slowly. "All right—all right, Mr. Greedy Boy. But you don't have to be cussing me, cause I don't take that kind of shit off nobody." As the elevator started downward, it felt to Rob like the Oglethorpe Hotel was falling down around him and the whole wide world was coming up toward him a million miles an hour. In a quick flash it came to him—the big giant neon sign on top of the hotel—He'd seen it more than a thousand times—HOTEL OGLETHORPE—and the sign underneath the great big sign—*210 rooms and baths. 30 rooms on each floor—all outside rooms.* He forgot about his fear, as his anger mounted and mounted, while the elevator went down down down, and his anger left the white woman up on the eighth floor and moved to the black man somewhere down on the first floor probably, and laughing at him. Elmo Thomas! And his damn Mr. Badcock in 831!

When the elevator reached the first floor, the operator pulled the door open with an angry bang, and Rob heard the gray-haired old man curse softly under his breath. "I'm sorry, Mister. I didn't mean any harm. I just almost got into some serious trouble upstairs with some crackers, and I wanted to come down real quick."

"Well how come you didn't say so in the first damn place?" the man said angrily.

When he reached the post he looked around all over the place for Elmo Thomas, but one of the other boys told him that Elmo had gotten off from work already. "This is his short day. Everybody have one short day in the week. He come in at eight and get off at four, and come back at eight tonight and work till midnight. That's so every man on the day shift can have at least four hours off during the week in the daytime. They really give a man a break in Hotel Oglethorpe," Hack Dawson said. "They even give you a raise every twenty-five years. I ain't been here but twenty-four yet." He laughed at Rob.

Rob had forgotten his anger for the moment, as he listened to

Hack Dawson, and just at that moment two white men came in with great big bags, and Hack took one and Rob took the other. And the stuff was on all over again. Just as Hack left Rob he smiled and said, "Did you get a great big old tip? How was Mr. Badcock in Room 831?"

When Rob knocked off at eight o'clock that night he went down in the second basement to the locker room, where the colored help kept their clothes, and he changed his clothes. All the bellboys on his shift were down there waiting for him. "How's Mr. Badcock in 831?" Bruh Robinson asked him. "He was a bad sonofabitch when I ran into him about a year ago."

Rob didn't say a word. He undressed quietly.

"I remember the first time I waited on old man Badcock about twenty-four years ago," Hack Dawson said. "He was a living ass, I mean to tell you. He tipped me with a hundred dollar bill. The only trouble—it was Confederate money."

The other men in the locker room howled and stomped their feet.

Elmo Thomas winked his eye and said, "Why donchall leave my buddy alone?" as he walked quickly out of the locker and headed upstairs to take his post.

"What's your name, son?" the elevator operator asked.

"Rob Youngblood."

He straightened up from lacing his shoes. "Y'all know what I know, y'all better leave Youngblood alone. He was hotter than six boxes of matches when he came down on that elevator. I thought he was going to give me a whupping right there on the spot."

All of the men laughed. Rob looked at the old man and smiled.

Bruh Robinson came over to where Rob was sitting. "The boys don't mean no harm," he said. "They play that joke on every new man come to work at the hotel. Don't pay it no rabbit-ass mind."

Rob looked up at Bruh and glanced around at the other men, and he thought about himself up on the eighth floor looking for Mr. Badcock and 831, serious and anxious and scared half to death, and the white woman named Livonia, and it hadn't been funny to him at all, but somehow he laughed, and he couldn't help from laughing. And he said to Bruh Robinson—"Man, you get the hell out of my face."

And Rob dressed quietly listening to the men talking to each other about first one thing and then another. They dressed slowly, taking their time, relaxing after that 12-hour shift.

"How much did you make today in tips, Youngblood?"

Rob hesitated before he muttered, "A dollar and a quarter." He had counted it just before he left the post. It was exactly ninety-five cents.

"A dollar and a quarter!" somebody exclaimed.

"You must not've been rooming nothing but Georgia snakes all day long," Bruh Robinson said. "That's the one thing I hate about this job. You got to depend on tips to get along. Depend on somebody giving you something. Got to depend on whether a cracker like the way you smile or not."

"Now ain't that just like a colored man. Ain't never satisfied," Hack Dawson said. "Boy, even if you don't get no tips at all, the bossman pays you *three* whole dollars every two weeks. What more do you want?"

The men chuckled and laughed.

Ellis Jordan, a middle-aged bellboy said, "Bruh, where your boy tonight? He ain't come in yet. You know who I'm talking about—Talmadge's buddy."

At that moment Gus came into the locker room on the run. "Look out everybody," Bruh Robinson said. "Here comes the one and only, and he's running late."

"That's me," Fat Gus said, pulling off his clothes as he went quickly toward his locker. Rob watched Fat Gus, didn't say a word to him.

Gus had taken off all of his clothes excepting his drawers.

"What's the latest word you heard from the Governor?" Ellis Jordan asked.

"He better get his big ass upstairs to the post," Bruh Robinson said, laughing at Gus. "Talmadge ain't gon help him none if Mister Ogle get a holt of his ass." The colored workers called the owner of the hotel Mr. Ogle behind his back. His real name was Otis Holloway.

"Mr. Ogle ain't scared of me," Fat Gus said, "and I damn sure ain't scared of Mr. Ogle." He turned toward Bruh and he glanced at Rob, but he didn't recognize who he was at first. He looked back at Rob again.

"Well kiss my Aunty in the country," he said. He came quickly across the floor toward Rob. "What the hell you doing around here?"

Rob looked up at him and smiled. He really wasn't fat anymore —he had grown out of it. And he wasn't slim either. He was chunky and stout. "What you think I'm doing? The same thing you doing."

"Well, kiss my Aunty in the country," he repeated. "You working for Mr. Ogle too—Ain't that a bitch." He turned to the rest of the men. "I'm telling y'all now. This is my real cut-buddy. I don't want nobody messing with him. If y'all don't start no shit, it ain't gon be none."

"I thought Eugene Talmadge was your cut-buddy," Ellis said.

Gus said, "Oh yeah—I got something tell y'all about that boy in Atlanta."

The men chuckled and gathered around Gus. "You better get ready and get upstairs," Rob said.

"That's all right," Gus said. "They glad to see me whenever I get there." He walked toward his locker to get his bellboy uniform, talking as he went. "Anyhow old Eugene got tired of Rob Youngblood and them other Negroes up there in New York City and Chicago and them other places up there always talking about what a no-good skunk he is, and how bad the colored man is treated in Georgia. Old Eugene bought him some time on a national hook-up, one of them radio hook-ups that go out all over the world."

The men chuckled and giggled. Fat Gus had stopped dressing.

"He went way into the backwoods—way back in the woods— Skunk Nellie, Georgia or some kind of damn Georgia—"

"Skunk Nellie, Georgia," Ellis repeated and laughed out loud. The other men giggled.

"He found him a poor old Negro and he had him tied up and brought him all the way back to Atlanta. He told the old Negro they wanted him to go over the radio and speak to the world and President Roosevelt and tell everybody how Nigrahs were treated in the great state of Georgia. And when he finished speaking over the radio they were going to untie him and sit him down to the biggest meal he ever ate and just as much corn licker as he could drink. They brought the old Negro into the radio station, and when the time came, they introduced him, and the poor old man just stood before the mike but didn't say a mumbling word. They kept whispering to him to speak up and tell the rest of the country how he felt. One of Gene's henchmen grabbed his arm and started

**342**

twisting it. Finally the poor old Negro man opened his mouth and spoke before that mike in a little biddy whisper, and all he said was—HELP—"

The men laughed and howled and stomped their feet. Rob laughed so hard his stomach started to hurt. "Boy, you sure is hard on your buddy Eugene," Ellis said.

The door to the locker room opened and the laughing stopped suddenly. Deacon Jenkins came in. "Gus, you better get up there to the post in a hurry. You fifteen minutes late already. If you don't want to work, just say so."

"All right," Fat Gus said. "I'll be upstairs before a cat can lick his hindparts."

Deacon Jenkins muttered under his breath, and he waited around till Gus was ready, and he followed Gus out of the locker room. He turned at the door and he spoke to Rob. "Wait for me, Pee Wee, till I get back downstairs. I ain't gon be long."

"All right, Deacon Jenkins."

"Old Leroy sure is hard on Gus," Bruh Robinson said after Gus and the Deacon had left.

"He just doing his job," Will Turner said.

The locker room door opened again, and a medium sized cracker walked in. "How you boys getting along?" he said friendly-like. "Y'all right this time?"

"Just fine, Mr. Baker," Will Turner said, the other men silent. Roy Baker was the chef on the day-time shift.

Mr. Baker's eyes roved around the locker room till they rested on Rob, and Rob felt warm in the collar already. "You the new boy, ain'tcha?"

Rob grunted and began to feel around in his locker like he was looking for something. Maybe he would always be a boy and never a man.

"You the one been way up there in New York City. I bet you done told all the boys about it."

Rob didn't say a word. He felt his whole body growing warmer and warmer.

"They tell me nigrah men go round with white women and all lacka dat up there in New York. What about it, boy?"

Rob felt his hand trembling as he locked his locker.

"Come on now, boy, tell us all about it," the cracker said pleasantly.

**343**

Rob didn't say a word. He walked past the cracker and out of the room, and the other men followed him. Will Turner said, "Good-night, Mr. Baker." Somebody had to say it.

"So long, boys. We'll get together and talk sometime about New York City."

## CHAPTER TWO

IT HAD BEEN a whole two weeks of running and walking and lifting and smiling and yes-sirring and yes-mamming and being called boy and sometimes worse, and he hadn't got used to anything. And backaches and his poor feet hurting like his toes had the toothache. He had time or energy for nothing but work. He didn't even have time for Ida Mae Raglin. The way he figured she didn't want to see him anyhow. It was Saturday night and he had just received his three dollars for the first two weeks and a couple of dollars in his pockets from tips he had earned the last couple of days, and he was colored-folks rich. He came downstairs to the locker room.

"Old Youngblood got an ass-hole of money," Ellis Jordan said as Rob came in. All the other men looked at Rob and laughed. All the men called him Youngblood now, even Fat Gus.

"What you gon do with all that money, Youngblood? You got somewhere to dump it? You got a old lady?" Elmo Thomas winked his eye at the others.

Ellis Jordan said, "What you talking about? Man, Youngblood got more women than you can shake a stick at."

"With all that money he got he can have more womens than he can shake two sticks at."

Ellis said, "Man I can see you don't know the kind of fellow Youngblood is. He don't mess with no women that you got dump your money to. He goes around with them society women."

"It don't make no never mind society or not," Elmo said. "A woman is a woman and all a woman loves you for is the do-re-me, especially a colored woman. She ain't got no affection at all. I know what I'm talking about."

Rob sat there lacing his shoes, his feet still aching, listening to the men, and he thought about Mama and Daddy, and how hard both of them worked and the kind of love they had for each

**344**

other, do-re-me or no do-re-me. And he thought about Miss Lulabelle out there in the Quarters, Fat Gus's mother. And he wanted to say something about women in general and especially the colored ones, but they were older than he was, every one of these men. He looked over where Elmo was sitting, and he felt a warmth and an anger growing in his collar and he just had to say it. "Is that all Miss Josie love your father for?—the do-re-me?"

"Uh—Uh—" Ellis Jordan said. "Ooo—wee—Old Youngblood do play rough. Elmo don't play that stuff, Youngblood."

"I don't play it either," Rob said heatedly. "And don't nobody get the wrong idea."

"Youngblood ain't playing," Fat Gus said. "I can state you that."

"I don't play any dozens," Youngblood continued. "But it makes me mad to hear you all sit around here all the time talking against women. I'm talking about your mother, Elmo. She's a woman. Is she just out for the do-re-me? I mean it. Is she?"

"I don't mean women like my mother. I'm talking about these mor-dren women. They don't make them like Mama no more."

"Right now," Rob argued, "there's more colored women in Crossroads, Georgia, working and bringing home the bacon and holding the family together than there is men-folks."

"You right about that," Fat Gus said.

"I ain't talking about them kind of women," Elmo said. "I mean mor-dren women, man—mordren women. I done told you that."

"You said *women,* man. You said especially colored women."

"You just don't understand, Youngblood. You too young. Ain't had no experience."

"Experience—" Gus said, looking slyly at Rob. "Y'all don't know nothing about all the pretty women crazy about Youngblood. All kind of women. If the New York women love him like the Georgia ones, he musta been a really sweet daddy up there. A pie-back from way back."

The men laughed at Gus, but they looked at Rob with a different tone in their eyes. "Old Youngblood's a dog," Ellis said. "He's really a hound."

Rob felt the heat moving around in his face. "That's nothing but a whole heap of stuff Gus is talking about. But all the same, if we don't hold up our own women and respect them, who else is going to do it? Not any of these Georgia crackers."

"You tell 'em about that mess," Fat Gus said. "If it don't be for my mother, ain't no telling what would of 'come of my family." He went out of the locker room door heading upstairs where he should have been ten minutes earlier. The door reopened. He came back and stood in the doorway. "Don't do nothing I wouldn't do, Youngblood. Don't let them lead you astray tonight. If you can't be good, do be careful. Tell you like the preacher told the congregation—Don't do what I do. Do what I say do." He waved his big hand and closed the door behind him.

"Fat Gus is a mess and a big pile of it."

"That cracker been messing with you lately, Youngblood?" Ellis Jordan asked.

"Not lately," Rob said. Two or three times a week Roy Baker would run into Rob. He would either come down to the locker room at knocking-off time, or corner him in the kitchen with all the other white men looking and listening, or bump into him in one of the downstairs corridors, and the question would always be the same with slight variations. "I hear tell up there in New York colored boys mess around with white women. Tell me all about it, boy, or tell us all about it. Come on now—what about it, boy?" He hadn't spoken to the cracker yet, but every time the cracker pulled this on him, he felt that the cracker had spied on him, and knew what was going on inside of him. Maybe Roy Baker even knew about him and Betty Jane and was just playing with him like Skippy used to do with the rats and the mice he used to catch around the house.

"You better watch that cracker," Will Turner said seriously. "He don't mean you no good. He's picking at you, and he's doing it for a reason."

Ellis said, "He can kiss my assets. Well what you gon do, Youngblood? Where you gon take us? It's all on you tonight."

"I don't know anything about taking you anywhere." All week long they had been kidding him and warning him that payday night was his night to take the boys out and set them up to at least one drink. It was expected of every new boy on his first payday.

"It's Youngblood's night to shine," Bruh Robinson shouted. "We'll show you, Youngblood. You just lead the way," Ellis Jordan said.

When they had finished dressing they left the locker room and they filed out silently past the white watchman. Rob didn't notice the other two white men till he was right up on them. They stood there laughing and talking with the watchman. Rob recognized Roy Baker's voice. The cracker turned toward him just as he was passing.

"Hello there, New York City." He laughed at Rob. "When you going to tell us all about it, boy?"

"Cut it out, Roy. Leave the boy alone," the other cracker said. Rob recognized him as Oscar Jefferson.

He kept walking with the other men past the three crackers, but he saw Roy turn on Oscar angrily. "You keep the hell outa my business, Oscar. Goddammit—brother-in-law or no brother-in-law, don't try to tell me how to mess with niggers!"

Rob and the other men kept walking down the alley behind the big hotel.

"That cracker sure is got a hard-on for you," Ellis said.

"I'm just going to be able to take just so much of his stuff," Rob said. "One of these day he's going to catch me wrong, and it's going to be Too-Bad-Jim. I'm going to forget all about what color he is."

"Don't let that cracker make you lose your temper, Young-blood," Will Turner pleaded. "That's just what he wants you to do."

"Goddamn these crackers," Ellis said. "We going to see Miss Bessie Mae tonight. Lead the way, Youngblood."

Rob followed the men down the alley across Washington Street all the way to Harlem Avenue, and they crossed over the avenue, and halfway down another alley they came to a dimly-lighted shack. Ellis Jordan knocked on the door.

"Who that?" A woman's voice. "You that," Ellis said.

The door cracked cautiously at first, then opened, and the men walked in.

"Might've known who it was," the woman said. "I must've forgot it was payday night on Mr. Ogle's plantation."

"Don't you worry about Mr. Ogle," Ellis said, patting her lightly on her behind. "We got his waters on, jumping and buck-jumping."

Bessie was black and beautiful and when she smiled her beautiful smile, her soft eyes smiled, and she seemed to help brighten the dimly-lit room. "Keep your hands where they belong," she said with a good-natured firmness.

"Ain't that's what I'm doing?" Ellis asked her, but he didn't pat her on the behind again.

The men stood around the table in the center of the room gazing at the flame in the kerosene lamp. A slight breeze came in through the open window. "Well, what's it going to be, boys?" Bessie Mae asked. She winked an eye at Youngblood.

"It's all left up to Youngblood," Ellis said. "We following his lead tonight."

"That's right," Elmo said, "you ain't met Mr. Youngblood from New York City."

"How I'm going to meet him? Ain't nobody introduced us." She smiled at Rob.

"Mr. Youngblood meet Miss Bessie Mae Brown, the prettiest woman in this here town."

"Please to meet you," she said, smiling up into his face and squeezing his hand. "You're not Joe Youngblood's boy, are you? Of course you are. You just like your mother."

"Yes, mam."

"Don't be yes-mamming me, boy. I ain't that much older than you, and you five times bigger than I ever was. Do I look like an old woman to you?"

"No, mam, I mean, you certainly don't."

"Well alright then, baby-face. You sure are just like Laurie Lee Youngblood. That's how come you got such a pretty head on your shoulders."

"Old Youngblood's a mess," Bruh Robinson said. "Trying to make time with the lady already."

"He ain't trying," Ellis said. "He making it. Bring us a pint, Bessie Mae. Youngblood's paying for it."

She said, "That's what I'm here for." And she went into the other room. Rob watched her walk and she certainly didn't walk like an old woman either.

"She going to bring us some of that Harlem Alley Lightning. P-P-P—You know what that mean, Youngblood? Piss, Potash and Pepper. That's what it's made of."

Bessie Mae came back in the room with a pint milk bottle filled with colorless whiskey. She set it down in the middle of the table and she went out of the room again and she brought back a tray with a pitcher of ice water and six glasses on it. "All right, boys, just help yourself. That'll be just one half of a dollar since I know you so good." Rob reached self-consciously into his pocket and he gave the lady a dollar and she gave him his change. The men stood there pouring up their drinks with serious looks on their faces like they were taking communion in church. Rob

**348**

watched them staring at their drinks as if they expected the colorless liquid to tell them something. It was the first time he had been in a liquor joint in Crossroads, Georgia. He glanced at Bessie Mae and her smile told him not to be so serious.

"All right, baby face," she said, pushing the whiskey toward him, "pour your own trouble. We all waiting for you to take the poison off."

He poured some of the whiskey into his glass, his hands trembling slightly, and they all held their glasses out in front of them and Bruh Robinson said—"To Youngblood." And they put the glasses up to their mouths, and they didn't take them down till the glasses were empty. The whiskey felt like nothing he had imagined when it reached his throat, cutting off his breath like pieces of ground-up glass and burning its way down to the pit of his stomach, but he kept the glass up to his mouth just like the others till there was nothing left, and he thought the lining of his stomach was on fire and his eyes ran water. He reached quickly for the pitcher of ice water and poured himself a glassful.

Elmo pointed at Youngblood and laughed. "Old Youngblood built him a fire and now he's putting it out. Ain't that a damn shame?"

They all laughed at Youngblood. "I'm telling you, boy," Ellis said, "this whiskey so bad it'll make you talk back to your mama."

They pulled up chairs and sat there around the table drinking and talking, Youngblood sipping on his second drink, pretending he was drinking as much as the others. "Bring us another pint, Bessie Mae," Ellis Jordan said. "This one's on me. It ain't every day in the week you get to sit and drink with high-tone people from New York City."

Bessie Mae looked at Rob and laughed. "You telling me? Are you telling me?" There was beautiful rhythm in the way she walked. It was a pleasure to watch her.

Ellis Jordan laughed. "She truly built for speed—ain't she Youngblood? And heavy duty!"

She came back with the second pint, and they sat around drinking and laughing and talking. "Youngblood playing possum," Ellis said. "He ain't drinking no licker. He still sipping on that second glass."

"Leave him alone," Bessie Mae said.

"Youngblood just don't like this bad-ass whiskey you sell. They don't sell no white lightning in New York City. They sell that seal stuff, don't they Youngblood? They been selling seal whiskey ever since Mr. Roosevelt took his seat. I sure do wish he was president of Georgia."

"One of these days Georgia gon come back into the Union," Bruh Robinson said.

Ellis Jordan stared across the table at Youngblood. "How you like your job, Youngblood?"

"I like it all right," Rob said. The room was getting hotter and hotter every time he took a sip of Miss Bessie Mae's white lightning, hot and close, and the cigarette smoke getting in his eyes. He thought about Ida Mae and he wished she were there with him, but Ida Mae wouldn't come to Bessie Mae's place.

Hack Dawson took a big gulp of whiskey and he stared at Youngblood. "Three dollars a week—twice a month. Mr. Ogle sure is good to his black children."

"Drink that licker up and have another one, Youngblood. Don't be no chinch," Ellis said.

"You just leave Baby Face right alone," Bessie Mae said.

"Twelve hours a day, seven days a week," Hack Dawson said. He took another drink. "One day a week you get off at four o'clock and come back at eight and work till midnight. Mr. Ogle is such a nice man. Anybody'll tell you—He's cheap but he's sweet. He'll tell you his ownself."

Rob looked around at all of them. He and Bruh Robinson had known each other almost as long as they had known themselves. He glanced at Bessie Mae, and his eyes traveled quickly to the other men, and he wondered if ten or fifteen or twenty years from now, he and Bruh and Fat Gus would be coming here in Harlem Alley and lapping up rot gut whiskey and laughing and talking about Mister Ogle and first one thing and then another. A shudder passed over his shoulder. He wasn't going to work at Hotel Oglethorpe all of his life. He was going to college just as soon as he could spell able. He had discussed it with Richard Myles and Dr. Riley and they had friends in Washington, D.C., and Richmond, Virginia, and New York City, and places like that and they were going to see just what could be done. Rob met one of Richard's friends in New York last summer, a Negro man, who was an important lawyer and argued a lot of those civil rights cases. Rob had been deeply impressed with the man, and he had thought about it all summer long—If he could go to college he would become a lawyer and work in the South on civil rights cases. Lord knows they were needed. He would finish law school, and he would come back home and marry Ida Mae and he would serve his people—He and Ida Mae. . . .

Somebody knocked on the door and they all got quiet and Bessie Mae went to the door and said who that, and she cracked the door and stood there talking softly to two men in overalls, and she went with them to the back of the house, and a few minutes later she came back with them and let them out the front door again.

The third pint of white lightning was on the table now, and Ellis was drinking and talking and talking and drinking and getting a little tipsy. His voice was louder than it usually was. "Youngblood, whiskey is the enemy of mankind. You hear what I say. Don't never form the habit of drinking. You listen to me. Don't drink no licker, no home brew, no wine no nothing. It's the worst habit in the whole wide world. Not even no Bevo."

"Hush your mouth, Ellis Jordan. You talking like a fool," Bessie Mae said.

Hack Dawson had pulled off his shoes. "Walking walking walking," he said. "I bet I done walked a million miles all over old man Ogle's chinch harbor."

"Them ain't no chinches, man," Bruh Robinson said. "Them Georgia snakes that live at Hotel Oglethorpe. Them nickel-tippers is the ones that work you the hardest. A snake is a sonofagun."

"Have a drink, Youngblood, goddammit," Ellis shouted.

"Leave Baby Face alone."

Hack Dawson shook his head. He stretched his legs toward Youngblood and looked at his feet. "Boy, sometimes my feet hurt so bad I'm scared to put them down on the floor. I don't know whether I'm coming or going. Talk about some bad puppies. My feet bad enough to carry a pistol. Picking em up and putting em down—Shooting em in and turning around. Twelve hours a day seven days a week."

Rob looked from Hack Dawson's weary eyes to Bruh Robinson, and he thought about many years ago when they were just kids in swimming out at Cracker Rayburn's and later in the shack as the rain poured down outside, and the feeling of being together and the importance of being together, always together, and the sun shining and the rain still raining. He thought about what Richard Myles always said about colored folks sticking together because you couldn't fight these crackers by yourself, and his Mama believed it and his Daddy did too, and maybe if they got together at the hotel they could get a few changes made.

"Boy, don't you never drink none of this Harlem Alley lightning, you hear what I say?" Ellis Jordan shouted to Rob. "I had a boy. He woulda been just about your age. A couple of years older. You 'member Bubber. He was a good boy and smart in school. Ask any of them teachers out at the school. They'll tell you about Bubber. Bubber wanted to be a doctor. That's how come he run away from home. Bubber ain't no doctor, lessen they got colleges up yonder, in Heaven. Somebody come through here about two years ago. Say Bubber got killed on a freight train. One of them railroad dicks beat him to death."

Hack Dawson laughed bitterly. "Man, you crazy. Even if they is got colleges in Heaven, they don't allow no black boys to go to them. You ought to know that."

Bruh Robinson laughed. "Hack, you ought to be shame of yourself. You reckin a colored man catch hell up in Heaven too?"

"So you like your job at the hotel," Hack said to Rob, "honh, Youngblood? You like them eighty-four hours a week and all that money two times a month. I believe they got laws in Washington against what Mr. Ogle putting down. Roosevelt done passed some laws up there. I know he is. Mr. Ogle just think he got a bunch of ignorant Negroes, and he can do anything."

"*Think* it?" Ellis Jordan asked. "You kidding?"

"One of these days Georgia gon come into the Union," Bruh Robinson said.

Rob thought about the union he had been a member of for almost three whole months in New York City.

"Man, Georgia ain't never gon come into the Union," Ellis said.

Rob looked from one to the other of their serious faces. "That's what we need at the hotel—a union. Mr. Ogle would sit up and take notice then. I bet anybody."

Will Turner had been nodding. He woke up quickly. "Union? You crazy, Youngblood? You come around that hotel talking about some kind of damn union, Mr. Ogle kick your hindparts off the job so fast, it'll make your head swim."

352

"He doesn't need to know anything about it till we get it to rolling. Be too late then. All we'd have to do is stick together."

"Man, you ain't in no New York City. These Negroes down here ain't gon stick together. Tell him about it, Ellis. Tell him what I say."

Ellis nodded his head. "Don't drink no whiskey—no wine—no home brew—no no-nothing—You hear what I say, Youngblood. I'm gon whup your ass if I catch you doing it. That's one thing about me, anybody'll tell you, I don't drink."

"Watch your language, Mr. Jordan," Bessie Mae said. "Don't you know I run a respectable joint? You better respect me and Youngblood."

Bruh Robinson laughed. "Not since swallowing came in style. You sure don't drink."

"How do you know they won't stick together?" Youngblood argued. "You all ever tried to organize a union at the hotel?"

Will Turner laughed. "Man these Negroes don't know nothing about no union."

"We can learn. That's one sure thing. You all always fussing about conditions at the hotel, this and that, I bet you one thing—it isn't ever going to change, unless we get together and do something about it. The man isn't ever going to give you a blessed thing just out of the goodness of his heart. He finds out just how much stuff you'll take and that's exactly how much he'll give you."

Bessie Mae reached out and patted Youngblood gently on his big hands. "Y'all better listen to Baby Face. Y'all better listen to the man from New York City. He talks more sense than all y'all put together. Y'all old heads better listen to Youngblood."

"I wish we could get a union at the hotel, but what about the crackers?" Hack Dawson said. "They ain't gon join no union with colored. This ain't New York."

"If they don't want to join," Rob said, feeling his whiskey, "let them stay the hell out. Shame on them."

"Yeah, but you can't do without them."

"I can do without them," Ellis mumbled. "I can do without crackers each and every day in the week. I don't even eat soda crackers."

"It'll be just like that factory union that was round here, only the other way round. They wouldn't let the colored join they union, and when they went on strike, Old Man Cross hired colored

**353**

to break the strike and after it was broke the colored was laid off. The crackers didn't get no kind of raise. What good did that do? Ask your Daddy, Youngblood. He knows about it."

"I don't see what that's got to do with us getting together at the hotel," Bruh Robinson said.

"You don't see. It's got a whole heap to do with it. Ain't no crackers gon join our union, even if we had one. And if we start any stuff with Mr. Ogle, the crackers'll take sides with him instead of us. And we'll be right out on our hindparts. That's what I'm talking about."

Rob looked across the table through the thickness of the cigarette smoke and the whiskey fumes. He stared at Hack Dawson and his tired-looking eyes and the broad forehead and his hair getting scarce, and he knew Hack Dawson was speaking the truth. Yet and still conditions were terrible, and they had always been terrible, and they wouldn't get better unless the men got together and did something about it. But times were tight and jobs were scarce, and if a man got fired, there wasn't any telling when he would be able to find another job. "When I see Leroy, I mean Deacon Jenkins tomorrow, I'm going to ask him what he thinks about it," Rob said. "We got to do something."

"Ask Deacon Jenkins? Ask Leroy? Man, you might as well go to the *man,* and say Mr. Ogle, do you think it's a good idea for us boys to organize us a union."

Rob had sipped the second drink down to the last drop, and he was slightly drunk, what with the closeness and the smoke his head felt woozy. "What you mean—I might as well go to Mr. Ogle as to go to Deacon Jenkins?"

"Man, the Deacon is Mr. Ogle's favorite colored man. He pays him four fifty every two weeks and he lets him go to church every Sunday and prayer meeting through the week. What more could Leroy ask for?"

Rob didn't say a word. He couldn't say a word. He had always respected the Deacon. He used to think Deacon Jenkins could do no wrong. He remembered the many Saturday afternoons, when he was a kid, and they used to meet Deacon Jenkins in the Big Store or coming from the Big Store, and the Deacon would kid him about how fast he was growing and first one thing and then another, and he would always give him and Jenny Lee a nickel apiece. He remembered the Deacon in church, his pride and dignity.

**354**

"Deacon Jenkins isn't any Uncle Tom," he said angrily. "Can't nobody make me believe that about him. I've known the Deacon all of my life."

Hack Dawson shook his head, didn't say a word.

"It's getting late," Rob said as he got to his feet. "I got to go home."

"Wait a minute, Youngblood. All of us going directly," Ellis said. "Just as soon as we finish this pint on the table."

Bessie Mae looked up at Rob and said, "You put me in mind of that new prize fighter they got up there in Detroit and New York. Did anybody ever mistake you for Joe Louis up there?"

"Stop teasing the boy," Hack Dawson said.

"Shut your mouth," Bessie Mae said. "You just jealous, that's all. Did you ever see Joe Louis fight up there, honey bunch? That's one thing I want to do before I die. See him knock out one of them crackers."

"I didn't see him fight," Rob told her. "Cost too much money."

"You reckin he gon ever win the heavyweight belt?" she asked.

"He's the best that ever did it," Rob said.

And when all of them were ready to go, she came to the door with them, and she came up to Youngblood and kissed him gently on his cheek. She smiled up into his serious face. "Let that be a lesson to you, Baby Face. Stay the hell outa Harlem Alley. It ain't no place for sweet little boys like you. Next time you here I ain't gonna let you off so easy. It's gon be too-bad-Jim."

He didn't say a word, as he went out of the house with the rest of the men, all of them laughing except Youngblood.

The weeks seemed to gallop like wild race horses, even though the individual days at the hotel were long and dragged out, and each day seemed to be longer than the one before. He hadn't gone back to Bessie Mae's again—wasn't ever going back. The Monday following the Saturday night he and the other men were down in the Alley, Deacon Jenkins had spoken to him, as they walked together on the way home that night.

"I heard about you and the other boys down to Bessie Mae's the other night, Pee Wee. I might have knowed they was going to take you down there on your first payday, but I forgot all about it."

The old man's voice trailed off. Rob didn't say a word. The old man continued. "The boys down at the hotel is all good fellows, but they ain't your kind, Pee Wee, and that's something you got to understand. I told your mother I would see after you down at the hotel. That's how come I'm talking to you like this."

It was a night in October and a breeze in the air, but the trees were still as green as grass and the grass was green on Jeff Davis Boulevard. "What you mean, Deacon Jenkins?"

"You know, what I mean, Pee Wee. They're nice fellers, but they're kinda low class. They ain't got no education like you got. They don't go to church. They don't do nothing but work and drink licker. A couple of them boys go down to Bessie Mae's every night to get a nip before going home. Can't do without it."

Rob felt an uneasy anger move around inside of him, but he had the greatest respect for the Deacon. Was it true what Hack Dawson had said the other night? "One thing, Deacon Jenkins," he said, "they don't hardly have time to go to church. All of us work twelve hours a day every day the Good Lord sends." He hated that part of the job worst than anything else. You couldn't go anywhere, do anything. By the time you got home every night, it was almost nine o'clock, and by the time you got ready to go anywhere it was too darn late. If only there was one day off in the week, or even a half day.

"I'm just telling you, Pee Wee, cause I told your mother I would look out for you. They all right, but they ain't in your class. They're a bunch of licker heads."

The job was beating him down to his socks. He was too tired to do anything but try to relax when he got home. He would talk to the folks, especially Mama, and he would do a little reading, till his head got groggy. He hadn't seen Richard Myles hardly at all since he started to work, not to mention Ida Mae, but he was always thinking about her—day and night. One Thursday he got to studying about her on the job, and when he got off work he went by Miss Sarah's and told her to tell Ida Mae he was coming to see her on Saturday night. And all day Friday and Saturday on the job and off, he thought about her and he just couldn't wait for Saturday night to come. And after he knocked off work he went downstairs to get ready in a hurry. The other fellows left him, because they didn't have to wash up like he did. They were going straight home. Just as he was about to leave, Deacon Jenkins came downstairs, and he said that they had just got word that Hack Dawson's mother was mighty sick and Hack had to stay home with her. The Deacon asked Rob would he cover the next four hours for Hack. Rob was dead tired and he wanted desperately to see Ida Mae, but he thought about Hack and Miss Johnnie Mae, and the others who were already gone, and he wanted to see Ida Mae very very bad, but he couldn't say no to Hack Dawson.

One Friday morning he woke early with Miss Sweetening very much on his mind, and he had dreamed about her all night long, all kinds of crazy dreams. He just had to see her, had to work out some way of seeing her regularly, job or no job, but there wasn't any way. He had heard rumors of Biff Roberts courting her by long distance from Howard University, but more than that and ten times worse he had heard rumors of Mr. Benjamin Blake, the principal of Pleasant Grove School.

He left home even earlier than usual that morning, and he went by Richard Myles and asked him could he use his car that afternoon and night, and Richard agreed, and when he got to work, he asked the men if one of them would work from eight to twelve for him that night. It was his day to get off at four, but he would have to come back at eight and work till twelve, unless he got somebody to cover for him.

The men stood in the locker room getting ready for work. They looked at each other. Elmo Thomas signified. "Old Youngblood really wants to do him some heavy courting tonight."

"Leave him alone," Ellis Jordan said. "I'll do it, Youngblood. Don't worry about a thing." Hack Dawson didn't come in that day. His mother had taken sick again and his wife wasn't well.

The hours from eight to four that day were the longest he had ever experienced. At four he left the post in the lobby and went down to the locker room on the run. He washed up in a hurry and put on his tan Sunday-go-to-meeting suit and was long gone. He caught the bus for Pleasant Grove and stopped at Monroe Terrace where Richard and Josephine lived in Josephine's house. He got the car and left in a hurry as if he were in a crazy race with an unseen something. He drove out Georgia Avenue to Cross County Road. He loved to get behind the wheel and push push push and feel the earth move swiftly out from under him in the other direction. He had to get out there to the school before she started home for the week-end, because that's the way he had planned it. They would go for a ride or drive up to Macon to the movies or a dance. They would do anything they wanted to do. And she would be surprised to see him. It was a half hour ride from town to the Booker T. School, but Rob made it in eighteen minutes. He parked in the school yard and he jumped out of the car and slammed the door. He wanted to see Miss Sweetening bad bad bad. He had to keep himself under control to keep from breaking into a run. He walked through the one-story, one-room, wooden frame school house, but he didn't see Miss Sweetening or anybody else. He saw a man in overalls in the backyard behind the school house with a hoe in his hand. He told Rob the school teacher had gone over to the house.

Rob didn't go back to the car. He walked toward the side of the house from the school yard. He didn't see the big green Buick parked in the front till he had almost reached the gate, and it might be anybody's Buick in the world, but as he opened the gate he spied Mr. Blake sitting on the porch of the wooden-frame house partially hidden by the thick green ivy that reached from the tar paper roof down to the railings of the porch. He moved a couple of steps toward the house and he stopped in his tracks, as if Joe Louis had struck him a blow and paralyzed him. He felt his whole body going warm with an unexpected shame and anger. If he could back up quietly and slip away without anybody knowing he had ever been there, he felt like doing so. Because suddenly and for the very first time he was really unsure of himself and his relationship with Ida Mae. Greater than that was the feeling of betrayal. Mr. Blake could offer her everything and what could he offer, a hotel bellboy? He heard Mr. Blake move around on the porch and clear his throat and he knew he had been seen, and he started walking toward the front porch again.

Mr. Blake stood up and shook his hand. "How are you, Robert?"

"I'm all right, Mr. Blake. How're you this evening?"

"I reckin I have no cause to complain," he said, his eyes glancing nervously toward the front door. And the two of them stood staring into each other's eyes, Rob a whole head taller than Mr. Blake. They could hear footsteps coming down the hall in the house, as they stood waiting.

When she came to the door with a small suitcase in her hand, she had the most beautiful smile on her face, and she looked just the way she had looked in the dream he had dreamed the night before, and his heart stopped beating as the smile left her face, and now a worried or an angry look had settled in her big brown eyes, and perspiration just above her lips. She put the suitcase down.

"Hello, Rob," she said finally, and what he thought she left unsaid was—What the devil are you doing way out here?

"Hello, Ida Mae," he said, and then nothing was said for more than a minute which seemed like an hour, and why did she stand there staring at him like he was a bear to be scared of or something? And he heard Mr. Blake clear his throat, and he felt he just had to say something, Rob Youngblood did.

"I had Richard Myles's car," he said, "and I was driving out this way and I just thought I would drop in on you," he said, suffering all of a sudden from the terrible heat. "Like I said I was going to do one of these days," he added.

"I'm so glad you came, Rob," Ida Mae said, but her eyes didn't say so.

"I though maybe I could give you a ride home—but—but—" He was sweating all over. How could he, a hard working man, compete with a man like Mr. Blake, respectable, well-off principal of the Pleasant Grove School? But how could she go for a man like Blake? How could she do it? He was older than her father would have been, and fat and slick and Uncle Tom. But he was educated and stood for something, and with Mr. Blake in Ida Mae's corner, she wouldn't have to spend another term at the country school. He could have her transferred to town.

She smiled the thinnest kind of smile and she turned to Mr. Blake and the bottom fell out of Rob's stomach, as she gave Mr. Blake her bag, and told him to take it to the car and wait for her, and he took the bag without question, like he was one of the pupils in her class, as all kinds of wild thoughts raced through Youngblood's mind.

"Let's sit in the swing for a minute, Rob," she said.

"All right, Miss Sweetening." He tried to laugh.

They sat in the swing and the swing squeaked out a signifying note, and the nearness of her tantalized him, as did the cool fall breeze that came across the porch and was suddenly hot and unbearable. He stared fiercely into the space across the porch, but he knew that she glanced at his face quickly and away again, and he knew there was worry in her big brown eyes. He didn't say a word.

"I thought you never were going to get around to coming out here and seeing our little country school," she said.

"A man out of work and looking for a job doesn't have any

time at all on the side, and a bellboy doesn't have as much time as a man out of work. A big old important school principal has plenty of time," he made himself say, "especially if he has a great big car."

She stood up and he could see the anger flashing in her eyes. He didn't want to make her angry! "You don't have to be that way, Rob Youngblood. What you expect me to do? Sit at home till the great handsome man from New York makes up his mind to pay poor little me a visit? Do you think all a woman is supposed to do is wait on the man? Just because you're a man you think you can just pick up and run all over the country, and I'm a woman, so I'm supposed to just sit and wait and twiddle my thumbs? I hate that about you," she said, almost like he painfully remembered her saying I hate that about you when she was younger and he was younger, standing at the gate to her house after they had walked home from school together, just as they stood there now on the front porch of the little country house facing each other. But it was different and he knew it was a great big difference, for they had both taken up the role of men and women now, and she was a school teacher and he was a bellboy. And yet he didn't want it to be different at all, and he forgot about Mr. Blake, older than his father, and standing out on the sidewalk near the big green Buick, and he forgot she was a country school teacher and that country people always keep an eye on their school teacher, especially if she's a woman. He forgot time and he forgot place, unaware of people walking the street, and there were only Rob Youngblood and Ida Mae Raglin like there had always been since he could remember, and nobody else, and he wanted to bring her into his arms and tell her he loved her and would always love her and to blot out all the trouble and confusion that had risen between them. He reached out quickly, and before she knew it, his arms were around her, and his lips seeking hers, and she pulled away from him, and vaguely he heard Mr. Blake from the sidewalk exclaim—"Miss Raglin! Miss Raglin!" And Ida Mae's voice—"Rob Youngblood! Are you losing your mind?" A leaf turning brown fell gently onto the porch between him and her.

"I'm sorry, Ida Mae. I really am sorry." She stood there away from him looking up at him and he thought she surely was going to cry, and he fighting hard to keep himself from crying.

She shook her head. "I'm sorry too, Rob. I honestly and truly

**360**

am sorry. Good-bye, Rob." She turned from him quickly and walked across the porch and down the steps.

He didn't even say good-bye. He watched her go swiftly down the walk to the gate and get into the big green car with the man, and the motor starting up and the car making a U turn and heading back to Crossroads. He didn't move from the porch till they were almost out of sight. Then he walked like a man sleep-walking till he got to Richard's car. He didn't turn and head back to Crossroads. He drove like fury toward Macon, and far to his left the sun was setting in glorious streaks of red and yellow. He had made a fool of himself before Ida Mae and in front of Mr. Blake, and it was all his fault, and he didn't blame Ida Mae in the least, but how could she mess around with a fat little old Uncle Tom man like Mr. Blake? She probably thought he was going to be a bell-hop the balance of his days, scuffling like a slave. Well that showed how much she really knew about him. He was going to college—maybe next year. Mr. Myles was working on a scholarship for him and Dr. Riley too, and one of them was bound to come through. But in spite of everything he didn't believe there was really anything between Ida Mae and Mr. Blake. He was going to be a lawyer. A civil rights lawyer or a labor lawyer. He drove till night began to fall all over the countryside, even as the leaves turning brown kept falling. He slowed down and he turned into a path that led to some white man's great big plantation, and he backed out onto the highway again and he headed toward Crossroads. Might as well take Richard Myles's car to him and go on back to work. But as he approached the lights of the country town that used to be a great big city to him just a few months ago, he thought about Ida Mae and Benjamin Blake and he became angrier and angrier, unreasonably angry with Ida Mae Raglin, better known as Miss Sweetening, and he thought maybe that was what Mr. Blake called her when they were alone. He was so mad with Mr. Blake he could hardly see the highway before him. Taking advantage of a young girl like Ida Mae, a baby to him, taking advantage of his position in the town and taking unfair advantage of Rob Youngblood. He slowed down as he reached the town and he thought to himself—Why should he go back to work and have to explain to the boys what had happened?—make up a lie? Why shouldn't he make a night of it? Ida Mae—Miss Sweetening wasn't letting any dust settle under her feet. He thought about how some of the men talked about women down at the hotel. Maybe they were right. Where would he go? Maybe to the picture show. Didn't need any car to go to the picture show. Wasn't anything playing anyhow but a cowboy picture. A great excitement had grabbed hold of him, and he could hear his own breathing, as he turned into Harlem Avenue. He would show Miss Sweetening. When he got to Harlem Alley, he turned up the long dark alley to Bessie Mae's house. He stood for awhile on her porch before he knocked. He could feel his heart beating way up in his temples. He was just stopping by to have a little talk with her, he argued with himself. And anyhow she was younger than Mr. Blake was, a whole lot younger, he made himself reason, basing everything on the comparison between Blake and Bessie Mae. He knocked on the door and the thought came to him suddenly that his hotel buddies might be sitting in there, but he quickly dismissed the thought, as a different kind of panic seized hold of him as he waited for pretty Miss Bessie Mae Brown, shamefacedly waited.

"Who's that?"

He lost his voice for a moment. "Youngblood," he muttered.

"Who?"

"Youngblood." What was the matter with Bessie Mae's ears?

The door cracked open. "Oh," she said, "Mr. Baby Face Youngblood from New York City. Joe Louis the Second. Come right in."

She closed the door and she put her arm in his and they walked toward the table in the center of the dimly-lit room. "What can I do for you, Prettier-Than-Me?"

"I just dropped by to see how you were getting along—that's all." He told himself he sounded like a fool.

"Well that's just fine," she said, "and I sure am glad to have you, doll baby. The last time you were here, you set up the house. This time everything is on me. Just name it and you can have it," she said. He stood tall and silent, staring at her, ashamed of himself for having come, but he had come and that was a natural fact. She laughed. "What's the matter, doll baby? Somebody got you all excited and heated up before you got to Mama?"

He felt like a little biddy boy and a damn fool too and at that moment he hated her guts. "I want a drink," he said.

"All right, doll baby. Anything you say. Everything's on Mama."

She brought a bottle of brown-colored whiskey and set it on the table. "This is my special special brand," she said. "I don't use that Harlem Alley Lightning when I'm entertaining company." And they sat across the little table from each other, he looking at Bessie Mae with her soft-tone, sometimes sleepy-looking eyes and down at the table and thinking about Ida Mae and wondering where she was and what she was doing, and she would be really surprised if she knew where he was this very minute, and it was all her fault, but it wasn't her fault, and he knew that it wasn't. He got drunk real quick and his head going around like a merry-go-round. He got drunk and bold and he smelled his pee. And he would show Ida Mae. He looked across the table at Bessie Mae and she got prettier and prettier under his gaze, and when she stared at him, he didn't drop his eyes like he had been doing. He would show Ida Mae.

She smiled at him knowingly. "What's the matter, doll baby?"

"You know what's the matter," he said. He got to his feet and went around the table to her, and he pulled her clumsily to her feet, and he tried to kiss her, and she let him have his way for a moment.

Then she pulled away from him abruptly. "It's time for you to go, Baby Sweet," she said.

"Go?" he said in a husky voice. "Go? I just got here." He came toward her and pulled her into his arms again, but she pulled away from him, as he mumbled something about him loving her, and he felt the greatest kind of shame—ridiculous shame.

She went around to the other side of the table. "Be shame of yourself," she said with a teasing understanding smile. "Talking about love. I'm old enough to be your mother. What you need is a good cold glass of ice water. One of them white gals up to the hotel must been picking at you. Got you all heated up and you come down here to take it out on Mama. No, Baby Sweet, Mama ain't robbing the cradle tonight."

He stared across the table at her, as she poured up a glass of ice water for him. "I haven't been at the hotel since four o'clock. I got off for tonight."

"What's the matter, Baby Sweet? Your girl friend must've turn you down. You must be got one of these nice-nasty little girls— scared to live. Turned you down and you come a-running to Mama." She laughed at the serious look on his face. "Come on now, Baby Sweet. Drink the ice water Mama made for you."

He stared at her. How in the hell did she know so much? "You don't like me," he said.

"I do like you, doll baby. I think you the prettiest and the sweetest boy in Crossroads, Georgia, and the smartest too."

"Then why?—How come?"

"Cause you don't want to be messed up with Mama. You want to make something out of yourself. I got too much respect for your mother and father to have anything to do with you. I ain't in the cradle-snatching business yet. Mama ain't that hard up yet awhile."

He was ready to go now, because she had sobered him up completely. He was ready to go, but he wasn't quite ready. "I'm a man," he said. Why didn't he just say good-night and leave?

"I could make a fool out of myself," she said, "and call myself falling in love with you and set you up in some kind of shady business, but it would be the ruination of both of us. You wouldn't go for it anyhow. Cause you got too much of the real stuff in you. I know what I'm talking about. Ever since I went to that Jubilee thing a few years ago, and seen you and heard you. I knew you had it in you, boy. You ain't gon be at that hotel long. You just marking a little time right long in now."

He picked up the glass of ice water and he drank it down. He was ready to go but he didn't know how. She went toward him and put her arm in his and led him to the door. And when they reached the door they turned to each other, his face red hot with a godawful shame.

"Deacon Jenkins wanted to bet me *anything* you wouldn't come back to see me. But he wouldn't bet me nothing cause he ain't a gambling man. I told him he didn't know from nothing."

"Deacon Jenkins!"

"Don't get the wrong idea, Baby. He didn't come down here. I met him on the Avenue a couple of weeks ago. And don't worry, cause I ain't gon tell him you were here. I ain't gon tell nobody. Ain't nobody's business but mine and your'ns."

She reached up and kissed him lightly on his lips. "Don't you come back to see Mama no more, you hear, doll baby? Cause Mama might not be able next time to resist the temptation." She laughed. "Mama should take the bad boy cross her knee right now and give him a spanking he'll never forget."

He started to speak but it never came out.

"All kidding aside, Youngblood. Whatever trouble you having with your girl friend, it ain't gon be solved by coming down here in Harlem Alley. That's all there is to it. Your father knows that. I ain't never seen him in Harlem Alley."

He looked down into her face, her soft friendly understanding eyes, and he started to say—Thank you, mam, but he mumbled good-night, and he went out of the door into the cool night air, which cut into his hot dampish body like an old buggy whip. And he was sorry he had come, awfully ashamed, but somehow, he wasn't exactly sorry.

## CHAPTER THREE

HE CAME DOWN to the locker room thankful that the day had finally come to an end. It was one of his worst days, and the days were getting worse and worse and the *man* was getting meaner and meaner. And the newspapers kept saying things were getting better or going to get better, but outside the hotel Bad Times were everywhere, and everybody knew the Depression had gone no place at all. That morning he had been sent up to 315 to check out a party that had asked specifically for him—Number 7—That was his number. But when he had gotten up there Mr. Oakley was nowhere to be seen, and Mrs. Oakley came to the door in her panties and brassiere and stood there talking to him as if she were fully dressed. Her husband was Mr. Robert Lee Oakley the Third, President of the Middle Georgia Life Insurance Company, the biggest insurance company in South and Central Georgia. Everybody knew he was a real big cracker.

She said, "What you want, boy?" And she looked at him as if she didn't see him, and he looked past her as if she didn't exist. This happened to him at least a couple of times a week, white women coming to the door in varied degrees of undress, sometimes in their birthday suits. One of the fellows told him—"You get used to that, man." But he had never gotten used to it and never would.

Mrs. Oakley looked him up and down, systematically undressing him with her light green eyes. "Mr. Oakley sent for me," he said angrily. And what in the hell was the matter with these rich white women? They had the world in a jug, but every one he had seen at the hotel seemed poor and cheap and hungry as a wolf—dressed-up whores. They didn't have one-tenth of the dignity that Bessie Mae had.

"I'm so sorry," she said. "He just this minute stepped out. Come on in and wait. He'll be back directly." She raised her arms and stretched her young pink body like an old nervous dog and she yawned out loud.

He stepped back quickly out of the door. "No, mam, I'll come back when he gets back. We're so busy downstairs." And he left before she could utter a word.

And later that day Mr. Oakley sent for him again, but he wouldn't go back. He told Hack Dawson about what happened, and Hack went in his place. "They after you, Youngblood, cause you young and good-looking. A old bad-feet man like me ain't got nothing to worry about." Hack Dawson was only forty years old.

Sometimes Rob thought about Ruby Cross—Mrs. Cross Jr.— and he could see her again wilting and helpless under the fire of Mama's great fury and sinking into the chair and sliding to the floor near the hearth, and he couldn't imagine it had really happened. Mrs. Cross Junior—Mr. George Cross Junior's wife. Biggest crackers in Crossroads, Georgia. Sometimes he thought about Betty Jane Cross—He would never forget her—She was a part of his life, a part that had to be even thought about in secret, but nevertheless a part. He sometimes wondered where she was and what she was doing, and what had happened between her and her mother that day he had left them in Mr. Jim Bradford's room. White womanhood—Southern white womanhood. Two things every cracker born agreed upon—Keep the Negro down and protect white womanhood. Some folks said that white women were the cause of the Negro's condition. A lot of colored folks believed it to be a natural fact. But sometimes Youngblood wondered. Most of the time he seriously doubted it.

That same afternoon about one o'clock, all the bellboys were called together in the manager's office. He sat behind his desk as the eight men stood waiting on him. There were chairs, and Youngblood's feet were aching, and he started to sit down, but he saw that the rest of the men were standing and he stood too.

"Boys," the manager said. "I hear tell you got some kind of complaints on your mind." He was a great big giant of a white man. Looked like he should have been somewhere pushing a plow. He looked uncomfortable in his pretty blue suit. His cattish-gray eyes traveled from one to the other of them "If y'all got something on y'all's mind, if something around here you think ain't quite right, just tell us all about it. We don't want no unhappy employees walking around pouting every day and toting a grudge."

Mr. Bussey paused and looked around, but nobody bit.

"Come on now, boys, speak your piece or forever hold it."

Rob listened for the other men to speak up. They were always grumbling about this and that down in the locker. Now was the time to speak but nobody did. He felt his whole body grow warm with anger. They were older than he, they had been there longer. Why in the hell didn't they open their mouths? The white man's gray eyes traveled from face to face and it seemed to Rob he was daring them to speak. "Come on, boys," the white man said. "Ain't nothing to be scared of."

Rob Youngblood wasn't scared. He felt sweat breaking out all over his body. Goddamn his buddies! He didn't want to be the one to speak first. "Sir—" he began and he felt Ellis Jordan's foot come down heavily upon his poor aching toes and they felt like needles were sticking in them.

Mr. Bussey looked up at Youngblood. "Did you start to say something, boy?"

"No, sir." He hated this cracker and he hated himself.

"Somebody started to say something—one of you boys. Which one was it?"

"No, sir," Rob said. "I just cleared my throat—that's all."

He looked around at all of them. "Well all right then. Leroy got something to tell you all. Give him your undivided attention."

Youngblood felt a certain kind of numbness as Deacon Jenkins came forward, his old wrinkled face drawn tight as a trap drum, and nothing here resembled the proud confident air of the leader in the Pleasant Grove Baptist Church.

"Come on, Leroy. Come on 'round here by me where they can hear you good fashion." The Deacon walked behind the desk. He pulled a piece of paper out of his pocket. He looked up at the men and quietly down at the paper again. "Boys, I been asked to 'nounce a few changes in rules and regulations." Rob looked down at the floor. He looked up at the Deacon again and he closed his eyes. He wanted to turn and walk out of the room.

"Number One—There will be no more split shifts. Every boy will work twelve straight hours a day."

Rob felt a hatred for this Bussey cracker burning so hot inside of him he had to breathe out loud to let off the steam. It was as if the cracker had ordered Leroy to pull down his pants in front of the men. That was how Rob felt.

"Number Two—When a boy has to get off for one or two hours, he will not take it on his own and get another boy to cover for him as has been the practice. He will go to the Head Bellboy with his problem or come to the Manager.

"Number Three—There is too much getting to work late. From now on when a boy is late fifteen minutes or more, fifty cents will be deducted from his wages.

"Number Four—There will be no more loitering of the boys in the locker room. After you get off from work, you will promptly get dressed and leave the premises."

Deacon Jenkins looked up from the paper he had been reading. His face had broken out in an awful sweat. He glanced at the men and especially at Rob and sideways at the cracker. Rob watched Deacon Jenkins and felt like crying. He hated the Deacon for what he had let the cracker make him do, and yet he sympathized with the Deacon, and it was very confusing the way he felt.

"All right, Leroy. Thank you very much. Any questions, boys?"

The office rang out loud with the silence.

"All right, boys. Get back to work. And remember we expect every employee to live up to the rules and regulations of Hotel Oglethorpe. We got the best staff of any in Georgia, and we're right proud of it, and By God we aim to keep it that way. And we ain't gon tolerate no agitating and grumbling like a bunch of Communists among the employees. You got anything on your mind, be man enough to come right up to Leroy and me."

Rob thought to himself—How could they be men when they were nothing but boys? Boys—boys—boys—day and night and all the time—They were always boys. Didn't make any difference how old they were or who they were or what they were.

"All right, boys, get back to work," Mr. Bussey said and Youngblood smiled an arrogant smile.

They walked sullenly out of the room, but they didn't start grumbling till they were well out of hearing distance. Rob didn't want to hear them then.

At exactly eight o'clock he left his post in the main lobby. He wanted to get away from the hotel with no messing around. Just before eight o'clock two new guests arrived, and the bellboy relieving Rob took care of one, after he was checked in, and the other one looked around the lobby as he was being checked in, and the only other bellboy he saw was Rob walking swiftly across the wide lobby with his aching feet heading for the stairway to the basement.

The new guest shouted, "Hey, nigger, come here and get my bags." The cracker was dressed up like a million dollars and surrounded by bags brought into the lobby by a taxicab driver. Youngblood kept walking as if he were deaf. "Hey you nigger, come back here and get my bags." He turned to the clerk. "What's the matter with that nigger?"

The clerk ran out from behind the desk. "Just a minute, sir." He ran across the lobby. "Hey, boy. Hey Youngblood." He caught up with Rob just before he reached the stairs. Rob turned to face him. Rob's eyes narrow, mean and dangerous as he stared at the clerk.

"What's the matter with you boy?"

"Ain't nothing the matter with me." The white clerk was a young city-looking cracker with sandy hair almost as tall as Rob in height.

"Didn't you hear the guest calling you? What's the matter? You deaf?"

"I didn't hear anybody calling me. My name is Youngblood."

"You must've heard him."

"I didn't hear anybody calling me."

"You need to give them ears of yours a good washing then. Come on now, boy, and take care of the guest."

"It's time for me to knock off. It's way past time."

"That's all right, Youngblood. It's just about five minutes after eight. You take care of Mr. Cayton. He gives a real big tip. Gus ain't come in yet—a triflin rascal. Don't forget to wash them ears out when you get home, boy."

Rob had gone back to the desk bursting wide open with a dangerous anger, and had sweated over the four big bags, had to listen to the expensive-looking cracker run his mouth, and had done this and that for the cracker and after it was over the cracker had thrown him a dime and he had wanted to throw it back into the cracker's face, but had left it on the floor outside the cracker's suite.

It had been one of his worst days, but now it was over and he wanted to get down to the locker room, and get his other clothes on without a word to anybody and be long-gone. None of the men had left when he got downstairs.

"Where you been, Youngblood? I b'lieve you trying to make all the money. You one of them real greedy boys."

Rob didn't say a word, didn't even look in Elmo's direction. He went straight to his locker. He undressed quietly. The other men had already dressed and were waiting on him.

"We waiting on you, Youngblood," Ellis Jordan said.

"What you waiting on me for?"

"We want to talk things over."

"Talk what things? What good does it do to talk, beat up your gums all the time down here in the locker room and lose your voice when you get in front of Mr. Charlie?"

"We don't want to talk about it in here. We want to wait till we get outside."

"You can wait if you want to," Youngblood said. "I haven't got hold of your feet."

They waited, and just about that time Roy Baker came through the locker room. "Howdy boys," the long tall lanky cracker said.

"How you Mr. Roy," Will Turner replied.

"Just fine I thank you." He let his eyes wander lazily around the room till they rested on Youngblood. "There my buddy is." The silence was deafening. The water dripping in the toilet next to the locker sounded like pistol shots.

Youngblood laced up his shoes, watched the long legs of the cracker coming toward him. "Boy, we ain't never had that little talk about New York City, is we? Come on now, boy. Ain't no hard feelings. I just want to learn all about it. I ain't never heard tell of nothing like that before."

Rob didn't even look up. The cracker stood over him looking down at him, his face turning red and his neck and his ears, and the air in the locker room smelled heavy and dangerous.

Will Turner said, "Youngblood ain't feeling so forty today, Mr. Roy. He got a terrible headache."

Another one of the men cleared his throat and it sounded so loud.

"Is he sure 'nough?" Mr. Roy said. "Well it ain't gon hurt his head none to talk a little bit I don't reckin. He musta keep a headache all the damn time. I ain't never heard him say nothing. What's the matter, boy, the cat got your tongue?" He rolled himself a cigarette, and he spat little pieces of extra tobacco on the floor near Youngblood, and Youngblood could feel the sweat hop up all over his back like something alive. White woman-hood—White womanhood—The cracker aimed it at him like a double-barreled shotgun.

"I bet the cat didn't have your tongue when you was way up there in New York City. Tell me boy, is it true what I heard tell? Do the colored go around with white women up there and all lacka dat?"

Rob stood up and faced the cracker. He felt like smashing him in his red ugly face. Everything that had been happening all day long crowded in on him, and all the other days and this was about the millionth time the cracker had asked him this question. And he didn't know what he was going to do. His dark narrow eyes stared into the eyes of the gray-eyed cracker. The cracker shuffled his feet and batted his eyes.

"Come on now, boy, don't be like that. Is it true what I heard? Do colored boys mess around with white women up there and all lacka dat?"

There was a moment of silence, a great big silence. "Yes," Rob said, "and all lacka dat." Mocking the cracker's manner of speaking. And he walked past the cracker out of the locker room and the other men followed.

They walked quickly without looking back past the watchman and out into the night. Halfway down the alley he turned to the men. "You all want to talk?"

"Unh-hunh," Ellis said. "Wanna have a little bull session."

"Where you want to go?"

"Let's go down to Bessie Mae," Elmo suggested. "She's stuck on old Youngblood."

Youngblood felt the warm blood rushing to his cheeks. But he wasn't in the mood for any foolishness. "Why don't you come out to my house?" he said.

"That's a good idea, Youngblood," Ellis said, "if your Mama don't mind."

They walked all the way to Pleasant Grove and Youngblood's house. Laughing and talking. A funny kind of laughing that wasn't really funny.

"Boy, old Youngblood sure enough told that cracker a thing or two. Lord Lord Lord, Fat Gus shoulda been there."

"Gus better start getting to work on time," Youngblood said.

"That cracker gon sure have it in for you," Will Turner said. "You better watch your step."

"And he better watch his step," Youngblood said, but he didn't feel one half as brave as he sounded. It wouldn't do any good to let the men know that his body was warm all over with fear. Now that he was out in the air thinking about it, he was much more afraid than he had been in the locker room. The more he thought about it, the more frightened he became. Anything could happpen at any moment. Anything could happen to him or Daddy or Jenny Lee or even Mama, or all of them together. He was getting to be too damn hotheaded. And he had to go back to the hotel to work every day. Anyhow, wasn't any need to be scared right this minute, because the fellows were with him.

When they got to the house all the men said howdy do Miss Laurie Lee and How you Laurie Lee and Howdy Joe and Howdy Jenny Lee, and the Youngbloods said just fine how're you, and Rob told Laurie Lee that the fellows wanted to have a little meeting to talk a little business about down at the hotel and would it be all right. And Bruh Robinson with his shame-faced eyes on Jenny Lee Youngblood.

Mama said to Rob, "You all just make yourself right at home. Where you want to be in here or in the kitchen?"

Rob said, "In the kitchen, Mama. We can sit around the table."

She said, "That'll be just fine." And she looked for chairs.

Rob said, "Sit down, Mama. We can take care of everything."

Joe Youngblood said, "Rob, you'll have to bring a couple of boxes out of the backyard."

They sat around the clumsy wooden scrubbed-colorless table on chairs and on boxes and Rob sat a-straddle one of his mother's ironing horses. They sat around the table and they stared at each other. Ellis pulled out a cigarette. "Is it all right to smoke, Youngblood? Ask your mother."

"I guess it's all right," Youngblood said. "Go ahead and smoke."

Ellis lit the cigarette. His hand was shaking. "Well, Youngblood, it's like this here. Things are bad at the hotel, and they ain't getting better."

"They bad enough, but they getting more worse," Bruh Robinson said.

"Yeah," Ellis said, staring through the cigarette smoke at Bruh. He looked around at Rob again. "Yeah," he repeated. "Like today in Bussey's office. Anybody can see things gon be rough. So we figured we might get our heads together and see what we can do before things really gets rough. I reckin you know about them cutting the boys over at the Rob Lee from three dollars to two dollars." The Rob Lee was the other big hotel in Crossroads, Georgia. It wasn't quite as big as Hotel Oglethorpe.

Will Turner said, "It musta not be so bad at the Oglethorpe after all then. They ain't cut our wages."

Hack Dawson laughed. "Will, you sure is crazy about the man."

"I ain't crazy about the man. Facts is facts," Will Turner said.

Rob readjusted his bottom on the ironing horse.

"I know you were steaming up and boiling over in the manager's office this afternoon, Youngblood, but the reason I stepped on your feet was—wasn't no need you speaking up then and showing the cracker your hand. The first one that spoke woulda got his head chopped off."

"You oughta know better'n to be stepping on the man's feet, Ellis," Bruh Robinson said. "Two things a colored man kill you quick about. Don't mess with his feet and his something-to-eat." All the men laughed including Youngblood.

"It isn't going to do any good for us to beat up our gums among each other," Rob said, "and get before the man and lose our voice."

"I know it don't do no good. That ain't what I mean, Youngblood. I mean before we talk up to that man we got to get together and see what it is we gon say. I ain't scared of no Bussey, but ain't no needa being no fool."

Rob shook his head up and down. He could still feel the effects of Ellis Jordan stepping on his toes that morning with those big feet of his.

"You see what I mean, doncha, Youngblood?"

"Yes, indeed," Youngblood said. "You mean we need a union."

"Old Youngblood sure is crazy about the union," Elmo said.

"You bet not come around that hotel talking about no union," Will Turner said.

"Y'all be quiet," Hack Dawson said. "Let Youngblood talk. He had experience up north in the union."

Rob looked around at the men at the table, all of them old enough to be his father excepting Bruh Robinson and maybe Elmo. "I didn't have that much experience," he said. "But I tell you one thing I learned. I learned that a colored man isn't going to get anywhere on the job doing things on his own. Isn't any working man going to get anywhere, let alone a colored one. But if they get together and stay together, the man just got to sit up and take notice. We want to cut down on these hours we work. We want some split shifts. We want more money. We're not going to get anything unless we're together. And if the Rob Lee gets away with cutting the wages over there, Mr. Ogle going to pull the same thing on us just as sure as Heaven's happy. He isn't in the hotel business for his health and your health either."

"You talk a whole heap of sense, Youngblood," Bruh Robinson said. "I declare you do."

"Mr. Ogle ain't gon let y'all have no union," Will Turner said. "Negroes ain't gon stick together nohow. Don't tell me nothing—I know these Georgia Negroes."

"Don't pay no attention to Will," Hank said. "Keep right on talking, Youngblood."

"Don't try to hush me up. I got just as much right to talk as anybody else," Will said.

"Yeah," Hack said, "but you don't never be talking about nothing. Come on, Youngblood."

"If we organize all the Negroes at the hotel, the waiters and the maids and the elevator operators, what's he going to do? He can't fire us all."

"What's gon keep him from doing it?" Hack asked. "A cracker'll do anything he big and white enough to do."

Ellis Jordan laughed. "And he real big and very very white."

The other men laughed. "He sure can't pass for colored no shape, form or fashion," Bruh Robinson said.

"That's what I'm talking about," Will said, like he was over in the Amen corner.

"He might be big and white, but he isn't big enough to run that hotel all by his lonesome," Youngblood said. "Man if all the colored folks at that hotel stuck together it would scare Mr. Ogle's britches off. They scared of you when you're together. You haven't ever seen a cracker jump on a big bunch of Negroes. That's the one thing they don't want you to do. Get together and stay together."

"Tell em about it, Youngblood," Bruh Robinson said.

"Yeah," Hack said, "but you done forgot one thing. That's the crackers. Them in the kitchen, the pantry maids and all—the clerks. They ain't gon join up with us and you know it, Youngblood. And the man will use them to kick us in the teeth. I seen it happen, Youngblood. I done told you about it."

Youngblood sighed. "We have to see what we can do with the crackers too. Some of them might come in with us," he argued, not really believing it. "But if we take it real easy at first and get all of *our* folks together, sort of ease up on the *man,* we ought to get the Negroes in the other three hotels to come in with us, especially the Rob Lee."

"Old Youngblood wanna organize everybody in the world," Bruh said.

"Ain't gon organize nobody," Will said. "Negroes don't know nothing about no union. They ain't studying about sticking together."

They talked far into the night and sometimes tempers got short and hot, but they didn't come to any kind of conclusions. They talked and they talked and the conversation jumped from one subject to another. President Roosevelt was a better President than Abraham Lincoln—and they ended up debating about who was the toughest prize fighter ever lived—Jack Johnson, Jack Dempsey or young Joe Louis. What they did agree to do was to sound out the other colored folks at the hotel about getting together and do it on the Que-Tee, all except Leroy.

Every minute on the job for the next few days he ran himself ragged, at the same time waiting for something to happen with Roy Baker. He was nervous and jumpy as a cat, upstairs on the floor, in the corridors, down in the locker, staying out of the kitchen as much as possible. But he didn't run into Roy Baker anywhere, and every night when he left the job he would leave in the company of the other men. But on Friday night he was caught upstairs rooming a guest at quitting time and it was eight thirty before he got down and the men were gone. He walked past the watchman and turned left up the alley, and he had walked halfway up the alley before he realized that he was being followed, and even then he wasn't sure. He could hear the footsteps quicken behind him, coming closer and closer, catching up with him, and maybe he should break into a run, but the cracker might shoot him in the back. It probably wasn't any cracker at all—probably one of the boys—but all of the boys had left before he did. He kept walking but he glanced quickly behind him and even though the glimpse was a quick one he could tell it was a white face, and immediately his body, already growing warm grew hot, and the cracker seemed determined to catch up with him before he reached the end of the alley, and Rob was scared but even more than that he was tired of running—all day long he was on the run, because the pressure was on and increasing every day, and if you didn't keep running they would get another boy to run in your place, so it was run run run and never stop running.

"Youngblood—Youngblood—"

Rob's heart flip-flopped and he turned quickly to face the cracker. "What you want with me?" And he looked the cracker square in the face, but his mind wouldn't recognize the cracker at first.

"Howdy, Youngblood. I just want to talk a few minutes with you."

"Howdy, Mr. Jefferson." He felt a relief flow through his body that he could not explain. What the hell did this funny-acting white man want with him?

They stood facing each other in the darkness of the alley. He was a whole head taller than this powerfully-built cracker. "What you want, Mr. Jefferson?"

Oscar Jefferson looked quickly up and down the alley. "Can't we walk while we talk?"

"I reckin we can." All kinds of questions running through his head.

They started to walk up the alley together and they reached the street and crossed over the street and continued up the alley again before the white man spoke. "You better watch your step, Youngblood."

"What you mean, Mr. Jefferson, watch my step?"

"They got it in for you down at the hotel."

"Got it in for me? What they? Who?"

"Roy Baker got it in for you, but I wasn't talking about him. I'm talking about the boss—Mr. Bussey—you know him, the manager—whatever they call him."

Rob could feel the tension throbbing at his temples, and nervous thoughts jumping around in his head. What was Oscar Jefferson up to? "Why should Mr. Baker have it in for me? I haven't ever done anything to him. And I don't see what he could have against me. I always do my work jam up to a tee. He can ask Leroy."

"It ain't got nothing to do with that," Oscar said. "As far as Roy Baker is concerned, he's just a damn fool and ain't gon never be nothing else but. He's my brother-in-law, I ought to know. But with Mr. Bussey, that's a different story."

"What about Mr. Bussey?"

"Mr. Bussey done heard tell you stirring up trouble amongst the colored boys at the hotel. Trying to get them join up into one of them there unions."

Rob kept walking up the alley not saying a word, because he couldn't think of anything to say. How in the hell did Mr. Bussey know about him talking to the boys about the union? How did Oscar Jefferson know? He glanced sideways at Oscar and straight ahead up the dark alley again. He had hoped Oscar Jefferson was a friendly cracker. Friendly cracker—There was no such thing. New York City had made a fool out of him. "Mr. Bussey hears a whole heap of things, I reckin," Rob said finally.

They had reached the end of the alley now and there was no extension of it across Cherry Street, and the middle-aged white man and the young colored man acknowledged the fact as they stopped walking and turned toward each other.

"Well I just thought you ought to know about it," Oscar said. "Cause they gon be watching you like a hawk watching a chicken."

Rob stared at the friendly-faced, anxious-eyed white man. "Well, it just goes to show you how people go around telling lies on a man, and give other people the wrong impression."

"Well I just thought you ought to know about a thing like that," Oscar repeated. "It sure don't hurt none."

Rob looked into the white man's face again, and he wanted desperately to trust this white man with the friendly face and the eyes that were crying out loud to be trusted, but how could he trust him in Crossroads, Georgia?

He said, "Thank you, Mr. Jefferson."

"You welcome, Youngblood. I reckin twan't nothing any man oughtn't do." The cracker looked down at his white hand in the darkness, and he brought it up slowly and held it toward Youngblood. He stood looking at the cracker's hand. It was the strangest thing that ever happened to Rob, like a dream while he was fully awake—talking to a white man like that in Oglethorpe Alley way down in Georgia—

He stared hard at the red-faced cracker. Was Oscar the man he was looking for? He had spoken easily at his house the other night about trying to get some of the whites to come in with them and

**377**

form a union. Maybe the time to start was right now with Oscar Jefferson. He should have mentioned it when they were in the alley. He couldn't talk to this white man about any union on big Cherry Street with all the white folks looking at him. And besides he couldn't trust Oscar Jefferson, didn't care if he did say howdy Joe to Daddy that day in the payline. Didn't care if he did like the Jubilee program. Didn't care if he did tell Roy Baker to leave him alone—He was still a white man in Georgia. He was still a cracker and couldn't be trusted. He wanted to trust him, this plain-faced friendly-looking white man, but something wouldn't let him. They stood facing each other in an awkward silence, as staring white folks passed them by. He took Oscar's white hand in his limp brown one and said, "Goodnight Mr. Jefferson," and he turned and walked up Cherry Street, cussing himself for being so chicken.

The next Saturday afternoon Oscar was walking along Mulberry Street where the poor white working men and women and children gathered every Saturday and wagon-loads of people who came from the country. Every week he took a stroll on Mulberry Street amongst his kind of folks when he got his two hours off on Saturday afternoon. The workingmen stores with their windows filled with week-end bargains and easy credit and brand-new overalls and lumber jackets and heavy high-topped brogan shoes and the sharp warm smell of horse dung freshly deposited near the edge of the sidewalk. He stared into some of their lean hungry faces, and he was one of them and he knew he was one of them, and he always had been and he couldn't get away from it. He looked about him as he walked up the street, stared into the faces of the poor white trash. Just like his Ma used to tell his Pa they were all white trash except the Charlie Wilcoxes. White trash white trash—he hated the word, but it was true—it was true— It was the gospel truth. He had worked almost ever since he came in the world, but he was still white trash, and niggers were niggers —Negroes were Negroes—

One Monday he had heard about the Jubilee and had made up his mind to go without fail. Sitting there in that auditorium, listening to those colored children singing and to young Youngblood talk (the only thing about Rob Youngblood that looked like Little Jim was his height), Oscar had been carried away and a feeling ran through him like new-found religion, and he felt like crying and he felt like shouting.

Two Sundays later his preacher had eaten dinner at Oscar's house, and that man could eat. After dinner the big fat preacher had sat there at the table belching and apologizing, and Oscar had stared at him long and hard.

"Rev. Culpepper, is colored pe—is niggers going to Heaven?" He looked away from the preacher, felt his face growing hot. He knew the answer.

Reverend Culpepper belched and one of the younger children snickered. He wiped his mouth with the back of his hand. "Excuse me, folkses. Brother Jefferson, I reckin some black ones gon get in the gate."

"How come we don't let them come into our church?"

The preacher looked up at the grayish white ceiling and cleared his throat. He looked around at everybody seated at the table. "You see, Brother Jefferson, just like it says in the Good Book. Some was meant to be hewers of wood and drawers of water, and that means the niggers. They were meant to be separate and serve the white man. That's why God made them black. It's in the Bible. See what I mean?"

Oscar looked into Reverend Culpepper's serious face and shook his head. Reverend Culpepper was a Christian-hearted God-fearing man. Everybody gave him credit for that.

Walking along lost in his thoughts, he reached the point where Mulberry ran across Cherry Street. Halfway across the intersection he was startled by the sudden loud blasting of an automobile horn and he jumped just in time. He turned around angrily.

Mr. Mack honked his horn again like the street belonged to him and he laughed and waved at Oscar. "Goddamn, boy, you ought to've moved thatta way when you was on the job and you'd never been laid off."

Oscar had lost his job at the mill about six months after the strike had ended. Mr. Mack had come over to him while he was hard at work and sweating like a horse, and had slapped Oscar on his behind, and Oscar had turned quickly and knocked Mr. Mack down and cussed him out. That's when his job ended. He came home that evening and he looked at all of his raggedy children and he looked at Jessie Belle and after he ate supper he went for a walk way out in the woods, and he cried like a baby all by himself. . . .

He looked for work and he looked for work but he couldn't find any, and his children were hungry and his wife was sick, and he didn't have money to pay the rent. He got so desperate he went to his brother-in-law to see about a job. He and his brother-in-law, Roy Baker, had never set horses. Roy worked as a hotel chef and thought he was a big shot. Nobody could touch him with a ten-foot pole. But Oscar got tired of walking every day from place to place and his children getting hungrier and his wife getting sicker, so he swallowed his pride and he went to his brother-in-law friendly-like, and his brother-in-law got him the job at the Oglethorpe Hotel.

Poor white trash poor white trash—Everywhere he looked on Mulberry Street was poor white trash. He thought about his oldest boy—Junior Jefferson—his favorite, the only one he ever talked to about his old plantation days and him and Little Jim. Junior was going on seventeen and getting old before his time. Already he had that lean, worried, red-faced look about him. Every day his feet pounded the pavement looking for a job that never showed up. Already Junior looked like poor white trash because that's what he was. And it didn't matter what Reverend Culpepper said the Good Book said, didn't no colored folks ever serve Oscar Jefferson, and he was as white as any other white man. Even Reverend Culpepper didn't have any colored servants. He worked in the same factory where Oscar used to work.

## CHAPTER FOUR

Time moved on and the *man* got meaner, and Rob and Bruh and Ellis and Fat Gus and Hack spoke to some of the rest of the folks about getting together, and some seemed scared, and very very scared, as if you had told them to go up on big Oglethorpe Street or Jeff Davis Boulevard in the middle of the day and slap a cracker without any reason, but everybody was interested, the scared ones included. Most of them thought the time wasn't quite ripe. Don't be too hasty, y'all. Not yet awhile. You got to be cautious where crackers concerned. Willabelle said she was ready any time any place. Will Turner said, "Take it easy. Ain't nobody going nowhere. We still get a dollar more than over at the Rob Lee. Wait till the *man* show *his* hand first." But Rob was impatient and he didn't want to wait, but he had to.

Fat Gus worked on the day shift now. He came by the house for Rob every morning just before seven thirty and he would whistle for Rob like he used to do when they were kids a long time ago. De-De-De-De——Dee to the tune of "I Love My Baby." And they would walk to work together. Rob wondered why Gus came so far out of his way from the Quarters every morning just to walk to work with him, because there was a much nearer route to the hotel for Gus. Rob didn't have long to wonder about it. Jenny Lee left for her job around the same time and went in their direction for five or six blocks, and after the second or third morning, Gus didn't hardly say more than good morning to Rob for the first five blocks. He and Jenny Lee would talk talk talk till they reached Orange Street and she would turn to the right and they would continue down Jeff Davis Boulevard. And it wasn't long before the men down at the hotel heard about it, and they signified and teased Fat Gus and Youngblood too. "No wonder Old Gus and Youngblood such good buddies, the fat sneaky rascal," Elmo said.

It was spring again and in the mornings when Rob got up he could hear spring singing all around his house, yelling out loud. The birds coming north and going north again and singing about it, and the crickets and the locusts and everything in an attitude of change, and greenness everywhere, a shining bright greenness, and he could smell the new springtime in the blossoming flowers and the wetness of the dew-kissed mornings. He could see it in Gus and Jenny Lee the way they walked and talked every morning and the way they laughed and the way they were starting to look at one another, and the way Gus stopped by the house some evenings on the way from work, as tired as he was—just dropped by. And he could feel it in Robert Youngblood, he could taste the springtime. Every night as tired as he always was, his thoughts always went to see Ida Mae Raglin, and when he woke up every morning he thought about her, and even on the job. Soon one Saturday morning about half past five he woke up with Miss Sweetening on his mind and spring in his soul and running all through him Miss Sweetening and spring, and he rolled and he tumbled and he pulled his long legs up and he stretched them till they reached beyond his pallet, but he could not fall back to sleep. He got up and slipped into his pants and shoes and tiptoed to the back door and down the back steps. He looked up at the sky and over to the east of the town where a new day was breaking, a day that had never been along this road before, and the sun coming up like a bright red platter over a mountain of red and yellow and it seemed to be dancing and shouting hallelujah, and what you gonna name this new born baby—it didn't seem right just to call it Saturday. He threw up his arms and let himself stretch and his whole body trembled, and he heard the spring-time in his backyard and he saw it and he smelled and tasted it. When he went back into the house he folded up his pallet and he washed himself up, and after breakfast he got an early start. He told Jenny Lee to tell Gus that he had left early because he had to make a stop before he got to work.

"So soon in the morning?" Jenny Lee said, smiling at her brother. Signifying.

"Got to tend to some business," Rob said.

"The early bird catches the worm—doesn't it, baby," Mama said.

"Old Fat Gus sure is an early bird," Rob said. "And somebody I know sure seem to like it."

"If I call their right name will you whistle?" Mama said.

"Onh onh," Rob said. "You aren't going to get Youngblood in no mess like that. I can't whistle anyhow. But Fat Gus can whistle. I bet a great big fat man Fat Gus can whistle." He kissed his mother and he gave Jenny Lee a smack on her cheek, and he went out into the new spring morning where the rhythm was jumping.

His feet took him quickly toward the house where Ben Raglin lived and Mrs. Sarah Raglin lived and pretty Miss Ida Mae Raglin Sweetening spent her week-ends. He reached the house and he knocked on the door, and as he stood there waiting, he could feel his heart knocking against his ribs, and he hoped she would be the one to come to the door. The door opened and there she stood. She looked surprised at first, but after a terrible anxious moment for him he saw her burst right out into a beautiful smile and her eyes were smiling and her lips were smiling and her whole face smiled. "Well—well—well—you really are the stranger." She seemed to be singing.

"Good morning, Ida Mae. How're you this morning? And Miss Sarah and Ben?"

"Just fine, Rob, I thank you. Everybody just fine. You're look-ing like the picture of health this morning. How're your folks?"

"They're all right, I reckin. I guess I'm the worst."

She laughed and spring was all over her and inside of her, and he wanted to take her into his arms right then and there. "Won't you come in and have breakfast with us?" she said. "Mama and I were kind of lazy this morning. We were just fixing to sit down to the table. Ben left the house looking for work a good while ago."

"No thank you, Ida Mae. I can't stay a minute. Got to get downtown to the man's job. I just wanted to know are you going to be busy tonight." He could feel himself swallowing all down through his body.

She said, "I'm sorry, Rob. I have a date—an engagement—already. I'm going up to a concert in Macon."

He said, "Maybe I can get Mr. Myles' car and take you up there. How about that? I like concerts." His voice was anxious. His eyes were desperate.

She looked up into his face, her big eyes filled with a deep concern. "I've already arranged to go with someone else, Rob."

"Oh," he said.

"I'm sorry, Rob. I didn't know you were coming around."

He said, "That's all right, Miss Sweetening." He made himself smile. "We'll get together one of these days I reckin. Give my best to Miss Sarah and Ben." He turned and started across the porch and down the steps. He didn't see the green vines climbing from the porch railings up to the top of the porch, nor did he smell the sweet honeysuckles, nor see the first flowers of spring in the yard nor the rosebushes, nor the lilies in bloom. Spring had died for him almost before she had a chance to be born.

"Rob—Rob."

He turned quickly toward her again. Maybe he had only imagined she called him.

"Are you busy tomorrow evening, Rob?"

"You know I work till eight o'clock, Ida Mae."

"Why don't you come as soon as you get off. If you can get Mr. Myles' car, we can go for a ride, or we can do anything we want to do. And then afterwards you can drive me out to the school."

He walked back up on the porch and held her hands in his and he smiled deeply down into her eyes. "All right, Miss Sweetening. I'll be seeing you tomorrow night." He heard the musical stroke of the city hall clock from way downtown and it told him that it was already a quarter to eight, and he would have to run all the way to the job . . . That night he went by Richard Myles' to pay him a visit and to see about borrowing the car for Sunday night, but Richard had driven to Atlanta for the weekend.

Sunday was a bright and beautiful day like you grew to expect most Sundays to be. Rob worked in a kind of frenzy all day long, watching the clock in the lobby and hoping when eight o'clock came he would not be caught upstairs rooming a guest, because he was going to quit at eight o'clock no matter where he happened to be. He had just roomed a guest and went back downstairs to the post and he looked up at the clock and it was only one-fifteen and he had thought surely it must be at least six, and he didn't know how he was going to make it with practically seven more hours to go. At about two thirty he was on his way downstairs and he knew it must be eight o'clock already, and he wanted to be away from the hotel and with Ida Mae so desperately, that he could feel it in his limbs and taste it in his mouth and his head began to throb and he just wouldn't wait any longer. He looked for Leroy and told him that he had an awful headache and he believed he had a fever and he couldn't work any longer and could he please get off for the rest of the day, and Leroy said he would see about it, and when he saw Rob a few minutes later he said Okay. "Tell your mother take good care of you."

Rob was the funniest sick man Leroy had ever seen. Leroy shook his head and smiled to himself. Before Rob was out of his sight he broke into a run and down the steps and washing up and getting dressed and his face a pleasing beaming brown as if he had run right out from under the headache. He got to Ida Mae's a little after three, and she hadn't expected him before eight thirty, but she was ready and waiting.

Side by side they walked out the Big Road with spring and the Cross County Woods on both sides of them, he grown into a lanky six-feet-two tall handsome brown boy, already a hard-working man, with a face that looked so much like his mother's, the narrow eyes with the long black eyelashes that seemed to look into the depths of everything and the prominent nose and sensitive mouth, and she was five-feet-six and relatively tall and long waisted and long-legged too, and her eyes still big and brown and anxious and pretty like they always were and her mouth her curvy lips and her nose and her roundish face just as he had always remembered it.

He remembered when they were kids in the first grade and

**384**

second grade and third grade and he had always sort-of-loved her. Puppy love, the grown folks called it. He remembered them getting older and she getting prettier and noticed and picked at by the older boys and the painful jealousy that he had silently suffered. He remembered the day when he had run away from home or had tried to, and she had wanted to know what his trouble was and to share it with him and he had wanted to tell her but his pride and his love for his mother hadn't let him do it. He remembered walking home from school every day with her and carrying her books, and especially the day she wrote him that letter about Betty Jane Cross.

They stopped walking and he looked down into her warm brown face and her big eyes and he took hold of both of her hands. "Let's leave the road and walk into my woods a piece. It's really pretty this time of the year."

"I don't know, Rob. You know how they talk about women school teachers. We have to watch every move we make. Especially out there in the country. You don't know."

"I know what you mean, Ida Mae. It makes you wonder sometimes doggonit why people so mean and doggone backward."

She laughed ironically. "This old world sure is hard on colored folks and women."

He squeezed her hand. "Do you want to go for a walk in the Youngblood Woods, Miss Sweetening?"

They both looked at the great big glittering greenness of the Cross County Woods. "I want to go for a walk in *your* woods, Rob, but—"

"Let's go then," he said, "and don't worry about a thing. The world doesn't need know about it at all. My friends in the woods won't tell a living soul outside."

She laughed. "Let's go."

They walked and they talked and they listened. The grass grew wild and green here and tall on each side of them and the big trees and the little trees and the in-between trees, green and glittering, and birds singing and wild flowers growing and noisy crickets and grasshoppers and all kinds of unseen creatures running through the deep grass, and a lady robin-redbreast busy as a bee building a nest in a poplar tree and a mockingbird making all kind of funny pretty sounds and two gray squirrels playing ten-ten-double ten. And they were completely taken in by the woods, and everything else was entirely forgotten. She felt a wild and drunk kind of freedom. They walked till they came to a spot, underneath a sparkling spruce tree, that had been cleared away some time before probably for a picnic.

"Let's sit down and rest a little while, Miss Sweetening. I had it cleared off just for us."

"Thank you, Mr. Youngblood. I sure do appreciate your hospitality."

They sat down and she lay back and stretched her slim body and looked up into the spruce tree and through the bright green needles up at the wide blue vastness hovering just above the top of the trees. She breathed deeply and the plumpish softness of her bosom pushed her yellow blouse in and out like a woman asleep and breathing deeply, and her face a much darker brown than he remembered it used to be; dark and warm and brown her arms. "Rob! Rob! It's so wonderful out here in your woods. It's so beautiful and it smells so nice and ripe and green, it's a pleasure to breathe, I declare it is." The trees stood still in the afternoon heat, and heavy with bright green leaves. The leaves motionless as if holding their breaths for something to happen.

He next to her and looking down into her face, and her eyes alive with so much happiness and freedom. "Are you glad you came?" his husky voice asked her.

"Rob! Rob!" was all she said, and she reached out and took his hand and squeezed it hard, and he took her quickly into his arms and he kissed her fiercely and he kissed her tenderly—her soft sweet curvy lips, her eyes her nose her cheeks her ears, and he felt her body trembling in his arms and his body trembled. He stopped kissing her for a moment and she reached up and put her hands behind his neck and pulled his lips back to hers.

"Why did you stay away so long, Rob?"

"I don't know. I guess I'm just crazy as a bedbug."

"You went up to great big old New York City and you didn't write me but two or three old little biddy letters. I thought maybe you had gotten sweet on one of those up-the-country girls."

Shaking his head like he wanted it to fall off the top of his body. He couldn't say a word.

"Then you come back home and you come to see me once or twice and then I don't see you anymore. I thought maybe you were going with Willabelle Braxton. She works at the hotel."

"That's a great big hotel," he said. "I hardly ever see Willabelle. And even if I did, it wouldn't make any difference."

"How come you stayed away so long, Rob?"

"After that day I made a fool out of myself out to your school in the country, I thought you didn't want to see me anymore. And everybody said Mr. Blake was sweet on you."

She looked at Rob and she laughed and shook her head. "You made me so mad that day in the country, but you looked so pitiful and sweet when I left you on the porch. Like a little biddy old baby boy."

"Everybody says you sweet on Mr. Blake," he said. He had not wanted to say it.

She started to speak. Her soft lips curved into a circle like they always had a way of doing when she talked. And his mind made a ridiculous picture of Mr. Blake, old and balding and getting fatter by the day, and he was afraid of what she was going to say and her mouth nice and curvingly round always looked even sweeter than ever when she talked. "How could you Ida Mae?" he shouted softly to her and smothered her lips with the fiercest kind of an agonized kiss and the words she was speaking never were heard.

And now he held her closely and her sweet breath caressing his warm face and the breathing softness of her plump bosom against chest. "Do you believe what everybody says?" she asked him.

"I was so jealous I didn't know what to believe."

"But did you believe it?"

"I didn't believe it, sweetheart, till I drove out that Friday to bring you back home. After that I didn't know what to believe."

"Listen, Rob, Ben Blake is old enough to be my father. And anyhow he isn't the kind of man I could ever like. But he has been nice to me, and he said he would come for me that time and drive me home, and he got there before you did. What was I supposed to do—tell him never mind? You have to be nice to people, Rob, don't you?"

He didn't say anything at first. If she only knew how stupid he really had been that night—down in Harlem Alley! When he did speak to her he said, "I love you, Ida Mae."

She said, "He's taken me around a couple of places. He took me to the concert in Macon last night. But it doesn't mean a thing."

Rob repeated in a husky voice, "I love you, Ida Mae."

"Do you really love me, Rob Youngblood?"

"Yes yes yes—you know I love you." He reached around desperately inside of his mind for words, more powerful words, to make her understand the mighty size and power of his love for her, but there were no such words, so he merely repeated, "I love you, darling."

She smiled and said, "I love you too darling. I reckin I always have loved you since I can remember."

She lay with her head in his lap, and he looked down into her big happy eyes and he watched her curving lips rounding out her mouth when she said I love you darling, and he felt a greater happiness than ever before, and his whole being overflowing with a great gladness and love for her and he leaned forward and kissed her lips gently and his silly tears fell onto her face. She kissed his eyes till they were dry of his tears and damp with her kisses.

"I wanted to tell you I loved you many many times when I was a girl in school, but they say the girl's supposed not to be so forward and wait for the boy to say it first, and I always wanted you to be my feller since I-don't-know-when. It didn't make any sense to me, darling, but the main reason I didn't tell you, was I didn't think you were studying about me. Because all the little girls were truly crazy about Rob Youngblood. Even that old white girl out to the Crosses."

He felt an angry uneasiness flow through his body when she mentioned the Crosses. He looked around at the listening trees as if they were long tall white-sheeted crackers moving in on them. He laughed nervously. "You ought to stop that stuff," he said. "Wasn't any other girls studying about me."

"Humph," she said. "Tell that to somebody don't know any better. What about Willabelle Braxton? She still stuck on you."

They talked about his trip to New York and his experience in the union and his job in the restaurant and the tall skyscrapers and the subways and the pretty picture shows that allowed colored people. They didn't notice the shadiness falling softly and quietly onto the woods as time slipped by swiftly and unnoticed. They talked about her school and she said if she taught there next year, she was going to teach Negro history the way Mr. Myles had taught it to them, and he stopped her curving lips with a kiss. And she told him about the night of spiritual singing that was being planned, and the program around it like Jubilee Night. She told him about the children she taught and the little boy named Harold who was big for his age and reminded her of

Rob when he was that age, and she didn't believe in having pets in her school, but in his case she just couldn't help showing a teeny bit of preference. He kissed her again. "I never did like a teacher who believed in pets," he said mockingly. "You better watch that kind of stuff, woman." And he told her about the work at the hotel and the running and the waiting and the mamming and the sirring, but he didn't tell her about the part the white women played in their negligees and their birthday suits. It crossed his mind time and again, but he left it unsaid. He told her about his talk with the boys about getting together and about Oscar Jefferson.

"You better watch your step, darling," she said, her big eyes filled with concern for him.

"We got to do something," he said. "If we don't, it's going to get worse. Old man Ogle going to get away with anything he's big and white and ugly enough to get away with. And nothing's going to stop him but us colored folks down there getting together. Let the man know how much stuff you'll take, that's how much he'll give you."

And westward the sun was going down and shadows falling softly all over the woods, but by this time Rob saw nothing but the love and the springtime in Ida Mae's eyes, deafened to the many noises of the woods because he heard nothing but the music in Ida Mae's voice. And her breathing long and labored and so was his and his legs aching and a nervous quiver in the bottom of his stomach and a fever running all through his body. They lay full length on the grass and he pulled her to him and they kissed and he began to caress her womanly softness with an awkward roughness that was sometimes tender, her softness growing firm underneath his touch.

"No, Rob—No!" And she turned away from him.

And even though he didn't want to offend her, at that moment his love was so overwhelming it demanded of her that she be a woman instead of a schoolteacher, because somehow he knew she didn't really want to turn away from him. And he pulled her around into his arms again and his lips seized hers and she fought against him for the slightest moment and she uttered Oh God! And going limp in his arms and then her arms desperately around him as if she would never again turn him loose and her long soft body hard against his and the breath against breath, and love was so rough and love was so tender and love was so painful and love

**389**

was so sweet, and young love at that, and the shadows falling faster now all over Youngblood's woods. . . .

He felt so happy he couldn't say a word, as she lay in his arms, and he felt like shouting for joy. He was surprised when the sobs shook her bosom up against him and her hot salty tears fell upon his face.

"What's the matter, darling? You're crying."

She shook her head and she wiped her eyes on his shirt.

"What's the matter?" He had been so completely carried away, he could not imagine why she was crying.

"Nothing's the matter," she said and she turned away from him.

"Ida Mae, honey, there must be something the matter."

"Suppose something happens?" he heard her mumble. "Suppose something happens?"

"Something happens?"

"You know what I mean, Rob. Suppose I get pregnant?" She turned back to him. "I'd be so scared, Rob. I wouldn't know what in the world to do."

He put his arms around her again. "Don't cry, baby. Don't be scared. It wouldn't be just you, darling. It would be both of us— you *and* me." He kissed her lips, kissed her eyes, big and brown and wet with sweet salty tears.

She shook her head.

"What's the matter, darling?"

She didn't say anything, wiped her face again on his shirt tail.

"Ida Mae, what's the matter?"

"If something did happen, I'm the one they would low-rate, Rob. Everybody in town would put the blame on me—just because I'm a woman. They would kick me out of the school system so fast it would make your head swim." She pulled away from him and looked up into his confused face and her eyes flashed with anger as if he were to blame for everything. He didn't know what to say. They had been so supremely happy a few moments before, it didn't seem possible that they were the same people. And yet he knew she was telling the gospel truth. Because he remembered painfully little Theresa Gaines. She had been the nicest quietest little girl in the whole school. Sitting in school one day quiet and innocent, and a few days later like a clap of thunder, the whole town was talking and scandalizing her

**390**

name, as if she had committed first degree murder. She was this and she was that and she ought to be ashamed of herself, a shameless hussy, and all this because poor little Theresa was going to have a baby. She was expelled from school and everybody tried to see how mean they could be. Hardly anybody said anything against Skinny Johnson who had made her pregnant and had gotten nervous and left town on a freight train. Rob had heard Old Lady Sarah say to Mama—"These little hot-tail gals these days can't keep they dress down." And Mama had blessed the old woman out. "What about the boy?" Mama asked. "What about Skinny? I haven't heard anybody say a word against him" . . . "He couldn't've did it if she didn't let him and give him encouragement," old Lady Sarah said. "Aah Lord, Sarah," Mama said, "I can just imagine Skinny needed a whole heap of encouragement. I reckin little Theresa just plumb took advantage of him. Poor Skinny—Poor Skinny." That night Mama went to see Theresa, and her father was fixing to put her out and Mama gave him a blessing out and made him ashamed of the way he had turned against his own daughter. Later that night Mama spoke to Rob and Jenny Lee. "Women don't have no bed of roses in this old world. I want you both to understand that, especially you, Rob. Don't ever take advantage of a woman, son. And if you do make a slip, be man enough to take up the responsibility. Poor little Theresa don't know which way to turn. That boy's done his devilment and left her to suffer. Isn't anybody she can turn to, not even to God." Daddy had puffed on his smelly old pipe and looked straight at Rob. "There ain't a finer person on God's green earth, Rob, than your Mama, and you know that, and your Mama is a woman. So if you ever in life, tomorrow or a hundred years from now, get it into your head to mistreat a woman just 'cause this old world give you more privileges, just think about your Mama. Woman—woman—woman—GreatGodAlmighty!" And they had sat there shaking their heads, Rob and Big Sister. . . .

Ida Mae was sitting away from him now and crying again and there was a terrible fear in her eyes. He would never take advantage of Ida Mae Raglin. Never! Never! He drew her to him again and he said to her in a strange husky voice, "Nothing's going to happen. Nothing's going to happen, Ida Mae. We're going to get married anyhow sooner or later. So if something does happen, it'll just mean sooner instead of later."

"But we're so young, Rob," she said.

It was as if she had stared into his mind. He too had been thinking that they were very young to be talking about babies and children. And wanting to go to college and becoming a lawyer. He made himself laugh. "We're old enough to know better," he said. "If we're old enough to make a family we're old enough to keep it together." He tried to think of something else to say to her to make it all right, because it had been so sweet and beautiful and wonderful all afternoon in Youngblood's woods and he didn't want it to end like this. He reached around desperately in his mind for the words that would make her know exactly how it was. But the only thing he came up with was—"I love you, sweetheart. You know I love you." And that was what she wanted to hear again and again because Ida Mae Raglin truly did love Rob Youngblood.

## CHAPTER FIVE

WHEN HE GOT to work the following day the men kidded him about his headache. Elmo said, "Old Youngblood must've went to the best doctor in town. He sure look healthy as a dog today."

"That kind of doctor is good for what ails you," Ellis said, "honh, Youngblood? Old Youngblood look as happy as a monkey eating ground-peas."

He had been working for about an hour when the *man* sent for him. He thought about the warning Oscar Jefferson had given him that night going up the alley a few weeks before. Mr. Bussey was going to give him his walking papers. It couldn't be anything else. He went into the office and stood waiting for Mr. Bussey to say something to him. The sloppy looking white man had his head bent over a pile of paper and he didn't look up when Youngblood entered, but he knew that Youngblood was there all right. Rob knew that he knew. After a couple of minutes he glanced up at Youngblood, and he looked down again and reached for his telephone. Rob felt his whole body going hot with anger and his fear was forgotten. He sat down in one of the chairs in the office. To hell with Mr. Bussey—his feet were tired.

Minutes passed before the white man looked up again, and when he did look up he stared at Youngblood as if he didn't recognize who he was or why he was there. He tried to stare Rob up from the chair, but Rob wouldn't move.

Finally Mr. Bussey spoke to him. "Come over here by the desk, Youngblood. I don't like to shout so everybody know our business."

Youngblood got up and came toward the desk and stood there tall and angry and dangerous and waiting.

"How you like your job, Youngblood?"

"It's all right, Mr. Bussey."

"You got any complaints?"

He wanted to say he had a million complaints, but he thought about what Ellis had said about it wouldn't do any good for one person to complain. He would just get fired and what good would that do? Within fifteen minutes some poor colored bastard would happily step in and fill his place. "No, sir," he said.

"Are you sure about that, boy?"

"Yes, sir."

"Boy I heard tell there is a strange colored person in town riding around in a brand new Packard car. You know anything about it?"

"No, sir."

"Somebody told me it's a big good-looking colored woman, some say it's a man. You sure you don't know nothing about it? You ain't heard nothing?"

What was this cracker driving at?—A stranger in a car? "No, sir, I don't know a thing about it. I haven't heard a word."

"I believe he's one them union racketeers. What you think?"

"I don't know a thing about it."

"Boy, you better not know nothing about it. That's the one thing a colored man better stay away from if he aiming to keep out of trouble. Them union racketeers is the worst thing in the world for a colored man to mess with, especially in Georgia, all that social equality and messing with white women."

Rob didn't say a word. He hoped his face didn't give away how angry he was.

"That ain't all I heard," the cracker said. "I heard you were studying about joining one of these unions."

Rob looked the cracker in the eye without batting an eyelash. "You did?"

Mr. Bussey said, "That's just what I heard. I ain't got nothing to do with it, Youngblood, but it ain't nothing but something to take your money." He pounded the desk with his big red fist. "You don't have to pay a penny, not one red copper to get a job here or to keep it after you get it. It's highway robbery and you don't have to do it! And NLRB or no NLRB I won't stand for it!"

Rob stood there watching Mr. Bussey with a blank look on his face. He wanted to burst out laughing at the cracker.

"There ain't gonna be no union at the hotel, Youngblood. I tell you right now. You might as well get them New York ideas outa your head. You can tell the boys. And if we find out who the strange colored man is we fix him so he wish he never heard of Crossroads, Georgia. You hear me, Youngblood?"

"I hear you, Mr. Bussey."

That evening when he knocked off work he told the boys about it down in the locker room. The men had serious looks on their faces.

"How come he told you all this mess, Youngblood? How come he picked you out? You the youngest one here," Ellis Jordan said.

The men looked around at each other thoughtfully.

"How the hell do I know?" Youngblood said.

"You better be careful," Will Turner said. "We better let that union mess die down for a while."

"What you mean die down?" Fat Gus said. "It ain't never been born yet."

"And it ain't gon never be born if Mr. Ogle have anything to say about it."

"If we want to get together and form us a union, Mr. Bussey or Mr. Ogle or anybody else don't have a damn thing to do with it," Youngblood said.

"I still can't figure out why the man picked on you, Youngblood—lessen some white mouth been to him beating up they gums." Ellis Jordan looked around at the rest of the men who had already dressed for the street and were standing around with frowns and worried looks on their faces. "A sonofabitch that'll carry stories to the white man is lower than a rattlesnake."

Bruh Robinson coughed. "You mighty right."

Will wiped perspiration from his wrinkled brow.

Hack Dawson smiled an ironical smile. "Goddamn—Goddamn—"

They all looked worried.

**394**

Rob went to see Richard Myles that night and they talked far into the night about conditions at the hotel which were growing worse every day and about unions. Richard told Rob that he had to go back to Atlanta over the week-end to an NAACP meeting, and he thought that there might be a union up there interested in organizing hotel workers, and he would go by and have a talk with them. Richard Myles made some lemonade and they sat around in the little living room drinking lemonade and eating tea cakes that Josephine had made and the three of them sat around talking about unions and the NAACP and the south in general. He couldn't seem to keep his embarrassed eyes off Josephine Myles who was three or four months with child and poking out slightly. He thought about Ida Mae and last Sunday in Youngblood woods and Great God Almighty he hoped she wasn't pregnant but it had been truly wonderful and no other day in his whole life had been as wonderful.

"When we going to form an NAACP in Crossroads?" Rob asked. He looked at Richard and glanced at Josephine and he remembered when they were Miss Josephine and Mr. Myles to him and they were his teachers before they hardly even knew each other, but he was a man now, a hard working man.

"That's just the thing we're working on now," Josephine said.

"Well, you all just let me know when you ready. I can get the folks at the hotel to join."

"We'll let you know soon enough," Richard said. "Don't worry about a thing." Richard told him about the couple of times he had gotten together with Dr. Riley and a couple of other teachers out at the white University and discussed the forming of an NAACP in Crossroads, and the time he had been to dinner at Dr. Riley's. "He's a pretty nice cracker," Richard said, smiling at Rob. Rob thought about his Daddy and Oscar Jefferson and laughed out loud. Richard said, "Dr. Riley's old man was a missionary. The American Missionary Association sent him down here from Vermont to teach at Talladega. And I reckon Dr. Riley considers himself dedicated to his father's work. I told him the colored didn't need any missionaries. He needed to work on these uncivilized white folks, because they were the most ignorant and unscientific and barbarous people on the face of the earth."

"No you didn't." Rob laughed and he glanced at Josephine.

"He naturally told him," Josephine said, and all of them laughed.

"He's really a pretty nice fellow though," Richard said seriously, "and he likes a good philosophical discussion, and Josephine and I really do engage him. He asks for it and we give it to him."

"He's got a face that looks like Abraham Lincoln," Josephine said.

When he left them that night he felt a little better about things but he still couldn't figure out how Mr. Bussey knew he had been the first to say something to the men about getting together. As he walked through the spring night he could see them sitting on the couch together, Josephine and Richard, and there was a new kind of glowing beauty about Miss Josephine that was never there before, and he was glad that they had married and he wondered about the new kind of toughness he could feel in Richard Myles these days, gradually growing like newly-found muscles, and how much like down-home-folks he was talking, or maybe Rob had become accustomed to his up-the-country brogue. He thought about himself and Ida Mae and marriage and children, and he thought about college and becoming a lawyer, and he thought about the fellows down at the hotel, and he wondered who the stool pigeon was.

The next Sunday there was a great big spread in the Sunday *Telegram* that talked about anti-American, Yankee influences that had come into town and stirring up the workers and especially the colored workers, and it warned that things were nice and peaceful in Crossroads, Georgia between colored and white and it was going to stay that way and Crossroads wasn't going to stand for any stirring up trouble by a bunch of union racketeers. And if any foreign elements were discovered in town they would be dealt with in the good old southern tradition. Rob read the editorial with a nervous excitement and everybody wondered what it was all about.

The next morning at the hotel, he roomed a very well-to-do looking white man, and the man worked him half to death ordering this, that and the other thing for him and his elegant young wife. "Boy, take these suits and see to them getting pressed, and take these things to the laundry for Miss Peavy and bring me a set-up of ice and soda, and be quick about it." And after he had finished running all over the world for Mr. and Mrs. Peavy, Mr. Peavy, a great big handsome giant of a rich-looking cracker, who reminded Youngblood of Mr. Cross Jr., gave Rob a quarter and had the nerve to ask him for fifteen cents change.

Youngblood stood looking at the cracker, the sweat from the last hour and a half of work draining from him all over his body. He put his hands in his pocket and jingled the nickels and dimes that were there. He looked from Mr. Peavy to pretty Miss Peavy and back to Mr. Peavy again.

"I don't have any change, Mr. Peavy."

"You sure you ain't got no change, boy?"

"Yes, sir."

"Let him have the whole quarter, Ronald. It won't break you. And he looks like such a nice boy. We worked him hard enough to give him a quarter." Her sleepy-looking eyes roamed all over Youngblood.

"Times too hard to be tipping a great big old quarter. That boy got change."

"Aw give it to him, Ronald. He's a nice boy."

Youngblood watched the man and his wife like they were two white folks in a Hollywood movie. He was so mad he could feel the sweat dripping from his eye brows into his eyes. He handed the quarter back to the cracker.

"That's all right, Mr. Peavy. Times is so hard, I know you can't afford it. I wouldn't want your whole family to suffer just for one lousy dime." And he turned quickly and left the white folks standing in the middle of the room.

The next day at the hotel they cut everybody's wages a dollar all down the line. And the place was buzzing, and there were angry looks everywhere and grumbling and swearing under their breaths, and there was fear and distrust, and even some of the white men grumbled. That evening in the locker room, the men were quietly dressing. Hack Dawson looked up. "What we going to do, Youngblood? You told us it would happen."

Youngblood looked at Hack. Everything was quiet, waiting for his answer, all fearful angry eyes on Rob Youngblood. He felt his youth bearing down on him in comparison with their age and experience and he thought about the future, and him and Ida Mae, and college and law, and the editorial in the Sunday *Telegram,* and what did he know to tell these people?

"Don't ask me," he said in an anger that he didn't himself understand. "All of you all worked here way longer than I have."

"Yeah, but Youngblood, goddamn, we got to do something."

Fat Gus looked around at the rest of the men. "Youngblood told you asses what to do a long time ago—Get together and make up a goddamn union. Y'all wanted to wait and see. I reckin you done seen enough by now goddammit."

"We still get more than over at the Rob Lee," Will Turner said. "It sure could be a whole heap worser. You know what was in the Sunday's paper, and them people won't fooling."

"I can't stand this cut," Hack said. "Too many mouths to be fed at my house. Tips getting littler and littler every day. Some of these snakes put up such a poor mouth when you rooming them you feel like putting your hand in your pockets and giving them a tip steada the other way round."

Rob had to smile. It reminded him of the guests he had roomed yesterday morning—Mr. and Mrs. Peavy.

Bruh Robinson looked at Rob and he looked at Gus and glanced at Will. "Old Will ain't never gon be for no union. He too damn scared of the white folks."

"Ain't nobody scared of the white folks," Will said.

"Will ain't scared of the white folks," Gus said. "He just wouldn't take a good healthy shit if Mr. Charlie told him not to. He'd walk around with a load in his britches. But he ain't scared —onh-onh—not much."

The men laughed bitterly.

"You better watch what you say, Gus Mackey. I don't have to take no stuff off no young ass nigger like you."

"Oh," Fat Gus said, staring at Will with an evil grin on his face. "I see what you mean, Mr. Turner. You don't take no shit offa no young ass nigger like me. You just lets Mr. Charlie shit all over you. Excuse me—please, sir, but my mother didn't have no *nigger* babies, even if your mother did."

"Goddammit—I done told you to cut it out!" He picked up the wooden stool he had been sitting on and walked toward Gus. His face covered with perspiration and his arms trembling. Gus stood up and waited.

"Take it easy, Will, you and Gus."

"Don't tell him nothing," Gus said. "Don't tell Uncle Tom a goddamn thing. Let the devil fool him."

"You see?" Will shouted. "You see? I don't have to take that kind of stuff. I'll try my best to crucify him." He swung at Gus with the stool and Gus ducked and the blow glanced off his shoulders, and Gus closed in on Will and hit him once in the stomach and once on the jaw and the stool skidded to the other side of the locker room. Rob jumped between Gus and Will puffing and blowing like horses. "Turn me loose goddammit!" Bruh Robinson was holding Will Turner and Rob held Gus.

"That's what we always do," Rob said. "Fight each other instead of Mr. Charlie."

Gus tried to pull away from Rob. "Turn me loose, Youngblood. I mean it goddammit! That old Uncle Tom tried to hit me on the head with that stool. I'll kill him dead as he got to die."

Rob pulled Fat Gus away to a corner of the locker room, and he turned to the rest of them. "You see?" he said angrily. "You see how quick we are to fight each other—instead of the *man?* Mr. Charlie can do anything he wants to, all we do is grumble to each other. That doesn't make Mr. Ogle's business bad—It just tickles him to death. Go ahead, kill each other." He turned and walked out the locker room.

When he got home Richard Myles had been there and left word for him to come by his house. He was so angry and upset about the hotel and the fellows at the hotel, he didn't feel like seeing Richard Myles or anybody else. But he went.

When he got there he was introduced to a man who looked to be about the size and the age of his father, only Jim Collins wasn't as stout as Joe Youngblood. He was long and rangy, and his eyes were deep and seemed to watch you closely, taking everything in. Richard introduced Jim to Rob, and Rob was impressed with the warm handshake and the serious watchful eyes.

"Mr. Collins is a union organizer," Richard told Rob.

Rob looked quickly into the man's face again, and he felt a swift excitement beating at his temples. He looked at Richard as if he had probably not heard him correctly. Union organizer!

Richard Myles laughed. "That's what I said, Rob, union organizer. You know any workers who need to be organized?"

"Do I?"

They sat down and began to talk and Rob could not keep his eyes away from the man's face and the warmth of his face and the strength of his eyes—and—and union organizer! In Crossroads, Georgia! He felt a chill spread over his back.

"The people I'm talking about work at a hotel," Rob said hesitantly.

"There ain't no hotel workers' union around that's interested in organizing colored workers," Jim Collins said. "Not that I know of. Our union is mainly interested in factory workers."

"Oh—." Rob was plainly disappointed.

"But if there are workers raring to be organized and nobody else to organize you, we might be able to give you a hand."

"I don't know how raring they are," Rob said.

"Is the work hard?" Jim asked with a warm friendly smile.

"Yes, sir."

"Is the boss mean?"

"Mean as a rattlesnake."

"Oh," Jim said. "Then he must pay them extra high wages."

"No, sir, he doesn't. He used to pay three dollars and a half every two weeks, but just the other day he cut us to two and a half dollars. We have to depend mostly on tips, and the people aren't tipping what they used to tip. They don't do anything but talk to the bell boys about how hard times are."

Richard and Josephine sat listening to Jim and Rob. "It seems to me they should be raring for the union, Rob," Josephine said. "If things are so bad."

"Some of them are scared," Rob said. "Scared of losing their jobs and the way things are, they're scared they wouldn't be able to get another one."

"Yeah," Jim said. "And the way they figure, the fellow on the other job don't do as well as they do at the hotel, as bad as it is. And beside they don't know exactly what a union is."

"Some of them are ready," Rob said, wondering how Jim Collins, who didn't know any of the folks at the hotel, could know so much about them. "Some of them already said they were ready."

"How many workers at the hotel?" Jim asked.

"I don't know—between seventy five and a hundred." Rob looked at the long lanky figure sitting opposite him and he glanced around the room, and Josephine and Richard were really sitting there with them and it wasn't any dream, and he still couldn't believe that he was talking to a union organizer in Crossroads, Georgia—a colored organizer.

"How many colored?"

"Don't know exactly—More than half."

"Any white workers interested?"

"I don't know." And then he thought about Oscar Jefferson, and he thought about that night walking up the alley with Oscar, and Oscar in the payline and at the Jubilee and Oscar in the cracker union. "There is one white feller—kind of half decent. Can't quite figure him out yet. He might be interested but you can't ever tell about a cracker in Georgia." He turned to Richard

Myles. "You know the one—He spoke to you that Jubilee night at the auditorium. Oscar Jefferson."

"He seems pretty nice," Richard said. "He looks like the one we're looking for."

Jim interrupted. "Oscar Jefferson—Oscar Jefferson—" A big frown wrinkling the middle of his forehead. "You say his name is Oscar Jefferson?"

"Yes, sir," Rob said. "What's the matter?"

Jim smiled. "Nothing," he said. "I was just wondering if he was any kin to Old Thomas Jefferson or Jefferson Davis."

Rob looked at Jim and he looked around at the others and laughed.

They changed the subject, talked about the NAACP and Josephine said they were organizing a program for a couple of Sundays away at the Lincoln Theatre, and they expected to form a chapter in Crossroads, Georgia and they changed the subject again and they talked about Dr. Riley and Joe and Laurie and Eugene Talmadge and Franklin Delano Roosevelt, and all of them agreeing that President Roosevelt was turning out to be a pretty good president.

And Richard and Josephine served cinnamon buns and coffee and they talked some more. Because Jim Collins was easy to talk with and after awhile it was very cozy and very comfortable and it felt like kin folks. When the spirit moved him this Jim Collins fellow could talk talk talk and carry you completely away with his talk, but he could listen too. And he loved to listen.

Finally he told Rob he was on his way to south Georgia and could be in town only two more days, and could Rob have a few of the boys come over to Richard's on the following night. "Just a few," he cautioned Rob. "Just four or five that you can really trust." Rob said all right.

"How about Oscar Jefferson?" Richard suggested.

"Bring that friendly cracker along," Jim said. "We'll see what he's made of."

"The cracker?" Rob said. "The friendly cracker? I—I—I'm not sure of him."

"You sure of every last one of the colored workers?" Jim asked.

"Not exactly." Rob thought about the fact that one of the men had probably gone to the boss already and he wasn't sure which —but a colored man.

"Bring him along," Jim said, "if he'll come. It can't do no

**401**

harm. Somebody gon always carry tales to the *man,* even if you don't have nary a white man for miles around."

Richard said, "Bring him along. We might really have something here."

And so the next day five of them came along with Rob. Bruh Robinson and Gus and Hack Dawson and Ellis Jordan and Willabelle Braxton. And they sat there after they had met Jim Collins looking him over and laughing and talking. At about five after nine the doorbell rang, and everything got uneasily quiet, as they sat there staring at each other. Richard Myles opened the door and Oscar walked in. Bruh Robinson's mouth hung open in amazement. The other men from the hotel just sat there staring in surprise at the cracker. Richard said, "Come right in and have a sit-down." As if it was nothing at all unusual

He introduced Oscar to the other workers and they all gave him a stiff how-de-do, excepting Rob, who shook his hand. Rob looked at Gus and in his mind he could hear Gus saying to himself—What the hell kinda party is this?

And finally Jim got up to meet Oscar Jefferson and Oscar had not seen him sitting in a comfortable chair at the other end of the room. "Mr. Oscar Jefferson, meet Mr. Jim Collins."

And everybody could see Oscar's face and his red neck growing redder, as he stood like a man paralyzed at first and unable to bring his reddish white hand up to the black hand that reached out toward him. "Jim Collins! Jim Collins?"

The organizer's voice ran softly in the room. "How's old man Wilcox's plantation, boy?" he said to Oscar Jefferson.

Oscar's hand went up to meet the black man's. "Little Jim!" he muttered. "Little Jim—Little Jim!"

The other folks in the room looked on in amazement. It was the most curious sight in the world in Crossroads, Georgia.

"I'm a whole heap bigger than you ever were," Jim said. "Where you get that Little Jim stuff from?"

And Oscar Jefferson started to laugh and he couldn't stop laughing and he stood there laughing till the tears rolled down his cheeks and his face growing redder and redder every second. He looked around at the faces of the other folks in the room, and he wiped his eyes with the back of his hand. "Excuse me, folks," Oscar said. "It's been such a long time since I seen this boy."

"Boy?" Jim Collins said.

"Mr. Kil—I mean Mr. Collins."

**402**

"That's more like it," Jim said. He turned to the others. "Well let's get down to the case on the docket."

They started to talk, and Jim would ask them questions about this and that, but they were hesitant about their answers, and they threw distrustful glances at Oscar Jefferson, and they were not getting anywhere at all.

And finally Jim said, "Don't worry about Oscar. He's all right. I've known him since he was knee-high to a mosquito. He's with us I reckin. He better be."

And Fat Gus was glad to hear Jim say this, and so was Ellis Jordan and Willabelle and Hack and Bruh, because already they had a world of confidence in this tall black man, and they tried to loosen up in front of Oscar, but they just couldn't do it.

Finally Jim said excuse me a minute, and he called Oscar to a corner of the room and buzz buzz buzz and Oscar's face getting redder and redder and Jim Collins' hand on Oscar's shoulder and more buzz buzz, and finally Oscar left. And the folks opened up. He told them there was no hotel workers' union that he knew about in this region and they would have to organize themselves. He suggested that they have some union membership cards mimeographed and to get as many workers signed as possible, do it quietly, sound them out before asking them to sign. Then when a lot of them had signed, call them together. He told them they wouldn't have any easy time.

"Nobody don't ever have no easy time organizing a union, and especially in Georgia, but it can be done. And once you get started just stick together, don't care what comes.

"You didn't bring but one woman with you, Youngblood," he said, smiling at Willabelle. "Better get the women folks lined up just as quick as you can. They be the back-bone of the organization. I know what I'm talking about."

And then he told them that they should try to get some of the white workers if it were possible, and he told them he had known Oscar Jefferson ever since he was knee-high to a grasshopper, and Oscar used to be a straight-thinking white man when he was a boy, and he looked around at them and he could see the doubt and confusion written on their faces.

He stopped talking for a moment and looked from one to the other of them. "What's the matter?" he asked. "Y'all know something about Oscar that ain't been said?"

Nobody said a word.

"Y'all know something about Oscar I don't know?"

"We know he's a cracker," Fat Gus said. "But you know that. He sure can't pass for colored."

"He's a worker too," Jim Collins said. "Don't forget that."

"He was a cracker before he was a worker," Ellis said. "And I bet he ain't forgot that either. They don't ever forget it." Ellis lowered his eyes from the penetrating stare of Jim Collins. He looked at Rob. "Youngblood, I'm surprised at you—asking that cracker to come. We ain't gon never succeed in nothing unless we keep the crackers outa our business. You can't trust a white man no shape, form or fashion, especially down here in Georgia."

"You right about that," Hack Dawson said. "Yet and still, you got to have the white that works at the hotel on your side, or else you ain't gon amount to a hill of beans."

Richard Myles said, "He must be interested or else he wouldn't have come."

Jim Collins just listened.

"He too damn innerested," Ellis said.

Rob said, "We need the white workers at the hotel to join up with us, just like Hack already been telling us. And if there's one cracker in town that can be trusted a little biddy bit, it's Oscar Jefferson." Rob told them about his Daddy and that day in the payline and Oscar Jefferson, and Jubilee Night and the auditorium and Oscar and the cracker union and about that night a couple of weeks ago in Oglethorpe's alley. "We ought to give him a try and see what happens."

"I reckin so," Fat Gus said. "Ain't much we can lose."

"All right," Ellis said. "But I'm sure gon say I told you so."

Willabelle said, "The way I see it—the more join up the better it'll be. If we don't use the crackers against Mr. Ogle, Mr. Ogle'll use them against us."

"That's it, Sister," Jim Collins said. "That's the gospel truth."

"I knew you weren't going to go against Rob Youngblood," Fat Gus said to Willabelle underneath his breath. "If he said jump off the top of Hotel Oglethorpe, you'd be for it."

"Humph," she said.

"I know it's the truth. Youngblood could lead you by the nose all over Creation."

Jim Collins said, "Well, I tell you what let's do. I'm meeting with Oscar tomorrow night. I'm gon sound him out good fashion.

Maybe you should come over too, Youngblood, and you too, Sister—Sister—"

"Willabelle Braxton."

"Sister Willabelle. We'll sound him out, and if he sound all right, we'll get him to see how many crackers he can bring along with him."

"That's okay with me."

"I say we ought to keep the crackers out of our business."

But all of them were carried away with Jim Collins, even Ellis and Gus and Hack, and they seemed to want the evening to last on and on, just sit and talk about anything and everything, and let it grow late. But finally it ended and he said goodbye and good luck to them, and except for Willabelle and Rob Youngblood, maybe they would never see him again.

The next night they met at Richard Myles again with Oscar Jefferson, and they put it on the line with him, especially Jim Collins. He talked with Oscar just like he was talking to another colored man. Oscar said he didn't know how many, but he thought he could bring along a few white ones, he didn't know how many. It wouldn't be an easy job.

Jim said, "Humph—the colored workers ain't gon be easy either. Ain't no workers easy."

Oscar said, "I know that, but the white ones gon be a whole heap harder."

"How come?" Jim asked him. "They need a union just as bad as anybody else don't they?"

"I reckin they do."

"Reckin? Is the man giving them shares in the corporation?"

Rob and Willabelle and Richard and Josephine sat there fascinated, uncomfortable for the poor friendly cracker, marveling at the long tall colored man's boldness.

"They need the union all right," Oscar said. His face was reddening.

"What's the matter then? They ain't got as much sense as the Negroes got?"

"I don't know what the matter is." His voice was trembling with white folks' anger.

"This ain't nothing to be mad about, man," Jim said gently. "It's just one of the things that's always puzzled me—How long it gon be before the poor white folks catch on to people like Talmadge and old man Wilcox and the man that owns the hotel pulling the wool over their eyes?" He stared at Oscar long and hard. "Well, anyhow, it ain't your fault, Oscar, but doggonnit you ought to do your level best to see how many workers you can get to go along with the Negro workers. And they won't be doing the colored no favor neither. It'll be for their own damn good. Excuse me, ladies."

"I'll do what I can, Jim," Oscar said.

"Good—good—good—" Jim said. "And keep in close touch with Youngblood and Sister Willabelle and the rest of them." He smiled and he stretched wearily his long trembling legs. "I wish I had a nip of that good old Georgia corn they used to make on old man Wilcox's plantation." His eyes wandered around the room at the rest of them. He went and sat on the couch next to Oscar and he put his arms around the white man's shoulders and squeezed them hard and Rob could see the red coloration oozing around in the white man's face. "Me and old Oscar figured it out a long time ago—this colored and white business. Didn't we Oscar? Boy, it's a many a time I wondered about you and what you was doing—many a time."

They stayed so late that when they left, the buses had stopped running into Pleasant Grove and Rob walked all the way to Rockingham Quarters with Willabelle, and they talked about the folks at the hotel getting together and forming a union and they talked in wonderment about Oscar Jefferson, who was a poor white cracker, and always had been and talked like one and couldn't be mistaken for anything else but.

"I don't know," Willabelle said. "You just can't figure a cracker like that out no way you might try. He's just a plain every day cracker and he act like he don't think he's any better than anybody else. He musta be got something up his sleeve."

"I don't know, Willabelle. I think he's really the pure in heart. He's just got more sense than the rest of the crackers. He acts more like a human being than he does a cracker." Willabelle laughed. "I reckin so."

"That Jim Collins is about the roughest stud this side of nowhere, I'll tell anybody. He's truly great," Rob said.

They were at the top of Madison Hill and looking down on The Quarters which was entirely dark except for a few scattered dim lights in a few houses and looking like lightning bugs with their blinkers not working. When they reached the ditches he helped her across them, even though he knew that she could handle them as well as he, maybe more easily, because she was more used to them. And when he touched her like this he knew that her body was excited and tense. Though not a word or a movement gave her away, he knew. Because somehow he had always known how pretty Miss Willabelle Braxton felt about Rob Youngblood.

And as they walked through the dark Quarters now between the black shacks standing trembly in soft shaky shadows on each side of them, he thought about the time he had come to see her and Fat Gus had left them and the feeling he had had for her that day and she for him. They stood briefly in her tiny front yard, and even in the darkness he could see the few pitiful flowers she had planted there.

They walked up on her porch and it cried out loud enough to wake up the dead, let alone Miss Ella Mae, and the softer he walked the more noise the floor made. She turned to him near the front door, and she looked up into his face, and they stood there awkwardly in the yellow moonlight and they didn't say anything. Her soft black eyes, her dark warm face. When she spoke he could hear a tremble in her voice.

"I never will forget Mr. Jim Collins," she said, "and Oscar Jefferson is something to think about. I'm really glad you asked me to come."

"I'm glad you came," he said. "Get it first hand about building a union."

And everything got quiet again. He could hear the soft snoring of Willabelle's mother.

"Thank you, Mr. Youngblood, for walking me home."

"Wasn't anything, Willabelle."

"It's the first time you ever walked me home, I do believe."

"I reckin it is," he said and he thought about Ida Mae and the many times he had walked her home from school, carried her books, and it was very late and long past midnight and they both had to make Mr. Ogle's time early in the morning, and Willabelle Braxton had soft pretty eyes and was sweet on him, very very sweet, always had been, but he was in love with Ida Mae Raglin.

His deep husky voice came out of the darkness. "We got a great big job to do—building up a union."

"You mighty right, Rob."

He put his hand out and took her hand and held it tight and "Good-night, Willabelle."

"Good-night, Youngblood."

## CHAPTER SIX

BIG SISTER MAKING the last-minute morning preparations in front of the big mirror.

Mama getting ready for a long day of ironing white folks' clothes.

Rob taking a quick look at the *Morning Telegram*.

Daddy left the house before day in the morning, humming one of his favorite tunes—Walk Together Children.

Gus Mackey's crazy whistle. He had whistled the same whistle for the last six years, and Rob couldn't whistle any kind of whistle.

And both of them, Jenny Lee and Rob, kissing Mama good-bye for all day long.

"You think he's going to win tonight?" Mama asked.

"He ain't going to skip it. He's going to whip that peck till he knows not one."

"I don't know," Mama said. "That's a might big cracker he's fighting."

"That doesn't make any difference," Rob said. "The good Lord makes 'em, and Joe Louis don't pick 'em." Joe Louis was one of his favorite people, big and powerful and whipping every white man that came before him right down to the ground or down to the canvas, and every time Rob saw his name or heard his name, he felt a great pride as if Joe Louis were a full blood relative.

Fat Gus whistled again.

It wasn't any later than seven thirty, but the air was hot and heavy already and there wasn't much air to be hot and heavy. August was almost a thing of the past.

"How-do, Miss Youngblood," Fat Gus said with a mocking bow. "How're you, Mr. Youngblood? How you good folkses doing this beautiful sunshiny summertime morning?"

Jenny Lee Youngblood said, "Just fine." Just like she always said every morning. "How're you, Mr. Mackey?"

And they hardly spoke to Rob again till she left them at Orange

Street, and Gus said to her—"I'm coming by for you tonight, Jenny Lee, and take you over to Sadie's house to listen to the fight."

"All right, Gus. That'll be just fine."

Gus bowed to her like a real southern gentleman. "I'll see you tonight, Miss Youngblood."

"All right, Mr. Mackey."

And now they walked down Jeff Davis Boulevard, Rob and Gus, and they had started to walk faster as they always did after the first five blocks of courting. "Where you gon listen to the fight, Youngblood?" Gus asked him. "Why don't you come on over to Sadie's with us."

"I got to work tonight. They having a fight party up in Mr. Oakley's suite. Mr. Oakley asked for me to work on the party. He asked for Number Seven."

"He's a well-off cracker. You ought to make a nice taste of change. But you better watch out, because they gon be one evil bunch of peckerwoods, when Joe knock that cracker on his ass. They gon be evil and drunk and that's a bad combination."

"I sure could use a nice taste of change," Rob said, thinking about his Daddy, who had been a hard-working man since he was a little boy, years before Rob was even thought about, and out of work for the last two or three months.

"I sure do hope Joe wins," Rob said. "They say that cracker is sixty pounds heavier and strong as a bull."

"Man, Joe Louis is smart. He gon out-box him and out-fox him and then he gon out-fight him. Whenever Joe get in that ring with a cracker, he thinks about all the mean things crackers done against Negroes. He thinks about the lynchings, he thinks about the jim crow and the Ku Klux Klan and he thinks about how nice Negroes been to white folks too goddamn long and the more he thinks the madder he gets and the harder he hits. And it don't make no never mind how big the cracker is. Cause the bigger he is the more there is for old Joe to hit. Joe subject to haul off and hit that cracker tonight and knock him into the middle of next damn week."

Rob looked at Gus and he stopped walking and started to laugh and he laughed and he laughed and he couldn't stop laughing and the people on the street stared at them and what made it funnier than it actually was was the serious look on Gus Mackey's face. Rob always felt a quiet smouldering anger when he read in the sport columns of the *Telegram* and even in the Atlanta papers, that Joe was powerful, but sort of on the unintelligent side, brutish and unskilled. Rob thought of Joe as powerful and skillful and quiet and thoughtful and nobody's dumbbell, without education but a whole lot of mother wit.

"It's just like that Mr. Jim Collins said and I believe it's the truth. Sometimes you got to just whip some sense in these peckerwoods' heads else they ain't gon ever learn."

"You can say that again."

Like all the mornings of late Rob felt good and full of summertime till he reached the hotel, and then the big rich building seemed to reach out and pull him in and swallow him up and all the others and everybody worked under a feverish tension as if Mr. Ogle were spying on you from the walls of the hotel and the corridors and even up from the deep plushy carpet and eyes and ears that followed you everywhere like a picture on the wall. They had not gotten very far with forming the union, because the workers were scared to death of losing their jobs. A few had signed up, but most of them hadn't. That morning he met Bill Brinson in the colored lavatory washing his hands. Bill was a few years older than Youngblood. He had always been the kind of a fellow that didn't take any stuff off of anybody including white folks. A medium-sized black man with light brown eyes. He had just been transferred from the night shift to the day.

Rob walked up to Bill with one hand in his pocket fingering one of the mimeographed union cards. He always kept a few in his pocket. "What you know, Bill?"

"Don't know it, Youngblood. What you know good?"

"Don't know a thing good," Rob said softly. "I know the work is getting harder and the boss getting meaner. That's one thing I know."

"You ain't no lying man," Bill said. "That Mr. Ogle is a natural ass. Run your goddamn tongue out. I didn't have to do nothing. I just come in here to catch my breath."

"What you think of him cutting our pay?" Rob asked.

"It's a damn shame. Wasn't paying us a goddamn thing in the first place. It's a sin and a shame."

"Some of the folks want to do something about it," Rob said.

"Ain't nothing can be done," Bill said, his eyes traveling from the wash bowl to Youngblood and back again. "You have to like it or lump it. The man'll tell you quick, if you don't like it he'll get somebody'll be crazy about it."

"Some folks figured on getting together and doing something

about it. Not one single man by himself. Do something about the cut, the long hours and the shifts, one day off and all like that."

Bill laughed weakly. "You crazy man. Ain't nothing can be done." A slight uneasiness moving around in Bill's face now, wrinkling his brow, deepening his light brown eyes.

"Would you be against it?" Rob asked.

"Be against what?" Washing his hands over and over, unaware he was washing his hands.

"Against getting together and figuring out something and doing something about it. Together, I mean."

"I got to be for it," Bill said against his obvious will. He wiped his hands and he looked desperately as if he wanted to dash past Rob and be out of the lavatory, but he also wanted to stay a little longer and to hear what else Rob had to say.

Rob stared at Bill. He felt the mimeographed cards in his pocket. He could almost see the thoughts running around in Bill Brinson's head, the doubts and the fears, and Bill was a good guy, everybody knew it, not easily frightened. But it was time now to put up or shut up, it was time now to take his hand out of his pocket and have a union card in it and hand it to Bill. Rob hesitated, because he was tired of the excuses and the hemming and the hawing that some of the guys had given him when this point was reached. He was almost embarrassed.

Rob cleared his throat. "I thought you'd be for it." He took his hand slowly out of his pocket empty-handed. He cleared his throat again. "Some of the folks thinking about getting together and forming a union. They figured that's the only way to make Mr. Ogle get up off it."

"A union?" Bill said. His eyes glanced nervously toward the lavatory door as if he expected Mr. Ogle or the devil himself to come through it any minute. "What kind of old union?"

"A union union. What you mean what kind? You know what a union is. It gets us together and it speaks right up to the man in favor of us, and the man can't pick us off one at a time 'cause it's all of us."

"Sounds inneresting," Bill said worriedly.

"Would you be interested?" Youngblood asked.

Bill looked at Youngblood and he looked at the door and back at Youngblood again. "Course I would. But I'm in a real big hurry right now. I been off the job too long. They be coming in here looking for me directly."

He didn't want to push Bill any further at the moment, but he made himself do it. "Look here," Rob said, reaching in his pocket and bringing out a card and handing it to Bill.

Bill stared at the card in Youngblood's hand like it was a rattle-snake. "What's that?"

"A card—a union card. All you got to do is to sign it and that means you're for forming a union at the hotel, and we get a heap of us signed up, we're going to get together and form us a union."

"Who behind all this?"

"Nobody but us. What you mean?" Rob asked.

"You know what I mean. Ain't no racketeers behind it?"

Rob wanted to say—I'm one of the ones behind it. Do I look like a racketeer to you? "Of course no racketeers are behind it or in front of it either. Nobody behind it but the folks that work at the hotel. *We* are behind it."

"The *Telegram* say—"

"The *Telegram*'s mouth ain't no damn prayer book," Rob said.

"I know it ain't," Bill said. "But where there's a whole heap of smoke you can look for the fire."

"Look at it this way," Rob said heatedly. "You might say the *Telegram* is in the same union with Mr. Ogle and all the other rich white folks and they have gotten together and trying to scare us out of forming a union."

"How many men done already signed?"

"Quite a few," Rob lied, his face growing warmer.

"Sign up the rest of them, then come back to me and then I'll sign."

"If everybody waited on the other fellow," Rob argued, "nobody ever would get signed up."

Bill smiled sheepishly. "Gimme that goddamn card. How you learn to argue so good?"

Rob handed him the card. "Goddamn," Rob said, with an easy laugh, "a man with as much gumption and mother wit as you got, we counting on you to help get some of the others signed up."

He smiled at Rob, looked down at the strange-to-him looking card. "I got to study about it a little, Youngblood. Can't rush into nothing. I got to get back to the job. Been gone too goddamn long."

"Come on now, Bill. Aren't you going to sign?" He handed Bill a pencil that he carried around with him, but Bill didn't take it.

"Course I'm gonna sign. But don't rush me, Youngblood. I wanna study it a little bit. But you know I'm gonna sign. I got to do it." He put the card in his pocket and walked out of the lavatory.

**412**

Rob watched him go and he heaved a sigh of deep satisfaction
. . . and he wondered if Bill Brinson really would sign. He should
have pushed him a little further to sign then and there. It was just
like this with all the other workers, even many times worse, like
being in a chicken yard covered with chickens and pulling their
teeth out one by one. Right after Jim Collins had left town a few
of them had gotten together with Richard and Josephine and Reverend Ledbetter at the church and they had discussed at length
what would go on the card, Gus and Willabelle and Bruh and
Ellis and Richard and Josephine and Reverend Ledbetter, and it
should be this and it should be that and it should be the other. And
Richard cut the stencil and they ran it off on the church's mimeo-
graph machine. And the first few days he had approached the folks
at the hotel with all kinds of enthusiasm, sometimes even without
enough discretion. It was like he had gotten some kind of new religion and wanted to spread the good thing Jim Collins had left
with all of the folks. But after the first few days and the questions
that his folks at the hotel had asked, and the doubts and the fears
and two or three (Get away from me, man, I don't wanna hear no
kinda talk like that. You trying to get me in trouble) angry re-
fusals, his spirit and enthusiasm went up and down like an elevator.
Sometimes he wasn't sure whether his folks would ever get together. But he never gave up.

Youngblood tried to take it easy during the day because it would
be a long day for him with a half an hour off at seven thirty then
back to work Mr. Oakley's prize fight party. But there was no way
in the world he could take it easy, because the pressure was on
Leroy to keep the boys stepping lively every damn minute or get
another boy. Running smiling sirring mamming seeing-and-not-
seeing white missey's birthday garments, cussing sweating lifting,
stealing a minute to whisper to somebody about forming a union,
running smiling sirring cussing-under-breath, mamming sweating
all day long.

That afternoon about four o'clock he met Bill Brinson coming
up one of the corridors, and Bill didn't say a word. He just handed
the union card back to Rob and kept on walking down the carpeted
hall. Rob took it and put it quickly in his pocket with the other
unsigned ones. He had shot another blank. Well maybe he was
wrong about the whole damn thing. Maybe the union was really
bad for the folks at the hotel. Maybe the thing to do was to take
it easy—wait, hope and pray—but Mr. Ogle wouldn't let you
take it easy goddammit! He felt the worst kind of helpless anger

toward Bill Brinson, as he watched him disappear at the other end of the hall. "I got to do it—I got to be for it," Bill Brinson had told him just to git rid of him.

It wasn't worth the effort to take off his uniform when seven thirty came. It was hardly worth it to leave the hotel at all for a lousy half an hour. But he left and he was glad to leave, and it was hotter outside in the summertime night than in the hotel, a quiet dampish sticky kind of heat, but after all those suffocating hours of Hotel Oglethorpe he didn't mind it at all. He walked down to Harlem Avenue and he got himself a soft drink at a hot dog stand. He said hello to this one and he stopped to speak to that one, but mostly he walked along Harlem Avenue toward the outskirts of the city—walking and thinking. Wondering how long he would be at the hotel. Thinking about Ida Mae and getting married, and next year this time maybe he would be up north somewhere, because he was going to college and he was going to be a lawyer, a civil rights lawyer, but what about the folks at the hotel and making up a union, and the folks didn't want any union at the hotel, and he would probably be fired anyhow. He had sent to Washington for a copy of the National Labor Relations Act and Rules and Regulations and he had read it through and through, fancy language and all, Section this and Section that, and it was against the law for an employer to fire a worker for union activities, but he had sense enough to know that these big crackers in Georgia didn't care anything about any National Labor Relations Act or any other Act, especially when it came to the rights of a Negro. The courthouse clock bonged into the middle of his thoughts, telling him that it was eight o'clock, and already he was a half of a second late getting back to the job. He turned and started running back up Harlem Avenue. He slowed down to a trot, and after he had trotted for a couple of blocks puffing and blowing and his poor feet aching, he thought to himself—Goddamn running like a fool back to the job. He would get there when he got there, and if they weren't glad to see him, it would be just too bad about them.

When he got back to the hotel he went right up to Mr. Oakley's suite, and Mrs. Oakley greeted him at the door, and she told him to come right in and he went in and started to get things ready for the party, wondering anxiously to himself where in the hell was Mr. Oakley. Young Mrs. Oakley had a million things written down on a piece of paper for him to do. He went for the liquor, he brought up loads and loads of ice and soda. He was tired and he took a quick drink when Mrs. Oakley wasn't looking. He went to the kitchen and he checked with the waiter about bringing up food. He helped Mrs. Oakley move the furniture about. He did the moving, she did the telling in her nice dangerously-friendly voice and walking around with a transparent housecoat over her sheer slip and leaning innocently onto his shoulders while she pondered what had to be done about the chair over here and the couch over there, and he painfully aware of her expensive perfume. He tried to keep out of the suite, going downstairs for something or the other on the slightest pretense till the other folks came or at least Mr. Oakley.

The time he came back from the big kitchen downstairs she said, "All right now, you can take it easy. I think we're all set."

He said, "All right, Mrs. Oakley, I'll go back downstairs to catch my breath for a few minutes. When Mr. Oakley and the rest of them get here and you need me just call for Number 7."

She looked up into his worried face. "Why should you go to all that trouble? You can sit right here and catch your breath."

"No, mam, I rather go downstairs for a minute. I just remembered I left something down there." He was a man as much as she was a woman, and he hated this business of making up stupid excuses, and acting like an uncle-tom monkey all the time.

"You just remembered," she said in a mocking tone. "Well, I just remembered you were almost a half an hour late getting here, and you supposed to stay right here on the job till the party is over. That's the way I remember it. So get to work and make me two scotch highballs while I put on my dress, and don't you leave 'cause I got something else for you to do."

She went to the bedroom and he went to the kitchen and made the highballs and he brought them out and set them on a cocktail table, and he went back into the kitchen and waited till she called him.

She stood in the middle of the room in a long Fifth Avenue New Yorkish gown and she had both of the highballs in her hand and she handed one of them to Rob. "Drink up, Number 7," she said. "It'll put a little pep in you, and you sure gonna need it. You got a long hard night ahead of you."

He took the glass and started toward the kitchen. "Well, what you going to say, Number 7?"

He turned around toward her again feeling a new heat move around in his collar. "What you mean?" he asked her.

**415**

"You know, I give you a highball and you just take it and turn away. What's the matter? Don't you have any manners? What you going to say?"

"Thank you, mam." He felt a great humiliating relief.

"You welcome, sir, Mister Number 7," she said and laughed. "What you going back into the kitchen for? Nothing out here is going to bite you. Sit down, Mr. Number 7, sit down."

He heard all kinds of danger signals ringing in his head. And for the first time a doubt entered his head that scared him to death. Maybe there was no such thing as a prize fight party for tonight. Maybe this was all something Mrs. Oakley made up in the name of Mr. Oakley. Maybe Mr. Oakley wasn't even in town. But there had to be a party. He was just letting his imagination run away with him. He looked at Mrs. Oakley with her light green eyes and her new-blonde hair, and week before last she had been a brunette, and sometimes a redhead, but always glamorous—Hollywood style. He started to say—I got to go back to the kitchen, please mam, there's something I got to do in there—but he was tired of the ducking and the dodging, tired of the Amos and Andy excuses that white folks expected, sick and tired of sounding like a jackass, helping to make them think they were superior. He took a big drink of the scotch highball and he sank down into the cushiony couch, and he felt his weariness coming down on him and tired tired tired and goddamn the white folks.

She sat across from him in an easy chair and she pulled her long dress up to her knees, and she stared at Youngblood and he stared back at her, and he looked her up and down, and forgotten at the moment was the danger involved in being alone in a hotel room with the wife of a rich white man. He stared arrogantly into her eyes, let his eyes roam all over her, including those places where her dress pulled tightly over her young restless body, and her knees gleaming white, and her legs with no stockings. He wanted to laugh, because he could look her up and down and have not the slightest feeling of desire for her, and he knew that she thought he was burning with desire.

"What's your name, Number 7?" she asked

"My name is Number 7," he said.

"No, I mean what's your real name?"

He started to say Colored folks don't have any real names—We just have nicknames—but he thought about it and he said, "My name is Jesse James."

"Jesse James," she said with a short laugh. "Jesse James—I'll bet you're a real bad man all right. Your folks have such romantic names."

He stared at her. Jesse James—Romantic names. She didn't know a goddamn thing about his folks.

She looked at him and she smiled at him with a conscious coyness. "What you thinking about, Jesse James?"

"Nothing, Mrs. Oakley."

"I bet I know what you're thinking about."

He kept staring at her and he wondered why every white woman in the U.S.A. thought every black man did nothing but go around dreaming of the time he could get in the bed with her great white body. He felt a little drunk. He stood up and looked down upon her, and he wanted to say to her—Old white whore, you're a goddamn liar. I don't want no goddamn part of you. You couldn't even make my courage rise. But instead he said, "I'll be back when the party begins." And before she could open her mouth he had opened the door and was gone. He didn't get very far, because he bumped into Mr. Oakley in the hall with some other people coming to the party. "You the boy gon help with the party?" he asked Youngblood.

"Yes, sir," Youngblood said. "I'm the man."

"Well, where you think you going?"

"I was just going downstairs for a minute."

"Ain't got no time to be going downstairs," the big rich good-looking robust white man said. "Let's get the party going."

Youngblood went back to Mr. Oakley's suite with them and the party got started without any messing around. He served them a round of highballs and they started yapping about any and everything, and they started playing jazz records on a phonograph, and more people came, men and women, and more highballs all the way around.

"Hey, boy. Where's that boy?" Rob was in the kitchen and pretended not to hear.

Mr. Oakley came into the kitchen. "Didn't you hear me calling you, boy?"

"No, sir."

"What's your name?"

"My name is Youngblood."

"Where's the food, Youngblood? We ain't got no food."

"It's down in the kitchen. I have to go and get it."

"Don't you go nowhere. Call down to the kitchen and let them send it up and be quick about it."

A waiter brought the food up and helped Youngblood set it up buffet style, and everybody was stuffing and drinking and laughing and talking and cussing and the music playing real loud—*and the music go round and round—whoa oo whoa whoa oo whoa and it comes out here—*

He gobbled down some of the food in the kitchen and he took another drink when no one was looking, and he came back into the room and he stood with his back to one of the windows watching the white folks having a ball, as if he were getting material for a book he was writing.

"Hey," somebody yelled, "what about the fight?"

"Goddamn the fight," another man yelled. "Let's have a good time. You wanna fight? Let's me and you fight." He was a round chubby man and when he laughed he shook all over.

"I'll bet the nigger wins," a white woman shouted.

"Costelli gon crucifix that nigger."

Rob watched all of them with a certain kind of deliberate detachment, as if they were a bunch of ignoramuses making fools of themselves for his benefit and because they didn't know any goddamn better. He thought about what Richard had said to Dr. Riley about who was uncivilized. And these were the people who were supposed to be better than his people, and superior to his people, and even a whole lot of his own people believe it, bcause these were the great big well-to-do crackers. He went into the kitchen.

"Youngblood—Youngblood, come in here," Mr. Oakley called out. "Turn on this damn radio and get the fight. It's past ten o'clock."

He turned the radio on and the fight had already started.

"Boy, you look like Joe Louis your own self," a white man said.

"He certainly do," a white woman said. "Look just like him. Just like Joe Louis."

Rob went and stood near the window again. He wished they would be quiet because he wanted to hear the fight even if they didn't.

THIS IS THE BEGINNING OF THE THIRD ROUND, SPORTS FANS, AND SO FAR COSTELLI HAS REALLY GIVEN A GOOD ACCOUNT OF HIMSELF. HE'S ALL OVER THE RING AS BIG AS HE IS. A SHORT LEFT

**418**

BY LOUIS—A LEFT AND A RIGHT AND ANOTHER LEFT BY COS-
TELLI————

Youngblood could hear the voices in the room competing with
the radio.

"Get him, Costelli! Thatta baby! I knew you could do it!"

"I'm still betting on the nigger—Anybody wanna take it—"

IT'S MIDWAY IN THE FOURTH ROUND, LADIES AND GENTLEMEN,
AND NOBODY EXPECTED IT TO GO THIS LONG EXCEPT THE COSTELLI
FAITHFULS, BUT COSTELLI IS AS STRONG AS A BULL, AND LOUIS
SEEMS WORRIED, AS COSTELLI DELIVERS A LEFT AND A RIGHT TO
THE MIDSECTION AND A RIGHT TO THE JAW OF LOUIS—AND HE
CROWDS THE BROWN BOMBER INTO THE ROPES, AND LOUIS LOOKS
TIRED—VERY VERY TIRED.

He could hear the crackers yelling and whooping it up out on
Oglethorpe Street where they stood in front of the *Daily Telegram*
Building getting the blow-by-blow description of the fight. But
Rob wasn't worried about Joe Louis losing the fight. Joe was just
giving the fans a little run for their money. Rob kept telling himself
he wasn't worried. Joe would take care of the Costelli cracker all in
due time.

In Mr. Oakley's room the party went on and on even as Youngblood watched and listened, and the people looked strange to him
as if they came from another planet, or maybe he came from
another planet, and he could see them and knew all about them,
but they didn't know a thing about him. He saw one of them with
a blue dress on stagger toward him and his body grew warm and
alert and tense, and before he knew it she was almost on top of
him, her black hair flopping all over her face. "I'm for Joe Louis,"
she said. "I'm for Joe Louis. And you sure do fuflavor Louis.
You look just like him. You—"

A little sawed-off cracker came up behind her and pulled her
back to the white folks' party.

HE'S LEANING HEAVILY ON LOUIS—THAT'S BEEN HIS TACTIC,
LADIES AND GENTLEMEN, THROUGHOUT THE FIGHT—WEARING
THE YOUNGER MAN DOWN AND AND AND HE'S CROWDING LOUIS
AND LOUIS IS IN TROUBLE!

The crackers were jumping up and down in the room and
raising hell out on Oglethorpe Street and Youngblood was worried.

**419**

COSTELLI HAS THROWN ALL CAUTION TO THE WIND—HE'S
MOVING IN FOR THE KILL AND THE BROWN BOMBER FROM DETROIT
IS IN SERIOUS TROUBLE—HIS LEGS ARE WOBBLING! HIS LEGS ARE
WOBBLING! A LEFT! A RIGHT! ANOTHER LEFT! AND A RIGHT! AND
HE'S DOWN! HE'S DOWN!

Youngblood heard one mighty shout go up down on the street
in front of the *Telegram* as if all the crackers in town had assembled, and he felt his heart in the bottom of his stomach and
his face filling up, and the noise drowned out the radio, and the
crackers in the room with him going crazy.

—HE'S TRYING TO GET UP! HE'S TRYING TO GET UP! BUT HE
CAN'T MAKE IT! JUST CAN'T MAKE IT! HE FALLS FLAT ON HIS
FACE AND LOUIS IS STANDING IN A NEUTRAL CORNER WITH THAT
POKER-FACE EXPRESSION—

And everything got suddenly quiet in the room and down on
the street, and he was startled by an even more powerful roar
coming all the way from Harlem Avenue, a continuous roar
gaining every second.

FIVE SIX SEVEN EIGHT NINE TEN! Rob felt so good he felt like
crying. IT'S ALL OVER FOLKS AND THE BROWN BOMBER LIGHTNING
STRUCK AGAIN—JOE LOUIS WINNER BY A KNOCKOUT—ONE MINUTE
AND FIFTY SECONDS OF THE SEVENTH—

Somebody clicked the radio off. "Goddamn nigger done it
again!"
"All right goddammit, you owe me fifty dollars. Pay me the
money."
The white woman started toward Youngblood again. "You look
just like him, boy. I swear before God!"
"Come back here, woman," the short cracker shouted.
Rob had a feeling of great pride on being identified with Joe
Louis, even though he knew he looked nothing like Joe except that
he was big and brown and Negro.
"Jack Dempsey woulda whipped that nigger with one hand
tied behind him," a big black-haired white man said and he glared
at Youngblood.
"That's all right about Jack Dempsey. Just pay me my fifty
dollars. That's what you do."
"I don't see how you can bet on a nigger beating a white man,

Gil," a brown-haired cracker with a red mustache said. "I swear to my Jesus, it don't seem natural."

"I don't see that either," a white woman with red hair said.

The room was filled with cussing and swearing and cigar smoke and cigarette smoke and whiskey smells and angry drunken white people and down on the street was quiet as a graveyard and a continuous roar from Harlem Avenue.

"That's right, Gil. Goddamn, how can a white man bet on a nigger against another white man?"

"Easy enough—just put up the money," Gil said uneasily.

"Lessen he's a sonofabitching nigger-lover."

"You better watch what you say, Ned Lumpkin. I don't take that shit off nobody's body."

"The prize fight's over," Mrs. Oakley shouted. "Let's have a party. Make them break it up, Robert Lee."

The prize fight was over and Youngblood thought about his people all over Georgia rejoicing, maybe all over the country, and he wanted to be out of this hotel away from these crackers and down on Harlem Avenue with his kind of people, but he had to stay till the party was over. He could feel now the hate for colored folks thick in the room all mixed up with the too-much-whiskey, and some of the crackers drunkenly aware of his presence and staring at him as if he were really Joe Louis.

"You here betting on a nigger to whup a white man. If they don't find a white man to beat that Louis nigger in a hurry, niggers all over everywhere gon git outa hand. A nigger ain't got no business being allowed to whup a white man under no kind of circumstances."

"You just pay me fifty dollars. That's all I want out of you."

The big black-haired white man counted five ten-dollar bills to the man named Gil. His dark angry eyes roamed around the smoke-filled room and rested on Youngblood. "Come here, boy."

Youngblood's body grew rigid with tension, but he didn't move, pretended not to hear.

"Hey, you, boy, come here goddammit, you hear me!"

"Leave the boy alone, Ned."

"Boy, don't you hear a white man calling you?" another cracker shouted in a drunken mumble-jumble.

"You see what I mean?" the man that lost the money said. "Just cause Joe Louis won the fight, this boy here getting out of hand already. Goddammit, you bellboy, come here this minute.

You still working on this party, ain't you? What kind of parties do you give, Robert Lee Oakley?"

Out on the street there was the blast of a police siren going down Oglethorpe Street toward Harlem Avenue.

"Come over here, Yu-Youngblood. See what the gentleman wants."

Youngblood came toward the white folks, his fists balled up so tight that his fingers hurt. "What you want, Mr. Oakley?"

"This gentleman here wants you. Maybe he wants some ice or some more whiskey."

Youngblood turned to the dark-haired white man. They stared at each other as the room got suddenly quiet. Somebody nervously cleared his drunken throat.

"How you like the fight, boy?"

"You want me to bring you some soda, sir—and maybe some ice?"

"Hell, naw, I don't want no soda. I just want you to answer my question."

"What question?"

"How you like the fight—You heard what I said."

"I liked it all right."

"Don't you feel bad about that nigger beating the white man?"

Rob could feel the sweat breaking out all over his body. He didn't take his eyes off this dark-haired cracker one minute, but he could see the white faces of everybody in the room, sitting and standing. "I don't know what you talking about," he said to the cracker. "I thought you were talking about the Louis-Costelli fight."

"That's the one I'm talking about, boy. Don't you feel bad about the white man getting beat?"

Youngblood could feel his heart thumping in the back of his head.

"Aw leave the boy alone, Ned. You lost your fifty dollars fair and square," Mrs. Oakley said. "Let's have a goddamn party."

"Don't you feel bad about a white man getting beat, boy?"

"No, sir, I don't know what color Costelli is. Joe Louis is my favorite fighter."

"He's my favorite too. Joe Louis—the Brown Bomber—Yippee!—and you look just like him—Ex-ex-excuse me, I'm drrrunk—"

Rob never did take his eyes off the cracker. The cracker stood

**422**

up and walked close to Youngblood and stared him in the face. Rob could feel his liquored breath. "You try to be slick, don't you, boy? Trying to make a fool out of Ned Lumpkin. I ought to kick you square in the ass."

Rob didn't say a word.

"Oughten I to kick your ass?"

"Leave the boy alone."

"Kick his black ass, Ned, goddammit!" the red-haired white woman yelled. "Teach him some manners!"

"Oughten I to make you bend over and kick you square in the ass?"

"Make him pull his pants down!" the red-headed woman yelled.

"No, sir. I don't think that would be the right thing to do."

The white man buckled slightly at the knees. "I ought to make you bend over and let everybody give you a swift kick in your black ass! That's what I ought to do."

"Gone do it, Ned! Let me get my high heel slippers on! Who seen my slippers?"

"No, sir, Mister, you definitely wrong. Ain't nobody going to kick Rob Youngblood tonight."

"Do it, Ned! That nigger been had his eyes on me all night long!"

The man lunged at Youngblood. Youngblood stepped out of the way and the man pushed past him. Rob looked around for Mr. Oakley. "Mr. Oakley, I'm going to have to be leaving. You can pay me off now or give it to me tomorrow. It doesn't make any difference."

Mrs. Oakley's hoarse whiskeyed voice lighted up the room. "Get the hell out of my place, Ned Lumpkin. You always trying to break up a party. Get the hell outa here and don't ever come back."

Ned Lumpkin straightened up and staggered back toward Youngblood. "Whassa matter with you, Susie Mae? I'm just trying to have a little fun—liven up the party."

"Get out of my place."

Rob stepped out of his way. He turned to Mrs. Oakley again. "Whassa goddamn matter with you, Susie Mae? You act like a goddamn nigger-lover."

She slapped the dark-haired cracker's face so hard it sounded like bursting a big paper bag filled up with air. He staggered to the couch stunned and astonished. "Goddamn nigger-lover!"

She turned around quickly. "Are you going to stand for this drunken bum insulting your wife, Robert Lee Oakley? Throw his ass outa here!"

Youngblood stood there with a certain transfixed fascination. He had almost forgotten his own situation. He almost laughed out loud at these goddamn people as he saw Mr. Oakley tussling with Ned Lumpkin all the way to the door, both of them drunk, and somebody opened the door and Mr. Oakley pushed Ned Lumpkin out into the hall and he fell on his face, and Mr. Oakley slammed the door locked.

As Rob stood there watching the white folks, the rich white folks, he put his hand in his pocket and absent-mindedly pulled out the blank union card Bill Brinson had given him, and unaware of the white folks, he stared at the card and it wasn't a blank card at all, it had three names signed on it including Bill Brinson's.

Mr. Oakley came back from the door toward his wife, but on a second thought he walked over to where Youngblood stood with a smile on his face like he was enjoying a great big joke on all of these white folks.

"All right, boy," Mr. Oakley said loudly enough for everybody to hear, "next time don't be so goddamn sassy around white folks —Joe Louis or no goddamn Joe Louis."

Youngblood looked at the cracker and his sense of humor played tricks on him again and he had to struggle hard to keep a serious look on his face. Joe Louis and Bill Brinson and Joe Louis. He went into the kitchen. And the party went on and on. And he would come out every now and then and bring soda and ice and open up more bottles of liquor and the crackers got sloppier and sloppier drunk and loud and wrong and started to get fresh with each other's wives and a boisterous crap game over in a corner and a couple of small-sized fights over the honor of southern womanhood, and a couple of times the dark-haired lady stumbled into the kitchen looking for Joe Louis, but each time the sawed-off cracker would follow her and drag her back into the other room.

"If you don't stop going into the kitchen, I'm gon have to whup that nigger for making passes at you."

The party broke up about two thirty in the morning and most of the crackers left tips for Youngblood on a tray on the table before they staggered out. But after the party ended Youngblood couldn't leave because he had to clean up. And Mrs. Oakley

**424**

followed him around staggering after him, trying to help him, and leaning up against him to keep from falling down.

"It's late, Susie Mae," Mr. Oakley said. "Go in the bedroom and get undressed and go to bed."

"No-sir-ree—I'm going help Jesse James straighten up everything. He got to go home and go to bed too."

And Mr. Oakley's face already whiskey red turning redder and his brown eyes watching every movement she made and—"Come on Susie Mae, I told you now. Go in the bedroom an' go to bed like a good girl. He doesn't need any help."

"No-sir-ree—No-sir-ree—Jesse James need plenty of help—"

The drunken white woman was getting on Youngblood's nerves which by this time were stretched tight and thin and as sharp as a razor. He wished she would get lost and stop following him around, because he wanted to finish and get his money and be long gone.

He stooped over to pick up some cigarette butts from the thick carpet and when he straightened up, she stumbled and she threw her arms around him to keep from falling, and his whole body froze. "Thanksha, Jesse James. Thanksha verra mush."

Mr. Oakley almost leaped across the room and grabbed hold of her. "All right Youngblood, get your money and get out. I can get the goddamn place cleaned up tomorrow." He gestured towards the pile of bills over on the tray, and he reached in his pocket and gave Youngblood a twenty dollar bill.

Youngblood took the money from the white man. "Yes, sir," and he went to the table and he nervously picked the other money up, and he mumbled goodnight and he was long gone.

He reached Harlem Avenue where a couple of places stayed open all night. The street was black dark and empty, not a single street light on, and everything closed up tight as Dick's hatband, and Rob walked up dark Harlem Avenue, his heart beating wildly, wondering what the hell it was all about. He was halfway up the block when—

"Hey, man, you better come outa the street."

Rob's heart jumped quickly and he almost started to break into a run.

"Come on over here a minute, man. I ain't gon bite you. I ain't no white folks."

Rob stared through the darkness at the shadowy figure standing in a doorway. He walked cautiously toward the doorway, and he stopped when he was about five feet away. "Who're you?" he asked.

"I ain't nobody but Larry McGruder. You know me, Youngblood. I live up over the barber shop. I'm the shoeshine boy."

Rob stood in the doorway with the hunch-backed colored man. "Man, you should've said who you were in the first place." Rob laughed.

The other man chuckled. "What you doing out here this time of night?"

"Been working on a party at the hotel. Where is everybody? How come Sporting Life and the other place closed up?"

"Man, ain't you heard? After Joe Louis whupped that cracker, some crackers came down here wanted to turn Harlem Avenue out. Boy, some young Negroes started kicking asses and taking names. Some Negroes tried to get on the bus to Pleasant Grove and the bus driver wouldn't let them on, and they turned the damn bus over and upside down. All the police in town came down here and ran everybody off the streets and out of the places, closed up everything. Made everybody and his brother go home. About a half an hour later the street lights went off. Man, I'm telling you. These crackers is a bitch. I just came down to get a little fresh air. Man, I'm telling you! They sure don't like to see a colored man get ahead. As far as I'm concerned that Joe Louis is one of the greatest men in the world."

Rob looked down at the hunch-back, a million thoughts going around in his head.

The hunch-back seemed to be reading his mind. "Youngblood, you got to walk all the way out to Pleasant Grove by your lonesome. You better spend the night with me. I ain't got much room but one of us can sleep on the floor."

Rob smiled bitterly. He had slept on a pallet on the floor all of his life. It was the one thing he was going to do with his party money—buy himself a cot. Sleeping in the same room with his sister all of these years. Now it would be two beds in the kitchen. He looked down at the man again, made his mind up quickly. "No, thank you, Mr. McGruder. I'm going on home, I reckin. Thank you just the same."

And he walked out into the night beginning the long dark lonely journey. He would go by way of as many alleys as possible and he would try to stay out of the way of the white folks and the police and the police cars, but he was going home, because home was where he lived. As he walked through the coolish night of the early morning he thought proudly of the mighty Joe Louis, as a chill danced over the middle of his back and out toward his shoulders, and he reckoned that the crackers were really scared of Joe, because he was proving every time he fought that the white wasn't any damn better than the colored or any other people. Just give everybody an equal chance. He walked past the back of Hotel Oglethorpe again and on up the alley, and somehow or other he thought about Oscar Jefferson, and wondering what he had done tonight, and what did he think about the mighty Joe Louis? And Bill Brinson and Oscar Jefferson and the mighty Joe Louis. . . .


## CHAPTER SEVEN

THAT MONDAY MORNING wasn't any different from any other morning. It was a morning in late August and hot and sunshiny with no air stirring. It was just like any other August morning except that Daddy had breakfast with the rest of the family instead of eating early before day and leaving early on his way to the job or on his way to look for a job as was the case recently. He looked around at his family—Rob almost as big as his Daddy, at seventeen years old a hard-working man, and all kinds of sense up in his handsome head, and he was always thinking about Rob here lately—wanted him to go on to college and become a lawyer. There wasn't one single Negro lawyer in Crossroads, and colored folks sure could use a good colored lawyer, and Rob would be a good one and serve his people. But how could he think about sending Rob to college when he, the father, didn't have any kind of a job. Big Sister—Teeny Weeny Bits he used to call her. It didn't seem like she was eighteen years old already. It hurt him to think that as hard as he and Laurie had worked all of their lives the only job Jenny Lee could find was in the white folks' house working like a slave for practically nothing. Well if he got himself a regular job real soon, maybe he and Laurie Lee could set a little something aside and Jenny Lee could go to that teaching school down in Forsythe like she wanted to do. First thing for him to do was to get himself a steady job and cut out all of these wild crazy dreams. He looked across the table at Laurie and even though there was more gray in her hair than there used to be she seemed to him more beautiful than ever, and sometimes he felt toward her like a young boy courting his first sweetheart.

"Boy, they tell me you a real courting man these days," he said to Rob.

"That's what they say," Rob answered.

"She's a fine young woman," Joe said seriously. "A mighty fine young woman." He turned his head toward Jenny Lee. "And what's this I been hearing about you and that fat-head Mackey boy, Big Sister?"

"He's a fine young man," Jenny Lee said. "A mighty fine young man."

Mama laughed. "Tell him about it, Jenny Lee Youngblood."

Joe looked across the table at Mama and smiled. "How you doing, Madame Chairman?" His pride for her made his soft eyes beam. One night last week they had all attended a meeting of the NAACP at the Lodge Hall, and everybody had been there, including a few white folks—workers, teachers, doctors, all kind of colored folks. And it had been a good meeting with singing and speeches and also refreshments. They talked about the poll tax and votes for colored people. They talked about lynching and somebody mentioned the Scottsboro Boys. Laurie Lee talked about the jim crow schools and how they crippled the colored children, the generations coming. "It's a sin and a shame, a first-class scandal. And one of these days they just got to go. We got to get rid of them." And when they had started to set up a temporary committee to get things a-rolling, everybody had looked around at each other, till finally somebody got up and nominated Richard Myles and he declined and nominated Sister Laurie Lee Youngblood to be the temporary chairman, and in a great burst of pride and confusion Joe got to his feet and seconded the nomination, and some of the brothers and sisters patted their feet and said Amen. Richard Myles was elected the temporary secretary, and Ida Mae Raglin had come all the way from summer school in Forsythe to be at the meeting and she was elected to the temporary committee and so was Dr. Jamison, and Dr. Riley from the University, who brought along two other white teachers. They launched a membership campaign and gave everybody membership cards.

Mama stared back at Daddy across the table and she shook her head and laughed out loud. "Lord, man, you're really a mess.

All those people at the meeting and you had to jump up and second the nomination for your own wife. Lord Savior have mercy."

"What's wrong with that?" Joe said. "That's just the way I felt about it."

He turned his mischievous eyes to the boy again. "How you doing with building that union? Y'all gon be able to get them colored folks together, or y'all just gon talk about it for the next five or six years?"

Rob looked at Daddy. He hadn't seen him in such a good mood in a long time. "We're doing pretty good. Signed up quite a few. I signed up eleven myself, and Gus signed up quite a few, and so has Hack and Ellis and Bruh and Bill Brinson, and that Willabelle's signed all the womenfolks and a few men too. Even old Oscar Jefferson gave us four cards the other night. Four white folks. One of them was his own boy, Junior."

"Great God Almighty, boy, that's good. That's really good. Y'all on the march."

"I told you about Richard Myles. He gave a little social get together at his place the other night for the folks. About fifteen came. He talked to them about building the union at the hotel. I did too and so did Reverend Ledbetter."

"That's what I'm talking about."

"We're going to call all of them together next Tuesday at the church and form us a union and see how many we got signed up. Before Mr. Ogle knows anything he's going to have hell—the devil on his hands."

"Oscar Jefferson—Son, that's really fine. If y'all get that thing together and be successful, it'll be an inspiration to the men at the mills, and if I ever get a job back there one of these old rainy days, me and Ray Morrison and Jack Linwood'll do the same thing." He looked around the table into all of their faces, his black face beaming. "I done come to realize that colored ain't gon get nowhere at all lessen they get together and stay together. Boy, if y'all be successful in forming a union in Crossroads, Georgia, and with white in it, too, y'alla be unbeatable, and y'alla go down in history just as sure as you're born."

"I don't know about going down in history but we're definitely going to form a union. Because we just got to do it."

"That's what I'm talking about," Joe said. "Sometime I used to think life wasn't worth living. I used to think this old world must be coming to an end, but now I know that it's just begun. Whatcha got to do is just walk together children."

*Walk together children*
*Doncha get weary*
*There's a great camp meeting*
*In the Promised Land . . .*

"Talk—talk—talk," Jenny Lee kidded, but her big brown eyes kind-of told everybody that she was moved by her Daddy's spirit.

"I want to see how many NAACP people you all going to sign up," Rob said to all of them and especially to Daddy. "Don't worry about the union."

"Don't *you* worry about the mule going blind," Laurie Lee said. Daddy and Big Sister laughed at Rob.

"All right, Madame Chairman."

After the children left for work, Joe piddled around the house for more than a half an hour, trying to make up his mind not to do the rounds of the factory gates today, because he was feeling good for some reason or other, and he didn't want to change his feelings by standing around amongst a gang of evil-hearted crackers and hearing the man say *Sorry, boy—No work today,* and wearing out his shoe leather and his poor tired feet. But at about half past eight or a little before, he went out in the backyard and kissed Laurie Lee good-bye and he went out looking for work just like he had done all the other mornings, because he was Joe Youngblood.

He went straight to his old plant that hot Monday morning and landed a job just like that. It wasn't the same job he used to have and he had a different foreman, but it was the same kind of work. His new foreman was Mr. Mack, the cracker in charge of the colored payline every Saturday afternoon. Joe loved him like a rattlesnake.

It had been hot all night long the night before and it was 99 now before nine in the morning, but Joe Youngblood felt nothing but gladness, didn't feel any heat. He had a job! He was going back to work. The depression was over!

He reported to Platform Number 11 that same morning and he looked up at the great big barrels of turpentine and he glanced around quickly at the little white buildings and the big white buildings and the long red smoke stacks, he smelled the fresh turpentine, and everything sweet and familiar to him like good home-cooking. And the barrels didn't look heavy to him and he had forgotten that the work was hard—had come near killing him once-upon-a-time. Joe Youngblood stood there smiling all over. Maybe Jenny Lee could go to that teaching school down in Forsythe after all and maybe that boy could go on to college and get to be a lawyer like he wanted to be. Wild crazy dreams in the broad open daytime. He heard somebody walking quietly up behind him. He turned.

The little white man walked over to Joe and Joe stood waiting.

"Good morning, Joe."

"Howdy, Mr. Mack."

"Just come over to welcome you back on the job and to let you know I'm the boss around here."

"Yes, sir." Joe smiled at the cracker a friendly smile.

"Well I'm just telling you, we ain't gon stand for no stuff out of you. Too many people outside of that gate just crying for work."

Joe wouldn't stop smiling. "You don't have to worry, Mr. Mack. I'm gon do my work good. I always did. Ain't nobody in the whole plant work any harder than Joe Youngblood."

"I know that, boy. That's how come we hired you again. But I ain't talking about that."

"What you talking about?" He wanted to start off on the right foot with Mr. Mack because he just had to keep this job. He had had his taste of being out of work and the taste was as bitter as the gall from a chicken and he just couldn't stand it.

The white man stared up into Joe's face, trying to read his mind. "You know what I mean. We ain't gon stand for no biggedness out you, you understand?"

"Yes, sir, Mr. Mack, I see what you mean."

The cracker stood there looking at Joe as if what Joe said might have a double meaning missed by him. "All right, boy," he finally said. "Get to work. You know what to do."

"Yes, sir." He wasn't going to let a little sawed-off cracker dampen his spirits.

But every day that first week Mr. Mack would pick at Joe, and Joe would say yes sir or no sir and smile at Mr. Mack, as if Mr. Mack were making a fool of himself, till Mr. Mack got so he couldn't stand to see Joe smile, but the fool kept coming. Joe had made up his mind he was going to keep this job. And at home every night Joe Youngblood was himself again, he and Laurie like two young lovers.

The first week back on the job passed quickly, and before he knew it was Saturday and he was standing in the old familiar payline and the sun beating down through the buildings like it was mad at him, but it couldn't make Joe Youngblood mad, because he was thinking about his family and Laurie Lee and Jenny Lee and Rob and what he could do with his money to make them happy—*Walk together children*—*Doncha get tired*—He wanted to buy Laurie Lee a brand-new Sunday-go-to-meeting dress. He wanted to buy Jenny Lee a new pair of shoes, and get the boy some little something. Maybe he would get a phonograph for the house. Make everybody happy. He had to smile at his own foolish thoughts. His money wasn't almost long enough to buy all those things. He would do good if he could pay the rent and buy Laurie Lee a nice handkerchief.

The line inched along. Jack Linwood standing in front of Joe. "It's a mighty fine day for the race," he said to Joe.

"What race?" Joe asked him.

"The human race."

"That's a mighty big race." Joe Youngblood laughed. "And we gon win it one of these days."

"We just got to win it in the long damn run," Jack said.

"I hope that run ain't too damn long," Joe said.

"When the moon goes down and the sun comes up we got to do it."

"That sun ain't never coming up unless we do something to help it along. It ain't fair to ask the Good Lord to do everything nohow. He keeps too busy."

"Joe Youngblood, you better hush your mouth." Jack looked around and laughed out loud.

"That's right," Joe said. "The Good Book backs me up in that. It says the Lord help them that help themselves, and if we don't get together and help ourselves, it's shame on us."

"You right about that."

"Well, if I'm right about that, how come I didn't see you at the Hall the other night at the NAACP?"

"Man, I wanted to come," Jack said with a shame-faced smile, "but I just couldn't make it."

"Well, if you wanted to come and just couldn't make it, I'm gon sign you up just as soon as the man pays you off, so don't get in no hurry and run away."

"You know me, Joe Youngblood, you know me."

They talked like that till they got smack up to the pay counter. And Jack got paid off, and Joe said, "Don't run away. I'll be right with you. You know I got some business to transact with you."

"You know me," Jack said.

Joe laughed. "That's just it, man, I know you."

And now he turned to face the paymaster, Mr. Mack, his foreman on the job every day.

And it was "Howdy, Joe."

"Good evening, Mr. Mack." Both of them smiling.

"Ain't seen you in this line in a hell of time. You glad to be back?"

"Yes sir, indeed." And watching Mr. Mack skin back his jaws in a smile he was suddenly reminded of another line and another Saturday afternoon and Mr. Mack and Joe Youngblood, and the sun coming down through the big ugly buildings became all at once unbearably hot. And he tried to keep the smile on his face but it wouldn't hold still.

Mr. Mack kept smiling as he counted out the money to himself. "You doing all right," he said. "Been a good boy all week long." He pushed the money toward Joe and it was just as Joe had suddenly known it would be and had hoped it wouldn't. It was all in nickels and dimes and quarters, and it hadn't been like this since that Saturday in the payline a long time ago.

Joe didn't have to count it, because he knew already what the story would be. But it had come to him so suddenly and had happened so quickly he didn't have time to think about he shouldn't do this and he shouldn't do that. Mr. Mack hadn't pulled this trick on him in he-couldn't-remember how many years. He had told himself all week long that he was going to keep this job didn't care what, but when he thought of that and Laurie and the children, it was too damn late. He had begun to count the money with his trembling hands and there wasn't any turning back for him.

"Come on, Joe. Be a good boy now, and go on about your business. I'm in a hurry."

That's the kind of opportunity Mr. Mack gave Joe to save his black face, but Joe didn't take it, kept right on counting, and the cracker's face turned redder and redder.

Joe didn't count it but once. Mr. Mack had cut him a dollar and a half short! "Mr. Mack, give me my money." Joe was so angry he barely thought about the danger involved, and Joe's face wore that dangerous smile.

"Nigger, you don't get away from here this very minute they gon have to tote your black ass away."

"Mr. Mack, I ain't gon let you and no damn body else cheat me outa my hard-earned money."

Joe remembered about Mr. Mack's gun just as he saw the cracker's hand dive under the counter, and as the cracker's hand came up with it, gleaming like pine needles, in that brief instant Joe knew the time had come and the race was run. He threw his fist like a flash of lightning and struck the cracker on the side of the head and the cracker went one way, the gun went the other, and Joe heard Mr. Mack's head strike the cement floor inside of the pay house and it seemed to strike fire, and Joe heard somebody's voice, probably Jack Linwood, cry—"What's the matter, Joe!" And Joe turned to run, leaving the money on the counter. And before he had gone five steps a gun started talking from the white pay counter—*Once! Twice!* And Joe went down with two bloody holes in his back, as the crackers looked on and the Negroes too, and it had all happened so quick and sudden, nobody else had time to say a word, let alone move or do something about it. Jack Linwood kneeled down and turned Joe gently over and looked into his soft dark eyes.

The cracker named Lem Davis stood behind the counter with the gun still in his hand. "I had to do it," he shouted. "I had to do it! It was self-defense. He was running amuck. He done killed Mack Turner—he'da kilt me too."

Ray Morrison ran up from the back of the line. "GreatGod-Almighty—Joe Youngblood!"

More colored men moved out of the line and stood around Joe's body.

"Git him away from here, y'all," Lem Davis shouted, waving his big pistol. "Get him away from here and be quick about it."

Ray looked up from Joe and stared at the cracker. And evil-hearted colored men stared at the cracker with murder in their eyes. Crackers had already gone into the colored pay-shed and taken Mr. Mack away.

"All right all you niggers—go on home. We closing down the nigger payline. Pay you next week sometime. Go on home, every last one of you."

"He's still breathing! He's still breathing!" Ray Morrison shouted.

**434**

They took Joe's body through the plant gate and they sent for an automobile and they sent word to Laurie Lee, and when the man came with the automobile they took Joe to the City Hospital, but they wouldn't let him in. "We heard all about what happened. Take him away from here."

They argued and persuaded but it did no good, because there was no room in the Colored Ward for Joe Youngblood. And when they drove him home through Peckerwood Town, the white folks and children threw rocks at the car, broke a couple of windows. When they reached the house a crowd of colored people were standing on the sidewalk and all in the front yard looking at the house. They took Joe still bleeding up the ramshackle steps. Somebody said, "She gone to the hospital. She thought he was there." But Laurie Lee had been so excited she had left the door unlocked. They took him in the house and lay him on the bed in the front room, and Big Sister came running up the steps behind them yelling and screaming. "What happened to my Daddy! What happened to my Daddy!"

Ray looked at her with a helpless look. "Cracker tried to kill him," was all that he said to her.

She stood away from the bed, afraid to look. "But he ain't dead!" she shouted to him. "He ain't dead, is he, Uncle Ray?"

"No, baby doll, your Daddy ain't dead. You stay here with him and I'm going to bring Dr. Jamison back."

Mama came in a few minutes later, and she didn't cry till she saw him lying long and motionless on their bed. "Joe! Joe! Joe! Oh Lord Savior Have Mercy!" She ran to him and put her arms around his neck and she cried wet tears onto his dark calm face, his eyes soft and motionless. "Joe! Joe!"

She felt Jenny Lee's steady hand on her shoulder. "Don't cry, Mama. Ain't no need of you falling to pieces. We're going to need all of our strength to pull Daddy through."

She shook her head and she turned and looked up into Jenny Lee's face, which was calm now because she wanted her mother to be calm. "Anybody go for the doctor?" Laurie Lee asked.

"Uncle Ray did, Mama. He went for Dr. Jamison."

Rob heard about it down on the job when he came downstairs from rooming a guest. Fat Gus told him. He looked for Leroy and he told Leroy what had happened and he had to go home. Leroy said, "Go ahead, boy. I understand. I'll be by after I get off. Lord Have Mercy!"

He walked swiftly out of the back of the hotel and when he

reached the alley he broke into a run. He had to get down to Harlem Avenue in a hurry and catch one of the two colored taxis. When he got to the Avenue the place was almost as empty as it had been early that morning after the Joe Louis fight. And the colored folks who had not left already were piling into cars.

"You better come on in a hurry, Youngblood," he heard a woman's voice call out from an automobile.

He walked toward the car and he saw it was already filled with Negroes.

"Come on, get in, Baby Face," she said. "You can sit in my lap or I can sit in yours. Don't be bashful. Ain't got no time to be messing around."

He got in the car and Bessie Mae sat in his lap and they started quickly and other cars were leaving jammed with Negroes. "How's your Daddy, Youngblood?" Bessie asked.

"I don't know. That's what I'm doing now—going home to find out." He was afraid to think about it, didn't want to talk about it.

They dodged the main thoroughfares, took a zigzaggy route that would allow them to meet as few white people as possible, because white people were already gathering in town with guns and pistols and sticks and shouting "nigger!"

"Gon be hot times in the old town tonight," Bessie Mae said. "The law came down on Harlem Avenue and made every loving colored brother's sister's child git for home. Closed up everything. Talking about it was going to be trouble and they were trying to keep it from getting out of hand."

Bessie was the only woman in the car. Nobody said another word after that as they rode around the edge of Peckerwood Town and some children threw great big rocks at the car and ran behind it calling names.

"Nice friendly people." Bessie Mae broke the silent tension inside of the car. One of the men cussed. Bessie Mae turned around to Robby. "Your Daddy gon be all right, Baby Sweet. A Negro is tough. Can't kill him just dry along so. Especially your Daddy. If a Negro wasn't tough the whole race would've been wiped out a long time ago."

They were home now, in Pleasant Grove, Colored Town, and it was a hot day but people were busy closing windows and pulling down shades, getting ready for rough and stormy weather. They turned into Middle Avenue, and Rob was nearly home. His heart began to beat up against his ribs and his face filling up, and he had tried not to think about it, but he just couldn't help it. His Daddy might already be no more. Dead—dead—Dead. He had seen his Daddy in the picture of health that morning and now he might be gone forever. Murdered by the *goddamn white man.* It was always the white man cheating, stealing, murdering the colored. He looked around him at the others in the car. Maybe it was a dream, but he hadn't dreamed the grim looks on their faces, nor the worried looks of the black and brown faces up and down Middle Avenue, nor the houses with the shades pulled down in red-hot August.

In front of his house the people stood with anxious and angry faces and he was afraid to look at his house for fear the crepe might already have been posted. He mumbled good-bye to the people in the car and they told him they hoped it wasn't too serious, but he knew that they knew it was plenty serious, everything was. He walked with his head down through the crowd on the sidewalk and standing in his front yard and up the steps he went and into the house. In the front room he saw Dr. Jamison bent over the still body of his Daddy and Jenny Lee standing there tight-lipped and wide-eyed and helping the doctor, and he looked around the room unconsciously for Mama. He tiptoed over toward the bed, his heart in his throat, and the doctor straightened up.

"How—" Rob began and his voice choked off.

The doctor had a round black face and he looked at Rob from dark calm eyes and wrinkled brow. "It's going to be a tough fight, Rob. It'll be mostly up to God and Joe Youngblood, and you and I both know Joe Youngblood's going to carry his end of it. He's a fighting man. Always has been."

"Yes, sir," was all Rob said.

Dr. Jamison was a middle-height efficient-looking man. He stared at Rob. "You can look at him for a minute, if you want to, but he won't see you. He's still unconscious."

Rob nodded his head up and down and went toward the bed where his father lay still as a dead man. He gazed upon the giant in the bed who was his father and the eyes that did not see stared back at him, dark and calm as they always were. His Daddy's face was calm and relaxed, telling nothing of the struggle that the doctor had mentioned, and yet he knew his Daddy was fighting like never before. He wanted to cry out fight a little harder. Fight!

**437**

Fight! He felt Jenny Lee's hand on his shoulder, and she a grown woman now if never before, leading him from the bed. He looked down into her face and he saw a strength and a calmness there that he had never noticed in her before.

"Where's Mama?" he whispered.

She nodded her head toward the other room, and then he heard his Mama.

"Who's that in there, Jenny Lee? Who's that in there? Is that my baby? Oh, Good Lord, son! Jesus have mercy!"

He bit his lips and went into the kitchen where Mama lay in Jenny Lee's bed. Miss Sarah, Ida Mae's mother, sat near the bed fanning Mama and trying to keep her quiet. Miss Lulabelle was doing something over by the stove. Rob went to his mother.

"There's my baby! There's my baby. Come here, Robby! Come here, darling! I can't stand it, Rob! Your Daddy! Your Daddy ain't never did nothing to nobody but treat them right. And I can't stand it! Let him live, Lord! Let him live, Jesus! Ain't no better man than him in all the world!"

He wanted to do what they said a man was expected to do, wanted to go to her and take her in his arms and comfort her, give her strength. But as he sat on the side of the bed—"Excuse me, Miss Sarah"—and took her in his arms, and looking into her face and realizing sharply that his mother was no longer the young woman he thought she somehow would always be, and her eyes filled with fear and misery and tears, he couldn't stop his own face from filling up and he must not cry here he must wait till he got by himself so no one could see him, because he wasn't supposed to have easy tears, but he thought about the good man in the next room battling for his life and he looked at his mother and he bit his lips and now he was filling up all through his body and up through his throat and his face so full now, he turned his head suddenly away from her and walked quickly to the back door and out into the yard.

The tall mannish boy stood near the back fence crying like a baby.

"Have yourself a good cry, honey. It ain't nothing to be ashamed about." He wiped his face on his shirt sleeves and he turned and Miss Lulabelle, tall, strong and bony, handed him a big white towel. "Sometimes it takes strength to cry, honey. Some strong people cry, some strong people don't. Your Mama ain't no weak woman, I can state you that. And that Jenny Lee is something. She just took right over. The doctor said he wanted one of the womenfolks to help him and she stepped forward and said I'm woman enough. And she sure is that."

After a while Rob didn't hardly hear Miss Lulabelle but he felt her strength and kindness and goodness. He wiped his face with the towel and he walked back into the room where his mother lay weeping. He took her into his arms again.

"Baby—Rob—Baby! Your Daddy—your Daddy!"

He kissed her wet eyes. "The doctor said Daddy has a fighting chance, Mama. And you know Daddy is a fighting man. So there isn't any use to you acting like a little old crybaby, cause everybody knows you're the fightenest woman in the State of Georgia. And besides you don't want Daddy to hear you crying. He's got enough to worry about already."

He made her give him a weak smile through her tears and he took the white towel Miss Lulabelle had given him and wiped her face. She said, "Where's Big Sister?"

"In the front room taking care Daddy, assisting the doctor. I didn't know that woman was a first-class nurse but she certainly is. And if you don't cut this foolishness out we're going to have you on our hands."

She started to get up out of the bed.

"Sit still, sweetheart," he said, "and try your best to relax."

"I'm alright now, Rob. How you expect me to relax anyhow and your Daddy in there battling for his life. I got to be with him." She got up and Rob followed her into the next room.

And they stood there, the three Youngbloods, silently watching the busy doctor, and the fourth Youngblood, stretched out on his and Laurie Lee's marriage bed, saw nothing at all. And the strength coming back to the mother's face and the tears no longer flowing.

And the heavy ugly footsteps coming up the front steps and quiet in the room and suddenly Bam! Bam! Bam! and Open up *in the name of the law!* And the shocked looks on everybody's face, including Jenny Lee's. And the door opened before anybody inside could move and the Law walked in, all six of them, big and white and red-faced and blue-suits and gun-toting and evil. And Skinny McGuire was one of these Laws.

They crowded into the room with their guns in their hands. "We want to talk with this Youngblood nigger—Joe Youngblood," the leader of the pack who was a lieutenant said. "We got another carload of police outside, so don't start no monkey business."

Mama and Big Sister moved instinctively toward the cops, and

Rob pulled them back and stepped in front of them. "What's the matter?" he said to the lieutenant. "What do you want?"

"You one of the Youngbloods?" the cop said.

"That's right," Rob said.

"What kin you to Joe Youngblood?"

"He's my father."

"We just want to take him down and talk to him a little bit."

"Take him down!"

"Yes," the calm-faced officer said. "Take him down to the lock-up and ask him a few questions."

Rob stared into the relaxed face of the freckled-faced officer as if to find out if the cracker was serious. "My father lying there battling for his life and you talking about take him down to some lock—you talking about moving him?"

The doctor came forward. "Officer, this man can't possibly be moved. He hasn't even gained consciousness yet."

"What you mean—can't possibly? Who're you anyhow?"

"I'm Dr. Jamison, officer—I—"

"He's a doctor, Lieutenant. I know him. Howdy, doc," Skinny McGuire said.

"What you mean—can't possibly?" the lieutenant repeated.

"I mean, officer, that Mr. Youngblood cannot be moved without risking his very life. He's still unconscious." One thing bad about Dr. Jamison, he was educated up north and he hadn't gotten it out of him as long as he had been back. He talked too precise and proper around white folks.

The lieutenant looked at the doctor without batting an eyelash. "That's all right, doc, we'll bring him to."

"If you move him now you'll sign his death warrant. He'll die before you get him down to the courthouse. He can't be moved."

"He will be moved, doc."

"He'll be moved after all three of us are stretched out dead," Laurie Lee said softly.

"That ain't no nice way to talk, Aunty. We just might haul off and take all y'all down for obstructing justice."

"Don't lose no more time with these biggedy niggers, Lieutenant," another officer of the law said. "Take all of them down."

The lieutenant looked Laurie Lee up and down. Skinny McGuire cleared his throat. "Lieutenant, kin I speak to you a minute." And they went over into a corner and talked in low arrogant tones, and one of the cops, big young plug-ugly with a flat broken nose, stared brazenly at Jenny Lee Youngblood and she felt like spitting in his ugly face.

The lieutenant came back and spoke to Dr. Jamison. "You say he'll die if we move him, doc?"

"Positively——I mean—yes, sir."

"Suppose we talk to him here right now?"

"Impossible——I mean he's still unconscious."

The lieutenant looked around at the faces of the Youngbloods. "All right, doc, I'm gon take your word for it, but we're coming back and you better have him conscious by then."

"I certainly am doing all within my power to make him conscious."

The lieutenant smiled. "You work hard like a nigger, doc, saving his life, and he might not appreciate it after all, cause as soon as he's able he gon be facing a charge of assault and battery with intent to murder." One of the officers laughed out loud with a gun in his hand. And when they went out of the door he was still laughing but he cut it off short as they went down the steps.

Rob walked to the door and he saw the colored people, his people, still out on the sidewalk keeping close watch over 346 Middle Avenue where Joe Youngblood lay between life and death. There was a quiet in the room for a brief moment after the law left, a thoughtful silence. Laurie Lee looked at Joe's quiet black face for a moment and was it possible that he was going to leave her and never return? Was he going to die? She remembered the other times that death had struck her loved ones down—Mama first and then Big Mama—but Joe Youngblood wasn't going to die. She thought about what the cracker lieutenant had said about coming back again to take Joe to the lock-up. And white folks white folks seemed all around her and ganging up on her and closing in on her, and she felt like screaming. She looked at the doctor and she motioned for them all to come into the kitchen.

"Sit down," she said in a soft quiet voice. And they sat down around the big table and they looked at Laurie Lee.

"You all think they coming back to take Joe down to the lock-up?"

"Is the sun coming up in the morning?" Jenny Lee said.

Laurie Lee looked sideways at her daughter. "I don't know whether it is or not, sugar pie. It just might not come up at all. You can't ever tell." She stared at Big Sister and she looked at the doctor and she looked at Rob and she looked at the two women

**441**

sitting on the side of Big Sister's bed. "They'll be back, won't they?"

"They'll be back, Mama," Rob said. "You can count on that."

"I think they'll be back, Mrs. Youngblood," the doctor said.

"They'll be back here just as sure as Heaven's happy," Miss Lulabelle said.

Laurie Lee sounded like she was arguing quietly with herself. "They'll come back and the next time they will really take him down to the lock-up, unconscious or no, or try to make him talk here. And they would handle Joe rough any whichaway, and he couldn't take that kind of rough treatment right long in now—could he Doctor?"

"No, mam," the doctor said. The round-faced doctor with the serious eyes stared at the woman as if she were a sudden revelation to him.

"We'll have to move him ourself then before they come back," she said as if she had discussed it at length with them and had reached a collective agreement. "We would move him nice and gentle. We wouldn't move him rough."

"Where would we move him to, Mama?" Jenny Lee asked.

"Move him out to the Quarters, baby darling," Lulabelle said. "I bet anything they wouldn't find him then. Not till we were ready for them. Be like being in the Good Lord's hands—Almost. Lord Have Mercy, forgive me, Jesus."

Lauree Lee looked at the doctor. Dr. Jamison's eyes batted a tenth of a second and he hesitated and Laurie Lee saw it. "We could use my car," he said.

"You better stay out of this part of it, Doctor. These crackers might take your license away."

"But I'm the doctor. He's my patient. I'm responsible for—"

"This part we'll be responsible for, Doctor, if you don't mind."

"I could get Richard to let me use his car," Rob said.

"Yes," Mama said softly. "We wouldn't move him till right after dark. The night can't see quite as good as the daytime."

Lulabelle said, "I know one thing—Y'all better get something to eat inside of you."

Laurie Lee looked toward the room where her husband lay and then at Lulabelle and she smiled wearily. "Aah Lord, Lulabelle— I ain't got no stomach for something to eat right now. It wouldn't go down. Give the doctor and the children something, and you and Sarah eat."

People came all afternoon and knocked softly on the door and asked how Joe was, and was there anything they could do—and all afternoon they came and they went, and some of the people Laurie never knew before. And Ray Morrison came back, and Richard Myles.

And Laurie Lee went in the kitchen with them, and she looked at Richard Myles, and he felt like a blood relation to her, and she wanted to ask him like she would a brother or maybe a son, where had he been and why had he taken so long to come?

Richard looked into her deep narrow eyes. "I would have been here a long time ago," he said, "but I was out of town, and I didn't hear about it till I reached Atlanta. I turned right around and headed right back."

"God bless you, Richard," she said, her face filling up again and she felt like crying all over again but she wouldn't cry. She put one arm around Richard Myles and one around Ray. And Rob stood looking at all three of them and he came to his mother and kissed her on her cheek.

Under the cover of early darkness they took the big man softly and tenderly in Richard's car, Dr. Jamison following. But Joe's body was jarred many times, because the road was rough and rocky and they didn't dare drive with the headlights on. Lulabelle had gone ahead to make preparations, and when they got to the Quarters, they took Joe to Willabelle Braxton's. She and her mother had moved in with some other people to make way for the Youngbloods.


## CHAPTER EIGHT

IT WAS A nervous jumpy kind of a night all over Crossroads, Georgia. Hot and nervous. Angry nervous white folks all afternoon gathering by the hundreds in the downtown districts, some half-scared—On Cherry Street, Jeff Davis Boulevard, Oglethorpe Street, standing in front of the big white Post Office and the Cross County Courthouse.

The radio blasting all afternoon every hour on the hour about the rumblings of war in Europe and the ominous danger of Hitler and the Nazis, and something mentioning the pennant race in the American and the National Leagues, and everytime and especially the horrible story of the Big Black Burly Negro that ran amuck at Plant Number 9 and had to be shot down like a wild dangerous beast by a courageous and trigger-thinking paymaster by the name of Lemuel Davis. AND FEELING IS HIGH, FELLOW CITIZENS, FEELING IS DANGEROUSLY HIGH, SO KEEP YOUR WOMEN AND CHILDREN OFF THE STREET. JUST AS A PRECAUTION. THE MAYOR AND THE POLICE HAVE PLEDGED TO KEEP VIOLENCE AT A MINIMUM BUT THE CITIZENS ARE FIGHTING MAD WITH RIGHTEOUS INDIGNATION, AND GOD ONLY KNOWS WHAT'S GOING ON AMONG THE COLORED FOLKS OUT IN PLEASANT GROVE AND ROCKINGHAM QUARTERS. ALL POLICE IN THE CROSS COUNTY AREA HAVE BEEN ALERTED. STAY TUNED TO WCMI, FELLOW CITIZENS, FOR FURTHER DEVELOPMENTS —THIS IS YOUR CITIZEN STATION, WCMI, CROSS MILLS, INCORPORATED, CROSSROADS, GEORGIA IN THE COUNTY OF CROSS—

Within an hour after it happened it seemed that someone had blown a great big bugle and mobilized all the white folks in town and the outlying countryside. With guns and pistols, concealed and out in the open, and knives and sticks and angry looks and hateful looks and scared worried looks and looks of confusion. The afternoon sun beating down on red-faced crackers in brand-new overalls and sun-burned farmers in wagons and trucks on their regular Saturday trip into town and some crackers dressed up in business suits. White folks everywhere cussing and grumbling and laughing and talking and *"Let's git the nigger"—"What nigger?"—"Where is he?"—"What happened?"—"He's running amuck—Let's git him Goddammit!"*

A little white boy stood with his white-haired, no-teeth grandmama across the plaza from the courthouse watching the excitement. "What happened, Grandma? The men going to war? Where's my papa?"

"The nigger! The nigger!" the grandmother shouted.

The little boy's white face puzzled and anxious.

A little after dark that night some people dressed up in white regalia went up and down Harlem Avenue, men, women and children, and they smashed store windows and broke down doors and they yelled and they whooped and they carried on, and they broke into the colored places of business, which had been closed up hours before, barber shops and hot dog stands and pool rooms and restaurants, and they turned over barber chairs and smashed the mirrors and upset tables and counters and all in all they had a good white-folks' time till the police came.

"All right boys, the party's over. Let's go home."

**444**

The police rounded all of them up and chased them away from Harlem Avenue.

"If you all spent more time keeping these bad ass niggers in line, we wouldn't have all this trouble," a man in a white hood argued with an officer.

"All right, Otis," the officer said good-naturedly. "You just go on now, and stay out of the way of the police whatever you do. We got our orders."

It was a restless night in Rockingham Quarters. It was hot and sticky and grown folks weren't thinking about going to sleep and babies crying and the children excited. And groups of angry people getting together all over the Quarters and talking about it.

Elwood Dailey stood on his porch with his double-barreled shotgun. "We ought to go over to Peckerwood Town and kill off a few of em."

"You goddamn right," Sam Billings said. "Wait a minute till I get back."

People were stirring all over the Quarters. Angry—uneasy and hot and bothered.

Ray Morrison and Fat Gus went around from house to house, rounding up the men-folks. They gathered in the darkness of Fat Gus's backyard. They came on the run, some with guns and pistols and knives. And the women-folks came without being invited and some of the children.

And Ray Morrison told them that the white folks might be coming for Joe that night. "And we got to be ready for them when they get here."

"I'm already ready," somebody said.

"They already been down on Harlem Avenue raising hell," Ray continued, "and if they come out here looking for trouble we gon damn sure give it to them. This is one time we gon stick together. Am I right or wrong?"

The folks in the yard nodding their heads in the darkness and mumbling and grumbling and already restless. Lightning bugs blinking off and on and mosquitoes biting.

"We ain't gon mess with the law, is we? I mean crackers is one thing, but the law, that's different."

"What's the difference?" Ray asked.

"Ain't no difference," Fat Gus said. "A cracker is a cracker don't care what kind of uniform he wear."

"Are we gon stick together or ain't we?" Ray demanded.

"We gon stick!"

"You mighty right."

"I just want to get me just one peckerwood before I die."

"All y'all didn't bring them, go back home and get your guns and your pistols and any other kind of weapon and meet back up here in a hurry. We ain't got no time to waste. Ain't no telling what the crackers up to."

"I ain't got to go back nowhere. I had mine on me since this afternoon."

"Me too, goddammit!"

"I'm ready to fight!"

They ran off in the dark in every direction, and all over the Quarters they were reaching in dresser drawers and up in the closet and under the mattress and everywhere else, and when they came back, Gus went with four of them and took them to stand guard around Willabelle Braxton's house where Joe Youngblood was and the rest of the Youngbloods, and Ray took the others out to the edges of the Quarters and especially that part that almost touched the tip of Peckerwood Town.

"Let em come. Let em come—goddammit. We ready for em."

In the front room of Willabelle's house Jenny Lee took the kerosene lamp from the table and held it over the bed for the doctor. The doctor straightened up. "Thank you, Miss Youngblood. You can put it back on the table now."

He walked back and forth in the room for a minute, Jenny Lee watching him anxiously, and then he went into the other room, the kitchen, where Rob and Laurie Lee and Richard and Willabelle and Lulabelle sat around the big kitchen table.

Mama and Rob looked up at the Doctor. Richard Myles asked the question for them. "How is he Doctor?" The damp heat seemed to be moving around like something alive. Everybody sweating.

"He—" the doctor began. An automobile came noisily up to the house and stopped. Everything got unnaturally quiet. The flame from the kerosene lamp in the middle of the table seemed to stop flickering, holding its breath.

A voice outside the door called out the challenge. "Who's that?"

"Reverend Ledbetter."

"Well all right then."

Nobody moved from the table. They heard the Reverend walk up on the porch and into the front room and he paused there for a couple of minutes before he came into the kitchen. Laurie Lee nodded to the minister. "So glad—so glad you came, Reverend Ledbetter. Lord have mercy on our souls."

"Praise the Lord, Sister Youngblood. Praise the Good Lord." He nodded to the rest of them. "There is no other place for me to be at this hour, Sister Youngblood." He got down on his knees and the others bowed their heads as he offered a silent prayer. Laurie Lee was so nervous and disturbed she couldn't keep her head down. When he finished praying he stood up again and they gave him a seat at the table. The doctor got up and started his nervous pacing again.

"How is he, Brother Jamison?" the minister asked. "How is Deacon Youngblood?"

The doctor hesitated, looked around the table at their anxious faces. "Tell us the truth," Laurie Lee said. "We got to know the truth."

"It's hard to tell," the doctor said. "He was shot in the back by two bullets and one of them isn't so serious, but the other seems to be lodged somewhere in the thorax—the chest—and could be dangerous, very dangerous. He's not bleeding so much outwardly, but there's probably a lot of inward bleeding. That's why he continues to get weaker—doesn't gain consciousness."

"What does it mean, Doctor? How is my husband?"

"I have to go to my office and get my equipment for blood transfusion." He stared at Laurie Lee. "I have to get a portable X-ray machine from somewhere. He has to have an operation." He gazed at Reverend Ledbetter. "God only knows."

Richard Myles got up from the table. "Well let's get going, Dr. Jamison."

"I was going to use my car," the doctor said.

"They might be on the look-out for your car, Doctor. I'll drive my car. You just tell me where you want to go."

They drove off into the dark hot night up the dusty road. On each side of the road the lightning bugs turned their lights on and off on and off and the crickets yelling, and before they reached the edge of Rockingham Quarters Richard Myles clicked his car lights off as the car moved past colored men lying in ditches and standing behind trees with guns and rifles, as if war had been declared.

The car found its way cautiously and painfully through Pleasant Grove toward Monroe Terrace. Pleasant Grove was dark as the blackest night. It was lights out everywhere. They finally reached the Terrace and came to a stop in front of Dr. Jamison's. The doctor got out. "You need any help, Doctor?"

"No, thanks. I can handle it easily. You just keep the motor running." The doctor laughed a short nervous laugh.

Richard leaned back heavily upon the back of the seat and he stretched his nervous body and he looked about him in the hot quiet darkness and he thought about the Youngbloods, and he had come to feel like a part of the family, and Joe Youngblood his father and brother. An automobile came slowly up the street as someone in the car flashed a big beam of light up against the houses, and Richard Myles kneeled down on the floor of his car and he could hear his own breathing and he hoped that the doctor wouldn't come out of his house at this very moment. He saw a wave of light pass over his car and he held his breath and the car passed on and he still knelt on the floor of the car. He raised and watched it go out of sight. The doctor came out of his house and down his steps with a satchel in each hand and he got into the car.

"What's the next stop, Doctor?"

"I need a portable X-ray machine. Got to see what's happening inside of Joe. Davis has one, but I don't know when that man will be home. I haven't seen him all day long." The doctor lit a cigarette and pulled hard on it.

"You mean to say, there isn't one white doctor in Crossroads, Georgia with a speck of humanity?"

"They need humanity and a little bit of guts to go along with it," the doctor said. "Any white man that takes sides with us right now is asking for it. Let's try Dr. Blackstone. Can't do any harm. Turn right on Chestnut Street."

Dr. Blackstone met Dr. Jamison at the door.

"What you want, Jamison?" the white doctor asked. "Come in a minute." He was big around the middle and very white faced and partially bald. They stood in the vestibule facing each other.

"I want to borrow your portable X-ray machine, Dr. Blackstone."

The doctor shook his sweaty head from side to side. "Don't ever lend it out, Jamison. Wouldn't lend it to anybody."

"But a man is dying, Dr. Blackstone. I just have to have one."

"What man's dying? What's his name?" His bald head reflected the light from the ceiling.

"Joe Youngblood," Dr. Jamison said and wished quickly that

**448**

he hadn't, but he was weary and desperate and at intervals he wasn't as sharp as usual, almost like a drunken man.

"That's what I thought," Dr. Blackstone said. "No-sir-ree. Even if I was of a mind to lend it to you, I wouldn't for him."

He looked the white doctor in his light brown eyes. He was tired and desperate and powerfully angry. Angry with himself for giving it away, as well as with the doctor. "Why Dr. Blackstone? Why wouldn't you? He's a man and in danger of losing his life, and you're a doctor."

"If you leave now," Dr. Blackstone said, "I'll forget all about it. I won't remember you ever came. That's just because I like your spirit." Dr. Blackstone's face and head were shining with bubbles of perspiration.

"But what about the X-ray machine?"

"No! No!" Dr. Blackstone shouted. "Go on now. Go on about your business, and be thankful to God that I don't report you— you wouldn't be able to practice in Georgia anymore."

Dr. Jamison left with the painful realization that Dr. Blackstone was the nicest white doctor in town, particularly as far as Negroes were concerned. But he went to see two more white doctors and they both refused him. As he left the third doctor he knew he had to get back to the Quarters, X-ray machine or no X-ray machine. "I may have lost my patient already—while I run around in the dark like a fool chasing the southern medical profession."

Suddenly Richard could see Joe's quiet face and his soft dark eyes, and he felt an overwhelming despair and helplessness, and all of a sudden out of desperation he thought about Dr. Riley. He said, "Just a minute. I know somebody. Let's make one last stab at it." And they crept, lights off, through the western part of town toward the University and they stopped in front of Dr. Riley's cottage. Dr. Riley said, "Well, this *is* a surprise," as he invited the two men into his house. Before the lanky soft-spoken white man could ask them to have a seat, Richard said, "I might as well get to the point, Dr. Riley. As you must have guessed, this is no social visit." The pink-faced white man cleared his throat and smiled nervously. "We need your portable X-ray machine to save a man's life—Joe Youngblood's. The father of the young man you think has such great promise." Richard nodded his head toward the other doctor. "You know Dr. Jamison."

"Yes, of course. You gentlemen have a seat." He reminded Richard more than ever of how Abraham Lincoln might have looked when he was a young man, but he had a voice that was a cross between a Harvard accent and a Georgia drawl, soft and sweet. "Thanks, Doctor, but we really don't have time," Richard said. "It's touch and go—life or death."

"Well, of course I make a practice, Professor, of never lending it out. I just don't do it. It doesn't belong to me anyhow. It's University property." The ugly friendly-faced white man cleared his throat again, his big blue eyes nervous and worried.

"That's all right, Doctor," Richard said quietly. "We appreciate that. We'll take you along and you can operate it. Dr. Jamison needs professional help anyhow."

Dr. Riley looked around the room as if he expected another unexpected visitor. He went to his desk and got his pipe but he never did light it. "I couldn't possibly do that, Professor. I'm all tied up. I'm making a speech in Atlanta tomorrow. I was just preparing it." His broad pink forehead turning red and covered with sweat. His forehead seemed to be actually expanding like it would pop wide open from thinking so fiercely.

Richard had been sitting. He got up again. "This is a man's life, Doctor. A damn good man. Don't tell me about any speech you have to make in Atlanta. I was supposed to be in Atlanta too. You have a duty here. In the medical profession you take an oath. Everybody does."

"You know where I stand on the race question, Professor. I'm with you one hundred percent. That isn't the point at all."

"It is precisely the point, Doctor. And I want you to feel guilty about it. Joe was lynched by your kind of people and your duty is out in Rockingham Quarters."

He stared at Richard with his big blue eyes. His quiet voice had an angry tremble. "Well, of course I couldn't do it anyhow. It's just impossible. I would lose my job at the University." He tried to hide his white-folks anger.

"Lose your job—And Joe Youngblood might lose his life. And what do you think might happen to Dr. Jamison? He might lose his license to practice anywhere." Richard knew he was hitting below the belt, but the soft quiet face of Joe Youngblood urged him on, and if Roderick Riley had a soft spot he intended to find it. He turned to Dr. Jamison. "Dr. Riley isn't one of these everyday crackers, Doctor. I want you to know that. His father was a great Christian missionary, and he's more enlightened and dedicated than his father was."

Dr. Riley pulled his lounging jacket more closely about him and strode angrily toward the front door. "See here, Myles, I won't tolerate any more of your insults. I won't be pushed around, by God!"

Richard didn't move, his voice raised higher. "He's making a courageous intelligent speech tomorrow, Dr. Jamison, at the interracial conference. You understand? He's going to speak at a Negro church about better relations between the races. I should go back to Atlanta tomorrow myself and make me a speech and run him off the platform."

The red-faced white man turned from the door. He looked at Dr. Jamison and back at Richard. "You're not being fair, Myles. You know what will happen if I—"

"I know I'm not being fair, Doctor, but those crackers weren't fair to Joe this afternoon. You're not needed in Atlanta tomorrow like you're needed here right now."

"Myles, doggonnit, I—"

"You're a sensible sensitive human being, Doctor. And more than just Joe's life is at stake here. Your own integrity is on the block. You're not like that mob downtown. I know you're not. And I'm just demanding that you live up to who you really are."

Dr. Riley looked from Dr. Jamison to Richard. "All right, Professor, you can use the machine."

"Thanks, Doctor, but we need you too, not just the machine."

"Yes, I understand," the doctor said softly.

Richard breathed a deep heavy sigh. "I knew you would, Doctor."

They went back through the night to Rockingham Quarters, and when they reached the house, the doctors went in to look after Joe and later they went out to the kitchen and Dr. Jamison spoke to everybody. "Joe needs blood and a whole lot of it. I want you to go out and tell as many as possible to come and offer their blood to Joe. We have to work fast."

The folks went out of the kitchen in a hurry. The doctor and Jenny Lee set things up for the business of blood-type testing and blood transfusions. They laid their equipment out on the table, and they pulled the cot over from the other side of the room and placed it near to Joe.

The people lined up, Richard Myles in the lead, and his was type O, the same as Joe, and the doctors tested twenty more people and only got three others with Joe's blood-type.

At about one o'clock Joe's soft eyes moved and he looked around and he tried to stir and his soft eyes smiled when they took in Big Sister and they asked for Mama and Rob, and Mama came in the room and looked at Joe smiling with his eyes and trying to talk and a fierce hope gripped at her heart and she didn't want to cry—didn't want to cry . . . Laurie could see the battle he was waging, could feel it inside of her, and recognition gone now—fading—fading—consciousness gone . . . And Rob watched the big man losing ground and the man was his father, but it was more than that, the man was his friend and more than that, the man was a man, the man was Joe Youngblood, and what made it especially painful to Rob was the helpless feeling, because Rob and Mama and Jenny Lee couldn't even give blood to Daddy.

But all night long the people came and they felt like brothers and sisters to Rob, especially the men that worked with him, like Ellis and Bruh and even Elmo.

And they took pictures and located the bullets and the internal bleeding and they made preparations for the operation. Dr. Jamison told Jenny Lee she should get herself some rest, but she insisted on sticking right with it, and she held the lamp when it had to be held, and she handed them things as they worked on her father, and sometimes she stood there watching them and she couldn't see because her eyes filled with tears and spilling down her cheeks but she didn't leave the bed. And the doctors working, both of them desperately working, and heat and dampness moving around in the room and the hospital smell and no breeze stirring and flies and mosquitoes and lightning bugs, and the doctors messing around inside of her Daddy and blood blood blood red blood everywhere and her Daddy's blood, and how could he live with all this bleeding? Her Daddy! Her Daddy! The doctors sweating like real working men—But how could he live? Oh God! Oh God! She felt her face filling up and the awful bitterness in her mouth and her poor head reeling, but she had to stay with it . . . she had to stay with it . . . She couldn't let him down . . . She swallowed the bitter gall in her mouth because she had to stay with it. . . .

Oscar Jefferson wasn't able to sleep. It was too damn hot for anybody to sleep, he told himself, but Jessie Belle was sleeping, and he could hear the children in the next room snoring. Ever since he had heard the news on the job at the hotel he hadn't been able to think of anything else for any length of time. His mind had been filled with mixed up pictures of Joe Youngblood and Jim Collins and Little Jim as he used to be and young Rob Youngblood and Mr. Mack. All afternoon long as he messed with the food at the hotel he had thought of hardly anything else, and the rest of them talked about nothing except how the niggers were getting out of hand, and Roy Baker throwing glances at him for the rest of the day as if he were to blame for all that had happened.

The night was hotter than he ever remembered and he had a dull stubborn pain in the back of his head and he turned from one side of the bed to another. The stale sleepish smell of the room, the dampish heat, the soft even breathing of Jessie Belle lying next to him, the air that didn't move around at all, the loud snoring from the other room, and Little Jim standing firm inside of his conscience and Rob Youngblood and Joe Youngblood and Junior Jefferson and Mr. Mack—all of it getting together and ganging up on him to keep him awake.

His old man and Charlie Wilcox and the plantation and what it did to his mother and the Kilgrow family, and he remembered the night he and his old man had fought all over the house and the kitchen floor and later down in the colored quarters down in the Bottom and Little Jim's mother doctoring on him and giving him food, and sleeping next to Little Jim and talking far into the night and Little Jim and Big Jim with their guns cocked and ready. And he remembered the other night a few weeks ago when Jim had been at the teacher's house and the boys at the hotel had been afraid to talk in front of him because he was a white man. He remembered what Jim had told him when he took him aside. "They want to trust you, Oscar—awful bad—but they just can't do it right long in now. Goddammit you got to prove yourself first. You got to make them know it. As far as they're concerned you're just another white cracker. You might be spying on them for all they know." Jim had smiled bitterly down into Oscar's face. "They just like I told you about me and my Daddy scumpteen years ago —If you act right they'll go more than half way but they gonna always keep their guns cocked and ready."

He got up and walked barefoot out through the backroom where the boys were snoring louder than ever and out on the back porch he got a dipper of water from the bucket and he drank it down and it cooled him off for a half of a minute but he went and lay down again and he couldn't fall asleep. Two shots in the back at very close range. Maybe Joe was already dead. And the radio said that Mr. Mack was out of danger—an honery bastard! Mr. Mack and Joe—Joe and Mr. Mack—and white and black and black and white—And nobody had to tell him what had happened in the payline. He knew what had happened just as if he had witnessed the whole damn thing like he had witnessed it that other time when he had seen Mr. Mack trying to cheat Joe Youngblood. He got up again and he slipped on his clothes and he went and stood in his backyard looking up at the sky where the bright full moon had started downward. He wondered what time it was. He was a white man and he didn't have any business being bothered about colored. He was white and the Youngbloods were black and Mr. Mack and Mr. Lem were white, and he, Oscar Jefferson, was white. That evening a little after dark they had come for him with their shotguns and rifles and great big sticks, and it was—"Come on, Oscar, we got to teach some niggers a lesson" and—"Goddammit, Oscar, you act like a nigger-lover." But he had not gone with them and he had stood in his front yard and watched them go up the road laughing and talking like they were going on a picnic. And he had remembered another time when he was a boy on the plantation, and they had told him come on Oscar, let's go nigger-hunting, and he hadn't gone that time either—His mother! His mother! Little Jim! Little Jim! The same kind of people had asked him to go, including his father and brothers, and they had had a wonderful time, wiping out the whole Kilgrow family that night, except Little Jim . . . He had not noticed that two of his own boys had slipped off with the rest till he saw them way up the road. "Sonny and Jim, come back here this minute!" And when they had come back, he told them—"If air one of you put they feet out this house tonight I'm gon kill you just as sure as you got to die." The older boy, Junior, who had been standing quietly near the edge of the yard, had come toward his father. "I wouldn't go, Pa. You didn't have to tell me. I wouldn't go out tracking down poor niggers ain't done nothing to me."

Oscar looked about him in the darkness of the backyard and he figured it must be getting on toward morning, and if he were going he better get started. It was so quiet in Crossroads, Georgia, you wouldn't think anything at all had happened or was going to happen. It was so quiet at that moment Oscar could hear the chickens stirring uneasily in the backyards all over town. He had better get going. He started around the side of the house.

"Where you going, Pa?"

**454**

He turned and stared through the fading darkness at his oldest son standing in the backyard in his shorts with his thing sticking out. Junior had always been closer to him than the rest of the children. When he was a little boy he used to want to go everywhere his Daddy went. He was his father's son. The only one his father could talk to.

"I couldn't sleep, son. I'm going for a walk."

"Can I go with you?"

"Ain't no needa that, Junior. I'm just going for a little old walk. I be back directly."

"I'm going with you, Pa."

He looked through the dark at the white naked form of the seventeen-year-old boy who everybody said was his spitting image. "Well, hurry up then, and put on your britches." Why in the hell did Junior have to wake up? He was always a light sleeper just like Oscar.

They walked up the red dusty road toward the Quarters. They walked in silence, and yet there was a strong communion from one to the other. Junior was his father's height already and the same broad shoulders but not quite as chunky in the middle of him. "Where we going, Pa?" he finally said.

"We going out to the Quarters."

"Wha—What we going out there for?"

"We going looking for Joe Youngblood."

Junior stopped in the middle of the road and he stared at his father.

"We ain't going on account of that, son. You know we ain't. We going to see if there's anything we can do."

"How come you got that there gun bulging out your britches?"

"Ain't no telling what kind of help they might need, son. You got to be ready." The words rang in his head—guns cocked and ready.

"Suppose some white folks meet us on the way?"

"I don't know, son. I just don't know. We'll have to cross that bridge when we get to it."

"Oh," Junior said and they started to walk again through the early morning darkness and the chickens getting up all over town and talking about it and lightning bugs blinking like the middle of the night and a few dogs howling.

"Son," Oscar said to Junior. "Look at it thissa way. Ain't a meaner skunk in all cf Cross Woods than old man Mack Turner

**455**

lessen it's one by the name of Lem Davis. And ain't a nicer set of folks on God's green earth than the Youngblood family, white or colored. And look at it thissa way too. Ever since I come to work at the Mills, Mack Turner been riding my ass. He the very one that fired me. I'd look like a damn fool to pick up and join a bunch of poor don't-know-no-better crackers to track down Joe Youngblood 'cause he wouldn't let Mack cheat him out of his hard-earned pay."

The boy said, "Oh."

"Goddammit Mack Turner ain't no friend of mine, I don't give a damn what color he is," he said angrily as if the boy had disagreed with him but he was really having it out with himself as well as explaining it to the boy and the boy understood what was happening.

They walked together through the just-before-day-in-the-morning darkness, and he wanted to explain to Junior why he had to do more than just not-go-with-the-other-poor-crackers—like he had done when he was a boy, and also that morning at the factory gate. He was a grown man now and a man who had grown. But he couldn't explain it, because he didn't even know how to explain it to himself. The just-before-day noises were ringing all about them. He desperately hoped that they wouldn't run into any other white folks. He thought about the other two white men who had signed for the union at the hotel, and he was glad he had not seen them among the suckers who had passed his house last evening. They might have been in another such gang, but anyhow he was glad he hadn't seen them. He looked sideways at the strong set expression on Junior's face. He had told Junior the story of Little Jim Kilgrow for the hundredth time the first night he had come home from the colored teacher's house.

The boy finally broke the silence between them. "We be coming to the Quarters before long now." His husky voice trembled.

"That's right," Oscar said.

The sleepy-head men lay in the ditches and stood behind trees and on the front porches hidden by the trees and they gazed toward the east where the trouble had come from and might come again and they watched the darkness begin to lift on that side of town where the night met the daybreak and redness taking shape in the midst of the darkness.

Last night they had stared at the dark dusty road so long till they were almost able to see in the darkness. But it had not been necessary when the trouble did come. Suddenly off in the dark distance they had seen torch light and the white-robed figures of the Ku Klux Klan, and crackers in overalls with shotguns and rifles. And time wasn't taken to consult Ray Morrison or Fat Gus Mackey, because the men were tired and nervous and jumpy and fingers automatically pressed on triggers and even more suddenly than the white folks appeared on the road, the quiet of the night was broken by gun fire. Bang-Bang-Bang-Bang—Screaming through the night and Ziing—Bop, and kicking up dust. And the white hooded figures and torch lights on the road scattered and scampered back the way they came from as the dust did fly. And the guns kept barking a long time after nothing could be seen. And the men had waited for four nervous sleepy and wideawake hours, but nothing else had happened. And day would break soon.

"Who the hell is that coming up the road?" Ray Morrison asked from the front porch of one of the shacks on the edge of the Quarters. "You see what I see?" He walked down off the porch down into the yard. The sleepiness quickly left everybody's eyes. All eyes squinted down the dusty road that led to the horizon where it wouldn't be long before the sun would be rising. It was as if the two figures had risen up out of the mist instead of the sun. "They look like a couple of peckerwoods to me."

Elwood Dailey sat on the side of a ditch and he looked long and hard down the barrel of his rifle. "I got em covered, Ray. Should I bust a cap in they asses, somebody?"

"Naw, wait a minute, Ellie. Wait till they get up here. I just want to find out how crazy a cracker can be. Coming out here amongst a whole bunch of evil colored folks all by their lonesome. Let's see what they got to say for they self."

"I say blow them to hell and back. They don't never listen to nothing we got to say."

"You mighty right. It might be a goddamn trick anyhow."

"Come on Ray, let me get just a little piece of them. I don't mean the whole damn hog."

The men laughed. "All right then, go ahead—I don't give a damn—Wait a minute—Here's Youngblood. What's the matter, Rob?"

"Daddy needs more blood, Uncle Ray. He's just got to have it."

Ray stared at Rob and he looked around at the men. "Y'all heard what Rob said? Joe needs more blood."

"I ain't the right type. Doc already tested me."

"Me neither."

"Me neither."

The men with serious guilty looks on their faces, as if they had deliberately picked for themselves the wrong type of blood.

"All of us been tested, Rob," Ray said. "How's Joe doing?"

"Not so good, Uncle Ray. He's just got to have blood."

"I wish to God he could use my blood." Ray stared at Rob.

Rob turned to leave. "I'll be over there directly, Rob. Maybe I can find somebody."

Elwood Dailey's voice shouted—"Whoa there, white folks. What the hell you want?"

The two men halted. The older man spoke. "We don't want nothing. We want to find Joe Youngblood."

"If y'all don't get your asses back to Peckerwood Town where you belongs we'll find you Joe Youngblood."

"We want to help. Ain't that young Youngblood going there?" the white man asked. "Youngblood—Youngblood!" Youngblood didn't hear him. He was thinking so hard on where he could get more blood for his Daddy. He turned in between two shacks, walking quickly away out of hearing distance.

"Ain't that Youngblood?" Oscar asked desperately, his face going red with white folks' anger. "Wasn't that Youngblood?"

"You didn't hear him answer."

"These niggers don't want nobody to help them," the young cracker said to the older man. "Let's go home."

Elwood cocked his rifle and said, "I should blow both of you crackers to hell and back. Blow the goddamn top of your heads off. Least I would do is to let you see it coming, 'stead of shooting you in the back like you did Joe Youngblood."

"Cut out all the damn who-shot-John. Do what you gon do," Ray Morrison said. "They didn't talk it over with Joe like that."

Elwood aimed his rifle directly between Oscar's eyebrows, and the red color drained from the white men's faces.

A man came up the road from the other end of the Quarters with a pistol. When he spied the two white men he broke into a run. "Y'all got two crackers—Y'all got two crackers." He ran up to them all out of breath. He came to a stop and he stared at the white men. "Oscar Jefferson!"

"Ellis Jordan," the cracker shouted.

"What the hell you doing out here?"

All of them looked at the two white men like they were freaks in a sideshow, and Oscar remembered he was white and they ought to be tickled to death he had come, and the color coming back into his face now, and to hell with these sassy niggers, and he put his shaking hand on his hip where the handle of his gun was, but he also remembered Mr. Mack was a white man, but Joe Youngblood and Rob and Jim Whatever-he-called-himself-now were all black men, and Jim had told him—Goddammit, Oscar, you got to prove yourself first. You got to make them know you mean what you say. You might be spying on them for all they know. His body grew warm and he felt embarrassed before his boy.

"We come to help, but it sure don't look like we're needed at all."

"You better take your hand off that goddamn pistol, else you ain't gon be able to help no damn body." He turned to Ellis. "You know this cracker?"

"Course I know Oscar Jefferson. He work at the hotel. He's a pretty nice old cracker. You know him, doncha, Ray?"

"I don't know *no* cracker. I just know his name is Oscar Jefferson."

"How is Joe?" Oscar asked.

"He's mighty bad off," Ellis answered. "They giving him blood transfusions again."

"Where is he?" Oscar asked.

"Whatcha want to know that for?"

"Don't tell him, Ellis. Don't tell the cracker."

The blood in Oscar's face made his cheeks run redder than red. He wanted to turn back but he didn't know how, and Elwood still had his gun aimed at him.

Ray looked contemptuously at the two crackers. "Why don't you give your blood, Mr. White Folks? You heard the man say they were giving Mr. Youngblood blood." All of them stared at the stocky-shouldered crackers.

Oscar could feel his entire body running hot and cold. He looked straight ahead of him but he could see Junior's frightened face turning white. When he had started for the Quarters earlier with Junior, he had not let the question of how they would help when they got there bother him at all. The thing was to go—And after he got there, to do what was needed. But giving his blood, a white man's blood, and letting it mix with a black man's blood was more than he had counted on.

"These crackers don't wanna help nobody," Elwood said. "They up to some kind of trick or something. They looking for trouble."

"Well, what you gon do, Mr. White Folks?" Ray said. "Piss or git off the goddamn pot."

He didn't really want to give blood to a Negro, but he knew that he should, and these Negroes made it so hard for him to refuse or agree. "We gon give blood," Oscar said with a tremble in his voice, "if the doctor say okay."

"Is white blood any different from colored?" Elwood asked uneasily.

"Man, blood is blood," Ray said. "I'm surprised at you."

"You better watch them crackers. I still don't trust them."

"What the hell harm can two white men do all by their lonesome?"

Oscar and Junior walked quietly and quickly in the midst of four Negroes toward Willabelle's house. Ray went up on the porch with the two white men and into the house. Richard Myles was on the cot next to Joe giving blood again. Joe had come out of it again and he wanted to say something but he could do nothing but mumble to himself. The two white peckerwoods stood in the colored folks' house along with the others who came to give blood.

Ray said to Dr. Jamison, "They want to give blood, doc."

Dr. Jamison stared hard and long at the white men. "Is it all right, doc?" Oscar asked. "Do white blood mix with colored?"

The doctor looked at the other doctor. Mama came in from the kitchen. Richard Myles sat up on the cot. "There's no white blood and there's no black blood," Dr. Riley said. "All blood is red-blood. The only difference is in the different types. Blood doesn't know any color line."

Oscar's tongue slipped over his lip. "I'm ready to be tested." He turned to the boy. "How about you, son?"

The boy cleared his throat, lost his voice for a second, and when he found it, it trembled slightly. "I'm ready too."

"Stand over there, till we get around to you," Dr. Jamison said in a forced casualness. "There's a couple here ahead of you."

And when they got to them, they tested Oscar first. He stood there straight as a post, his lips slightly trembling and the blood running to and from his serious face. And when it was Junior's turn he stepped forward and clamped his bottom lip with his upper teeth and he winced slightly as the doctor sent the needle into his arm and sucked out the blood. And now they were testing the red blood on the slides, and Dr. Jamison looked at Oscar and shook his head, "No, yours won't do," and the man couldn't hide the shame-faced relief that the headshake gave him. Young Jefferson stared at his father and he turned toward the doctor and watched him examine his blood on the slide, and his tongue slipped noiselessly over his lip.

The doctor looked up and around at the boy. "You have the right kind of blood, young man."

The white boy's face turned whiter and whiter. He looked at his father.

"You ready, young man?" The doctor's voice was calm and cool.

The boy didn't move. His eyes asked his father—What must I do? What must I do? You got me into this—What must I do? The white man stared back at his son and Junior knew it was left up to him. He was his own man now if never before.

And the boy moved slowly forward, the color draining from all over his face, and they lay the pale-face chunky-shouldered white boy down beside the big black man, and Joe's soft eyes weakly smiling and his eyelashes fluttering and his mouth working, painfully, but nothing came out. And the white boy stretched out next to the black man and the blood from Junior flowing into Joe. And the red coming back to the white boy's cheeks. And when they were finished Junior got to his feet but his head felt dizzy and his legs were shaky and he lay down again to get himself together. And when he got up the next time, Laurie came over and shook his hands and said, God bless you, like she had done with most of the others who had given Joe blood. Everybody acted especially casual as if nothing out of the ordinary had happened at all, except that Dr. Riley put his arms around both of them as if they were his long lost brothers. And Oscar went awkwardly with Junior through the kitchen like the others had done and they gave Junior water from a wooden dipper and he went into the backyard.

Rob walked over to them and shook their hands, and Fat Gus said, "Howdy, Oscar."

And Oscar said, "Howdy—y'all know Junior."

They stood around talking about this and that, most of the time Rob's narrow eyes heavily on the back door of the house where his father lay, and other people coming up and listening to the talk and joining in the talk, and the embarrassment gradually wearing away, and even Gus Mackey wasn't ill at ease around these two crackers, and Bill Brinson stood there and Elmo Thomas and Willabelle Braxton.

"Damn," Elmo said quietly, "Mr. Ogle better bring his hotel way out here if he want his guests to be waited on."

Fat Gus with a serious smile on his face. "Far as I'm concerned, Oscar, you and Junior all right with me. Y'all members of the club. One of these days there'll be more like you."

Junior blushed like a ten-year-old cracker.

After a while Oscar said they had better be going, because both of them had to go to work that morning. And they shook everybody's hand all the way around and they went back through the house to say good-bye, and afterwards they walked down the dusty road heading out of the Quarters facing the sun that had already risen. And all kinds of doubts and confusions and good feelings too and new understandings ran through their minds, but they felt closer together, father and son, than ever before.

The folks in Willabelle's backyard could see them come into view and out again in the spaces between the shacks till they finally disappeared. Fat Gus, watching them, shook his head. "They all right. Them two crackers all right with me. I just hope they don't snag they pants up the road a piece."

The hotel fellows gradually drifted away, because they had to go home and get ready for work. It was about four hours later, about nine o'clock that bright Sunday morning, when a dark cloud passed suddenly between the sun and the earth, and a low grumbling thunder from away over yonder and a slight flash of lightning, and an anxious frown on Youngblood's brow, as he stood with some folks near a sycamore tree in Willabelle's back-yard, and somehow or other he felt like a boy again and at the same time a full grown man. And at that moment a shout went out from the house that could be heard all over the Quarters and his heart leaped in him and his stomach turned over, and another shout and another shout and he wanted to run toward the house where the shouts came from but he couldn't move an inch, and he stood there near the sycamore tree as some of the people he had been talking to went toward the house, but he couldn't move yet as the shouting died away and got louder again and he stood there crying unaware of the people unaware of the tears.

"Oh, my God! Rob! Rob! Daddy is gone! Daddy's gone! Oh, Lordy Have Mercy!"

Rob wiped his eyes and he walked toward the house and up the back steps and through the kitchen where people were standing eyes wet with tears, and "Rob! Robby! Rob! We ain't got no more Daddy! Ain't got no more Daddy," and he walked in the death room just as Jenny Lee sank down to the floor and the doctors picked her up and took her to the other cot, and he made his eyes look toward the bed where the white sheet covered the big man's body no more of this world, and he couldn't believe it because it couldn't be true, and he looked around for his mother and he saw her standing over on the side, her brown face turned to the color of ashes, but it couldn't be true that his Daddy was dead—His Daddy dead! And it was the first time he had seen Ida Mae since the whole thing happened. She standing there with her arms around Mama.

He went to them and he put his arms around both of them. "Oh, Rob—Rob!" Ida Mae wept softly and she kissed his cheek. "I got here just as soon as I could. I left Forsythe just as soon as I got the word what happened."

He felt his mother give in at the knees as he stood between them. "It's all over, son," he heard Mama whisper. "It's all over now." As if she were calling for the end of the world.

He didn't say a word, he couldn't say a word, but in the ears of his mind he could hear his Daddy—It's just begun—just last Monday morning at the breakfast table—It's just begun—And they took Mama, he and Ida Mae, into the kitchen and they sat her down, and Ida Mae fanned Mama's face with a paper fan. Rob slipped his arms tenderly from around her shoulders and he went back into the next room and over to the bed where his dead father lay and he pulled the sheet from over his head, and gazed down through the tears that were falling again upon the black face relaxed and the soft smiling eyes, and Daddy had died with his eyes wide open. And he heard Reverend Ledbetter's melodious voice like off in a distance.

"The Lord giveth—The Lord taketh away—Blessed be the name of the Lord. . . ."

And he could hear his mother from the next room shout— "No, Jesus, No! I can't stand it! I just can't stand it!"

Later he heard Dr. Jamison mumble to the other doctor, "It's a damn shame, Dr. Riley. He didn't have to die. He wouldn't've died either, if they had taken him in at the City hospital when he first got shot." The white doctor shook his big head sadly.

Reverend Ledbetter came and he sat down at the kitchen table where Laurie Lee sat now staring into space and Ida Mae and Richard and Rob sat too, every one of their eyes wet. "God bless you and yours, Sister Youngblood. I have to be going now. Got to go home and get ready for eleven o'clock service."

All of them looked anxiously into the little preacher's face except Laurie Lee. "You're going to have services in church this morning? What about the crackers?" Richard asked.

The Reverend looked up through the shingled roof. There was a rumble of thunder away to the east. He looked back in their faces. "Unless the Lord strikes the church with some of his lightning and sets it on fire. If that doesn't happen we're going to have it this morning and every Sunday morning. The Master hasn't given me any sign to the contrary."

Nobody said a word. "Well I got to get going," he said. "God bless all of you. I'll be back this evening."

Laurie Lee looked up. "Be careful, Reverend Ledbetter."

"Just a minute, Reverend Ledbetter," Richard said and he went quickly out of the kitchen door. And he got some of the men to go home with Reverend Ledbetter. The preacher and the men stood in front of Willabelle's house near the preacher's car.

"I tell you, boys," Reverend Ledbetter said sternly, "I appreciate it, Lord knows I do. But I believe my protection ought to be in the hands of the Good Lord this Sabbath morning."

"It still won't hurt for us to go along with you," Richard said.

The minister looked at Richard and he looked at the anxious looks on the men's faces and he studied long. "All right then, Brother Myles. All right. Our folks always did believe in a practical religion from way back yonder. We always did believe in helping the Lord take care of his children."

When he got home he telephoned all the preachers in town and asked them to speak in their pulpits that morning about Joe Youngblood. And later that morning near the end of the services at Pleasant Grove Baptist Church, he spoke to his congregation about a God-fearing man named Joseph Youngblood, a great fearless black soldier in the Army of the Lord, smitten down in the full bloom of life by the Pharisees. And the Church said Amen. And he called on all within the sound of God's voice to

**464**

come to the funeral at the Pleasant Grove Baptist Church and bring *everybody*, and he didn't know what the exact day of the funeral would be, but it would be announced later, and everybody should come even if they had to leave the job for a few short hours. And the sun glittering brightly on the stained-glass windows with the pictures of Jesus and the people fanning with paper fans the black and brown and light skin faces, and the patting of feet and the wiping of eyes all over the church and—Just last Sunday he was sitting over there with the family—and the shaking of heads, and somebody shouted over in the Amen corner and down near the middle of the second aisle. And the congregation said, *Amen.*

## CHAPTER NINE

JOE YOUNGBLOOD'S FUNERAL was held on a Wednesday afternoon at four o'clock, and the people came from all over the county, all over the state. Colored folks came, and a few white people. They started gathering in the church yard about half past two and before three thirty the church was packed and all downstairs in the Sunday School part, and out in the yard and out on the street, and the sun shone all day long that day.

About four fifteen the big gray hearse pulled up and behind the hearse was the Youngblood family and in front of the hearse the six pall bearers in a big black car and big cars small cars all around the block. The pall bearers took the long gray casket up the church steps. And Rob went up the steps with Mama on one arm and Ida Mae on the other, all of them dressed in black, and Jenny Lee with Augustus Mackey, and Dale Barksdale and Bertha Barksdale from Tipkin, Georgia, and even Laurie Lee's Cousin Mark all the way from Detroit, Michigan, and Richard Myles and Josephine Myles, and Lulabelle Mackey and Sarah Mae Raglin and Benjamin Raglin, and Willabelle Braxton and Ella Mae Braxton and a whole host of other friends and relations. But all of it had an unreal quality to Rob, because he had not yet accepted the fact that his Daddy was dead. All week long ever since it happened he had gone through the motions like a man in a stupor.

That Sunday morning at Willabelle's house when the undertakers first came, he had been the one to talk with them, along with Richard Myles. Then at one point Mama had come into the room and said to everybody in a soft quiet manner, "Let's get ready. We're going to move him back home."

"How about taking the body to the undertaker parlor, Miss Laurie?" Mr. Mansion said.

"I want you to take him to Three Forty-Six, Middle Avenue," Mama said softly and firmly.

"But Miss Laurie Lee—"

"If you don't we will," Mama said quietly. "I want him at home where he's supposed to be." Mama spoke just like Daddy was still alive.

"Yes, Mam, Miss Laurie."

They took him home and embalmed him there and people started coming Sunday evening, and all day Monday, and all day Tuesday the people came to see the family, and was there anything at all that they could do? Just say the word—and to view the body and express their sorrow and anger as well. And flowers came and telegrams too from the Deacon Board of Pleasant Grove Baptist, from the Willing Workers' Club and the Douglass Lodge and the NAACP of Georgia and the Crossroads NAACP, and from Mr. and Mrs. Cross Jr. a mountain of flowers. And also from the workers at the hotel and Dr. Riley from the University.

And they found out that the Klan had burned a cross in their front yard sometime Saturday night and the neighbors had destroyed it and moved it away.

Monday night Oscar and Junior had come and brought some flowers, and when they were leaving they told Rob and Gus they would be at the funeral, but Gus had followed them down the steps and out into the darkness of Middle Avenue. After he walked about a half of a block with them he stopped, and they stopped, waiting. "Excuse me, Oscar," Gus said, "but I don't think you ought to go to the funeral—you and Junior."

"How come, Gus?"

"Well it's like this here—You don't have to prove nothing to nobody by coming to the funeral."

Oscar waved his hand at a buzzing mosquito. The hot sticky night lay heavy and damp on his face and his neck.

"We ain't trying to prove nothing," Junior said.

"It ain't that," Gus said. "It ain't that at all. If a whole heap of white folks were gon be there it would be something else." He paused. "But goddammit, Oscar, we want y'all to bring some more of them white workers at the hotel into the union, but if y'all go to the funeral, y'all ain't gon be able to touch em with a ten foot pole."

Oscar and Junior stood there staring at Gus, not saying a word.

"Good-night, Oscar and you too, Junior," Gus finally said. "Think it over a little bit." And when Gus had gone back to the house he had told Rob about it. And then they remembered the union meeting that had been called for the following night, and Gus said it would naturally have to be put off, and he and Bruh would go around and tell everybody and give them a new date. "What you think about Tuesday week?" And Rob thought hard and long but not too long about Tuesday week. He looked around in the backyard at the lightning bugs blinking like crazy and he smelled the washbench, sour and soapy, and he should be ashamed of himself thinking about holding some kind of union meeting tomorrow night and his Daddy lying dead in the front room, but he remembered his Daddy at the breakfast table just last Monday morning and he knew what Daddy had thought of the union and Walk Together Children and maybe he should ask Mama about it, but he was a man now and growing faster than ever before and reaching desperately and angrily for his Daddy's height. "No, Gus, don't put off any meeting. You and Bruh and ask Bill to help you—go around and tell everybody the meeting isn't off. Tell all of them to be there. Tell them all to keep it on the Que-tee." And Gus and Rob had argued quietly about it, till finally Gus said, "Okay—okay. But you don't have to be there. Every little thing will be taken care of."

And now they were sitting in the jam-packed church and it was hot and sticky and fans were waving all over the place and the white-robed choir was singing sweetly:

> *When they ring those golden bells for you and me*
> *Can't you hear those bells a-ringing*
> *Can't you hear the angels singing*
> *'Tis the glory hallelujah jubilee*
> *In that far off sweet forever*
> *When we cross that shining river*
> *And they ring those golden bells for you and me. . . .*

And the warm sweet voices dying away now, singing the chorus softer and softer, and handkerchiefs out all over the church, and he was supposed to be with Mama and give her support, and

Mama's nails digging into his shoulders through his dark suit, and it was Daddy lying in that long gray casket with mountains of flowers surrounding him, and he couldn't keep denying it.

Last night Mama seemed to suddenly realize that Daddy was dead. She had gone into his death room filled with the sad sweet scent of flowers and death, and she had opened the casket and gazed upon her lover, and suddenly it came to her that this night was their very last together. It was as if she didn't really think of him as dead, but that on tomorrow he was going on a long and endless journey and never return. And the years they had shared together were the only years she remembered now, and all of the years had been hard years but all of them had been good years too, and she would never hear his soft deep laughter nor the soft booming thunder of his voice, and he would never call her Lil Bits again nor sing that song Walk Together Children, and the bitterest part was they would never walk together again— Walk together—never—never—And the never never never part of it reached right out and seized her heart and twisted it till the pain was unbearable and Mama woke everybody up in the house. Nobody was asleep. *"Oh—Lord! Oh—Lord!* Our last night together! Our last night together! I want to go with you, Joe! I want to go with you, Joe! Lord have mercy! Don't leave me behind!"

Rob and Miss Lulabelle tried to quiet her down. "Joe is dead, darling," Miss Lulabelle said. "Joe is dead, Laurie Lee. He wouldn't want you to break yourself up like this. Now lie down, honey and try to get some rest, and behave yourself."

"All right, Lulabelle, all right. I'm going to lie down."

But then she seemed to suddenly remember and she went into the front room and she took the biggest bunch of flowers there, and she dragged them through the kitchen as Rob and Lulabelle Mackey watched and she threw Mrs. Cross Junior's beautiful expensive spray into the backyard. "They killed my Joe! They killed my Joe, the two-faced devils, and then have the nerve to send flowers to him! We don't want no flowers from them! We don't need them! We don't need them!"

"Take hold of yourself, Laurie Lee Youngblood. Please, sugar pie," Miss Lulabelle said.

"They tried to kill you too," Mama said to Rob. "We don't need them. All right, Lulabelle, I'll be quiet." And then Mama looked up into Rob's face and it was—"Oh, Rob! Oh, Rob, darling! My children ain't got no more Daddy!" And Jenny Lee who had been trying to sleep next door at Miss Jessie Mae's ran into the kitchen.

And now the remarks of the Grand Worthy Chancellor of the Frederick Douglass Lodge of Georgia. "Joseph Youngblood, a charter member. . . ."

And then Willabelle dressed in white got up and walked up on the rostrum and sang.

*When you come to the end of your journey . . .*
*. . . He'll understand and say—well done. . . .*

Rob was so filled up now he didn't hardly know where he was or what he was doing, but he wondered why his mind kept moving and wouldn't stay put, wouldn't concentrate on his Daddy's funeral. This was his Daddy's funeral! He was thinking of the night Joe Louis beat Costelli and afterwards down on Harlem Avenue talking to the man, Larry McGruder, who lived up above the barber shop. Monday night after Daddy died and things had gotten quiet and peaceful between the two races, the little hunchback man had gone back to live over the barber shop again, and late that night about three in the morning a bunch of crackers had broken into his room and taken him to the woods and they beat him and flogged him and left him for dead, but he hadn't died.

And Miss Sallie Roundtree, Chairman of the Deaconess Board, reading the Obituary:—

"Joseph Youngblood was born in eighteen hundred and ninety-eight in Glenville, Georgia . . . one of church's most faithful members ever since. . . . Installed as a deacon. . . . Joseph Youngblood married Laurie Lee Barksdale from Tipkin, Georgia. . . . They lived together as man and wife until he passed—two devoted children. . . . Joseph and Laurie Lee lived a full happy life together. . . ."

He saw Mama wipe the tears from her eyes as more tears followed, and Daddy was dead! Daddy was dead! And he was supposed to give Mama strength.

The organ played and the choir sang softly, softer and softer —one verse only—and all over the church the people humming:

*Oh Freedom—Oh Freedom*
*Oh-oh Freedom over me*
*And before I be a slave*
*I'll be buried in my grave*

*And go home to my LORD*
*And be free. . . .*

And Rob, seated between Mama and Ida Mae and listening
now to the remarks of the NAACP by Josephine Rollins Myles,
who was almost bursting wide open with child, could feel Mama
strengthening even as his arm was about her shoulders, and she
seemed to be tapping the strength of some unseen power as the
funeral services went on and on and on. . . .

"NAACP in the sight of God dedicates itself to the principles
by which Joseph Youngblood lived . . . for which he died . . .
and under the leadership of his lifelong companion, Laurie Youngblood, and others like her we shall bring together the colored
people of Crossroads and the State of Georgia . . . the hundreds
and the thousands . . . and the decent-thinking white people. . . ."

And the tears no longer flowing from his mother's eyes. Getting
stronger and stronger and somehow transferring some of her
secret strength to Rob, and he was the one who was supposed
to keep her from falling apart.

And the reading of telegrams from all over the country, and
it seemed that everybody in the whole world knew about Joe
Youngblood.

Vaguely Rob saw Reverend Ledbetter rise and walk slowly
forward as the choir sang softly, *Abide with Me—Fast Falls the
Eventide.* And he saw Reverend Ledbetter open his Holy Bible,
and Rob's eyes came down and rested on the long gray casket
again with the flowers everywhere and he thought about his
father, working in the mills and the time he broke his back at the
mills and his Daddy's soft friendly eyes and playing ball with
Daddy in the vacant lot, and "Son, your mother is the wonderfullest
woman in the whole wide world," and Daddy in the payline
standing up to the crackers, and the other Monday morning at
the breakfast table talking about building a union at the hotel and
everything else, and many of the workers had taken time off to
come to the funeral—Mr. Ogle couldn't hold them—

After Gus had left him the other night he had thought hard
about it—the union meeting—and had taken it to bed with him—
the union and Daddy—and he hadn't slept a wink, and all the
next day thinking about it, even as he went about helping in the
final preparations for his Daddy's funeral, and he didn't understand how he could think of anything else but his Daddy dead.

**470**

And finally that night he knew what he would do, and what his Daddy would want him to do, and he told Jenny Lee and she agreed and now he wished he had told Mama too, but he had told her afterwards. He went late to the meeting and things got quiet when he walked in, and it looked like all the folks who worked at the hotel were there, the colored folks, except Leroy and Will and a few other backsliders, and even Oscar and Junior were there along with a couple of other crackers they brought. They discussed and fussed and argued and talked. Almost everybody said something. "We better watch our step at first. Mr. Ogle ain't gon like it a bit." And—"Shame on Mr. Ogle. We ain't getting together for his benefit." And—"Yet and still we got to be careful. He right about that." And they took a pledge like in a secret order. Rev. Ledbetter gave it to them. Everybody joined the union except two or three colored and they had to think about it just a little bit longer. And the youngest one there was elected the chairman— Young Youngblood. And Hack Dawson treasurer and Willabelle secretary and Oscar and Gus on the Executive Committee, and all through it all he had a funny feeling he could hear his Daddy's booming laughter, he could see him smiling and Walk Together Children. And they would build the union strong, get everybody in.

But his Daddy was dead! His Daddy was dead, and he was attending his Daddy's funeral. And the next time Rob looked up toward the pulpit again his eyes were wet, and he was aware of Reverend Ledbetter reading from the Holy Bible.

"I take my text from the written word of the Gospel according to Saint John, the eleventh chapter and the twenty-fifth verse ———'Jesus said unto her, I am the resurrection and the life: He that believeth on me, though he die, yet shall he live' . . ." He slowly closed the Holy Bible.

"Though he die, yet shall he live—yet shall he live. And though Deacon Youngblood has passed on to that land where all is peace and time stands still, though he has died, yet shall he live. Yet shall he live in the hearts of his devoted family, in the spirit of Pleasant Grove Baptist Church, in the Deacon Board, praise the Lord. Joseph Youngblood lives in all of us. His spirit lives in the Frederick Douglass Lodge of Georgia. His spirit lives in the National Association for the Advancement of Colored People. His spirit lives wherever men and women come together to serve our Lord and Savior, Jesus Christ, and the cause of freedom. . . ."

"Amen—Amen!"

"Joe Youngblood! Joe Youngblood! Have Mercy, Jesus!"

"Yes, My Lord!"

"And brothers and sisters, I say to you this afternoon with a heart full of sorrow, for Deacon Youngblood was a man I looked upon as a brother and friend in the fullest sense, and yet I say to you and particularly to the grief-stricken family— this is not the time for tears—and yet we do cry, dear Lord, for we are human beings, weak and unknowing, down here on Your bountiful earth and we do not always understand the complexities of Thy infinite wisdom. We do not understand, oh merciful Savior, the reason that our brother and brave Christian soldier was smitten down by the enemy in the heat of the day just as the battle is about to begin—

"But Oh make a joyful noise unto God all the earth—this is a day for rejoicing and hallelujah and reaffirmations and rededications—for who is there among us can say that Joe Youngblood has died in vain? Who can say he has not left with us a strength and spirit and determination that will bring together the God-fearing, freedom-loving people of Crossroads, Georgia and the whole State of Georgia. This then is the reason—This is the purpose. The Lord works in mysterious ways His wonders to perform—Glory to His Name.

"Joseph Youngblood has gone to sing in that heavenly choir with John Brown and Harriet Tubman and Fred Douglass and Sojourner Truth and Abraham Lincoln, but his truth is marching on!

"Sleep on, dear brother—sleep on, Brother Youngblood, and take your rest—and rest you in the firmest knowledge that we shall carry on and on till that great morning when the stone the builders rejected is become the head of the corner. . . .

"Sleep on, Brother Youngblood. Though you die, yet shall you live—yet shall you live. . . ."

The tears fell now, unnoticed, from Rob's eyes, and all of the tears were not tears of sorrow—The remarks of the various people about his Daddy, and especially the sermon of Reverend Ledbetter and the feeling and spirit of all his folks packing the hot stuffy church and standing along the sides and in the back and down in the Sunday School and out in the church yard and the faces at last night's union meeting and especially his mother next to him now and the man in the casket and Harriet Tubman and John Brown and Frederick Douglass lifted him up to a greater

**472**

understanding and a firm determination that Daddy's life shall not have been given in vain—And yet he cried—He heard Miss Hannah begin the introduction on the organ—Nearer My God To Thee—but he didn't want to hear any sad songs now. Let them play a Jubilee—

*Neer—row my God to Thee*
*Neer—row to Thee*
*Neer—row my God to Thee*
*Neer—row to Thee*

And now the undertakers uncovering the body for the people to see for the last last time, and first came the family. And when Rob rose with Mama on one side and Ida Mae on the other, her eyes filled with tears, he felt his knees give in for a moment, and Mama's hand tightened on his arm, and he had to fight hard to steady himself, as they moved toward the casket. They stood for a moment looking down on his calm quiet face, his eyes sealed now finally in death, but they seemed to be smiling like they always smiled, and he looked so natural just like he was asleep, and the realization that this was the last time they would ever look upon him was too much to bear. He felt his mother's shoulders shaking now and the sobs came forth from her small heavy bosom. "Lord, have mercy! Lord, have mercy! No more Joe, Jesus—No more Joe!"

And he said softly, "Mama . . . Mama . . ." but he couldn't say more, because he had to fight so hard to keep himself from crying. And Jenny Lee walked up with Gus Mackey and she looked at her father long and hard and she wiped her eyes and she looked some more, and she said very quietly—"No more Daddy. . . ." And the family moved away and made way for the others to view the body, and the heat and the dampness and the sweet awful smell of the beautiful flowers, and the choir still singing in almost a whisper, *Safe in the arms of Jesus—Safe on His gentle breast* . . . and people weeping all over the church . . . and anger now on most of their faces. . . .

Outside the procession has started toward Lincoln Cemetery. And the long line of cars all kinds of descriptions and over a thousand people on foot. They reach the pavement now of the business section and down Jeff Davis Boulevard they march, quietly and solemn . . .

**473**

The sun beat down like the middle of the day. White folks standing along the sidewalks and looking out of the office buildings at the angry, dangerous-looking-faces-gleaming-with-sweat of the colored people in the line of march.

"Shouldn't let them march through town like this—stopping up the traffic," an important-looking white man said to another.

"They sure is a mean looking bunch, and great-day-in-the-morning, so many of em! Enough to scare you half to death—"

"They look like soldiers going off to war—" the white lady said to the tall white gentleman in the palm beach suit. . . .

"I sure am sorry I saw this sight," the gentleman said. "I'm the worst sleeper in the whole wide world. Tonight when I'm asleep I'll be hearing black feet marching all over Georgia."

And one cracker said to another cracker, "I ought to have my shotgun. You sure would see some black birds scatter."

And the other cracker said, "You better say you reckin." And he shook his head from side to side.

And all along the way the white folks stood with looks of awe and concern on their faces as the colored folks marched slow and unsmiling and four abreast through the heart of the town and all along the way colored folks joining and swelling the ranks. Men and women and children.

At Hotel Oglethorpe a cook left the kitchen without anybody knowing and the stocky-shouldered middle-aged white man went quietly in his white uniform out past the watchman. "I be back directly." And his heart beat faster as he walked up the alley and turned right on Cherry Street and walked quickly in his cook's uniform toward Jeff Davis Boulevard and he stood there on the edge of the sidewalk till it all passed by. The courthouse clock went bong and he wiped his eyes and looked up quickly and it was six thirty and he realized he had been off the job forty-five minutes and he hurried back to work.

And out at the cemetery hundreds and hundreds of people everywhere. . . .

And

*Ashes to ashes*
*Dust to dust*

And she saw them lower him into the ground, and it was all over now, she thought to herself. And Mama leaned heavily against Rob and she started to say, It's all over, son. It's all over now. . . . But she looked around her and she saw all the faces, people they knew and people they didn't know . . . black and brown and light-skin faces, all of them angry . . . and somehow she felt a union of strength with them because they were her people and she was angry too. She looked at Rob and her eyes sought out Jenny Lee Youngblood and her mind made a picture of Joe Youngblood at the breakfast table on a Monday morning— *I used to think that this old world was coming to an end, but now I know that it just begun and all we got to do is walk together children. . . .*

She felt Rob's arm tighten around her shoulders and Rob Youngblood and Jenny Lee Youngblood and Joe! Joe! Joe! and Richard Myles and Ray Morrison and Ida Mae and Lulabelle and Gus and Willabelle and Sarah Mae and Ellis Jordan and Leroy Jenkins and Benjamin Raglin and Hack Dawson and—So many many people . . . all her folks . . . and over on the outer edge of the crowd she saw Dr. Riley and Junior Jefferson.

"It's just begun, son," she whispered to Rob.

"What you say, Mama?" And Rob a man now a full grown man, growing bigger and bigger.

Reverend Ledbetter came over to where they were standing, and he took the widow into his arms. "Don't be disheartened, Sister Youngblood. You have two of the finest children in the whole State of Georgia. A fine young man and fine young woman, and Richard Myles he's your youngun too. And look all around you at your brothers and sisters, thousands of them, and, Great GodAlmighty, fighting mad, and we're going to make them pay one day soon, the ones that're responsible. There's going to be a reckoning day right here in Georgia and we're going to help God hurry it up."

And people coming over, strangers and friends, and shaking their hands, and hugging and kissing and giving them strength, and over in the west the sun going down, and the moon would come up and the moon would go down and tomorrow the sun would come up again.